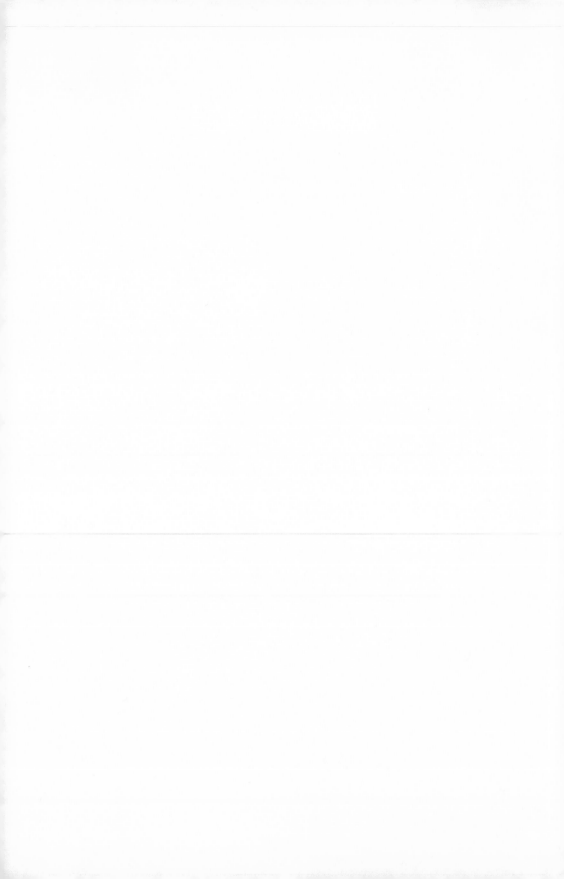

WILDERNESS
TALES

WILDERNESS TALES

Forty Stories of the North American Wild

EDITED WITH AN INTRODUCTION
AND COMMENTARY BY

DIANA FUSS

ALFRED A. KNOPF   NEW YORK   2023

THIS IS A BORZOI BOOK
PUBLISHED BY ALFRED A. KNOPF

Introduction and commentary copyright © 2023 by Diana Fuss

www.aaknopf.com

Knopf, Borzoi Books, and the colophon are registered
trademarks of Penguin Random House LLC.

Permissions appear at the end of the book.

Library of Congress Cataloging-in-Publication Data
Names: Fuss, Diana, 1960– editor.
Title: Wilderness tales : forty stories of the North American wild /
edited with an introduction and commentary by Diana Fuss.
Description: New York : Alfred A. Knopf, 2023. |
Includes bibliographical references.
Identifiers: LCCN 2022017630 (print) | LCCN 2022017631 (ebook) |
ISBN 9780593318973 (hardcover) | ISBN 9780593318980 (ebook)
Subjects: LCSH: Nature stories, American. | Ecofiction, American. | Frontier and
pioneer life—North America—Fiction. | Outdoor life—North America—Fiction. |
Short stories, American. | Short stories, Canadian. | Short stories, Mexican. |
LCGFt: Nature fiction. | Short stories.
Classification: LCC PS648.N32 W55 2023 (print) | LCC PS648.N32 (ebook) |
DDC 813/.6—dc23/eng/20220809
LC record available at https://lccn.loc.gov/2022017630
LC ebook record available at https://lccn.loc.gov/2022017631

Jacket art by Neil Gower
Jacket flap illustrations by Mark Edward Geyer
Jacket design by John Gall
Illustrations by Mark Edward Geyer

Manufactured in the United States of America
First Edition

To Linda Courtney, sister and friend,
and to her remarkable extended brood,
Pamela Kapitulik, Jeffrey Stylos, Joseph Stylos,
Melissa Stylos, and Cameron Johnson,
who are among the most resourceful people on the planet
and its most faithful custodians

Contents

Introduction

Fifteen years ago, while hiking the Storm Point trail on the northern rim of Yellowstone Lake, my hiking partner and I turned a blind corner and unexpectedly came upon two rutting bison pumped with testosterone and competing over a female. The bull facing us, already swinging its massive head, instantly charged, sending us sprinting back around the corner and down the trail, with a drop to the lake on one side of us and a forest of lodgepole trees, fallen branches, and brambles on the other.

I often wonder what would have happened that day if we had not had the good fortune to run straight into an experienced park ranger. Would we have tried to climb a straggly tree (bad idea), leapt over the cliff (even worse idea), or taken our chances with the brambles and branches? This low brush, offering no substantial cover, seemed to me the worst option, but the ranger knew what we did not: bison fear losing their footing, and so they take great care with thickets. When she yelled, "Into the woods—now!" we followed her, leaping and stumbling into the brush. To be sure, there is no outrunning a bison. But there is outthinking one. As the enraged bison slowly started to pick its way through the small but dense area of bushes and trees, we eventually broke free and sprinted across an open meadow, thankful to have been saved by a savvy ranger well versed in bison behavior. Such encounters are a sobering reminder that one is rarely prepared for the reality of life in the wild, even on a well-traveled hiking path in America's first and best-loved national park.

Attitudes toward the North American wild have changed over time, with the Yellowstone caldera a good case in point. After John Colter left the Lewis and Clark Expedition in 1806 and soon after crossed the Yellowstone River, he saw a landscape of "stinking water" and "hot spring brimstone." In the mid-1830s, trapper Osborne Russell described the Yellowstone area in starkly different terms, as a place of "wild romantic splendor" that seemed to "support the heavens." Cornelius Hedges, a member of the 1870 Washburn Expedition into Yellowstone, shared both views; he understood why less scientific men might perceive its hot springs and geysers as an "infernal" place in which to hold "unhallowed carnival," though he also pronounced himself astonished and awed by its "grandeur" and "beauties." By the time my grandfather, Joseph Fuss, served in the early 1920s as a summer yarder hauling garbage and chopping wood at the Yellowstone Lake Hotel, he saw only a "wonder of nature" and a "grand site." For centuries the many Indigenous tribes who lived near or passed through the Yellowstone area—among them the Kiowa, Bannocks, Blackfeet, Crow, Nez Perce, and Shoshones—viewed its thermal features and imposing mountains as places of immense spiritual power to be both feared and revered. Now, after decades of exploding tourism, park custodians worry that Yellowstone's enthusiastic visitors might be "loving it to death."

All these complex historical attitudes toward the wild can also be found in our fictional stories about life in the wilderness. Indeed, a vast archive of North American wilderness tales, stretching from the birth of the short-story form in the early nineteenth century to the emergence of "eco-fiction" in the twenty-first century, has not merely reflected shifting cultural views of the wild but in turn has helped to shape, promote, and sometimes challenge those perceptions. Across two centuries, the wilderness short story has evolved from early tales of mystery and suspense, to classic tales of danger and survival, to modern tales of retreat and solitude, to contemporary tales of endangerment and apocalypse, together mapping a deep fascination with stories about North America's wild.

In a time defined by ecological crisis—climate change, environmental degradation, species extinction—why publish a collection of fictional wilderness stories? Why not simply let science carry the burden of explaining why wilderness matters? For the simple reason that fictional works can accomplish what numbers and data alone cannot:

they educate our emotions, creating human interest, empathy, and awareness. Whether read individually or together, the stories in this fiction anthology speak to more than just our intellect. They offer visceral reading experiences suggesting why we should care about the wild and why we might worry about its disappearance.

As the wilds of North America continue to vanish, it can be difficult to comprehend the sheer weight of what has happened to them. During the European conquest of the continent, settlers viewed the immensity of its natural features—forests, deserts, mountains, rivers, marshes—not just as dangerous forces against which they often felt compelled to protect themselves but also as economic resources and opportunities. Now wilderness environments, along with the many natural life-forms they support, have themselves become the things that are most endangered and in need of protection. At this moment in time, wilderness tales have morphed from stories about how we survive within the wild into stories about how we survive without it.

The absence of any collections devoted to the wilderness short story is curious given the long-standing visibility of these tales. From their early appearance in the new mass-market magazines of the 1800s to their prominence in internet short fiction and environmental literature sites today, short stories about the wild have endured in popularity and importance for two centuries. Indeed, they constitute one of North America's oldest and most resilient literary genres.

LITERARY HISTORY

The North American wilderness tale historically emerged during a revolution in publishing: the rapid rise of periodical culture. In the first half of the nineteenth century, the explosion of cheap, consumable, and transportable magazines and journals proved to be the perfect vehicles for generating and sustaining a literary form also new to the scene, the literary sketch or tale, soon known as the short story.

Wilderness short stories became a distinct literary genre during America's antebellum period in magazines such as Boston's *New-England Magazine* (Nathaniel Hawthorne's 1835 "Young Goodman Brown") and the *Atlantic Monthly* (Harriet Prescott Spofford's 1860 "Circumstance"), as well as in books and newspapers (Frederick Douglass's 1853 "The Heroic Slave" appeared both in the abolitionist anthol-

ogy *Autographs for Freedom,* for which it was commissioned, and in
the author's own abolitionist newspaper, *Frederick Douglass's Paper*).
Capitalizing on the curiosity and wanderlust of educated and increasingly urbanized East Coast audiences, many magazines, newspapers,
and story collections fed the growing enthusiasm for tales of human
endurance, whether on mountain or plain, forest or desert, marshland
or tundra. Influenced by a history of religious revivals, frontier expeditions, and gold rushes, wilderness tales offered both the romance and
the realism of human encounters with the wild that few metropolitan
readers were likely ever to have experienced firsthand.

Upon the inauguration of railway mail service in the 1860s, the
national audience for monthly magazines, and thus for short stories
of all kinds, increased dramatically. Seizing the opportunity to build
their subscription base, magazines broadened their content for more
geographically diverse though still largely genteel audiences. Closely
following the transcontinental journey of pioneers—a movement that
claimed ever larger land and water areas for farming and industry—the
emergent wilderness genre worked to buttress the ideology of western
expansion by concealing its damaging effects, both on natural environments and Indigenous peoples. In a very real sense, the North American wilderness tale fully came to life only when wilderness itself began
to recede.

After the Civil War, and in the continued absence of a national newspaper, the two most successful monthly magazines, *Harper's Magazine*
and the *Atlantic,* transported their stories west, south, and eventually
southwest across America, as well as north into newly self-governing
Canada, securing an even larger audience for wilderness short stories.
In 1868 a new magazine out of San Francisco, the *Overland Monthly,*
reversed directions and brought exciting tales of the West, both real
and fictional, back to the East. By the turn of the twentieth century,
magazines, riding a wave of increased interest, advertisers, and readers,
finally secured for the wilderness tale not just national but international
prominence. Readers living and working in crowded cities developed
an abiding interest in adventure stories set in the North American wild.
No longer in touch with the continent's undeveloped regions, these
city dwellers enthusiastically responded to tales of how to survive there.

Already by 1900 two authors were becoming famous for their wilderness tales: the American writer Jack London and the Canadian writer

Charles G. D. Roberts. While neither author can be said to have created the North American wilderness short story (that distinction goes to Washington Irving), they did more than any of their predecessors to exploit its commercial potential and to secure its future. London and Roberts together popularized and consolidated the genre by turning wilderness fiction into a staple for well-established magazines aimed at adults (*Scribner's Magazine,* the *Century Magazine,* the *Saturday Evening Post*), along with new magazines marketed to younger readers (*Youth's Companion,* the *American Boy*). Jack London managed to reach both audiences: his 1902 tale "To Build a Fire" was published in *Youth's Companion* six years before reappearing, in a substantially revised form, in the *Century Magazine,* where it sat comfortably alongside Roberts's tale "The Vagrants of the Barren." It was London's and Roberts's stories of the frozen North, each published in the *Century Magazine* in 1908, that set the benchmark for almost every survival wilderness tale to follow.

Today, wilderness tales continue to circulate widely, and much more immediately, in internet periodicals. In their online presence they are never more than a click away. EcoLit Books identifies sixty-five active websites for anyone interested in reading or writing about wilderness, animals, or ecology. In the current era of the Anthropocene or "Great Acceleration," in which human activity has altered the very surface of the earth and the air we breathe, the traditional wilderness tale has morphed into a many-headed beast, with tentacles in climate change, land conservation, species protection, earth science, and environmental justice. This anthology ends by focusing on the most dramatic new chapters in the history of wilderness literature: stories about endangerment, extinction, climates, and futures. As environmental catastrophes become no longer possible to ignore, we are entering a historical moment where the only stories about wilderness left to tell appear to be stories of its continued demise.

WHAT IS WILDERNESS?

One likely explanation for why no anthology of wilderness short stories has been published before might well be long-standing historical, cultural, and political disagreements over the definition or meaning of wilderness. In its earliest usage recorded in the Oxford English Dictionary, the word *wilderness,* derived from the Old English *wild(d)éornes,* denoted "wild or uncultivated land"—and soon expanded to encompass "a wild or uncultivated region or tract of land, uninhabited, or inhabited only by wild animals." Disagreement over the specific meaning and character of North America's wilderness is a conversation on the one hand as old as the European colonization of the continent, and on the other hand as recent as the contentious debates over America's Wilderness Act of 1964, which controversially identified "wilderness" as unpopulated and uncultivated land: "an area where earth and its community of life are untrammeled by man, where man himself is a visitor who does not remain."

Such a strict legal definition was news to anyone already living in the newly designated wilderness areas, for whom the concept of wilderness as a place without people reinforced old colonial assumptions. To Indigenous communities, the notion of an "empty" and "unspoiled" land, a geographical terrain that nonnative settlers alternately viewed with dread and awe, was never a wilderness. It was simply where they lived, loved, struggled, thrived, and died. As many historians have argued, most notably Roderick Frazier Nash in his 1967 book *Wilderness and the American Mind,* wilderness has never been so much a place as a collection of feelings or attitudes about that place. Wilderness is an idea or state of mind about the wild, with a complicated and difficult history entangled in religious persecution, manifest destiny, settler colonialism, and environmental exploitation. Put another way, "wild" denotes unsettled terrains and their wildlife, while "wilderness" encompasses the changing stories we tell about them.

The first dictionary in North America, Noah Webster's *A Compendious Dictionary of the English Language* (1806), follows the British wordsmith Samuel Johnson in defining wilderness as "a track of solitude and savageness." Later, in his *American Dictionary of the English Language* (1828), Webster, a proud New Englander, offers a more expansive definition of wilderness tailored to what he knew of the North American landscape. He first identifies wilderness as "a desert; a tract of land or region uncultivated and uninhabited by human beings, whether a forest or a wide barren plain," before adding, erroneously, that "in the United States, it is applied only to a forest." While writers at the time did indeed describe North America's deep woods as wilderness, the term had been in common usage for centuries to name any "vast" or

"boundless" region in which one might become lost or "bewildered"—
including the ocean, Webster's second definition of "wilderness."

Most North American wilderness tales fall broadly into three main
categories: Gothic, Romance, and Environment. The majority of early
tales lean toward Wilderness Gothic, dramatizing the power of the wild
to mystify and terrify. Especially prominent in the nineteenth century,
Gothic stories depict wilderness as haunting, dangerous, and unholy,
more "Devil's Den" than "Edenic Garden." Invoking the terrors of first
contact with the New World, they draw their power from religious
notions of wilderness as a place of trial, hardship, sin, and temptation.
Depicting wilderness as a moral and spiritual wasteland, these stories
stage their dramatic action in desolate settings haunted by evil spirits or
populated by wild beasts. In works like *The Scarlet Letter* and "Young
Goodman Brown," Hawthorne's dangerous New England forest con-
veys (in order to critique) earlier views of wilderness as "unconverted,"
"heathen," and "frightful." Hawthorne's primeval forest serves as an
allegorical reflection of the dark heart of Puritanism.

Wilderness Romance, in contrast, captures the transcendent side of
the wild, emphasizing its natural virtues and restorative effects. Embracing the continent's uncultivated landscapes as its most distinctive feature, nineteenth-century Romantics spoke of the wonders rather than
the perils of the North American wild. As people began to appreciate
the grandeur and beauty of nature, wilderness became less forbidding
and more inviting. For a transcendentalist like Henry David Thoreau,
it presented a means to resist the deadening influence of civilization
by offering an opportunity to live simply and deeply, as he explains in
Walden: "I went to the woods because I wished to live deliberately, to
front only the essential facts of life." Thoreau's college commonplace
book suggests he may have been inspired to go to the woods by James
Fenimore Cooper's Leatherstocking novels, a sequence of frontier tales
composed between 1823 and 1841 that romanticize and idealize the wild,
celebrating their sublimity and nobility.

More recent short stories that focus on the ecology of the wild
constitute a third major historical movement: Wilderness Environment. Often dystopic or elegiac in tone, environmental fiction envisions a world increasingly devoid of wild places, plants, animals, and
even people. These stories offer cautionary warnings about a vanishing

wild and an imperiled planet, posing serious ethical and political questions for both our present and our future. In doing so they sometimes incorporate strains of both the Gothic and the Romance traditions of wilderness literature, presenting lyrical descriptions of the wild directly alongside terrifying visions of its destruction. But whereas in earlier traditions of wilderness fiction the wild is abundantly present, in today's environmental tales it typically is not. Saving or bringing back the wild may be the central point or purpose of the story, but wilderness is rarely the setting. Dusty ghost towns, flooded coastal cities, or disease-ravaged suburbs are more likely locales for the new wilderness tale, its characters forever searching for ways to adapt and survive. The fear or fascination that distinguished earlier literary treatments of the wild still inhabit the inventive worlds of environmental fiction, but they generally take a back seat to the compelling existential questions posed by the realities of wildlife endangerment, species extinction, and climate change.

At the same time, environmental concerns are not just the purview of contemporary wilderness fiction. Cooper's Leatherstocking Romance fictions fiercely oppose the excesses of pioneer settlement and the reckless despoiling of the continent's forests and prairies. Ernest Hemingway's most famous short story, "Big Two-Hearted River," indicts on its very first page the charred landscape left behind by slash-and-burn logging companies in Michigan's Upper Peninsula. And William Faulkner's many fictional works set in the environs of Mississippi's Tallahatchie River offer moving laments to the ruined natural landscapes of the industrial New South. The contemporary stories that conclude this anthology do more than bring readers into the present or the future. They simultaneously extend an invitation to reconsider a number of classic literary works in light of their own early environmental concerns.

If the literary-historical movements of Gothic, Romance, and Environment do not necessarily exclude one another, they also do not sufficiently capture the full cultural diversity of responses to the North American wild. For enslaved African Americans, feelings about wilderness were much more complicated. In their communities, the continent's wild landscapes were viewed neither as a promised land nor as an eternal hell. Early African American songs and spirituals, which often endowed the American wild with moral and religious significance, saw bewildering forests and dismal swamps as places of trial but also of freedom. Wilderness offered remote environments outside the plantation to meet, to worship, or to hide, with some slaves preferring to escape into the dangerous depths of the wild than to remain in bondage. The institution of slavery is itself a Gothic horror story, standing in stark contrast to the founding myths of Wilderness Romance in particular. As transcendentalists wrote encomiums to the deep woods, fugitive slaves were hunted down in them. As landscape painters celebrated the picturesque beauty of trees, Black people were whipped against their trunks and lynched from their branches.

Similarly, Indigenous peoples of North America, from Mexico to the Bering Strait, also dismissed the view of wilderness as either strictly malevolent or wholly benevolent. For these storytellers the continent's dark forests, vast plains, deep canyons, tangled marshes, open deserts, rapid rivers, imposing mountains, and icy glaciers offer occasions to change the narrative by substituting new tales about the wild or by exploding the concept of wilderness altogether. Focusing on the harmony and interdependency between communities and environments, both Native creation myths and human-animal transformation tales directly counter the standard wilderness endurance plot in which individual actors must prove themselves against an antagonistic or indifferent wild. Indigenous writers frequently invoke legends and folktales to move Native peoples and histories out of the background and into the foreground, repeatedly reminding us that not all depictions of the wild draw on Anglo-European conceptions of wilderness. These stories force a consideration of the cultural work wilderness tales perform, and for whom. To study the full range and diversity of wilderness tales is to recognize that such stories may tell us as much if not more about ourselves, and about the historical or cultural contexts in which the stories emerged, than about anything intrinsic to the actual wild places of North America.

ANTHOLOGY

This anthology features a total of forty short stories organized into ten different thematic sections. Brief introductions anchor each of the sections, with each tale preceded by an author and story introduction. Seeking to underscore the notable variety of wilderness tales while simultaneously highlighting their natural groupings, I have elected not to list the forty short stories in order of their publication dates. Instead I have gathered and organized the best of the wilderness tales by theme, turning to chronology only within individual sections to create a "then and now" format.

The structure of the anthology reflects how certain attitudes toward the wild developed over time, both culturally and creatively. The volume begins with tales of Suspense and Terror (where the wilderness short story historically takes root) and concludes with stories on Climates and Futures (where the genre imaginatively reinvents itself today). Its sequencing of tales invites readers to explore how wilderness tales encode specific historical periods or events and express different cultural beliefs or perspectives. Theme sections make it possible to see the precise ways wilderness stories speak to and spark off one another in a shared desire to answer, through the elastic medium of fiction, the question of what wilderness may mean and why it compels us.

A heat map of locations featured in the anthology's selection of short stories reveals the broad and shifting climatological zones embraced by North American wilderness tales, as interests shift from cool Northern forests and humid Southern wetlands to frozen tundra, temperate prairies, and arid deserts. Yet across anthology sections a story's landmarks can feel uncannily familiar. Tales decades or even centuries apart are drawn back to the same natural or geological features: rocks, woods, and trees; lakes, rivers, and oceans; hills, mountains, and valleys; grass, sand, and ice. In the end it is these signifiers of wildness, the very solid and not so solid ground we inhabit, that define a wilderness tale most. Given the current reality and damaging effects of climate change on Earth's surface, we might well wonder: Does the wilderness short story have a future?

As some of the most recent stories in this volume suggest, if the wilderness tale does ultimately survive the destruction of its subject, it will likely linger on in the mode of historical fiction, fantasy fiction, or speculative fiction. Most wilderness stories today carry a distinctly mournful tone. And their purpose is clear: to remind us of what we have lost, what we continue to lose, and why. Tales of our vanishing wilderness pose the question: When will the domain of the wild be beyond all possible recovery, and who will we be without it? I very much hope that this story anthology, which tracks the emergence and evolution of the

North American wilderness tale, does not simultaneously and ironically presage its end.

That said, I do detect distant tremors of a new kind of wilderness story seeking to emerge, narratives capable of pointing us in another direction. As local and global efforts to conserve and protect remaining wilderness areas intensify, it is now reasonable to ask not whether the literary wilderness tale *has* a future, but whether this adaptive genre can *show* us the future—indeed, many possible, achievable, reparative futures. Plotting and inspiring different paths forward, the wilderness tale may still have a critical job: imagining spaces, places, and conditions where wilderness endures, wildlife recovers, and people thrive. Perhaps a time will come when it will be possible to add to this book of wilderness tales a new final section, one that bears the more aspirational or hopeful title Restoration and Revival.

WILDERNESS
TALES

PART I

SUSPENSE AND TERROR

Inspired in part by the European Gothic novel—a genre preoccupied with sin and guilt, criminality and sexuality, madness and violence—the first American wilderness short stories sought to provoke in readers feelings of suspense, even terror. But unlike European Gothic literature, which set its mysterious plots in medieval castles and abbeys, North American writers took as their prime Gothic setting the wilderness itself, substituting for the ancient interiors and secret passageways of European architecture the natural and unmapped wilds of the New World. From the beginning, Wilderness Gothic has been deeply rooted in the thicketed forests of the North and the dense swamps of the South. Southern plantation owners spoke of a wilderness filled with evil spirits and dangerous creatures to deter enslaved people from escaping into nearby woods and swamps, while New England ministers initially populated their descriptions of wilderness with devils, witches, and "savages" to dramatize the Calvinist doctrine of innate human depravity. By the nineteenth century these haunted landscapes offered writers of the new short-story form powerful symbolic settings in which to explore the terrors of the unknown while also crucially providing something more: moral frameworks for excavating the all-too-human horrors that transpired in the wild—real historical events too indelible to be buried or silenced.

"Rip Van Winkle"

WASHINGTON IRVING

Washington Irving (1783–1859) was raised in Manhattan in the late eighteenth century, but it was not until an outbreak of yellow fever forced him north, up the Hudson River to Tarrytown, New York, that he found the landscapes that would serve as the inspiration for his most enduring fiction. "Of all the scenery of the Hudson," Irving wrote in his later years, "the Kaatskill Mountains had the most witching effect on my boyish imagination." Irving drew on the area's Dutch folktales and ghost stories to compose his two most famous works, "The Legend of Sleepy Hollow" and "Rip Van Winkle," the latter reportedly written in a single night. Both are New World tales with Gothic plots set in the past, and both appear in Irving's serialized work *The Sketchbook of Geoffrey Crayon, Gent.* (1819–20), America's first short-story collection. Irving died at the age of seventy-six and was buried in Tarrytown Cemetery, renamed Sleepy Hollow Cemetery at Irving's suggestion. A mixture of both the Gothic and the Romance wilderness traditions, Washington Irving's "Rip Van Winkle" tells the story of American literature's most famous woodland rambler, a man who loves to tell tales of ghosts, witches, and Indians and who one day escapes with his dog, Wolf, into the sublime "fairy mountains" of the Catskills. A story about wilderness storytelling, Irving's "Rip Van Winkle" introduces the theme that will define nearly every wilderness tale for the next two hundred years: wilderness may be a place, but it is also a dream, an imaginative projection of human fears and fantasies.

"Rip Van Winkle"

WASHINGTON IRVING

I

Whoever has made a voyage up the Hudson must remember the Kaatskill Mountains. They are a branch of the great Appalachian family, and are seen away to the west of the river, swelling up to a noble height, and lording it over the surrounding country. Every change of season, every change of weather, indeed, every hour of the day, produces some change in the magical hues and shapes of these mountains, and they are regarded by all the goodwives, far and near, as perfect barometers.

At the foot of these fairy mountains the traveler may have seen the light smoke curling up from a village, whose shingle roofs gleam among the trees, just where the blue tints of the upland melt away into the fresh green of the nearer landscape. It is a little village of great age, having been founded by some of the Dutch colonists in the early times of the province, just about the beginning of the government of the good Peter Stuyvesant (may he rest in peace!), and there were some of the houses of the original settlers standing within a few years, built of small yellow bricks brought from Holland, having latticed windows and gable fronts, surmounted with weathercocks.

In that same village, and in one of these very houses, there lived, many years since, while the country was yet a province of Great Britain, a simple, good-natured fellow, of the name of Rip Van Winkle. He was a descendant of the Van Winkles who figured so gallantly in the chivalrous days of Peter Stuyvesant, and accompanied him to the siege of Fort Christina. He inherited, however, but little of the martial character of his ancestors. I have observed that he was a simple, good-natured man; he was, moreover, a kind neighbor and an obedient, henpecked husband.

Certain it is that he was a great favorite among all the goodwives of the village, who took his part in all family squabbles; and never failed, whenever they talked those matters over in their evening gossipings, to lay all the blame on Dame Van Winkle. The children of the village, too, would shout with joy whenever he approached. He assisted at their sports, made their playthings, taught them to fly kites and shoot marbles, and told them long stories of ghosts, witches, and Indians. Whenever he went dodging about the village, he was surrounded by a troop of them, hanging on his skirts, clambering on his back, and playing a thousand tricks on him; and not a dog would bark at him throughout the neighborhood.

The great error in Rip's composition was a strong dislike of all kinds of profitable labor. It could not be from the want of perseverance; for he would sit on a wet rock, with a rod as long and heavy as a lance, and fish all day without a murmur, even though he should not be encouraged by a single nibble. He would carry a fowling piece on his shoulder for hours together, trudging through woods and swamps, and up hill and down dale, to shoot a few squirrels or wild pigeons. He would never refuse to assist a neighbor even in the roughest toil, and was a foremost man at all country frolics for husking Indian corn, or building stone fences; the women of the village, too, used to employ him to run their errands, and to do such little odd jobs as their less obliging husbands would not do for them. In a word, Rip was ready to attend to anybody's business but his own; but as to doing family duty, and keeping his farm in order, he found it impossible.

His children, too, were as ragged and wild as if they belonged to nobody. His son Rip promised to inherit the habits, with the old clothes, of his father. He was generally seen trooping like a colt at his mother's heels, equipped in a pair of his father's cast-off breeches, which he had much ado to hold up with one hand, as a fine lady does her train in bad weather.

Rip Van Winkle, however, was one of those happy mortals, of foolish, well-oiled dispositions, who take the world easy, eat white bread or brown, whichever can be got with least thought or trouble, and would rather starve on a penny than work for a pound. If left to himself, he would have whistled life away in perfect contentment; but his wife kept continually dinning in his ear about his idleness, his carelessness, and the ruin he was bringing on his family. Morning, noon, and night, her tongue was incessantly going, and everything he said or did was sure to produce a torrent of household eloquence. Rip had but one way of replying to all lectures of the kind, and that, by frequent use, had grown into a habit. He shrugged his shoulders, shook his head, cast up his eyes, but said nothing. This, however, always provoked a fresh volley from his wife; so that he was fain to draw off his forces, and take to the outside of the house—the only side which, in truth, belongs to a henpecked husband.

Rip's sole domestic adherent was his dog Wolf, who was as much henpecked as his master; for Dame Van Winkle regarded them as companions in idleness, and even looked upon Wolf with an evil eye, as the cause of his master's going so often astray. True it is, in all points of spirit befitting an honorable dog, he was as courageous an animal as ever scoured the woods; but what courage can withstand the ever-enduring and all-besetting terrors of a woman's tongue? The moment Wolf entered the house his crest fell, his tail drooped to the ground or curled between his legs, he sneaked about with a gallows air, casting many a sidelong glance at Dame Van Winkle, and at the least flourish of a broomstick or ladle he would fly to the door with yelping precipitation.

Times grew worse and worse with Rip Van Winkle as years of matrimony rolled on. A tart temper never mellows with age, and a sharp tongue is the only edged tool that grows keener with constant use. For a long while he used to console himself, when driven from home, by frequenting a kind of perpetual club of sages, philosophers, and other idle personages of the village, which held its sessions on a bench before a small inn, designated by a rubicund portrait of His Majesty George III. Here they used to sit in the shade of a long, lazy summer's day, talking listlessly over village gossip, or telling endless sleepy stories about nothing. But it would have been worth any statesman's money to have heard the profound discussions which sometimes took place, when by chance an old newspaper fell into their hands from some passing traveler. How solemnly they would listen to the contents, as drawled out by Derrick Van Bummel, the schoolmaster—a dapper, learned little man, who was not to be daunted by the most gigantic word in the dictionary—and how sagely they would deliberate upon public events some months after they had taken place!

The opinions of this junto were completely controlled by Nicholas Vedder, a patriarch of the village, and landlord of the inn, at the door of which he took his seat from morning till night, just moving sufficiently to avoid the sun, and keep in the shade of a large tree; so that the neighbors could tell the hour by his movements as accurately as by a sundial.

It is true, he was rarely heard to speak, but smoked his pipe incessantly. His adherents, however (for every great man has his adherents), perfectly understood him, and knew how to gather his opinions. When anything that was read or related displeased him, he was observed to smoke his pipe vehemently, and to send forth short, frequent, and angry puffs; but, when pleased, he would inhale the smoke slowly and tranquilly, and emit it in light and placid clouds, and sometimes, taking the pipe from his mouth, and letting the fragrant vapor curl about his nose, would nod his head in approbation.

From even this stronghold the unlucky Rip was at length routed by his termagant wife, who would suddenly break in upon the tranquility of the assemblage, and call the members all to naught; nor was that august personage, Nicholas Vedder himself, sacred from the daring tongue of this terrible virago, who charged him with encouraging her husband in habits of idleness.

Poor Rip was at last reduced almost to despair; and his only alternative, to escape from the labor of the farm and clamor of his wife, was to take gun in hand and stroll away into the woods. Here he would sometimes seat himself at the foot of a tree, and share the contents of his wallet with Wolf, with whom he sympathized as a fellow-sufferer in persecution. "Poor Wolf," he would say, "thy mistress leads thee a dog's life of it; but never mind, my lad, whilst I live thou shalt never want a friend to stand by thee." Wolf would wag his tail, look wistfully in his master's face; and if dogs can feel pity, I verily believe he reciprocated the sentiment with all his heart.

In a long ramble of the kind on a fine autumnal day, Rip had unconsciously scrambled to one of the highest parts of the Kaatskill Mountains. He was after his favorite sport of squirrel-shooting, and the still solitudes had echoed and reechoed with the reports of his gun. Panting and fatigued, he threw himself, late in the afternoon, on a green knoll, covered with mountain herbage, that crowned the brow of a precipice. From an opening between the trees he could overlook all the lower country for many a mile of rich woodland. He saw at a distance the lordly Hudson, far, far below him, moving on its silent but majestic course, with the reflection of a purple cloud, or the sail of a lagging bark, here and there sleeping on its glassy bosom, and at last losing itself in the blue highlands.

On the other side he looked down into a deep mountain glen,

wild and lonely, the bottom filled with fragments from the overhanging cliffs, and scarcely lighted by the reflected rays of the setting sun. For some time Rip lay musing on this scene; evening was gradually advancing; the mountains began to throw their long blue shadows over the valleys; he saw that it would be dark long before he could reach the village, and he heaved a heavy sigh when he thought of encountering the terrors of Dame Van Winkle.

As he was about to descend, he heard a voice from a distance, hallooing, "Rip Van Winkle! Rip Van Winkle!" He looked round, but could see nothing but a crow winging its solitary flight across the mountain. He thought his fancy must have deceived him, and turned again to descend, when he heard the same cry ring through the still evening air: "Rip Van Winkle! Rip Van Winkle!"—at the same time Wolf bristled up his back, and giving a low growl, skulked to his master's side, looking fearfully down into the glen. Rip now felt a vague apprehension stealing over him; he looked anxiously in the same direction, and perceived a strange figure slowly toiling up the rocks, and bending under the weight of something he carried on his back. He was surprised to see any human being in this lonely and unfrequented place; but supposing it to be someone of the neighborhood in need of his assistance, he hastened down to yield it.

On nearer approach he was still more surprised at the singularity of the stranger's appearance. He was a short, square-built old fellow, with thick bushy hair, and a grizzled beard. His dress was of the antique Dutch fashion—a cloth jerkin strapped round the waist, and several pair of breeches, the outer one of ample volume, decorated with rows of buttons down the sides. He bore on his shoulder a stout keg that seemed full of liquor, and made signs for Rip to approach and assist him with the load. Though rather shy and distrustful of this new acquaintance, Rip complied with his usual alacrity, and relieving one another, they clambered up a narrow gully, apparently the dry bed of a mountain torrent.

As they ascended, Rip every now and then heard long, rolling peals, like distant thunder, that seemed to issue out of a deep ravine, or rather cleft, between lofty rocks, toward which their rugged path conducted. He paused for an instant, but supposing it to be the muttering of one of those transient thundershowers which often take place in mountain heights, he proceeded. Passing through the ravine, they came to a hollow, like a small amphitheater, surrounded by perpendicular precipices, over the brinks of which trees shot their branches, so that you only caught glimpses of the azure sky and the bright evening cloud. During the whole time Rip and his companion had labored on in silence; for though the former marveled greatly, what could be the object of carrying a keg of liquor up this wild mountain, yet there was something strange and incomprehensible about the unknown that inspired awe and checked familiarity.

On entering the amphitheater new objects of wonder presented themselves. On a level spot in the center was a company of odd-looking personages playing at ninepins. They were dressed in a quaint, outlandish fashion; some wore short doublets, others jerkins, with long knives in their belts, and most of them had enormous breeches, of similar style with that of the guide's. Their visages, too, were peculiar: one had a large head, broad face, and small, piggish eyes; the face of another seemed to consist entirely of nose, and was surmounted by a white sugar-loaf hat, set off with a little red cock's tail. They all had beards, of various shapes and colors. There was one who seemed to be the commander. He was a stout old gentleman, with a weather-beaten countenance; he wore a laced doublet, broad belt and hanger, high-crowned hat and feather, red stockings, and high-heeled shoes, with roses in them. The whole group reminded Rip of the figures in an old Flemish painting, in the parlor of Dominie Van Shaick, the village parson, which had been brought over from Holland at the time of the settlement.

What seemed particularly odd to Rip was that, though these folks were evidently amusing themselves, yet they maintained the gravest faces, the most mysterious silence, and were, withal, the most melancholy party of pleasure he had ever witnessed. Nothing interrupted the stillness of the scene but the noise of the balls, which, whenever they were rolled, echoed along the mountains like rumbling peals of thunder.

As Rip and his companion approached them, they suddenly desisted from their play, and stared at him with such fixed, statue-like gaze, and such strange, uncouth countenances, that his heart turned within him, and his knees smote together. His companion now emptied the contents of the keg into large flagons, and made signs to him to wait upon the company. He obeyed with fear and trembling; they quaffed the liquor in profound silence, and then returned to their game.

By degrees Rip's awe and apprehension subsided. He even ventured, when no eye was fixed upon him, to taste the beverage, which he found had much of the flavor of excellent Hollands. He was naturally a thirsty soul, and was soon tempted to repeat the draught. One taste provoked another; and he repeated his visits to the flagon so often that at length his senses were overpowered, his eyes swam in his head, his head gradually declined, and he fell into a deep sleep.

II

On waking he found himself on the green knoll whence he had first seen the old man of the glen. He rubbed his eyes—it was a bright, sunny morning. The birds were hopping and twittering among the bushes, and the eagle was wheeling aloft, and breasting the pure mountain breeze. "Surely," thought Rip, "I have not slept here all night." He recalled the occurrences before he fell asleep. The strange man with a keg of liquor—the mountain ravine—the wild retreat among the rocks—the woebegone party at ninepins—the flagon—"Oh! that flagon! that wicked flagon!" thought Rip; "what excuse shall I make to Dame Van Winkle?"

He looked round for his gun, but in place of the clean, well-oiled fowling piece, he found an old firelock lying by him, the barrel encrusted with rust, the lock falling off, and the stock worm-eaten. He now suspected that the grave revelers of the mountain had put a trick upon him and, having dosed him with liquor, had robbed him of his gun. Wolf, too, had disappeared, but he might have strayed away after a squirrel or partridge. He whistled after him, and shouted his name, but all in vain; the echoes repeated his whistle and shout, but no dog was to be seen.

He determined to revisit the scene of the last evening's gambol, and if he met with any of the party, to demand his dog and gun. As he rose to walk, he found himself stiff in the joints, and wanting in his usual activity. "These mountain beds do not agree with me," thought Rip, "and if this frolic should lay me up with a fit of the rheumatism, I shall have a blessed time with Dame Van Winkle." With some difficulty he got down into the glen; he found the gully up which he and his companion had ascended the preceding evening; but to his astonishment a mountain stream was now foaming down it, leaping from rock to rock, and filling the glen with babbling murmurs. He, however, made shift to scramble up its sides, working his toilsome way through thickets of birch, sassafras, and witch hazel, and sometimes tripped up or entangled by the wild grapevines that twisted their coils from tree to tree, and spread a kind of network in his path.

At length he reached to where the ravine had opened through the cliffs to the amphitheater; but no traces of such opening remained. The rocks presented a high, impenetrable wall, over which the torrent came tumbling in a sheet of feathery foam, and fell into a broad, deep basin, black from the shadows of the surrounding forest. Here, then, poor Rip was brought to a stand. He again called and whistled after his dog; he was only answered by the cawing of a flock of idle crows sporting high in the air about a dry tree that overhung a sunny precipice; and who, secure in their elevation, seemed to look down and scoff at the poor man's perplexities. What was to be done?—the morning was passing away, and Rip felt famished for want of his breakfast. He grieved to give up his dog and gun; he dreaded to meet his wife; but it would not do to starve among the mountains. He shook his head, shouldered the rusty firelock, and, with a heart full of trouble and anxiety, turned his steps homeward.

As he approached the village he met a number of people, but none whom he knew, which somewhat surprised him, for he had thought himself acquainted with everyone in the country round. Their dress, too, was of a different fashion from that to which he was accustomed. They all stared at him with equal marks of surprise, and whenever they cast their eyes upon him, invariably stroked their chins. The constant recurrence of this gesture induced Rip, involuntarily, to do the same, when, to his astonishment, he found his beard had grown a foot long!

He had now entered the skirts of the village. A troop of strange children ran at his heels, hooting after him, and pointing at his gray beard. The dogs, too, not one of which he recognized for an old acquaintance, barked at him as he passed. The very village was altered; it was larger and more populous. There were rows of houses which he had never seen before, and those which had been his familiar haunts had disappeared. Strange names were over the doors—strange faces at the windows—everything was strange. His mind now misgave him; he began to doubt whether both he and the world around him were not bewitched. Surely this was his native village, which he had left but the day before. There stood the Kaatskill Mountains—there ran the silver Hudson at a distance—there was every hill and dale precisely as it had always been. Rip was sorely perplexed. "That flagon last night," thought he, "has addled my poor head sadly!"

It was with some difficulty that he found the way to his own house, which he approached with silent awe, expecting every moment to hear the shrill voice of Dame Van Winkle. He found the house gone to decay—the roof fallen in, the windows shattered, and the doors off the hinges. A half-starved dog that looked like Wolf was skulking about it. Rip called him by name, but the cur snarled, showed his teeth, and passed on. This was an unkind cut indeed. "My very dog," sighed Rip, "has forgotten me!"

He entered the house, which, to tell the truth, Dame Van Winkle had always kept in neat order. It was empty, forlorn, and apparently abandoned. He called loudly for his wife and children—the lonely chambers rang for a moment with his voice, and then all again was silence.

III

He now hurried forth, and hastened to his old resort, the village inn—but it, too, was gone. A large, rickety wooden building stood in its place, with great gaping windows, some of them broken and mended with old hats and petticoats, and over the door was painted, "The Union Hotel, by Jonathan Doolittle." Instead of the great tree that used to shelter the quiet little Dutch inn of yore, there now was reared a tall, naked pole, with something on the top that looked like a red nightcap, and from it was fluttering a flag, on which was a singular assemblage of stars and stripes; all this was strange and incomprehensible. He recognized on the sign, however, the ruby face of King George, under which he had smoked so many a peaceful pipe; but even this was singularly changed. The red coat was changed for one of blue and buff, a sword was held in the hand instead of a scepter, the head was decorated with a cocked hat, and underneath was painted in large characters, GENERAL WASHINGTON.

There was, as usual, a crowd of folk about the door, but none that Rip recollected. The very character of the people seemed changed. There was a busy, bustling tone about it, instead of the accustomed drowsy tranquility. He looked in vain for the sage Nicholas Vedder, with his broad face, double chin, and long pipe, uttering clouds of tobacco smoke instead of idle speeches; or Van Bummel, the schoolmaster, doling forth the contents of an ancient newspaper. In place of these, a lean fellow, with his pockets full of handbills, was haranguing vehemently about rights of citizens—elections—members of congress—Bunker's Hill—heroes of seventy-six—and other words, which were a perfect jargon to the bewildered Van Winkle.

The appearance of Rip, with his long, grizzled beard, his rusty fowling piece, his uncouth dress, and an army of women and children at his heels, soon attracted the attention of the tavern politicians. They crowded round him, eyeing him from head to foot with great curiosity. The orator bustled up to him, and, drawing him partly aside, inquired "On which side he voted?" Rip stared in vacant stupidity. Another short but busy little fellow pulled him by the arm, and, rising on tiptoe, inquired in his ear, "Whether he was Federal or Democrat?" Rip was equally at a loss to comprehend the question; when a knowing, self-important old gentleman, in a sharp cocked hat, made his way through the crowd, putting them to the right and left with his elbows as he passed, and planting himself before Van Winkle, with one arm akimbo, the other resting on his cane, his keen eyes and sharp hat penetrating, as it were, into his very soul, demanded, in an austere tone, "What brought him to the election with a gun on his shoulder, and a mob at his heels; and whether he meant to breed a riot in the village?"—"Alas! gentlemen," cried Rip, somewhat dismayed, "I am a poor, quiet man, a native of the place, and a loyal subject of the king, God bless him!"

Here a general shout burst from the bystanders—"A tory! a tory! a spy! a refugee! hustle him! away with him!" It was with great difficulty that the self-important man in the cocked hat restored order; and having assumed a tenfold austerity of brow, demanded again of the unknown culprit, what he came there for, and whom he was seeking! The poor man humbly assured him that he meant no harm, but merely came there in search of some of his neighbors.

"Well—who are they? Name them."

Rip bethought himself a moment, and inquired, "Where's Nicholas Vedder?"

There was a silence for a little while, when an old man replied, in a thin, piping voice, "Nicholas Vedder! why, he is dead and gone these eighteen years! There was a wooden tombstone in the churchyard that used to tell all about him, but that's rotten and gone, too."

"Where's Brom Dutcher?"

"Oh, he went off to the army in the beginning of the war; some say he was killed at the storming of Stony Point; others say he was drowned in a squall at the foot of Anthony's Nose. I don't know; he never came back again."

"Where's Van Brummel, the schoolmaster?"

"He went off to the wars, too, was a great militia general, and is now in congress."

Rip's heart died away at hearing of these sad changes in his home and friends and finding himself thus alone in the world. Every answer puzzled him, too, by treating of such enormous lapses of time, and of matters which he could not understand: war—congress—Stony Point. He had no courage to ask after any more friends, but cried out in despair, "Does nobody here know Rip Van Winkle?"

"Oh, Rip Van Winkle!" exclaimed two or three, "oh, to be sure! that's Rip Van Winkle yonder, leaning against the tree."

Rip looked, and beheld a precise counterpart of himself, as he went up the mountain—apparently as lazy and certainly as ragged. The poor fellow was now completely confounded. He doubted his own identity, and whether he was himself or another man. In the midst of his bewilderment, the man in the cocked hat demanded who he was, and what was his name.

"God knows," exclaimed he, at his wits' end; "I'm not myself—I'm somebody else—that's me yonder—no—that's somebody else got into my shoes—I was myself last night, but I fell asleep on the mountain, and they've changed my gun, and everything's changed, and I'm changed, and I can't tell what's my name, or who I am!"

The bystanders began now to look at each other, nod, wink significantly, and tap their fingers against their foreheads. There was a whisper, also, about securing the gun, and keeping the old fellow from doing mischief, at the very suggestion of which the self-important man in the cocked hat retired with some precipitation. At this critical moment a fresh, comely woman pressed through the throng to get a peep at the gray-bearded man. She had a chubby child in her arms, which, frightened at his looks, began to cry. "Hush, Rip," cried she, "hush, you little fool; the old man won't hurt you." The name of the child, the air of the mother, the tone of her voice, all awakened a train of recollections in his mind. "What is your name, my good woman?" asked he.

"Judith Gardenier."

"And your father's name?"

"Ah, poor man, Rip Van Winkle was his name, but it's twenty years since he went away from home with his gun, and never has been heard of since—his dog came home without him; but whether he shot himself, or was carried away by the Indians, nobody can tell. I was then but a little girl."

Rip had but one question more to ask; but he put it with a faltering voice:

"Where's your mother?"

"Oh, she, too, had died but a short time since; she broke a blood-vessel in a fit of passion at a New England peddler."

There was a drop of comfort, at least, in this intelligence. The honest man could contain himself no longer. He caught his daughter and her child in his arms. "I am your father!" cried he—"Young Rip Van Winkle once—Old Rip Van Winkle now! Does nobody know poor Rip Van Winkle?"

All stood amazed until an old woman, tottering out from among the crowd, put her hand to her brow, and peering under it in his face for a moment, exclaimed, "Sure enough! it is Rip Van Winkle—it is himself! Welcome home again, old neighbor. Why, where have you been these twenty long years?"

Rip's story was soon told, for the whole twenty years had been to him but as one night. The neighbors stared when they heard it; some were seen to wink at each other, and put their tongues in their cheeks: and the self-important man in the cocked hat, who when the alarm was over had returned to the field, screwed down the corners of his mouth, and shook his head—upon which there was a general shaking of the head throughout the assemblage.

It was determined, however, to take the opinion of old Peter Vanderdonk, who was seen slowly advancing up the road. He was a descendant of the historian of that name, who wrote one of the earliest accounts of the province. Peter was the most ancient inhabitant of the village, and well versed in all the wonderful events and traditions of the neighborhood. He recollected Rip at once, and corroborated his story in the most satisfactory manner. He assured the company that it was a fact, handed down from his ancestor the historian, that the Kaatskill Mountains had always been haunted by strange beings. It was affirmed that the great Hendrick Hudson, the first discoverer of the river and country, kept a kind of vigil there every twenty years, with his crew of the *Half-moon;* being permitted in this way to revisit the scenes of his enterprise, and keep a guardian eye upon the river and the great city called by his name. His father had once seen them in their old Dutch dresses playing at ninepins in a hollow of the mountain; and he himself had heard, one summer afternoon, the sound of their balls, like distant peals of thunder.

To make a long story short, the company broke up and returned to the more important concerns of the election. Rip's daughter took him home to live with her; she had a snug, well-furnished house, and a stout, cheery farmer for a husband, whom Rip recollected for one of the urchins that used to climb upon his back. As to Rip's son and heir, who was the ditto of himself, seen leaning against the tree, he was employed to work on the farm; but showed an hereditary disposition to attend to anything else but his business.

"Young Goodman Brown"

NATHANIEL HAWTHORNE

Nathaniel Hawthorne (1804–1864) was born in Salem, Massachusetts, lived most of his life in the towns of Concord and Lenox, Massachusetts, and spent part of his childhood in what he later described as Maine's "primeval woods." His most discussed short story, "Young Goodman Brown," which appeared in the *New-England Magazine* in 1835, and his most widely taught novel, *The Scarlet Letter* (1850), each draw on earlier Puritan fantasies of wilderness. In Hawthorne's allegorical fiction, the New World is a dismal place of terror and temptation, and New England's dark woods are full of shadows, phantoms, and wickedness—more nightmares than dreamscapes. His story collections *Twice-Told Tales* (1837) and *Mosses from an Old Manse* (1846), along with his novels *The House of the Seven Gables* (1851), *A Romance* (1851), *The Blithedale Romance* (1852), and *The Marble Faun* (1860), further established his reputation as America's most original Gothic Romance writer. If there are demons in the woods, Hawthorne suggests in "Young Goodman Brown," they are monsters of our own making, apparitions of colonial America's most horrific moral transgressions, including the hanging of witches and the killing of Indigenous peoples. Hawthorne's richly symbolic tales repeatedly turn New England's mysterious woods into a living metaphor for the darkest recesses of the human mind. The author died suddenly in New Hampshire, where he had gone to convalesce among the White Mountains.

"Young Goodman Brown"

NATHANIEL HAWTHORNE

Young Goodman Brown came forth at sunset into the street at Salem village; but put his head back, after crossing the threshold, to exchange a parting kiss with his young wife. And Faith, as the wife was aptly named, thrust her own pretty head into the street, letting the wind play with the pink ribbons of her cap while she called to Goodman Brown.

"Dearest heart," whispered she, softly and rather sadly, when her lips were close to his ear, "prithee put off your journey until sunrise and sleep in your own bed to-night. A lone woman is troubled with such dreams and such thoughts that she's afeard of herself sometimes. Pray tarry with me this night, dear husband, of all nights in the year."

"My love and my Faith," replied young Goodman Brown, "of all nights in the year, this one night must I tarry away from thee. My journey, as thou callest it, forth and back again, must needs be done 'twixt now and sunrise. What, my sweet, pretty wife, dost thou doubt me already, and we but three months married?"

"Then God bless you!" said Faith, with the pink ribbons; "and may you find all well when you come back."

"Amen!" cried Goodman Brown. "Say thy prayers, dear Faith, and go to bed at dusk, and no harm will come to thee."

So they parted; and the young man pursued his way until, being about to turn the corner by the meeting-house, he looked back and saw the head of Faith still peeping after him with a melancholy air, in spite of her pink ribbons.

"Poor little Faith!" thought he, for his heart smote him. "What a wretch am I to leave her on such an errand! She talks of dreams, too. Methought as she spoke there was trouble in her face, as if a dream had warned her what work is to be done tonight. But no, no; 't would kill her to think it. Well, she's a blessed angel on earth; and after this one night I'll cling to her skirts and follow her to heaven."

With this excellent resolve for the future, Goodman Brown felt himself justified in making more haste on his present evil purpose. He had taken a dreary road, darkened by all the gloomiest trees of the forest, which barely stood aside to let the narrow path creep through, and closed immediately behind. It was all as lonely as could be; and there is this peculiarity in such a solitude, that the traveller knows not who may be concealed by the innumerable trunks and the thick boughs overhead; so that with lonely footsteps he may yet be passing through an unseen multitude.

"There may be a devilish Indian behind every tree," said Goodman Brown to himself; and he glanced fearfully behind him as he added, "What if the devil himself should be at my very elbow!"

His head being turned back, he passed a crook of the road, and, looking forward again, beheld the figure of a man, in grave and decent attire, seated at the foot of an old tree. He arose at Goodman Brown's approach and walked onward side by side with him.

"You are late, Goodman Brown," said he. "The clock of the Old South was striking as I came through Boston, and that is full fifteen minutes agone."

"Faith kept me back a while," replied the young man, with a tremor in his voice, caused by the sudden appearance of his companion, though not wholly unexpected.

It was now deep dusk in the forest, and deepest in that part of it where these two were journeying. As nearly as could be discerned, the second traveller was about fifty years old, apparently in the same rank of life as Goodman Brown, and bearing a considerable resemblance to him, though perhaps more in expression than features. Still they might have been taken for father and son. And yet, though the elder person was as simply clad as the younger, and as simple in manner too, he had an indescribable air of one who knew the world, and who would not have felt abashed at the governor's dinner table or in King William's court, were it possible that his affairs should call him thither. But the only thing about him that could be fixed upon as remarkable was his staff, which bore the likeness of a great black snake, so curiously wrought that it might almost be seen to twist and wriggle itself like a living serpent. This, of course, must have been an ocular deception, assisted by the uncertain light.

"Come, Goodman Brown," cried his fellow-traveller, "this is a dull pace for the beginning of a journey. Take my staff, if you are so soon weary."

"Friend," said the other, exchanging his slow pace for a full stop, "having kept covenant by meeting thee here, it is my purpose now to return whence I came. I have scruples touching the matter thou wot'st of."

"Sayest thou so?" replied he of the serpent, smiling apart. "Let us walk on, nevertheless, reasoning as we go; and if I convince thee not thou shalt turn back. We are but a little way in the forest yet."

"Too far! too far!" exclaimed the goodman, unconsciously resuming his walk. "My father never went into the woods on such an errand, nor his father before him. We have been a race of honest men and good Christians since the days of the martyrs; and shall I be the first of the name of Brown that ever took this path and kept—"

"Such company, thou wouldst say," observed the elder person, interpreting his pause. "Well said, Goodman Brown! I have been as well acquainted with your family as with ever a one among the Puritans; and that's no trifle to say. I helped your grandfather, the constable, when he lashed the Quaker woman so smartly through the streets of Salem; and it was I that brought your father a pitch-pine knot, kindled at my own hearth, to set fire to an Indian village, in King Philip's war. They were my good friends, both; and many a pleasant walk have we had along this path, and returned merrily after midnight. I would fain be friends with you for their sake."

"If it be as thou sayest," replied Goodman Brown, "I marvel they never spoke of these matters; or, verily, I marvel not, seeing that the least rumor of the sort would have driven them from New England. We are a people of prayer, and good works to boot, and abide no such wickedness."

"Wickedness or not," said the traveller with the twisted staff, "I have a very general acquaintance here in New England. The deacons of many a church have drunk the communion wine with me; the select-men of diverse towns make me their chairman; and a majority of the Great and General Court are firm supporters of my interest. The governor and I, too—but these are state secrets."

"Can this be so?" cried Goodman Brown, with a stare of amazement at his undisturbed companion. "Howbeit, I have nothing to do with the governor and council; they have their own ways, and are no rule for a simple husbandman like me. But, were I to go on with thee, how should I meet the eye of that good old man, our minister, at Salem village? Oh, his voice would make me tremble both Sabbath day and lecture day."

Thus far the elder traveller had listened with due gravity; but now burst into a fit of irrepressible mirth, shaking himself so violently that his snake-like staff actually seemed to wriggle in sympathy.

"Ha! ha! ha!" shouted he again and again; then composing himself, "Well, go on, Goodman Brown, go on; but, prithee, don't kill me with laughing."

"Well, then, to end the matter at once," said Goodman Brown, considerably nettled, "there is my wife, Faith. It would break her dear little heart; and I'd rather break my own."

"Nay, if that be the case," answered the other, "e'en go thy ways, Goodman Brown. I would not for twenty old women like the one hobbling before us that Faith should come to any harm."

As he spoke he pointed his staff at a female figure on the path, in whom Goodman Brown recognized a very pious and exemplary dame, who had taught him his catechism in youth, and was still his moral and spiritual adviser, jointly with the minister and Deacon Gookin.

"A marvel, truly, that Goody Cloyse should be so far in the wilderness at nightfall," said he. "But with your leave, friend, I shall take a cut through the woods until we have left this Christian woman behind. Being a stranger to you, she might ask whom I was consorting with and whither I was going."

"Be it so," said his fellow-traveller. "Betake you to the woods, and let me keep the path."

Accordingly the young man turned aside, but took care to watch his companion, who advanced softly along the road until he had come within a staff's length of the old dame. She, meanwhile, was making the best of her way, with singular speed for so aged a woman, and mumbling some indistinct words—a prayer, doubtless—as she went. The traveller put forth his staff and touched her withered neck with what seemed the serpent's tail.

"The devil!" screamed the pious old lady.

"Then Goody Cloyse knows her old friend?" observed the traveller, confronting her and leaning on his writhing stick.

"Ah, forsooth, and is it your worship indeed?" cried the good dame. "Yea, truly is it, and in the very image of my old gossip, Goodman Brown, the grandfather of the silly fellow that now is. But—would your worship believe it?—my broomstick hath strangely disappeared, stolen, as I suspect, by that unhanged witch, Goody Cory, and that, too, when I was all anointed with the juice of smallage, and cinquefoil, and wolf's bane."

"Mingled with fine wheat and the fat of a new-born babe," said the shape of old Goodman Brown.

"Ah, your worship knows the recipe," cried the old lady, cackling aloud. "So, as I was saying, being all ready for the meeting, and no horse to ride on, I made up my mind to foot it; for they tell me there is a nice young man to be taken into communion to-night. But now your good worship will lend me your arm, and we shall be there in a twinkling."

"That can hardly be," answered her friend. "I may not spare you my arm, Goody Cloyse; but here is my staff, if you will."

So saying, he threw it down at her feet, where, perhaps, it assumed life, being one of the rods which its owner had formerly lent to the Egyptian magi. Of this fact, however, Goodman Brown could not take cognizance. He had cast up his eyes in astonishment, and, looking down again, beheld neither Goody Cloyse nor the serpentine staff, but his fellow-traveller alone, who waited for him as calmly as if nothing had happened.

"That old woman taught me my catechism," said the young man; and there was a world of meaning in this simple comment.

They continued to walk onward, while the elder traveller exhorted his companion to make good speed and persevere in the path, discoursing so aptly that his arguments seemed rather to spring up in the bosom of his auditor than to be suggested by himself. As they went, he plucked a branch of maple to serve for a walking stick, and began to strip it of the twigs and little boughs, which were wet with evening dew. The moment his fingers touched them they became strangely withered and dried up as with a week's sunshine. Thus the pair proceeded, at a good free pace, until suddenly, in a gloomy hollow of the road, Goodman Brown sat himself down on the stump of a tree and refused to go any farther.

"Friend," said he, stubbornly, "my mind is made up. Not another step will I budge on this errand. What if a wretched old woman do choose to go to the devil when I thought she was going to heaven: is that any reason why I should quit my dear Faith and go after her?"

"You will think better of this by and by," said his acquaintance, composedly. "Sit here and rest yourself a while; and when you feel like moving again, there is my staff to help you along."

Without more words, he threw his companion the maple stick, and was as speedily out of sight as if he had vanished into the deepening gloom. The young man sat a few moments by the roadside, applauding himself greatly, and thinking with how clear a conscience he should meet the minister in his morning walk, nor shrink from the eye of good old Deacon Gookin. And what calm sleep would be his that very night, which was to have been spent so wickedly, but so purely and sweetly now, in the arms of Faith! Amidst these pleasant and praiseworthy meditations, Goodman Brown heard the tramp of horses along the road, and deemed it advisable to conceal himself within the verge of the forest, conscious of the guilty purpose that had brought him thither, though now so happily turned from it.

On came the hoof tramps and the voices of the riders, two grave old voices, conversing soberly as they drew near. These mingled sounds appeared to pass along the road, within a few yards of the young man's hiding-place; but, owing doubtless to the depth of the gloom at that particular spot, neither the travellers nor their steeds were visible. Though their figures brushed the small boughs by the wayside, it could not be seen that they intercepted, even for a moment, the faint gleam from the strip of bright sky athwart which they must have passed. Goodman Brown alternately crouched and stood on tiptoe, pulling aside the branches and thrusting forth his head as far as he durst without discerning so much as a shadow. It vexed him the more, because he could have sworn, were such a thing possible, that he recognized the voices of the minister and Deacon Gookin, jogging along quietly, as they were wont to do, when bound to some ordination or ecclesiastical council. While yet within hearing, one of the riders stopped to pluck a switch.

"Of the two, reverend sir," said the voice like the deacon's, "I had rather miss an ordination dinner than to-night's meeting. They tell me that some of our community are to be here from Falmouth and beyond, and others from Connecticut and Rhode Island, besides several of the Indian powwows, who, after their fashion, know almost as much deviltry as the best of us. Moreover, there is a goodly young woman to be taken into communion."

"Mighty well, Deacon Gookin!" replied the solemn old tones of the minister. "Spur up, or we shall be late. Nothing can be done, you know, until I get on the ground."

The hoofs clattered again; and the voices, talking so strangely in the empty air, passed on through the forest, where no church had ever been gathered or solitary Christian prayed. Whither, then, could these holy men be journeying so deep into the heathen wilderness? Young Goodman Brown caught hold of a tree for support, being ready to sink down on the ground, faint and overburdened with the heavy sickness of his heart. He looked up to the sky, doubting whether there really was a heaven above him. Yet there was the blue arch, and the stars brightening in it.

"With heaven above and Faith below, I will yet stand firm against the devil!" cried Goodman Brown.

While he still gazed upward into the deep arch of the firmament and had lifted his hands to pray, a cloud, though no wind was stirring, hurried across the zenith and hid the brightening stars. The blue sky was still visible, except directly overhead, where this black mass of cloud was sweeping swiftly northward. Aloft in the air, as if from the depths of the cloud, came a confused and doubtful sound of voices. Once the listener fancied that he could distinguish the accents of towns-people of his own, men and women, both pious and ungodly, many of whom he had met at the communion table, and had seen others rioting at the tavern. The next moment, so indistinct were the sounds, he doubted whether he had heard aught but the murmur of the old forest, whispering without a wind. Then came a stronger swell of those familiar tones, heard daily in the sunshine at Salem village, but never until now from a cloud of night. There was one voice of a young woman, uttering lamentations, yet with an uncertain sorrow, and entreating for some favor, which, perhaps, it would grieve her to obtain; and all the unseen multitude, both saints and sinners, seemed to encourage her onward.

"Faith!" shouted Goodman Brown, in a voice of agony and desperation; and the echoes of the forest mocked him, crying, "Faith! Faith!" as if bewildered wretches were seeking her all through the wilderness.

The cry of grief, rage, and terror was yet piercing the night, when the unhappy husband held his breath for a response. There was a scream, drowned immediately in a louder murmur of voices, fading into far-off laughter, as the dark cloud swept away, leaving the clear and silent sky above Goodman Brown. But something fluttered lightly down through the air and caught on the branch of a tree. The young man seized it, and beheld a pink ribbon.

"My Faith is gone!" cried he, after one stupefied moment. "There is no good on earth; and sin is but a name. Come, devil; for to thee is this world given."

And, maddened with despair, so that he laughed loud and long, did Goodman Brown grasp his staff and set forth again, at such a rate that he seemed to fly along the forest path rather than to walk or run. The road grew wilder and drearier and more faintly traced, and vanished at length, leaving him in the heart of the dark wilderness, still rushing onward with the instinct that guides mortal man to evil. The whole forest was peopled with frightful sounds—the creaking of the trees, the howling of wild beasts, and the yell of Indians; while sometimes the wind tolled like a distant church bell, and sometimes gave a broad roar around the traveller, as if all Nature were laughing him to scorn. But he was himself the chief horror of the scene, and shrank not from its other horrors.

"Ha! ha! ha!" roared Goodman Brown when the wind laughed at him.

"Let us hear which will laugh loudest. Think not to frighten me with your deviltry. Come witch, come wizard, come Indian powwow, come devil himself, and here comes Goodman Brown. You may as well fear him as he fear you."

In truth, all through the haunted forest there could be nothing more frightful than the figure of Goodman Brown. On he flew among the black pines, brandishing his staff with frenzied gestures, now giving vent to an inspiration of horrid blasphemy, and now shouting forth such laughter as set all the echoes of the forest laughing like demons around him. The fiend in his own shape is less hideous than when he rages in the breast of man. Thus sped the demoniac on his course, until, quivering among the trees, he saw a red light before him, as when the felled trunks and branches of a clearing have been set on fire, and throw up their lurid blaze against the sky, at the hour of midnight. He paused, in a lull of the tempest that had driven him onward, and heard the swell of what seemed a hymn, rolling solemnly from a distance with the weight of many voices. He knew the tune; it was a familiar one in the choir of the village meeting-house. The verse died heavily away, and was lengthened by a chorus, not of human voices, but of all the sounds of the benighted wilderness pealing in awful harmony together.

Goodman Brown cried out, and his cry was lost to his own ear by its unison with the cry of the desert.

In the interval of silence he stole forward until the light glared full upon his eyes. At one extremity of an open space, hemmed in by the dark wall of the forest, arose a rock, bearing some rude, natural resemblance either to an altar or a pulpit, and surrounded by four blazing pines, their tops aflame, their stems untouched, like candles at an evening meeting. The mass of foliage that had overgrown the summit of the rock was all on fire, blazing high into the night and fitfully illuminating the whole field. Each pendent twig and leafy festoon was in a blaze. As the red light arose and fell, a numerous congregation alternately shone forth, then disappeared in shadow, and again grew, as it were, out of the darkness, peopling the heart of the solitary woods at once.

"A grave and dark-clad company," quoth Goodman Brown.

In truth they were such. Among them, quivering to and fro between gloom and splendor, appeared faces that would be seen next day at the council board of the province, and others which, Sabbath after Sabbath, looked devoutly heavenward, and benignantly over the crowded pews, from the holiest pulpits in the land. Some affirm that the lady of the governor was there. At least there were high dames well known to her, and wives of honored husbands, and widows, a great multitude, and ancient maidens, all of excellent repute, and fair young girls, who trembled lest their mothers should espy them. Either the sudden gleams of light flashing over the obscure field bedazzled Goodman Brown, or he recognized a score of the church members of Salem village famous for their especial sanctity. Good old Deacon Gookin had arrived, and waited at the skirts of that venerable saint, his revered pastor. But, irreverently consorting with these grave, reputable, and pious people, these elders of the church, these chaste dames and dewy virgins, there were men of dissolute lives and women of spotted fame, wretches given over to all mean and filthy vice, and suspected even of horrid crimes. It was strange to see that the good shrank not from the wicked, nor were the sinners abashed by the saints. Scattered also among their pale-faced enemies were the Indian priests, or powwows, who had often scared their native forest with more hideous incantations than any known to English witchcraft.

"But where is Faith?" thought Goodman Brown; and, as hope came into his heart, he trembled.

Another verse of the hymn arose, a slow and mournful strain, such as the pious love, but joined to words which expressed all that our nature can conceive of sin, and darkly hinted at far more. Unfathomable to mere mortals is the lore of fiends. Verse after verse was sung; and still the chorus of the desert swelled between like the deepest tone of a mighty organ; and with the final peal of that dreadful anthem there came a sound, as if the roaring wind, the rushing streams, the howling beasts, and every other voice of the unconcerted wilderness were mingling and according with the voice of guilty man in homage to the prince of all. The four blazing pines threw up a loftier flame, and obscurely discovered shapes and visages of horror on the smoke wreaths above the impious assembly. At the same moment the fire on the rock shot redly forth and formed a glowing arch above its base, where now appeared a figure. With reverence be it spoken, the figure bore no slight similitude, both in garb and manner, to some grave divine of the New England churches.

"Bring forth the converts!" cried a voice that echoed through the field and rolled into the forest.

At the word, Goodman Brown stepped forth from the shadow of the trees and approached the congregation, with whom he felt a loathful brotherhood by the sympathy of all that was wicked in his heart. He could have well-nigh sworn that the shape of his own dead father beckoned him to advance, looking downward from a smoke wreath, while a woman, with dim features of despair, threw out her hand to warn him back. Was it his mother? But he had no power to retreat one step, nor to resist, even in thought, when the minister and good old Deacon Gookin seized his arms and led him to the blazing rock. Thither came also the slender form of a veiled female, led between Goody Cloyse, that pious teacher of the catechism, and Martha Carrier, who had received the devil's promise to be queen of hell. A rampant hag was she. And there stood the proselytes beneath the canopy of fire.

"Welcome, my children," said the dark figure, "to the communion of your race. Ye have found thus young your nature and your destiny. My children, look behind you!"

They turned; and flashing forth, as it were, in a sheet of flame, the fiend worshippers were seen; the smile of welcome gleamed darkly on every visage.

"There," resumed the sable form, "are all whom ye have reverenced from youth. Ye deemed them holier than yourselves, and shrank from your own sin, contrasting it with their lives of righteousness and prayer-ful aspirations heavenward. Yet here are they all in my worshipping assembly. This night it shall be granted you to know their secret deeds: how hoary-bearded elders of the church have whispered wanton words to the young maids of their households; how many a woman, eager for widows' weeds, has given her husband a drink at bedtime and let him sleep his last sleep in her bosom; how beardless youths have made haste to inherit their fathers' wealth; and how fair damsels—blush not, sweet ones—have dug little graves in the garden, and bidden me, the sole guest to an infant's funeral. By the sympathy of your human hearts for sin ye shall scent out all the places—whether in church, bedcham-ber, street, field, or forest—where crime has been committed, and shall exult to behold the whole earth one stain of guilt, one mighty blood spot. Far more than this. It shall be yours to penetrate, in every bosom, the deep mystery of sin, the fountain of all wicked arts, and which inexhaustibly supplies more evil impulses than human power—than my power at its utmost—can make manifest in deeds. And now, my children, look upon each other."

They did so; and, by the blaze of the hell-kindled torches, the wretched man beheld his Faith, and the wife her husband, trembling before that unhallowed altar.

"Lo, there ye stand, my children," said the figure, in a deep and solemn tone, almost sad with its despairing awfulness, as if his once angelic nature could yet mourn for our miserable race. "Depending upon one another's hearts, ye had still hoped that virtue were not all a dream. Now are ye undeceived. Evil is the nature of mankind. Evil must be your only happiness. Welcome again, my children, to the com-munion of your race."

"Welcome," repeated the fiend worshippers, in one cry of despair and triumph.

And there they stood, the only pair, as it seemed, who were yet hesitating on the verge of wickedness in this dark world. A basin was hollowed, naturally, in the rock. Did it contain water, reddened by the lurid light? or was it blood? or, perchance, a liquid flame? Herein did the shape of evil dip his hand and prepare to lay the mark of bap-tism upon their foreheads, that they might be partakers of the mystery of sin, more conscious of the secret guilt of others, both in deed and thought, than they could now be of their own. The husband cast one look at his pale wife, and Faith at him. What polluted wretches would the next glance show them to each other, shuddering alike at what they disclosed and what they saw!

"Faith! Faith!" cried the husband, "look up to heaven, and resist the wicked one."

Whether Faith obeyed he knew not. Hardly had he spoken when he found himself amid calm night and solitude, listening to a roar of the wind which died heavily away through the forest. He staggered against the rock, and felt it chill and damp; while a hanging twig, that had been all on fire, besprinkled his cheek with the coldest dew.

The next morning young Goodman Brown came slowly into the street of Salem village, staring around him like a bewildered man. The good old minister was taking a walk along the graveyard to get an appetite for breakfast and meditate his sermon, and bestowed a blessing, as he passed, on Goodman Brown. He shrank from the venerable saint as if to avoid an anathema. Old Deacon Gookin was at domestic worship, and the holy words of his prayer were heard through the open window. "What God doth the wizard pray to?" quoth Goodman Brown. Goody Cloyse, that excellent old Christian, stood in the early sunshine at her own lattice, catechizing a little girl who had brought her a pint of morning's milk. Goodman Brown snatched away the child as from the grasp of the fiend himself. Turning the corner by the meeting-house, he spied the head of Faith, with the pink ribbons, gazing anxiously forth, and bursting into such joy at sight of him that she skipped along the street and almost kissed her husband before the whole village. But Goodman Brown looked sternly and sadly into her face, and passed on without a greeting.

Had Goodman Brown fallen asleep in the forest and only dreamed a wild dream of a witch-meeting?

Be it so if you will; but, alas! it was a dream of evil omen for young Goodman Brown. A stern, a sad, a darkly meditative, a distrustful, if not a desperate man did he become from the night of that fearful dream. On the Sabbath day, when the congregation were singing a holy psalm, he could not listen because an anthem of sin rushed loudly upon his ear and drowned all the blessed strain. When the minister spoke from the pulpit with power and fervid eloquence, and, with his hand on the open Bible, of the sacred truths of our religion, and of saint-like lives and triumphant deaths, and of future bliss or misery unutterable, then did Goodman Brown turn pale, dreading lest the roof should thunder down upon the gray blasphemer and his hearers. Often, waking suddenly at midnight, he shrank from the bosom of Faith; and at morning or eventide, when the family knelt down at prayer, he scowled and muttered to himself, and gazed sternly at his wife, and turned away. And when he had lived long, and was borne to his grave a hoary corpse, followed by Faith, an aged woman, and children and grandchildren, a goodly procession, besides neighbors not a few, they carved no hopeful verse upon his tombstone, for his dying hour was gloom.

"The Heroic Slave"

FREDERICK DOUGLASS

Frederick Douglass (1818–1895) was born into slavery, near Tucka-hoe Creek in Talbot County, Maryland, and became the most renowned Black abolitionist and orator of the nineteenth century. After the failure of an early plan to escape north to freedom on foot, Douglass finally succeeded in 1838, disguised as a sailor, eventually reaching New York by train, ferry, and steamboat. In Massachusetts he became a preacher and a lecturer, and in Rochester, New York, a newspaperman. He founded *Frederick Douglass's Paper* (formerly the *North Star*) where his story "The Heroic Slave" appeared in serialized form in 1853, after its initial appearance the same year in Julia Griffiths's abolitionist anthology *Autographs for Freedom*. By then Douglass was a respected antislavery writer, author of *Narrative of the Life of Frederick Douglass* (1845), an autobiography of his childhood years and escape from slavery that he later expounded on in two more memoirs, *My Bondage and My Freedom* (1855) and *Life and Times of Frederick Douglass* (1881, rev. 1892). "The Heroic Slave," the only short story the antislavery reformer wrote, is a partly fictionalized account of the extraordinary real-life Madison Washington, a freedom seeker like Douglass and the leader of a successful 1841 slave-ship rebellion. Douglass greatly admired Madison Washington and wanted to spread the word of his heroism: his daring escape to Canada, his later thwarted attempt to rescue the wife and child he left behind in Virginia, his recapture by slave traders who put him on the slave ship *Creole* to be sold at a New Orleans slave market, and his dramatic role in commandeering the ship and sailing it to the Bahamas, where Madison and other enslaved Africans eventually secured their freedom. Douglass's absorbing journey narrative, composed of four parts, accompanies its hero into forest and swamp, through fire and hurricane, across lake and ocean, in a yearslong quest for freedom. Excerpted here, from parts one and two, is Madison's tale of his time in Virginia's Great Dismal Swamp, a forested wetlands that, despite its dangers, had long served as a refuge, and even a home, for individuals escaping bondage.

"The Heroic Slave"

FREDERICK DOUGLASS

In the spring of 1835, on a Sabbath morning, within hearing of the solemn peals of the church bells at a distant village, a Northern traveller through the State of Virginia drew up his horse to drink at a sparkling brook, near the edge of a dark pine forest. While his weary and thirsty steed drew in the grateful water, the rider caught the sound of a human voice, apparently engaged in earnest conversation.

Following the direction of the sound, he descried, among the tall pines, the man whose voice had arrested his attention. "To whom can he be speaking?" thought the traveller. "He seems to be alone." The circumstance interested him much, and he became intensely curious to know what thoughts and feelings, or, it might be, high aspirations, guided those rich and mellow accents. Tieing his horse at a short distance from the brook, he stealthily drew near the solitary speaker; and, concealing himself by the side of a huge fallen tree, he distinctly heard the following soliloquy:—

"What, then, is life to me? it is aimless and worthless, and worse than worthless. Those birds, perched on yon swinging boughs, in friendly conclave, sounding forth their merry notes in seeming worship of the rising sun, though liable to the sportsman's fowling-piece, are still my superiors. They *live free,* though they may die slaves. They fly where they list by day, and retire in freedom at night. But what is freedom to me, or I to it? I am a *slave,*—born a slave, an abject slave,—even before I made part of this breathing world, the scourge was platted for my back; the fetters were forged for my limbs. How mean a thing am I. That accursed and crawling snake, that miserable reptile, that has just glided into its slimy home, is freer and better off than I. He escaped my blow, and is safe. But here am I, a man,—yes, *a man!*—with thoughts and wishes, with powers and faculties as far as angel's flight above that hated reptile,—yet he is my superior, and scorns to own me as his master, or to stop to take my blows. When he saw my uplifted arm, he darted beyond my reach, and turned to give me battle. I dare not do as much as that. I neither run nor fight, but do meanly stand, answering each heavy blow of a cruel master with doleful wails and piteous cries. I am galled with irons; but even these are more tolerable than the consciousness, the *galling* consciousness of cowardice and indecision. Can it be that I *dare* not run away? *Perish the thought,* I *dare* do any thing which may be done by another. When that young man struggled with the waves *for life,* and others stood back appalled in helpless horror, did I not plunge in, forgetful of life, to save his? The raging bull from whom all others fled, pale with fright, did I not keep at bay with a single pitchfork? Could a coward do that? *No,—no,—*I wrong myself,—I am no coward. *Liberty* I will have, or die in the attempt to gain it. This working that others may live in idleness! This cringing submission to insolence and curses! This living under the constant dread and apprehension of being sold and transferred, like a mere brute, is *too* much for me. I will stand it no longer. What others have done, I will do. These trusty legs, or these sinewy arms shall place me among the free. Tom escaped; so can I. The North Star will not be less kind to me than to him. I will follow it. I will at least make the trial. I have nothing to lose. If I am caught, I shall only be a slave. If I am shot, I shall only lose a life which is a burden and a curse. If I get clear, (as something tells me I shall,) liberty, the inalienable birth-right of every man, precious and priceless, will be mine. My resolution is fixed. *I shall be free.*"

At these words the traveller raised his head cautiously and noiselessly, and caught, from his hiding-place, a full view of the unsuspecting speaker. Madison (for that was the name of our hero) was standing erect, a smile of satisfaction rippled upon his expressive countenance, like that which plays upon the face of one who has but just solved a difficult problem, or vanquished a malignant foe; for at that moment he was free, at least in spirit. The future gleamed brightly before him, and his fetters lay broken at his feet. His air was triumphant.

Madison was of manly form. Tall, symmetrical, round, and strong. In his movements he seemed to combine, with the strength of the lion, a lion's elasticity. His torn sleeves disclosed arms like polished iron. His face was "black, but comely." His eye, lit with emotion, kept guard under a brow as dark and as glossy as the raven's wing. His whole appearance betokened Herculean strength; yet there was nothing savage or forbidding in his aspect. A child might play in his arms, or dance on his shoulders. A giant's strength, but not a giant's heart was in him. His broad mouth and nose spoke only of good nature and kindness.

But his voice, that unfailing index of the soul, though full and melodious, had that in it which could terrify as well as charm. He was just the man you would choose when hardships were to be endured, or danger to be encountered,—intelligent and brave. He had the head to conceive, and the hand to execute. In a word, he was one to be sought as a friend, but to be dreaded as an enemy.

As our traveller gazed upon him, he almost trembled at the thought of his dangerous intrusion. Still he could not quit the place. He had long desired to sound the mysterious depths of the thoughts and feelings of a slave. He was not, therefore, disposed to allow so providential an opportunity to pass unimproved. He resolved to hear more; so he listened again for those mellow and mournful accents which, he says, made such an impression upon him as can never be erased. He did not have to wait long. There came another gush from the same full fountain; now bitter, and now sweet. Scathing denunciations of the cruelty and injustice of slavery; heart-touching narrations of his own personal suffering, intermingled with prayers to the God of the oppressed for help and deliverance, were followed by presentations of the dangers and difficulties of escape, and formed the burden of his eloquent utterances; but his high resolution clung to him,—for he ended each speech by an emphatic declaration of his purpose to be free. It seemed that the very repetition of this, imparted a glow to his countenance. The hope of freedom seemed to sweeten, for a season, the bitter cup of slavery, and to make it, for a time, tolerable; for when in the very whirlwind of anguish,—when his heart's cord seemed screwed up to snapping tension, hope sprung up and soothed his troubled spirit. Fitfully he would exclaim, "How can I leave her? Poor thing! what can she do when I am gone? Oh! oh! 't is impossible that I can leave poor Susan!"

A brief pause intervened. Our traveller raised his head, and saw again the sorrow-smitten slave. His eye was fixed upon the ground. The strong man staggered under a heavy load. Recovering himself, he argued thus aloud: "All is uncertain here. To-morrow's sun may not rise before I am sold, and separated from her I love. What, then, could I do for her? I should be in more hopeless slavery, and she no nearer to liberty,—whereas if I were free,—my arms my own,—I might devise the means to rescue her."

This said, Madison cast around a searching glance, as if the thought of being overheard had flashed across his mind. He said no more, but, with measured steps, walked away, and was lost to the eye of our travel-ler amidst the wildering woods.

Long after Madison had left the ground, Mr. Listwell (our travel-ler) remained in motionless silence, meditating on the extraordinary revelations to which he had listened. He seemed fastened to the spot, and stood half hoping, half fearing the return of the sable preacher to his solitary temple. The speech of Madison rung through the cham-bers of his soul, and vibrated through his entire frame. "Here is indeed a man," thought he, "of rare endowments,—a child of God,—guilty of no crime but the color of his skin,—hiding away from the face of humanity, and pouring out his thoughts and feelings, his hopes and res-olutions to the lonely woods; to him those distant church bells have no grateful music. He shuns the church, the altar, and the great congrega-tion of christian worshippers, and wanders away to the gloomy forest, to utter in the vacant air complaints and griefs, which the religion of his times and his country can neither console nor relieve. Goaded almost to madness by the sense of the injustice done him, he resorts hither to give to his pent up feelings, and to debate with himself the feasibility of plans, plans of his own invention, for his own deliverance. From this hour I am an abolitionist. I have seen enough and heard enough, and I shall go to my home in Ohio resolved to atone for my past indifference to this ill-starred race, by making such exertions as I shall be able to do, for the speedy emancipation of every slave in the land."

Five years after the foregoing singular occurrence, in the winter of 1840, Mr. and Mrs. Listwell sat together by the fireside of their own happy home, in the State of Ohio. The children were all gone to bed. A sin-gle lamp burnt brightly on the centre table. All was still and comfort-able within; but the night was cold and dark; a heavy wind sighed and moaned sorrowfully around the house and barn, occasionally bring-ing against the clattering windows a stray leaf from the large oak trees that embowered their dwelling. It was a night for strange noises and for strange fancies. A whole wilderness of thought might pass through one's mind during such an evening. The smouldering embers, partak-ing of the spirit of the restless night, became fruitful of varied and fan-tastic pictures, and revived many bygone scenes and old impressions. The happy pair seemed to sit in silent fascination, gazing on the fire.

Suddenly this *reverie* was interrupted by a heavy growl. Ordinarily such an occurrence would have scarcely provoked a single word, or excited the least apprehension. But there are certain seasons when the slightest sound sends a jar through all the subtle chambers of the mind; and such a season was this. The happy pair started up, as if some sudden danger had come upon them. The growl was from their trusty watch-dog.

"What can it mean? certainly no one can be out on such a night as this," said Mrs. Listwell.

"The wind has deceived the dog, my dear; he has mistaken the noise of falling branches, brought down by the wind, for that of the footsteps of persons coming to the house. I have several times to-night thought that I heard the sound of footsteps. I am sure, however, that it was but the wind. Friends would not be likely to come out at such an hour, or such a night; and thieves are too lazy and self-indulgent to expose themselves to this biting frost; but should there be any one about, our brave old Monte, who is on the lookout, will not be slow in sounding the alarm."

Saying this they quietly left the window, whither they had gone to learn the cause of the menacing growl, and re-seated themselves by the fire, as if reluctant to leave the slowly expiring embers, although the hour was late. A few minutes only intervened after resuming their seats, when again their sober meditations were disturbed. Their faithful dog now growled and barked furiously, as if assailed by an advancing foe. Simultaneously the good couple arose, and stood in mute expectation. The contest without seemed fierce and violent. It was, however, soon over,—the barking ceased, for, with true canine instinct, Monte quickly discovered that a friend, not an enemy of the family, was coming to the house, and instead of rushing to repel the supposed intruder, he was now at the door, whimpering and dancing for the admission of himself and his newly made friend.

Mr. Listwell knew by this movement that all was well; he advanced and opened the door, and saw by the light that streamed out into the darkness, a tall man advancing slowly towards the house, with a stick in one hand, and a small bundle in the other. "It is a traveller," thought he, "who has missed his way, and is coming to inquire the road. I am glad we did not go to bed earlier,—I have felt all the evening as if somebody would be here to-night."

The man had now halted a short distance from the door, and looked prepared alike for flight or battle. "Come in, sir, don't be alarmed, you have probably lost your way."

Slightly hesitating, the traveller walked in; not, however, without regarding his host with a scrutinizing glance. "No, sir," said he, "I have come to ask you a greater favor."

Instantly Mr. Listwell exclaimed, (as the recollection of the Virginia forest scene flashed upon him,) "Oh, sir, I know not your name, but I have seen your face, and heard your voice before. I am glad to see you. *I know all.* You are flying for your liberty,—be seated,—be seated,—banish all fear. You are safe under my roof."

This recognition, so unexpected, rather disconcerted and disquieted the noble fugitive. The timidity and suspicion of persons escaping from slavery are easily awakened, and often what is intended to dispel the one, and to allay the other, has precisely the opposite effect. It was so in this case. Quickly observing the unhappy impression made by his words and action, Mr. Listwell assumed a more quiet and inquiring aspect, and finally succeeded in removing the apprehensions which his very natural and generous salutation had aroused.

Thus assured, the stranger said, "Sir, you have rightly guessed, I am, indeed, a fugitive from slavery. My name is Madison,—Madison Washington my mother used to call me. I am on my way to Canada, where I learn that persons of my color are protected in all the rights of men; and my object in calling upon you was, to beg the privilege of resting my weary limbs for the night in your barn. It was my purpose to have continued my journey till morning; but the piercing cold, and the frowning darkness compelled me to seek shelter; and, seeing a light through the lattice of your window, I was encouraged to come here to beg the privilege named. You will do me a great favor by affording me shelter for the night."

"A resting-place, indeed, sir, you shall have; not, however, in my barn, but in the best room of my house. Consider yourself, if you please, under the roof of a friend; for such I am to you, and to all your deeply injured race."

While this introductory conversation was going on, the kind lady had revived the fire, and was diligently preparing supper; for she, not less than her husband, felt for the sorrows of the oppressed and hunted ones of earth, and was always glad of an opportunity to do them a service. A bountiful repast was quickly prepared, and the hungry and toil-worn bondman was cordially invited to partake thereof. Gratefully he acknowledged the favor of his benevolent benefactress; but appeared scarcely to understand what such hospitality could mean. It was the first time in his life that he had met so humane and friendly a greeting at the hands of persons whose color was unlike his own; yet it was impossible for him to doubt the charitableness of his new friends, or the genuineness of the welcome so freely given; and he therefore, with many thanks, took his seat at the table with Mr. and Mrs. Listwell, who, desirous to make him feel at home, took a cup of tea themselves, while urging upon Madison the best that the house could afford.

Supper over, all doubts and apprehensions banished, the three drew around the blazing fire, and a conversation commenced which lasted till long after midnight.

"Now," said Madison to Mr. Listwell, "I was a little surprised and alarmed when I came in, by what you said; do tell me, sir, *why* you thought you had seen my face before, and by what you knew me to be a fugitive from slavery; for I am sure that I never was before in this neighborhood, and I certainly sought to conceal what I supposed to be the manner of a fugitive slave."

Mr. Listwell at once frankly disclosed the secret; describing the place where he first saw him; rehearsing the language which he (Madison) had used; referring to the effect which his manner and speech had made upon him; declaring the resolution he there formed to be an abolitionist; telling how often he had spoken of the circumstance, and the deep concern he had ever since felt to know what had become of him; and whether he had carried out the purpose to make his escape, as in the woods he declared he would do.

"Ever since that morning," said Mr. Listwell, "you have seldom been absent from my mind, and though now I did not dare to hope that I should ever see you again, I have often wished that such might be my fortune; for, from that hour, your face seemed to be daguerreotyped on my memory."

Madison looked quite astonished, and felt amazed at the narration to which he had listened. After recovering himself he said, "I well remember that morning, and the bitter anguish that wrung my heart; I will state the occasion of it. I had, on the previous Saturday, suffered a cruel lashing; had been tied up to the limb of a tree, with my feet chained together, and a heavy iron bar placed between my ankles. Thus suspended, I received on my naked back forty stripes, and was kept in this distressing position three or four hours, and was then let down, only to have my torture increased; for my bleeding back, gashed by the cow-skin, was washed by the overseer with old brine, partly to augment my suffering, and partly, as he said, to prevent inflammation. My crime was that I had stayed longer at the mill, the day previous, than it was thought I ought to have done, which, I assured my master and the overseer, was no fault of mine; but no excuses were allowed. 'Hold your tongue, you impudent rascal,' met my every explanation. Slaveholders are so imperious when their passions are excited, as to construe every word of the slave into insolence. I could do nothing but submit to the agonizing infliction. Smarting still from the wounds, as well as from the consciousness of being whipt for no cause, I took advantage of the absence of my master, who had gone to church, to spend the time in the woods, and brood over my wretched lot. Oh, sir, I remember it well,—and can never forget it."

"But this was five years ago; where have you been since?"

"I will try to tell you," said Madison. "Just four weeks after that Sabbath morning, I gathered up the few rags of clothing I had, and started, as I supposed, for the North and for freedom. I must not stop to describe my feelings on taking this step. It seemed like taking a leap into the dark. The thought of leaving my poor wife and two little children caused me indescribable anguish; but consoling myself with the reflection that once free, I could, possibly, devise ways and means to gain their freedom also, I nerved myself up to make the attempt. I started, but ill-luck attended me; for after being out a whole week, strange to say, I still found myself on my master's grounds; the third night after being out, a season of clouds and rain set in, wholly preventing me from seeing the North Star, which I had trusted as my guide, not dreaming that clouds might intervene between us.

"This circumstance was fatal to my project, for in losing my star, I lost my way; so when I supposed I was far towards the North, and had almost gained my freedom, I discovered myself at the very point from which I had started. It was a severe trial, for I arrived at home in great destitution; my feet were sore, and in travelling in the dark, I had dashed my foot against a stump, and started a nail, and lamed myself. I was wet and cold; one week had exhausted all my stores; and when I landed on my master's plantation, with all my work to do over again,—

hungry, tired, lame, and bewildered,—I almost cursed the day that I was born. In this extremity I approached the quarters. I did so stealthily, although in my desperation I hardly cared whether I was discovered or not. Peeping through the rents of the quarters, I saw my fellow-slaves seated by a warm fire, merrily passing away the time, as though their hearts knew no sorrow. Although I envied their seeming contentment, all wretched as I was, I despised the cowardly acquiescence in their own degradation which it implied, and felt a kind of pride and glory in my own desperate lot. I dared not enter the quarters,—for where there is seeming contentment with slavery, there is certain treachery to freedom. I proceeded towards the great house, in the hope of catching a glimpse of my poor wife, whom I knew might be trusted with my secrets even on the scaffold. Just as I reached the fence which divided the field from the garden, I saw a woman in the yard, who in the darkness I took to be my wife; but a nearer approach told me it was not she. I was about to speak; had I done so, I would not have been here this night; for an alarm would have been sounded, and the hunters been put on my track. Here were hunger, cold, thirst, disappointment, and chagrin, confronted only by the dim hope of liberty. I tremble to think of that dreadful hour. To face the deadly cannon's mouth in warm blood unterrified, is, I think, a small achievement, compared with a conflict like this with gaunt starvation. The gnawings of hunger conquers by degrees, till all that a man has he would give in exchange for a single crust of bread. Thank God, I was not quite reduced to this extremity.

"Happily for me, before the fatal moment of utter despair, my good wife made her appearance in the yard. It was she; I knew her step. All was well now. I was, however, afraid to speak, lest I should frighten her. Yet speak I did; and, to my great joy, my voice was known. Our meeting can be more easily imagined than described. For a time hunger, thirst, weariness, and lameness were forgotten. But it was soon necessary for her to return to the house. She being a house-servant, her absence from the kitchen, if discovered, might have excited suspicion. Our parting was like tearing the flesh from my bones; yet it was the part of wisdom for her to go. She left me with the purpose of meeting me at midnight in the very forest where you last saw me. She knew the place well, as one of my melancholy resorts, and could easily find it, though the night was dark.

"I hastened away, therefore, and concealed myself, to await the arrival of my good angel. As I lay there among the leaves, I was strongly tempted to return again to the house of my master and give myself up; but remembering my solemn pledge on that memorable Sunday morning, I was able to linger out the two long hours between ten and midnight. I may well call them long hours. I have endured much hardship; I have encountered many perils; but the anxiety of those two hours, was the bitterest I ever experienced. True to her word, my wife came laden with provisions, and we sat down on the side of a log, at that dark and lonesome hour of the night. I cannot say we talked; our feelings were too great for that; yet we came to an understanding that I should make the woods my home, for if I gave myself up, I should be whipped and sold away; and if I started for the North, I should leave a wife doubly dear to me. We mutually determined, therefore, that I should remain in the vicinity. In the dismal swamps I lived, sir, five long years,—a cave for my home during the day. I wandered about at night with the wolf and the bear,—sustained by the promise that my good Susan would meet me in the pine woods at least once a week. This promise was redeemed, I assure you, to the letter, greatly to my relief. I had partly become contented with my mode of life, and had made up my mind to spend my days there; but the wilderness that sheltered me thus long took fire, and refused longer to be my hiding-place.

"I will not harrow up your feelings by portraying the terrific scene of this awful conflagration. There is nothing to which I can liken it. It was horribly and indescribably grand. The whole world seemed on fire, and it appeared to me that the day of judgment had come; that the burning bowels of the earth had burst forth, and that the end of all things was at hand. Bears and wolves, scorched from their mysterious hiding-places in the earth, and all the wild inhabitants of the untrodden forest, filled with a common dismay, ran forth, yelling, howling, bewildered amidst the smoke and flame. The very heavens seemed to rain down fire through the towering trees; it was by the merest chance that I escaped the devouring element. Running before it, and stopping occasionally to take breath, I looked back to behold its frightful ravages, and to drink in its savage magnificence. It was awful, thrilling, solemn, beyond compare. When aided by the fitful wind, the merciless tempest of fire swept on, sparkling, creaking, cracking, curling, roaring, outdoing in its dreadful splendor a thousand thunderstorms at once. From tree to tree it leaped, swallowing them up in its lurid, baleful glare; and leaving them leafless, limbless, charred, and lifeless behind. The scene was overwhelming, stunning,—nothing was spared,—cattle, tame and wild, herds of swine and of deer, wild beasts of every name and kind,— huge night-birds, bats, and owls, that had retired to their homes in lofty tree-tops to rest, perished in that fiery storm. The long-winged buzzard and croaking raven mingled their dismal cries with those of the count- less myriads of small birds that rose up to the skies, and were lost to the sight in clouds of smoke and flame. Oh, I shudder when I think of it! Many a poor wandering fugitive, who, like myself, had sought among wild beasts the mercy denied by our fellow men, saw, in helpless consternation, his dwelling-place and city of refuge reduced to ashes forever. It was this grand conflagration that drove me hither; I ran alike from fire and from slavery."

After a slight pause, (for both speaker and hearers were deeply moved by the above recital,) Mr. Listwell, addressing Madison, said, "If it does not weary you too much, do tell us something of your journey- ings since this disastrous burning,—we are deeply interested in every- thing which can throw light on the hardships of persons escaping from slavery; we could hear you talk all night; are there no incidents that you could relate of your travels hither? or are they such that you do not like to mention them."

"For the most part, sir, my course has been uninterrupted; and, considering the circumstances, at times even pleasant. I have suffered little for want of food; but I need not tell you how I got it. Your moral code may differ from mine, as your customs and usages are different. The fact is, sir, during my flight, I felt myself robbed by society of all my just rights; that I was in an enemy's land, who sought both my life and my liberty. They had transformed me into a brute; made merchan- dise of my body, and, for all the purposes of my flight, turned day into night,—and guided by my own necessities, and in contempt of their conventionalities, I did not scruple to take bread where I could get it."

"And just there you were right," said Mr. Listwell; "I once had doubts on this point myself, but a conversation with Gerrit Smith, (a man, by the way, that I wish you could see, for he is a devoted friend of your race, and I know he would receive you gladly,) put an end to all my doubts on this point. But do not let me interrupt you."

"I had but one narrow escape during my whole journey," said Madison.

"Do let us hear of it," said Mr. Listwell.

"Two weeks ago," continued Madison, "after travelling all night, I was overtaken by daybreak, in what seemed to me an almost interminable wood. I deemed it unsafe to go farther, and, as usual, I looked around for a suitable tree in which to spend the day. I liked one with a bushy top, and found one just to my mind. Up I climbed, and hiding myself as well as I could, I, with this strap, (pulling one out of his old coat-pocket,) lashed myself to a bough, and flattered myself that I should get a *good night's* sleep that day; but in this I was soon disappointed. I had scarcely got fastened to my natural hammock, when I heard the voices of a number of persons, apparently approaching the part of the woods where I was. Upon my word, sir, I dreaded more these human voices than I should have done those of wild beasts. I was at a loss to know what to do. If I descended, I should probably be discovered by the men; and if they had dogs I should, doubtless, be *'treed.'* It was an anxious moment, but hardships and dangers have been the accompaniments of my life; and have, perhaps, imparted to me a certain hardness of character, which, to some extent, adapts me to them. In my present predicament, I decided to hold my place in the tree-top, and abide the consequences. But here I must disappoint you; for the men, who were all colored, halted at least a hundred yards from me, and began with their axes, in right good earnest, to attack the trees. The sound of their laughing axes was like the report of as many well-charged pistols. By and by there came down at least a dozen trees with a terrible crash. They leaped upon the fallen trees with an air of victory. I could see no dog with them, and felt myself comparatively safe, though I could not forget the possibility that some freak or fancy might bring the axe a little nearer my dwelling than comported with my safety.

"There was no sleep for me that day, and I wished for night. You may imagine that the thought of having the tree attacked under me was far from agreeable, and that it very easily kept me on the look-out. The day was not without diversion. The men at work seemed to be a gay set; and they would often make the woods resound with that uncontrolled laughter for which we, as a race, are remarkable. I held my place in the tree till sunset,—saw the men put on their jackets to be off. I observed that all left the ground except one, whom I saw sitting on the side of a stump, with his head bowed, and his eyes apparently fixed on the ground. I became interested in him. After sitting in the position to which I have alluded ten or fifteen minutes, he left the stump, walked directly towards the tree in which I was secreted, and halted almost under the same. He stood for a moment and looked around, deliberately and reverently took off his hat, by which I saw that he was a man in the evening of life, slightly bald and quite gray. After laying down his hat carefully, he knelt and prayed aloud, and such a prayer, the most fervent, earnest, and solemn, to which I think I ever listened. After reverently addressing the Almighty, as the all-wise, all-good, and the common Father of all mankind, he besought God for grace, for strength, to bear up under, and to endure, as a good soldier, all the hardships and trials which beset the journey of life, and to enable him to live in a manner which accorded with the gospel of Christ. His soul now broke out in humble supplication for deliverance from bondage. 'O thou,' said he, 'that hearest the raven's cry, take pity on poor me! O deliver me! O deliver me! in mercy, O God, deliver me from the chains and manifold hardships of slavery! With thee, O Father, all things are possible. Thou canst stand and measure the earth. Thou hast beheld and drove asunder the nations,—all power is in thy hand,—thou didst say of old, "I have seen the affliction of my people, and am come to deliver them,"—Oh look down upon our afflictions, and have mercy upon us.' But I cannot repeat his prayer, nor can I give you an idea of its deep pathos. I had given but little attention to religion, and had but little faith in it; yet, as the old man prayed, I felt almost like coming down and kneel by his side, and mingle my broken complaint with his.

"He had already gained my confidence; as how could it be otherwise? I knew enough of religion to know that the man who prays in secret is far more likely to be sincere than he who loves to pray standing in the street, or in the great congregation. When he arose from his knees, like another Zacheus, I came down from the tree. He seemed a little alarmed at first, but I told him my story, and the good man embraced me in his arms, and assured me of his sympathy.

"I was now about out of provisions, and thought I might safely ask him to help me replenish my store. He said he had no money; but if he had, he would freely give it me. I told him I had *one dollar;* it was all the money I had in the world. I gave it to him, and asked him to purchase some crackers and cheese, and to kindly bring me the balance; that I would remain in or near that place, and would come to him on his return, if he would whistle. He was gone only about an hour. Meanwhile, from some cause or other, I know not what, (but as you shall see very wisely,) I changed my place. On his return I started to meet him; but it seemed as if the shadow of approaching danger fell upon my spirit, and checked my progress. In a very few minutes, closely on the heels of the old man, I distinctly saw *fourteen men,* with something like guns in their hands."

"Oh! the old wretch!" exclaimed Mrs. Listwell, "he had betrayed you, had he?"

"I think not," said Madison, "I cannot believe that the old man was to blame. He probably went into a store, asked for the articles for which I sent, and presented the bill I gave him; and it is so unusual for slaves in the country to have money, that fact, doubtless, excited suspicion, and gave rise to inquiry. I can easily believe that the truthfulness of the old man's character compelled him to disclose the facts; and thus were these blood-thirsty men put on my track. Of course I did not present myself; but hugged my hiding-place securely. If discovered and attacked, I resolved to sell my life as dearly as possible.

"After searching about the woods silently for a time, the whole company gathered around the old man; one charged him with lying, and called him an old villain; said he was a thief; charged him with stealing money; said if he did not instantly tell where he got it, they would take the shirt from his old back, and give him thirty-nine lashes.

"'I did *not* steal the money,' said the old man, 'it was given me, as I told you at the store; and if the man who gave it me is not here, it is not my fault.'

"'Hush! you lying old rascal; we'll make you smart for it. You shall not leave this spot until you have told where you got that money.'

"They now took hold of him, and began to strip him; while others went to get sticks with which to beat him. I felt, at the moment, like rushing out in the midst of them; but considering that the old man would be whipped the more for having aided a fugitive slave, and that, perhaps, in the *melée* he might be killed outright, I disobeyed this impulse. They tied him to a tree, and began to whip him. My own flesh crept at every blow, and I seem to hear the old man's piteous cries even now. They laid thirty-nine lashes on his bare back, and were going to repeat that number, when one of the company besought his comrades to desist. 'You'll kill the d—d old scoundrel! You've already whipt a dollar's worth out of him, even if he stole it!' 'O yes,' said another, 'let him down. He'll never tell us another lie, I'll warrant ye!' With this, one of the company untied the old man, and bid him go about his business.

"The old man left, but the company remained as much as an hour, scouring the woods. Round and round they went, turning up the underbrush, and peering about like so many bloodhounds. Two or three times they came within six feet of where I lay. I tell you I held my stick with a firmer grasp than I did in coming up to your house tonight. I expected to level one of them at least. Fortunately, however, I eluded their pursuit, and they left me alone in the woods.

"My last dollar was now gone, and you may well suppose I felt the loss of it; but the thought of being once again free to pursue my journey, prevented that depression which a sense of destitution causes; so swinging my little bundle on my back, I caught a glimpse of the *Great Bear* (which ever points the way to my beloved star,) and I started again on my journey. What I lost in money I made up at a hen-roost that same night, upon which I fortunately came."

"But you did'nt eat your food raw? How did you cook it?" said Mrs. Listwell.

"O no, Madam," said Madison, turning to his little bundle;—"I had the means of cooking." Here he took out of his bundle an old-fashioned tinder-box, and taking up a piece of a file, which he brought with him, he struck it with a heavy flint, and brought out at least a dozen sparks at once. "I have had this old box," said he, "more than five years. It is the *only* property saved from the fire in the dismal swamp. It has done me good service. It has given me the means of broiling many a chicken!"

It seemed quite a relief to Mrs. Listwell to know that Madison had, at least, lived upon cooked food. Women have a perfect horror of eating uncooked food.

By this time thoughts of what was best to be done about getting Madison to Canada, began to trouble Mr. Listwell; for the laws of Ohio were very stringent against any one who should aid, or who were found aiding a slave to escape through that State. A citizen, for the simple act of taking a fugitive slave in his carriage, had just been stripped of all his property, and thrown penniless upon the world. Notwithstanding this, Mr. Listwell was determined to see Madison safely on his way to Canada. "Give yourself no uneasiness," said he to Madison, "for if it cost my farm, I shall see you safely out of the States, and on your way to a land of liberty. Thank God that there is *such* a land so near us! You will spend to-morrow with us, and to-morrow night I will take you in my carriage to the Lake. Once upon that, and you are safe."

"Thank you! thank you," said the fugitive; "I will commit myself to your care."

For the *first* time during *five* years, Madison enjoyed the luxury of resting his limbs on a comfortable bed, and inside a human habitation. Looking at the white sheets, he said to Mr. Listwell, "What, sir! you don't mean that I shall sleep in that bed?"

"Oh yes, oh yes."

After Mr. Listwell left the room, Madison said he really hesitated whether or not he should lie on the floor; for that was *far* more comfortable and inviting than any bed to which he had been used.

We pass over the thoughts and feelings, the hopes and fears, the plans and purposes, that revolved in the mind of Madison during the day that he was secreted at the house of Mr. Listwell. The reader will be content to know that nothing occurred to endanger his liberty, or to excite alarm. Many were the little attentions bestowed upon him in his quiet retreat and hiding-place. In the evening, Mr. Listwell, after treating Madison to a new suit of winter clothes, and replenishing his exhausted purse with five dollars, all in silver, brought out his two-horse wagon, well provided with buffaloes, and silently started off with him to Cleveland. They arrived there without interruption, a few minutes before sunrise the next morning. Fortunately the steamer *Admiral* lay at the wharf, and was to start for Canada at nine o'clock. Here the last anticipated danger was surmounted. It was feared that just at this point the hunters of men might be on the look-out, and, possibly, pounce upon their victim. Mr. Listwell saw the captain of the boat; cautiously sounded him on the matter of carrying liberty-loving passengers, before he introduced his precious charge. This done, Madison was conducted on board. With usual generosity this true subject of the emancipating queen welcomed Madison, and assured him that he should be safely landed in Canada, free of charge. Madison now felt himself no more a piece of merchandise, but a passenger, and, like any other passenger, going about his business, carrying with him what belonged to him, and nothing which rightfully belonged to anybody else.

Wrapped in his new winter suit, snug and comfortable, a pocket full of silver, safe from his pursuers, embarked for a free country, Madison gave every sign of sincere gratitude, and bade his kind benefactor farewell, with such a grip of the hand as bespoke a heart full of honest manliness, and a soul that knew how to appreciate kindness. It need scarcely be said that Mr. Listwell was deeply moved by the gratitude and friendship he had excited in a nature so noble as that of the fugitive. He went to his home that day with a joy and gratification which knew no bounds. He had done something "to deliver the spoiled out of the hands of the spoiler," he had given bread to the hungry, and clothes to the naked; he had befriended a man to whom the laws of his country forbade all friendship,—and in proportion to the odds against his righteous deed, was the delightful satisfaction that gladdened his heart. On reaching home, he exclaimed, *"He is safe,—he is safe,—he is safe,"*—and the cup of his joy was shared by his excellent lady. The following letter was received from Madison a few days after.

"WINDSOR, CANADA WEST, DEC. 16, 1840.

My dear Friend,—for such you truly are:—

Madison is out of the woods at last; I nestle in the mane of the British lion, protected by his mighty paw from the talons and the beak of the American eagle. I AM FREE, and breathe an atmosphere too pure for *slaves,* slave-hunters, or slave-holders. My heart is full. As many thanks to you, sir, and to your kind lady, as there are pebbles on the shores of Lake Erie; and may the blessing of God rest upon you both. You will never be forgotten by your profoundly grateful friend,

MADISON WASHINGTON."

"Swamp Judgment"

N. B. YOUNG JR.

N.B. Young Jr. (1894–1993) was born in Tuskegee, Alabama, in 1894, next door to Booker T. Washington. He was the son of Nathan Benjamin Young, who was born into slavery and went on to become president of Florida A&M College and Missouri's Lincoln University. After receiving a special degree from Yale Law School, Young Jr. returned to Alabama, where he wrote a story for a magazine contest sponsored by the *Crisis,* cofounded in 1910 by W. E. B. DuBois as the official publication of the National Association for the Advancement of Colored People. Young's award-winning "Swamp Judgment" appeared in the quarterly magazine's June 1926 issue, as he began work both as a lawyer and as an organizer for the NAACP, provoking threats from the Ku Klux Klan. Shortly after, he moved to Missouri and founded the newspaper the *St. Louis American,* writing editorials for forty-two years while also becoming the first African American to serve as a St. Louis municipal court judge, again drawing harassment from the KKK. A talented musician in his youth, Young later became an artist in retirement, producing more than five hundred acrylic paintings before he died at the age of ninety-eight. Like Frederick Douglass before him, Young's tale of one man's desperate escape through snake-infested wetlands highlights the importance of swamps in African American history and literature. "Swamp Judgment," composed in the segregated Jim Crow era, exposes the racial violence and injustice haunting many African American stories set in the South, where wilderness has long evoked the nightmare of slavery and its violent aftermaths. By the time Young wrote his historical short fiction in the 1920s, 273 African Americans had been lynched in Alabama.

"Swamp Judgment"

N. B. YOUNG JR.

He was not sure that he had even reached the main stretch of the Big Swamp. Yet already it was a difficult task to keep a definite course in such a confusion of canebrake and undergrowth. And if he should be moving in a circle! The thought chilled him.

From the light streaks in the sky overhead he could reckon the way the sun was setting. That was his course—due west with the sun. Somewhere in that direction was the other side of Big Swamp—"thirty miles as the crow flies" he had always heard.

His strength was still with him, even his mended leg had but a tingle of pain in it. On the night he had been wounded in France he had crawled back to first aid, miles it seemed then. He could never forget the Argonne Forest and the chill rains, the spongy, shell-torn area, the thickets from behind which sputtered juts of death. Nor could he forget October ninth, 1918, while helping to drag a gun through the mire he went down, his left leg throbbing. And here it was another October and another torture. Several times already he had run into boggy stretches worse than anything he saw in France. As he jogged on, voracious mosquitoes struck him with unrelenting force and frogs sprang from under his feet. With every few steps he would turn to avoid the slimy green puddles set amid the crowding undergrowth like cankered eyes. The deeper in, the more tedious the passage; already his trousers were drenched and frazzled from the briers.

There was still enough light filtering through the dense foliage to allow him to keep bearing due west, which was the only way, his only hope of reaching Big Creek, the western boundary of Big Swamp. Then a few miles south and he would cross the Alabama line into Florida.

Something brought him to a halt. He lifted his head to make sure. It was the seven o'clock train into Andalusia and the only railroad within a hundred miles of the Big Swamp. There was no mistaking its whistle. It pushed him off to a new start. He had not covered as much ground as he had thought, hardly more than nine or ten miles into the swamp. With them on his trail by now, what if, moving in a circle, he should emerge right into their midst? He had lost his only weapon while fording Little Cedar River. It would be the beginning of the most terrible thing that could happen to him.

To increase his alarm the shadowy darkness had now a strangled grasp on the swamp; the mosquitoes were more desperate and their singing nagging to the ears. Mosquitoes had been biting him all his life, but none like these. Their stings even took his attention from the first pangs of pain in his old leg wound. With them plaguing his face and hands he could not stop and rest if he wanted to. But regardless of the mosquitoes he would have to rest some before he was out of the swamp. Once already he had sprawled in the ooze and twice he had avoided the fangs of a sluggish cotton-mouth moccasin. However, he had the same feeling about snake bite as he had about dying in France. It happened or it didn't happen.

As long as he could keep going his leg would not get stiff, and if he kept his bearing the better his chances of getting through. He had often thought the trenches overrun with vermin had been the very bottom of earthly anguish, but now he knew the batter-like ooze in its dank surrounding was worse. Yet, what he was fleeing from would out-torture both experiences.

The thoughts of what he was escaping kindled a new sheath of strength in him. The black swamp night had conquered. Overhead through the occasional break in the foliage no stars were visible, they are seldom visible in the swamp because of the miasmal fog that hangs in the tops of the dense growth. A deep ancestral instinct alone must keep him moving westward through the drenched jungle. At times he was forced to pause to get his bearing and each time the grim cold fingers of the swamp began to play up and down his back. The denim shirt and blue jumper coat so ample the day before were now but a tissue against the subtle hammock cold.

He moved on, splashing heavily through ankle-deep slush. How it would be possible for them to follow his trail his mind never questioned. He knew they *would* follow at all cost and overtake him if he didn't keep moving. With torches and hounds they would gain an advantage through the night anyway.

At last a dry stretch beneath his feet to recharge his determination. But not very long. A lightning cry of a lost soul nearby caused him to fall to a crouching position. Nothing so unphysical could more pierce human flesh than such a cry. Again it shattered him and he was aware of the soft rustling of a great pair of wings past his head. Frozen, he waited for his senses to thaw. The great hoot-owl, winged panther of the night, was on its rampage. He waited for another shivering cry only to hear a feeble screeching of some unlucky prey alarmed from its warm rut into the tallons of death. Strangely, he remembered he had long ago believed that the swamp meant death. Now he knew it.

Discounting the whirl of pestering mosquitoes, the low silence of the swamp was on again. This time it took an effort to get his leg into motion, but it had to be done or else he would fall victim to other harbingers of death pressing upon him through the swamp night . . .

The first faint bit of light found him crowding on, now by sheer grit. And with the cold fingering at his very vitals he suddenly realized that he needed food as well as rest. But the swamp had little to offer, the water was certain poison, the density of growth bore no edible fruit and the boggy, infested ground was no place upon which to drop one's body. However, the leg was dragging him and he had to stop.

An ancient moss-draped cypress offered a place between its protruding knees to snatch the imperative rest. Raking together the scattered bits of drenched moss and humus he dropped onto it and into a sleep . . .

Not until the sun's rays came down perpendicular did he stir. There was a nettle-like tickling in his face which he brushed at with his hand unaware of the spider and the web she had attached to him. Another sweep of hand carried the trap, its maker and impaneled prey into ruin.

He came up with a start. His hands and face were punctured with mosquito bites, his lower limbs numb and his eyes filled with a shimmering of mud, roots and leaves. For some minutes he lay back prone recollecting slowly the desperate escape he had made. After he had seen his wife and children knocked down when they refused to tell where he was, he had stepped out from his hiding and pulled the trigger of the old army automatic until it refused to spit fire, running away amid a shower of whizzing bullets. And what was it all about? His memory was yet dulled; all that came to him was that his overlord had come to collect for rations gotten at the plantation commissary when only a week before he had turned in three bales of cotton and cleared everything up . . . And when they had come back for him with the long blacksnake whip he had toppled over two of them . . .

A kingfisher rattled its metallic cry as it darted above him; a moment later the echo of it came back. He sat up with a jerk. His eyes were wide open, his dry lips drawn back, his hands twitching. The blurred rattle of the kingfisher he heard again, but something else had undeniably reached his ears—the distant "yelp, yelp—yelp, yelp."

They were coming fast. He tried to raise his body and floundered. His leg was stone. He must get himself up in a few minutes or else—

"Yelp, yelp—yelp, yelp," steady and approaching. The bloodhounds were perhaps leading by half a mile or more. "Yelp, yelp—yelp, yelp"—they came in bolder, as does the baying of bloodhound when the trail becomes surer.

Not able to raise himself he had drawn his body to a crawling position and found that with his hands he could drag his body. From their yelping the dogs were closing in rapidly and unless he could get to his feet he would in short be surrounded. Again he attempted to place his weight on his leg and the result was a flattening of himself in the mud. He determined to catch his breath and make one more effort; if he could gain his feet he could drag on and possibly cross the dogs by circling his trail, giving him time to make his escape.

Then, in less than a stone's throw came a victorious "yelp, yelp, yelp" throated by the lead dog and echoed by the others. They were coming upon him without seeing him. "Whoopee, whoopee," sounded a human voice to the rear of the dogs and he realized they were too near now even for hope. Already he could hear the rustling of undergrowth.

Out of unmixed fear and not counting the griping pain in his leg he began rolling over and over through the slush. The lead hound had come within sight of him now and was baying to the tallest cypress his finding. The whole swamp seemed to be suddenly alive from all directions. "Whoopee, whoopee," echoed in other voices. Three shots rang in succession. That was the signal. In a few minutes they would have a rope around his neck ready to drag him back over those hellish miles he had struggled through. The choking hemp rope, the jeers, the agony, the fagots piled ready for the match—as they passed his mental eye there was a physical squelching.

He had rolled himself against a cypress sapling just off the edge of a stagnant pool of greenish water and was ready to shut his eyes to it all when a slow vibration in the scum of water caught his attention. When he realized what it was he did not flinch, he was smiling and did not know it.

To his back now voices were heard amid the baying of the dogs. One glance back and he pushed his ebon leg right out at the wavering head—

The water-moccasin is sloven of body but quick in thrust of its deadly fangs, carrying the deadliest attack in the swamp. And the swamp had not deceived him. It meant death.

PART 2

WOMEN AND PANTHERS

Gothic themes characterize what at first appear to be the strangest subgenre in the history of wilderness literature: tales of courtship, marriage, or motherhood featuring women and panthers. Once common in the forests and wetlands of North America, panthers native to the continent (spotted jaguars, brown bobcats, tan cougars, brown-silver Canada lynx) appear in early wilderness fiction as silent and savage nocturnal predators. Though rarely seen, panthers and their uncanny cries alarmed early colonists on the Eastern Seaboard and later terrified settlers on the western frontier. Called "Indian devils" in New England, these mysterious and stealthy creatures of the night appear in American fiction as spectral embodiments of the fears and phantasms accompanying European colonial encounters with the unfamiliar landscapes and peoples of the New World. Articulating distinctly White anxieties during the period of Indian Removal and Native American uprisings, as well as chattel slavery and post–Civil War Reconstruction, nineteenth-century wilderness fiction both racialized and often sexualized the panther. Early women-and-panther stories register not just a widespread pioneer terror of wild beasts but also an irrational fear of African American and Native American bodies—bodies feared to be lurking in the woods, waiting to attack unprotected White women.

"A Panther Tale"

JAMES FENIMORE COOPER

James Fenimore Cooper (1789–1851), the second youngest of twelve children, was raised a Quaker in the New York frontier settlement Cooperstown, founded by his father at the southern tip of Otsego Lake. As his older brothers began to pass away, Cooper turned to fiction writing to support their widows and his own large family. The forest, lakes, and rivers in and around Cooperstown provided both inspiration and setting for Cooper's immensely popular 1823 novel *The Pioneers*, which spawned four more historical wilderness novels—*The Last of the Mohicans* (1826), *The Prairie* (1827), *The Pathfinder* (1840), and *The Deerslayer* (1841)—together known as Cooper's *Leatherstocking Tales*. Through his protagonist, Natty Bumppo—a wilderness scout who in the series also goes under the names Leatherstocking, Hawkeye, Pathfinder, and Deerslayer—the irascible and opinionated Cooper found a suitable mouthpiece for his complaints about the country's Edenic landscapes succumbing to the "march of civilization." Alarmed by the continent's vanishing wilderness areas (though less so by the fate of those displaced from their ancestral lands), Cooper put out a call to protect wild places from pioneer settlement and agriculture, which made him at the time not just America's first popular homegrown novelist but also its first dedicated wilderness conservation writer. The public fascination in the nineteenth century with women-and-panther tales begins with Cooper, in an episode excerpted on the following pages from *The Pioneers*. Cooper's dramatic tale of two frontierswomen's encounter in the woods with a female panther would be memorialized by multiple American landscape artists for years after. Later in life, Cooper repurchased the Cooperstown home where he was raised, and he died there having composed more than thirty novels, mostly historical romances or nautical adventures that sought to keep alive an idealized mythic view of wilderness that in the end could survive only in fiction.

"A Panther Tale"

JAMES FENIMORE COOPER

By this time they had gained the summit of the mountain, where they left the highway, and pursued their course under the shade of the stately trees that crowned the eminence. The day was becoming warm, and the girls plunged more deeply into the forest, as they found its invigorating coolness agreeably contrasted to the excessive heat they had experienced in the ascent. The conversation, as if by mutual consent, was entirely changed to the little incidents and scenes of their walk, and every tall pine, and every shrub or flower, called forth some simple expression of admiration.

In this manner they proceeded along the margin of the precipice, catching occasional glimpses of the placid Otsego, or pausing to listen to the rattling of wheels and the sounds of hammers that rose from the valley, to mingle the signs of men with the scenes of nature, when Elizabeth suddenly started, and exclaimed:

"Listen! there are the cries of a child on this mountain! Is there a clearing near us, or can some little one have strayed from its parents?"

"Such things frequently happen," returned Louisa. "Let us follow the sounds; it may be a wanderer starving on the hill."

Urged by this consideration, the females pursued the low, mournful sounds, that proceeded from the forest, with quick and impatient steps. More than once, the ardent Elizabeth was on the point of announcing that she saw the sufferer, when Louisa caught her by the arm, and pointing behind them, cried:

"Look at the dog!"

Brave had been their companion, from the time the voice of his young mistress lured him from his kennel, to the present moment. His advanced age had long before deprived him of his activity; and when his companions stopped to view the scenery, or to add to their bouquets, the mastiff would lay his huge frame on the ground and await their movements, with his eyes closed, and a listlessness in his air that ill accorded with the character of a protector. But when, aroused by this cry from Louisa, Miss Temple turned, she saw the dog with his eyes keenly set on some distant object, his head bent near the ground, and his hair actually rising on his body, through fright or anger. It was most probably the latter, for he was growling in a low key, and occasionally showing his teeth, in a manner that would have terrified his mistress, had she not so well known his good qualities.

"Brave!" she said, "be quiet, Brave! What do you see, fellow?"

At the sounds of her voice, the rage of the mastiff, instead of being at all diminished, was very sensibly increased. He stalked in front of the ladies, and seated himself at the feet of his mistress, growling louder than before, and occasionally giving vent to his ire by a short, surly barking.

"What does he see?" said Elizabeth; "there must be some animal in sight."

Hearing no answer from her companion, Miss Temple turned her head and beheld Louisa, standing with her face whitened to the color of death, and her finger pointing upward with a sort of flickering, convulsed motion. The quick eye of Elizabeth glanced in the direction indicated by her friend, where she saw the fierce front and glaring eyes of a female panther, fixed on them in horrid malignity, and threatening to leap.

"Let us fly," exclaimed Elizabeth, grasping the arm of Louisa, whose form yielded like melting snow.

There was not a single feeling in the temperament of Elizabeth Temple that could prompt her to desert a companion in such an extremity. She fell on her knees by the side of the inanimate Louisa, tearing from the person of her friend, with instinctive readiness, such parts of her dress as might obstruct her respiration, and encouraging their only safeguard, the dog, at the same time, by the sounds of her voice.

"Courage, Brave!" she cried, her own tones beginning to tremble, "courage, courage, good Brave!"

A quarter-grown cub, that had hitherto been unseen, now appeared, dropping from the branches of a sapling that grew under the shade of the beech which held its dam. This ignorant but vicious creature approached the dog, imitating the actions and sounds of its parent, but exhibiting a strange mixture of the playfulness of a kitten with the ferocity of its race. Standing on its hind-legs, it would rend the bark of a tree with its fore-paws, and play the antics of a cat; and then, by lashing itself with its tail, growling, and scratching the earth, it would attempt the manifestations of anger that rendered its parent so terrific.

All this time Brave stood firm and undaunted, his short tail erect, his body drawn backward on its haunches, and his eyes following the movements of both dam and cub. At every gambol played by the latter, it approached nigher to the dog, the growling of the three becoming more horrid at each moment, until the younger beast, over-leaping its intended bound, fell directly before the mastiff. There was a moment of fearful cries and struggles, but they ended almost as soon as commenced, by the cub appearing in the air, hurled from the jaws of Brave, with a violence that sent it against a tree so forcibly as to render it completely senseless.

Elizabeth witnessed the short struggle, and her blood was warming with the triumph of the dog, when she saw the form of the old panther in the air, springing twenty feet from the branch of the beech to the back of the mastiff. No words of ours can describe the fury of the conflict that followed. It was a confused struggle on the dry leaves, accompanied by loud and terrific cries. Miss Temple continued on her knees, bending over the form of Louisa, her eyes fixed on the animals with an interest so horrid, and yet so intense, that she almost forgot her own stake in the result. So rapid and vigorous were the bounds of the inhabitant of the forest, that its active frame seemed constantly in the air, while the dog nobly faced his foe at each successive leap. When the panther lighted on the shoulders of the mastiff, which was its constant aim, old Brave, though torn with her talons, and stained with his own blood, that already flowed from a dozen wounds, would shake off his furious foe like a feather, and, rearing on his hind-legs, rush to the fray again, with jaws distended, and a dauntless eye. But age, and his pampered life, greatly disqualified the noble mastiff for such a struggle. In everything but courage, he was only the vestige of what he had once been. A higher bound than ever raised the wary and furious beast far beyond the reach of the dog, who was making a desperate but fruitless dash at her, from which she alighted in a favorable position, on the back of her aged foe. For a single moment only could the panther remain there, the great strength of the dog returning with a convulsive effort. But Elizabeth saw, as Brave fastened his teeth in the side of his enemy, that the collar of brass around his neck, which had been glittering throughout the fray, was of the color of blood, and directly that his frame was sinking to the earth, where it soon lay prostrate and helpless. Several mighty efforts of the wild-cat to extricate herself from the jaws of the dog followed, but they were fruitless, until the mastiff turned on his back, his lips collapsed, and his teeth loosened, when the short convulsions and stillness that succeeded announced the death of poor Brave.

Elizabeth now lay wholly at the mercy of the beast. There is said to be something in the front of the image of the Maker that daunts the hearts of the inferior beings of his creation; and it would seem that some such power, in the present instance, suspended the threatened blow. The eyes of the monster and the kneeling maiden met for an instant, when the former stooped to examine her fallen foe; next, to scent her luckless cub. From the latter examination it turned, however, with its eyes apparently emitting flashes of fire, its tail lashing its sides furiously, and its claws projecting inches from her broad feet.

Miss Temple did not or could not move. Her hands were clasped in the attitude of prayer, but her eyes were still drawn to her terrible enemy—her cheeks were blanched to the whiteness of marble, and her lips were slightly separated with horror. The moment seemed now to have arrived for the fatal termination, and the beautiful figure of Elizabeth was bowing meekly to the stroke, when a rustling of leaves behind seemed rather to mock the organs than to meet her ears.

"Hist! hist!" said a low voice, "stoop lower, gal; your bonnet hides the creatur's head."

It was rather the yielding of nature than a compliance with this unexpected order, that caused the head of our heroine to sink on her bosom; when she heard the report of the rifle, the whizzing of the bullet, and the enraged cries of the beast, who was rolling over on the earth, biting its own flesh, and tearing the twigs and branches within its reach. At the next instant the form of the Leatherstocking rushed by her, and he called aloud:

"Come in, Hector! come in, old fool; 'tis a hard-lived animal, and may jump agin."

Natty fearlessly maintained his position in front of the females, notwithstanding the violent bounds and threatening aspect of the wounded panther, which gave several indications of returning strength and ferocity, until his rifle was again loaded, when he stepped up to the enraged animal, and, placing the muzzle close to its head, every spark of life was extinguished by the discharge.

The death of her terrible enemy appeared to Elizabeth like a resurrection from her own grave. There was an elasticity in the mind of our heroine that rose to meet the pressure of instant danger, and the more direct it had been, the more her nature had struggled to overcome them. But still she was a woman. Had she been left to herself in her late extremity, she would probably have used her faculties to the utmost, and with discretion, in protecting her person; but, encumbered with her inanimate friend, retreat was a thing not to be attempted. Notwithstanding the fearful aspect of her foe, the eye of Elizabeth had never shrunk from its gaze, and long after the event her thoughts would recur to her passing sensations, and the sweetness of her midnight sleep would be disturbed, as her active fancy conjured, in dreams, the most trifling movements of savage fury that the beast had exhibited in its moment of power.

We shall leave the reader to imagine the restoration of Louisa's senses, and the expressions of gratitude which fell from the young women. The former was effected by a little water, that was brought from one of the thousand springs of those mountains, in the cap of the Leatherstocking; and the latter were uttered with the warmth that might be expected from the character of Elizabeth. Natty received her vehement protestations of gratitude with a simple expression of good-will, and with indulgence for her present excitement, but with a carelessness that showed how little he thought of the service he had rendered.

"Well, well," he said, "be it so, gal; let it be so, if you wish it—we'll talk the thing over another time. Come, come—let us get into the road, for you've had terror enough to make you wish yourself in your father's house agin."

This was uttered as they were proceeding, at a pace that was adapted to the weakness of Louisa, toward the highway; on reaching which the ladies separated from their guide, declaring themselves equal to the remainder of the walk without his assistance, and feeling encouraged by the sight of the village which lay beneath their feet like a picture, with its limpid lake in front, the winding stream along its margin, and its hundred chimneys of whitened bricks.

The reader need not be told the nature of the emotions which two youthful, ingenuous, and well-educated girls would experience at their escape from a death so horrid as the one which had impended over them, while they pursued their way in silence along the track on the side of the mountain; nor how deep were their mental thanks to that Power which had given them their existence, and which had not deserted them in their extremity; neither how often they pressed each other's arms as the assurance of their present safety came, like a healing balm, athwart their troubled spirits, when their thoughts were recurring to the recent moments of horror.

Leatherstocking remained on the hill, gazing after their retiring figures, until they were hidden by a bend in the road, when he whistled in his dogs, and shouldering his rifle, he returned into the forest.

"Circumstance"

HARRIET PRESCOTT SPOFFORD

Harriet Prescott Spofford (1835–1921) was for most of her life a resident of Newburyport and Amesbury, Massachusetts, having come of age in Calais, Maine, home to the Passamaquoddy long before Euro-American settlers arrived in the area in the late eighteenth century. Though her father, Joseph N. Prescott, left his family to seek fortune in the West (eventually helping found Oregon City, the western terminus of the Oregon Trail), Harriet Prescott Spofford spent her life in New England, writing and submitting, at first anonymously, hundreds of magazine short stories to financially support her extended family. Though she also wrote poetry, essays, and novels (beginning with *Sir Rohan's Ghost: A Romance* in 1860), today Spofford is remembered for her early detective, supernatural, and Gothic short stories. Among the best of these tales, "The Amber Gods," "In a Cellar," and "Circumstance" all appear in Spofford's first story collection, *The Amber Gods, and Other Stories* (1863). Spofford claimed that "Circumstance" was based on a real event: her great-grandmother's nocturnal encounter with a panther in the wilds of eastern Maine. Her story of a frontierswoman who attempts to mesmerize a panther with her singing (until her voice goes hoarse) was a success when it appeared in 1860 in the *Atlantic,* helping to secure for the young writer further story commissions and a loyal readership. Among her readers was the poet Emily Dickinson, who famously declared she did not have the constitution for such nerve-racking tales: "I read Miss Prescott's 'Circumstance,'" she admitted, "but it followed me in the Dark—so I avoided her." After considerable success publishing her fiction, Spofford married local lawyer and minor poet Richard S. Spofford Jr., who purchased a small island between Newburyport and Amesbury, where the couple lived in an old converted inn. With a commanding view of the powerful Merrimack River, which flowed around the island, Spofford continued to write regularly, having distinguished herself over a sixty-year writing career as one of the most prolific and popular authors of magazine fiction.

"Circumstance"

HARRIET PRESCOTT SPOFFORD

She had remained, during all that day, with a sick neighbor,—those eastern wilds of Maine in that epoch frequently making neighbors and miles synonymous,—and so busy had she been with care and sympathy that she did not at first observe the approaching night. But finally the level rays, reddening the snow, threw their gleam upon the wall, and, hastily donning cloak and hood, she bade her friends farewell and sallied forth on her return. Home lay some three miles distant, across a copse, a meadow, and a piece of woods,—the woods being a fringe on the skirts of the great forests that stretch far away into the North. That home was one of a dozen log-houses lying a few furlongs apart from each other, with their half-cleared demesnes separating them at the rear from a wilderness untrodden save by stealthy native or deadly panther tribes.

She was in a nowise exalted frame of spirit,—on the contrary, rather depressed by the pain she had witnessed and the fatigue she had endured; but in certain temperaments such a condition throws open the mental pores, so to speak, and renders one receptive of every influence. Through the little copse she walked slowly, with her cloak folded about her, lingering to imbibe the sense of shelter, the sunset filtered in purple through the mist of woven spray and twig, the companionship of growth not sufficiently dense to band against her, the sweet homefeeling of a young and tender wintry wood. It was therefore just on the edge of the evening that she emerged from the place and began to cross the meadowland. At one hand lay the forest to which her path wound; at the other the evening star hung over a tide of failing orange that slowly slipped down the earth's broad side to sadden other hemispheres with sweet regret. Walking rapidly now, and with her eyes wide-open, she distinctly saw in the air before her what was not there a moment ago, a winding-sheet,—cold, white, and ghastly, waved by the likeness of four wan hands,—that rose with a long inflation, and fell in rigid folds, while a voice, shaping itself from the hollowness above, spectral and melancholy, sighed,—"The Lord have mercy on the people! The

Lord have mercy on the people!" Three times the sheet with its corpse-covering outline waved beneath the pale hands, and the voice, awful in its solemn and mysterious depth, sighed, "The Lord have mercy on the people!" Then all was gone, the place was clear again, the gray sky was obstructed by no deathly blot; she looked about her, shook her shoulders decidedly, and, pulling on her hood, went forward once more.

She might have been a little frightened by such an apparition, if she had led a life of less reality than frontier settlers are apt to lead; but dealing with hard fact does not engender a flimsy habit of mind, and this woman was too sincere and earnest in her character, and too happy in her situation, to be thrown by antagonism, merely, upon superstitious fancies and chimeras of the second-sight. She did not even believe herself subject to an hallucination, but smiled simply, a little vexed that her thought could have framed such a glamour from the day's occurrences, and not sorry to lift the bough of the warder of the woods and enter and disappear in their sombre path. If she had been imaginative, she would have hesitated at her first step into a region whose dangers were not visionary; but I suppose that the thought of a little child at home would conquer that propensity in the most habituated. So, biting a bit of spicy birch, she went along. Now and then she came to a gap where the trees had been partially felled, and here she found that the lingering twilight was explained by that peculiar and perhaps electric film which sometimes sheathes the sky in diffused light for many hours before a brilliant aurora. Suddenly, a swift shadow, like the fabulous flying-dragon, writhed through the air before her, and she felt herself instantly seized and borne aloft. It was that wild beast—the most savage and serpentine and subtle and fearless of our latitudes—known by hunters as the Indian Devil, and he held her in his clutches on the broad floor of a swinging fir-bough. His long sharp claws were caught in her clothing, he worried them sagaciously a little, then, finding that ineffectual to free them, he commenced licking her bare arm with his rasping tongue and pouring over her the wide streams of his hot, foetid breath. So quick had this flashing action been that the woman had had no time for alarm; moreover, she was not of the screaming kind: but now, as she felt him endeavoring to disentangle his claws, and the horrid sense of her fate smote her, and she saw instinctively the fierce plunge of those weapons, the long strips of living flesh torn from her bones, the agony, the quivering disgust, itself a worse agony,—while by her side, and holding her in his great lithe embrace, the monster crouched, his white tusks whetting and gnashing, his eyes glaring through all the darkness like balls of red fire,—a shriek, that rang in every forest hollow, that startled every winter-housed thing, that stirred and woke the least needle of the tasselled pines, tore through her lips. A moment afterward, the beast left the arm, once white, now crimson, and looked up alertly.

She did not think at this instant to call upon God. She called upon her husband. It seemed to her that she had but one friend in the world; that was he; and again the cry, loud, clear, prolonged, echoed through the woods. It was not the shriek that disturbed the creature at his relish; he was not born in the woods to be scared of an owl, you know; what then? It must have been the echo, most musical, most resonant, repeated and yet repeated, dying with long sighs of sweet sound, vibrated from rock to river and back again from depth to depth of cave and cliff. Her thought flew after it; she knew, that, even if her husband heard it, he yet could not reach her in time; she saw that while the beast listened he would not gnaw,—and this she *felt* directly, when the rough, sharp, and multiplied stings of his tongue retouched her arm. Again her lips opened by instinct, but the sound that issued thence came by reason. She had heard that music charmed wild beasts,—just this point between life and death intensified every faculty,—and when she opened her lips the third time, it was not for shrieking, but for singing.

A little thread of melody stole out, a rill of tremulous motion; it was the cradle-song with which she rocked her baby;—how could she sing that? And then she remembered the baby sleeping rosily on the long settee before the fire,—the father cleaning his gun, with one foot on the green wooden rundle—the merry light from the chimney dancing out and through the room, on the rafters of the ceiling with their tassels of onions and herbs, on the log walls painted with lichens and festooned with apples, on the king's-arm slung across the shelf with the old pirate's-cutlass, on the snow-pile of the bed, and on the great brass clock,—dancing, too, and lingering on the baby, with his fringed-gentian eyes, his chubby fists clenched on the pillow, and his fine breezy hair fanning with the motion of his father's foot. All this struck her in one, and made a sob of her breath, and she ceased.

Immediately the long red tongue thrust forth again. Before it touched, a song sprang to her lips, a wild sea-song, such as some sailor might be singing far out on trackless blue water that night, the shrouds whistling with frost and the sheets glued in ice,—a song with the wind in its burden and the spray in its chorus. The monster raised his head and flared the fiery eyeballs upon her, then fretted the imprisoned claws a moment and was quiet; only the breath like the vapor from some hell-pit still swathed her. Her voice, at first faint and fearful, gradually lost its quaver, grew under her control and subject to her modulation; it rose on long swells, it fell in subtile cadences, now and then its tones pealed out like bells from distant belfries on fresh sonorous mornings. She sung the song through, and, wondering lest his name of Indian Devil were not his true name, and if he would not detect her, she repeated it. Once or twice now, indeed, the beast stirred uneasily, turned, and made the bough sway at his movement. As she ended, he snapped his jaws together, and tore away the fettered member, curling it under him with a snarl,—when she burst into the gayest reel that ever answered a fiddle-bow. How many a time she had heard her husband play it on the homely fiddle made by himself from birch and cherrywood! how many a time she had seen it danced on the floor of their one room, to the pat-ter of wooden clogs and the rustle of homespun petticoat! how many a time she had danced it herself!—and did she not remember once, as they joined clasps for eight-hands-round, how it had lent its gay, bright measure to her life? And here she was singing it alone, in the forest, at midnight, to a wild beast! As she sent her voice trilling up and down its quick oscillations between joy and pain, the creature who grasped her uncurled his paw and scratched the bark from the bough; she must vary the spell; and her voice spun leaping along the projecting points of tune of a hornpipe. Still singing, she felt herself twisted about with a low growl and a lifting of the red lip from the glittering teeth; she broke the hornpipe's thread, and commenced unravelling a lighter, livelier thing, an Irish jig. Up and down and round about her voice flew, the beast threw back his head so that the diabolical face fronted hers, and the torrent of his breath prepared her for his feast as the anaconda slimes his prey. Franticly she darted from tune to tune; his restless movements followed her. She tired herself with dancing and vivid national airs, growing feverish and singing spasmodically as she felt her horrid tomb yawning wider. Touching in this manner all the slogan and keen clan cries, the beast moved again, but only to lay the disengaged paw across her with heavy satisfaction. She did not dare to pause; through the clear cold air, the frosty starlight, she sang. If there were yet any tremor in the tone, it was not fear,—she had learned the secret of sound at last; nor could it be chill,—far too high a fever throbbed her pulses; it was nothing but the thought of the log-house and of what might be passing within it. She fancied the baby stirring in his sleep and moving his pretty lips,—her husband rising and opening the door, looking out after her, and wondering at her absence. She fancied the light pouring through the chink and then shut in again with all the safety and comfort and joy, her husband taking down the fiddle and playing lightly with his head inclined, playing while she sang, while she sang for her life to an Indian Devil. Then she knew he was fumbling for and finding some shining fragment and scoring it down the yellowing hair, and unconsciously her voice forsook the wild wartunes and drifted into the half-gay, half-melancholy Rosin the Bow.

Suddenly she woke pierced with a pang, and the daggered tooth penetrating her flesh;—dreaming of safety, she had ceased singing and lost it. The beast has regained the use of all his limbs, and now, standing and raising his back, bristling and foaming, with sounds that would have been like hisses but for their deep and fearful sonority, he withdrew step by step toward the trunk of the tree, still with his flaming balls upon her. She was all at once free, on one end of the bough, twenty feet from the ground. She did not measure the distance, but rose to drop herself down, careless of any death, so that it were not this. Instantly, as if he scanned her thoughts, the creature bounded forward with a yell and caught her again in his dreadful hold. It might be that he was not greatly famished; for, as she suddenly flung up her voice again, he settled himself composedly on the bough, still clasping her with invincible pressure to his rough, ravenous breast, and listening in a fascination to the sad, strange U-la-lu that now moaned forth in loud, hollow tones above him. He half closed his eyes, and sleepily reopened and shut them again.

What rending pains were close at hand! Death! and what a death! worse than any other that is to be named! Water, be it cold or warm, that which buoys up blue icefields, or which bathes tropical coasts with currents of balmy bliss, is yet a gentle conqueror, kisses as it kills, and draws you down gently through darkening fathoms to its heart. Death at the sword is the festival of trumpet and bugle and banner, with glory ringing out around you and distant hearts thrilling through yours. No gnawing disease can bring such hideous end as this; for that is a fiend bred of your own flesh, and this—is it a fiend, this living lump of appetites? What dread comes with the thought of perishing in flames! but fire, let it leap and hiss never so hotly, is something too remote, too alien, to inspire us with such loathly horror as a wild beast; if it have a life, that life is too utterly beyond our comprehension. Fire is not half ourselves; as it devours, arouses neither hatred nor disgust; is not to be known by the strength of our lower natures let loose; does not drip our blood into our faces from foaming chaps, nor mouth nor slaver above us with vitality. Let us be ended by fire, and we are ashes, for the winds to bear, the leaves to cover; let us be ended by wild beasts, and the base, cursed thing howls with us forever through the forest. All this she felt as she charmed him, and what force it lent to her song God knows. If her voice should fail! If the damp and cold should give her any fatal hoarseness! If all the silent powers of the forest did not conspire to help her! The dark, hollow night rose indifferently over her; the wide, cold air breathed rudely past her, lifted her wet hair and blew it down again; the great boughs swung with a ponderous strength, now and then clashed their iron lengths together and shook off a sparkle of icy spears or some long-lain weight of snow from their heavy shadows. The green depths were utterly cold and silent and stern. These beautiful haunts that all the summer were hers and rejoiced to share with her their bounty, these heavens that had yielded their largess, these stems that had thrust their blossoms into her hands, all these friends of three moons ago forgot her now and knew her no longer.

Feeling her desolation, wild, melancholy, forsaken songs rose thereon from that frightful aerie,—weeping, wailing tunes, that sob among the people from age to age, and overflow with otherwise unexpressed sadness,—all rude, mournful ballads,—old tearful strains, that Shakespeare heard the vagrants sing, and that rise and fall like the wind and tide,—sailor-songs, to be heard only in lone mid-watches beneath the moon and stars,—ghastly rhyming romances, such as that famous one of the Lady Margaret, when

> *"She slipped on her gown of green*
> *A piece below the knee,—*
>
> *And 't was all a long cold winter's night*
> *A dead corse followed she."*

Still the beast lay with closed eyes, yet never relaxing his grasp. Once a half-whine of enjoyment escaped him,—he fawned his fearful head upon her; once he scored her cheek with his tongue: savage caresses that hurt like wounds. How weary she was! and yet how terribly awake! How fuller and fuller of dismay grew the knowledge that she was only prolonging her anguish and playing with death! How appalling the thought that with her voice ceased her existence! Yet she could not sing forever; her throat was dry and hard; her very breath was a pain; her mouth was hotter than any desert-worn pilgrim's;—if she could but drop upon her burning tongue one atom of the ice that glittered about her!—but both of her arms were pinioned in the giant's vise. She remembered the winding-sheet, and for the first time in her life shivered with spiritual fear. Was it hers? She asked herself, as she sang, what sins she had committed, what life she had led, to find her punishment so soon and in these pangs,—and then she sought eagerly for some reason why her husband was not up and abroad to find her. He failed her,—her one sole hope in life; and without being aware of it, her voice forsook the songs of suffering and sorrow for old Covenanting hymns,—hymns with which her mother had lulled her, which the class-leader pitched in the chimney-corners,—grand and sweet Methodist hymns, brimming with melody and with all fantastic involutions of tune to suit that ecstatic worship,—hymns full of the beauty of holiness, steadfast, relying, sanctified by the salvation they had lent to those in worse extremity than hers,—for they had found themselves in the grasp of hell, while she was but in the jaws of death. Out of this strange music, peculiar to one character of faith, and than which there is none more beautiful in its degree nor owning a more potent sway of sound, her voice soared into the glorified chants of churches. What to her was death by cold or famine or wild beasts? "Though He slay me, yet will I trust in him," she sang. High and clear through the frore fair night, the level moonbeams splintering in the wood, the scarce glints of stars in the shadowy roof of branches, these sacred anthems rose,—rose as a hope from despair, as some snowy spray of flower-bells from blackest mould. Was she not in God's hands? Did not the world swing at his will? If this were in his great plan of providence, was it not best, and should she not accept it?

"He is the Lord our God; his judgments are in all the earth."

Oh, sublime faith of our fathers, where utter self-sacrifice alone was true love, the fragrance of whose unrequired subjection was pleasanter than that of golden censers swung in purple-vapored chancels!

Never ceasing in the rhythm of her thoughts, articulated in music as they thronged, the memory of her first communion flashed over her. Again she was in that distant place on that sweet spring morning. Again the congregation rustled out, and the few remained, and she trembled to find herself among them. How well she remembered the devout, quiet faces, too accustomed to the sacred feast to glow with their inner joy! how well the snowy linen at the altar, the silver vessels slowly and silently shifting! and as the cup approached and passed, how the sense of delicious perfume stole in and heightened the transport of her prayer, and she had seemed, looking up through the windows where the sky soared blue in constant freshness, to feel all heaven's balms dripping from the portals, and to scent the lilies of eternal peace! Perhaps another would not have felt so much ecstasy as satisfaction on that occasion; but it is a true, if a later disciple, who has said, "The Lord bestoweth his blessings there, where he findeth the vessels empty."

"And does it need the walls of a church to renew my communion?" she asked. "Does not every moment stand a temple four-square to God? And in that morning, with its buoyant sunlight, was I any dearer to the Heart of the World than now?—'My beloved is mine, and I am his,'" she sang over and over again, with all varied inflection and profuse tune. How gently all the winter-wrapt things bent toward her then! into what relation with her had they grown! how this common dependence was the spell of their intimacy! how at one with Nature had she become! how all the night and the silence and the forest seemed to hold its breath, and to send its soul up to God in her singing! It was no longer despondency, that singing. It was neither prayer nor petition. She had left imploring, "How long wilt thou forget me, O Lord? Lighten mine eyes, lest I sleep the sleep of death! For in death there is no remembrance of thee,"—with countless other such fragments of supplication. She cried rather, "Yea, though I walk through the valley of the shadow of death, I will fear no evil: for thou art with me; thy rod and thy staff, they comfort me,"—and lingered, and repeated, and sang again, "I shall be satisfied, when I awake, with thy likeness."

Then she thought of the Great Deliverance, when he drew her up out of many waters, and the flashing old psalm pealed forth triumphantly:—

"The Lord descended from above,
and bow'd the heavens hie:

And underneath his feet he cast
the darknesse of the skie.

On cherubs and on cherubins
full royally he road:

And on the wings of all the winds
came flying all abroad."

She forgot how recently, and with what a strange pity for her own shapeless form that was to be, she had quaintly sung,—

"O lovely appearance of death!
What sight upon earth is so fair?

Not all the gay pageants that breathe
Can with a dead body compare!"

She remembered instead,—"In thy presence is fulness of joy; at thy right hand there are pleasures forevermore. God will redeem my soul from the power of the grave: for he shall receive me. He will swallow up death in victory." Not once now did she say, "Lord, how long wilt thou look on; rescue my soul from their destructions, my darling from the lions,"—for she knew that the young lions roar after their prey and seek their meat from God. "O Lord, thou preservest man and beast!" she said.

She had no comfort or consolation in this season, such as sustained the Christian martyrs in the amphitheatre. She was not dying for her faith; there were no palms in heaven for her to wave; but how many a time had she declared,—"I had rather be a doorkeeper in the house of my God, than to dwell in the tents of wickedness!" And as the broad rays here and there broke through the dense covert of shade and lay in rivers of lustre on crystal sheathing and frozen fretting of trunk and limb and on the great spaces of refraction, they builded up visibly that house, the shining city on the hill, and singing, "Beautiful for situation, the joy of the whole earth, is Mount Zion, on the sides of the North, the city of the Great King," her vision climbed to that higher picture where the angel shows the dazzling thing, the holy Jerusalem descending out of heaven from God, with its splendid battlements and gates of pearls, and its foundations, the eleventh a jacinth, the twelfth an amethyst,—with its great white throne, and the rainbow round about it, in sight like unto an emerald: "And there shall be no night there,—for the Lord God giveth them light," she sang.

What whisper of dawn now rustled through the wilderness? How the night was passing! And still the beast crouched upon the bough, changing only the posture of his head, that again he might command her with those charmed eyes;—half their fire was gone; she could almost have released herself from his custody; yet, had she stirred, no one knows what malevolent instinct might have dominated anew. But of that she did not dream; long ago stripped of any expectation, she was experiencing in her divine rapture how mystically true it is that "he that dwelleth in the secret place of the Most High shall abide under the shadow of the Almighty."

Slow clarion cries now wound from the distance as the cocks caught the intelligence of day and re-echoed it faintly from farm to farm,—sleepy sentinels of night, sounding the foe's invasion, and translating that dim intuition to ringing notes of warning. Still she chanted on. A remote crash of brushwood told of some other beast on his depredations, or some night-belated traveller groping his way through the narrow path. Still she chanted on. The far, faint echoes of the chanticleers died into distance, the crashing of the branches grew nearer. No wild beast that, but a man's step,—a man's form in the moonlight, stalwart and strong,—on one arm slept a little child, in the other hand he held his gun. Still she chanted on.

Perhaps, when her husband last looked forth, he was half ashamed to find what a fear he felt for her. He knew she would never leave the child so long but for some direst need,—and yet he may have laughed at himself, as he lifted and wrapped it with awkward care, and, loading his gun and strapping on his horn, opened the door again and closed it behind him, going out and plunging into the darkness and dangers of the forest. He was more singularly alarmed than he would have been willing to acknowledge; as he had sat with his bow hovering over the strings, he had half believed to hear her voice mingling gayly with the instrument, till he paused and listened if she were not about to lift the latch and enter. As he drew nearer the heart of the forest, that intimation of melody seemed to grow more actual, to take body and breath, to come and go on long swells and ebbs of the night-breeze, to increase with tune and words, till a strange shrill singing grew ever clearer, and, as he stepped into an open space of moonbeams, far up in the branches, rocked by the wind, and singing, "How beautiful upon the mountains are the feet of him that bringeth good tidings, that publisheth peace," he saw his wife,—his wife,—but, great God in heaven! How? Some mad exclamation escaped him, but without diverting her. The child knew the singing voice, though never heard before in that unearthly key, and turned toward it through the veiling dreams. With a celerity almost instantaneous, it lay, in the twinkling of an eye, on the ground at the father's feet, while his gun was raised to his shoulder and levelled at the monster covering his wife with shaggy form and flaming gaze,—his wife so ghastly white, so rigid, so stained with blood, her eyes so fixedly bent above, and her lips, that had indurated into the chiselled pallor of marble, parted only with that flood of solemn song.

I do not know if it were the mother-instinct that for a moment lowered her eyes,—those eyes, so lately riveted on heaven, now suddenly seeing all life-long bliss possible. A thrill of joy pierced and shivered through her like a weapon, her voice trembled in its course, her glance lost its steady strength, fever-flushes chased each other over her face, yet she never once ceased chanting. She was quite aware, that, if her husband shot now, the ball must pierce her body before reaching any vital part of the beast,—and yet better that death, by his hand, than the other. But this her husband also knew, and he remained motionless, just covering the creature with the sight. He dared not fire, lest some wound not mortal should break the spell exercised by her voice, and the beast, enraged with pain, should rend her in atoms; moreover, the light was too uncertain for his aim. So he waited. Now and then he examined his gun to see if the damp were injuring its charge, now and then he wiped the great drops from his forehead. Again the cocks crowed with the passing hour,—the last time they were heard on that night. Cheerful home sound then, how full of safety and all comfort and rest it seemed! What sweet morning incidents of sparkling fire and sunshine, of gay household bustle, shining dresser, and cooing baby, of steaming cattle in the yard, and brimming milk-pails at the door! What pleasant voices! What laughter! What security! And here—

Now, as she sang on in the slow, endless, infinite moments, the fervent vision of God's peace was gone. Just as the grave had lost its sting, she was snatched back again into the arms of earthly hope. In vain she tried to sing, "There remaineth a rest for the people of God,"—her eyes trembled on her husband's, and she could only think of him, and of the child, and of happiness that yet might be, but with what a dreadful gulf of doubt between! She shuddered now in the suspense; all calm forsook her; she was tortured with dissolving heats or frozen with icy blasts; her face contracted, growing small and pinched; her voice was hoarse and sharp,—every tone cut like a knife,—the notes became heavy to lift,— withheld by some hostile pressure,—impossible. One gasp, a convulsive effort, and there was silence,—she had lost her voice.

The beast made a sluggish movement,—stretched and fawned like one awaking,—then, as if he would have yet more of the enchantment, stirred her slightly with his muzzle. As he did so, a sidelong hint of the man standing below with the raised gun smote him; he sprung round furiously, and, seizing his prey, was about to leap into some unknown airy den of the topmost branches now waving to the slow dawn. The late moon had rounded through the sky so that her gleam at last fell full upon the bough with fairy frosting; the wintry morning light did not yet penetrate the gloom. The woman, suspended in mid-air an instant, cast only one agonized glance beneath,—but across and through it, ere the lids could fall, shot a withering sheet of flame,—a rifle-crack, half-heard, was lost in the terrible yell of desperation that bounded after it and filled her ears with savage echoes, and in the wide arc of some eternal descent she was falling;—but the beast fell under her.

I think that the moment following must have been too sacred for us, and perhaps the three have no special interest again till they issue from the shadows of the wilderness upon the white hills that skirt their home. The father carries the child hushed again into slumber, the mother follows with no such feeble step as might be anticipated. It is not time for reaction,—the tension not yet relaxed, the nerves still vibrant, she seems to herself like some one newly made; the night was a dream; the present stamped upon her in deep satisfaction, neither weighed nor compared with the past; if she has the careful tricks of former habit, it is as an automaton; and as they slowly climb the steep under the clear gray vault and the paling morning star, and as she stops to gather a spray of the red-rose berries or a feathery tuft of dead grasses for the chimney-piece of the log-house, or a handful of brown cones for the child's play,—of these quiet, happy folk you would scarcely dream how lately they had stolen from under the banner and encampment of the great King Death. The husband proceeds a step or two in advance; the wife lingers over a singular foot-print in the snow, stoops and examines it, then looks up with a hurried word. Her husband stands alone on the hill, his arms folded across the babe, his gun fallen,—stands defined as a silhouette against the pallid sky. What is there in their home, lying below and yellowing in the light, to fix him with such a stare? She springs to his side. There is no home there. The log-house, the barns, the neighboring farms, the fences, are all blotted out and mingled in one smoking ruin. Desolation and death were indeed there, and beneficence and life in the forest. Tomahawk and scalping-knife, descending during that night, had left behind them only this work of their accomplished hatred and one subtle foot-print in the snow.

For the rest,—the world was all before them, where to choose.

"The Eyes of the Panther"

AMBROSE BIERCE

A mbrose Bierce (1842–1914?) was born in the Ohio settlement of Horse Cave Creek but spent most of his childhood in Walnut Creek, another frontier settlement in the deep forest of Northern Indiana. As a young man Bierce enlisted in the Union Army and saw action in several Civil War battles, including one of its bloodiest, the Battle of Shiloh. After surviving a severe head wound late in the war, Bierce traveled to San Francisco to become a newspaper journalist and a magazine fiction writer. The haunting tone of his short memoir, *What I Saw of Shiloh* (1881), a dramatic account of all "the phantoms of a blood-stained period," found creative outlet not just in his war stories ("An Occurrence at Owl Creek" remains his most celebrated work) but also in his horror fiction, satirical fables, and supernatural tales. Recently Bierce's work has garnered renewed attention as a progenitor of today's "weird fiction," supernatural stories partly inspired by Edgar Allan Poe's tales of the macabre, but with an emphasis less on Gothic horror and more on strange fantasy. Bierce's "The Eyes of the Panther," which appeared in the *San Francisco Examiner* (October 17, 1897), brings the fantasy of a woman's nighttime wilderness encounter with a voracious panther much further than Harriet Prescott Spofford's "Circumstance" ever dared. Likely based on American folklore, this cross-species story of mesmerism and seduction has been adapted twice—for a 1989 television episode and a 2007 short movie thriller. At the age of seventy-one, Bierce, while touring Mexico during the Mexican Revolution, became the stuff of legend himself. After writing in a letter that he was leaving for an unknown destination, he was never heard from again, thus becoming American literature's most famous missing person.

"The Eyes of the Panther"

AMBROSE BIERCE

I. ONE DOES NOT ALWAYS MARRY WHEN INSANE

A man and a woman—nature had done the grouping—sat on a rustic seat, in the late afternoon. The man was middle-aged, slender, swarthy, with the expression of a poet and the complexion of a pirate—a man at whom one would look again. The woman was young, blonde, graceful, with something in her figure and movements suggesting the word *"lithe."* She was habited in a gray gown with odd brown markings in the texture. She may have been beautiful; one could not readily say, for her eyes denied attention to all else. They were gray-green, long and narrow, with an expression defying analysis. One could only know that they were disquieting. Cleopatra may have had such eyes.

The man and the woman talked.

"Yes," said the woman, "I love you, God knows! But marry you, no. I cannot, will not."

"Irene, you have said that many times, yet always have denied me a reason. I've a right to know, to understand, to feel and prove my fortitude if I have it. Give me a reason."

"For loving you?"

The woman was smiling through her tears and her pallor. That did not stir any sense of humor in the man.

"No; there is no reason for that. A reason for not marrying me. I've a right to know. I must know. I will know!"

He had risen and was standing before her with clenched hands, on his face a frown—it might have been called a scowl. He looked as if he might attempt to learn by strangling her. She smiled no more—merely sat looking up into his face with a fixed, set regard that was utterly without emotion or sentiment. Yet it had something in it that tamed his resentment and made him shiver.

"You are determined to have my reason?" she asked in a tone that was entirely mechanical—a tone that might have been her look made audible.

"If you please—if I'm not asking too much."

Apparently this lord of creation was yielding some part of his dominion over his co-creature.

"Very well, you shall know: I am insane."

The man started, then looked incredulous and was conscious that he ought to be amused. But, again, the sense of humor failed him in his need and despite his disbelief he was profoundly disturbed by that which he did not believe. Between our convictions and our feelings there is no good understanding.

"That is what the physicians would say," the woman continued—"if they knew. I might myself prefer to call it a case of 'possession.' Sit down and hear what I have to say."

The man silently resumed his seat beside her on the rustic bench by the wayside. Over-against them on the eastern side of the valley the hills were already sunset-flushed and the stillness all about was of that peculiar quality that foretells the twilight. Something of its mysterious and significant solemnity had imparted itself to the man's mood. In the spiritual, as in the material world, are signs and presages of night. Rarely meeting her look, and whenever he did so conscious of the indefinable dread with which, despite their feline beauty, her eyes always affected him, Jenner Brading listened in silence to the story told by Irene Marlowe. In deference to the reader's possible prejudice against the artless method of an unpracticed historian the author ventures to substitute his own version for hers.

II. A ROOM MAY BE TOO NARROW FOR THREE, THOUGH ONE IS OUTSIDE

In a little log house containing a single room sparely and rudely furnished, crouching on the floor against one of the walls, was a woman, clasping to her breast a child. Outside, a dense unbroken forest extended for many miles in every direction. This was at night and the room was black dark: no human eye could have discerned the woman and the child. Yet they were observed, narrowly, vigilantly, with never even a momentary slackening of attention; and that is the pivotal fact upon which this narrative turns.

Charles Marlowe was of the class, now extinct in this country, of woodmen pioneers—men who found their most acceptable surroundings in sylvan solitudes that stretched along the eastern slope of the Mississippi Valley, from the Great Lakes to the Gulf of Mexico. For more than a hundred years these men pushed ever westward, generation after generation, with rifle and ax, reclaiming from Nature and her savage children here and there an isolated acreage for the plow, no sooner reclaimed than surrendered to their less venturesome but more thrifty successors. At last they burst through the edge of the forest into the open country and vanished as if they had fallen over a cliff. The woodman pioneer is no more; the pioneer of the plains—he whose easy task it was to subdue for occupancy two-thirds of the country in a single generation—is another and inferior creation. With Charles Marlowe in the wilderness, sharing the dangers, hardships and privations of that strange, unprofitable life, were his wife and child, to whom, in the manner of his class, in which the domestic virtues were a religion, he was passionately attached. The woman was still young enough to be comely, new enough to the awful isolation of her lot to be cheerful. By withholding the large capacity for happiness which the simple satisfactions of the forest life could not have filled, Heaven had dealt honorably with her. In her light household tasks, her child, her husband and her few foolish books, she found abundant provision for her needs.

One morning in midsummer Marlowe took down his rifle from the wooden hooks on the wall and signified his intention of getting game.

"We've meat enough," said the wife; "please don't go out to-day. I dreamed last night, O, such a dreadful thing! I cannot recollect it, but I'm almost sure that it will come to pass if you go out."

It is painful to confess that Marlowe received this solemn statement with less of gravity than was due to the mysterious nature of the calamity foreshadowed. In truth, he laughed.

"Try to remember," he said. "Maybe you dreamed that Baby had lost the power of speech."

The conjecture was obviously suggested by the fact that Baby, clinging to the fringe of his hunting-coat with all her ten pudgy thumbs was at that moment uttering her sense of the situation in a series of exultant goo-goos inspired by sight of her father's raccoon-skin cap.

The woman yielded: lacking the gift of humor she could not hold out against his kindly badinage. So, with a kiss for the mother and a kiss for the child, he left the house and closed the door upon his happiness forever.

At nightfall he had not returned. The woman prepared supper and waited. Then she put Baby to bed and sang softly to her until she slept. By this time the fire on the hearth, at which she had cooked supper, had burned out and the room was lighted by a single candle. This she afterward placed in the open window as a sign and welcome to the hunter if he should approach from that side. She had thoughtfully closed and barred the door against such wild animals as might prefer it to an open window—of the habits of beasts of prey in entering a house uninvited she was not advised, though with true female prevision she may have considered the possibility of their entrance by way of the chimney. As the night wore on she became not less anxious, but more drowsy, and at last rested her arms upon the bed by the child and her head upon the arms. The candle in the window burned down to the socket, sputtered and flared a moment and went out unobserved; for the woman slept and dreamed.

In her dreams she sat beside the cradle of a second child. The first one was dead. The father was dead. The home in the forest was lost and the dwelling in which she lived was unfamiliar. There were heavy oaken doors, always closed, and outside the windows, fastened into the thick stone walls, were iron bars, obviously (so she thought) a provision against Indians. All this she noted with an infinite self-pity, but without surprise—an emotion unknown in dreams. The child in the cradle was invisible under its coverlet which something impelled her to remove. She did so, disclosing the face of a wild animal! In the shock of this dreadful revelation the dreamer awoke, trembling in the darkness of her cabin in the wood.

As a sense of her actual surroundings came slowly back to her she felt for the child that was not a dream, and assured herself by its breathing that all was well with it; nor could she forbear to pass a hand lightly across its face. Then, moved by some impulse for which she probably could not have accounted, she rose and took the sleeping babe in her arms, holding it close against her breast. The head of the child's cot was against the wall to which the woman now turned her back as she stood. Lifting her eyes she saw two bright objects starring the darkness with a reddish-green glow. She took them to be two coals on the hearth, but with her returning sense of direction came the disquieting consciousness that they were not in that quarter of the room, moreover were too high, being nearly at the level of the eyes—of her own eyes. For these were the eyes of a panther.

The beast was at the open window directly opposite and not five paces away. Nothing but those terrible eyes was visible, but in the dreadful tumult of her feelings as the situation disclosed itself to her understanding she somehow knew that the animal was standing on its hinder feet, supporting itself with its paws on the window-ledge. That signified a malign interest—not the mere gratification of an indolent curiosity. The consciousness of the attitude was an added horror, accentuating the menace of those awful eyes, in whose steadfast fire her strength and courage were alike consumed. Under their silent questioning she shuddered and turned sick. Her knees failed her, and by degrees, instinctively striving to avoid a sudden movement that might bring the beast upon her, she sank to the floor, crouched against the wall and tried to shield the babe with her trembling body without withdrawing her gaze from the luminous orbs that were killing her. No thought of her husband came to her in her agony—no hope nor suggestion of rescue or escape. Her capacity for thought and feeling had narrowed to the dimensions of a single emotion—fear of the animal's spring, of the impact of its body, the buffeting of its great arms, the feel of its teeth in her throat, the mangling of her babe. Motionless now and in absolute silence, she awaited her doom, the moments growing to hours, to years, to ages; and still those devilish eyes maintained their watch.

Returning to his cabin late at night with a deer on his shoulders Charles Marlowe tried the door. It did not yield. He knocked; there was no answer. He laid down his deer and went round to the window. As he turned the angle of the building he fancied he heard a sound as of stealthy footfalls and a rustling in the undergrowth of the forest, but they were too slight for certainty, even to his practised ear. Approaching the window, and to his surprise finding it open, he threw his leg over the sill and entered. All was darkness and silence. He groped his way to the fire-place, struck a match and lit a candle. Then he looked about. Cowering on the floor against a wall was his wife, clasping his child. As he sprang toward her she rose and broke into laughter, long, loud, and mechanical, devoid of gladness and devoid of sense—the laughter that is not out of keeping with the clanking of a chain. Hardly knowing what he did he extended his arms. She laid the babe in them. It was dead—pressed to death in its mother's embrace.

III. THE THEORY OF THE DEFENSE

That is what occurred during a night in a forest, but not all of it did Irene Marlowe relate to Jenner Brading; not all of it was known to her. When she had concluded the sun was below the horizon and the long summer twilight had begun to deepen in the hollows of the land. For some moments Brading was silent, expecting the narrative to be carried forward to some definite connection with the conversation introducing it; but the narrator was as silent as he, her face averted, her hands clasping and unclasping themselves as they lay in her lap, with a singular suggestion of an activity independent of her will.

"It is a sad, a terrible story," said Brading at last, "but I do not understand. You call Charles Marlowe father; that I know. That he is old before his time, broken by some great sorrow, I have seen, or thought I saw. But, pardon me, you said that you—that you—"

"That I am insane," said the girl, without a movement of head or body.

"But, Irene, you say—please, dear, do not look away from me—you say that the child was dead, not demented."

"Yes, that one—I am the second. I was born three months after that night, my mother being mercifully permitted to lay down her life in giving me mine."

Brading was again silent; he was a trifle dazed and could not at once think of the right thing to say. Her face was still turned away. In his embarrassment he reached impulsively toward the hands that lay closing and unclosing in her lap, but something—he could not have said what—restrained him. He then remembered, vaguely, that he had never altogether cared to take her hand.

"Is it likely," she resumed, "that a person born under such circumstances is like others—is what you call sane?"

Brading did not reply; he was preoccupied with a new thought that was taking shape in his mind—what a scientist would have called an hypothesis; a detective, a theory. It might throw an added light, albeit a lurid one, upon such doubt of her sanity as her own assertion had not dispelled.

The country was still new and, outside the villages, sparsely populated. The professional hunter was still a familiar figure, and among his trophies were heads and pelts of the larger kinds of game. Tales variously credible of nocturnal meetings with savage animals in lonely roads were sometimes current, passed through the customary stages of growth and decay, and were forgotten. A recent addition to these popular apocrypha, originating, apparently, by spontaneous generation in several households, was of a panther which had frightened some of their members by looking in at windows by night. The yarn had caused its little ripple of excitement—had even attained to the distinction of a place in the local newspaper; but Brading had given it no attention. Its likeness to the story to which he had just listened now impressed him as perhaps more than accidental. Was it not possible that the one story had suggested the other—that finding congenial conditions in a morbid mind and a fertile fancy, it had grown to the tragic tale that he had heard?

Brading recalled certain circumstances of the girl's history and disposition, of which, with love's incuriosity, he had hitherto been heedless—such as her solitary life with her father, at whose house no one, apparently, was an acceptable visitor and her strange fear of the night, by which those who knew her best accounted for her never being seen after dark. Surely in such a mind imagination once kindled might burn with a lawless flame, penetrating and enveloping the entire structure. That she was mad, though the conviction gave him the acutest pain, he could no longer doubt; she had only mistaken an effect of her mental disorder for its cause, bringing into imaginary relation with her own personality the vagaries of the local myth-makers. With some vague intention of testing his new "theory," and no very definite notion of how to set about it he said, gravely, but with hesitation:

"Irene, dear, tell me—I beg you will not take offence, but tell me—"

"I have told you," she interrupted, speaking with a passionate earnestness that he had not known her to show—"I have already told you that we cannot marry; is anything else worth saying?"

Before he could stop her she had sprung from her seat and without another word or look was gliding away among the trees toward her father's house. Brading had risen to detain her; he stood watching her in silence until she had vanished in the gloom. Suddenly he started as if he had been shot; his face took on an expression of amazement and alarm: in one of the black shadows into which she had disappeared he had caught a quick, brief glimpse of shining eyes! For an instant he was dazed and irresolute; then he dashed into the wood after her, shouting: "Irene, Irene, look out! The panther! The panther!"

In a moment he had passed through the fringe of forest into open ground and saw the girl's gray skirt vanishing into her father's door. No panther was visible.

IV. AN APPEAL TO THE CONSCIENCE OF GOD

Jenner Brading, attorney-at-law, lived in a cottage at the edge of the town. Directly behind the dwelling was the forest. Being a bachelor, and therefore, by the Draconian moral code of the time and place denied the services of the only species of domestic servant known there-about, the "hired girl," he boarded at the village hotel, where also was his office. The woodside cottage was merely a lodging maintained—at no great cost, to be sure—as an evidence of prosperity and respect-ability. It would hardly do for one to whom the local newspaper had pointed with pride as "the foremost jurist of his time" to be "homeless," albeit he may sometimes have suspected that the words "home" and "house" were not strictly synonymous. Indeed, his consciousness of the disparity and his will to harmonize it were matters of logical inference, for it was generally reported that soon after the cottage was built its owner had made a futile venture in the direction of marriage—had, in truth, gone so far as to be rejected by the beautiful but eccentric daughter of Old Man Marlowe, the recluse. This was publicly believed because he had told it himself and she had not—a reversal of the usual order of things which could hardly fail to carry conviction.

Brading's bedroom was at the rear of the house, with a single win-dow facing the forest.

One night he was awakened by a noise at that window; he could hardly have said what it was like. With a little thrill of the nerves he sat up in bed and laid hold of the revolver which, with a forethought most commendable in one addicted to the habit of sleeping on the ground floor with an open window, he had put under his pillow. The room was in absolute darkness, but being unterrified he knew where to direct his eyes, and there he held them, awaiting in silence what further might occur. He could now dimly discern the aperture—a square of lighter black. Presently there appeared at its lower edge two gleaming eyes that burned with a malignant lustre inexpressibly terrible! Brading's heart gave a great jump, then seemed to stand still. A chill passed along his spine and through his hair; he felt the blood forsake his cheeks. He could not have cried out—not to save his life; but being a man of courage he would not, to save his life, have done so if he had been able. Some trepidation his coward body might feel, but his spirit was of sterner stuff. Slowly the shining eyes rose with a steady motion that seemed an approach, and slowly rose Brading's right hand, holding the pistol. He fired!

Blinded by the flash and stunned by the report, Brading nevertheless heard, or fancied that he heard, the wild, high scream of the panther, so human in sound, so devilish in suggestion. Leaping from the bed he hastily clothed himself and, pistol in hand, sprang from the door, meeting two or three men who came running up from the road. A brief explanation was followed by a cautious search of the house. The grass was wet with dew; beneath the window it had been trodden and partly leveled for a wide space, from which a devious trail, visible in the light of a lantern, led away into the bushes. One of the men stumbled and fell upon his hands, which as he rose and rubbed them together were slippery. On examination they were seen to be red with blood.

An encounter, unarmed, with a wounded panther was not agreeable to their taste; all but Brading turned back. He, with lantern and pistol, pushed courageously forward into the wood. Passing through a difficult undergrowth he came into a small opening, and there his courage had its reward, for there he found the body of his victim. But it was no panther. What it was is told, even to this day, upon a weather-worn headstone in the village churchyard, and for many years was attested daily at the graveside by the bent figure and sorrow-seamed face of Old Man Marlowe, to whose soul, and to the soul of his strange, unhappy child, peace. Peace and reparation.

"The Midnight Zone"

LAUREN GROFF

Lauren Groff (b. 1978) is the author of two acclaimed short-story collections, *Delicate Edible Birds* (2009) and *Florida* (2018), as well as four highly regarded novels, *The Monsters of Templeton* (2008), *Arcadia* (2012), *Fates and Furies* (2015), and *Matrix* (2021). Based on Groff's hometown of Cooperstown, New York, her first novel, *The Monsters of Templeton,* cannily invokes James Fenimore Cooper's *The Pioneers,* Cooper's "women and panther" episode serving as a historical predecessor to Groff's own panther tale, "The Midnight Zone," appearing almost two centuries later in the *New Yorker* (May 23, 2016). Though much of Groff's early work is set in Western New York, her recent stories favor Florida, a place she describes in interviews as reptilian, dangerous, and teeming. "The Midnight Zone" features a woman left alone with her young children, this time in a remote marshland dwelling in the Florida Keys, a lone panther pacing outside. Eschewing the racial and sexual fears that mark nineteenth-century panther tales, Groff's modern story captures the spectral return of the rare Florida panther, one of the first animals protected by the 1973 Endangered Species Act and the only breeding population left in America today. Groff included "The Midnight Zone" in her book *Florida,* which went on to win the Story Prize for best short-story collection of the year and which was also shortlisted for the National Book Award for Fiction. Groff currently resides in Gainesville, Florida, with her husband and two children.

"The Midnight Zone"

LAUREN GROFF

It was an old hunting camp shipwrecked in twenty miles of scrub. Our friend had seen a Florida panther sliding through the trees there a few days earlier. But things had been fraying in our hands, and the camp was free and silent, so I walked through the resistance of my cautious husband and my small boys, who had wanted hermit crabs and kites and wakeboards and sand for spring break. Instead, they got ancient sinkholes filled with ferns, potential death by cat.

One thing I liked was how the screens at night pulsed with the tender bellies of lizards.

Even in the sleeping bag with my smaller son, the golden one, the March chill seemed to blow through my bones. I loved eating, but I'd lost so much weight by then that I carried myself delicately, as if I'd gone translucent.

There was sparse electricity from a gas-powered generator and no internet and you had to climb out through the window in the loft and stand on the roof to get a cell signal. On the third day, the boys were asleep and I'd dimmed the lanterns when my husband went up and out and I heard him stepping on the metal roof, a giant brother to the raccoons that woke us thumping around up there at night like burglars.

Then my husband stopped moving, and stood still for so long I forgot where he was. When he came down the ladder from the loft, his face had blanched.

Who died? I said lightly, because if anyone was going to die it was going to be us, our skulls popping in the jaws of an endangered cat. It turned out to be a bad joke, because someone actually had died, that morning, in one of my husband's apartment buildings. A fifth-floor occupant had killed herself, maybe on purpose, with aspirin and vodka and a bathtub. Floors four, three, and two were away somewhere with beaches and alcoholic smoothies, and the first floor had discovered the problem only when the water of death had seeped into the carpet.

My husband had to leave. He'd just fired one handyman and the other was on his own Caribbean adventure, eating buffet food to the sound of cruise-ship calypso. Let's pack, my husband said, but my rebel-liousness at the time was like a sticky fog rolling through my body and never burning off, there was no sun inside, and so I said that the boys and I would stay. He looked at me as if I were crazy and asked how we'd manage with no car. I asked if he thought he'd married an incompetent woman, which cut to the bone, because the source of our problems was that, in fact, he had. For years at a time I was good only at the things that interested me, and since all that interested me was my work and my children, the rest of life had sort of inched away. And while it's true that my children were endlessly fascinating, two petri dishes growing human cultures, being a mother never had been, and all that seemed assigned by default of gender I would not do because it felt insulting. I would not buy clothes, I would not make dinner, I would not keep schedules, I would not make playdates, never ever. Motherhood meant, for me, that I would take the boys on monthlong adventures to Europe, teach them to blast off rockets, to swim for glory. I taught them how to read, but they could make their own lunches. I would hug them as long as they wanted to be hugged, but that was just being human. My husband had to be the one to make up for the depths of my lack. It is exhausting, living in debt that increases every day but that you have no intention of repaying.

Two days, he promised. Two days and he'd be back by noon on the third. He bent to kiss me, but I gave him my cheek and rolled over when the headlights blazed then dwindled on the wall. In the banish-ing of the engine, the night grew bold. The wind was making a low, inhuman muttering in the pines, and, inspired, the animals let loose in call-and-response. Everything kept me alert until shortly before dawn, when I slept for a few minutes until the puppy whined and woke me. My older son was crying because he'd thrown off his sleeping bag in the night and was cold but too sleepy to fix the situation.

I made scrambled eggs with a vengeful amount of butter and ched-dar, also cocoa with an inch of marshmallow, thinking I would stupefy my children with calories, but the calories only made them stronger.

Our friend had treated the perimeter of the clearing with panther deterrent, some kind of synthetic superpredator urine, and we felt safe-ish near the cabin. We ran footraces until the dog went wild and leapt up and bit my children's arms with her puppy teeth, and the boys screamed with pain and frustration and showed me the pink stripes on their skin. I scolded the puppy harshly and she crept off to the porch to watch us with her chin on her paws. The boys and I played soccer. We rocked in the hammock. We watched the circling red-shouldered hawks. I made my older son read *Alice's Adventures in Wonderland* to the little one, which was a disaster, a book so punny and Victorian for modern children. We had lunch, then the older boy tried to make fire by rubbing sticks together, his little brother attending solemnly, and they spent the rest of the day constructing a hut out of branches. Then dinner, singing songs, a bath in the galvanized-steel horse trough some-one had converted to a cold-water tub, picking ticks and chiggers off with tweezers, and that was it for the first day.

There had been a weight on us as we played outside, not as if some-thing were actually watching but because of the possibility that some-thing could be watching when we were so far from humanity in all that Florida waste.

The second day should have been like the first. I doubled down on the calories, adding pancakes to breakfast, and succeeded in making the boys lie in pensive digestion out in the hammock for a little while before they ricocheted off the trees.

But in the afternoon the one light bulb sizzled out. The cabin was all dark wood and I couldn't see the patterns on the dishes I was wash-ing. I found a new bulb in a closet, dragged over a stool from the bar area, and made the older boy hold the spinning seat as I climbed aboard. The old bulb was hot, and I was passing it from hand to hand, holding the new bulb under my arm, when the puppy leapt up at my older son's face. He let go of the stool to whack at her, and I did a quarter spin, then fell and hit the floor with my head, and then I surely blacked out.

After a while, I opened my eyes. Two children were looking down at me. They were pale and familiar. One fair, one dark; one small, one big.

Mommy? the little boy said, through water.

I turned my head and threw up on the floor. The bigger boy dragged a puppy, who was snuffling my face, out the door.

I knew very little except that I was in pain and that I shouldn't move. The older boy bent over me, then lifted an intact light bulb from my armpit, triumphantly; I a chicken, the bulb an egg.

The smaller boy had a wet paper towel in his hand and he was patting my cheeks. The pulpy smell made me ill again. I closed my eyes and felt the dabbing on my forehead, on my neck, around my mouth. The small child's voice was high. He was singing a song.

I started to cry with my eyes closed and the tears went hot across my temples and into my ears.

Mommy! the older boy, the solemn dark one, screamed, and when I opened my eyes both of the children were crying, and that was how I knew them to be mine.

Just let me rest here a minute, I said. They took my hands. I could feel the hot hands of my children, which was good. I moved my toes, then my feet. I turned my head back and forth. My neck worked, though fireworks went off in the corners of my eyes.

I can walk to town, the older boy was saying, through wadding, to his brother, but the nearest town was twenty miles away. Safety was twenty miles away and there was a panther between us and there, but also possibly terrible men, sinkholes, alligators, the end of the world. There was no landline, no umbilical cord, and small boys using cell phones would easily fall off such a slick, pitched metal roof.

But what if she's all a sudden dead and I'm all a sudden alone? the little boy was saying.

Okay, I'm sitting up now, I said.

The puppy was howling at the door.

I lifted my body onto my elbows. Gingerly, I sat. The cabin dipped and spun and I vomited again.

The big boy ran out and came back with a broom to clean up. No! I said. I am always too hard on him, this beautiful child who is so brilliant, who has no logic at all.

Sweetness, I said, and couldn't stop crying, because I'd called him Sweetness instead of his name, which I couldn't remember just then. I took five or six deep breaths. Thank you, I said in a calmer voice. Just throw a whole bunch of paper towels on it and drag the rug over it to keep the dog off. The little one did so, methodically, which was not his style; he has always been adept at cheerfully watching other people work for him.

The bigger boy tried to get me to drink water, because this is what we do in our family in lieu of applying Band-Aids, which I refuse to buy because they are just flesh-colored landfill.

Then the little boy screamed, because he'd moved around me and seen the bloody back of my head, and then he dabbed at the cut with the paper towel he had previously dabbed at my pukey mouth. The paper disintegrated in his hands. He crawled into my lap and put his face on my stomach. The bigger boy held something cold on my wound, which I discovered later to be a beer can from the fridge.

They were quiet like this for a very long time. The boys' names came back to me, at first dancing coyly out of reach, then, when I seized them in my hands, mine.

I'd been a soccer player in high school, a speedy and aggressive midfielder, and head trauma was an old friend. I remembered this constant lability from one concussive visit to the emergency room. The confusion and the sense of doom were also familiar. I had a flash of my mother sitting beside my bed for an entire night, shaking me awake whenever I tried to fall asleep, and I now wanted my mother, not in her diminished current state, brittle retiree, but as she had been when I was young, a small person but gigantic, a person who had blocked out the sun.

I sent the little boy off to get a roll of dusty duct tape, the bigger boy to get gauze from my toiletry kit, and when they wandered back I duct-taped the gauze to my head, already mourning my long hair, which had been my most expensive pet.

I inched myself across the room to the bed and climbed up, despite the sparklers behind my eyeballs. The boys let the forlorn puppy in, and when they opened the door they also let the night in, because my fall had taken hours from our lives.

It was only then, when the night entered, that I understood the depth of time we had yet to face. I had the boys bring me the lanterns, then a can opener and the tuna and the beans, which I opened slowly, because it is not easy, supine, and we made a game out of eating, though the thought of eating anything gave me chills. The older boy brought over Mason jars of milk. I let my children finish the entire half gallon of ice cream, which was my husband's, his one daily reward for being kind and good, but by this point the man deserved our disloyalty, because he was not there.

It had started raining, at first a gentle thrumming on the metal roof.

I tried to tell my children a cautionary tale about a little girl who fell into a well and had to wait a week until firefighters could figure out a way to rescue her, something that maybe actually took place back in the dimness of my childhood, but the story was either too abstract for them or I wasn't making much sense, and they didn't seem to grasp my need for them to stay in the cabin, to not go anywhere, if the very worst happened, the unthinkable that I was skirting, like a pit that opened just in front of each sentence I was about to utter. They kept asking me if the girl got lots of toys when she made it out of the well. This was so against my point that I said, out of spite, Unfortunately, no, she did not.

I made the boys keep me awake with stories. The younger one was into a British television show about marine life, which the older one maintained was babyish until I pretended not to believe what they were telling me. Then they both told me about cookie-cutter sharks, who bore perfect round holes in whales, as if their mouths were cookie cutters. They told me about a fish called the humuhumunukunukuāpua'a, a beautiful name that I couldn't say correctly, even though they sang it to me over and over, laughing, to the tune of "Twinkle Twinkle, Little Star." They told me about the walking catfish, which can stay out of water for days and days, meandering about in the mud. They told me about the sunlight, the twilight, and the midnight zones, the three depths of water, where there is transparent light, then a murky, darkish light, then no light at all. They told me about the World Pool, in which one current goes one way, another goes another way, and where they meet they make a tornado of air, which stretches, my little one said, from the midnight zone, where the fish are blind, all the way up up up to the birds.

I had begun shaking very hard, which my children, sudden gentlemen, didn't mention. They piled all the sleeping bags and blankets they could find on me, then climbed under and fell asleep without bathing or toothbrushing or getting out of their dirty clothes, which, anyway, they sweated through within an hour.

The dog did not get dinner but she didn't whine about it, and though she wasn't allowed to, she came up on the bed and slept with her head on my older son's stomach, because he was her favorite, being the biggest puppy of all.

Now I had only myself to sit vigil with me, though it was still early, nine or ten at night.

I had a European novel on the nightstand that filled me with dimness and fret, so I tried to read *Alice's Adventures in Wonderland,* but it was incomprehensible with my scrambled brains. Then I looked at a hunting magazine, which made me remember the Florida panther. I hadn't truly forgotten about it, but could manage only a few terrors at a time, and others, when my children had been awake, were more urgent. We had seen some scat in the woods on a walk three days earlier, enormous scat, either a bear's or the panther's, but certainly a giant predator's. The danger had been abstract until we saw this bodily proof of existence, and my husband and I led the children home, singing a round, all four of us holding hands, and we let the dog off the leash to circle us joyously, because, as small as she was, it was bred in her bones that in the face of peril she would sacrifice herself first.

The rain increased until it was deafening and still my sweaty children slept. I thought of the waves of sleep rushing through their brains, washing out the tiny unimportant flotsam of today so that tomorrow's heavier truths could wash in. There was a nice solidity to the rain's pounding on the roof, as if the noise were a barrier that nothing could enter, a stay against the looming night.

I tried to bring back the poems of my youth, and could not remember more than a few floating lines, which I put together into a strange, sad poem, Blake and Dickinson and Frost and Milton and Sexton, a tag-sale poem in clammy meter that nonetheless came alive and held my hand for a little while.

Then the rain diminished until all that was left were scattered clicks from the drops falling from the pines. The batteries of one lantern went out and the light from the remaining lantern was sparse and thwarted. I could hardly see my hand or the shadow it made on the wall when I held it up. This lantern was my sister; at any moment it, too, could go dark. I feasted my eyes on the cabin, which in the oncoming black had turned into a place made of gold, but the shadows seemed too thick now, fizzy at the edges, and they moved when I shifted my eyes away from them. It felt safer to look at the cheeks of my sleeping children, creamy as cheeses.

It was elegiac, that last hour or so of light, and I tried to push my love for my sons into them where their bodies were touching my own skin.

The wind rose again and it had personality; it was in a sharpish, meanish mood. It rubbed itself against the little cabin and played at the corners and broke sticks off the trees and tossed them at the roof so they jigged down like creatures with strange and scrabbling claws. The wind rustled its endless body against the door.

Everything depended on my staying still, but my skin was stuffed with itches. Something terrible in me, the darkest thing, wanted to slam my own head back against the headboard. I imagined it over and over, the sharp backward crack, and the wash and spill of peace.

I counted slow breaths and was not calm by two hundred; I counted to a thousand.

The lantern flicked itself out and the dark poured in.

The moon rose in the skylight and backed itself across the black.

When it was gone and I was alone again, I felt the dissociation, a physical shifting, as if the best of me were detaching from my body and sitting down a few feet distant. It was a great relief.

For a few moments, there was a sense of mutual watching, a wait for something definitive, though nothing definitive came, and then the bodiless me stood and circled the cabin. The dog moved and gave a soft whine through her nose, although she remained asleep. The floors were cool underfoot. My head brushed the beams, though they were ten feet up. Where my body and those of my two sons lay together was a black and pulsing mass, a hole of light.

I passed outside. The path was pale dirt and filled with sandspur and was cold and wet after the rain. The great drops from the tree branches left a pine taste in me. The forest was not dark, because darkness has nothing to do with the forest—the forest is made of life, of light—but the trees moved with wind and subtle creatures. I wasn't in any single place. I was with the raccoons of the rooftop, who were now down fiddling with the bicycle lock on the garbage can at the end of the road, with the red-shouldered hawk chicks breathing alone in the nest, with the armadillo forcing its armored body through the brush. I hadn't realized that I'd lost my sense of smell until it returned hungrily now; I could smell the worms tracing their paths under the pine needles and the mold breathing out new spores, shaken alive by the rain.

I was vigilant, moving softly in the underbrush, and the palmettos' nails scraped down my body.

The cabin was not visible, but it was present, a sore at my side, a feeling of density and airlessness. I couldn't go away from it, I couldn't return, I could only circle the cabin and circle it. With each circle, a terrible, stinging anguish built in me and I had to move faster and faster, each pass bringing up ever more wildness. What had been built to seem so solid was fragile in the face of time because time is impassive, more animal than human. Time would not care if you fell out of it. It would continue on without you. It cannot see you; it has always been blind to the human and the things we do to stave it off, the taxonomies, the cleaning, the arranging, the ordering. Even this cabin with its perfectly considered angles, its veins of pipes and wires, was barely more stable than the rake marks we made in the dust that morning, which time had already scrubbed away.

The self in the woods ran and ran, but the running couldn't hold off the slow shift. A low mist rose from the ground and gradually came clearer. The first birds sent their questions into the chilly air. The sky developed its blue. The sun emerged.

The drawing back was gradual. My older son opened his brown eyes and saw me sitting above him.

You look terrible, he said, patting my face, and my hearing was only half underwater now.

My head ached, so I held my mouth shut and smiled with my eyes and he padded off to the kitchen and came back with peanut-butter-and-jelly sandwiches, with a set of Uno cards, with cold coffee from yesterday's pot for the low and constant thunder of my headache, with the dog whom he'd let out and then fed all by himself.

I watched him. He gleamed. My little son woke but didn't get up, as if his face were attached to my shoulder by the skin. He was rubbing one unbloodied lock of my hair on his lips, the way he did after he nursed when he was a baby.

My boys were not unhappy. I was usually a preoccupied mother, short with them, busy, working, until I burst into fun, then went back to my hole of work; now I could only sit with them, talk to them. I could not even read. They were gentle with me, reminded me of a golden retriever I'd grown up with, a dog with a mouth so soft she would go down to the lake and steal ducklings and hold them intact on her tongue for hours until we noticed her sitting unusually erect in the corner, looking sly. My boys were like their father; they would one day be men who would take care of the people they loved.

I closed my eyes as the boys played game after game after game of Uno.

Noon arrived, noon left, and my husband did not come.

At one point, something passed across the woods outside like a shudder, and a hush fell over everything, and the boys and the dog all looked at me and their faces were like pale birds taking flight, but my hearing had mercifully shut off whatever had occasioned such swift terror over all creatures of the earth, save me.

When we heard the car from afar at four in the afternoon, the boys jumped up. They burst out of the cabin, leaving the door wide open to the blazing light, which hurt my eyes. I heard their father's voice, and then his footsteps, and he was running, and behind him the boys were running, the dog was running. Here were my husband's feet on the dirt drive. Here were his feet heavy on the porch.

For a half breath, I would have vanished myself. I was everything we had fretted about, this passive Queen of Chaos with her bloody duct-tape crown. My husband filled the door. He is a man born to fill doors. I shut my eyes. When I opened them, he was enormous above me. In his face was a thing that made me go quiet inside, made a long slow sizzle creep up my arms from the fingertips, because the thing I read in his face was the worst, it was fear, and it was vast, it was elemental, like the wind itself, like the cold sun I would soon feel on the silk of my pelt.

PART 3

FIRE AND ICE

Survival plots constitute the most gripping tales in the history of wilderness fiction, for the simple reason that their suspenseful scenarios and all-too-human predicaments are so entirely, strikingly plausible. These twentieth-century tales of survival in the wild feature rugged individualists—prospectors, backwoodsmen, trappers, hunters—all seeking to carve out livelihoods by intrepidly harnessing the resources of North America's western frontier. A year after the 1899 land rush on Oklahoma—a land grab that further displaced Indigenous peoples from their ancestral lands to bring settlement and agriculture even farther west—the U.S. Census Bureau declared the frontier "closed." But the allure of an open and wild frontier, already in the nineteenth century a literary site for mythologizations of heroic frontier masculinity, continues in the twentieth century in a much more realist vein, as writers like Jack London and Charles G. D. Roberts introduce the psychological wilderness story. Protagonists of what we might call classic wilderness survival tales are only erstwhile Daniel Boones and Davy Crocketts, early populist frontiersmen encountered by later writers mainly as larger-than-life figures in American folklore. Battling not just the harsh elements but their own minds, fiction's new wilderness frontiersmen learn humility in the face of Nature's indifference, finding their fates depend more on circumstance or chance than on their own survival skills.

"To Build a Fire"

JACK LONDON

Jack London (1876–1916) was a laborer, oyster pirate, seaman, seal hunter, factory worker, prospector, correspondent, traveler, rancher, and fiction writer. At the age of twenty-one, London joined the Klondike Gold Rush the year after gold was discovered there, keeping a travel diary of his trip into the Yukon, Canada's westernmost territory. Of his roughly two hundred short stories, nearly eighty are Klondike tales, including two of his best naturalistic stories, "To Build a Fire" and "Love of Life." The Yukon's subarctic clime and boreal forest also form the backdrop to London's two most famous novels, *The Call of the Wild* (1903) and *White Fang* (1906), books in which he continues to explore Darwinian themes of the will to live and the survival of the fittest. London knew all too well from his own experience that nothing can quite prepare you for the unpredictability of the wild. In the bitter Northern winter of 1897–98, fewer than one in three eager prospectors ("stampeders") ultimately managed to complete the dangerous hike over the Chilkoot Pass and up the Yukon River to find shelter in Dawson City. London was one who persevered, and although he never found gold, he did return south a year later with a trove of story ideas. The author composed his first and lesser-known 1902 version of "To Build a Fire" for the boy's magazine *Youth's Companion*. Six years later he revised and significantly expanded the story, explaining to his publisher at *Century Magazine* that he was motivated to offer a more adequate tale, one suitable for an adult audience. The second and superior 1908 version of "To Build a Fire," reprinted here, remains one of the most famous and widely anthologized short stories by a North American writer. During his time in the Yukon, London contracted scurvy, one of many factors that contributed to his early death at the age of forty. Before he died he had published more than fifty books and cemented his reputation as wilderness literature's most adventurous and commercially successful author.

"To Build a Fire"

JACK LONDON

Day had broken cold and grey, exceedingly cold and grey, when the man turned aside from the main Yukon trail and climbed the high earth-bank, where a dim and little-travelled trail led eastward through the fat spruce timberland. It was a steep bank, and he paused for breath at the top, excusing the act to himself by looking at his watch. It was nine o'clock. There was no sun nor hint of sun, though there was not a cloud in the sky. It was a clear day, and yet there seemed an intangible pall over the face of things, a subtle gloom that made the day dark, and that was due to the absence of sun. This fact did not worry the man. He was used to the lack of sun. It had been days since he had seen the sun, and he knew that a few more days must pass before that cheerful orb, due south, would just peep above the sky-line and dip immediately from view.

The man flung a look back along the way he had come. The Yukon lay a mile wide and hidden under three feet of ice. On top of this ice were as many feet of snow. It was all pure white, rolling in gentle undulations where the ice-jams of the freeze-up had formed. North and south, as far as his eye could see, it was unbroken white, save for a dark hair-line that curved and twisted from around the spruce-covered island to the south, and that curved and twisted away into the north, where it disappeared behind another spruce-covered island. This dark hair-line was the trail—the main trail—that led south five hundred miles to the Chilcoot Pass, Dyea, and salt water; and that led north seventy miles to Dawson, and still on to the north a thousand miles to Nulato, and finally to St. Michael on Bering Sea, a thousand miles and half a thousand more.

But all this—the mysterious, far-reaching hair-line trail, the absence of sun from the sky, the tremendous cold, and the strangeness and weirdness of it all—made no impression on the man. It was not because he was long used to it. He was a newcomer in the land, a *chechaquo,* and this was his first winter. The trouble with him was that he was without imagination. He was quick and alert in the things of life, but only in the things, and not in the significances. Fifty degrees below zero meant eighty-odd degrees of frost. Such fact impressed him as being cold and uncomfortable, and that was all. It did not lead him to meditate upon his frailty as a creature of temperature, and upon man's frailty in general, able only to live within certain narrow limits of heat and cold; and from there on it did not lead him to the conjectural field of immortality and man's place in the universe. Fifty degrees below zero stood for a bite of frost that hurt and that must be guarded against by the use of mittens, ear-flaps, warm moccasins, and thick socks. Fifty degrees below zero was to him just precisely fifty degrees below zero. That there should be anything more to it than that was a thought that never entered his head.

As he turned to go on, he spat speculatively. There was a sharp, explosive crackle that startled him. He spat again. And again, in the air, before it could fall to the snow, the spittle crackled. He knew that at fifty below spittle crackled on the snow, but this spittle had crackled in the air. Undoubtedly it was colder than fifty below—how much colder he did not know. But the temperature did not matter. He was bound for the old claim on the left fork of Henderson Creek, where the boys were already. They had come over across the divide from the Indian Creek country, while he had come the roundabout way to take a look at the possibilities of getting out logs in the spring from the islands in the Yukon. He would be into camp by six o'clock; a bit after dark, it was true, but the boys would be there, a fire would be going, and a hot supper would be ready. As for lunch, he pressed his hand against the protruding bundle under his jacket. It was also under his shirt, wrapped up in a handkerchief and lying against the naked skin. It was the only way to keep the biscuits from freezing. He smiled agreeably to himself as he thought of those biscuits, each cut open and sopped in bacon grease, and each enclosing a generous slice of fried bacon.

He plunged in among the big spruce trees. The trail was faint. A foot of snow had fallen since the last sled had passed over, and he was glad he was without a sled, travelling light. In fact, he carried nothing but the lunch wrapped in the handkerchief. He was surprised, however, at the cold. It certainly was cold, he concluded, as he rubbed his numbed nose and cheek-bones with his mittened hand. He was a warm-whiskered man, but the hair on his face did not protect the high cheek-bones and the eager nose that thrust itself aggressively into the frosty air.

At the man's heels trotted a dog, a big native husky, the proper wolf-dog, grey-coated and without any visible or temperamental difference from its brother, the wild wolf. The animal was depressed by the tremendous cold. It knew that it was no time for travelling. Its instinct told it a truer tale than was told to the man by the man's judgment. In reality, it was not merely colder than fifty below zero; it was colder than sixty below, than seventy below. It was seventy-five below zero. Since the freezing-point is thirty-two above zero, it meant that one hundred and seven degrees of frost obtained. The dog did not know anything about thermometers. Possibly in its brain there was no sharp consciousness of a condition of very cold such as was in the man's brain. But the brute had its instinct. It experienced a vague but menacing apprehension that subdued it and made it slink along at the man's heels, and that made it question eagerly every unwonted movement of the man as if expecting him to go into camp or to seek shelter somewhere and build a fire. The dog had learned fire, and it wanted fire, or else to burrow under the snow and cuddle its warmth away from the air.

The frozen moisture of its breathing had settled on its fur in a fine powder of frost, and especially were its jowls, muzzle, and eyelashes whitened by its crystalled breath. The man's red beard and moustache were likewise frosted, but more solidly, the deposit taking the form of ice and increasing with every warm, moist breath he exhaled. Also, the man was chewing tobacco, and the muzzle of ice held his lips so rigidly that he was unable to clear his chin when he expelled the juice. The result was that a crystal beard of the color and solidity of amber was increasing its length on his chin. If he fell down it would shatter itself, like glass, into brittle fragments. But he did not mind the appendage. It was the penalty all tobacco-chewers paid in that country, and he had been out before in two cold snaps. They had not been so cold as this, he knew, but by the spirit thermometer at Sixty Mile he knew they had been registered at fifty below and at fifty-five.

He held on through the level stretch of woods for several miles, crossed a wide flat of n——heads, and dropped down a bank to the frozen bed of a small stream. This was Henderson Creek, and he knew he was ten miles from the forks. He looked at his watch. It was ten o'clock. He was making four miles an hour, and he calculated that he would arrive at the forks at half-past twelve. He decided to celebrate that event by eating his lunch there.

The dog dropped in again at his heels, with a tail drooping discouragement, as the man swung along the creek-bed. The furrow of the old sled-trail was plainly visible, but a dozen inches of snow covered the marks of the last runners. In a month no man had come up or down that silent creek. The man held steadily on. He was not much given to thinking, and just then particularly he had nothing to think about save that he would eat lunch at the forks and that at six o'clock he would be in camp with the boys. There was nobody to talk to and, had there been, speech would have been impossible because of the ice-muzzle on his mouth. So he continued monotonously to chew tobacco and to increase the length of his amber beard.

Once in a while the thought reiterated itself that it was very cold and that he had never experienced such cold. As he walked along he rubbed his cheek-bones and nose with the back of his mittened hand. He did this automatically, now and again changing hands. But rub as he would, the instant he stopped his cheek-bones went numb, and the following instant the end of his nose went numb. He was sure to frost his cheeks; he knew that, and experienced a pang of regret that he had not devised a nose-strap of the sort Bud wore in cold snaps. Such a strap passed across the cheeks, as well, and saved them. But it didn't matter much, after all. What were frosted cheeks? A bit painful, that was all; they were never serious.

Empty as the man's mind was of thoughts, he was keenly observant, and he noticed the changes in the creek, the curves and bends and timber-jams, and always he sharply noted where he placed his feet. Once, coming around a bend, he shied abruptly, like a startled horse, curved away from the place where he had been walking, and retreated several paces back along the trail. The creek he knew was frozen clear to the bottom—no creek could contain water in that arctic winter—but he knew also that there were springs that bubbled out from the hillsides and ran along under the snow and on top the ice of the creek. He knew that the coldest snaps never froze these springs, and he knew likewise their danger. They were traps. They hid pools of water under the snow that might be three inches deep, or three feet. Sometimes a skin of ice half an inch thick covered them, and in turn was covered by the snow. Sometimes there were alternate layers of water and ice-skin, so that when one broke through he kept on breaking through for a while, sometimes wetting himself to the waist.

That was why he had shied in such panic. He had felt the give under his feet and heard the crackle of a snow-hidden ice-skin. And to get his feet wet in such a temperature meant trouble and danger. At the very least it meant delay, for he would be forced to stop and build a fire, and under its protection to bare his feet while he dried his socks and moccasins. He stood and studied the creek-bed and its banks, and decided that the flow of water came from the right. He reflected awhile, rubbing his nose and cheeks, then skirted to the left, stepping gingerly and testing the footing for each step. Once clear of the danger, he took a fresh chew of tobacco and swung along at his four-mile gait.

In the course of the next two hours he came upon several similar traps. Usually the snow above the hidden pools had a sunken, candied appearance that advertised the danger. Once again, however, he had a close call; and once, suspecting danger, he compelled the dog to go on in front. The dog did not want to go. It hung back until the man shoved it forward, and then it went quickly across the white, unbroken surface. Suddenly it broke through, floundered to one side, and got away to firmer footing. It had wet its forefeet and legs, and almost immediately the water that clung to it turned to ice. It made quick efforts to lick the ice off its legs, then dropped down in the snow and began to bite out the ice that had formed between the toes. This was a matter of instinct. To permit the ice to remain would mean sore feet. It did not know this. It merely obeyed the mysterious prompting that arose from the deep crypts of its being. But the man knew, having achieved a judgment on the subject, and he removed the mitten from his right hand and helped tear out the ice-particles. He did not expose his fingers more than a minute, and was astonished at the swift numbness that smote them. It certainly was cold. He pulled on the mitten hastily, and beat the hand savagely across his chest.

At twelve o'clock the day was at its brightest. Yet the sun was too far south on its winter journey to clear the horizon. The bulge of the earth intervened between it and Henderson Creek, where the man walked under a clear sky at noon and cast no shadow. At half-past twelve, to the minute, he arrived at the forks of the creek. He was pleased at the speed he had made. If he kept it up, he would certainly be with the boys by six. He unbuttoned his jacket and shirt and drew forth his lunch. The action consumed no more than a quarter of a minute, yet in that brief moment the numbness laid hold of the exposed fingers. He did not put the mitten on, but, instead, struck the fingers a dozen sharp smashes against his leg. Then he sat down on a snow-covered log to eat. The sting that followed upon the striking of his fingers against his leg ceased so quickly that he was startled, he had had no chance to take a bite of biscuit. He struck the fingers repeatedly and returned them to the mitten, baring the other hand for the purpose of eating. He tried to take a mouthful, but the ice-muzzle prevented. He had forgotten to build a fire and thaw out. He chuckled at his foolishness, and as he chuckled he noted the numbness creeping into the exposed fingers. Also, he noted that the stinging which had first come to his toes when he sat down was already passing away. He wondered whether the toes were warm or numbed. He moved them inside the moccasins and decided that they were numbed.

He pulled the mitten on hurriedly and stood up. He was a bit frightened. He stamped up and down until the stinging returned into the feet. It certainly was cold, was his thought. That man from Sulphur Creek had spoken the truth when telling how cold it sometimes got in the country. And he had laughed at him at the time! That showed one must not be too sure of things. There was no mistake about it, it *was* cold. He strode up and down, stamping his feet and threshing his arms, until reassured by the returning warmth. Then he got out matches and proceeded to make a fire. From the undergrowth, where high water of the previous spring had lodged a supply of seasoned twigs, he got his fire-wood. Working carefully from a small beginning, he soon had a roaring fire, over which he thawed the ice from his face and in the protection of which he ate his biscuits. For the moment the cold of space was outwitted. The dog took satisfaction in the fire, stretching out close enough for warmth and far enough away to escape being singed.

When the man had finished, he filled his pipe and took his comfortable time over a smoke. Then he pulled on his mittens, settled the ear-flaps of his cap firmly about his ears, and took the creek trail up the left fork. The dog was disappointed and yearned back toward the fire. This man did not know cold. Possibly all the generations of his ancestry had been ignorant of cold, of real cold, of cold one hundred and seven degrees below freezing-point. But the dog knew; all its ancestry knew, and it had inherited the knowledge. And it knew that it was not good to walk abroad in such fearful cold. It was the time to lie snug in a hole in the snow and wait for a curtain of cloud to be drawn across the face of outer space whence this cold came. On the other hand, there was keen intimacy between the dog and the man. The one was the toil-slave of the other, and the only caresses it had ever received were the caresses of the whip-lash and of harsh and menacing throat-sounds that threatened the whip-lash. So the dog made no effort to communicate its apprehension to the man. It was not concerned in the welfare of the man; it was for its own sake that it yearned back toward the fire. But the man whistled, and spoke to it with the sound of whip-lashes, and the dog swung in at the man's heels and followed after.

The man took a chew of tobacco and proceeded to start a new amber beard. Also, his moist breath quickly powdered with white his moustache, eyebrows, and lashes. There did not seem to be so many springs on the left fork of the Henderson, and for half an hour the man saw no signs of any. And then it happened. At a place where there were no signs, where the soft, unbroken snow seemed to advertise solidity beneath, the man broke through. It was not deep. He wetted himself half-way to the knees before he floundered out to the firm crust.

He was angry, and cursed his luck aloud. He had hoped to get into camp with the boys at six o'clock, and this would delay him an hour, for he would have to build a fire and dry out his foot-gear. This was imperative at that low temperature—he knew that much; and he turned aside to the bank, which he climbed. On top, tangled in the underbrush about the trunks of several small spruce trees, was a high-water deposit of dry fire-wood—sticks and twigs principally, but also larger portions of seasoned branches and fine, dry, last-year's grasses. He threw down several large pieces on top of the snow. This served for a foundation and prevented the young flame from drowning itself in the snow it otherwise would melt. The flame he got by touching a match to a small shred of birch-bark that he took from his pocket. This burned even more readily than paper. Placing it on the foundation, he fed the young flame with wisps of dry grass and with the tiniest dry twigs.

He worked slowly and carefully, keenly aware of his danger. Gradu-ally, as the flame grew stronger, he increased the size of the twigs with which he fed it. He squatted in the snow, pulling the twigs out from their entanglement in the brush and feeding directly to the flame. He knew there must be no failure. When it is seventy-five below zero, a man must not fail in his first attempt to build a fire—that is, if his feet are wet. If his feet are dry, and he fails, he can run along the trail for half a mile and restore his circulation. But the circulation of wet and freezing feet cannot be restored by running when it is seventy-five below. No matter how fast he runs, the wet feet will freeze the harder.

All this the man knew. The old-timer on Sulphur Creek had told him about it the previous fall, and now he was appreciating the advice. Already all sensation had gone out of his feet. To build the fire he had been forced to remove his mittens, and the fingers had quickly gone numb. His pace of four miles an hour had kept his heart pumping blood to the surface of his body and to all the extremities. But the instant he stopped, the action of the pump eased down. The cold of space smote the unprotected tip of the planet, and he, being on that unprotected tip, received the full force of the blow. The blood of his body recoiled before it. The blood was alive, like the dog, and like the dog it wanted to hide away and cover itself up from the fearful cold. So long as he walked four miles an hour, he pumped that blood, willy-nilly, to the surface; but now it ebbed away and sank down into the recesses of his body. The extremities were the first to feel its absence. His wet feet froze the faster, and his exposed fingers numbed the faster, though they had not yet begun to freeze. Nose and cheeks were already freezing, while the skin of all his body chilled as it lost its blood.

But he was safe. Toes and nose and cheeks would be only touched by the frost, for the fire was beginning to burn with strength. He was feeding it with twigs the size of his finger. In another minute he would be able to feed it with branches the size of his wrist, and then he could remove his wet foot-gear, and, while it dried, he could keep his naked feet warm by the fire, rubbing them at first, of course, with snow. The fire was a success. He was safe. He remembered the advice of the old-timer on Sulphur Creek, and smiled. The old-timer had been very serious in laying down the law that no man must travel alone in the Klondike after fifty below. Well, here he was; he had had the accident; he was alone; and he had saved himself. Those old-timers were rather womanish, some of them, he thought. All a man had to do was to keep his head, and he was all right. Any man who was a man could travel alone. But it was surprising, the rapidity with which his cheeks and nose were freezing. And he had not thought his fingers could go lifeless in so short a time. Lifeless they were, for he could scarcely make them move together to grip a twig, and they seemed remote from his body and from him. When he touched a twig, he had to look and see whether or not he had hold of it. The wires were pretty well down between him and his finger-ends.

All of which counted for little. There was the fire, snapping and crackling and promising life with every dancing flame. He started to untie his moccasins. They were coated with ice; the thick German socks were like sheaths of iron half-way to the knees; and the moccasin strings were like rods of steel all twisted and knotted as by some conflagration. For a moment he tugged with his numbed fingers, then, realizing the folly of it, he drew his sheath-knife.

But before he could cut the strings, it happened. It was his own fault or, rather, his mistake. He should not have built the fire under the spruce tree. He should have built it in the open. But it had been easier to pull the twigs from the brush and drop them directly on the fire. Now the tree under which he had done this carried a weight of snow on its boughs. No wind had blown for weeks, and each bough was fully freighted. Each time he had pulled a twig he had communicated a slight agitation to the tree—an imperceptible agitation, so far as he was concerned, but an agitation sufficient to bring about the disaster. High up in the tree one bough capsized its load of snow. This fell on the boughs beneath, capsizing them. This process continued, spreading out and involving the whole tree. It grew like an avalanche, and it descended without warning upon the man and the fire, and the fire was blotted out! Where it had burned was a mantle of fresh and disordered snow.

The man was shocked. It was as though he had just heard his own sentence of death. For a moment he sat and stared at the spot where the fire had been. Then he grew very calm. Perhaps the old-timer on Sulphur Creek was right. If he had only had a trail-mate he would have been in no danger now. The trail-mate could have built the fire. Well, it was up to him to build the fire over again, and this second time there must be no failure. Even if he succeeded, he would most likely lose some toes. His feet must be badly frozen by now, and there would be some time before the second fire was ready.

Such were his thoughts, but he did not sit and think them. He was busy all the time they were passing through his mind, he made a new foundation for a fire, this time in the open, where no treacherous tree could blot it out. Next, he gathered dry grasses and tiny twigs from the high-water flotsam. He could not bring his fingers together to pull them out, but he was able to gather them by the handful. In this way he got many rotten twigs and bits of green moss that were undesirable, but it was the best he could do. He worked methodically, even collecting an armful of the larger branches to be used later when the fire gathered strength. And all the while the dog sat and watched him, a certain yearning wistfulness in its eyes, for it looked upon him as the fire-provider, and the fire was slow in coming.

When all was ready, the man reached in his pocket for a second piece of birch-bark. He knew the bark was there, and, though he could not feel it with his fingers, he could hear its crisp rustling as he fumbled for it. Try as he would, he could not clutch hold of it. And all the time, in his consciousness, was the knowledge that each instant his feet were freezing. This thought tended to put him in a panic, but he fought against it and kept calm. He pulled on his mittens with his teeth, and threshed his arms back and forth, beating his hands with all his might against his sides. He did this sitting down, and he stood up to do it; and all the while the dog sat in the snow, its wolf-brush of a tail curled around warmly over its forefeet, its sharp wolf-ears pricked forward intently as it watched the man. And the man, as he beat and threshed with his arms and hands, felt a great surge of envy as he regarded the creature that was warm and secure in its natural covering.

After a time he was aware of the first far-away signals of sensation in his beaten fingers. The faint tingling grew stronger till it evolved into a stinging ache that was excruciating, but which the man hailed with satisfaction. He stripped the mitten from his right hand and fetched forth the birch-bark. The exposed fingers were quickly going numb again. Next he brought out his bunch of sulphur matches. But the tremendous cold had already driven the life out of his fingers. In his effort to separate one match from the others, the whole bunch fell in the snow. He tried to pick it out of the snow, but failed. The dead fingers could neither touch nor clutch. He was very careful. He drove the thought of his freezing feet, and nose, and cheeks, out of his mind, devoting his whole soul to the matches. He watched, using the sense of vision in place of that of touch, and when he saw his fingers on each side the bunch, he closed them—that is, he willed to close them, for the wires were down, and the fingers did not obey. He pulled the mitten on the right hand, and beat it fiercely against his knee. Then, with both mittened hands, he scooped the bunch of matches, along with much snow, into his lap. Yet he was no better off.

After some manipulation he managed to get the bunch between the heels of his mittened hands. In this fashion he carried it to his mouth. The ice crackled and snapped when by a violent effort he opened his mouth. He drew the lower jaw in, curled the upper lip out of the way, and scraped the bunch with his upper teeth in order to separate a match. He succeeded in getting one, which he dropped on his lap. He was no better off. He could not pick it up. Then he devised a way. He picked it up in his teeth and scratched it on his leg. Twenty times he scratched before he succeeded in lighting it. As it flamed he held it with his teeth to the birch-bark. But the burning brimstone went up his nostrils and into his lungs, causing him to cough spasmodically. The match fell into the snow and went out.

The old-timer on Sulphur Creek was right, he thought in the moment of controlled despair that ensued: after fifty below, a man should travel with a partner. He beat his hands, but failed in exciting any sensation. Suddenly he bared both hands, removing the mittens with his teeth. He caught the whole bunch between the heels of his hands. His arm-muscles not being frozen enabled him to press the hand-heels tightly against the matches. Then he scratched the bunch along his leg. It flared into flame, seventy sulphur matches at once! There was no wind to blow them out. He kept his head to one side to escape the strangling fumes, and held the blazing bunch to the birch-bark. As he so held it, he became aware of sensation in his hand. His flesh was burning. He could smell it. Deep down below the surface he could feel it. The sensation developed into pain that grew acute. And still he endured it, holding the flame of the matches clumsily to the bark that would not light readily because his own burning hands were in the way, absorbing most of the flame.

At last, when he could endure no more, he jerked his hands apart. The blazing matches fell sizzling into the snow, but the birch-bark was alight. He began laying dry grasses and the tiniest twigs on the flame. He could not pick and choose, for he had to lift the fuel between the heels of his hands. Small pieces of rotten wood and green moss clung to the twigs, and he bit them off as well as he could with his teeth. He cherished the flame carefully and awkwardly. It meant life, and it must not perish. The withdrawal of blood from the surface of his body now made him begin to shiver, and he grew more awkward. A large piece of green moss fell squarely on the little fire. He tried to poke it out with his fingers, but his shivering frame made him poke too far, and he disrupted the nucleus of the little fire, the burning grasses and tiny twigs separating and scattering. He tried to poke them together again, but in spite of the tenseness of the effort, his shivering got away with him, and the twigs were hopelessly scattered. Each twig gushed a puff of smoke and went out. The fire-provider had failed. As he looked apathetically about him, his eyes chanced on the dog, sitting across the ruins of the fire from him, in the snow, making restless, hunching movements, slightly lifting one forefoot and then the other, shifting its weight back and forth on them with wistful eagerness.

The sight of the dog put a wild idea into his head. He remembered the tale of the man, caught in a blizzard, who killed a steer and crawled inside the carcass, and so was saved. He would kill the dog and bury his hands in the warm body until the numbness went out of them. Then he could build another fire. He spoke to the dog, calling it to him; but in his voice was a strange note of fear that frightened the animal, who had never known the man to speak in such way before. Something was the matter, and its suspicious nature sensed danger—it knew not what danger but somewhere, somehow, in its brain arose an apprehension of the man. It flattened its ears down at the sound of the man's voice, and its restless, hunching movements and the liftings and shiftings of its forefeet became more pronounced; but it would not come to the man. He got on his hands and knees and crawled toward the dog. This unusual posture again excited suspicion, and the animal sidled mincingly away.

The man sat up in the snow for a moment and struggled for calmness. Then he pulled on his mittens, by means of his teeth, and got upon his feet. He glanced down at first in order to assure himself that he was really standing up, for the absence of sensation in his feet left him unrelated to the earth. His erect position in itself started to drive the webs of suspicion from the dog's mind; and when he spoke peremptorily, with the sound of whip-lashes in his voice, the dog rendered its customary allegiance and came to him. As it came within reaching distance, the man lost his control. His arms flashed out to the dog, and he experienced genuine surprise when he discovered that his hands could not clutch, that there was neither bend nor feeling in the fingers. He had forgotten for the moment that they were frozen and that they were freezing more and more. All this happened quickly, and before the animal could get away, he encircled its body with his arms. He sat down in the snow, and in this fashion held the dog, while it snarled and whined and struggled.

But it was all he could do, hold its body encircled in his arms and sit there. He realized that he could not kill the dog. There was no way to do it. With his helpless hands he could neither draw nor hold his sheath-knife nor throttle the animal. He released it, and it plunged wildly away, with tail between its legs, and still snarling. It halted forty feet away and surveyed him curiously, with ears sharply pricked forward. The man looked down at his hands in order to locate them, and found them hanging on the ends of his arms. It struck him as curious that one should have to use his eyes in order to find out where his hands were. He began threshing his arms back and forth, beating the mittened hands against his sides. He did this for five minutes, violently, and his heart pumped enough blood up to the surface to put a stop to his shivering. But no sensation was aroused in the hands. He had an impression that they hung like weights on the ends of his arms, but when he tried to run the impression down, he could not find it.

A certain fear of death, dull and oppressive, came to him. This fear quickly became poignant as he realized that it was no longer a mere matter of freezing his fingers and toes, or of losing his hands and feet, but that it was a matter of life and death with the chances against him. This threw him into a panic, and he turned and ran up the creek-bed along the old, dim trail. The dog joined in behind and kept up with him. He ran blindly, without intention, in fear such as he had never known in his life. Slowly, as he ploughed and floundered through the snow, he began to see things again—the banks of the creek, the old timber-jams, the leafless aspens, and the sky. The running made him feel better. He did not shiver. Maybe, if he ran on, his feet would thaw out; and, anyway, if he ran far enough, he would reach camp and the boys. Without doubt he would lose some fingers and toes and some of his face; but the boys would take care of him, and save the rest of him when he got there. And at the same time there was another thought in his mind that said he would never get to the camp and the boys; that it was too many miles away, that the freezing had too great a start on him, and that he would soon be stiff and dead. This thought he kept in the background and refused to consider. Sometimes it pushed itself forward and demanded to be heard, but he thrust it back and strove to think of other things.

It struck him as curious that he could run at all on feet so frozen that he could not feel them when they struck the earth and took the weight of his body. He seemed to himself to skim along above the surface and to have no connection with the earth. Somewhere he had once seen a winged Mercury, and he wondered if Mercury felt as he felt when skimming over the earth.

His theory of running until he reached camp and the boys had one flaw in it: he lacked the endurance. Several times he stumbled, and finally he tottered, crumpled up, and fell. When he tried to rise, he failed. He must sit and rest, he decided, and next time he would merely walk and keep on going. As he sat and regained his breath, he noted that he was feeling quite warm and comfortable. He was not shivering, and it even seemed that a warm glow had come to his chest and trunk. And yet, when he touched his nose or cheeks, there was no sensation. Running would not thaw them out. Nor would it thaw out his hands and feet. Then the thought came to him that the frozen portions of his body must be extending. He tried to keep this thought down, to forget it, to think of something else; he was aware of the panicky feeling that it caused, and he was afraid of the panic. But the thought asserted itself, and persisted, until it produced a vision of his body totally frozen. This was too much, and he made another wild run along the trail. Once he slowed down to a walk, but the thought of the freezing extending itself made him run again.

And all the time the dog ran with him, at his heels. When he fell down a second time, it curled its tail over its forefeet and sat in front of him facing him curiously eager and intent. The warmth and security of the animal angered him, and he cursed it till it flattened down its ears appeasingly. This time the shivering came more quickly upon the man. He was losing in his battle with the frost. It was creeping into his body from all sides. The thought of it drove him on, but he ran no more than a hundred feet, when he staggered and pitched headlong. It was his last panic. When he had recovered his breath and control, he sat up and entertained in his mind the conception of meeting death with dignity. However, the conception did not come to him in such terms. His idea of it was that he had been making a fool of himself, running around like a chicken with its head cut off—such was the simile that occurred to him. Well, he was bound to freeze anyway, and he might as well take it decently. With this new-found peace of mind came the first glimmerings of drowsiness. A good idea, he thought, to sleep off to death. It was like taking an anaesthetic. Freezing was not so bad as people thought. There were lots worse ways to die.

He pictured the boys finding his body next day. Suddenly he found himself with them, coming along the trail and looking for himself. And, still with them, he came around a turn in the trail and found himself lying in the snow. He did not belong with himself any more, for even then he was out of himself, standing with the boys and looking at himself in the snow. It certainly was cold, was his thought. When he got back to the States he could tell the folks what real cold was. He drifted on from this to a vision of the old-timer on Sulphur Creek. He could see him quite clearly, warm and comfortable, and smoking a pipe.

"You were right, old hoss; you were right," the man mumbled to the old-timer of Sulphur Creek.

Then the man drowsed off into what seemed to him the most comfortable and satisfying sleep he had ever known. The dog sat facing him and waiting. The brief day drew to a close in a long, slow twilight. There were no signs of a fire to be made, and, besides, never in the dog's experience had it known a man to sit like that in the snow and make no fire. As the twilight drew on, its eager yearning for the fire mastered it, and with a great lifting and shifting of forefeet, it whined softly, then flattened its ears down in anticipation of being chidden by the man. But the man remained silent. Later, the dog whined loudly. And still later it crept close to the man and caught the scent of death. This made the animal bristle and back away. A little longer it delayed, howling under the stars that leaped and danced and shone brightly in the cold sky. Then it turned and trotted up the trail in the direction of the camp it knew, where were the other food-providers and fire-providers.

"The Vagrants of the Barren"

CHARLES G. D. ROBERTS

Charles G. D. Roberts (1860–1943) was born before Canada was a nation, and he died during the middle of World War II. He was a professor, a hunter, a fisherman, and a nature lover, but also later in life a denizen of New York, Paris, London, and Toronto. He was a prolific writer, producing a dozen collections of poetry and more than forty works of fiction. Along with fellow Canadian Ernest Thompson Seton, Roberts is now remembered for his wilderness and animal tales that appeared in numerous illustrated collections across his career, from *Earth's Enigma* (1896) and *Around the Camp Fire* (1896), to *The Kindred of the Wild* (1902) and *Children of the Wild* (1913), to *Eyes of the Wilderness* (1933) and *Further Animal Stories* (1935). Author of Canada's first commercial travel guide, Appleton's *Canadian Guide-Book: The Tourist's and Sportsman's Guide to Eastern Canada and Newfoundland* (1891), Roberts's wilderness short stories take place in Eastern rather than Western Canada, though they nonetheless provoked comparisons to Jack London's Yukon survival tales. Both writers sought to test the power of human and animal endurance against unforgiving natural environments. A Maritimer in his youth, Roberts drew on his years in Westcock, New Brunswick, spent exploring the nearby woodlands and the Tantramar tidal salt marsh on the Bay of Fundy. One of his best tales, "The Vagrants of the Barren," appeared in 1908 in *Century Magazine* and again as the lead story in Roberts's *The Backwoodsmen* (1909). It follows the hardships that beset an Eastern Canadian woodsman suddenly left out in the bitter cold, with little to protect him, after a fire destroys his remote wilderness cabin. In recognition of his international reputation and contribution to Canadian letters, Roberts was knighted in 1935 by King George V.

"The Vagrants of the Barren"

CHARLES G. D. ROBERTS

With thick smoke in his throat and the roar of flame in his ears, Pete Noël awoke, shaking as if in the grip of a nightmare. He sat straight up in his bunk. Instantly he felt his face scorching. The whole cabin was ablaze. Leaping from his bunk, and dragging the blankets with him, he sprang to the door, tore it open, and rushed out into the snow.

But being a woodsman, and alert in every sense like the creatures of the wild themselves, his wits were awake almost before his body was, and his instincts were even quicker than his wits. The desolation and the savage cold of the wilderness had admonished him even in that terrifying moment. As he leaped out in desperate flight, he had snatched with him not only the blankets, but his rifle and cartridge-belt from where they stood by the head of the bunk, and also his larrigans and great blanket coat from where they lay by its foot. He had been sleeping, according to custom, almost fully clothed.

Outside in the snow he stood, blinking through scorched and smarting lids at the destruction of his shack. For a second or two he stared down at the things he clutched in his arms, and wondered how he had come to think of them in time. Then, realizing with a pang that he needed something more than clothes and a rifle, he flung them down on the snow and made a dash for the cabin, in the hope of rescuing a hunk of bacon or a loaf of his substantial woodsman's bread. But before he could reach the door a licking flame shot out and hurled him back, half blinded. Grabbing up a double handful of snow, he buried his face in it to ease the smart. Then he shook himself, coolly carried the treasures he had saved back to a safe distance from the flames, and sat down on the blankets to put on his larrigans.

His feet, clothed only in a single pair of thick socks, were almost frozen, while the rest of his body was roasting in the fierce heat of the conflagration. It wanted about two hours of dawn. There was not a breath of air stirring, and the flames shot straight up, murky red and clear yellow intertwisting, with here and there a sudden leaping tongue of violet white. Outside the radius of the heat the tall woods snapped sharply in the intense cold. It was so cold, indeed, that as the man stood watching the ruin of his little, lonely home, shielding his face from the blaze now with one hand then with the other, his back seemed turning to ice.

The man who lives alone in the great solitude of the forest has every chance to become a philosopher. Pete Noël was a philosopher. Instead of dwelling upon the misfortunes which had smitten him, he chose to consider his good luck in having got out of the shack alive. Putting on his coat, he noted with satisfaction that its spacious pockets contained matches, tobacco, his pipe, his heavy clasp-knife, and his mittens. He was a hundred miles from the nearest settlement, fifty or sixty from the nearest lumber-camp. He had no food. The snow was four feet deep, and soft. And his trusty snow-shoes, which would have made these distances and these difficulties of small account to him, were help- ing feed the blaze. Nevertheless, he thought, things might have been much worse. What if he had escaped in his bare feet? This thought reminded him of how cold his feet were at this moment. Well, the old shack had been a good one, and sheltered him well enough. Now that it would shelter him no longer, it should at least be made to contribute something more to his comfort. Piling his blankets carefully under the shelter of a broad stump, he sat down upon them. Then he filled and lighted his pipe, leaned back luxuriously, and stretched out his feet to the blaze. It would be time enough for him to "get a move on" when the shack was quite burned down. The shack was home as long as it lasted.

When the first mystic greyness, hard like steel and transparent like glass, began to reveal strange vistas among the ancient trees, the fire died down. The shack was a heap of ashes and pulsating, scarlet embers, with here and there a flickering, half-burned timber, and the red-hot wreck of the tiny stove sticking up in the ruins. As soon as the ruins were cool enough to approach, Pete picked up a green pole, and began poking earnestly among them. He had all sorts of vague hopes. He par- ticularly wanted his axe, a tin kettle, and something to eat. The axe was nowhere to be found, at least in such a search as could then be made. The tins, obviously, had all gone to pieces or melted. But he did, at least, scratch out a black, charred lump about the size of his fist, which gave forth an appetizing smell. When the burnt outside had been care- fully scraped off, it proved to be the remnant of a side of bacon. Pete fell to his breakfast with about as much ceremony as might have sufficed a hungry wolf, the deprivation of a roof-tree having already taken him back appreciably nearer to the elemental brute. Having devoured his burnt bacon, and quenched his thirst by squeezing some half-melted snow into a cup of birch-bark, he rolled his blankets into a handy pack, squared his shoulders, and took the trail for Conroy's Camp, fifty miles southwestward.

It was now that Pete Noël began to realize the perils that confronted him. Without his snowshoes, he found himself almost helpless. Along the trail the snow was from three to four feet deep, and soft. There had been no thaws and no hard winds to pack it down. After floundering ahead for four or five hundred yards he would have to stop and rest, half reclining. In spite of the ferocious cold, he was soon drenched with sweat. After a couple of hours of such work, he found himself consumed with thirst. He had nothing to melt the snow in; and, needless to say, he knew better than to ease his need by eating the snow itself. But he hit upon a plan which filled him with self-gratulation. Lighting a tiny fire beside the trail, under the shelter of a huge hemlock, he took off his red cotton neckerchief, filled it with snow, and held it to the flames. As the snow began to melt, he squeezed the water from it in a liberal stream. But, alas! the stream was of a colour that was not enticing. He realized, with a little qualm, that it had not occurred to him to wash that handkerchief since—well, he was unwilling to say when. For all the insistence of his thirst, therefore, he continued melting the snow and squeezing it out, till the resulting stream ran reasonably clear. Then patiently he drank, and afterward smoked three pipefuls of his rank, black tobacco as substitute for the square meal which his stomach was craving.

All through the biting silent day he floundered resolutely on, every now and then drawing his belt a little tighter, and all the while keeping a hungry watch for game of some kind. What he hoped for was rabbit, partridge, or even a fat porcupine; but he would have made a shift to stomach even the wiry muscles of a mink, and count himself fortunate. By sunset he came out on the edge of a vast barren, glorious in washes of thin gold and desolate purple under the touch of the fading west. Along to eastward ran a low ridge, years ago licked by fire, and now crested with a sparse line of ghostly rampikes, their lean, naked tops appealing to the inexorable sky. This was the head of the Big Barren.

With deep disgust, and something like a qualm of apprehension, Pete Noël reflected that he had made only fifteen miles in that long day of effort. And he was ravenously hungry. Well, he was too tired to go farther that night; and in default of a meal, the best thing he could do was sleep. First, however, he unlaced his larrigans, and with the thongs made shift to set a clumsy snare in a rabbit track a few paces back among the spruces. Then, close under the lee of a black wall of fir-trees standing out beyond the forest skirts, he clawed himself a deep trench in the snow. In one end of this trench he built a little fire, of broken deadwood and green birch saplings laboriously hacked into short lengths with his clasp-knife. A supply of this firewood, dry and green mixed, he piled beside the trench within reach. The bottom of the trench, to within a couple of feet of the fire, he lined six inches deep with spruce-boughs, making a dry, elastic bed.

By the time these preparations were completed, the sharp-starred winter night had settled down upon the solitude. In all the vast there was no sound but the occasional snap, hollow and startling, of some great tree overstrung by the frost, and the intimate little whisper and hiss of Pete's fire down in the trench. Disposing a good bunch of boughs under his head, Pete lighted his pipe, rolled himself in his blankets, and lay down with his feet to the fire.

There at the bottom of his trench, comforted by pipe and fire, hidden away from the emptiness of the enormous, voiceless world outside, Pete Noël looked up at the icy stars, and at the top of the frowning black rampart of the fir-trees, touched grimly with red flashes from his fire. He knew well—none better than he—the savage and implacable sternness of the wild. He knew how dreadful the silent adversary against whom he had been called, all unprepared, to pit his craft. There was no blinking the imminence of his peril. Hitherto he had always managed to work, more or less, *with* nature, and so had come to regard the elemental forces as friendly. Now they had turned upon him altogether and without warning. His anger rose as he realized that he was at bay. The indomitable man-spirit awoke with the anger. Sitting up suddenly, over the edge of the trench his deep eyes looked out upon the shadowy spaces of the night with challenge and defiance. Against whatever odds, he declared to himself, he was master. Having made his proclamation in that look, Pete Noël lay down again and went to sleep.

After the fashion of winter campers and of woodsmen generally, he awoke every hour or so to replenish the fire; but toward morning he sank into the heavy sleep of fatigue. When he aroused himself from this, the fire was stone grey, the sky overhead was whitish, flecked with pink streamers, and rose-pink lights flushed delicately the green wall of the fir-trees leaning above him. The edges of the blankets around his face were rigid and thick with ice from his breathing. Breaking them away roughly, he sat up, cursed himself for having let the fire out, then, with his eyes just above the edge of the trench, peered forth across the shining waste. As he did so, he instinctively shrank back into concealment. An eager light flamed into his eyes, and he blessed his luck that the fire had gone out. Along the crest of the ridge, among the rampikes, silhouetted dark and large against the sunrise, moved a great herd of caribou, feeding as they went.

Crouching low in his trench, Pete hurriedly did up his blankets, fixed the pack on his back, then crawled through the snow into the shelter of the fir-woods. As soon as he was out of sight, he arose, recovered the thongs of his larrigans from the futile snare, and made his way back on the trail as fast as he could flounder. That one glance over the edge of his trench had told his trained eye all he needed to know about the situation.

The caribou, most restless, capricious, and far-wandering of all the wilderness kindreds, were drifting south on one of their apparently aimless migrations. They were travelling on the ridge, because, as Pete instantly inferred, the snow there had been partly blown away, partly packed, by the unbroken winds. They were far out of gunshot. But he was going to trail them down even through that deep snow. By tireless persistence and craft he would do it, if he had to do it on his hands and knees.

Such wind as there was, a light but bitter air drawing irregularly down out of the north-west, blew directly from the man to the herd, which was too far off, however, to catch the ominous taint and take alarm. Pete's first care was to work around behind the herd till this danger should be quite eliminated. For a time his hunger was forgotten in the interest of the hunt; but presently, as he toiled his slow way through the deep of the forest, it grew too insistent to be ignored. He paused to strip bark from such seedlings of balsam fir as he chanced upon, scraping off and devouring the thin, sweetish pulp that lies between the bark and the mature wood. He gathered, also, the spicy tips of the birch-buds, chewing them up by handfuls and spitting out the residue of hard husks. And in this way he managed at least to soothe down his appetite from angry protest to a kind of doubtful expectancy.

At last, after a couple of hours' hard floundering, the woods thinned, the ground sloped upward, and he came out upon the flank of the ridge, a long way behind the herd, indeed, but well around the wind. In the trail of the herd the snow was broken up, and not more than a foot and a half in depth. On a likely-looking hillock he scraped it away carefully with his feet, till he reached the ground; and here he found what he expected—a few crimson berries of the Wintergreen, frozen, but plump and sweet-fleshed. Half a handful of these served for the moment to cajole his hunger, and he pressed briskly but warily along the ridge, availing himself of the shelter of every rampike in his path. At last, catching sight of the hindmost stragglers of the herd, still far out of range, he crouched like a cat, and crossed over the crest of the ridge for better concealment.

On the eastern slope the ridge carried numerous thickets of under-brush. From one to another of these Pete crept swiftly, at a rate which should bring him, in perhaps an hour, abreast of the leisurely moving herd. In an hour, then, he crawled up to the crest again, under cover of a low patch of juniper scrub. Confidently he peered through the scrub, his rifle ready. But his face grew black with bitter disappointment. The capricious beasts had gone. Seized by one of their incomprehensible vagaries—Pete was certain that he had not alarmed them—they were now far out on the white level, labouring heavily southward.

Pete set his jaws resolutely. Hunger and cold, each the mightier from their alliance, were now assailing him savagely. His first impulse was to throw off all concealment and rush straight down the broad-trodden trail. But on second thought he decided that he would lose more than he would gain by such tactics. Hampered though they were by the deep, soft snow, he knew that, once frightened, they could travel through it much faster than they were now moving, and very much faster than he could hope to follow. Assuredly, patience was his game. Slipping furtively from rampike to rampike, now creeping, now worm-ing his way like a snake, he made good time down to the very edge of the level. Then, concealment no more possible, and the rear of the herd still beyond gunshot, he emerged boldly from the covert of a clump of saplings and started in pursuit. At the sight of him, every antlered head went up in the air for one moment of wondering alarm; then, through a rolling white cloud the herd fled onward at a speed which Pete, with all his knowledge of their powers, had not imagined possible in such a state of the snow. Sullen, but not discouraged, he plodded after them.

Noël was now fairly obsessed with the one idea of overtaking the herd. Every other thought, sense, or faculty was dully occupied with his hunger and his effort to keep from thinking of it. Hour after hour he plodded on, following the wide, chaotic trail across the white silence of the barren. There was nothing to lift his eyes for, so he kept them automatically occupied in saving his strength by picking the easiest steps through the ploughed snow. He did not notice at all that the sun no longer sparkled over the waste. He did not notice that the sky had turned from hard blue to ghostly pallor. He did not notice that the wind, now blowing in his teeth, had greatly increased in force. Suddenly, however, he was aroused by a swirl of fine snow driven so fiercely that it crossed his face like a lash. Lifting his eyes from the trail, he saw that the plain all about him was blotted from sight by a streaming rout of snow-clouds. The wind was already whining its strange derisive menace in his face. The blizzard had him.

As the full fury of the storm swooped upon him, enwrapping him, and clutching at his breath, for an instant Pete Noël quailed. This was a new adversary, with whom he had not braced his nerves to grapple. But it was for an instant only. Then his weary spirit lifted itself, and he looked grimly into the eye of the storm. The cold, the storm, the hunger, he would face them all down, and win out yet. Lowering his head, and pulling a flap of his blanket coat across his mouth to make breathing easier, he plunged straight forward with what seemed like a new lease of vigour.

Had the woods been near, or had he taken note of the weather in time, Pete would have made for the shelter of the forest at once. But he knew that, when last he looked, the track of the herd had been straight down the middle of the ever-widening barren. By now he must be a good two miles from the nearest cover; and he knew well enough that, in the bewilderment of the storm, which blunted even such woodcraft as his, and blurred not only his vision, but every other sense as well, he could never find his way. His only hope was to keep to the trail of the caribou. The beasts would either lie down or circle to the woods. In such a storm as this, as he knew well enough, no animal but man himself could hunt, or follow up the trail. There was no one but man who could confront such a storm undaunted. The caribou would forget both their cunning and the knowledge that they were being hunted. He would come upon them, or they would lead him to shelter. With an obstinate pride in his superiority to the other creatures of the wilderness, he scowled defiantly at the storm, and because he was overwrought with hunger and fatigue, he muttered to himself as he went, cursing the elements that assailed him so relentlessly.

For hours he floundered on doggedly, keeping the trail by feeling rather than by sight, so thick were the cutting swirls of snow. As the drift heaped denser and denser about his legs, the terrible effort, so long sustained, began to tell on him, till his progress became only a snail's pace. Little by little, in the obstinate effort to conserve strength and vitality, his faculties all withdrew into themselves, and concentrated themselves upon the one purpose—to keep going onward. He began to feel the lure of just giving up. He began to think of the warmth and rest he could get, the release from the mad chaos of the wind, by the simple expedient of burrowing deep into the deep snow. He knew well enough that simple trick of the partridge, when frost and storm grow too ferocious for it. But his wiser spirit would not let him delude himself. Had he had a full stomach, and food in his pockets, he might, perhaps, safely have emulated this cunning trick of the partridge. But now, starving, weary, his vitality at the last ebb, he knew that if he should yield to the lure of the snow, he would be seen no more till the spring sun should reveal him, a thing of horror to the returning vireos and blackbirds, on the open, greening face of the barren. No, he would not burrow to escape the wind. He laughed aloud as he thought upon the madness of it; and went butting and plunging on into the storm, indomitable.

Suddenly, however, he stopped short, with a great sinking at his heart. He felt cautiously this way and that, first with his feet, fumbling through the deep snow, and then with his hands. At last he turned his back abruptly to the wind, cowered down with his head between his arms to shut out the devilish whistling and whining, and tried to think how or when it had happened. He had lost the trail of the herd!

All his faculties stung to keen wakefulness by this appalling knowledge, he understood how it happened, but not where. The drifts had filled the trail, till it was utterly blotted off the face of the plain; then he had kept straight on, guided by the pressure of the wind. But the caribou, meanwhile, had swerved, and moved off in another direction. Which direction? He had to acknowledge to himself that he had no clue to judge by, so whimsical were these antlered vagrants of the barren. Well, he thought doggedly, let them go! He would get along without them. Staggering to his feet, he faced the gale again, and thought hard, striving to remember what the direction of the wind had been when last he observed it, and at the same time to recall the lay of the heavy-timbered forest that skirted this barren on two sides.

At length he made up his mind where the nearest point of woods must be. He saw it in his mind's eye, a great promontory of black firs jutting out into the waste. He turned, calculating warily, till the wind came whipping full upon his left cheek. Sure that he was now facing his one possible refuge, he again struggled forward. And as he went, he pictured to himself the whole caribou herd, now half foundered in the drift, labouring toward the same retreat. Once more, crushing back hunger and faintness, he summoned up his spirit, and vowed that if the beasts could fight their way to cover, he could. Then his woodcraft should force the forest to render him something in the way of food that would suffice to keep life in his veins.

For perhaps half an hour this defiant and unvanquishable spirit kept Pete Noël going. But as the brief northern day began to wane, and a shadow to darken behind the thick, white gloom of the storm, his forces, his tough, corded muscles and his tempered nerves, again began to falter. He caught himself stumbling, and seeking excuse for delay in getting up. In spite of every effort of his will, he saw visions—thick, protecting woods close at one side or the other, or a snug log camp, half buried in the drifts, but with warm light flooding from its windows. Indignantly he would shake himself back into sanity, and the delectable visions would vanish. But while they lasted they were confusing, and presently when he aroused himself from one that was of particularly heart-breaking vividness, he found that he had let his rifle drop! It was gone hopelessly. The shock steadied him for some minutes. Well, he had his knife. After all, that was the more important of the two. He ploughed onward, once more keenly awake, and grappling with his fate.

The shadows thickened rapidly; and at last, bending with the insane riot of the storm, began to make strange, monstrous shapes.

Unravelling these illusions, and exorcising them, kept Pete Noël occupied. But suddenly one of these monstrous shapes neglected to vanish. He was just about to throw himself upon it, in half delirious antagonism, when it lurched upward with a snort, and struggled away from him. In an instant Pete was alive in every faculty, stung with an ecstasy of hope. Leaping, floundering, squirming, he followed, open knife in hand. Again and yet again the foundered beast, a big caribou bull, buried halfway up the flank, eluded him. Then, as his savage scramble at last over took it, the bull managed to turn half about, and thrust him violently in the left shoulder with an antler-point. Unheeding the hurt, Noël clutched the antler with his left hand, and forced it inexorably back. The next moment his knife was drawn with practised skill across the beast's throat.

Like most of our eastern woodsmen, Pete Noël was even finicky about his food, and took all his meat cooked to a brown. He loathed underdone flesh. Now, however, he was an elemental creature, battling with the elements for his life. And he knew, moreover, that of all possible restoratives, the best was at his hand. He drove his blade again, this time to the bull's heart. As the wild life sighed itself out, and vanished, Pete crouched down like an animal, and drank the warm, red fluid streaming from the victim's throat. As he did so, the ebbed tide of warmth, power, and mastery flooded back into his own veins. He drank his fill; then, burrowing half beneath the massive body, he lay down close against it to rest and consider.

Assured now of food to sustain him on the journey, assured of his own ability to master all other obstacles that might seek to withstand him, Pete Noël made up his mind to sleep, wrapping himself in his blankets under the shelter of the dead bull. Then the old hunter's instinct began to stir. All about him, in every momentary lull of the wind, were snortings and heavy breathings. He had wandered into the midst of the exhausted herd. Here was a chance to recoup himself, in some small part, for the loss of his cabin and supplies. He could kill a few of the helpless animals, hide them in the snow, and take the bearings of the spot as soon as the weather cleared. By and by he could get a team from the nearest settlement, and haul out the frozen meat for private sale when the game warden chanced to have his eyes shut.

Getting out his knife again, he crept stealthily toward the nearest heavy breathing. Before he could detect the beast in that tumultuous gloom, he was upon it. His outstretched left hand fell upon a wildly heaving flank. The frightened animal arose with a gasping snort, and tried to escape; but, utterly exhausted, it sank down again almost immediately, resigned to this unknown doom which stole upon it out of the tempest and the dark. Pete's hand was on it again the moment it was still. He felt it quiver and shrink beneath his touch. Instinctively he began to stroke and rub the stiff hair as he slipped his treacherous hand forward along the heaving flank. The heavings grew quieter, the frightened snortings ceased. The exhausted animal seemed to feel a reassurance in that strong, quiet touch.

When Pete's hand had reached the unresisting beast's neck, he began to feel a qualm of misgiving. His knife was in the other hand, ready for use there in the howling dark; but somehow he could not at once bring himself to use it. It would be a betrayal. Yet he had suffered a grievous loss, and here, given into his grasp by fate, was the compensation. He hesitated, arguing with himself impatiently. But even as he did so, he kept stroking that firm, warm, living neck; and through the contact there in the savage darkness, a sympathy passed between the man and the beast. He could not help it. The poor beasts and he were in the same predicament, together holding the battlements of life against the blind and brutal madness of storm. Moreover, the herd had saved him. The debt was on his side. The caress which had been so traitorous grew honest and kind. With a shamefaced grin Pete shut his knife, and slipped it back into his pocket.

With both hands, now, he stroked the tranquil caribou, rubbing it behind the ears and at the base of the antlers, which seemed to give it satisfaction. Once when his hand strayed down the long muzzle, the animal gave a terrified start and snort at the dreaded man smell so violently invading its nostrils. But Pete kept on soothingly and firmly; and again the beast grew calm. At length Pete decided that his best place for the night, or until the storm should lift, would be by the warmth of this imprisoned and peaceable animal. Digging down into the snow beyond the clutches of the wind, he rolled himself in his blankets, crouched close against the caribou's flank, and went confidently to sleep.

Aware of living companionship, Noël slept soundly through the clamour of the storm. At last a movement against his side disturbed him. He woke to feel that his strange bedfellow had struggled up and withdrawn. The storm was over. The sky above his upturned face was sharp with stars. All about him was laboured movement, with heavy shuffling, coughing, and snorting. Forgetful of their customary noise-lessness, the caribou were breaking gladly from their imprisonment. Presently Pete was alone. The cold was still and of snapping intensity; but he, deep in his hollow, and wrapped in his blankets, was warm. Still drowsy, he muffled his face and went to sleep again for another hour.

When he roused himself a second time he was wide awake and refreshed. It was just past the edge of dawn. The cold gripped like a vise. Faint mystic hues seemed frozen for ever into the ineffable crystal of the air. Pete stood up, and looked eastward along the tumbled trail of the herd. Not half a mile away stood the forest, black and vast, the trail leading straight into it. Then, a little farther down toward the right he saw something that made his heart leap exultantly. Rising straight up, a lavender and silver lily against the pallid saffron of the east, soared a slender smoke. That smoke, his trained eyes told him, came from a camp chimney; and he realized that the lumbermen had moved up to him from the far-off head of the Ottanoonsis.

"Trees Are Lonely Company"

HOWARD O'HAGAN

Howard O'Hagan (1902–1982) was raised in the Western Rockies, in Alberta and Vancouver, sites he turned to repeatedly in his writing. Initially O'Hagan worked as a mountain guide for many years, then as a recruiter and publicist for two Canadian railroads. Perhaps because he wrote of the Canadian West, or because his output was comparatively small, O'Hagan's reputation was slow to grow. His most productive period, between the 1930s and the 1960s, produced both his novel *Tay John* (1939), which Michael Ondaatje has classified as one of the earliest instances of mythic realism in Canadian literature, and his nonfiction book *Wilderness Men* (1958), described in Stuart Keate's contemporaneous *New York Times* book review as "a series of corking adventure stories" written with "a healthy admiration for men who can hunt and fight in 60-below weather." O'Hagan's *The Woman Who Got on at Jasper Station and Other Stories* (1963) collects his magazine fiction from across more than two decades, and includes the tale "Trees Are Lonely Company," which won the University of Western Ontario's 1959 President's Medal for best short story of the year after appearing in the *Tamarack Review.* Narrated by fur trapper "Wilderness Jake," O'Hagan's story explores the possibility that life in the wilderness may be not only a physical trial but also a psychological one. Like the mountain legends of the Canadian Rockies captured in O'Hagan's nonfiction, their fictional counterparts (also trappers, guides, hunters, and Mounties) are fundamentally lone wolves. And yet it is the short-story characters who emerge in the end as decidedly more human than heroic. O'Hagan died at the age of eighty, before he could complete a promised autobiography about his own adventures as a mountain man.

"Trees Are Lonely Company"

HOWARD O'HAGAN

It has been an open fall—but now, in mid-November, in the valley of the Moose, wind blew, snow flew—and with every stride he made, downriver towards the railroad, Jake Iverson, the burly, black-bearded trapper, was remembering the green grass. Green as springtime it had been, up there around the pool.

Breaking trail ahead, legs, snowshoes, swinging from his hips in tireless rhythm, was Felix Lemprière, also a trapper and a guide. Behind Jake, rifle ready in the crook of his arm, came Corporal Dallison of the Royal Canadian Mounted Police. Last in the procession was a big, wolf-like dog, ears laid back, tail held level and uncurving.

Heads down, wordless, the three men pushed through the storm. Sometimes a moosehide mittened hand would reach out, as if the ever shifting, ever receding snow were a curtain which, by a gesture, could be parted. Breaths rose, mingled, and were whipped away by the wind.

Incident by incident, timed to the creak of snowshoes, Jake recalled again what had brought him to where he was with a rifle pointed hot against him. It was the green grass. That was what "they" would be asking—why had he failed to notice the green growing grass? A mountain man, and he had failed to heed the grass when it was green . . .

There, in the upper valley, five days ago, all the willows had long ago shed their leaves. Even those around the pool were barren and the grass everywhere was scorched yellow by the frost. All the grass, that is, except the grass on the water's edge by the pool. That had been green, green as grass in May. And he had seen that it was green, although, at the time, he had paid it small attention. He had been busy and moving around a lot.

Nor was it as if he knew the river well. His cabin and Clem's, his partner's, was away back, a week's travel back on the Muddy. Usually, they came up the Muddy, down the Jackpine, up the Smokey and over the summit behind Mount Robson to reach the railroad. On this occasion, they had turned off from the Smokey over Moose Pass. Jake had not been along there for four or five years. But Clem had wanted to learn about the country, so they had come over the pass, down the Moose.

And anyway, not giving full notice to the green grass—that was no sign there was anything wrong, Jake argued to himself. Look, another man, less sharp, would have taken the money. It came to just over eleven dollars—a five, two twos, a couple of ones and some coppers. No silver, just the coppers. Not enough to be much good to anyone. Not enough to buy a winter's grubstake. And that's what they were coming out for, two trappers coming down the river to Red Pass to buy their grub. Of course, Tom Boylan, the storekeeper there, would have "staked" them, so the money wasn't so important after all.

If he had taken the money, he would have committed theft. And "they" would never pin a theft on him—not on old Jake Iverson, "Wilderness Jake," thirty years in the mountains and on speaking terms with most of the trees along the windings of every creek from the mouth of the Canoe at the Big Bend in British Columbia, north to where the Smokey joins the Arctic-flowing Peace in Alberta. Jake could even address some of the trees by name, like Jessie, for instance, the lone-growing birch by the footlog over Chatterbox creek. Roots washed by the stream, she reminded him of a maiden, especially in the spring when her leaves were newly out, a maiden touching toes to the water. And there was Natalie, a school-marm tree, standing on the edge of Starvation Flats. Up on the North Forks, where Whitehorn creek empties into it, was old Maude. Shutting his eyes, he could still hear her groan, and her old joints creak, when the wind blew down from the icefields. There were many other trees, with names, and nameless. But none of them, he repeated to himself, when he spoke had ever answered him back.

Naturally, being the man he was, and with all those trees in the Moose valley peering over his shoulder, he wasn't going to take Clem's money. "Clem Rawlings" was the full name, a lean young man with red hair and a moustache not so red as his hair. He was a fast traveller, proud of his long toes and high arched feet. He never wore boots. He wore moose-hide moccasins. Clem had been a great one too for writing letters which he carried down with him when they came out to the railroad, letters to correspondence schools. One day he wanted to be a salesman and the next he was set to pull up stakes and become a blacksmith. He wasn't content to be just a trapper. It used to trouble Jake's nerves at times, in the cabin or around the campfire, the way Clem would talk of what he was going to do with himself. At other times they both became sullen and unspeaking. They had lived together so closely that each had become his companion's conscience and until one could speak only if he reviled the other.

Even so, Jake wouldn't take Clem's money. No one would ever be able to say that old Jake was a thief or that he spent what was not his own. So, instead of lifting the money, he had stuffed stones into the pockets on top of it and tied the trouser cuffs with rope and unbuckled the belt around Clem's waist and shoved more stones into the trouser tops and buckled them tight again.

He did not search the pockets of the mackinaw or shirt. They held papers, envelopes from Clem's letter writing. The shirt, like the woollen underwear, was red. Clem believed that red kept out the cold. No, Jake let the shirt and mackinaw be. Then he dragged Clem across the clearing. One of the socks, trailing through the hot coals of the campfire, began to smoke. He dragged Clem across the clearing and through the low fringe of willows to the clay bank of the river and slipped him into the pool made by a back eddy. It took all his strength for the stones added weight to Clem's small, wiry body, so that Jake was scarcely aware of the grass among the willow roots, the grass which ran around the water's lip like a half circle of low burning green flame. Clem, his flat, pale eyes staring, mouth open as if he shouted, sank feet first. As he went down, his long red hair streamed from his scalp, as though a breeze blew up from below him. Afterwards, bubbles rose to the surface. Jake strained to see, but he could not see bottom, nor where Clem lay, through the clear, swirling water. The pool was very deep.

Jake dropped Clem's rifle in after him. This gave him pain because it was a good rifle, a .303 Savage with a telescope sight. But it was Clem's rifle, as the money was his and Jake would not use it. Going back to the campfire, he gathered up Clem's bedroll, pack-sack and the snowshoes he had been toting on his back against the coming of snow. Because this stuff would not easily sink, he cached it in the bush, under a log and dead branches, half a mile back from the trail. Returning, he scattered the bough bed, and swept up with a spruce branch, obliterating from the clearing all traces of the morning's business.

It was now coming on to noon and he was tired from what he had done. Before pulling out, he sat against a stump to have a smoke, staring down the valley. It was a calm, blue mountain morning and he could see as far as to where the valley narrowed and between two tall peaks, that were like a gateway, fell into the Fraser along which the railroad ran. During the night it had snowed. Though the snow, failing a wind, still clung to spruce and balsam on the slopes, the sun had thawed it in the valley bottom. That was all to the good, Jake considered. The thaw would dim his and Clem's tracks, the tracks of two men, coming down the river. Not that anyone would have been apt to see them. Except for grizzly hunters in the spring, few people travelled the trail up the Moose.

Out in midstream, as he watched, cakes of ice were floating down from the headwaters. Any day now, with a quick drop in temperature, which would occur if the snow held off, ice would bind the river. Of course, he had small cause for worry. A body weighted with stones, like Clem's, would not likely rise to the surface, ice or no ice. For all that, the ice, and snow upon the ice, would be a seal upon his efforts.

Jake was mulling this over, ready to knock out his pipe and be on his way, when, still looking down the river, he saw what sent a chill clean through him and made bristle of the hair upon the nape of his neck. Only a quarter of a mile away, coming around a bend, he saw a policeman. He knew it was a policeman, a Mounted Policeman at that, by the muskrat cap he was wearing with the flaps tied up and the yellow striped breeches. Another man was with him. They were afoot, rifles in their hands, snowshoes tied upon their packs.

At first Jake would not accept the evidence of his eyes. He rubbed them until the tears ran. He thought that he was already shaking hands with the willows. That was an idea Clem had had—that if a man stayed out too long in the mountains, he would surely go out to shake hands with the willows. Damn Clem. Damn him and his ideas. Why wouldn't Clem leave him alone?

If it hadn't been for his ideas . . . Still, it wasn't only his ideas. Sure, he talked a lot about them. He'd talk when Jake was tired after a day on the trail and the fire in the stove had burned down and the logs of the cabin were cracking in the cold. Jake might doze off for a few minutes and wake up and Clem continued to talk. He read magazines and newspapers, hid them in his pack when they were coming in from the railroad. That used to make Jake angry, for they had all they could do to pack in the grub they needed. It was in the magazines that Clem found the correspondence school advertisements which he wrote away about. His pockets were always full of papers, envelopes, pencils. He never studied, because by the time he got back an application form from one outfit to make him a salesman, he was in touch with another one that was going to show him how to be a mechanic.

But it was what he read in the magazine articles that he liked to talk about at night. The night before the last one, when they were sitting around their fire on the far side of Moose Pass on Calumet creek, he was talking about penguins. He had read that there were penguins on some place called the Falkland Islands. He was all set to go down to the Coast and sign on a ship so that he could see the penguins. On his way back, he was going to stop off in South America and go up in the high mountains there and trap chinchillas. Lots of money in chinchillas, he told Jake, as if Jake didn't know. But the money was in raising them, not in trapping them. Jake had had to listen, though all the while he knew Clem would do nothing about what he was talking about. No, he would stay and trap marten and lynx and silver fox, if they were lucky and trapped anything at all. You don't get rich being a trapper.

Sometimes when Clem was talking, Jake in impatience would rise up in the middle of one of his sentences and go out of the cabin, or leave the warm circle of the campfire, to walk in the forest among his friends, the trees. He would look up at them, at their heads, proud against the stars, nodding now here, now there, in guarded converse of their own. He would listen, half afraid of what he might hear. When no word came to him, he would return, relieved, soothed, to find Clem asleep or, more likely, still awake and ready to go on talking about his plans and ideas. It wasn't his ideas alone. It was more than that. Perhaps it was just the way they met up, a bit more than two years before. It was as though Clem had been sent, as though "they" had sent him, although Jake did not get to figuring along that line until some time later. Clem appeared beside his campfire one evening up on Sheep creek which flows into the Smokey. Walked out of the bush, stood beside the fire and there he was—a little fellow with moose-hide moccasins, red shirt, red hair, reddish moustache, pale blue eyes. He had a rifle, a bedroll, a pot, but no frying pan. He was travelling south, living off the country. His father, he said, was a homesteader down at Hudson Hope below the canyon on the Peace. Probably Clem had been reading and Hudson Hope was too small to hold him. So he started south to the railroad through the mountains. Only, he didn't go on farther south. Not then. He moved in with Jake to his cabin on the Muddy. Nothing was said. It was just taken for granted. At first it sat well. Jake had been alone so long, it seemed it would be good to have a partner for a change. Trees make a lonely sort of company.

Clem was young, not more than twenty-five, and he weighed no more than a hundred and thirty—Jake topped the scales at two hundred—but he was a moose for work and for travel. He took over the cooking, baked cakes and bread in place of bannock, roasted the meat instead of frying it. On the trail he carried the heavier pack. He got into camp before Jake and, when Jake pulled in, the spruce boughs were laid for the bed, wood cut for the night, supper hot and ready to be eaten. That's the way it was, day after day, night after night for the better part of two years until, finally, it began to get Jake down. He commenced to feel old. He felt he wasn't carrying as much, travelling as fast, working as hard as he should. Of course, when a man is over fifty, he has to expect to slow down a bit, but he doesn't want to have to remember it every waking hour of the day.

This Clem with his red hair, and those flat, blue eyes—they seemed to have no lashes—who never tired, was like Jake had been in his youth—first into camp, carrying the heaviest load. When Jake faced him across the campfire, it was as if he regarded himself of thirty years before and if Clem looked at him and grinned, Jake knew he was making fun, telling him he wasn't the man he used to be. Clem was doing what he did to show that the older man could do it no more. Even his ideas—these things he talked about—Jake had had ideas too. He had been going to see the world, but he had learned that the world was wide, a wide, wide place. He had put off from month to month, from year to year, what he was to do and each year, though maybe he was in a different valley, he was doing what he had been doing before—making snares for rabbits, notching trees for marten traps, canning moose or caribou for his winter's meat.

But it was when they came out to town, out to Red Pass on the railroad; that Jake became really suspicious. Clem went off talking to people—to railroaders, to other trappers, to strangers. Then it occurred to Jake that "they" had sent Clem up to spy. Sure, he had appeared from the other direction—from the north. That was probably part of the scheme, trying to fool old Jake. Jake, trusting no one, least of all the bankers in town, kept his money, more than a thousand dollars in five and ten dollar bills rolled in a yellow slicker, cached beyond the clearing of his cabin on the Muddy in a hole in a rock wall, plugged with a stone. No one knew where it was but himself. Clem never knew, or so Jake had thought. Jake went out there only when Clem was away hunting or running the trap-line. When snow was on the ground, he would approach the cache by indirection so that, though it was only half a mile back from the cabin, to reach it he would often travel four or five miles over muskeg, through forest and along frozen streams. Not so much as a blaze marked the spot. Well, maybe "they" were after the money. Maybe they just wanted to watch old Jake, see what he was up to and they had picked Clem for the job.

At any rate, if he was watching Jake, Jake was watching him. That's the way it was this last night when they camped beside the backwater on the Moose, two days' journey up from the railroad, going into town for their grub. They had finished supper. They were drinking their tea and Clem was still talking about those God-forsaken penguins on the Falkland Islands. Jake bore it as long as he could. Then he rose and once more walked out among the trees, a little distance back from the fire. These, in the Moose valley, were stranger trees. He did not know their names. Yet he spoke a word. As he lifted his head to listen, it seemed to him that in response, up there in the thousand-needled branches, there was movement, a rustling, something less than sound, the echo of a whisper, a sigh that might have been his name.

He felt gooseflesh climb upon his shoulders. The next minute, in the chill night, he was sweating. Fearful of showing his back to the darkness, he retreated in slow, careful steps backward to the fire. In its welcome light, he turned about, confronting Clem, who looked up to regard him—as it appeared to Jake—in a peculiar manner. Jake straddled his legs, wiped a hand across his forehead.

Clem, sitting with his back against a spruce tree, now glanced away and up towards the mountains. It was quiet, just the fire purring, the river flowing, the earth rolling beneath the stars.

Then Clem stared at Jake again, in the same peculiar manner, wrinkling his brows. In a moment he had spoken. For no reason at all, he declared to Jake, who stood above him across the campfire, "You know," he said, "a man has to be out here only so long until he begins to shake hands with the willows." He said nothing about the trees and the ghosts within them. He was too wise for that.

He spoke once more, to ask without warning, "Know what I would do if I had a thousand dollars?"

Suddenly, in a flash of flame behind his eyes, the entire progress of events became apparent to Jake: why Clem had stumbled on to his camp, that day on Sheep creek, why Clem had been trying to run him into the ground by making him travel faster than was his wont and why, in Red Pass, Clem was constantly whispering about him to strangers. Clem had discovered where the thousand odd dollars were hidden behind the cabin on the Muddy. Otherwise, why should he have said "a thousand dollars," no more, no less? He had discovered the money, but he had been afraid to take it for if he had had it on him, he would not have spoken as he did. No—he was waiting for his chance, biding his time.

A thousand dollars—a lonely lifetime's savings, every penny earned from trap-line, lumber-camp or mine. It was the dust of the years, watered with sweat and heavy with toil.

If Clem had been slower in saying what he did, if Jake had had a chance to think some more, or if he had not been standing with his partner squatting vulnerable across the fire, or if, though no wind blew, the murmur of the forest from behind him had not risen until it was a roar between his ears . . . As it was, Jake acted in self-defence and in the only fashion that he knew. He did not hesitate. He sprang, his boots scattering hot coals into Clem's face, and his fingers, those long fingers, strong as spruce roots, were around the other's throat. Soon, rolling into the fire, Jake smelt scorched woollen clothing. Then he felt the pulse in Clem's throat, beating against his fingertips like a marten's heart, but slower, when, bending over the trap, he squeezed in the chest, squeezed out the life, gently so as not to injure the fur. He had not meant to hang on so long as he had. He had merely intended to teach Clem a lesson, to teach him to keep his nose out of another man's affairs. But when he loosened his grip, Clem did not move, he did not speak, although his lips were parted as if he tried to. He lay there all night long. A light scuff of snow fell upon his cheeks, his open eyes. It did not melt. Jake sat by the fire and listened. He heard only the stilled tumult of the mountains. It was as if a great shout had come out of them and he waited, listening for the echo. It never came though, later, he was to start up from sleep, believing that he was about to hear it.

He did not touch Clem again until the morning. He had done what he had had to do. It had been himself or Clem. Now, by noon, he had finished with his task when, coming up the trail towards him, he saw the policeman and the other man. It was no vision, he realized, after rubbing his eyes. They were real enough, coming around the bend a quarter of a mile away. Jake had no time to jump the trail and take to the bush. His fire was still smoking, his gear was about it—but with no sign of anything that had belonged to Clem. Then, growing calmer, he thought that if "they" were after him, they would get him, no mistake about it. But why should they be after him? What did any of them know about him and Clem? No one could be asking questions as soon as this. He had met Mounted Policemen on the trail before. He had met them down the Smokey, checking up on the Indians at Grande Cache. Also, sometimes they came in after poachers. Jasper Park, a Dominion government game preserve, was just to the east of Moose valley.

Jake recognized the man with the policeman. He was Felix Lemprière, a French-Canadian, thickset man, wearing a buck-skin shirt, a tall black hat and a purple neckerchief. Soon he and the policeman were sitting around the fire which Jake had built up for them, eating their lunch of bully beef, bread and tea. With them was the big, wolf-like dog. He sat back a bit, panting, tongue lolling. The dog seemed to smile, as if he knew everything that Jake did and a bit more besides. But then, Jake figured, dogs don't talk.

The Mounted Policeman asked Jake a surprising question. He was young. He was new to that reach of country. Jake had not seen him before. He had only one eye, a black patch over the other one, the left one. The good eye was brown and it seemed to size Jake up, cool and steady, like an eye along a rifle barrel. Squatted on a log, he looked up, holding his tin mug in his hand, his breath puffing from his mouth in the cold air as if he were slowly burning up inside. He looked up at Jake and said, "I'm Corporal Dallison. I suppose you're Clem Rawlings?"

Jake, Clem Rawlings? Clem was so close to him, right at his elbow, so to speak, beyond the unleafed willows that, if it hadn't been for the water in his ears, he might have heard what was said. However, Clem wasn't listening anymore, Jake had not let Felix, the French-Canadian, go down to the pool for water for the tea. No, he had grabbed the billy and gone himself but, though he had had no breakfast, he drank none of the tea when it was made. Now, as the Corporal spoke, Felix sat on his heels looking into the fire. Felix and Jake had not spoken. They knew one another. They had met in Red Pass and along the trail. When there was need to speak, they would speak. If Felix had not been there, Jake might have permitted the Corporal to go on believing that he, Jake Iverson, was Clem Rawlings. The notion came to him, but he let it drop.

"No," he said, "Clem's my partner. I'm Jake Iverson."

"Oh!" the Corporal said, biting off a chunk of bread, "They told me there were two of you up here, but farther on, I thought . . . down the Smokey. I didn't know which was which."

Jake thought he should explain about Clem and why he was not with him. "He's gone over the head of Terrace creek," he said, nodding up the river. He was thankful again for the night's light fall of snow and the morning's thaw. The tracks of two men coming down would not show. "Up Terrace," he said, "and down the glacier to the summit behind Mount Robson. From there he told me he was crossing over the shoulder of Mount Whitehorn to the Swiftwater. He'll be coming down the Swiftwater about now and I'm on my way to Red Pass to meet him. We're going to stock up on grub."

"Lots of snow up high where he's gone. No good for glacier travel," Felix said, shaking his head.

"That's what I told him," Jake said, continuing to address the Corporal. "I told him he'd come to a bad end travelling alone across the ice. But he wanted to see the country, so he took his snowshoes and he's gone. That's how he is—bullheaded. You can't tell him nothing."

See? Jake was playing it crafty. If, later on, they went to look for Clem, they would go looking over the glacier and the high country behind Mount Robson. Wise old Jake. A man who wasn't lucid, bright as a dollar, would hardly have thought of that.

The Corporal and Felix sat around the fire a while longer. They talked about the weather and of how late the snow was in coming to the valley. The Corporal was not travelling to Grande Cache. No, he said, his lone eye impaling Jake upon its gaze as if the old trapper were a fly upon a pin, he was out to check up on poachers who had been taking fur out of Jasper Park, the game preserve over the divide to the east. Jake assured him that he and Clem did all their trapping on the

Muddy, miles distant to the north and west. But the Corporal's words brought a half smile to his bearded lips. Felix, the man travelling with the Corporal, was the best-known poacher in the country and it was him the Corporal had selected as his guide. Felix lifted a wary eye to Jake. Jake said nothing. Old Jake knew when to keep his mouth shut.

The dog was there too, bedded down now, chin on paws, but his eyes were open and seemed never to leave Jake's face. Jake was worried about the dog. If he got to frisking about, he might find Clem's bedroll and pack-sack only half a mile back in the bush and begin a yapping.

But the dog stayed by Felix, his master, and in a few minutes Felix and the Corporal fixed up their packs and were on their way up the valley. In a few days they would return down the Moose, or perhaps down the Snake Indian and come out in Alberta. It would depend upon snow conditions.

When the sounds of their going had perished and Jake was shuffling around the fire, something caused him to look behind. The dog stood on the edge of the clearing, one forepaw lifted, staring at him with black eyes large enough to put on the fire and boil moose meat in. Jake picked up a stick and threw it. The dog ran up the trail with a yelp, tail sucked under his belly.

Jake's plans were vague. Red Pass was two days' journey distant. When he arrived, he would have a likely tale to tell the boys in the beer parlour. Instead of sitting, as usual, by himself in the corner, he would join the group at the big table in the centre of the room. There he would say that he was concerned about Clem and would have to go up the Swiftwater to look for him. He would go in over the divides, far back from the Smokey where the Corporal might be, to his cabin in the Muddy. Then, with his thousand dollars, he would come down again, hop a freight at a lonely siding and go down to the Coast. From Vancouver, he would slip across the border to Seattle. Or he might simply head north, farther and farther into the mountains. No reason for alarm or hurry. It would be weeks, possibly months, before they set out to search for him or Clem.

But now, before starting downriver to Red Pass—he had told the Corporal that he was going there, and there he would have to go—he had a final job to do. The dog had made him apprehensive and, leaving the campfire, he went into the bush, picked up Clem's bedroll, pack-sack and snowshoes from where they were cached and carried them still farther back. He carried them to a rock slide, buried them under rocks. No dog nor man would find them there. It was the last move required to lock the door behind him.

It was dark when he returned to the campfire. In the dark it would be a bother to break camp, so he cut more wood, went upstream for his water and cooked a meal of bannock and bacon, rolled up in his blankets, slept the night. He was secure now. He could rest.

The morning broke bitter cold. No snow, no wind, but the heavy frost had come. The murmur of the sluggish river was distant because brittle ice had formed along its edges and only in midstream was it flowing freely. The chatter of a nearby creek was stilled. A weird, half-silence gripped the land as though God's fist had closed upon it.

But through the fringe of barren, frosted willows, Jake, rising from his blankets, saw the glint of open water with mist upon it. The pool had not frozen, though it was stirred by no strong current.

Strange that there was no ice upon the pool in whose depths rested the body and all the dreams of Clem, his partner. Then, pulling on his trousers, his boots, breath sifting grey from his nostrils, and parting the willows to look more closely, Jake saw again the green grass around the water's lip, and understood. The pool had not frozen, perhaps during the entire winter it would not freeze, because within it, bubbling up, was a warm spring of water. This kept the neighbouring grasses green. Such pools were not uncommon in the mountains. In winter, snow-shoeing up the rivers, a man had to be on guard against them. Still, he sensed that it was a long and sorry chance which had guided him to such a spot with Clem's body.

The snow would come and fall upon the ice which already half rimmed the pool. The waters of the pool would remain clear and open.

Under Jake's nose, pushed through the willows, a piece of paper floated. He leaned over, picked it up, took it with him as he turned to make his morning's fire. It was a sodden fragment of envelope, the pencil marks upon it now illegible from their long soaking, which, somehow released from the pocket of Clem's shirt or mackinaw, had risen to the surface. Doubtless, it had been addressed to one of the correspondence schools to which he had the habit of writing.

After gulping his breakfast, Jake returned to the pool. He gazed upon its placidity for long minutes before he saw the patch of wool, shredded from red underwear or shirt, which had lodged among willow roots. He picked it up and put it in the fire. He wondered—the phenomenon might be caused merely by the action of the water, or a mink, having swum under the ice from up or down the river, might be working down there in the pool, tearing at Clem's clothes to reach the white flesh beneath them. The belly was what it would go for.

Jake could not leave the pool—it seemed he would stay by it forever—while these grisly remnants of memory, of what had once been a man, were throughout the day, slowly and inexorably, upborne to his view. The Corporal and Felix might return this way. They would go to the pool for water for their tea. What they would find there would give them pause, cause them to think, to put two and two together. Jake cursed the green grass. On another part of the river, what was here revealed to sight, would have been hidden beneath ice and beneath snow, when the snow came. He cursed the thousand dollars behind his cabin on the Muddy. Yet he was thankful that, though his fear of the dog, and the need of burying Clem's gear farther from the trail, he had come back to filch from the pool this testimony of guilt.

He crouched in the willows for hours, body benumbed, eyes transfixed by the water's promise. Mechanically, as a piece of paper, a tatter of wool, a corner of a handkerchief, floated to the surface, he reached out for it with a branch of spruce, ground it in his fist, stuffed it in his pocket.

When night came and he could not see, he dozed by his fire and in the morning resumed his watch. Snow fell. It fell upon the forest and the willows and upon Jake's shoulders. It lay white upon the ice on the pool's rim. Into the pool each flake settled with a slight hiss and melted.

From the pool, steam rose as though in its warm depths, a man still breathed.

Jake, eyes wide and glaring, crouched beside the pool, heedless to snow, to cold, to time that was passing. When the snow ceased and the clouds lifted and the late sun shone up on the snow pink mountains, the pool was red, red as blood, lapping at his toes, and he could no longer see what floated there upon it.

It was then, or a day later, or two—he could not be certain, for time was absent with all timely things—that on their way back to the railroad, the Corporal and Felix Lemprière, ghostlike and wavering figures, were with him around the campfire and that he was pointing to the pool and babbling, "Blood. All of it, blood, Clem's blood."

Jake did that because now there was no cause for pretending. He had his wits about him. What he could see, the Corporal could see—though the Corporal at first, and until Jake led him back to the rockslide where he uncovered Clem's buried gear, was unbelieving.

Afterwards, seeing the big wolf-like dog, facing him by the campfire, Jake sprang to throttle him with his bare hands. Felix and the Corporal held him off.

Then Felix, under Jake's direction, sank a fishhook into the pool and pulled up a piece of Clem's trouser leg. Later the pool would be dragged with heavier tackle.

That was how it happened that, each bending his head to the driving snow, Jake had come down the Moose between the Corporal and the French-Canadian, the dog following behind.

Several times he had stopped to explain to the Corporal about the thousand dollars and of how Clem, with his fast travelling and nosing into his business, had persecuted him and to affirm that he, Jake, had done in self-defence only what any other man, with the same savvy, would have done. The Corporal had nodded in apparent agreement.

He and Felix had stood aside quietly too when Jake once stepped from the trail, took off his cap and bowed to a school-marm tree which, it seemed, he had met on his last trip down the Moose long ago. After speaking, Jake listened. Five nights before, as Clem's body lay beside the campfire, likewise he had listened, because at that time it was as though a great shout had come out of the mountains and he had waited to hear its echo. Now he thought, again he was about to hear that echo—from a tall spruce beyond the school-marm tree where the wind, in great gusts of snow, troubled the dark forest.

Jake shook his head. He turned down the trail, behind Felix, followed by the Corporal and the dog. This he could not explain to the Corporal—that Clem's voice was up there in the tree tops, calling to him, but in the howl of wind and groan of forest he could not distinguish what Clem was saying.

Nearing the railroad, though the snow still flew, it appeared to Jake that the green grass along the edge of the pool, now grew taller. It reached his knees, his waist, and higher, to engulf him. He put out a hand to fend it from his face.

Yet, as he stepped from the trail, climbed the embankment to stand upon the grade, the scene of where he was, was clear before him: the twin blue rails hurrying away to converge in the distance, the telegraph poles, weary with their burden, staggering into the storm. Instinctively, he dropped to one knee to untie a snowshoe, for here, between and beside the rails, the snow was packed and shallow and three men could walk abreast down the line and into Red Pass round the bend.

The Corporal, as if casually, knelt beside him. There was a quick click of metal. When Jake rose, his right wrist was handcuffed to the Corporal's left.

The three men, the prisoner in the middle, the dog behind, walked west down the track. They turned their backs upon the Moose where the legions of the wind howled and stamped and on whose upper reaches, into a pool half rimmed with grass, snowflakes fell and melted.

"The Wolfer"

WALLACE STEGNER

Wallace Stegner (1909–1993) was an American author, essayist, and teacher who lived in multiple states—among them Iowa, North Dakota, Montana, Utah, and California—though it was his six years growing up poor in Eastend, Saskatchewan, that haunt much of his best writing. The bitter winters of the Canadian Western prairies inspired several of his works: the semi-autobiographical novel *The Big Rock Candy Mountain* (1943), the memoir *Wolf Willow: A History, a Story, and a Memory of the Last Plains Frontier* (1962), and various essays in two collections: *The Sound of Mountain Water* (1969) and *Where the Bluebird Sings to the Lemonade Springs* (1992). Across a fifty-year writing career, Stegner won O. Henry first prize awards for three of his thirty-one short stories, as well as a Pulitzer Prize for his historical frontier novel *Angle of Repose* (1971) and a National Book Award for his marriage and memory novel *The Spectator Bird* (1976). The beauty and danger of frontier life in the West was Stegner's enduring theme. His passionate defense of wilderness in his 1960 "Wilderness Letter," a seminal document in the modern conservation movement, proved prescient: "Something will have gone out of us as a people if we ever let the remaining wilderness be destroyed, if we permit the last virgin forests to be turned into comic books and plastic cigarette cases; if we drive the few remaining members of the wild species into zoos and to extinction." In Stegner's most memorable wilderness short story, "The Wolfer," published in *Harper's Magazine* (October 1959), a Canadian Mountie recalls his pursuit of a missing wolf hunter across a frozen wilderness of ice and snow. As in all of Stegner's western narratives, a changing wild landscape operates much like a natural language, offering signs and warnings to those who know how to read them.

"The Wolfer"

WALLACE STEGNER

Yes, I saw a good deal of it, and I knew them all. It was my business to, and in those days it wasn't hard to know nearly every man between Willow Bunch and Fort Walsh, even the drifters; the women you could count on your two thumbs. One was Molly Henry at the T-Down Bar, the other was Amy Schulz, living with a reformed whiskey trader named Frost up on Oxarart Creek. I knew Schulz, too, and his miserable boy. At least I had seen him a good many times, and stopped with him a half-dozen times at one or another shack when I was out on patrol, and at least that many times had come within an ace of being eaten by his hound. Probably I knew him better than most people did, actually. Friends—that's another matter. He was about as easy to be friendly with as a wolverine.

Summers, he camped around in the Cypress Hills, hunting, but in winter he used the shacks that the cattle outfits maintained out along the Whitemud, on the patrol trail between the Hills and Wood Mountain. Two of them, at Stonepile and Pinto Horse Butte, were abandoned Mounted Police patrol posts—abandoned in the sense that no constables were stationed there, though we kept the barracks stocked with emergency supplies and always cut and stacked a few tons of prairie wool there in the fall. Both Schulz and I used the barracks now and then, for he as a wolfer and I as a Mountie covered pretty much the same territory. If the truth were known, I kept pretty close tab on him in my patrol book, because I was never entirely sure, after Amy left him, that he wouldn't go back up on Oxarart Creek and shoot Frost.

Probably I wronged him. I think he was glad to get rid of Amy; it freed him to be as wild as the wolves he hunted, with his snuffling adenoidal boy for a slave and daily killing for occupation and his staghound for friend and confidant. They were a pair; each was the only living thing that liked the other, I guess, and it was a question which had the edge in savagery. Yet love, too, of a kind. I have heard him croon and mutter to that thing, baby talk, in a way to give you the creeps.

Whenever I found Schulz at Stonepile or Pinto Horse I picked an upper bunk; if the hound got drooling for my blood in the night I wanted to be where he'd at least have to climb to get at me. There was no making up to him—he was Schulz's, body and soul. He looked at every other human being with yellow eyes as steady as a snake's, the hackles lifting between his shoulders and a rumble going away down in his chest. I'd hear him moving in the dark shack, soft and heavy, with his nails clicking on the boards. He wore a fighting collar studded with brass spikes, he stood as high as a doorknob at the shoulder, and he weighed a hundred and forty pounds. Schulz bragged that he had killed wolves single-handed. The rest of the pack, Russian wolfhounds and Russian-greyhound crosses, slept in the stable and were just dogs, but this staghound thing, which Schulz called Puma, was the physical shape of his own savagery: hostile, suspicious, deadly, unwinking. I have seen him stand with a foolish, passive smile on his face while that monster put his paws up on his shoulders and lapped mouth and chin and eyes with a tongue the size of a coal shovel.

He was a savage, a wild man. He hated civilization—which meant maybe two hundred cowpunchers and Mounties scattered over ten thousand square miles of prairie—but it was not civilization that did him in. It was the wild, the very savagery he trusted and thought he controlled. I know about that too, because I followed the last tracks he and his hound made in this country.

My patrol books would show the date. As I remember, it was toward the end of March 1907. The patrol was routine—Eastend, Bates Camp, Stonepile, the Warholes, Pinto Horse Butte, Wood Mountain, and return—but nothing else was routine that winter. With a month still to go, it was already a disaster.

Since November there had been nothing but blizzards, freezing fogs, and cold snaps down to forty below. One chinook—and that lasted only long enough to melt everything to mush, whereupon another cold snap came on and locked the country in a four-inch shell of ice. A lot of cattle that lay down that night never got up: froze in and starved there.

That time, just about Christmas, I passed the Warholes on a patrol and found a *métis* named Big Antoine and twenty of his Indian relatives trapped and half-starved. They had made a run for it from Wood Mountain toward Big Stick Lake when the chinook blew up, and got caught out. When I found them they hadn't eaten anything in two weeks except skin-and-bone beef that had died in the snow; they were seasoning it with fat from coyotes, the only thing besides the wolves that throve.

A police freighter got them out before I came back on my next trip. But the cowpunchers out in the range shacks were by that time just about as bad off. For weeks they had been out every day roping steers frozen into the drifts, and dragging them free; or they had been floundering around chasing cattle out of the deep snow of the bottoms and out onto the benches where the wind kept a little feed bare. They had got them up there several times, but they hadn't kept them there. The wind came across those flats loaded with buckshot, and the cattle turned their tails to it and came right back down to starve. At one point the two Turkey Track boys stationed at Pinto Horse had even tried to make a drag of poles, and drag bare a patch of hillside for the cattle to feed on. All they did was kill off their ponies. When I came by in March they had given up and were conducting a non-stop blackjack game in the barracks, and laying bets whether the winter would last till August, or whether it would go right on through and start over.

We had a little poker game that night. Whenever the talk died we could hear, through the logs and sod of the shack, the heavy hunting song of wolves drawn down from the hills for the big barbecue. It was a gloomy thing to hear. Say what you want about cowpunchers, they don't like failing at a job any better than other people. And they were sure failing. In November there had been close to seventy thousand head of cattle on that Whitemud range. At a conservative guess, half of them were dead already. If we didn't get a chinook in the next week, there wouldn't be a cow alive come spring.

I quit the game early to get some sleep, and for a joke pushed the deck over toward Curly Withers for a cut. "Cut a chinook," I said. He turned over the jack of diamonds. Then we went to the door for a look-see, and everything was wooled up in freezing fog, what nowadays they call a whiteout. You could have cut sheep out of the air with tin shears. "Some chinook," Curly said.

In the morning there was still no wind, but the air was clear. As I turned Dude down the trail and looked back to wave at the Turkey Track boys I had the feeling they were only six inches high, like carved figures in a German toy scene. The shack was braced from eaves to ground with icicles; the sky behind the quiver of heat from the stove-pipe jiggled like melting glass. Away down in the southeast, low and heatless, the sun was only a small painted dazzle.

It seemed mean and cowardly to leave those boys out there. Or maybe it was just that I hated to start another day of hard cold riding through all that death, with nobody to talk to. You can feel mighty small and lonesome riding through that country in winter, after a light snowfall that muffles noises. I was leading a packhorse, and ordinarily there is a good deal of jingle and creak and sound of company with two ponies, but that morning it didn't seem my noises carried ten feet.

Down in the river trough everything was still and white. Mainly the channel had a fur of frozen snow on it, but here and there were patches of black slick ice full of air bubbles like quarters and silver dollars. Depending on how the bends swung, drifts sloped up to the cutbanks or up to bars overgrown with snow-smothered rose bushes and willows. I crossed the tracks of three wolves angling upriver, side by side and bunched in clusters of four: galloping. They must have been running just for the hell of it, or else they had sighted an antelope or deer. They didn't have to gallop to eat beef.

Without wind, it wasn't bad riding, though when I breathed through my mouth the aching of my teeth reminded me that under the Christmas frosting the world was made of ice and iron. Now a dead steer among the rose bushes, untouched by wolves or coyotes. I cut a notch in a tally stick, curious about how many I would pass between Pinto Horse and Eastend. Farther on, a bunch of whitefaces lying and standing so close together they had breathed frost all over one another. If they hadn't been such skeletons they would have looked like farm-yard beasts in a crèche. They weren't trapped or frozen in, but they were making no move to get out—only bawled at me hopelessly as I passed. Two were dead and half drifted over. I cut two more notches.

In three hours I cut a good many more, one of them at a big wallow and scramble near the mouth of Snake Creek where wolves had pulled down a steer since the last snowfall. The blood frozen into the snow was bright as paint, as if it had been spilled only minutes before. Parts of the carcass had been dragged in every direction.

Those wolves rubbed it in, pulling down a beef within a half mile of where Schulz and his boy were camped at Stonepile. I wondered if he had had any luck yet—he hadn't had any at all last time I saw him—

and I debated whether to stop with him or go on to Bates and heat up a cold shack. The decision was for Bates. It was no big blowout to spend a night with the Schulzes, who were a long way from being the company the T-Down and Turkey Track boys were, and who besides were dirtier than Indians. Also I thought I would sleep better at Bates than I would at Stonepile, in an upper bunk with my hand on a gun while that hound prowled around in the dark and rumbled every time I rolled over. Sure Schulz had it trained, but all he had hold of it with was his voice; I would have liked a chain better.

Just to make a check on Stonepile for the patrol book, I turned up Snake Creek, and a little after noon I came up the pitch from the bottoms and surprised the Schulz boy standing bare-armed before the barracks door with a dishpan hanging from his hand. The dishpan steamed, his arm steamed, the sunken snow where he had flung the dishwater steamed. I was quite pleased with him, just then; I hadn't known he and his old man ever washed their dishes. He stood looking at me with his sullen, droop-lipped watchful face, one finger absentmindedly up his nose. Down in the stable the wolfhounds began to bark and whine and howl. I saw nothing of Schulz or the big hound.

"Howdy, Bud," I said. "How's tricks?"

He was sure no chocolate-box picture. His gray flannel shirt was shiny with grease, his face was pimply, long black hair hung from under the muskrat cap that I had never seen off his head. I think he slept in it, and I'll guarantee it was crawling. He never could meet a man's eyes. He took his finger out of his nose and said, looking past me, "Hello, Constable."

I creaked down. Dude pushed me from behind, rubbing the icicles off his nose. "Pa not around?" I said.

Something flickered in his eyes, a wet gray gleam. One eye socket and temple, I saw, were puffy and discolored—about a three-day-old black eye. He touched one cracked red wrist to his chapped mouth and burst out, "Pa went out yesterday and ain't come back!" With a long drag he blew his nose through his mouth and spit sideways into the snow. His eyes hunted mine and ducked away instantly. "And Puma got out!" he said—wailed, almost.

At that moment I wouldn't have trusted him a rope length out of my sight. He looked sneakily guilty, he had that black eye which could only be a souvenir from Daddy, he had fifteen years of good reasons for hating his old man. If Schulz and his hound were really missing, I had the conviction that I would find them dry-gulched and stuffed through the ice somewhere. Not that I could have blamed young Schulz too much. In the best seasons his old man must have been a bearcat to live with. In this one, when he had hunted and trapped all winter and never got a single wolf, he was a crazy man. The wolves walked around his traps laughing—they fed much too well to be tempted. They sat just out of rifle shot and watched him waste ammunition. And though he had the best pack of dogs in that country, he hadn't been able to run them for months because of the weather and the deep snow. Out on the flats the dogs could have run, but there were no wolves there; they were all down in the bottoms hobnobbing with the cattle. The last time I had passed through, Schulz had talked to me half the night like a man half-crazed with rage: red-faced, jerky-voiced, glassy-eyed. To make his troubles worse, he had headaches, he said; "bunches" on his head. A horse had fallen on him once.

So in a winter of complete hard luck, who made a better whipping boy than that sullen son of his? And who more likely, nursing his black eye and his grievance, to lie behind the cabin or stable and pot his father as he came up the trail?

It was a fine theory. Pity it wasn't sound. I told young Schulz to hold it while I turned the horses into the police haystack, and while I was down there I got a look around the stable and corrals. No bodies, no blood, no signs of a fight. Then up in the barracks, in the hot, close, tallowy-mousy room with muskrat and marten pelts on bows of red willow hanging from the ceiling and coyote and lynx hides tacked on the wall, and three spirals of last year's flypaper, black with last year's flies, moving in the hot air above the stove, I began asking him questions and undid all my nice imaginary murder.

I even began to doubt that anything would turn out to be wrong with Schulz or his hound, for it became clear at once that if Schulz was in trouble he was in trouble through some accident, and I didn't believe that the Schulzes had accidents. They might get killed, but they didn't have accidents. It was about as likely that he would freeze, or get lost, or fall through a rapid, or hurt himself with a gun, as it was that a wolf would slip and sprain his ankle. And if you bring up those bunches on his head, and the horse that he said fell on him, I'll bet you one thing. I'll bet you the horse got hurt worse than Schulz did.

Still, he was missing, and in that country and that weather it could be serious. He had left the barracks the morning before, on foot but carrying snowshoes, to check on some carcasses he had poisoned down by Bates Camp. Usually he didn't use poison because of the dogs. Now he would have baited traps with his mother, or staked out his snuffling boy, if he could have got wolves that way. He shut the wolfhounds in the stable and the staghound in the barracks and told the boy to keep them locked up. The staghound especially had to be watched. He was used to going everywhere with Schulz, and he might follow him if he were let out.

That was exactly what he did do. Young Schulz kept him in the barracks—it would have been like being caged with a lion—until nearly dark, when he went down to the stable to throw some frozen beef to the other dogs. He slid out and slammed the door ahead of the staghound's rush. But when he came back he wasn't so lucky. The dog was waiting with his nose to the crack, and when it opened he threw his hundred and forty pounds against the door and was gone. No one but Schulz would have blamed the boy—ever try to stop a bronc from coming through a corral gate, when you're there on foot and he's scared and ringy and wants to come? You get out of the way or you get trompled. That hound would have trompled you the same way. But Schulz wouldn't think of that. The boy was scared sick of what his father would do to him if and when he came back.

I thought that since the hound had *not* come back, he obviously must have found Schulz. If he had found him alive and unhurt, they would be back together before long. If he had found him hurt, he would stay with him, and with any luck I could find them simply by following their tracks. I asked the boy if he was afraid to stay alone two or three days, if necessary. He wasn't—it was exactly the opposite he was scared of. Also I told him to stay put, and not get in a panic and take off across a hundred miles of open country for Malta or somewhere; I would see to it that his old man laid off the horsewhip. Somebody—his old man, or me, or somebody—would be back within three days at the latest.

He stood in the doorway with his arms still bare, a tough kid actually, a sort of wild animal himself, though of an unattractive kind, and watched me with those wet little gleaming eyes as I rode off down Snake Creek.

I couldn't have had better trailing. The light snow two nights before had put a nice firm rippled coating over every old track. When I hit the river the channel was perfectly clean except for Schulz's moccasin tracks, and braided in among them the tracks of the hound. A wolf makes a big track, especially with his front feet—I've seen them nearly six inches each way—but that staghound had feet the size of a plate, and he was so heavy that in deep snow, even a packed drift, he sank way down. So there they went, the companionable tracks of a man and his dog out hunting. If I hadn't known otherwise I would have assumed that they had gone upriver together, instead of six hours apart.

The day had got almost warm. Under the north bank the sun had thawed an occasional rooty dark spot. I kneed Dude into a shuffle, the packhorse dragged hard and then came along. I could have followed that trail at a lope.

It led me four miles up the river's meanders before I even had to slow down, though I cut four more notches in the tally stick and saw two thin does and a buck flounder away from the ford below Sucker Creek, and took a snapshot with the carbine at a coyote, fatter than I ever saw a coyote, that stood watching me from a cutbank. My bullet kicked snow at the cutbank's lip and he was gone like smoke. Then a mile above Sucker Creek I found where Schulz had put on his snowshoes and cut across the neck of a bend. The hound had wallowed after him, leaving a trail like a horse.

The drifts were hard-crusted under the powder, but not hard-crusted enough, and the horses were in to their bellies half the time. They stood heaving while I got off to look at a little tent-like shelter with fresh snow shoveled over it. The hound had messed things up some, sniffing around, but he had not disturbed the set. Looking in, I found a marten in a No. 2 coyote trap, caught around the neck and one front leg. He wasn't warm, but he wasn't quite frozen either. I stuffed marten and trap into a saddlebag and went on.

The trail led out of the river valley and up a side coulee where among thin red willows a spring came warm enough from the ground to stay unfrozen for several feet. The wolfer had made another marten set there, and then had mushed up onto the bench and northwest to a slough where tules whiskered up through the ice and a half-dozen very high muskrat houses rose out of the clear ice farther out.

At the edge of the slough I got off and followed where man and hound had gone out on the ice. Where the ice was clear I could see the paths the rats make along the bottom. For some reason this slough wasn't frozen nearly as deep as the river, maybe because there were springs, or because of organic matter rotting in the water. The Royal Society will have to settle that sometime. All I settled was that Schulz had chopped through the ice in two places and set coyote traps in the paths, and had broken through the tops of three houses to make sets inside. He had a rat in one of the house sets. Since I seemed to be running his trapline for him, I put it in the other saddlebag.

Nothing, surely, had happened to Schulz up to here. The hound had been at every set, sniffing out the trail. That would have been pretty late, well after dark, when the fog had already shut off the half moon. It occurred to me as I got back on Dude and felt the icy saddle under my pants again that I would not have liked to be out there on that bare plain to see a wild animal like that hound go by in the mist, with his nose to his master's track.

From the slough the trail cut back to the river; in fifteen minutes I looked down onto the snowed-over cabin and buried corrals of Bates Camp. There had been nobody stationed in it since the T-Down fed its last hay almost two months before. No smoke from the stovepipe, no sign of life. My hope that I would find the wolfer holed up there, so that I could get out of the saddle and brew a pot of tea and eat fifty pounds or so of supper, went glimmering. Something had drawn him away from here. He would have reached Bates about the same time of day I reached it—between two and three in the afternoon—for though he was a tremendous walker he could not have covered eight miles, some of it on snowshoes, and set seven traps, in less than about four hours. I had then been on his trail more than two hours, and pushing it hard.

I found that he hadn't gone near the shack at all, but had turned down toward the corrals, buried so deep that only the top pole showed.

Wading along leading the horses, I followed the web tracks to the carcass of a yearling shorthorn half dug out of the snow.

There were confusing tracks all around—snowshoes, dog, wolf. The shorthorn had died with his tongue out, and a wolf had torn it from his head. The carcass was chewed up some, but not scattered. Schulz had circled it about six feet away, and at one place deep web tracks showed where he had squatted down close. I stood in the tracks and squatted too, and in front of me, half obscured by the dog's prints, I saw where something had rolled in the snow. Snagged in the crust was a long gray-black hair.

A wolf, then. This was one of the poisoned carcasses, and a wolf that rolled might be sick. Squatting in the quenched afternoon, Schulz would have come to his feet with a fierce grunt, darting his eyes around the deceptive shapes of snow and dusk, and he would not have waited a second to track the wolf to his dying place. The coyotes he ran or shot, and the marten and muskrat he trapped when nothing better offered, were nothing to him: it was wolves that made his wild blood go, and they had cheated him all winter.

For just a minute I let myself yearn for the cabin and a fire and a hot meal. But I still had an hour and a half of light good enough for trailing—about what Schulz himself had had—and after that maybe another half-hour of deceptive shadows, ghostly moonlight, phosphorescent snow, and gathering mist and dark. If he had got hurt somehow chasing the wolf, he might have survived one night: he couldn't possibly survive two. So I paused only long enough to put the packhorse in the stable and give him a bait of oats, and to light a fire to take a little of the chill out of the icy shack. Then I set the damper and took out on the trail again.

It was like a pursuit game played too long and complicated too far, to the point of the ridiculous—like one of those cartoons of a big fish swallowing a smaller fish swallowing a smaller fish swallowing a small fish. There went the sick wolf running from the heat of the strychnine in his guts, and after him the wolfer, implacable in the blue-white cold, and after him the great hound running silently, hours behind but gaining, loping hard down the river ice or sniffing out the first marten set. There went wildness pursued by hate pursued by love, and after the lot of them me, everybody's rescuer, everybody's nursemaid, the law on a tired horse.

Schulz never did catch up with that wolf. Probably it had never been sick at all, but had rolled in the snow in sassy contempt, the way a dog will kick dirt back over his scats. Up on the bench its tracks broke into the staggered pairs that showed it was trotting, and after a half mile or so another set of wolf tracks came in from the west, and the two went off together in the one-two-one of an easy lope.

Schulz quit, either because he saw it was hopeless or because the light gave out on him. I could imagine his state of mind. Just possibly, too, he had begun to worry. With darkness and fog and the night cold coming on, that open flat bare of even a scrap of sagebrush was no place to be. In an hour the freak windlessness could give way to a blizzard; a wind right straight off the North Pole, and temperatures to match, could light on him with hardly a warning, and then even a Schulz could be in trouble.

Above me, as I studied his tracks where he broke off the chase, a chip of moon was pale and blurry against a greenish sky; the sun over the Cypress Hills was low and strengthless. It would go out before it went down. And I was puzzled by Schulz. He must have been lost; he must have looked up from his furious pursuit and his furious reading of failure, and seen only misty dusk, without landmarks, moon, stars, anything, for instead of heading back for the river and the cabin he started straight eastward across the plain. So did I, because I had to.

It took him about a mile to realize his mistake, and it was easy to read his mind from his footprints, for there out in the middle of the empty snowflats they milled around a little and made an eloquent right angle toward the south. Probably he had felt out his direction from the drifts, which ran like shallow sea waves toward the southeast. I turned after him thankfully. But he hadn't gone back to Bates, and he hadn't gone back downriver to Stonepile. So where in hell *had* he gone? I worked the cold out of my stiff cheeks, and flapped my arms to warm my hands, and kicked old Dude into a tired trot across the packed flats.

In twenty minutes I was plowing down into the river valley again. The sun was blurring out, the bottoms were full of shadows the color of a gunbarrel, the snow was scratched with black willows. I judged that I was not more than a mile upriver from Bates. The plowing web tracks and the wallowing trail of the hound went ahead of me through deep drifts and across the bar onto the river ice, and coming after them, I saw under the opposite cutbank the black of a dead fire.

I stopped. There was no sign of life, though the snow, I could see, was much tracked. I shouted: "Schulz?" and the sound went out in that white desolation like a match dropped in the snow. This looked like the end of the trail, and because it began to look serious, and I didn't want to track things up until I got a chance to study them, I tied the horse in the willows and circled to come into the bend from below. When I parted the rose bushes to slide down onto the ice, I looked straight down on the body of Schulz's hound.

Dead, he looked absolutely enormous. He lay on his side with his spiked collar up around his ears. I saw that he had been dragged by it from the direction of the fire. He had bled a great deal from the mouth, and had been bleeding as he was dragged, for the snow along the drag mark had a filigree of red. On the back of his head, almost at his neck, was a frozen bloody patch. And along the trough where the body had been dragged came a line of tracks, the unmistakable tracks of Schulz's moccasins. Another set went back. That was all. It was as clear as printing on a page. Schulz had dragged the dead dog to the edge of the bank, under the overhanging bushes, and left him there, and not come back.

I tell you, I was spooked. My hair stood on end. I believe, and I know I looked quickly all around, in a fright that I might be under somebody's eyes or gun. On the frozen river there was not a sound. As I slid down beside the hound I looked both ways in the channel, half expecting to see Schulz's body too, or somebody else's. Nothing. Clean snow.

The hound's body was frozen rock hard. His mouth was full of frozen blood, and the crusted patch on the back of his neck turned out to be a bullet hole, a big one. He had been shot in the mouth, apparently by a soft-nosed bullet that had torn the back of his head off. And no tracks, there or anywhere, except those of Schulz himself. I knew that Schulz never used any gun but a .22, in which he shot long rifle cartridges notched so they would mushroom and tear a big internal hole and stop without making a second puncture in the hide. If he had shot the hound—and that was totally incredible, but who else could have?—a .22 bullet like that would not have gone clear through brain and skull and blown a big hole out the other side unless it had been fired at close range, so close that even in fog or half-dark the wolfer must have known what he was shooting at.

But I refused to believe what my eyes told me must be true. I could conceive of Schulz shooting his son, and I had already that day suspected his son of shooting *him*. But I could not believe that he would ever, unless by accident, shoot that dog. Since it didn't seem he could have shot it accidentally, someone else must have shot it.

It took me ten minutes to prove to myself that there were no tracks around there except the wolfer's. I found those, in fact, leading on upriver, and since I had looked at every footprint he made from Stonepile on, I knew these must be the ones he made going out. Instead of going home, he went on. Why?

Under the cutbank, in front of the fire, I found a hard path beaten in the snow where Schulz had walked up and down many times. The fire itself had never been large, but it had burned a long time; the coals were sunk deeply into the snow and frozen in their own melt. Schulz had evidently stayed many hours, perhaps all night, keeping the little fire going and walking up and down to keep from freezing. But why hadn't he walked a mile downriver and slept warm at Bates?

I might have followed to try to find out, but the light was beginning to go, and I was too cold and tired to think of riding any more of that crooked river that night. Still, just thinking about it gave me an idea. In any mile, the Whitemud ran toward every point of the compass, swinging and returning on itself. If Schulz had hit it after the fog closed in thick, he would have known that Bates lay downriver, but how would he know which way was downriver? There were no rapids in that stretch. There would have been no landmarks but bends and bars endlessly repeating, changing places, now on the right and now on the left. Some of the bends were bowknots that completely reversed their direction.

That might answer one question, but only one. I put myself in the path he had made, and walked up and down trying to see everything just as he had. I found the mark where he had stuck his rifle butt-down in the snow, probably to leave his arms free for swinging against the cold. There were hound tracks on the path and alongside it, as if the dog had walked up and down with him. At two places it had lain down in the snow off to the side.

That answered another question, or corroborated what I had guessed before: Schulz couldn't have shot the hound not knowing what it was; it had been there with him for some time.

Standing by the fire, I looked back at the deep tracks where Schulz, and after him the hound, had broken down off the bar onto the ice. The hound's tracks led directly to the fire and the path. I walked the path again, searching every foot of it. I found only one thing more: just where the path went along a streak of clear ice, where ice and snow joined in a thin crust, there were the deep parallel gouges of claws, two sets of them, close together. Would a heavy hound, rearing to put its front paws on a man's shoulders and its happy tongue in a man's face, dig that way, deeply, with its hind claws? I thought it would.

I stood at the spot where I thought Schulz and the hound might have met, and again studied the tracks and the places where the hound had lain down. In front of one of them was a light scoop, just the rippled surface taken off the new snow. Made by a tongue lapping? Maybe. By pure intensity of imagining I tried to reconstruct what might have happened. Suppose it went this way:

Suppose he fumbled down to the river with the visibility no more than fifty or a hundred feet, and could not tell which way it ran. The fact that he had lost himself up on the bench made that not merely possible, but probable. A fire, then, until daylight let him see. Willows yielded a little thin fuel, the tiny heat along leg or backside or on the turned stiff hands made the night bearable. But caution would have told anyone as experienced as Schulz that the night was long and fuel short—and at Pinto Horse the night before the thermometer had stood at fifteen below. He would have had to keep moving, the rifle stuck in a drift and his arms flailing and the felt cap he wore pulled down to expose only his eyes and mouth—a figure as savage and forlorn as something caught out of its cave at the race's dim beginning.

The sound of hunting wolves would have kept him company as it had kept us company in our social poker game, and it would have been a sound that for many reasons he liked less than we did. Except for that dark monotone howling there would have been no sound in the shrouded bend except the creak of his moccasins and the hiss of the fire threatening always to melt itself out—no other sound unless maybe the grating of anger in his own aching head, an anger lonely, venomous, and incurable, always there like the pressure of those "bunches" on his skull. I could imagine it well enough: too well. For the first time, that day or ever, I felt sorry for Schulz.

Endless walking through frozen hours; endless thinking; endless anger and frustration. And then—maybe?—the noise of something coming, a harsh and terrifying noise smashing in on his aloneness, as something big and fast plowed through the snowy brush and came scraping and sliding down the bank. Schulz would have reached the gun in one leap (I looked, but could find no sign to prove he had). Assuming he did: while he crouched there, a wild man with his finger on the trigger and his nerves humming with panic, here came materializing out of the white darkness a great bony shape whining love.

And been shot as it rushed up to greet Schulz, shot in the moment of fright when the oncoming thing could have been wolf or worse? It would have been plausible if it hadn't been for those hound tracks that went up and down along the path on the ice, and that place where the toenails had dug in as if the hound had reared to put its paws on the wolfer's shoulders. If there was ever a time when Schulz would have welcomed the hound, greeted it, talked to it in his mixture of baby talk, questions, and grunts of endearment, this would have been the time. The coming of the dog should have made the night thirty degrees warmer and hours shorter.

Surely the hound, having pursued him for ten miles or so, would have stuck close, kept him company in his pacing, stood with him whenever he built up the fire a little and warmed his feet and hands. But it had walked up and down the path only two or three times. Twice it had lain down. Once, perhaps, it had lapped up snow.

And this hound, following Schulz's tracks with blind love—and unfed all day, since it had escaped before the Schulz boy could feed it— had passed, sniffed around, perhaps eaten of, the carcass of the yearling at Bates Camp.

Suppose Schulz had looked up from his stiff pacing and seen the hound rolling, or feverishly gulping snow. Suppose that in the murk, out of the corner of his eye, he had seen it stagger to its feet. Suppose, in the flicker of the fire, its great jaws had been opening and closing and that foam had dripped from its chops. Suppose a tight moment of alarm and disbelief, a tableau of freezing man and crazed hound, the deadliest creature and his deadly pet. Suppose it started toward him. Suppose the wolfer spoke to it, and it came on; yelled his peremptory command of "Charge!" which usually dropped the dog as if it had been poleaxed—and the hound still came on. Suppose he yelled a cracking yell, and the hound lumbered into a gallop, charging him. The spring for the gun, the mitt snatched off between the teeth, the stiffened finger pulling the trigger, a snapshot from the waist: Schulz was a good shot, or a lucky one; he had had to be.

Suppose. I supposed it, I tell you, in a way to give myself goose-flesh. By the vividness of imagination or the freakishness of the fading light, the hound's tracks arranged themselves so that only those decisive, final ones were clear. They led directly from one of the places where it had lain down to the bloody scramble where it had died, and if I read them right they came at a scattering gallop. Standing in the path, Schulz would have fired with the hound no more than thirty feet away. Its momentum had carried it in a rolling plunge twenty feet closer. I stepped it off. When Schulz, with what paralysis in his guts and shaking in his muscles, lowered his gun and went up to the dead pet that his own poison had turned into an enemy, he had only three steps to go.

I went over to the hound and took off his collar, evidence, maybe, or a sort of souvenir. Dude was drooping in the willows with his head down to his knees. It was growing dark, but the fog that had threatened was evidently not going to come on; the moon's shape was in the sky.

What Schulz had done after the shooting of the hound was up for guesses. He had had to stay through the night until he knew which way was which. But then he had made those tracks upriver—whether heading for the T-Down for some reason, or wandering out of his head, or simply, in disgust and despair, starting on foot out of the country.

I would find out tomorrow. Right now it was time I got back to camp. When I led Dude down onto the ice and climbed on, the moon had swum clear, with a big ring around it. There was no aurora; the sky behind the thin remaining mist was blue-black and polished. Just for a second, when I took off a mitt and reached back to unbuckle the saddlebag and put the hound's collar inside, I laid my hand on the marten, stiff-frozen under soft fur. It gave me an unpleasant shock, somehow. I pulled my hand away as if the marten might have bitten me.

Riding up the channel, I heard the wind beginning to whine under the eaves of the cutbanks, and a flurry of snow came down on me, and a trail of drift blew eastward ahead of me down the middle of the ice. The moon sat up above me like a polished brass cuspidor in a high-class saloon, but that could be deceptive; within minutes the wrack of another storm could be blowing it under.

Then I rode out into an open reach, and something touched my face, brushed it and was gone, then back again. The willows shuddered in a gust. Dude's head came up, and so did mine, because that wind blew out of hundreds of miles of snowy waste as if it wafted across orange groves straight from Florida: instantly, in its first breath, there was a promise of incredible spring. I have felt the beginnings of many a chinook; I never felt one that I liked better than that one.

Before I reached Bates I was riding with my earlaps up and my collar open. I had heard a willow or two shed its load of snow and snap upright. The going under Dude's feet was no longer the squeaky dryness of hard cold, but had gone mushy.

By morning the coulees and draws would be full of the sound of water running under the sagged and heavied drifts; the rims of the river valley and patches of watery prairie might be worn bare and brown. There might be cattle on their feet again, learning again to bawl, maybe even working up toward the benches, because this was a wind they could face, and the prairie wool that had been only inches below their feet all winter would be prickling up into sight. Something—not much but something—might yet be saved out of that winter.

That night I went to bed full of the sense of rescue, happy as a boy scenting spring, eased of a long strain, and I never thought until morning, when I looked out with the chinook still blowing strong and saw the channel of the Whitemud running ten inches of water on top of the ice, that now I wouldn't be able to follow to their end the single line of tracks, by that time pursuing nothing and unpursued, that led upriver into ambiguity. By the time I woke up, Schulz's last tracks were on their way toward the Milk and the Missouri in the spring breakup; and so was his last fire; and so, probably was the body of his great hound; and so, for all I or anyone else ever found out, was he.

PART 4

ACCIDENT AND INJURY

Wilderness survival tales are replete with accidents and injuries. In the twentieth century, broken bodies and bewildered minds are especially common motifs in wilderness stories, their remote and often dangerous locales casting into high relief dramas of human fragility and fallibility. At the same time, if wilderness in the modern literary imagination often provides a place where characters must directly confront their very human weaknesses and vulnerabilities, it also offers a symbolic site of healing or repair where they can reclaim their strength and confidence. In short, wilderness stories are as likely to celebrate the resilience of bodies and minds as to shine a spotlight on their brittleness. Most stories of accidents in the wild feature injuries both physical and emotional. A plane crash in a glacier valley forces its two survivors to confront their present dangers and their past losses, or a sudden hiking mishap compels a personal reckoning by bringing the truth of a broken relationship into painful focus. As these tales imagine it, an emergency in the wild, with no one around to save you, sharpens bodily sensation, stimulates mental awareness, and provokes radical self-honesty. It also provides yet another reminder that nature may be wholly indifferent to your plight.

"Walking Out"

DAVID QUAMMEN

David Quammen (b. 1948) is a distinguished science and nature journalist who focuses on field biology, complex ecosystems, evolutionary history, and deadly viruses. His science writing, which has appeared in outlets like *National Geographic,* the *Atlantic, Harper's Magazine,* and the *New York Times Book Review,* has won numerous prizes, including three National Magazine Awards. A selection of influential essays from Quammen's popular "Natural Acts" column in *Outside* magazine appear in his *Natural Acts: A Sidelong View of Science and Nature* (1985, rev. 2008) and in its successor volume *The Flight of the Iguana* (1988). Drawing on his travels around the world to do research in remote locales (swamps, mountains, jungles), Quammen addresses a range of ecological themes in his nonfiction books: species extinction in *The Song of the Dodo* (1996), biological diversity in *The Reluctant Mr. Darwin* (2006), wild ecosystems in *Yellowstone: A Journey Through America's Wild Heart* (2016), and animal infections and emerging diseases in *Spillover* (2012) and *The Chimp and the River* (2015). The latter books foresaw the emergence of a virus where the animal-to-human viral spillover could not ultimately be contained, a virus like COVID-19. Best known for his science writing, Quammen is also a talented fiction writer, with three novels under his belt and a collection of short stories called *Blood Line: Stories of Fathers and Sons* (1988), which opens with the tale "Walking Out." Adapted for the screen in 2017, "Walking Out" follows an eleven-year-old boy as he reluctantly joins his father in Montana on a moose hunt. Quammen's affecting survival tale is one of many boys' coming-of-age stories that populate wilderness literature— stories in which adulthood must arrive on its own timetable. David Quammen resides in Bozeman, Montana, where he has lived for the past fifty years.

"Walking Out"

DAVID QUAMMEN

As the train rocked dead at Livingston he saw the man, in a worn khaki shirt with button flaps buttoned, arms crossed. The boy's hand sprang up by reflex, and his face broke into a smile. The man smiled back gravely, and nodded. He did not otherwise move. The boy turned from the window and, with the awesome deliberateness of a fat child harboring reluctance, began struggling to pull down his bag. His father would wait on the platform. First sight of him had reminded the boy that nothing was simple enough now for hurrying.

They drove in the old open Willys toward the cabin beyond town. The windshield of the Willys was up, but the fine cold sharp rain came into their faces, and the boy could not raise his eyes to look at the road. He wore a rain parka his father had handed him at the station. The man, protected by only the khaki, held his lips strung in a firm silent line that seemed more grin than wince. Riding through town in the cold rain, open topped and jaunty, getting drenched as though by necessity, was—the boy understood vaguely—somehow in the spirit of this season.

"We have a moose tag," his father shouted.

The boy said nothing. He refused to care what it meant, that they had a moose tag.

"I've got one picked out. A bull. I've stalked him for two weeks. Up in the Crazies. When we get to the cabin, we'll build a good roaring fire." With only the charade of a pause, he added, "Your mother." It was said like a question. The boy waited. "How is she?"

"All right, I guess." Over the jeep's howl, with the wind stealing his voice, the boy too had to shout.

"Are you friends with her?"

"I guess so."

"Is she still a beautiful lady?"

"I don't know. I guess so. I don't know that."

"You must know that. Is she starting to get wrinkled like me? Does

she seem worried and sad? Or is she just still a fine beautiful lady? You
must know that."

"She's still a beautiful lady, I guess."

"Did she tell you any messages for me?"

"She said . . . she said I should give you her love," the boy lied,
impulsively and clumsily. He was at once embarrassed that he had done it.

"Oh," his father said. "Thank you, David."

They reached the cabin on a mile of dirt road winding through
meadow to a spruce grove. Inside, the boy was enwrapped in the strong
syncretic smell of all seasonal mountain cabins: pine resin and insect
repellent and a mustiness suggesting damp bathing trunks stored in a
drawer. There were yellow pine floors and rope-work throw rugs and
a bead curtain to the bedroom and a cast-iron cook stove with none
of the lids or handles missing and a pump in the kitchen sink and old
issues of *Field and Stream,* and on the mantel above where a fire now
finally burned was a picture of the boy's grandfather, the railroad telegrapher, who had once owned the cabin. The boy's father cooked a dinner of fried ham, and though the boy did not like ham he had expected
his father to cook canned stew or Spam, so he said nothing. His father
asked him about school and the boy talked and his father seemed to
be interested. Warm and dry, the boy began to feel safe from his own
anguish. Then his father said:

"We'll leave tomorrow around ten."

Last year on the boy's visit they had hunted birds. They had lived
in the cabin for six nights, and each day they had hunted pheasant in
the wheat stubble, or blue grouse in the woods, or ducks along the
irrigation sloughs. The boy had been wet and cold and miserable at
times, but each evening they returned to the cabin and to the boy's
suitcase of dry clothes. They had eaten hot food cooked on a stove,
and had smelled the cabin smell, and had slept together in a bed. In six
days of hunting, the boy had not managed to kill a single bird. Yet last
year he had known that, at least once a day, he would be comfortable,
if not happy. This year his father planned that he should not even be
comfortable. He had said in his last letter to Evergreen Park, before the
boy left Chicago but when it was too late for him not to leave, that he
would take the boy camping in the mountains, after big game. He had
pretended to believe that the boy would be glad.

Last year his father had given him a 16-gauge over-and-under, and on the first morning they had practiced until the boy's shoulder was bruised. He had never before fired a gun. He hit a few coffee cans. Then they walked in the woods after blue grouse, and his father turned quickly, and the boy heard a rustle, and his father fired, and a blue grouse was dead in the bushes.

"Like that," his father said. "They're stupid, and slow. Not like a duck."

His father killed four blue grouse in five shots before he began to touch the boy's elbow and whisper, "There, David," instead of shooting. But the woods were thick and confused with bare alder bushes and everything was the same color and the blue grouse were faster than the boy could lift the gun. The ducks and pheasants were faster than the blue grouse. The boy's aim was not good. Sometimes he fired with his eyes closed, to see if it made any difference. It did not. So he gave up. Long before his father let him stop shooting, the boy had given up.

"It's hard, I know," his father said. "And then it gets easier. Eventually, you'll hit your first bird. You will. Then all of a sudden it gets very easy. But you have to keep trying. Don't close your eyes, David." The boy knew his father was lying. His father often said things were easy, when the boy knew they were not.

Then the boy hit his first grouse. The boy did not know whether he had hit it or not, but his father said that he had. He had hit it in the wing, and it faltered, and dropped. They went to the spot and searched the brush and the ground for an hour. Even his father could not find the crippled grouse, and they did not have a dog. The boy's father would not own a hunting dog. He had said that, since he was already alone, he did not want to give that much love to a creature who would only live fourteen or fifteen years. The bird must have run off and hidden itself to die, his father said.

The boy was disappointed at not finding the grouse. But his father, the boy could see, was even more disappointed. An hour seemed a very long time to keep looking.

"Just too bad we couldn't find that blue grouse you killed," his father had said at the station, when the boy left, and the boy was embarrassed. He understood how his father felt. So he had agreed to come back for hunting this year. His father did not mean to make everything difficult for the boy. He couldn't help it.

Now a deer or a moose would be a much bigger target than a blue grouse. But a deer is not slow, the boy knew, and is probably not stupid, he thought. He knew nothing about a moose except that it was stupid-looking. The boy wished again that they could have found the blue grouse he may have wounded last year, found it dead, and eaten it roasted in butter as they had the birds his father killed. That would have made a great difference to the boy now.

They would leave around ten the next day for the Crazy Mountains. The boy slept on the far edge of the bed, and did not let himself touch up against his father's warm body.

Then there was nothing, then more cold, and then the faint steady gray light of November dawn. The boy's father was up, and the stove was already making its warm noises. After breakfast they sighted in the boy's gun. They set up coffee cans on a fence in the meadow, and the boy hit a few. The rain had paused, so the boy was only drenched from the thighs down.

This year his father gave him a different gun. It was a lever-action Winchester .30-30, with open sights. It was a simple gun. It was older than the over-and-under, and it was probably a better gun, the boy could see, and it was certainly heavier and more powerful. This was just like the rifle with which he had killed his own first moose, when he was thirteen, the boy's father said. This was not the same rifle, but it was just like it. The boy's grandfather, the railroad telegrapher, had given him that gun. A boy should learn how to shoot with open sights, his father said, before he learns to depend on a telescope.

The Willys was loaded and moving by ten minutes to ten. For three hours they drove, through Big Timber, and then north on the highway, and then back west again on a logging road that took them winding and bouncing higher into the mountains. Thick cottony streaks of white cloud hung in among the mountain-top trees, light and dense dollops against the bulking sharp dark olive, as though in a black-and-white photograph. They followed the gravel road for an hour, and the boy thought they would soon have a flat tire or break an axle. If they had a flat, the boy knew, his father would only change it and drive on until they had the second, farther from the highway. Finally they crossed a creek and his father plunged the Willys off into a bed of weeds.

His father said, "Here."

The boy said, "Where?"

"Up that little drainage. At the head of the creek."

"How far is it?"

"Two or three miles."

"Is that where you saw the moose?"

"No. That's where I saw the sheepman's hut. The moose is farther. On top."

"Are we going to sleep in a hut? I thought we were going to sleep in a tent."

"No. Why should we carry a tent up there when we have a perfectly good hut?"

The boy couldn't answer that question. He thought now that this might be the time when he would cry. He had known it was coming.

"I don't much want to sleep in a hut," he said, and his voice broke with the simple honesty of it, and his eyes glazed. He held his mouth tight against the trembling.

As though something had broken in him too, the boy's father laid his forehead down on the steering wheel, against his knuckles. For a moment he remained bowed, breathing exhaustedly. But he looked up again before speaking.

"Well, we don't have to, David."

The boy said nothing.

"It's an old sheepman's hut made of logs, and it's near where we're going to hunt, and we can fix it dry and good. I thought you might like that. I thought it might be more fun than a tent. But we don't have to do it. We can drive back to Big Timber and buy a tent, or we can drive back to the cabin and hunt birds, like last year. Whatever you want to do. You have to forgive me the kind of ideas I get. I hope you will. We don't have to do anything that you don't want to do."

"No," the boy said. "I want to."

"Are you sure?"

"No," the boy said. "But I just want to."

They bushwhacked along the creek, treading a thick soft mixture of moss and humus and needles, climbing upward through brush. Then the brush thinned and they were ascending an open creek bottom, thirty yards wide, darkened by fir and cedar. Farther, and they struck a trail, which led them upward along the creek. Farther still, and the trail received a branch, then another, then forked.

"Who made this trail? Did the sheepman?"

"No," his father said. "Deer and elk."

Gradually the creek's little canyon narrowed, steep wooded shoulders funneling closer on each side. For a while the game trails forked and converged like a maze, but soon again there were only two branches, and finally one, heavily worn. It dodged through alder and willow, skirting tangles of browned raspberry, so that the boy and his father could never see more than twenty feet ahead. When they stopped to rest, the boy's father unstrapped the .270 from his pack and loaded it.

"We have to be careful now," he explained. "We may surprise a bear."

Under the cedars, the creek bottom held a cool dampness that seemed to be stored from one winter to the next. The boy began at once to feel chilled. He put on his jacket, and they continued climbing. Soon he was sweating again in the cold.

On a small flat where the alder drew back from the creek, the hut was built into one bank of the canyon, with the sod of the hillside lapping out over its roof. The door was a low dark opening. Forty or fifty years ago, the boy's father explained, this hut had been built and used by a Basque shepherd. At that time there had been many Basques in Montana, and they had run sheep all across this ridge of the Crazies. His father forgot to explain what a Basque was, and the boy didn't remind him.

They built a fire. His father had brought sirloin steaks and an onion for dinner, and the boy was happy with him about that. As they ate, it grew dark, but the boy and his father had stocked a large comforting pile of naked deadfall. In the darkness, by firelight, his father made chocolate pudding. The pudding had been his father's surprise. The boy sat on a piece of canvas and added logs to the fire while his father drank coffee. Sparks rose on the heat and the boy watched them climb toward the cedar limbs and the black pools of sky. The pudding did not set.

"Do you remember your grandfather, David?"

"Yes," the boy said, and wished it were true. He remembered a funeral when he was three.

"Your grandfather brought me up on this mountain when I was seventeen. That was the last year he hunted." The boy knew what sort of thoughts his father was having. But he knew also that his own home was in Evergreen Park, and that he was another man's boy now, with another man's name, though this indeed was his father. "Your grandfather was fifty years older than me."

The boy said nothing.

"And I'm thirty-four years older than you."

"And I'm only eleven," the boy cautioned him.

"Yes," said his father. "And someday you'll have a son and you'll be forty years older than him, and you'll want so badly for him to know who you are that you could cry."

The boy was embarrassed.

"And that's called the cycle of life's infinite wisdom," his father said, and laughed at himself unpleasantly.

"Why didn't he?" the boy asked, to escape the focus of his father's rumination.

"Why didn't who what?"

"Why was it the last year he hunted?"

"He was sixty-seven years old," his father said. "But that wasn't the reason. Because he was still walking to work at the railroad office in Big Timber when he was seventy-five. I don't know. We took a bull elk and a goat that year, I remember. The goat was during spring season and every inch of its hide was covered with ticks. I carried it down whole and after a mile I was covered with ticks too. I never shot another goat. I don't know why he quit. He still went out after birds in the wheat stubble, by himself. So it's not true that he stopped hunting completely. He stopped hunting with me. And he stopped killing. Once in every five or six times he would bring back a pheasant, if it seemed like a particularly good autumn night to have pheasant for supper. Usually he just went out and missed every shot on purpose. There were plenty of birds in the fields where he was walking, and your grandmother or I would hear his gun fire, at least once. But I guess when a man feels himself getting old, almost as old as he thinks he will ever be, he doesn't much want to be killing things anymore. I guess you might have to kill one bird in every ten or twenty, or the pheasants might lose their respect for you. They might tame out. Your grandfather had no desire to live among tame pheasants, I'm sure. But I suppose you would get a little reluctant, when you came to be seventy, about doing your duty toward keeping them wild. And he would not hunt with me anymore then, not even pheasants, not even to miss them. He said it was because he didn't trust himself with a partner, now that his hands were unsteady. But his hands were still steady. He said it was because I was too good. That he had taught me as well as he knew how, and that all I could learn from him now would be the bad habits of age, and those I would find for myself, in my turn. He never did tell me the real reason."

"What did he die of?"

"He was eighty-seven then," said his father. "Christ. He was tired."

The boy's question had been a disruption. His father was silent. Then he shook his head, and poured himself the remaining coffee. He did not like to think of the boy's grandfather as an eighty-seven-year-old man, the boy understood. As long as his grandfather was dead anyway, his father preferred thinking of him younger.

"I remember when I got my first moose," he said. "I was thirteen. I had never shot anything bigger than an owl. And I caught holy hell for killing that owl. I had my Winchester .30-30, like the one you're using. He gave it to me that year, at the start of the season. It was an old-looking gun even then. I don't know where he got it. We had a moose that he had stalked the year before, in a long swampy cottonwood flat along the Yellowstone River. It was a big cow, and this year she had a calf.

"We went there on the first day of the season and every hunting day for a week, and hunted down the length of that river flat, spaced apart about twenty yards, and came out at the bottom end. We saw fresh tracks every day, but we never got a look at that moose and the calf. It was only a matter of time, my father told me, before we would jump her. Then that Sunday we drove out and before he had the truck parked my hands were shaking. I knew it was that day. There was no reason why, yet I had such a sure feeling it was that day, my hands had begun shaking. He noticed, and he said: 'Don't worry.'

"I said: 'I'm fine.' And my voice was steady. It was just my hands.

" 'I can see that,' he said. 'But you'll do what you need to do.'

" 'Yessir,' I said. 'Let's go hunting.'

"That day he put me up at the head end of our cottonwood flat and said he would walk down along the riverbank to the bottom, and then turn in. We would come at the moose from both ends and meet in the middle and I should please not shoot my father when he came in sight. I should try to remember, he said, that he was the uglier one, in the orange hat. The shaking had left me as soon as we started walking, holding our guns. I remember it all. Before he went off I said: 'What does a moose look like?'

" 'What the hell do you mean, what does a moose look like?'

" 'Yes, I know,' I said. 'I mean, what is he gonna do when I see him? When he sees me. What color is he? What kind of thing is he gonna do?'

"And he said: 'All right. She will be black. She will be almost pitch black. She will not look to you very much bigger than our pickup. She is going to be stupid. She will let you get close. Slide right up to within thirty or forty yards if you can and set yourself up for a good shot. She will probably not see you, and if she does, she will probably not care. If you miss the first time, which you have every right to do, I don't care how close you get, if you miss the first time, she may even give you another. If you catch her attention, she may bolt off to me or she may charge you. Watch out for the calf when you come up on her. Worry her over the calf, and she will be mad. If she charges you, stand where you are and squeeze off another and then jump the hell out of the way. We probably won't even see her. All right?'

"I had walked about three hundred yards before I saw what I thought was a Holstein. It was off to my left, away from the river, and I looked over there and saw black and white and kept walking till I was just about past it. There were cattle pastured along in that flat but they would have been beef cattle, Herefords, brown and white like a deer. I didn't think about that. I went on looking everywhere else until I glanced over again when I was abreast and saw I was walking along sixty yards from a grazing moose. I stopped. My heart started pumping so hard that it seemed like I might black out, and I didn't know what was going to happen. I thought the moose would take care of that. Nothing happened.

"Next thing I was running. Running flat out as fast as I could, bent over double like a soldier would do in the field, running as fast but as quietly as I could. Running right at that moose. I remember clearly that I was not thinking anything at all, not for those first seconds. My body just started to run. I never thought, Now I'll scoot up to within thirty yards of her. I was just charging blind, like a moose or a sow grizzly is liable to charge you if you get her mad or confused. Who knows what I would have done. I wanted a moose pretty badly, I thought. I might have galloped right up to within five yards before I leveled, if it hadn't been for that spring creek.

"I didn't see it till I was in the air. I came up a little hillock and jumped, and then it was too late. The hillock turned out to be one bank of a spring-fed pasture seepage, about fifteen feet wide. I landed up to my thighs in mud. It was a prime cattle wallow, right where I had jumped. I must have spent five minutes sweating my legs out of that muck, I was furious with myself, and I was sure the moose would be gone. But the moose was still grazing the same three feet of grass. And by that time I had some of my sense back.

"I climbed the far bank of the mudhole and lay up along the rise where I could steady my aim on the ground. From there I had an open shot of less than forty yards, but the moose was now facing me head on, so I would probably either kill her clean or miss her altogether. My hands started shaking again. I tried to line up the bead and it was ridiculous. My rifle was waving all over that end of the woods. For ten minutes I lay there struggling to control my aim, squeezing the rifle tighter and tighter and taking deeper breaths and holding them longer. Finally I did a smart thing. I set the rifle down. I rolled over on my back and rubbed my eyes and discovered that I was exhausted. I got my breath settled back down in rhythm again. If I could just take that moose, I thought, I was not going to want anything else for a year. But I knew I was not going to do it unless I could get my hands to obey me, no matter how close I was. I tried it again. I remembered to keep breathing easy and low and it was a little better but the rifle was still moving everywhere. When it seemed like the trembling was about to start getting worse all over again I waited till the sights next crossed the moose and jerked off a shot. I missed. The moose didn't even look up.

"Now I was calmer. I had heard the gun fire once, and I knew my father had heard it, and I knew the moose would only give me one more. I realized that there was a good chance I would not get this moose at all, so I was more serious, and humble. This time I squeezed. I knocked a piece off her right antler and before I thought to wonder why a female should have any antlers to get shot at she raised her head up and gave a honk like eleven elephants in a circus-train fire. She started to run.

"I got off my belly and dropped the gun and turned around and jumped right back down into that mud. I was still stuck there when I heard her crash by on her way to the river, and then my father's shot.

"But I had wallowed myself out again, and got my rifle up off the ground, by the time he found me, thank God. He took a look at my clothes and said:

" 'Tried to burrow up under him, did you?'

"'No sir. I heard you fire once. Did you get her?'

"'Him. That was no cow and calf. That was a bull. No. No more than you.'

"He had been at the river edge about a hundred yards downstream from where the bull broke out. He took his shot while the bull was crossing the gravel bed and the shallows. The moose clambered right out into midstream of the Yellowstone and started swimming for his life. But the current along there was heavy. So the moose was swept down abreast with my father before he got halfway across toward the opposite shore. My father sighted on him as he rafted by, dog-paddling frantically and staying afloat and inching slowly away. The moose turned and looked at him, my father said. He had a chunk broken out of one antler and it was dangling down by a few fibers and he looked terrified. He was not more than twenty yards offshore by then and he could see my father and the raised rifle. My father said he had never seen more personality come into the face of a wild animal. All right, my father said the moose told him, Do what you will do. They both knew the moose was helpless. They both also knew this: my father could kill the moose, but he couldn't have him. The Yellowstone River would have him. My father lowered the gun. When he did, my father claimed, the moose turned his head forward again and went on swimming harder than ever. So that wasn't the day I shot mine.

"I shot mine the next Saturday. We went back to the cottonwood flat and split again and I walked up to within thirty yards of the cow and her calf. I made a standing shot, and killed the cow with one bullet breaking her spine. She was drinking, broadside to me. She dropped dead on the spot. The calf didn't move. He stood over the dead cow, stupid, wondering what in the world to do.

"The calf was as big as a four-point buck. When my father came up, he found me with tears flooding all over my face, screaming at the calf and trying to shoo him away. I was pushing against his flanks and swatting him and shouting at him to run off. At the sight of my father, he finally bolted.

"I had shot down the cow while she stood in the same spring seep where I had been stuck. Her quarters weighed out to eight hundred pounds and we couldn't budge her. We had to clean her and quarter her right there in the water and mud."

His father checked the tin pot again, to be sure there was no more coffee.

"Why did you tell me that story?" the boy said. "Now I don't want to shoot a moose either."

"I know," said his father. "And when you do, I hope you'll be sad too. But the other thing about a moose is, she makes eight hundred pounds of delicious meat. In fact, David, that's what we had for supper."

Through the night the boy was never quite warm. He slept on his side with his knees drawn up, and this was uncomfortable but his body seemed to demand it for warmth. The hard cold mountain earth pressed upward through the mat of fir boughs his father had laid, and drew heat from the boy's body like a pallet of leeches. He clutched the bedroll around his neck and folded the empty part at the bottom back under his legs. Once he woke to a noise. Though his father was sleeping between him and the door of the hut, for a while the boy lay awake, listening worriedly, and then woke again on his back to realize time had passed. He heard droplets begin to hit the canvas his father had spread over the sod roof of the hut. But he remained dry.

He rose to the smell of a fire. The tarp was rigid with sleet and frost. The firewood and knapsacks were frosted. It was that gray time of dawn before any blue and, through the branches above, the boy was unable to tell whether the sky was murky or clear. Delicate sheet ice hung on everything, but there was no wetness. The rain seemed to have been hushed by the cold.

"What time is it?"

"Early yet."

"How early?" The boy was thinking about the cold at home as he waited outside on 96th Street for his school bus. That was the cruelest moment of his day, but it seemed a benign and familiar part of him compared to this.

"Early. I don't have a watch. What difference does it make, David?"

"Not any."

After breakfast they began walking up the valley. His father had the .270 and the boy carried the old Winchester .30-30. The walking was not hard, and with this gentle exercise in the cold morning the boy soon felt fresh and fine. Now I'm hunting for moose with my father, he told himself. That's just what I'm doing. Few boys in Evergreen Park had ever been moose hunting with their fathers in Montana, he knew. I'm doing it now, the boy told himself.

Reaching the lip of a high meadow, a mile above the shepherd's hut, they had not seen so much as a magpie.

Before them, across hundreds of yards, opened a smooth lake of tall lifeless grass, browned by September drought and killed by the frosts and beginning to rot with November's rain. The creek was here a deep quiet channel of smooth curves overhung by the grass, with a dark surface like heavy oil. When they had come fifty yards into the meadow, his father turned and pointed out to the boy a large ponderosa pine with a forked crown that marked the head of their creek valley. He showed the boy a small aspen grove midway across the meadow, toward which they were aligning themselves.

"Near the far woods is a beaver pond. The moose waters there. We can wait in the aspens and watch the whole meadow without being seen. If he doesn't come, we'll go up another canyon, and check again on the way back."

For an hour, and another, they waited. The boy sat, and his buttocks drew cold moisture from the ground. He bunched his jacket around him with hands in the pockets. He was patient. His father squatted on his heels like a country man. Periodically, his father rose and inspected the meadow in all directions.

"He comes once in the morning, and again in the evening, I think. It looked from the tracks like he comes at least twice a day. But he may not show up for hours. You can't tell. If you could, it wouldn't be hunting. It would be shopping.

"He may even know that this is the last week of season. He may remember. So he'll be especially on his guard, and go somewhere else to drink. Somewhere less open." They waited in silence.

"But he may not be all that clever," his father added. "He may make a mistake."

The morning passed, and it was noon.

His father stood. He fixed his stare on the distant meadow, and like a retriever did not move. He said: "David."

The boy stood beside him. His father placed a hand on the boy's shoulder. The boy saw a large dark form rolling toward them like a great slug in the grass.

"Is it the moose?"

"No," said his father. "That is a grizzly bear, David. An old male grizzly."

The boy was impressed. He sensed an aura of power and terror and authority about the husky shape, even at two hundred yards.

"Are we going to shoot him?"

"No."

"Why not?"

"We don't have a permit," his father whispered. "And because we don't want to."

The bear plowed on toward the beaver pond for a while, then stopped. It froze in the grass and seemed to be listening. The boy's father added: "That's not hunting for the meat. That's hunting for the fear. I don't need the fear. I've got enough in my life already."

The bear turned and moiled off quickly through the grass. It disappeared back into the far woods.

"He heard us."

"Maybe," the boy's father said. "Let's go have a look at that beaver pond."

A sleek furred body lay low in the water. The boy thought at first it was a large beaver. It was too large. His father moved quickly ahead off the trail and said nothing. The boy saw that his father was not concerned to surprise it.

The carcass was swollen grotesquely with water and putrescence, and coated with glistening blowflies. His father did not touch it. Four days, his father guessed. He stood up to his knees in the sump. The moose had been shot at least eighteen times with a .22 pistol. One of its eyes had been shot out, and it had been shot twice in the jaw. Both of the quarters on the side that lay upward had been ruined with shots. The boy's father took the trouble of counting the holes in that side of the carcass, and probing one of the slugs out with his knife. It only made him angrier. He flung the lead away.

Nearby in the fresh mud was the lid from a can of wintergreen chewing tobacco.

For the next three hours, with his father withdrawn into a solitary and characteristic bitterness, the boy felt abandoned. He did not understand why a moose would be slaughtered with a light pistol and left to rot. His father did not bother to explain; like the bear, he seemed to understand it as well as he needed to. They walked on, but they did not really hunt.

They left the meadow for more pine, and now tamarack, naked tamarack, the yellow needles nearly all down and going where they coated the trail. The boy and his father hiked along a level path into another canyon, this one vast at the mouth and narrowing between high ridges of bare rock. They crossed and recrossed the shepherd's creek, which in this canyon was a tumbling freestone brook. The boy was miserably uneasy because his father had grown so quiet.

The boy's father tortured him when he spoke at the boy obscurely, both of them knowing that the boy could not hope to understand him, and that his father did not really care whether he did. But the boy preferred even that to his silences.

They wandered forward, deeper into the rock canyon, the boy following five yards behind his father, watching the cold, unapproachable rage that shaped the line of his father's shoulders. They climbed over deadfalls blocking the trail, skirted one boulder large as a cabin, and blundered into a garden of nettles that stung them fiercely through their trousers. They saw fresh elk scat, and bear, diarrhetic with late berries. The boy's father eventually grew bored with brooding. He showed the boy how to stalk. Before dusk that day they had shot an elk.

An open and gently sloped hillside, almost a meadow, ran for a quarter mile in quaking aspen, none over fifteen feet tall. The elk was above. The boy's father had the boy brace his gun in the notch of an aspen and gave him the first shot. The boy missed. The elk reeled and bolted down and his father killed it before it made cover. It was a five-point bull.

His father showed the boy how to approach a downed animal: from behind, so he could not lash out with his hooves. Get hold of his rack, in case he's not dead, the boy's father explained; reach forward and hook your fingers into the nostrils, he said; and then, suddenly, to the boy's utter shock, his father slit the elk's throat. The boy gagged.

They dressed the elk out and dragged it down the hill to the cover of large pines, near the stream. When they quartered the animal tomorrow, his father said, they would want water. They covered the body with fresh branches, and returned to the hut under twilight. The boy's father was satisfied and the boy was relieved. Again that evening, his father talked.

He talked about the former railroad telegrapher of Big Timber, Montana. He told of going to the station at 6:00 a.m. on school days to find the boy's grandfather bent forward and dozing over the key. He told of walking the old man back home for breakfast, and of his predictable insistence, against all fact, that the night had been busy, full of transmissions. He described how the boy's grandfather became subject to chronic, almost narcoleptic drowsiness after the boy's grandmother, still a young middle-aged woman, checked into the hospital for the last time and began dying. Then, until it faded to embers and the embers went gray, the boy's father stared at his memories, in the fire.

That night even the fetal position could not keep the boy warm. He shivered wakefully for hours. He was glad that the following day, though full of walking and butchery and oppressive burdens, would be their last in the woods. He heard nothing. When he woke, through the door of the hut he saw whiteness like bone.

Six inches had fallen, and it was still snowing. The boy stood about in the campsite, amazed. When it snowed three inches in Evergreen Park, the boy would wake before dawn to the hiss of sand trucks and the ratchet of chains. Here there had been no warning. The boy was not much colder than he had been yesterday, and the transformation of the woods seemed mysterious and benign and somehow comic. He thought of Christmas. Then his father barked at him.

His father's mood had also changed, but in a different way; he seemed serious and hurried. As he wiped the breakfast pots clean with snow, he gave the boy orders for other chores. They left camp with two empty pack frames, both rifles, and a handsaw and rope. The boy soon understood why his father felt the pressure of time: it took them an hour to climb the mile to the meadow. The snow continued. They did not rest until they reached the aspens.

"I had half a mind at breakfast to let the bull lie and pack us straight down out of here," his father admitted. "Probably smarter and less trouble in the long run. I could have come back on snowshoes next week. But by then it might be three feet deep and starting to drift. We can get two quarters out today. That will make it easier for me later." The boy was surprised by two things: that his father would be so wary in the face of a gentle snowfall and that he himself would have felt disappointed to be taken out of the woods that morning. The air of the meadow teemed with white.

"If it stops soon, we're fine," said his father.

It continued.

The path up the far canyon was hard climbing in eight inches of snow. The boy fell once, filling his collar and sleeves, and the gunsight put a small gouge in his chin. But he was not discouraged. That night they would be warm and dry at the cabin. A half mile and he came up beside his father, who had stopped to stare down at dark splashes of blood.

Heavy tracks and a dragging belly mark led up to the scramble of deepening red, and away. The tracks were nine inches long and showed claws. The boy's father knelt. As the boy watched, one shining maroon splotch the size of a saucer sank slowly beyond sight into the snow. The blood was warm.

Inspecting the tracks carefully, his father said, "She's got a cub with her."

"What happened?"

"Just a kill. Seems to have been a bird. That's too much blood for a grouse, but I don't see signs of any four-footed creature. Maybe a turkey." He frowned thoughtfully. "A turkey without feathers. I don't know. What I dislike is coming up on her with a cub." He drove a round into the chamber of the .270.

Trailing red smears, the tracks preceded them. Within fifty feet they found the body. It was half-buried. The top of its head had been shorn away, and the cub's brains had been licked out.

His father said, "Christ," and plunged off the trail. He snapped at the boy to follow closely.

They made a wide crescent through brush and struck back after a quarter mile. His father slogged ahead in the snow, stopping often to stand holding his gun ready and glancing around while the boy caught up and passed him. The boy was confused. He knew his father was worried, but he did not feel any danger himself. They met the trail again, and went on to the aspen hillside before his father allowed them to rest. The boy spat on the snow. His lungs ached badly.

"Why did she do that?"

"She didn't. Another bear got her cub. A male. Maybe the one we saw yesterday. Then she fought him for the body, and she won. We didn't miss them by much. She may even have been watching. Nothing could put her in a worse frame of mind."

He added: "If we so much as see her, I want you to pick the nearest big tree and start climbing. Don't stop till you're twenty feet off the ground. I'll stay down and decide whether we have to shoot her. Is your rifle cocked?"

"No."

"Cock it, and put on the safety. She may be a black bear and black bears can climb. If she comes up after you, lean down and stick your gun in her mouth and fire. You can't miss."

He cocked the Winchester, as his father had said.

They angled downhill to the stream, and on to the mound of their dead elk. Snow filtered down steadily in purposeful silence. The boy was thirsty. It could not be much below freezing, he was aware, because with the exercise his bare hands were comfortable, even sweating between the fingers.

"Can I get a drink?"

"Yes. Be careful you don't wet your feet. And don't wander anywhere. We're going to get this done quickly."

He walked the few yards, ducked through the brush at streamside, and knelt in the snow to drink. The water was painful to his sinuses and bitterly cold on his hands. Standing again, he noticed an animal body ahead near the stream bank. For a moment he felt sure it was another dead cub. During that moment his father called:

"David! Get up here right now!"

The boy meant to call back. First he stepped closer to turn the cub with his foot. The touch brought it alive. It rose suddenly with a high squealing growl and whirled its head like a snake and snapped. The boy shrieked. The cub had his right hand in its jaws. It would not release.

It thrashed senselessly, working its teeth deeper and tearing flesh with each movement. The boy felt no pain. He knew his hand was being damaged and that realization terrified him and he was desperate to get the hand back before it was ruined. But he was helpless. He sensed the same furious terror racking the cub that he felt in himself, and he screamed at the cub almost reasoningly to let him go. His screams scared the cub more. Its head snatched back and forth. The boy did not think to shout for his father. He did not see him or hear him coming.

His father moved at full stride in a slowed laboring run through the snow, saying nothing and holding the rifle he did not use, crossed the last six feet still gathering speed, and brought his right boot up into the cub's belly. That kick seemed to lift the cub clear of the snow. It opened its jaws to another shrill piggish squeal, and the boy felt dull relief on his hand, as though his father had pressed open the blades of a spring trap with his foot. The cub tumbled once and disappeared over the stream bank, then surfaced downstream, squalling and paddling. The boy looked at his hand and was horrified. He still had no pain, but the hand was unrecognizable. His fingers had been peeled down through the palm like flaps on a banana. Glands at the sides of his jaw threatened that he would vomit, and he might have stood stupidly watching the hand bleed if his father had not grabbed him.

He snatched the boy by the arm and dragged him toward a tree without even looking at the boy's hand. The boy jerked back in angry resistance as though he had been struck. He screamed at his father. He screamed that his hand was cut, believing his father did not know, and as he screamed he began to cry. He began to feel hot throbbing pain. He began to worry about the blood he was losing. He could imagine his blood melting red holes in the snow behind him and he did not want to look. He did not want to do anything until he had taken care of his hand. At that instant he hated his father. But his father was stronger. He all but carried the boy to a tree.

He lifted the boy. In a voice that was quiet and hurried and very unlike the harsh grip with which he had taken the boy's arm, he said:

"Grab hold and climb up a few branches as best you can. Sit on a limb and hold tight and clamp the hand under your other armpit, if you can do that. I'll be right back to you. Hold tight because you're going to get dizzy." The boy groped desperately for a branch. His father supported him from beneath, and waited. The boy clambered. His feet scraped at the trunk. Then he was in the tree. Bark flakes and resin were stuck to the raw naked meat of his right hand. His father said:

"Now here, take this. Hurry."

The boy never knew whether his father himself had been frightened enough to forget for that moment about the boy's hand, or whether his father was still thinking quite clearly. His father may have expected that much. By the merciless clarity of his own standards, he may have expected that the boy should be able to hold on to a tree, and a wound, and a rifle, all with one hand. He extended the stock of the Winchester toward the boy.

The boy wanted to say something, but his tears and his fright would not let him gather a breath. He shuddered, and could not speak. "David," his father urged. The boy reached for the stock and faltered and clutched at the trunk with his good arm. He was crying and gasping, and he wanted to speak. He was afraid he would fall out of the tree. He released his grip once again, and felt himself tip. His father extended the gun higher, holding the barrel. The boy swung out his injured hand, spraying his father's face with blood. He reached and he tried to close torn dangling fingers around the stock and he pulled the trigger.

The bullet entered low on his father's thigh and shattered the knee and traveled down the shin bone and into the ground through his father's heel.

His father fell, and the rifle fell with him. He lay in the snow without moving. The boy thought he was dead. Then the boy saw him grope for the rifle. He found it and rolled onto his stomach, taking aim at the sow grizzly. Forty feet up the hill, towering on hind legs, she canted her head to one side, indecisive. When the cub pulled itself up a snowbank from the stream, she coughed at it sternly. The cub trotted straight to her with its head low. She knocked it off its feet with a huge paw, and it yelped. Then she turned quickly. The cub followed.

The woods were silent. The gunshot still echoed awesomely back to the boy but it was an echo of memory, not sound. He felt nothing. He saw his father's body stretched on the snow and he did not really believe he was where he was. He did not want to move: he wanted to wake. He sat in the tree and waited. The snow fell as gracefully as before.

His father rolled onto his back. The boy saw him raise himself to a sitting position and look down at the leg and betray no expression, and then slump back. He blinked slowly and lifted his eyes to meet the boy's eyes. The boy waited. He expected his father to speak. He expected his father to say *Shinny down using your elbows and knees and get the first-aid kit and boil water and phone the doctor. The number is taped to the dial.* His father stared. The boy could see the flicker of thoughts behind his father's eyes. His father said nothing. He raised his arms slowly and crossed them over his face, as though to nap in the sun.

The boy jumped. He landed hard on his feet and fell onto his back. He stood over his father. His hand dripped quietly onto the snow. He was afraid that his father was deciding to die. He wanted to beg him to reconsider. The boy had never before seen his father hopeless. He was afraid.

But he was no longer afraid of his father.

Then his father uncovered his face and said, "Let me see it."

They bandaged the boy's hand with a sleeve cut from the other arm of his shirt. His father wrapped the hand firmly and split the sleeve end with his deer knife and tied it neatly in two places. The boy now felt searing pain in his torn palm, and his stomach lifted when he thought of the damage, but at least he did not have to look at it. Quickly the plaid flannel bandage began to soak through maroon. They cut a sleeve from his father's shirt to tie over the wound in his thigh. They raised the trouser leg to see the long swelling bruise down the calf where he was hemorrhaging into the bullet's tunnel. Only then did his father realize that he was bleeding also from the heel. The boy took off his father's boot and placed a half-clean handkerchief on the insole where the bullet had exited, as his father instructed him. Then his father laced the boot on again tightly. The boy helped his father to stand. His father tried a step, then collapsed in the snow with a blasphemous howl of pain. They had not known that the knee was shattered.

The boy watched his father's chest heave with the forced sighs of suffocating frustration, and heard the air wheeze through his nostrils. His father relaxed himself with the breathing, and seemed to be think-ing. He said, "You can find your way back to the hut."

The boy held his own breath and did not move.

"You can, can't you?"

"But I'm not. I'm not going alone. I'm only going with you."

"All right, David, listen carefully," his father said. "We don't have to worry about freezing. I'm not worried about either of us freezing to death. No one is going to freeze in the woods in November, if he looks after himself. Not even in Montana. It just isn't that cold. I have matches and I have a fresh elk. And I don't think this weather is going to get any worse. It may be raining again by morning. What I'm con-cerned about is the bleeding. If I spend too much time and effort trying to walk out of here, I could bleed to death.

"I think your hand is going to be all right. It's a bad wound but the doctors will be able to fix it as good as new. I can see that. I promise you that. You'll be bleeding some too, but if you take care of that hand, it won't bleed any more walking than if you were standing still. Then you'll be at the doctor's tonight. But if I try to walk out on this leg it's going to bleed and keep bleeding and I'll lose too much blood. So I'm staying here and bundling up warm and you're walking out to get help. I'm sorry about this. It's what we have to do.

"You can't possibly get lost. You'll just follow this trail straight down the canyon the way we came up, and then you'll come to the meadow. Point yourself toward the big pine tree with the forked crown. When you get to that tree you'll find the creek again. You may not be able to see it, but make yourself quiet and listen for it. You'll hear it. Follow that down off the mountain and past the hut till you get to the jeep."

He struggled a hand into his pocket. "You've never driven a car, have you?"

The boy's lips were pinched. Muscles in his cheeks ached from clenching his jaws. He shook his head.

"You can do it. It isn't difficult." His father held up a single key and began telling the boy how to start the jeep, how to work the clutch, how to find reverse and then first and then second. As his father described the positions on the floor shift the boy raised his swaddled right hand. His father stopped. He rubbed at his eye sockets, like a man waking.

"Of course," he said. "All right. You'll have to help me."

Using the saw with his left hand, the boy cut a small forked aspen. His father showed the boy where to trim it so that the fork would reach just to his armpit. Then they lifted him to his feet. But the crutch was useless on a steep hillside of deep grass and snow. His father leaned over the boy's shoulders and they fought the slope for an hour.

When the boy stepped in a hole and they fell, his father made no exclamation of pain. The boy wondered whether his father's knee hurt as badly as his own hand. He suspected it hurt worse. He said nothing about his hand, though several times in their climb it was twisted or crushed. They reached the trail. The snow had not stopped, and their tracks were veiled. His father said:

"We need one of the guns. I forgot. It's my fault. But you'll have to go back down and get it."

The boy could not find the tree against which his father said he had leaned the .270, so he went toward the stream and looked for blood. He saw none. The imprint of his father's body was already softened beneath an inch of fresh silence. He scooped his good hand through the snowy depression and was startled by cool slimy blood, smearing his fingers like phlegm. Nearby he found the Winchester.

"The lucky one," his father said. "That's all right. Here." He snapped open the breech and a shell flew and he caught it in the air. He glanced dourly at the casing, then cast it aside in the snow. He held the gun out for the boy to see, and with his thumb let the hammer down one notch.

"Remember?" he said. "The safety."

The boy knew he was supposed to feel great shame, but he felt little. His father could no longer hurt him as he once could, because the boy was coming to understand him. His father could not help himself. He did not want the boy to feel contemptible, but he needed him to, because of the loneliness and the bitterness and the boy's mother; and he could not help himself.

After another hour they had barely traversed the aspen hillside. Pushing the crutch away in angry frustration, his father sat in the snow. The boy did not know whether he was thinking carefully of how they might get him out, or still laboring with the choice against despair. The light had wilted to something more like moonlight than afternoon. The sweep of snow had gone gray, depthless, flat, and the sky warned sullenly of night. The boy grew restless. Then it was decided. His father hung himself piggyback over the boy's shoulders, holding the rifle. The boy supported him with elbows crooked under his father's knees. The boy was tall for eleven years old, and heavy. The boy's father weighed 164 pounds.

The boy walked.

He moved as slowly as drifting snow: a step, then time, then another step. The burden at first seemed to him overwhelming. He did not think he would be able to carry his father far.

He took the first few paces expecting to fall. He did not fall, so he kept walking. His arms and shoulders were not exhausted as quickly as he thought they would be, so he kept walking. Shuffling ahead in the deep powder was like carrying one end of an oak bureau up stairs. But for a surprisingly long time the burden did not grow any worse. He found balance. He found rhythm. He was moving.

Dark blurred the woods, but the snow was luminous. He could see the trail well. He walked.

"How are you, David? How are you holding up?"

"All right."

"We'll stop for a while and let you rest. You can set me down here." The boy kept walking. He moved so ponderously, it seemed after each step that he had stopped. But he kept walking.

"You can set me down. Don't you want to rest?"

The boy did not answer. He wished that his father would not make him talk. At the start he had gulped for air. Now he was breathing low and regularly. He was watching his thighs slice through the snow. He did not want to be disturbed. After a moment he said, "No."

He walked. He came to the dead cub, shrouded beneath new snow, and did not see it, and fell over it. His face was smashed deep into the snow by his father's weight. He could not move. But he could breathe. He rested. When he felt his father's thigh roll across his right hand, he remembered the wound. He was lucky his arms had been pinned to his sides, or the hand might have taken the force of their fall. As he waited for his father to roll himself clear, the boy noticed the change in temperature. His sweat chilled him quickly. He began shivering.

His father had again fallen in silence. The boy knew that his father would not call out or even mention the pain in his leg. The boy realized that he did not want to mention his hand. The blood soaking the outside of his flannel bandage had grown sticky. He did not want to think of the alien tangle of flesh and tendons and bones wrapped inside. There was pain, but he kept the pain at a distance. It was not *his* hand anymore. He was not counting on ever having it back. If he was resolved about that, then the pain was not his either. It was merely pain of which he was aware. His good hand was numb.

"We'll rest now."

"I'm not tired," the boy said. "I'm just getting cold."

"We'll rest," said his father. "I'm tired."

Under his father's knee, the boy noticed, was a cavity in the snow, already melted away by fresh blood. The dark flannel around his father's thigh did not appear sticky. It gleamed.

His father instructed the boy how to open the cub with the deer knife. His father stood on one leg against a deadfall, holding the Winchester ready, and glanced around on all sides as he spoke. The boy used his left hand and both his knees. He punctured the cub low in the belly, to a soft squirting sound, and sliced upward easily. He did not gut the cub. He merely cut out a large square of belly meat. He handed it to his father, in exchange for the rifle.

His father peeled off the hide and left the fat. He sawed the meat in half. One piece he rolled up and put in his jacket pocket. The other he divided again. He gave the boy a square thick with glistening raw fat.

"Eat it. The fat too. Especially the fat. We'll cook the rest farther on. I don't want to build a fire here and taunt Momma."

The meat was chewy. The boy did not find it disgusting. He was hungry.

His father sat back on the ground and unlaced the boot from his good foot. Before the boy understood what he was doing, he had relaced the boot. He was holding a damp wool sock.

"Give me your left hand." The boy held out his good hand, and his father pulled the sock down over it. "It's getting a lot colder. And we need that hand."

"What about yours? We need your hands too. I'll give you my—"

"No, you won't. We need your feet more than anything. It's all right. I'll put mine inside your shirt."

He lifted his father, and they went on. The boy walked.

He moved steadily through cold darkness. Soon he was sweating again, down his ribs and inside his boots. Only his hands and ears felt as though crushed in a cold metal vise. But his father was shuddering. The boy stopped.

His father did not put down his legs. The boy stood on the trail and waited. Slowly he released his wrist holds. His father's thighs slumped. The boy was careful about the wounded leg. His father's grip over the boy's neck did not loosen. His fingers were cold against the boy's bare skin.

"Are we at the hut?"

"No. We're not even to the meadow."

"Why did you stop?" his father asked.

"It's so cold. You're shivering. Can we build a fire?"

"Yes," his father said hazily. "We'll rest. What time is it?"

"We don't know," the boy said. "We don't have a watch."

The boy gathered small deadwood. His father used the Winchester stock to scoop snow away from a boulder, and they placed the fire at the boulder's base. His father broke up pine twigs and fumbled dry toilet paper from his breast pocket and arranged the wood, but by then his fingers were shaking too badly to strike a match. The boy lit the fire. The boy stamped down the snow, as his father instructed, to make a small oven-like recess before the fire boulder. He cut fir boughs to floor the recess. He added more deadwood. Beyond the invisible clouds there seemed to be part of a moon.

"It stopped snowing," the boy said.

"Why?"

The boy did not speak. His father's voice had sounded unnatural. After a moment his father said:

"Yes, indeed. It stopped."

They roasted pieces of cub meat skewered on a green stick. Dripping fat made the fire spatter and flare. The meat was scorched on the outside and raw within. It tasted as good as any meat the boy had ever eaten. They burned their palates on hot fat. The second stick smoldered through before they had noticed, and that batch of meat fell in the fire. The boy's father cursed once and reached into the flame for it and dropped it and clawed it out, and then put his hand in the snow. He did not look at the blistered fingers. They ate. The boy saw that both his father's hands had gone clumsy and almost useless.

The boy went for more wood. He found a bleached deadfall not far off the trail, but with one arm he could only break up and carry small loads. They lay down in the recess together like spoons, the boy nearer the fire. They pulled fir boughs into place above them, resting across the snow. They pressed close together. The boy's father was shivering spastically now, and he clenched the boy in a fierce hug. The boy put his father's hands back inside his own shirt. The boy slept. He woke when the fire faded and added more wood and slept. He woke again and tended the fire and changed places with his father and slept. He slept less soundly with his father between him and the fire. He woke again when his father began to vomit.

The boy was terrified. His father wrenched with sudden vomiting that brought up cub meat and yellow liquid and blood and sprayed them across the snow by the grayish-red glow of the fire and emptied his stomach dry and then would not release him. He heaved on pathetically. The boy pleaded to be told what was wrong. His father could not or would not answer. The spasms seized him at the stomach and twisted the rest of his body taut in ugly jerks. Between the attacks he breathed with a wet rumbling sound deep in his chest, and did not speak. When the vomiting subsided, his breathing stretched itself out into long bubbling sighs, then shallow gasps, then more liquidy sighs. His breath caught and froth rose in his throat and into his mouth and he gagged on it and began vomiting again. The boy thought his father would choke. He knelt beside him and held him and cried. He could not see his father's face well and he did not want to look closely while the sounds that were coming from inside his father's body seemed so unhuman. The boy had never been more frightened. He wept for himself, and for his father. He knew from the noises and movements that his father must die. He did not think his father could ever be human again.

When his father was quiet, he went for more wood. He broke limbs from the deadfall with fanatic persistence and brought them back in bundles and built the fire up bigger. He nestled his father close to it and held him from behind. He did not sleep, though he was not awake. He waited. Finally he opened his eyes on the beginnings of dawn. His father sat up and began to spit.

"One more load of wood and you keep me warm from behind and then we'll go."

The boy obeyed. He was surprised that his father could speak. He thought it strange now that his father was so concerned for himself and so little concerned for the boy. His father had not even asked how he was.

The boy lifted his father, and walked.

Sometime while dawn was completing itself, the snow had resumed. It did not filter down soundlessly. It came on a slight wind at the boy's back, blowing down the canyon. He felt as though he were tumbling forward with the snow into a long vertical shaft. He tumbled slowly. His father's body protected the boy's back from being chilled by the wind. They were both soaked through their clothes. His father was soon shuddering again.

The boy walked. Muscles down the back of his neck were sore from yesterday. His arms ached, and his shoulders and thighs, but his neck hurt him most. He bent his head forward against the weight and the pain, and he watched his legs surge through the snow. At his stomach he felt the dull ache of hunger, not as an appetite but as an affliction. He thought of the jeep. He walked.

He recognized the edge of the meadow but through the snow-laden wind he could not see the cluster of aspens. The snow became deeper

where he left the wooded trail. The direction of the wind was now vari-
able, sometimes driving snow into his face, sometimes whipping across
him from the right. The grass and snow dragged at his thighs, and he
moved by stumbling forward and then catching himself back. Twice he
stepped into small overhung fingerlets of the stream, and fell violently,
shocking the air from his lungs and once nearly spraining an ankle.
Farther out into the meadow, he saw the aspens. They were a hundred
yards off to his right. He did not turn directly toward them. He was
afraid of crossing more hidden creeks on the intervening ground. He
was not certain now whether the main channel was between him and
the aspen grove or behind him to the left. He tried to project from the
canyon trail to the aspens and on to the forked pine on the far side of
the meadow, along what he remembered as almost a straight line. He
pointed himself toward the far edge, where the pine should have been.
He could not see a forked crown. He could not even see trees. He could
see only a vague darker corona above the curve of white. He walked.

He passed the aspens and left them behind. He stopped several
times with the wind rasping against him in the open meadow, and
rested. He did not set his father down. His father was trembling uncon-
trollably. He had not spoken for a long time. The boy wanted badly to
reach the far side of the meadow. His socks were soaked and his boots
and cuffs were glazed with ice. The wind was chafing his face and making him dizzy. His thighs felt as if they had been bruised with a club.
The boy wanted to give up and set his father down and whimper that
this had gotten to be very unfair; and he wanted to reach the far trees.
He did not doubt which he would do. He walked.

He saw trees. Raising his head painfully, he squinted against the
rushing flakes. He did not see the forked crown. He went on, and
stopped again, and craned his neck, and squinted. He scanned a wide
angle of pines, back and forth. He did not see it. He turned his body
and his burden to look back. The snow blew across the meadow and
seemed, whichever way he turned, to be streaking into his face. He
pinched his eyes tighter. He could still see the aspens. But he could not
judge where the canyon trail met the meadow. He did not know from
just where he had come. He looked again at the aspens, and then ahead
to the pines. He considered the problem carefully. He was irritated that
the forked ponderosa did not show itself yet, but not worried. He was
forced to estimate. He estimated, and went on in that direction.

When he saw a forked pine it was far off to the left of his course. He turned and marched toward it gratefully. As he came nearer, he bent his head up to look. He stopped. The boy was not sure that this was the right tree. Nothing about it looked different, except the thick cakes of snow weighting its limbs, and nothing about it looked especially familiar. He had seen thousands of pine trees in the last few days. This was one like the others. It definitely had a forked crown. He entered the woods at its base.

He had vaguely expected to join a trail. There was no trail. After two hundred yards he was still picking his way among trees and dead-falls and brush. He remembered the shepherd's creek that fell off the lip of the meadow and led down the first canyon. He turned and retraced his tracks to the forked pine.

He looked for the creek. He did not see it anywhere near the tree. He made himself quiet, and listened. He heard nothing but wind, and his father's tremulous breathing.

"Where is the creek?"

His father did not respond. The boy bounced gently up and down, hoping to jar him alert.

"Where is the creek? I can't find it."

"What?"

"We crossed the meadow and I found the tree but I can't find the creek. I need you to help."

"The compass is in my pocket," his father said.

He lowered his father into the snow. He found the compass in his father's breast pocket, and opened the flap, and held it level. The boy noticed with a flinch that his right thigh was smeared with fresh blood. For an instant he thought he had a new wound. Then he realized that the blood was his father's. The compass needle quieted.

"What do I do?"

His father did not respond. The boy asked again. His father said nothing. He sat in the snow and shivered.

The boy left his father and made random arcs within sight of the forked tree until he found a creek. They followed it onward along the flat and then where it gradually began sloping away. The boy did not see what else he could do. He knew that this was the wrong creek. He hoped that it would flow into the shepherd's creek, or at least bring them out on the same road where they had left the jeep. He was very tired. He did not want to stop. He did not care any more about being warm. He wanted only to reach the jeep, and to save his father's life.

He wondered whether his father would love him more generously for having done it. He wondered whether his father would ever forgive him for having done it.

If he failed, his father could never again make him feel shame, the boy thought naively. So he did not worry about failing. He did not worry about dying. His hand was not bleeding, and he felt strong. The creek swung off and down to the left. He followed it, knowing that he was lost. He did not want to reverse himself. He knew that turning back would make him feel confused and desperate and frightened. As long as he was following some pathway, walking, going down, he felt strong.

That afternoon he killed a grouse. He knocked it off a low branch with a heavy short stick that he threw like a boomerang. The grouse fell in the snow and floundered and the boy ran up and plunged on it. He felt it thrashing against his chest. He reached in and it nipped him and he caught it by the neck and squeezed and wrenched mercilessly until long after it stopped writhing. He cleaned it as he had seen his father clean grouse and built a small fire with matches from his father's breast pocket and seared the grouse on a stick. He fed his father. His father could not chew. The boy chewed mouthfuls of grouse, and took the chewed gobbets in his hand, and put them into his father's mouth. His father could swallow. His father could no longer speak.

The boy walked. He thought of his mother in Evergreen Park, and at once he felt queasy and weak. He thought of his mother's face and her voice as she was told that her son was lost in the woods in Montana with a damaged hand that would never be right, and with his father, who had been shot and was unconscious and dying. He pictured his mother receiving the news that her son might die himself, unless he could carry his father out of the woods and find his way to the jeep. He saw her face change. He heard her voice. The boy had to stop. He was crying. He could not control the shape of his mouth. He was not crying with true sorrow, as he had in the night when he held his father and thought his father would die; he was crying in sentimental self-pity. He sensed the difference. Still he cried.

He must not think of his mother, the boy realized. Thinking of her could only weaken him. If she knew where he was, what he had to do, she could only make it impossible for him to do it. He was lucky that she knew nothing, the boy thought.

No one knew what the boy was doing, or what he had yet to do. Even the boy's father no longer knew. The boy was lucky. No one was watching, no one knew, and he was free to be capable.

The boy imagined himself alone at his father's grave. The grave was open. His father's casket had already been lowered. The boy stood at the foot in his black Christmas suit, and his hands were crossed at his groin, and he was not crying. Men with shovels stood back from the grave, waiting for the boy's order for them to begin filling it. The boy felt a horrible swelling sense of joy. The men watched him, and he stared down into the hole. He knew it was a lie. If his father died, the boy's mother would rush out to Livingston and have him buried and stand at the grave in a black dress and veil squeezing the boy to her side like he was a child. There was nothing the boy could do about that. All the more reason he must keep walking.

Then she would tow the boy back with her to Evergreen Park. And he would be standing on 96th Street in the morning dark before his father's cold body had even begun to grow alien and decayed in the buried box. She would drag him back, and there would be nothing the boy could do. And he realized that if he returned with his mother after the burial, he would never again see the cabin outside Livingston. He would have no more summers and no more Novembers anywhere but in Evergreen Park.

The cabin now seemed to be at the center of the boy's life. It seemed to stand halfway between this snowbound creek valley and the train station in Chicago. It would be his cabin soon.

The boy knew nothing about his father's will, and he had never been told that legal ownership of the cabin was destined for him. Legal ownership did not matter. The cabin might be owned by his mother, or sold to pay his father's debts, or taken away by the state, but it would still be the boy's cabin. It could only forever belong to him. His father had been telling him, *Here, this is yours. Prepare to receive it.* The boy had sensed that much. But he had been threatened, and unwilling. The boy realized now that he might be resting warm in the cabin in a matter of hours, or he might never see it again. He could appreciate the justice of that. He walked.

He thought of his father as though his father were far away from

him. He saw himself in the black suit at the grave, and he heard his
father speak to him from aside: *That's good. Now raise your eyes and tell
them in a man's voice to begin shoveling. Then turn away and walk slowly
back down the hill. Be sure you don't cry. That's good.* The boy stopped.
He felt his glands quiver, full of new tears. He knew that it was a lie.
His father would never be there to congratulate him. His father would
never know how well the boy had done.

He took deep breaths. He settled himself. Yes, his father would
know somehow, the boy believed. His father had known all along. His
father knew.

He built the recess just as they had the night before, except this
time he found flat space between a stone bank and a large fallen cottonwood trunk. He scooped out the snow, he laid boughs, and he made
a fire against each reflector. At first the bed was quite warm. Then the
melt from the fires began to run down and collect in the middle, forming a puddle of wet boughs under them. The boy got up and carved
runnels across the packed snow to drain the fires. He went back to sleep
and slept warm, holding his father. He rose again each half hour to feed
the fires.

The snow stopped in the night, and did not resume. The woods
seemed to grow quieter, settling, sighing beneath the new weight. What
was going to come had come.

The boy grew tired of breaking deadwood and began walking again
before dawn and walked for five more hours. He did not try to kill the
grouse that he saw because he did not want to spend time cleaning and
cooking it. He was hurrying now. He drank from the creek. At one
point he found small black insects like winged ants crawling in great
numbers across the snow near the creek. He stopped to pinch up and
eat thirty or forty of them. They were tasteless. He did not bother to
feed any to his father. He felt he had come a long way down the mountain. He thought he was reaching the level now where there might be
roads. He followed the creek, which had received other branches and
grown to a stream. The ground was flattening again and the drainage
was widening, opening to daylight. As he carried his father, his head
ached. He had stopped noticing most of his other pains. About noon
of that day he came to the fence.

It startled him. He glanced around, his pulse drumming suddenly,
preparing himself at once to see the long empty sweep of snow and

broken fence posts and thinking of Basque shepherds fifty years gone. He saw the cabin and the smoke. He relaxed, trembling helplessly into laughter. He relaxed, and was unable to move. Then he cried, still laughing. He cried shamelessly with relief and dull joy and wonder, for as long as he wanted. He held his father, and cried. But he set his father down and washed his own face with snow before he went to the door.

He crossed the lot walking slowly, carrying his father. He did not now feel tired.

The young woman's face was drawn down in shock and revealed at first nothing of friendliness.

"We had a jeep parked somewhere, but I can't find it," the boy said. "This is my father."

They would not talk to him. They stripped him and put him before the fire wrapped in blankets and started tea and made him wait. He wanted to talk. He wished they would ask him a lot of questions. But they went about quickly and quietly, making things warm. His father was in the bedroom.

The man with the face full of dark beard had used the radio to call for a doctor. He went back into the bedroom with more blankets, and stayed. His wife went from room to room with hot tea. She rubbed the boy's naked shoulders through the blanket, and held a cup to his mouth, but she would not talk to him. He did not know what to say to her, and he could not move his lips very well. But he wished she would ask him some questions. He was restless, thawing in silence before the hearth.

He thought about going back to their own cabin soon. In his mind he gave the bearded man directions to take him and his father home. It wasn't far. It would not require much of the man's time. They would thank him, and give him an elk steak. Later he and his father would come back for the jeep. He could keep his father warm at the cabin as well as they were doing here, the boy knew.

While the woman was in the bedroom, the boy overheard the bearded man raise his voice:

"He what?"

"He carried him out," the woman whispered.

"What do you mean, carried him?"

"Carried him. On his back. I saw."

"Carried him from where?"

"Where it happened. Somewhere on Sheep Creek, maybe."

"Eight miles?"

"I know."

"*Eight miles?* How could he do that?"

"I don't know. I suppose he couldn't. But he did."

The doctor arrived in half an hour, as the boy was just starting to shiver. The doctor went into the bedroom and stayed five minutes. The woman poured the boy more tea and knelt beside him and hugged him around the shoulders.

When the doctor came out, he examined the boy without speaking. The boy wished the doctor would ask him some questions, but he was afraid he might be shivering too hard to answer in a man's voice. While the doctor touched him and probed him and took his temperature, the boy looked the doctor directly in the eye, as though to show him he was really all right.

The doctor said:

"David, your father is dead. He has been dead for a long time. Probably since yesterday."

"I know that," the boy said.

"Selway"

PAM HOUSTON

Pam Houston (b. 1962) has been a bartender, a tour bus driver, a horse trainer, a ski instructor, a hunting guide, a river guide, and a professor of English at the University of California, Davis. Dubbed by one reviewer "the Rodeo Queen of American letters," Houston is the author of two novels, *Contents May Have Shifted* (2012) and *Sight Hound* (2005); a book of essays entitled *A Little More About Me* (1999); and two collections of short stories, *Waltzing the Cat* (1998) and *Cowboys Are My Weakness* (1992), winner of the 1993 Western States Book Award. Houston's strong female protagonists reshape the definition of wilderness through their own independent perspectives on the rugged landscapes and perilous terrains of the American West. Houston's short story "Selway" first appeared in *Mademoiselle* magazine under the title "The Call of the Wild Man"—a play on Jack London's most famous novel, *The Call of the Wild*—before it appeared, in its current form, in *Cowboys Are My Weakness*. Selway is a drainage river in the central Idaho Rocky Mountains and one of the first rivers earmarked for federal protection in the 1968 National Wild and Scenic Rivers System. Its unpolluted waters, remote location, forested canyons, and intense rapids make the Selway River one of the most magnificent if dangerous rivers in America. In 1993, using the money she made from selling her first story collection, Houston purchased a 120-acre ranch near the Rio Grande River headwaters in South Central Colorado, where she still lives. Her memoir, *Deep Creek: Finding Hope in the High Country* (2019)—winner of the Colorado Book Award and the High Plains Book Award—recounts a quarter century of her life on the ranch, raising Icelandic sheep and Irish wolfhounds while writing books at her kitchen table, all with a spectacular view of the Continental Divide and its surrounding twelve-thousand-foot peaks.

"Selway"

PAM HOUSTON

It was June the seventh and we'd driven eighteen hours of pavement and sixty miles of dirt to find out the river was at high water, the highest of the year, of several years, and rising. The ranger, Ramona, wrote on our permit, "We do not recommend boating at this level," and then she looked at Jack.

"We're just gonna go down and take a look at it," he said, "see if the river gives us a sign." He tried to slide the permit away from Ramona, but her short dark fingers held it against the counter. I looked from one to the other. I knew Jack didn't believe in signs.

"Once you get to Moose Creek you're committed," she said. "There's no time to change your mind after that. You've got Double Drop and Little Niagara and Ladle, and they just keep coming like that, one after another with no slow water in between."

She was talking about rapids. This was my first northern trip, and after a lazy spring making slow love between rapids on the wide desert rivers, I couldn't imagine what all the fuss was about.

"If you make it through the Moose Creek series there's only a few more real bad ones; Wolf Creek is the worst. After that the only thing to worry about is the takeout point. The beach will be under water, and if you miss it, you're over Selway Falls."

"Do you have a river guide?" Jack said, and when she bent under the counter to get one he tried again to slide the permit away. She pushed a small, multifolded map in his direction.

"Don't rely on it," she said. "The rapids aren't even marked in the right place."

"Thanks for your help," Jack said. He gave the permit a sharp tug and put it in his pocket.

"There was an accident today," Ramona said. "In Ladle."

"Anybody hurt?" Jack asked.

"It's not official."

"Killed?"

"The water's rising," Ramona said, and turned back to her desk.

. . .

At the put-in, the water crashed right over the top of the depth gauge. The grass grew tall and straight through the slats of the boat ramp.

"Looks like we're the first ones this year," Jack said.

The Selway has the shortest season of any river in North America. They don't plow the snow till the first week in June, and by the last week in July there's not enough water to carry a boat. They only allow one party a day on the river that they select from a nationwide lottery with thousands of applicants each year. You can try your whole life and never get a permit.

"Somebody's been here," I said. "The people who flipped today."

Jack didn't answer. He was looking at the gauge. "It's up even from this morning," he said. "They said this morning it was six feet."

Jack and I have known each other almost a year. I'm the fourth in a series of long-term girlfriends he's never gotten around to proposing to. He likes me because I'm young enough not to sweat being single and I don't put pressure on him the way the others did. They wanted him to quit running rivers, to get a job that wasn't seasonal, to raise a family like any man his age. They wouldn't go on trips with him, not even once to see what it was like, and I couldn't imagine that they knew him in any way that was complete if they hadn't known him on the river, if they hadn't seen him row.

I watched him put his hand in the water. "Feel that, baby," he said. "That water was snow about fifteen minutes ago."

I stuck my foot in the water and it went numb in about ten seconds. I've been to four years of college and I should know better, but I love it when he calls me baby.

Jack has taken a different high-water trip each year for the last fifteen, on progressively more difficult rivers. When a river is at high water it's not just deeper and faster and colder than usual. It's got a different look and feel from the rest of the year. It's dark and impatient and turbulent, like a volcano or a teenage boy. It strains against its banks and it churns around and under itself. Looking at its fullness made me want to grab Jack and throw him down on the boat ramp and make love right next to where the river roared by, but I could tell by his face he was trying to make a decision, so I sat and stared at the river and wondered if it was this wild at the put-in what it would look like in the rapids.

"If anything happened to you . . ." he said, and threw a stick out to the middle of the channel. "It must be moving nine miles an hour." He walked up and down the boat ramp. "What do you think?" he said.

"I think this is a chance of a lifetime," I said. "I think you're the best boatman you know." I wanted to feel the turbulence underneath me. I wanted to run a rapid that could flip a boat. I hadn't taken anything like a risk in months. I wanted to think about dying.

It was already early evening, and once we made the decision to launch, there were two hours of rigging before we could get on the water. On the southern rivers we'd boat sometimes for an hour after dark just to watch what the moon did to the water. On the Selway there was a rapid that could flip your boat around every corner. It wasn't getting pitch dark till ten-thirty that far north, where the June dusk went on forever, but it wasn't really light either and we wouldn't be able to see very far ahead. We told ourselves we'd go a tenth of a mile and make camp, but you can't camp on a sheer granite wall, and the river has to give you a place to get stopped and get tied.

I worked fast and silent, wondering if we were doing the right thing and knowing if we died it would really be my fault, because as much as I knew Jack wanted to go, he wouldn't have pushed me if I'd said I was scared. Jack was untamable, but he had some sense and a lot of respect for the river. He relied on me to speak with the voice of reason, to be life-protecting because I'm a woman and that's how he thinks women are, but I've never been protective enough of anything, least of all myself.

At nine-fifteen we untied the rope and let the river take us.

"The first place that looks campable," Jack said.

Nine miles an hour is fast in a rubber raft on a river you've never boated when there's not quite enough light to see what's in front of you. We were taking on water over the bow almost immediately, even though the map didn't show any rapids for the first two miles. It was hard for me to take my eyes off Jack, the way his muscles strained with every stroke, first his upper arms, then his upper thighs. He was silent, thinking it'd been a mistake to come, but I was laughing and bailing water and combing the banks for a flat spot and jumping back and forth over my seat to kiss him, and watching while his muscles flexed.

My mother says I thrive on chaos, and I guess that's true, because as hard a year as I've had with Jack I stayed with it, and I won't even admit by how much the bad days outnumbered the good. We fought like bears when we weren't on the river, because he was so used to fighting and I was so used to getting my own way. I said I wanted selfless devotion and he took a stand on everything from infidelity to salad dressing, and it was always opposite to mine. The one thing we had going for us, though, was the sex, and if we could stop screaming at each other long enough to make love it would be a day or sometimes two before something would happen and we'd go at it again. I've always been afraid to stop and think too hard about what great sex in bad times might mean, but it must have something to do with timing, that moment making love when you're at once absolutely powerful and absolutely helpless, a balance we could never find when we were out of bed.

It was the old Southern woman next door, the hunter's widow, who convinced me I should stay with him each time I'd get mad enough to leave. She said if I didn't have to fight for him I'd never know if he was mine. She said the wild ones were the only ones worth having and that I had to let him do whatever it took to keep him wild. She said I wouldn't love him if he ever gave in, and the harder I looked at my life, the more I saw a series of men—wild in their own way—who thought because I said I wanted security and commitment, I did. Sometimes it seems this simple: I tamed them and made them dull as fence posts and left each one for someone wilder than the last. Jack is the wildest so far, and the hardest, and even though I've been proposed to sixteen times, five times by men I've never made love to, I want him all to myself and at home more than I've ever wanted anything.

"Are you bailing? I'm standing in water back here," he said, so I bailed faster but the waves kept on crashing over the bow.

"I can't move this boat," he said, which I knew wasn't entirely true, but it was holding several hundred gallons of water times eight pounds a gallon, and that's more weight than I'd care to push around.

"There," he said. "Camp. Let's try to get to shore."

He pointed to a narrow beach a hundred yards downstream. The sand looked black in the twilight; it was long and flat enough for a tent.

"Get the rope ready," he said. "You're gonna have to jump for it and find something to wrap around fast."

He yelled *jump* but it was too early and I landed chest-deep in the water and the cold took my breath but I scrambled across the rocks to the beach and wrapped around a fallen trunk just as the rope went tight. The boat dragged the trunk and me ten yards down the beach before Jack could get out and pull the nose of it up on shore.

"This may have been real fuckin' stupid," he said.

I wanted to tell him how the water made me feel, how horny and crazy and happy I felt riding on top of water that couldn't hold itself in, but he was scared, for the first time since I'd known him, so I kept my mouth shut and went to set up the tent.

In the morning the tent was covered all around with a thin layer of ice and we made love like crazy people, the way you do when you think it might be the last time ever, till the sun changed the ice back to dew and got the tent so hot we were sweating. Then Jack got up and made coffee, and we heard the boaters coming just in time to get our clothes on.

They threw us their rope and we caught it. There were three of them, three big men in a boat considerably bigger than ours. Jack poured them coffee. We all sat down on the fallen log.

"You launched, late last night?" the tallest, darkest one said. He had curly black hair and a wide-open face.

Jack nodded. "Too late," he said. "Twilight boating."

"It's up another half a foot this morning," the man said. "It's supposed to peak today at seven."

The official forest service document declares the Selway unsafe for boating above six feet. Seven feet is off their charts.

"Have you boated this creek at seven?" Jack asked. The man frowned and took a long drink from his cup.

"My name's Harvey," he said, and stuck out his hand. "This is Charlie and Charlie. We're on a training trip." He laughed. "Yahoo."

Charlie and Charlie nodded.

"You know the river," Jack said.

"I've boated the Selway seventy times," he said. "Never at seven feet. It was all the late snow and last week's heat wave. It's a bad combination, but it's boatable. This river's always boatable if you know exactly where to be."

Charlie and Charlie smiled.

"There'll be a lot of holes that there's no way to miss. You got to punch through them."

Jack nodded. I knew Harvey was talking about boat flippers. Big waves that form in holes the river makes behind rocks and ledges and that will suck boats in and hold them there, fill them with water till they flip, hold bodies, too, indefinitely, until they go under and catch the current, or until the hole decides to spit them out. If you hit a hole with a back wave bigger than your boat perfectly straight, there's a half a chance you'll shoot through. A few degrees off in either direction, and the hole will get you every time.

"We'll be all right in this tank," Harvey said, nodding to his boat, "but I'm not sure I'd run it in a boat that small. I'm not sure I'd run it in a boat I had to bail."

Unlike ours, Harvey's boat was a self-bailer, inflatable tubes around an open metal frame that let the water run right through. They're built for high water, and extremely hard to flip.

"Just the two of you?" Harvey said.

Jack nodded.

"A honeymoon trip. Nice."

"We're not married," Jack said.

"Yeah," Harvey said. He picked up a handful of sand. "The black sand of the Selway," he said. "I carried a bottle of this sand downriver the year I got married. I wanted to throw it at my wife's feet during the ceremony. The minister thought it was pretty strange, but he got over it."

One of the Charlies looked confused.

"Black sand," Harvey said. "You know, black sand, love, marriage, Selway, rivers, life; the whole thing."

I smiled at Jack, but he wouldn't meet my eyes.

"You'll be all right till Moose Creek," Harvey said. "That's when it gets wild. We're gonna camp there tonight, run the bad stretch first thing in the morning in case we wrap or flip or tear something. I hope you won't think I'm insulting you if I ask you to run with us. It'll be safer for us both. The people who flipped yesterday were all experienced. They all knew the Selway."

"They lost one?" Jack said.

"Nobody will say for sure," Harvey said. "But I'd bet on it."

"We'll think about it," Jack said. "It's nice of you to offer."

"I know what you're thinking," Harvey said. "But I've got a kid now. It makes a difference." He pulled a picture out of his wallet. A baby girl, eight or nine months old, crawled across a linoleum floor.

"She's beautiful," I said.

"She knocks me out," Harvey said. "She follows everything with her finger; bugs, flowers, the TV, you know what I mean?"

Jack and I nodded.

"It's your decision," he said. "Maybe we'll see you at Moose Creek."

He stood up, and Charlie and Charlie rose behind him. One coiled the rope while the other pushed off.

Jack poured his third cup of coffee. "Think he's full of shit?" he said.

"I think he knows more than you or I ever will," I said.

"About this river, at least," he said.

"At least," I said.

In midday sunshine, the river looked more fun than terrifying. We launched just before noon, and though there was no time for sightseeing I bailed fast enough to let Jack move the boat through the rapids, which came quicker and bigger around every bend. The map showed ten rapids between the put-in and Moose Creek, and it was anybody's guess which of the fifty or sixty rapids we boated that day were the ones the forest service had in mind. Some had bigger waves than others, some narrower passages, but the river was continuous moving white water, and we finally put the map away. On the southern rivers we'd mix rum and fruit juice and eat smoked oysters and pepper cheese. Here, twenty fast miles went by without time to take a picture, to get a drink of water. The Moose Creek pack bridge came into sight, and we pulled in and tied up next to Harvey's boat.

"White fuckin' water," Harvey said. "Did you have a good run?"

"No trouble," Jack said.

"Good," Harvey said. "Here's where she starts to kick ass." He motioned with his head downriver. "We'll get up at dawn and scout everything."

"It's early yet," Jack said. "I think we're going on." I looked at Jack's face, and then Harvey's.

"You do what you want," Harvey said. "But you ought to take a look at the next five miles. The runs are obvious once you see them from the bank, but they change at every level."

"We haven't scouted all day," Jack said. I knew he wanted us to run alone, that he thought following Harvey would be cheating somehow, but I believed a man who'd throw sand at his new wife's feet, and I liked a little danger but I didn't want to die.

"There's only one way through Ladle," Harvey said. "Ladle's where they lost the girl."

"The girl?" Jack said.

"The rest of her party was here when we got here. Their boats were below Ladle. They just took off, all but her husband. He wouldn't leave, and you can't blame him. He was rowing when she got tossed. He let the boat get sideways. He's been wandering around here for two days, I guess, but he wouldn't get back in the boat."

"Jesus Christ," Jack said. He sat down on the bank facing the water.

I looked back into the woods for the woman's husband and tried to imagine a posture for him, tried to imagine an expression for his face. I thought about my Uncle Tim, who spent ten years and a lifetime of savings building his dream home. On the day it was completed he backed his pickup over his four-year-old daughter while she played in the driveway. He sold the house in three days and went completely gray in a week.

"A helicopter landed about an hour ago," Harvey said. "Downstream, where the body must be. It hasn't taken off."

"The water's still rising," Jack said, and we all looked to where we'd pulled the boats up on shore and saw that they were floating. And then we heard the beating of the propeller and saw the helicopter rising out over the river. We saw the hundred feet of cable hanging underneath it and then we saw the woman, arched like a dancer over the thick black belt they must use for transplanting wild animals, her long hair dangling, her arms slung back. The pilot flew up the river till he'd gained enough altitude, turned back, and headed over the mountain wall behind our camp.

"They said she smashed her pelvis against a rock and bled to death internally," Harvey said. "They got her out in less than three minutes, and it was too late."

Jack put his arm around my knees. "We'll scout at dawn," he said. "We'll all run this together."

Harvey was up rattling coffeepots before we had time to make love and I said it would bring us bad luck if we didn't but Jack said it would be worse than bad luck if we didn't scout the rapids. The scouting trail was well worn. Harvey went first, then Jack, then me and the two Charlies. Double Drop was first, two sets of falls made by water pouring over clusters of house-sized boulders that extended all the way across the river.

"You can sneak the first drop on the extreme right," Harvey said. "There's no sneak for the second. Just keep her straight and punch her through. Don't let her get you sideways."

Little Niagara was a big drop, six feet or more, but the run was pretty smooth and the back wave low enough to break through.

"Piece of cake," Harvey said.

The sun was almost over the canyon wall, and we could hear Ladle long before we rounded the bend. I wasn't prepared for what I saw. One hundred yards of white water stretched from shore to shore and thundered over rocks and logjams and ledges. There were ten holes the size of the one in Double Drop, and there was no space for a boat in between. The currents were so chaotic for such a long stretch there was no way to read which way they'd push a boat. We found some small logs and climbed a rock ledge that hung over the rapid.

"See if you can read this current," Harvey said, and tossed the smallest log into the top of the rapid. The log hit the first hole and went under. It didn't come back up. One of the Charlies giggled.

"Again," Harvey said. This time the log came out of the first hole and survived two more before getting swallowed by the biggest hole, about midway through the rapid.

"I'd avoid that one for sure," Harvey said. "Try to get left of that hole." He threw the rest of the logs in. None of them made it through. "This is big-time," he said.

We all sat on the rock for what must have been an hour. "Seen enough?" Harvey said. "We've still got No Slouch and Miranda Jane."

The men climbed down off the rock, but I wasn't quite ready to leave. I went to the edge of the ledge, lay flat on my stomach, and hung over until my head was so full of the roar of the river I got dizzy and pulled myself back up. The old Southern woman said men can't really live unless they face death now and then, and I know by men she didn't mean mankind. And I wondered which rock shattered the dead woman's pelvis, and I wondered what she and I were doing out here on this river when Harvey's wife was home with that beautiful baby and happy. And I knew it was crazy to take a boat through that rapid and I knew I'd do it anyway but I didn't any longer know why. Jack said I had to do it for myself to make it worth anything, and at first I thought I was there because I loved danger, but sitting on the rock I knew I was there because I loved Jack. And maybe I went because his old girlfriends wouldn't, and maybe I went because I wanted him for mine, and maybe it didn't matter at all why I went because doing it for me and doing it for him amounted, finally, to exactly the same thing. And even though I knew in my head there's nothing a man can do that a woman can't, I also knew in my heart we can't help doing it for different reasons. And just like a man will never understand exactly how a woman feels when she has a baby, or an orgasm, or the reasons why she'll fight so hard to be loved, a woman can't know in what way a man satisfies himself, what question he answers for himself, when he looks right at death.

My head was so full of the sound and the light of the river that when I climbed down off the bank side of the ledge I didn't see the elk carcass until I stepped on one of its curled hooves. It was a young elk, probably not dead a year, and still mostly covered with matted brown fur. The skull was picked clean by scavengers, polished white by the sun and grinning. The sound that came out of my mouth scared me as much as the elk had, and I felt silly a few minutes later when Harvey came barreling around the corner followed by Jack.

Harvey saw the elk and smiled.

"It startled me is all," I said.

"Jesus," Jack said. "Stay with us, all right?"

"I never scream," I said. "Hardly ever."

No Slouch and Miranda Jane were impressive rapids, but they were nothing like Ladle and both runnable to the left. On the way back to camp we found wild strawberries, and Jack and I hung back and fed them to each other and I knew he wasn't mad about me screaming. The boats were loaded by ten-thirty and the sun was warm. We wore life jackets and helmets and wet suits. Everybody had diver's boots but me, so I wore my loafers.

"You have three minutes in water this cold," Harvey said. "Even with a wet suit. Three minutes before hypothermia starts, and then you can't swim, and then you just give in to the river."

Harvey gave us the thumbs-up sign as the Charlies pushed off. I pushed off right behind them. Except for the bail bucket and the spare oar, everything on the boat was tied down twice and inaccessible. My job was to take water out of the boat as fast as I could eight pounds at a time, and to help Jack remember which rapid was coming next and where we had decided to run it.

I saw the first of the holes in Double Drop and yelled, "Right," and we made the sneak with a dry boat. We got turned around somehow after that, though, and had to hit the big wave backwards. Jack yelled, "Hang on, baby," and we hit it straight on and it filled the boat, but then we were through it and in sight of Little Niagara before I could even start bailing.

"We're going twelve miles an hour at least," Jack yelled. "Which one is this?"

"Niagara," I yelled. "Right center." The noise of the river swallowed my words and I only threw out two bucketfuls before we were over the lip of Niagara and I had to hold on. I could hear Ladle around the bend and I was throwing water so fast I lost my balance and that's when I heard Jack say, "Bail faster!" and that's when I threw the bail bucket into the river and watched, unbelieving, as it went under, and I saw Jack see it too but we were at Ladle and I had to sit down and hold on. I watched Harvey's big boat getting bounced around like a cork, and I think I closed my eyes when the first wave crashed over my face because the next thing I knew we were out of the heaviest water and Harvey was standing and smiling at us with his fist in the air.

I could see No Slouch around the bend and I don't remember it or Miranda Jane because I was kneeling in the front of the boat scooping armfuls of water the whole time.

We all pulled up on the first beach we found and drank a beer and hugged each other uncertainly, like tenants in an apartment building where the fires have been put out.

"You're on your own," Harvey said. "We're camping here. Take a look at Wolf Creek, and be sure and get to shore before Selway Falls." He picked up a handful of black sand and let it run through his fingers. He turned to me. "He's a good boatman, and you're very brave."

I smiled.

"Take care of each other," he said. "Stay topside."

We set off alone and it clouded up and started to rain and I couldn't make the topography match the river map.

"I can't tell where we are," I told Jack. "But Wolf Creek can't be far."

"We'll see it coming," he said, "or hear it."

But it wasn't five minutes after he spoke that we rounded a bend and were in it, waves crashing on all sides and Jack trying to find a way between the rocks and the holes. I was looking too, and I think I saw the run, fifty feet to our right, right before I heard Jack say, "Hang on, baby," and we hit the hole sideways and everything went white and cold. I was in the waves and underwater and I couldn't see Jack or the boat, I couldn't move my arms or legs apart from how the river tossed them. Jack had said swim down to the current, but I couldn't tell which way was down and I couldn't have moved there in that washing machine, my lungs full and taking on water. Then the wave spit me up, once, under the boat, and then again, clear of it, and I got a breath and pulled down away from the air and felt the current grab me, and I waited to get smashed against a rock, but the rock didn't come and I was at the surface riding the crests of some eight-foot rollers and seeing Jack's helmet bobbing in the water in front of me.

"Swim, baby!" he yelled, and it was like it hadn't occurred to me, like I was frozen there in the water. And I tried to swim but I couldn't get a breath and my limbs wouldn't move and I thought about the three minutes and hypothermia and I must have been swimming then because the shore started to get closer. I grabbed the corner of a big ledge and wouldn't let go, not even when Jack yelled at me to get out of the water, and even when he showed me an easy place to get out if I just floated a few yards downstream it took all I had and more to let go of the rock and get back in the river.

I got out on a tiny triangular rock ledge, surrounded on all sides by walls of granite. Jack stood sixty feet above me on another ledge.

"Sit tight," he said. "I'm going to go see if I can get the boat."

Then he was gone and I sat in that small space and started to shake.

It was raining harder, sleeting even, and I started to think about freezing to death in that space that wasn't even big enough for me to move around in and get warm. I started to think about the river rising and filling that space and what would happen when Jack got back and made me float downstream to an easier place, or what would happen if he didn't come back, if he died trying to get the boat back, if he chased it fifteen miles to Selway Falls. When I saw the boat float by, right side up and empty, I decided to climb out of the space.

I'd lost one loafer in the river, so I wedged myself between the granite walls and used my fingers, mostly, to climb. I've always been a little afraid of heights, so I didn't look down. I thought it would be stupid to live through the boating accident and smash my skull free-climbing on granite, but as I inched up the wall I got warmer and kept going. When I got to the top there were trees growing across, and another vertical bank I hadn't seen from below. I bashed through the branches with my helmet and grabbed them one at a time till they broke or pulled out and then I grabbed the next one higher. I dug into the thin layer of soil that covered the rock with my knees and my elbows, and I'd slip down an inch for every two I gained. When I came close to panic I thought of Rambo, as if he were a real person, as if what I was doing was possible, and proven before, by him.

And then I was on the ledge and I could see the river, and I could see Jack on the other side, and I must have been in shock, a little, because I couldn't at that time imagine how he could have gotten to the other side of the river, I couldn't imagine what would make him go back in the water, but he had, and there he was on the other side.

"I lost the boat," he yelled. "Walk downstream till you see it."

I was happy for instructions and I set off down the scouting trail, shoe on one foot, happy for the pain in the other, happy to be walking, happy because the sun was trying to come out again and I was there to see it. It was a few miles before I even realized that the boat would be going over the falls, that Jack would have had to swim one more time across the river to get to the trail, that I should go back and see if he'd made it, but I kept walking downstream and looking for the boat. After five miles my bare foot started to bleed, so I put my left loafer on my right foot and walked on. After eight miles I saw Jack running up the trail behind me, and he caught up and kissed me and ran on by.

I walked and I walked, and I thought about being twenty-one and hiking in mountains not too far from these with a boy who almost drowned and then proposed to me. His boots had filled with the water of a river even farther to the north, and I was wearing sneakers and have a good kick, so I made it across just fine. I thought about how he sat on the far bank after he'd pulled himself out and shivered and stared at the water. And how I ran up and down the shore looking for the shallowest crossing, and then, thinking I'd found it, met him halfway. I remembered when our hands touched across the water and how I'd pulled him to safety and built him a fire and dried his clothes. Later that night he asked me to marry him and it made me happy and I said yes even though I knew it would never happen because I was too young and free and full of my freedom. I switched my loafer to the other foot and wondered if this danger would make Jack propose to me. Maybe he was the kind of man who needed to see death first, maybe we would build a fire to dry ourselves and then he would ask me and I would say yes because by the time you get to be thirty, freedom has circled back on itself to mean something totally different from what it did at twenty-one.

I knew I had to be close to the falls and I felt bad about what the wrecked boat would look like, but all of a sudden it was there in front of me, stuck on a gravel bar in the middle of the river with a rapid on either side, and I saw Jack coming back up the trail toward me.

"I've got it all figured out," he said. "I need to walk upstream about a mile and jump in there. That'll give me enough time to swim most of the way across to the other side of the river, and if I've read the current right, it'll take me right into that gravel bar."

"And if you read the current wrong?" I said.

He grinned. "Then it's over Selway Falls. I almost lost it already the second time I crossed the river. It was just like Harvey said. I almost gave up. I've been running twelve miles and I know my legs'll cramp. It's a long shot but I've got to take it."

"Are you sure you want to do this?" I said. "Maybe you shouldn't do this."

"I thought the boat was gone," he said, "and I didn't care because you were safe and I was safe and we were on the same side of the river. But there it is asking me to come for it, and the water's gonna rise tonight and take it over the falls. You stay right here where you can see what happens to me. If I make it I'll pick you up on that beach just below. We've got a half a mile to the takeout and the falls." He kissed me again and ran back upriver.

The raft was in full sunshine, everything tied down, oars in place. Even the map I couldn't read was there, where I stuck it, under a strap.

I could see Jack making his way through the trees toward the edge of the river, and I realized then that more than any other reason for being on that trip, I was there because I thought I could take care of him, and maybe there's something women want to protect after all. And maybe Jack's old girlfriends were trying to protect him by making him stay home, and maybe I thought I could if I was there, but as he dropped out of sight and into the water I knew there'd always be places he'd go that I couldn't, and that I'd have to let him go, just like the widow said. Then I saw his tiny head in the water and I held my breath and watched his position, which was perfect, as he approached the raft: But he got off center right at the end, and a wave knocked him past the raft and farther down the gravel bar.

He got to his feet and went down again. He grabbed for a boulder on the bottom and got washed even farther away. He was using all his energy to stay in one place and he was fifty yards downriver from the raft. I started to pray then, to whomever I pray to when I get in real trouble, and it may have been a coincidence but he started moving forward. It took him fifteen minutes and strength I'll never know to get to the boat, but he was in it, and rowing, and heading for the beach.

Later, when we were safe and on the two-lane heading home, Jack told me we were never in any real danger, and I let him get away with it because I knew that's what he had to tell himself to get past almost losing me.

"The river gave us both a lesson in respect," he said, and it occurred to me then that he thought he had a chance to tame that wild river, but I knew I was at its mercy from the very beginning, and I thought all along that that was the point.

Jack started telling stories to keep himself awake: the day his kayak held him under for almost four minutes, the time he crashed his hang glider twice in one day. He said he thought fifteen years of high water was probably enough, and that he'd take desert rivers from now on.

The road stretched out in front of us, dry and even and smooth. We found a long dirt road, turned, and pulled down to where it ended at a chimney that stood tall amid the rubble of an old stone house. We didn't build a fire and Jack didn't propose; we rolled out our sleeping bags and lay down next to the truck. I could see the light behind the mountains in the place where the moon would soon rise, and I thought about all the years I'd spent saying love and freedom were mutually exclusive and living my life as though they were exactly the same thing.

The wind carried the smell of the mountains, high and sweet. It was so still I could imagine a peace without boredom.

"Pond Time"

GRETEL EHRLICH

Gretel Ehrlich (b. 1946) was born in Santa Barbara, California, on a horse ranch, and has lived most of her life in Wyoming. She writes essays, poetry, fiction, biography, and memoir, and is the only writer in this volume who has been struck by lightning (twice) and lived to tell the tale in her book *A Match to the Heart* (1994). Attracted early to the open land, arid valleys, and silent skies of the American West, so lyrically described in her nonfiction classic *The Solace of Open Spaces* (1985), Ehrlich has since been writing about climate change and its extreme weather effects on the world's most remote places. In *The Future of Ice: A Journey into Cold* (2004), Ehrlich travels from the tip of Tierra del Fuego to the top of the Spitsbergen archipelago to study heat, drought, cold, and blizzards. And in *In the Empire of Ice: Encounters in a Changing Landscape* (2010), she circumnavigates the Arctic Circle to write a prose elegy to its vanishing ice sheets and glaciers. Ehrlich's environmental writing also includes *This Cold Heaven: Seven Seasons in Greenland* (2001), where she traveled alone by dogsled to Greenland's northern icecap. Her most recent memoir, *Unsolaced: Along the Way to All That Is* (2021), again takes us from her ranch in Wyoming to points around the globe to chronicle the visible signs of global warming. Author of *John Muir: Nature's Visionary* (2000), a photobiography of America's best-known naturalist, Ehrlich was later awarded the 2010 Henry David Thoreau Prize for excellence in nature writing. Her 1998 short story "Pond Time," set in Southwest Alaska, draws on Ehrlich's lived knowledge of sublime landscapes to explore another key theme in her writing: the wilderness of the human heart.

"Pond Time"

GRETEL EHRLICH

Tengmiirvik. April. Or was it September? She couldn't remember. Madeleine saw five cliffs come apart and fall away and the ice on Newhalen River breaking into railroad-car-sized chunks, all upended, and the willow-choked path leading down to the water ablaze with red leaves. The footings of reality were loose, this she knew. They had been given to oblivion by fluctuating glaciers whose snouts pushed gravel forward and back. She likened ice to a single continent whose moving edge dealt blows to geology all winter, and by spring ate rock and was eaten by sun until the whole world opened into water. But other days, the bad days, she thought of ice as a bedcover being lifted from the gaunt body of her dead husband.

The cliffs were made of birds and the falling away was the birds flying from their resting places in the small clefts of rock walls. In the same way, what had appeared to be one thing turned out to be quite another when the plane bringing her there had to make an unexpected landing at a time in her life when she thought no more emergencies were possible. The engine failed; the palms of her hands grew moist and her first thought was, I'll get to be with Henry again, but instantly knew nothing is ever that easy. The air went coarse, the black grains straining to shoot the rapids of life's hourglass, and the ground heaved out of its flat aspect, taking on the complications of topography. Geography is destiny, she knew that; she knew she was geography's ant being hurtled toward rock, and she laughed, harder and harder, switching off the headset so the pilot couldn't hear.

They descended in slow motion, first circling, as if outlining the opened body of an animal. Caribou drank at the meltwater pond, their strong haunches pushing through tundra heath, their backs dappled with snow. One bull was neck deep in water and others walked the edge of the pond, stopping to drink, then graze, their coats dark brown, almost black at the hips, and their manes, butts, and chests the color of cream. She thought about the lichens and mosses they were eating, dredging snow with the broad blade of their brow tines—how neither plant has roots, absorbing water when there is some, lapsing into a near-death state of dormancy, then coming back to life, how both mosses and lichens are anchored precariously to rock by hairlike strands too delicate to see. She wondered why humans aren't made that way, why they are so heavily anchored to things, even death, and why, with a splash of life-giving moisture, Henry couldn't be reconstituted.

The bull rose out of the pond, his neck dripping, his back glistening in cool Alaskan sun, asymmetrical antlers tipping this way and that like dowsing rods as he searched for what would keep him alive in the winter to come. The caribou had splintered off from a large herd. Soon they would rejoin the others and travel together, stopping only for rutting season before continuing south. She said to the pilot, "I don't know where I'm going. Let's just follow the caribou." And he nodded.

Flying into the country, she had seen the jumbled Chigmit Mountains, hanging green lakes fed by cornices, and red brush lining white highways of ice. The plane roared over valleys that lay like vessels cut open; what the vessels had been holding was now lost. Valleys opened onto other valleys and celadon lakes turned aquamarine. Under them, a river oxbowed, making hard, hairpin turns. The plane aligned itself with a narrow cloud shaped like an arrow, pointing at what? She didn't know where to begin her search for a girl whose name she didn't know. Just keep going, she told the pilot, as if the plane were a taxi, and he laughed, because even if she'd wanted to stop, there was no place to land.

Below was the northern tip of Iliamna Lake, big and brutal as an ocean, and every rocky beach had its own bear rolling in wild rye, napping in sun and rain. Even the first snow, when it came, did not discourage the bears, the sparse flakes upturned and chaotic, lost in air.

They flew above thin, striated clouds through which she could see the reflections of other clouds in a long lake to the north, Lake Clark, and the old village site of Iliamna, abandoned when almost everyone there died of TB. Stunted spruce trees looked as if they had been pushed backward, off balance, but the land lifted up from valley floors like brown wings, and the gravel outlets of receding glaciers leaked floury water—streams seeking the sea.

Tengmiirvik means "bird place" in Central Yup'ik, a language she didn't know at all. She had come here because of the story Henry told her, and because of something she found out after he died. He had talked so softly she'd had to put her ear to his lips. His voice was faint because he was on his way somewhere. She had grown ravenous; before he left, she wanted to know everything he had to say.

"Attu," he whispered, and she nodded. He meant the Battle of Attu in 1942. "I had to kill someone," he said. "No, lots of men. We landed on the beach in a fog. Swirling fog and hundred-mile-per-hour winds. The Japanese were waiting for us. Only we couldn't see them. They'd dug tunnels in the mountains. Waited until we got real close—a few feet away. Then they attacked. Not guns, but bayonets. My face was cut with a point made from a piece of sharpened bamboo.

"I was taken prisoner and put on a ship to Otaru, Hokkaido. On the way, my appendix burst. A Japanese doctor on the ship saved my life. He operated on me secretly—he wasn't supposed to help the prisoners at all—and made me promise never to tell anyone. I haven't until now. After, he jumped overboard. Why did he have to do that? Now I'm jumping too."

The plane reeled, then smoothed out. Earlier she had opened the Yup'ik dictionary and saw the words, *cella maliggluku.* "I'm going in the direction of the universe." That's what Henry would have said if he'd known the language.

The other story went with the photograph she'd found of a Yup'ik woman and a small child. Accompanying it was a badly written note: "She got borne in the spring of the year May 1944 after you been heer since then Im missing you plese come.—A."

The Yup'ik woman was once Henry's lover and the child was his, though so many years had passed the child wasn't a child anymore. Madeleine wanted to see the girl, now a young woman, not from jealousy, though she felt some, but because the young woman was all she had left of Henry, the only flesh of his flesh anywhere.

Looking up from the photograph, she saw how mountains gentled into pond-dotted, barren country and wondered what she was doing there. Nothing would bring Henry back. No meeting would erase the watery nothingness of living on without him.

. . .

The plane was going to crash. It had floats, not wheels, and they made a beeline, a bear-line, really, following a grizzly trail toward a large pond. Trails crosshatched rock. She thought of those lines as grizzly script, directions in bear writing: this way to big trout, that way to good den, the other way to recent kill.

"Never before, never again. Take a deep seat, darlin'," the pilot said on the headset. It wasn't clear whether they would be hitting rock or water, whether they would crash and die or survive. Out of a perverse curiosity Madeleine turned up the headset to hear what the pilot would say as they came close to the end. But he was cool, as if the possibility of death had never occurred to him.

The plane was a Super Cub and her seat was directly behind the pilot's, a tiny slot into which her small body barely fit. "I can land this little bug anywhere," he said. "And you with it."

A bald eagle perched on a rock stared at them as they whizzed past and a grizzly loped out from under the noiseless plane, abandoning the trail, his back fat rolling. She spied the pond's glint ahead, flashing its Morse code: LAND HERE. Her knees pressed into the hard back of the pilot's seat as if pushing the plane forward. "You should see this place in May when the caribou are calving," the pilot had told her earlier. "It's ringed with grizzlies, wolves, and eagles, all waiting for one moment of carelessness when they can move in and snatch a calf." Now she thought of that ring of animals squeezing in tighter and tighter—like a noose—vanquishing life.

Carelessness was exactly what is bringing us down, she thought, this stranger and me. And the failed attention of a mechanic. Now she was falling through the hole he had created for them. The plane's angle was nauseatingly steep at first and death was the blunt point at the end of the dart, the ass on which you pinned life's wriggling tail. Death was always a kind of steepness, whether it was Henry's, or this pilot's, or her own, a vertigo whose free fall had no end.

What if her life was to be spared? She wasn't sure how she would feel about it. She was sure Henry was laughing at them, at the comedy that kept the pale human stories going, page after page, in helpless, endless variations on the theme of error.

It was error that had brought her here in the first place, error that

Henry had been captured and taken prisoner of war, error that when he had come home to eat, sleep, ride, and rest he still died, because he had traveled too far into starvation and horror to come back.

"Henry, catch me!" she said. The windshield of the airplane went black with oil.

If they survived the landing, they then would have to survive the night chasing the bear away, a bear who would be curious about the plane. Perhaps it was only curiosity that lets us live, she thought. Error curbed by wanting to know.

The pilot opened the side window and stuck his head out to see. At the last moment he flapped the flaps and the plane rose, then floated down into the earth's blue iris that had been watching them. Pond.

No time for anger, false melodrama. No time for death wishes. They went about the business of surviving. The pilot gave her orders and laughed; being alive seemed suddenly robust. He was small and compact, blond haired, his skin blotched dark red from twenty-four-hour-a-day sun and sun on ice. "I get crazy if I don't fly every day," he had told her before takeoff. "I always like to be leaving a place and coming to a new one, and I like all the decisions I have to make every moment while flying. It's a way of being alive, I guess."

From the plane he retrieved his short-handled ax, a rifle, which he loaded quickly, matches, a tarp, emergency food, four sleeping bags, flares, and assorted camping equipment. He zipped the sleeping bags together two by two, stuffing one set inside the other, and laid them on a doubled-up tarp on the ground under the wing of the plane. "We'll have to sleep together to stay warm," he said matter-of-factly, almost as if he was sorry, and she nodded as if it were a commonplace she'd anticipated. But it wasn't. The idea frightened her.

His name was Archer, but she tried to think of him simply as the pilot. He was impossible to fathom. Maybe all pilots are like that, she thought. Maybe that's how they stay aloft, by not letting anyone puncture them with questions or truths. He wasn't hardhearted. Quite the opposite. His blue eyes twinkled, but his shell was thick—she was sure he was as buoyant as his plane—and no heartbroken woman was going to ruin him.

Balancing on the plane's float, the pilot peered into the engine. It was beginning to get dark. He knew the problem was an oil line, but he couldn't see where it had disconnected. The plane wobbled like a rocking horse as he shifted his weight from one foot to the other, and the pond was a piece of night squeezed tight by tundra.

The bear would come back and they knew it. She had heard about the old trapper who had survived a plane crash but was eaten by a bear. The pilot told her they would have to take turns staying awake. She nodded. It wouldn't be hard for her. She was a rancher and, from years of calving heifers, knew how to sleep lightly.

When they had organized their camp, they walked to a small creek. "We're going fishing," the pilot announced, though he had no rod. The creek was twenty feet wide with clear, fast water and a gravelly bottom. It twisted through the caribou calving grounds and emptied into the lake. The lake was black and roiling. She could not see the other side and was glad they had not landed on it.

The pilot lay on his side and inched his arm down into the water. "These trout are some of the biggest in the world and live to be twelve or thirteen years old. I'll get an old slow one for dinner." She saw the water churn, then his other hand went in and came out empty. He grinned. "Almost," he said.

"Don't you ever get discouraged?" she asked.

"About what?" His innocence was a wall that repelled her.

He slid to a place where the stream bank hung over the water and tried again. This time he came up with a wriggling fish. When he bashed the fish's head on a rock, she turned her head away and wondered if she would be up to the rigors of survival.

"The Yup'ik don't like white people coming here to fish. They say it is not good to play with animals unless you need them. We're okay this time. We needed this food."

They cooked the trout on a stick over a smoky heather fire. He told her about *ircenrraq*, small people who were half animals—wolves or foxes—and whose songs are sometimes heard.

"They live in those hills over there," he said, pointing toward the dry ruffle to the northwest that eventually rose into mountains. He was smiling as he ate chunks of trout with his fingers. "Watch out," he said, "because if you spend the night with an *ircenrraq*, it will seem like just a few hours have passed but it will really have been a year. Also, they can tell the future."

She looked at him but said nothing. Then, "How do you know these things?"

He shrugged and watched with pleasure as she ate. "I live here."

"How long are we going to be here?" He shrugged again, pulling another chunk of pale meat from fragile bones.

They heard a noise. A slightly hunched-over bear appeared on the trail not far from the plane. The pilot handed Madeleine the coffeepot and a spoon. "Bang on it. Hard." The noise made the bear stop. He stood, sniffing the air full of cooked fish. She kept banging and the pilot lifted the rifle up, aiming just over the bear's head. He fired. The bear chuffed then hit the air with one paw, chasing bullets. Confused by the din, he turned and ambled off into the darkness.

"That worked out pretty good," the pilot said. "The bear's young. He's more curious than anything. The trouble is they can really tear up a little plane like this." She was sure he cared more about his plane than about her.

It had begun to get dark at night and it was dark when she woke. She had dozed off sitting by the fire, her head resting against his shoulder, and she was numb with fury and bewilderment. Henry had called to her in a dream: "Wake up!" he said in a voice from before he had become so sick, tinged with anger. She jerked awake suddenly to find the pilot sitting up with a rifle across his lap and the same expression of bemusement on his face.

"Stop looking like that!" she yelled at him.

"It's time for your watch," he said, handing her the rifle. "If the bear comes don't shoot him, just use the gun to make noise. Do you know how to use it?"

"Hell yes," she said.

He slid under the double layer of down, pulling his wool cap low over his forehead.

"I'm sorry," she said.

He saw that she was crying. "My husband died of starvation because he couldn't eat. He lost the will to live."

The pilot looked at her, then closed his eyes. During Madeleine's watch she fell asleep sitting up and another dream of Henry came: he was lying on top of his coffin beckoning to her. He had a smile on his face, the sweet, ironic dimpled smile that never failed to lure her to his side. Then everything began rattling as though in an earthquake, and she couldn't get to him. The earth kept coming apart the way the wall of birds had disintegrated and there was no passageway to him.

When the pilot woke, Madeleine was looking through the rifle's scope, peering into darkness at nothing.

No animals came. Madeleine slept. She felt Henry lying next to her and tried to hold him, but could not. It was like grabbing thin air. When her eyes opened, all that was visible was the pilot's gold hair and the bright rim of hills in the distance. She slept again, and this time was able to hold Henry close because there was something sticky on her arms. But the tighter she held him, the deeper she sank, and feared she would drown.

The pilot touched her arm and she woke. "You were moaning," he said. "Are you all right?" She couldn't speak, just nodded her head. In the north the hard spires of the aurora were searchlights, as if someone were looking for them.

"The Inuit say you have to make the path clear, you have to open the way from the land of the living to the land of the dead," the pilot said.

"How do I do that?" she asked.

"It's easy. As easy as shoveling snow from your front door."

A herd of caribou came close. Madeleine and the pilot could hear the animals' hooves on rock and the rubbing of muzzles over lichen. "The Yup'ik say it's best not to brood, not to follow your mind too closely, not to turn bad thoughts inside," the pilot said. "I'll tell you a story about caribou: 'A young woman went out to get some wood. Soon she became tired and fell asleep. Upon waking, she felt a great change in her life. Later on she discovered she was to have a child. When the time came she gave birth to a caribou. When the caribou was old enough, his mother sent him away from home to go and search for his own kind. Finally the child discovered a large band of caribou and joined the herd.'"

Madeleine slept and the pilot kept watch. The northern lights faded quickly. In the winter they would undulate in the sky like curtains, but it was still too early in the year and too warm for that.

The pond where they'd landed had begun to ice over. Now she knew it wasn't April, but September. Had she made a mistake or had she been there a long time? The pilot spent the morning trying to repair the plane's engine. At noon they caught another large trout—larger than she had ever seen.

He took the fish to where the creek emptied into the lake and cleaned it there so the guts would not attract the bear. There was no wind and the lake was as still as a window. But Madeleine didn't want to see out. She was happy being where she was. They added heather to the smoking fire and cooked the trout. Eating its flesh was like eating pure water.

After, Madeleine showed the picture of the woman and child to the pilot. He scrutinized it and turned it over as if the back might say something about when and where it was taken, but there was only a blank. He looked up. The ponds were half closed with white ice, half shaking in sunlight.

"When was this taken?" he asked. She told him. He was silent, then said, "The little girl—it's been a long time since she was a little girl— she was my wife. We lived in Newhalen."

"Where is she now?" Madeleine asked.

The pilot looked away, then spoke. "She and her mother drowned under the ice three years ago. The old woman hated snowmobiles and drove her own dogsled. It was spring and the ice wasn't good enough. Usually the dogs know and won't go on bad ice, but there was too much snow on top and it had formed a hard crust. They went down through the crust and kept going."

Madeleine's eyes traveled the sinuous route of the creek traversing barren lands whose ponds had no inlets or outlets, where black fish froze into the ice and lived, thawing out in spring. Everywhere she looked there was action going on, hand in hand with inaction: lichens dying from thirst and reviving in mist, Henry's dead hand in her live one, and Henry's child mixed with the seed of this man.

She found the tiny bottle of brandy from the airplane in her jacket. She poured a thimbleful into the bottle top and handed it to the pilot. He drank. She filled it again and drank the portion herself. They did this until the small bottle was empty.

The caribou that had been grazing near the pond had joined the larger herd. Madeleine and the pilot saw them trotting across the rock barrens, up into the hills where the *ircenrraq* lived. Clouds had covered the sun and it was cold. Madeleine crawled into the zipped-together sleeping bags and the pilot crawled in after her, once again apologizing for the intimate arrangement. The wing of the plane stuck out over them like sculpture, casting an elongated shadow that extended beyond their bodies. She lay stiffly in the soft cocoon.

In the old days women wore bird-skin shirts sewn with bird-bone needles. Madeleine wondered what the shirts felt like and whether they enabled a human to fly. The pilot put his arm over her shoulder because she was shaking—whether from cold or from sorrow he never knew, nor was she about to tell him. All she knew was that they were both alive.

For a long time they lay under the plane. On the hills that curved around them the red fire of autumn spread through brush. The plane was a shadow. It was a man hovering over her, a bird, like a condor, or maybe death. She liked best the story the pilot told her about the small beings called *amekaq,* who can travel through land as if it were water and leave no hole when they come out of the ground. She wished she could be one of them.

She dozed. Sometime later, claustrophobic and sweating, she struggled to free her arms. Her breathing came fast. The pilot lay beside her on his back. Was he the plane's shadow, arms outstretched to hold her, fallen to the ground? She knew she had been selfish, thinking she was the only one with a claim on sorrow. The pilot, this stranger with gold hair, had lost someone, too. In her sleep she had called out for Henry, and the pilot had said in a clear voice, Henry is dead. He had soothed her, stroked her neck, finally and wordlessly entered her, and she remembered that it had been amniotic, as though the rock ground and fiery hues of autumn brush had turned to water.

.   .   .

The bird cliffs fell away and no new ones came into being. The pilot was still asleep beside her. She touched the back of his neck, where his hair shone, and wondered if he was an *ircenrraq,* if he had made a whole year go by. She wondered if she could love him and what exactly that meant. She didn't know if she could stay with him; she didn't know if she could leave. Either way, it would be the same.

"I feel as if a lot of time has passed," she said. He jerked awake. When they sat up, they saw that the place where they had fallen to earth, with its lacework of lichen like memory's intricacy, had gone white with snow.

"Testimony of the Donkey"

ANNIE PROULX

Annie Proulx (b. 1935) is a native Northeasterner, born in Norwich, Connecticut. She eventually left New England for a life in Wyoming, a path followed by the protagonist of her first novel, *Postcards* (1992). From the beginning, Proulx's award-winning works have been defined by their careful attention to the beautiful and dangerous natural environments of North America. Her second novel, *The Shipping News* (1993), winner of both the Pulitzer Prize and the National Book Award, is set among the fishing villages of coastal Newfoundland. *Accordion Crimes* (1996) travels back and forth, from east to west and north to south, as a handmade accordion repeatedly changes hand. *That Old Ace in the Hole* (2002) brings us deep into the flatlands of the Texas and Oklahoma panhandle as big agribusiness seeks to displace small-town farms. And *Barkskins* (2016) follows the role played by two indentured servants and their descendants in the massive deforestation of the New World's northern woods. Proulx's historically informed and environmentally conscious writing distinguishes her shorter fiction as well. The short stories in three of her four collections—*Close Range* (1999), *Bad Dirt* (2004), and *Fine Just the Way It Is* (2008)—feature Wyoming landscapes, with the most famous story, "Brokeback Mountain," adapted into an opera and an Academy Award–winning film. The Wyoming wilderness plays a similarly unsentimental role in Proulx's hiking story "Testimony of the Donkey" (2008). In this striking tale, a young couple's mutual love of the outdoors determines the rocky path of their relationship. Proulx is the recipient of two lifetime achievement awards: the National Book Foundation's Medal for Distinguished Contribution to American Letters (2017) and the Library of Congress Prize for American Fiction (2018). She currently resides in Port Townsend, Washington.

"Testimony of the Donkey"

ANNIE PROULX

Traveler, there is no path. Paths are made by walking.

—ANTONIO MACHADO (1875–1939)

Marc was fourteen years older than Catlin, could speak three languages, was something of a self-declared epicure, a rock climber, an expert skier, a not-bad cellist, a man more at home in Europe than the American West, he said, but Catlin thought these differences were inconsequential although she had only been out of the state twice, spoke only American and played no instrument. They met and fell for each other in Idaho, where Marc was working as a volunteer on the fire line and Catlin was dishing up lasagna in the fire center cafeteria. After a few months they began to live together.

He had noticed her muscular legs as she strode along the counter snatching up pans empty of macaroni and cheese and asked her later if she would like to go hiking sometime. For the last two summers Catlin, against her parents' disapproval, had worked on an all-girl hay-stacking crew, and she had hiked Idaho's mountains since she was a child. She was strong and experienced. He knew an excellent trail, he said. She said yes but doubted he could show her any trail she had not hiked.

He picked her up at four on Sunday morning and drove north. By sunrise she had figured it out: "Seven Devils?" He nodded. And he was right. She had never been on the Dice Roll trail. It had a reputation for attracting tourists and she had always imagined it crowded by day-trippers tossing candy wrappers.

As they walked into the fragrant quietude of the pines she was suffused with euphoria, the old mountain trail excitement. Her earliest memory was of trying to clasp pollen-thick sunbeams streaming through stiff needles as she rode in the child carrier on her father's back. She associated the deep green canopy, the rough red bark with well-being. Marc smirked at her; he'd known she would like this trail. They moved in harmony. In midafternoon, her stomach growling with hunger, they reached a spectacular overlook into the chaos of Hell's Canyon. Marc's idea of lunch was two carrots, some string cheese, and some fishy paste they scooped out of the container with the carrots. It didn't matter. They had shown each other their lapsarian atavistic tastes, their need for the forest, for the difficult and solitary, for what her father had called "the eternal verities," but which she secretly thought might be ephemeral verities. Yet Catlin's sensibilities tingled with a faint apprehension. She had never expected to meet such a person. Where was the catch?

Their time together stretched into four years. Catlin regaled him with family stories—her sleepwalking grandmother, the alcoholic cousin who fell off a Ferris wheel, her father's steady withdrawal from the family, her mother's generous humor. She told him about her only previous lover, a rapscallion type studying meteorology but now in Iraq. Their affair had been nothing, she said; they had slept together only twice before admitting a growing dislike for each other. Marc was quiet about his past and Catlin took him on lover's faith. His fine black hair rose in a Mephistophelian aura around his head when the wind blew—it was longer than the locals liked it—and his face bore an arched Iberian nose and narrow eyes with black irises and heavy brows. But in contrast to his darkly handsome face, he was rather short, with thick arms and small hands. He looked a little vicious, like an old artist whose eye is offended by contemporary daubs.

Catlin had been a plump baby with a face like a small pancake. Her adult face was still baby-round with fleshy cheeks and acne scars that gave her a slightly tough streetwise look. The hay-stacking job had made her muscular, an inch taller and ten pounds heavier than Marc. She had man-size feet that had never known high heels. Beauty salon visits lightened and permed her limp blond hair into platinum waves that contrasted with her rough skin. She favored a blue-eyed, parted-lips look popularized by 1930s movie stars. She could hardly know that she resembled his mother.

At the end of the fire season they left Idaho for Lander, Wyoming, where Marc had the promise of a job with an outdoor climbing school. Housing was tight and they finally ended up in a drab single-wide trailer which Catlin said needed more color. She painted the walls cherry red, purple, orange. At a thrift store she found an old round table and sprayed it cobalt blue. A 1960s television set discovered in the shed behind the trailer became one of several shrines to her invented juju gods and fetishes—the Shrine of Never Falling, and the Shrine of Adventure.

"Very oriental," said Marc in a tone that meant nothing. He was thinking of Tibet. After a few months he quit the job at the climbing school, saying only that he couldn't deal with so many flaming egos, didn't like the career life, the business of climbing. Still, he continued to climb with Ed Glide, his only local friend. He switched back to what he had done before firefighting—freelance work updating information on African countries for travelers' guidebooks, keeping track of insurrections, changing tastes in music and clothing, the whims of dictators. As a child he had lived in Ivory Coast and Zaire, then, as near as Catlin could make out, had spent his adult years in four or five Mediterranean countries. When she asked about that time he talked about plantains in fufu and other dishes. She changed the Shrine of Never Falling to a Shrine of Information for Travelers.

Their landlord was Biff, an elongated, chain-smoking old cowboy with a sweat stain on his hat that resembled the battlements of Jericho. Biff thought he'd discovered the secret of wealth by renting out his dead ex-wife's trailer. He did not like Catlin's color scheme.

"How in hell can I rent this place now? Looks like a carnival." He was so thin he had to buy youth jeans. They were always too short. He stuffed the high-water ends into his run-down work boots.

"Well, you *are* renting it—to us."

"When you're gone," he said, rolling a fresh cigarette with maimed yellow fingers, squinting his triangular eyes against the smoke.

There was nothing to say to that. Only the day before she had asked Marc what he thought about building a cabin. She didn't want to say "house." It sounded too permanent. He only shrugged. That could mean anything. He had that evasive streak and it worried her. She asked once why he had come to Idaho and he answered that he had always wanted to be a cowboy. She had never seen him near a horse or a ranch. Was it a joke?

Catlin had been born and raised in Boise, the great-granddaughter of a Basque shepherd from the Pyrenees, and she sometimes told Marc that that made her European, although she had never been farther away from Idaho than Salt Lake City and Yellowstone Park.

The sheepherder ancestor had been ambitious. He became interested in the criminal physiognomy work of Bertillon and Galton and thought it was possible to make a composite photograph of the Universal Upright Man by overlaying photographs of respected men from every race. The project fell short when he could not find an Inuit, a Papuan, a Bushman, or other Idaho rarities to photograph and coalesce. He became cynical about doing good in the world and turned his attention to money, opening a clothing store in Boise, a store that burgeoned into three, enough to provide the family with modest wealth.

Catlin had an allowance from her parents and could have scraped by without working, but she thought it would demoralize Marc. In Wyoming she found a part-time job with the local tourism office and they set her to puzzling out scenic motor tours for massive campers and RVs. That brought about the Shrine of Wide Roads with No Traffic and No Hills.

They maintained the fiction of independence because each owned a vehicle. The real focus of their lives was neither work nor clutching love, but wilderness travel. As many days and weeks as they could manage they spent hiking the Big Horns, the Wind Rivers, exploring old logging roads, digging around ancient mining claims. Marc had a hundred plans. He wanted to canoe the Boundary Waters, to kayak down the Labrador coast, to fish in Peru. They snowboarded the Wasatch, followed wolf packs in Yellowstone's backcountry. They spent long weekends in Utah's Canyonlands, in Wyoming's Red Desert Haystacks looking for fossils. The rough country was their emotional center.

But it wasn't all joy; sometimes the adventures went to vinegar— once when the snow came in mid-October, four feet of dry powder on bare ground, snow so insubstantial they sank through it until their skis grated on rock.

"*Neige poudreuse*. Give it a few days to settle and make a base," he said. But it stayed cold and didn't pack, didn't settle, and that was it. The wind blew it around, wore it out. No more came in November, December, half of January. They were crazy with cabin fever, longing for snow. When Biff stopped by for the rent, he predicted, through a mouthful of chewing tobacco, a thousand-year drought.

"Happened before," he said. "Ask any Anasazi."

Then a line of storms moved in from the Pacific. Heavy snow and torrents of wind piled up seven-foot drifts. When they ran outside to load the skis and test the snow they could feel the tension, deep smothered sounds below indicating basal shifts.

"Today, no off *piste*," said Marc. "And we won't even try the trails. The old skid road is probably safe enough."

On the drive up the mountain it began to snow again, and they passed men straining to push a truck out of the ditch. They crawled along in whiteout conditions.

They started skiing up the old logging road but in less than twenty minutes found it blocked by an ocean of broken snow. Looking up the east slope of the hill they could see the avalanche track, sack-shaped like the gut of a deer.

"Not good," said Marc. "No point going any farther. There's that terrain trap past the bridge." They went home, Marc saying it was likely they could be called for avalanche rescue.

A violent wind battered the trailer half the night, the electric lights flickering. But the next morning the sky was milky blue. Marc squinted at it and sighed. They waited. By eleven the skin of cloud thickened. The left hand of the storm fell on them like a dropped rock. Marc's cell phone uttered an incongruous meadowlark call.

"Yes. Yes. Leaving now," he said. Search and Rescue needed them. He reminded Catlin to put her radio transceiver in her jacket zip pocket.

"So we won't be part of the problem." On the way he said that Ed Glide had remarked that the storm had brought out hundreds of people, who knew why? Well, because it had been a dry winter.

Catlin knew why. It was more than a dry winter. There was something about skiing in storms that thrilled certain people—climbers of dangerous rock at night, kayakers in ice-choked rivers, hikers who could not resist battering wind and hail.

At the trailhead excited people rushed around in the falling snow, shouting teenage snowboarders with huge packs on their backs, parents bellowing "Get back here" at their children, skiers slipping through the trees, all disappearing into the bludgeoning white.

Ed Glide, beard as coarse as the stuffing in antique chair seats, dark nostrils reminding one of the open doors of a two-car garage, was standing in front of the billboard trail map using a ski pole as a pointer. The fresh rescue group listened, stamped around to keep their feet warm. Ed was talking about the lost snowmobiler rescued at dawn, naked and curled up under a tree.

"There's a shitload of snow in the backcountry," he said. "And there's six damn kids on the Miner's trail. Snowshoes. They headed out this morning with one of the daddies to have a winter cookout at Horse Lake. There's that big cornice over the open slope along there. I doubt any of them's got enough sense to—" He had not finished the sentence when they all heard the heavy roar to the southwest. Even through the light snow they could see a vast cloud rising.

"Fuck!" shouted Ed. "That's it. Let's go! Go!"

A mile along the trail they met two of the boys on snowshoes, stumbling along and repeatedly falling, red faces clotted with snow and frozen tears. The gasping boys said the group had almost reached Horse Lake when Mr. Shelman said the snow was too deep for a cookout and they turned back. They had barely recrossed the bottom of the open slope when the avalanche came. The others were under the snow.

The search crew spent the rest of the day looking for signs of survivors, probing, shoveling. None of the boys or Mr. Shelman had carried a transceiver. Distraught parents came postholing to the site and some of them brought the family dog. Someone found a mitten. The search went on through the night. It took two days to dig out the bodies, and forever to get over the sense of failure and loss.

"Cookout! What a fiasco," said Marc. "Poor little kids." He meant the two survivors, already stained with guilt at being alive.

Their best times were always their explorations into the remnants of the vanishing wild. They treasured discovering new country. She thought sometimes that they were seeing the end of the old world. She knew Marc felt it too. They were in such harmony that they had never had an argument until the lettuce fight. They were leaving the next morning on a ten-day hike in the Old Bison range. The Jade trail had been closed for years but Marc relished the plan for an end run around the Forest Service. It was their practice to have a big dinner the night before they started an adventure, and then to eat sparingly in the wild, the feast a kind of Carnival before Lent. A little hunger, said Marc, makes the mind sharp. Catlin bought tomatoes, a head of lettuce, fillets of halibut at the local market. It was Marc's turn to make dinner. He was making aloko, an African dish of bananas cooked in palm oil with chile to accompany the fried halibut. And, of course, her salad.

Before he started cooking he took off his shirt, more efficient, he said, than putting on an apron. She knew it was because he didn't like the only apron in the house, a fire-engine red thing her mother had given her for a silly present. She said he would be burned by spattering grease. She said she didn't want to find chest hairs clinging to the lettuce.

"You worry too much," he said. The oily smell of frying banana spread through the trailer.

She sorted gear for the trip. Why did he still prefer those antique primitivo boots studded with hobnails? "Do you want a beer while you make the salad?"

"Isn't there any of that white wine left? Whatever it was." He was cutting a red onion—the slices too thick. If he was so continental why couldn't he cut an onion properly? She found an opened bottle of the wine in the refrigerator, poured him a glass and stood watching as he finished slicing, waved the knife with a flourish and began hacking the lettuce.

"You didn't wash it," she said. "And you're supposed to tear the leaves, not cut them."

"Babes, it's a clean lettuce, no dirt. Why wash it? Of course I would prefer a nice little endive, some mesclun, but what we've got is a big, tasteless, hard head of lettuce like a green cannonball. It deserves to be cut." There was no doubt that he despised iceberg lettuce.

"Well, that's all they had. It came from California. Who knows if they sprayed it, or whether the one who picked it had a disease or TB or peed on it?" Her voice spiraled upward. Catlin was inclined to an organic, vegetarian diet, a taste first professed when she was in her teens and designed to annoy her meat-and-potatoes parents, a diet even more difficult to uphold in beef-more-beef-and-potatoes Wyoming. She had considered herself sophisticated in food preferences until Marc. And although she usually gave in to him on whatever main dish he proposed, she insisted on the salad.

"Does everything have to be antiseptic? Does everything have to be done your way? It's only a salad, agreed, it is not a very good salad as we have only the most wretched of ingredients, but I'm making it, and you're eating it." He, of course, would sniffily ignore the salad, gobble the bananas and chile heaped on the fish.

"Oh no. I'm not eating that salad. It's probably full of hairs." He threw down the knife in exasperation.

There were a few more verbal jabs and then suddenly they were in a shouting match about fried bananas, Africa, Mexico, immigration policy, farm labor, olive trees, California. She said he was not only a filthy lettuce nonwasher but a foreign creep who would probably eat caterpillars. He was a freeloader (he was occasionally short on his share of the rent) and he couldn't even make a simple salad. He certainly didn't know how to slice an onion. And why wear those stupid hobnail boots that made him look like a nineteenth-century Matterhorn guide? Maybe he'd like a pair of lederhosen for his birthday? He said he *had* eaten caterpillars in Africa and they were packed with protein and tasty, that the boots had belonged to his grandfather who had been a climber on serious Himalayan expeditions after the Second World War, that she had become controlling, headstrong, egotistical, provincial and unpleasant. Then came accusations of sexual failure and repulsive habits, of ex-lovers, of cheating and lying, the horrible wholesome flax-seed cereal she favored, his addiction to smelly cheeses and bread that had to be made because it could not be bought, and again the wretched hobnail boots. It was less argument than bitter testimony, as when, on the last night of Carnaval in some towns in rural Spanish Galicia, a man presents the *testamento,* the rhymed and furious catalog of the village's sins in the past year, and fictionally apportions the body parts of a donkey to fit the sins. He had told her about this, and now he awarded her the donkey's flatulent gut as most expressive of her raving.

Hundreds of irritations and grievances each had kept closeted spouted from the volcanoes of their injured and insulted egos. Marc threw the salad bowl on the floor, the onion slices rolling on their broad edges. She threw his shirt in the salad. She poured olive oil on the shirt and said if he liked olive oil so much, why, here was plenty of it. She raced to the stove, seized the frying pan and dumped the banana-chile mess in the sink. When he tried to stop her she delivered him a head-ringing slap. She screamed imprecations but he was suddenly very quiet. The expression on his face was peculiar and familiar; anger and—yes, pleasure.

Then he recovered and as if to goad her began again. "You American bitch!" he said, almost conversationally, but his voice sharpening with each word. "You and this constipated place of white, narrow-minded Republicans with the same right-wing opinions. There's no diversity, there's no decent food, there's no conversation, there's no ideas, there's nothing except the scenery. And the Alps have more beautiful scenery than the Rockies." He folded his arms and waited.

"Well, it's good to hear what you really think. Why don't you clear out. Go fuck old fat-legs Julia!" Her voice was a diabolic screech. Yet even as she yelled she was embarrassed by the florid theatricality of the scene. And he wondered how could she know anything about Julia. He had never mentioned her. Julia was his mother.

His lips infolded, he stalked through the rooms collecting his remaining clothes, his books, the maligned hobnail boots, his GPS unit and climbing gear, his skis, his African mask collection, coldly packing everything into his truck. He said nothing while she continued to make caustic taunts. Striding through the kitchen he slipped on the olive oil and nearly fell. Humiliation deepened his anger. She noticed the bandage on his left hand was stained with pus and blood. A few days earlier, trying to strike flakes from a gleaming lump of obsidian Ed Glide had given him, he had driven a sliver deep into his hand. It must be infected, she thought with malicious joy.

The last thing he did was to rip down her poster of Big Train Johnson, the centerpiece of her Shrine to Idaho Baseball, showing the pitcher just after he'd hurled the ball, right-hand knuckles bent, an expression of mild curiosity on his plain face. Marc glared at her. It seemed to her he was presenting his face to get smacked again. She didn't move and abruptly he left.

Through the window she saw him get in his truck and drive away. South. Toward Denver, where, as he had said, there was more than one skin color, a cultural mix and an international airport.

She cleaned up the salad with his ruined shirt, crammed the greasy mess into a trash bag. Slowly she calmed and a brilliant thought came; she would hike the Jade trail without him. She didn't need him.

She slept only a few hours, waking twice to the knowledge that they had broken up. She got up with the first light, boiled a dozen eggs—good hiking trip food—and packed the Jeep. The phone rang as she was carrying out the last load.

"Catlin," he said quietly. "I've got two tickets to Athens on a flight tomorrow morning. I'm going to fight the wildfires in Greece. Will you come?"

"I've got other plans." She hung up, then pulled out the phone cord. She tossed her watch and cell phone in the silverware drawer and rushed out the door. Somewhere along the way, not from *him,* she had learned that discarding the technology sharpened the senses, led to deeper awareness.

On the road driving north she felt she was once again in her own life. For miles she listened to music by groups he despised, reveling in the sense of liberation. He favored Alpha Blondy or monotonous talking-drum music on long drives. She could not stop thinking about the breakup, and after a while even her favorite tunes seemed to develop talking-drum backgrounds. Silence was better. She recalled the strangely pleased expression on Marc's face after she hit him, familiar but impossible to place in context.

It was dusk when she reached the town at the edge of the Big Bison National Forest. She found a motel. She did not want to miss the sign-less trailhead in evening gloom. The wind came up in the night, occasionally lifting her from sleep. Each time she stretched, thinking how wonderful it was to have the whole bed to herself. It was not until the morning that she discovered she had left the topo map back at the trailer in her haste to get out. At the local hardware store she found another, compiled from aerial photographs taken in 1958. It was better than the forgotten map as the Jade trail was clearly marked.

She found some paper in the glove compartment—the receipt for the last oil change—and with an old pencil stub that had rolled around on the dash for a year she scrawled her name, "Jade Trail" and the date and left it on the seat.

Even in broad daylight the abandoned trail was difficult to find. Years before, the Forest Service had uprooted the sign and blocked off the entrance with fallen pines and boulders. Young lodgepole had grown up to shoulder height. The map showed that six miles north the trail flanked an unnamed mountain, then curled around half a dozen small glacier lakes. Marc had planned to fish those lakes. A disturbing thought came to her. He might not go to Athens but return to the trailer and find her gone, notice that all her camping gear was missing. He would know immediately that she had come up to hike the trail without him. He would follow her. She would have to watch and dodge.

The first mile was unpleasant; the trail was rocky and the soil a fine dust half an inch deep. It was clear that many hikers ignored the "Trail Closed" legend on the forest map and ventured up it for a mile or two before turning back. They had marked their passage with broken branches which clawed her arms.

Gradually the head-high trees disappeared as the trail led into the old forest. She walked soundlessly on the thick needle duff. The trail bent and opened onto views of forested slopes, showing thousands of deep red-orange trees killed by the mountain pine beetle infestation and drought. In open areas the trail was choked with seedlings reclaiming the ground. The young trees looked healthy and green, still untouched by the beetles. She wondered if the world was seeing the last of the lodgepole forests. If Marc had been with her they would have talked about this. The memory of his stained bandage came to her. He had determined to learn how to make stone projectile points. They had talked about prehistoric stone tools, and when he told her their edges were only a few microns thick and sharper than razors, she idly wondered aloud why terrorists did not arm themselves with chert knives that would escape airport detection.

"That's stupid," he said.

After several miles of level ground the trail began to climb and twist in a steep stairway of roots and rocks. Snowmelt had scoured it out to slick earth packed around bony flints. Around noon the trail broke into an explosion of wildflowers—columbine, penstemon, beautiful Clarkia, chickweed, and Indian paintbrush. Delighted by the alpine meadow and a few banks of snow packed into clefts on the north sides of slopes, she looked down at a small lake. The scene was exquisitely beautiful. But even here it was not as cool as she had expected. The sun was strong and a cloud of gnats and mosquitoes warped around her in elliptical flight. She ate her lunch sitting in the shade of a giant boulder. She did not miss Marc.

She looked west at Buffalo Hunter, the highest peak in the range. Its year-round snow cover was gone and the peak stood obscenely bare, a pale gray summit quivering in radiant heat. Rock that had not seen sunlight in hundreds of years lay exposed. Another hot, dry summer, the sky filling with wind-torn clouds and lightning but no rain. Occasionally a few drops rattled the air before the clouds dragged them away. Next month the Arizona monsoon would move in with blessed rain, but now the flatland below was parched, the grasses seeded out and withered to a brittle tan wire that cracked underfoot. In the mountains the heat was almost as intense as at lower elevations, and the earth lifeless gravel.

By late afternoon she was tired and reckoned she had hiked thirteen or fourteen miles. The Jade trail ran for another sixty-odd miles and came out on a dead trailhead near a mining ghost town. From the ruins to the main road was another four or five miles. She was sure she could do it easily in ten days. She pitched the little tent beside an unnamed glacier-melt lake. As she ate her hydrated tomato soup she watched trout rise to an evening hatch, the perfect circles spreading outward on the water, coalescing with other spreading circles. The setting sun illuminated the millions of flying insects as a glittering haze over the lake. Marc would have been down there matching the evening hatch, but he was probably in Greece by now. A gray jay, remembering the good old days when hikers had scattered bread crusts and potato chips along the trail, watched expectantly. She crumbled a cracker for him and gave him a name—Johnson, in honor of Big Train Johnson. The day left her a sky veneered with pink pearl, the black ridge against it serrated with pine tops like obsidian spear blades. She was not afraid of the dark and sat up listening to the night sounds until the last liquid smear of light in the west was gone. There was no moon.

She had slept on a stone and wakened stiff and aching in the vague morning. As soon as the sun came up the mountains began to heat, the few remaining snowdrifts melting to feed the gurgling rivulets that twisted through the alpine meadows. The snow patches lay in fantastic shapes, maps of remote archipelagoes, splatters of spilled yogurt, dirty legs, swan wings. There was no wind and the gnats and mosquitoes were bad enough that she slathered on insect repellent. She limbered up with a few bends and stretches, boiled water for tea, ate two of the boiled eggs in her pack and started off again. The eggs had picked up insect repellent from her fingers and the nasty smarting taste stayed in her mouth for a long time.

She hiked past half a dozen small lakes dimpled with rings from rising trout and thought of Marc. She could hear but not see a rushing stream under the willows, a stream that cascaded from the high melting snowbanks. Obscurant mountain willow grew thick wherever the water trickled. The shallow lakes, the color of brown khaki and denim blue, reflected the peaks and shrinking snowfields above. Some lakes were a profound, saturated blue shading out from tawny boulders at the edge to depths where the big fish rested in the coolest water. The waterlines marking shore boulders told that the lake levels once had been four or five feet higher.

The trail slanted steadily upward and was so badly overgrown that long sections melted into the general mountain terrain. Twice she lost it and had to scramble to a high point to see its continuation. She was close now to the height of land where the trail would run above tree line for seven or eight miles before starting down the west slope. This was country where great shelves and masses of shadowed rock displayed exquisite lichen worlds. She knew the lichen chemical factories broke down the rock into soil, some of them fanning across the stone like a stain, nitrogen-loving hot orange lichen where foxes had urinated. Marc had said once that lichens might have been the earth's first plants, that over millions of years they had converted the world's rock covering into the soil that allowed life; the lichens they saw were still devouring the mountains. On their hikes they had seen lichens in hundreds of shapes and colors—flames, antlers, specks and fiery dots, potato chips, caviar, blobs of jelly, corn kernels, green hair, tiny felt mittens, skin diseases, Lilliputian pink-rimmed cups. They always told each other that they were going to learn the lichens, and then, back home, never did.

The rocks themselves, wreathed to their knees in a foam of columbine blossom, were too beautiful to look at for long. One massive soft red rock, as large as three houses, was splotched with pea green lichen. She scratched at the lichen with her fingernail, but it was impervious to abrasion. Flowering plants grew on the rock's small ledges and shelves. This perfection of color and place, too rare and too much to absorb, induced a great sadness; she did not know why and thought it might be rooted in a primordial sense of the spiritual. In this wild place there were no signs of humans except the high mumble of an occasional jet. The solitude provoked existential thoughts, and she regretted the argument with Marc which fell steadily toward the importance of a fuzz of dust. But she was not unhappy to be alone. "Puts things in perspective, right, Johnson?" she said to the gray jay who was following her.

. . .

On the next day around noon she reached a church-size rock about a hundred feet from a tan lake, really more cliff than rock, an interlocking system of glistening pink house-size chunks of granite cracked and fractured into blocks and shelves so huge a few young pines had found enough soil to keep them alive. Their forcing roots would split the rock in time. The ground between the cliff and the lake was littered with a talus of fallen boulders. A few miles away bare scree-covered slopes protruded from the gnarled krummholz, marking the trail's maximum height. She did not want to hike up there in late afternoon, to be forced by darkness to camp in the lightning zone. Even now torn gray clouds slid over the naked peaks. The map showed the tallest as "Tolbert Mountain." The sun was halfway down the western sky. She would quit for the day and camp here. She eased off her backpack and let it drop heavily to the trail. It made a hard clank. The trail here crossed a vast sheet of granite half a mile wide. To be free from the familiar weight was a luxury and she stretched.

High up on the pink cliff she thought she saw writing—initials and a date? Early miners and travelers had left their marks everywhere. She decided to scramble up and see what it was; maybe Jim Bridger, John Fremont, or Jedediah Smith, or some other important historical figure. She felt a bitter dart of loss, like a thorn under the fingernail, that Marc wasn't with her. He would have shouted with joy at this beautiful trail and the pristine lakes, and he would have climbed directly to the inscription on the rock.

The bottom third of the cliff was a rubble of fallen breakstone encrusted with the nubby fabric of gray lichen. Then came fifty feet of climbable clean granite that gave way abruptly to an almost perpendicular wall of glinting stone bristling with jutting blocks. She was determined to get near enough to read the inscription, for she was sure the marks were weathered letters.

The climb was more difficult than it looked. Several stones at the bottom wobbled a little, but so near the ground they seemed hardly a concern. Above them was a tiny trail formed by rain and snow runoff snaking down from an upper jam of more broken blocks, just wide enough for her foot. She inched up the tiny path as far as the lowest block and managed to claw her way around its side, not looking down.

Now she was close enough to make out the letters daubed in black paint, JOSÉ 1931. Not a famous explorer after all—just some old Mexican sheepherder. So much for that.

Getting down was surprisingly awkward. Small rocks turned and slid beneath her feet. In one place she had to slide down a rough incline that rucked her pants uncomfortably up into her crotch. She was in a hurry to set up camp as soon as she got down. This would be the night to break out the pint of rum, maybe mix it with the bottle of cranberry juice she had lugged for days. She craved the thirst-quenching acidity.

Near the bottom she jumped eighteen inches onto the top stone in the jackstraw jumble. The stone swiveled as though it were on ball bearings. Her foot plunged down into the gap between it and another rock and with her weight off it, once more the huge stone shifted, pinning her leg. At first, while she struggled, she ignored the pain and thought of her situation as a temporary obstacle. Then, unable to move the rock or to pull out of its grip, she understood she was trapped.

It took a long time—several minutes—for her to grasp the situation because she was so furious. On the climb up that same block had shifted slightly with a stony rasp as though clearing its throat. Because it was less than two feet from the ground she had considered it inconsequential. She had not taken care. If Marc had been with her he would have said something like "Watch out for this rock." And if Marc was with her he could push or pry up the rock long enough for her to pull her leg out. If Marc was with her. If anyone was with her. She certainly knew the stupidity of hiking alone. She had climbed up there because that was what Marc would have done. So, in a causative way, he was there.

She kept trying to pull the rapidly swelling leg free. The rock pressed against her calf and knee. She could slightly move her ankle and foot. That was the only good news. As a child she had learned that those who did not give up lived, while those who quit trying died. And sometimes those who did not give up died anyway. She thought of her chances. If Marc went back to the trailer he would find the forgotten map on the kitchen table. He would see her camping gear was missing. He would know she was on the Jade trail and he would come. Unless, said her dark, inner voice, unless he was in Greece on some fire line. And if he was in Greece, would Forest Service personnel notice her jeep sitting there day after day? Would they see her note on the front seat, now six days old, and come looking? Those were her chances: to free herself; for Marc to come; for a Forest Service search and rescue. There was one more slender possibility. Another hiker or fisherman might take the closed trail. In the meantime she was mad thirsty. Her backpack was on the trail where she had dropped it, but because it was behind her she could not even see it. In it were the cranberry juice, food, the tiny stove, matches, a signal mirror—everything. In frustration she heaved at the rock which did not move.

As twilight advanced she cried angrily, raging at the tiny misstep that might cost her everything. Her tongue stuck to the roof of her dry mouth. Eventually, leaning against the cooling rock, she fell into a half doze, starting awake many times. Her trapped leg was numb. Thirst and the cold mountain air fastened onto her like leeches. Her neck ached, and she pulled her shoulders forward. She shivered, wrapped her arm around herself, but the shivering intensified until she was racked with deep, clenching shudders. Possible scenes rolled through her head. Could she get so cold the trapped leg would shrink enough to let her pull it out? She pulled again, the fiftieth time, and could feel the edge of the huge stone pressing down on the top of her kneecap. Could she summon the strength to pull the leg relentlessly up even if the edge of the rock cut or crushed the kneecap? She tried until the pain overwhelmed. The effort eased the shuddering for a few minutes, but soon her muscles were clenching violently again. She prayed for morning, remembered how hot it had been every day. She thought if she could just get warm she would get back some strength, and if she had water, after she drank, surely she could get the leg out. She could pour water—if she had it—down her leg and perhaps the water would provide enough lubrication to let her get free. As she thought about this she realized that urine might both warm her and lubricate the trapped leg. But the warmth was fleeting and any lubrication went unnoticed by the rock, which had now passed from inanimate object to malevolent personality.

Between shuddering spasms she fell into tiny snatches of sleep just a few seconds in duration. Finally the stars paled and the sky turned the color of crabapple jelly.

"Come on, come on," she begged the sun, which rose with interminable slowness. At last sunlight struck the ridge to the west, but she was still in cold shadow. An hour passed. She could hear birds. One perched on the edge of the cruel rock just out of her reach. If she could seize it she would bite its head off and drink the blood. But the air was slowly warming even if the sun rays were still not touching the rock. Her leg felt like a great pounding column. At last the blessed sun fell across her body, and gradually the shuddering slowed. The wonderful heat relaxed her and she nodded off for long minutes. But each time she snapped awake her thirst was a disease, enflaming every pore of her body, swelling her throat. She could feel her fat tongue thickening.

The sun's warmth, so pleasant and grateful, became heat, burning her exposed arms, her neck and face. The eagles screamed overhead. By noon her smarting skin and clamorous thirst overshadowed the injured leg. Her eyes were scratchy and hot, and she had to blink to see the distant scree cones that seemed to pulse in the heat. By sunset those naked peaks had changed to heaps of glowing metal shavings. Several times throughout the day she imagined Marc's approach and called out to him. A fox ran up toward the snowbank with something in its mouth.

Now she took new stock of the object that was imprisoning her. It was an irregularly shaped block of granite roughly three feet long and two feet high, the top a sloping table with a scooped declivity a foot or so long and perhaps two inches deep in the center. She could just reach the declivity with her fingers.

The sun notched down the sky, changing the rock shadows. A curious marmot ran to the top of the adjacent rock and stared at her, ran down beneath it, reappeared from a different direction. Johnson, the gray jay, flew in and out of her vision so often he seemed a floater. There was nothing to see but Johnson, the marmot, the dots of black lichen, the eagles in the sky. There was only one thing to think about. Then, as the sun declined, there was another: night and cold.

The rock lost its heat slowly but with cruel inevitability. The sun crashed below the horizon and immediately a stream of chill air flowed down from the snow slopes. At first the coolness felt good on her burned skin, but within the hour she was shivering. She knew what was coming and so did her body, which seemed to brace itself. Far overhead she heard the drone of a small plane engine. Her mind raced to think of a way she could signal a plane the next day. She had a reflecting mirror in her backpack. If only she had worn her watch; if only she had brought the cell phone. If only she was not alone. If only she and Marc had not quarreled. If only he would come. Now. She thought that the sounds of his approach she had imagined during the day must have been a fox raiding her backpack. The night dragged and she dozed woozily for longer periods, minutes instead of seconds, bent over at the waist, for the rock made a kind of slanting table at just the height to cripple cotton pickers and short-row hoers. The leg alternated between numbness and throbbing.

The morning was bitterly familiar. She felt she had been trapped here since infancy. Nothing before the rock was real. She was a mouse in a mousetrap. Everything was the same, the brightening sky, the yearning for the sun's heat. Her tongue filled her mouth and her fingers were stiff. She mistook the gray jay, Johnson, standing two feet away from her on the far edge of the rock, for a wolf. The dull peaks at the height of land were very like monstrous ocean waves, and she could see them swell and roll. The surface of the rock holding her in its grasp was fine-grained, lustrous, dotted with pinprick lichens. The sky bent over the rock. Something smelled bad. Was it her leg or her urine-soaked jeans. Again her drying eyes went to the ocean waves, back down to the rock, to Johnson, who had now taken the guise of the sleeve of her gray chenille bathrobe, to the surface of the rock, to her cramping hands and back again to the naked scree slopes. She had not known that dying could be so boring. She fell asleep for moments and dreamed about the granite mousetrap, built with such care by an unknown stonemason. She dreamed that her father had pulled up a chair nearby. He said that her leg was going to wither and drop off, but that she could make a nice crutch from a small pine and hop back down the trail. She dreamed that a rare butterfly landed on the rock and an entomologist who looked like Marc came for it, easily lifting the stone from her leg and showing her the special mountain wheelchair he had brought to get her down the slopes.

When she snapped back to consciousness the sky hunched over the rock, the slopes, the high snowbanks oozed and sagged, undulating in rhythm with the bald knobs. Time itself writhed and fluttered. Johnson the jay was making thick booming sounds such as no bird had ever before produced. He was a drum, an empty oil barrel on which someone was beating a message, a talking drum. She almost understood. The sun seemed to go up and down like a yo-yo, splitting her eyes with light, then disappearing. Something was happening. She could just make out tiny lichens, transparent, hopping on the stone, on the backs of her hands, on her head and arms. She opened her mouth and the lichens became rain falling on her roasted tongue. Immediately she felt a surge of gratification and pleasure. She cupped her hands to catch the rain but they were too stiff. The rain poured off her hair, dripped from the end of her nose, soaked her shirt, filled the declivity in the top of the rock with blessed water that she could not quite reach.

She drank the downpour, feeling strength and reason return. When the storm moved away her head was clearer. The hard blue sky pressed down and the sun began to pull in the moisture like someone reeling in a hose. She managed to get her shirt off and by making a feeble toss at the water-filled declivity, which held several cups of water, landed one sleeve in the precious puddle. She pulled it toward her and sucked the moisture from the sleeve, repeating the gesture until she had swallowed it all. Not far away she could hear one of the tiny mountain streams rattling through the stones. Her mind was lucid enough to realize that the rain might have only postponed one of the eternal verities. She could see other thunderheads to the east, but nothing to the northwest, the direction of the prevailing wind. The gray jay was not in her sight line.

She had sopped the declivity dry with her shirt, and now she pulled it back on against the burning sun. The gravelly soil had swallowed the rain. There was nothing to do but squint against the glittering world. The cycle started once more. Within an hour her thirst, which, before the storm, had begun to dim, returned with ferocity. Her entire body, her fingernails, her inner ears, the ends of her greasy hair, screamed for water. She bored holes in the sky looking for more rain.

In the night lightning teased in the distance but no more rain fell. The top of the imprisoning rock became a radiant plain under a sliver of ancient moonlight.

By morning the temporary jolt of strength and clarity was gone. She felt as though electricity was shooting up through the rock and into her torso, needles and pins and the numbness that followed was almost welcome, although she dimly knew what it meant. Apparitions swarmed from the snowbanks above, fountains and dervishes, streaming spigots, a helicopter with a waterslide, a crowd of garishly dressed people reaching down, extending their hands to her. All day a desiccating hot wind blew and made her nearly blind. She could not close her eyes. The sun was horrible and her tongue hung in her mouth like a metal bell clapper, clacking against her teeth. Her hands and arms had changed to black and gray leather, a kind of lichen. Her ears swarmed with rattling and buzzing and her shirt seemed made of a stiff metal that chafed her lizard skin.

In the long struggle to get her painful shirt off through the buzzing in her ears, through her cracking skin she heard Marc. He was wearing the hobnail boots and coming up the trail behind her. This was no illusion. She fought to clear her senses and heard it clearly, the hobnail boots sharply click-click-clicking up the granite section of trail. She tried to call his name, but "Marc" came out as a guttural roar, *"Maaaa . . . ,"* a thick and frightening primeval sound. It startled the doe and her half-grown fawns behind her, and they clattered down the trail, black hooves clicking over the rock out of sight and out of hearing.

PART 5

CATCH AND RELEASE

In the long tradition of wilderness tales, writers do not always represent wild places as forbidding environments. By the final decades of the nineteenth century a desire for fresh air and physical activity sent many men in particular into the great outdoors on hunting or fishing trips. Assisted by a burgeoning public interest in camping, as well as by an expanding railroad system that brought wild places within closer reach, the new cultural figure of the sportsman quickly migrates out of early fish-and-game magazines and into the pages of literary fiction. With no guns required, fishing took on the labor of restoring to the battle-weary a tentative sense of safety and serenity. As suffering men learned to become sportsmen, the abundant lakes, rivers, and streams of North America prepared veterans to reenter the cultural mainstream. In Ernest Hemingway's semi-autobiographical "Big Two-Hearted River," returning World War I vet Nick Adams retreats to Michigan's remote Upper Peninsula to engage in the simple rituals of hiking, camping, cooking, and fishing. This 1925 classic set the terms for the modern fishing tale, influencing countless other writers navigating the unsettling waters of postwar America. Rivers in literature can signify the passage of time, the inevitability of aging, or the depth of wisdom. As actual North American rivers like the Colorado River begin to run dry before they reach the sea, their dwindling currents carry downstream with them a storied history of the freshwater river as a vital source of human sustenance, renewal, and inspiration.

"Big Two-Hearted River"

ERNEST HEMINGWAY

Ernest Hemingway (1899–1961) was born in Oak Park, Illinois, where he became an avid camper and outdoorsman, learning the pastime of fly-fishing from his father at his family's Michigan summer cottage. By all accounts, Hemingway was by turns charismatic and shy, proud and insecure, anxious and reckless. The Hemingway legend portrays the Nobel Prize–winning author as a man who was "tough," "hard," "muscular," "masculine," "lean," and "athletic"—all terms routinely used by reviewers to describe his spare writing style. In truth, from the time he was a young child and cast a fishhook into his own back, Hemingway was plagued by repeated injuries and chronic pain, most from multiple automobile, motorcycle, and airplane crashes, and far too many from self-inflicted harms like baiting sharp-clawed circus lions or accidentally shooting himself in the leg. At the age of eighteen, working as an ambulance driver on the Italian front, Hemingway sustained serious injuries from a mortar attack, requiring the removal of countless pieces of shrapnel from his body, a story recounted in his World War I novel *A Farewell to Arms* (1929). Like many shell-shocked veterans returning home, Hemingway sought solace and renewal in fresh air and natural scenery, camping on Michigan's Upper Peninsula—the setting of his most famous short story, "Big Two-Hearted River" (1925). Here the writer's signature prose is as methodical and precise as the disciplined art of fly-fishing. While the story invites us to read it for its hidden depths, it also remains, almost a century after its publication, simply the best narrative dramatization of this wilderness sport ever written. In 1961, after suffering decades of concussions, illnesses, and bouts of deep depression, Hemingway took his own life, like his father, sister, and brother before him.

"Big Two-Hearted River"

ERNEST HEMINGWAY

I

The train went on up the track out of sight, around one of the hills of burnt timber. Nick sat down on the bundle of canvas and bedding the baggage man had pitched out of the door of the baggage car. There was no town, nothing but the rails and the burned-over country. The thirteen saloons that had lined the one street of Seney had not left a trace. The foundations of the Mansion House hotel stuck up above the ground. The stone was chipped and split by the fire. It was all that was left of the town of Seney. Even the surface had been burned off the ground.

Nick looked at the burned-over stretch of hillside, where he had expected to find the scattered houses of the town and then walked down the railroad track to the bridge over the river. The river was there. It swirled against the log spires of the bridge. Nick looked down into the clear, brown water, colored from the pebbly bottom, and watched the trout keeping themselves steady in the current with wavering fins. As he watched them they changed their positions again by quick angles, only to hold steady in the fast water again. Nick watched them a long time.

He watched them holding themselves with their noses into the current, many trout in deep, fast moving water, slightly distorted as he watched far down through the glassy convex surface of the pool, its surface pushing and swelling smooth against the resistance of the log-driven piles of the bridge. At the bottom of the pool were the big trout. Nick did not see them at first. Then he saw them at the bottom of the pool, big trout looking to hold themselves on the gravel bottom in a varying mist of gravel and sand, raised in spurts by the current.

Nick looked down into the pool from the bridge. It was a hot day. A kingfisher flew up the stream. It was a long time since Nick had looked into a stream and seen trout. They were very satisfactory. As the shadow of the kingfisher moved up the stream, a big trout shot upstream in a long angle, only his shadow marking the angle, then lost his shadow as he came through the surface of the water, caught the sun, and then, as he went back into the stream under the surface, his shadow seemed to float down the stream with the current unresisting, to his post under the bridge where he tightened facing up into the current.

Nick's heart tightened as the trout moved. He felt all the old feeling.

He turned and looked down the stream. It stretched away, pebbly-bottomed with shallows and big boulders and a deep pool as it curved away around the foot of a bluff.

Nick walked back up the ties to where his pack lay in the cinders beside the railway track. He was happy. He adjusted the pack harness around the bundle, pulling straps tight, slung the pack on his back, got his arms through the shoulder straps and took some of the pull off his shoulders by leaning his forehead against the wide band of the tump-line. Still, it was too heavy. It was much too heavy. He had his leather rod-case in his hand and leaning forward to keep the weight of the pack high on his shoulders he walked along the road that paralleled the rail-way track, leaving the burned town behind in the heat, and he turned off around a hill with a high, fire-scarred hill on either side onto a road that went back into the country. He walked along the road feeling the ache from the pull of the heavy pack. The road climbed steadily. It was hard work walking up-hill. His muscles ached and the day was hot, but Nick felt happy. He felt he had left everything behind, the need for thinking, the need to write, other needs. It was all back of him.

From the time he had gotten down off the train and the baggage man had thrown his pack out of the open car door things had been different. Seney was burned, the country was burned over and changed, but it did not matter. It could not all be burned. He hiked along the road, sweating in the sun, climbing to cross the range of hills that separated the railway from the pine plains.

The road ran on, dipping occasionally, but always climbing. Nick went on up. Finally the road after going parallel to the burnt hillside reached the top. Nick leaned back against a stump and slipped out of the pack harness. Ahead of him, as far as he could see, was the pine plain. The burned country stopped off at the left with a range of hills. On ahead islands of dark pine trees rose out of the plain. Far off to the left was the line of the river. Nick followed it with his eye and caught glints of the water in the sun.

There was nothing but the pine plain ahead of him, until the far blue hills that marked the Lake Superior height of land. He could hardly see them, faint and far away in the heat-light over the plain. If he looked too steadily they were gone. But if he only half-looked they were there, the far-off hills of the height of land.

Nick sat down against the charred stump and smoked a cigarette. His pack balanced on the top of the stump, harness holding ready, a hollow molded in it from his back. Nick sat smoking, looking out over the country. He did not need to get his map out. He knew where he was from the position of the river.

As he smoked, his legs stretched out in front of him, he noticed a grasshopper walk along the ground and up onto his woolen sock. The grasshopper was black. As he had walked along the road, climbing, he had started many grasshoppers from the dust. They were all black. They were not the big grasshoppers with yellow and black or red and black wings whirring out from their black wing sheathing as they fly up. These were just ordinary hoppers, but all a sooty black in color. Nick had wondered about them as he walked, without really thinking about them. Now, as he watched the black hopper that was nibbling at the wool of his sock with its fourway lip, he realized that they had all turned black from living in the burned-over land. He realized that the fire must have come the year before, but the grasshoppers were all black now. He wondered how long they would stay that way.

Carefully he reached his hand down and took hold of the hopper by the wings. He turned him up, all his legs walking in the air, and looked at his jointed belly. Yes, it was black too, iridescent where the back and head were dusty.

"Go on, hopper," Nick said, speaking out loud for the first time. "Fly away somewhere."

He tossed the grasshopper up into the air and watched him sail away to a charcoal stump across the road.

Nick stood up. He leaned his back against the weight of his pack where it rested upright on the stump and got his arms through the shoulder straps. He stood with the pack on his back on the brow of the hill looking out across the country, toward the distant river and then struck down the hillside away from the road. Underfoot the ground was good walking. Two hundred yards down the fire line stopped. Then it was sweet fern, growing ankle high, to walk through, and clumps of jack pines; a long undulating country with frequent rises and descents, sandy underfoot and the country alive again.

Nick kept his direction by the sun. He knew where he wanted to strike the river and he kept on through the pine plain, mounting small rises to see other rises ahead of him and sometimes from the top of a rise a great solid island of pines off to his right or his left. He broke off some sprigs of the heathery sweet fern, and put them under his pack straps. The chafing crushed it and he smelled it as he walked.

He was tired and very hot, walking across the uneven, shadeless pine plain. At any time he knew he could strike the river by turning off to his left. It could not be more than a mile away. But he kept on toward the north to hit the river as far upstream as he could go in one day's walking.

For some time as he walked Nick had been in sight of one of the big islands of pine standing out above the rolling high ground he was crossing. He dipped down and then as he came slowly up to the crest of the bridge he turned and made toward the pine trees.

There was no underbrush in the island of pine trees. The trunks of the trees went straight up or slanted toward each other. The trunks were straight and brown without branches. The branches were high above. Some interlocked to make a solid shadow on the brown forest floor. Around the grove of trees was a bare space. It was brown and soft underfoot as Nick walked on it. This was the over-lapping of the pine needle floor, extending out beyond the width of the high branches. The trees had grown tall and the branches moved high, leaving in the sun this bare space they had once covered with shadow. Sharp at the edge of this extension of the forest floor commenced the sweet fern.

Nick slipped off his pack and lay down in the shade. He lay on his back and looked up into the pine trees. His neck and back and the small of his back rested as he stretched. The earth felt good against his back. He looked up at the sky, through the branches, and then shut his eyes. He opened them and looked up again. There was a wind high up in the branches. He shut his eyes again and went to sleep.

Nick woke stiff and cramped. The sun was nearly down. His pack was heavy and the straps painful as he lifted it on. He leaned over with the pack on and picked up the leather rod-case and started out from the pine trees across the sweet fern swale, toward the river. He knew it could not be more than a mile.

He came down a hillside covered with stumps into a meadow. At the edge of the meadow flowed the river. Nick was glad to get to the river. He walked upstream through the meadow. His trousers were soaked with the dew as he walked. After the hot day, the dew had come quickly and heavily. The river made no sound. It was too fast and smooth. At the edge of the meadow, before he mounted to a piece of high ground to make camp, Nick looked down the river at the trout rising. They were rising to insects come from the swamp on the other side of the stream when the sun went down. The trout jumped out of water to take them. While Nick walked through the little stretch of meadow alongside the stream, trout had jumped high out of water. Now as he looked down the river, the insects must be settling on the surface, for the trout were feeding steadily all down the stream. As far down the long stretch as he could see, the trout were rising, making circles all down the surface of the water, as though it were starting to rain.

The ground rose, wooded and sandy, to overlook the meadow, the stretch of river and the swamp. Nick dropped his pack and rod case and looked for a level piece of ground. He was very hungry and he wanted to make his camp before he cooked. Between two jack pines, the ground was quite level. He took the ax out of the pack and chopped out two projecting roots. That leveled a piece of ground large enough to sleep on. He smoothed out the sandy soil with his hand and pulled all the sweet fern bushes by their roots. His hands smelled good from the sweet fern. He smoothed the uprooted earth. He did not want anything making lumps under the blankets. When he had the ground smooth, he spread his three blankets. One he folded double, next to the ground. The other two he spread on top.

With the ax he slit off a bright slab of pine from one of the stumps and split it into pegs for the tent. He wanted them long and solid to hold in the ground. With the tent unpacked and spread on the ground, the pack, leaning against a jack pine, looked much smaller. Nick tied the rope that served the tent for a ridgepole to the trunk of one of the pine trees and pulled the tent up off the ground with the other end of the rope and tied it to the other pine. The tent hung on the rope like a canvas blanket on a clothesline. Nick poked a pole he had cut up under the back peak of the canvas and then made it a tent by pegging out the sides. He pegged the sides out taut and drove the pegs deep, hitting them down into the ground with the flat of the ax until the rope loops were buried and the canvas was drum tight.

Across the open mouth of the tent Nick fixed cheesecloth to keep out mosquitoes. He crawled inside under the mosquito bar with various things from the pack to put at the head of the bed under the slant of the canvas. Inside the tent the light came through the brown canvas. It smelled pleasantly of canvas. Already there was something mysterious and homelike. Nick was happy as he crawled inside the tent. He had not been unhappy all day. This was different though. Now things were done. There had been this to do. Now it was done. It had been a hard trip. He was very tired. That was done. He had made his camp. He was settled. Nothing could touch him. It was a good place to camp. He was there, in the good place. He was in his home where he had made it. Now he was hungry.

He came out, crawling under the cheesecloth. It was quite dark outside. It was lighter in the tent.

Nick went over to the pack and found, with his fingers, a long nail in a paper sack of nails, in the bottom of the pack. He drove it into the pine tree, holding it close and hitting it gently with the flat of the ax. He hung the pack up on the nail. All his supplies were in the pack. They were off the ground and sheltered now.

Nick was hungry. He did not believe he had ever been hungrier. He opened and emptied a can of pork and beans and a can of spaghetti into the frying pan.

"I've got a right to eat this kind of stuff, if I'm willing to carry it," Nick said. His voice sounded strange in the darkening woods. He did not speak again.

He started a fire with some chunks of pine he got with the ax from a stump. Over the fire he stuck a wire grill, pushing the four legs down into the ground with his boot. Nick put the frying pan and a can of spaghetti on the grill over the flames. He was hungrier. The beans and spaghetti warmed. Nick stirred them and mixed them together. They began to bubble, making little bubbles that rose with difficulty to the surface. There was a good smell. Nick got out a bottle of tomato ketchup and cut four slices of bread. The little bubbles were coming faster now. Nick sat down beside the fire and lifted the frying pan off. He poured about half the contents out into the tin plate. It spread slowly on the plate. Nick knew it was too hot. He poured on some tomato ketchup. He knew the beans and spaghetti were still too hot. He looked at the fire, then at the tent; he was not going to spoil it all by burning his tongue. For years he had never enjoyed fried bananas because he had never been able to wait for them to cool. His tongue was very sensitive. He was very hungry. Across the river in the swamp, in the almost dark, he saw a mist rising. He looked at the tent once more. All right. He took a full spoonful from the plate.

"Chrise," Nick said, "Geezus Chrise," he said happily.

He ate the whole plateful before he remembered the bread. Nick finished the second plateful with the bread, mopping the plate shiny. He had not eaten since a cup of coffee and a ham sandwich in the station restaurant at St. Ignace. It had been a very fine experience. He had been that hungry before, but had not been able to satisfy it. He could have made camp hours before if he had wanted to. There were plenty of good places to camp on the river. But this was good.

Nick tucked two big chips of pine under the grill. The fire flared up. He had forgotten to get water for the coffee. Out of the pack he got a folding canvas bucket and walked down the hill, across the edge of the meadow, to the stream. The other bank was in the white mist. The grass was wet and cold as he knelt on the bank and dipped the canvas bucket into the stream. It bellied and pulled hard in the current. The water was ice cold. Nick rinsed the bucket and carried it full up to the camp. Up away from the stream it was not so cold.

Nick drove another big nail and hung up the bucket full of water. He dipped the coffee pot half full, put some more chips under the grill onto the fire and put the pot on. He could not remember which way he made coffee. He could remember an argument about it with Hopkins, but not which side he had taken. He decided to bring it to a boil. He remembered now that was Hopkins's way. He had once argued about everything with Hopkins. While he waited for the coffee to boil, he opened a small can of apricots. He liked to open cans. He emptied the can of apricots out into a tin cup. While he watched the coffee on the fire, he drank the juice syrup of the apricots, carefully at first to keep from spilling, then meditatively, sucking the apricots down. They were better than fresh apricots.

The coffee boiled as he watched. The lid came up and coffee and grounds ran down the side of the pot. Nick took it off the grill. It was a triumph for Hopkins. He put sugar in the empty apricot cup and poured some of the coffee out to cool. It was too hot to pour and he used his hat to hold the handle of the coffee pot. He would not let it steep in the pot at all. Not the first cup. It should be straight Hopkins all the way. Hop deserved that. He was a very serious coffee drinker. He was the most serious man Nick had ever known. Not heavy, serious. That was a long time ago. Hopkins spoke without moving his lips. He had played polo. He made millions of dollars in Texas. He had borrowed carfare to go to Chicago, when the wire came that his first big well had come in. He could have wired for money. That would have been too slow. They called Hop's girl the Blonde Venus. Hop did not mind because she was not his real girl. Hopkins said very confidently that none of them would make fun of his real girl. He was right. Hopkins went away when the telegram came. That was on the Black River. It took eight days for the telegram to reach him. Hopkins gave away his .22 caliber Colt automatic pistol to Nick. He gave his camera to Bill. It was to remember him always by. They were all going fishing again next summer. The Hop Head was rich. He would get a yacht and they would all cruise along the north shore of Lake Superior. He was excited but serious. They said good-bye and all felt bad. It broke up the trip. They never saw Hopkins again. That was a long time ago on the Black River.

Nick drank the coffee, the coffee according to Hopkins. The coffee was bitter. Nick laughed. It made a good ending to the story. His mind was starting to work. He knew he could choke it because he was tired enough. He spilled the coffee out of the pot and shook the grounds loose into the fire. He lit a cigarette and went inside the tent. He took off his shoes and trousers, sitting on the blankets, rolled the shoes up inside the trousers for a pillow and got in between the blankets.

Out through the front of the tent he watched the glow of the fire, when the night wind blew on it. It was a quiet night. The swamp was perfectly quiet. Nick stretched under the blanket comfortably. A mosquito hummed close to his ear. Nick sat up and lit a match. The mosquito was on the canvas, over his head. Nick moved the match quickly up to it. The mosquito made a satisfactory hiss in the flame. The match went out. Nick lay down again under the blanket. He turned on his side and shut his eyes. He was sleepy. He felt sleep coming. He curled up under the blanket and went to sleep.

II

In the morning the sun was up and the tent was starting to get hot. Nick crawled out under the mosquito netting stretched across the mouth of the tent, to look at the morning. The grass was wet on his hands as he came out. He held his trousers and his shoes in his hands. The sun was just up over the hill. There was the meadow, the river and the swamp. There were birch trees in the green of the swamp on the other side of the river.

The river was clear and smoothly fast in the early morning. Down about two hundred yards were three logs all the way across the stream. They made the water smooth and deep above them. As Nick watched, a mink crossed the river on the logs and went into the swamp. Nick was excited. He was excited by the early morning and the river. He was really too hurried to eat breakfast, but he knew he must. He built a little fire and put on the coffee pot.

While the water was heating in the pot he took an empty bottle and went down over the edge of the high ground to the meadow. The meadow was wet with dew and Nick wanted to catch grasshoppers for bait before the sun dried the grass. He found plenty of good grasshoppers. They were at the base of the grass stems. Sometimes they clung to a grass stem. They were cold and wet with the dew, and could not jump until the sun warmed them. Nick picked them up, taking only the medium-sized brown ones, and put them into the bottle. He turned over a log and just under the shelter of the edge were several hundred hoppers. It was a grasshopper lodging house. Nick put about fifty of the medium browns into the bottle. While he was picking up the hoppers the others warmed in the sun and commenced to hop away. They flew when they hopped. At first they made one flight and stayed stiff when they landed, as though they were dead.

Nick knew that by the time he was through with breakfast they would be as lively as ever. Without dew in the grass it would take him all day to catch a bottle full of good grasshoppers and he would have to crush many of them, slamming at them with his hat. He washed his hands at the stream. He was excited to be near it. Then he walked up to the tent. The hoppers were already jumping stiffly in the grass. In the bottle, warmed by the sun, they were jumping in a mass. Nick put in a pine stick as a cork. It plugged the mouth of the bottle enough, so the hoppers could not get out and left plenty of air passage.

He had rolled the log back and knew he could get grasshoppers there every morning.

Nick laid the bottle full of jumping grasshoppers against a pine trunk. Rapidly he mixed some buckwheat flour with water and stirred it smooth, one cup of flour, one cup of water. He put a handful of coffee in the pot and dipped a lump of grease out of a can and slid it sputtering across the hot skillet. On the smoking skillet he poured smoothly the buckwheat batter. It spread like lava, the grease spitting sharply. Around the edges the buckwheat cake began to firm, then brown, then crisp. The surface was bubbling slowly to porousness. Nick pushed under the browned under surface with a fresh pine chip. He shook the skillet sideways and the cake was loose on the surface. I won't try and flop it, he thought. He slid the chip of clean wood all the way under the cake, and flopped it over onto its face. It sputtered in the pan.

When it was cooked Nick regreased the skillet. He used all the batter. It made another big flapjack and one smaller one.

Nick ate a big flapjack and a smaller one, covered with apple butter. He put apple butter on the third cake, folded it over twice, wrapped it in oiled paper and put it in his shirt pocket. He put the apple butter jar back in the pack and cut bread for two sandwiches.

In the pack he found a big onion. He sliced it in two and peeled the silky outer skin. Then he cut one half into slices and made onion sandwiches. He wrapped them in oiled paper and buttoned them in the other pocket of his khaki shirt. He turned the skillet upside down on the grill, drank the coffee, sweetened and yellow brown with the condensed milk in it, and tidied up the camp. It was a good camp.

Nick took his fly rod out of the leather rod-case, jointed it, and shoved the rod-case back into the tent. He put on the reel and threaded the line through the guides. He had to hold it from hand to hand, as he threaded it, or it would slip back through its own weight. It was a heavy, double tapered fly line. Nick had paid eight dollars for it a long time ago. It was made heavy to lift back in the air and come forward flat and heavy and straight to make it possible to cast a fly which has no weight. Nick opened the aluminum leader box. The leaders were coiled between the damp flannel pads. Nick had wet the pads at the water cooler on the train up to St. Ignace. In the damp pads the gut leaders had softened and Nick unrolled one and tied it by a loop at the end to the heavy fly line. He fastened a hook on the end of the leader. It was a small hook, very thin and springy.

Nick took it from his hook book, sitting with the rod across his lap. He tested the knot and the spring of the rod by pulling the line taut. It was a good feeling. He was careful not to let the hook bite into his finger.

He started down to the stream, holding his rod, the bottle of grasshoppers hung from his neck by a thong tied in half hitches around the neck of the bottle. His landing net hung by a hook from his belt. Over his shoulder was a long flour sack tied at each corner into an ear. The cord went over his shoulder. The sack slapped against his legs.

Nick felt awkward and professionally happy with all his equipment hanging from him. The grasshopper bottle swung against his chest. In his shirt the breast pockets bulged against him with the lunch and his fly book.

He stepped into the stream. It was a shock. His trousers clung tight to his legs. His shoes felt the gravel. The water was a rising cold shock.

Rushing, the current sucked against his legs. Where he stepped in, the water was over his knees. He waded with the current. The gravel slid under his shoes. He looked down at the swirl of water below each leg and tipped up the bottle to get a grasshopper.

The first grasshopper gave a jump in the neck of the bottle and went out into the water. He was sucked under in the whirl by Nick's right leg and came to the surface a little way down stream. He floated rapidly, kicking. In a quick circle, breaking the smooth surface of the water, he disappeared. A trout had taken him.

Another hopper poked his face out of the bottle. His antennas wavered. He was getting his front legs out of the bottle to jump. Nick took him by the head and held him while he threaded the slim hook under his chin, down through his thorax and into the last segments of his abdomen. The grasshopper took hold of the hook with his front feet, spitting tobacco juice on it. Nick dropped him into the water.

Holding the rod in his right hand he let out line against the pull of the grasshopper in the current. He stripped off line from the reel with his left hand and let it run free. He could see the hopper in the little waves of the current. It went out of sight.

There was a tug on the line. Nick pulled against the taut line. It was his first strike. Holding the now living rod across the current, he brought in the line with his left hand. The rod bent in jerks, the trout pulling against the current. Nick knew it was a small one. He lifted the rod straight up in the air. It bowed with the pull.

He saw the trout in the water jerking with his head and body against the shifting tangent of the line in the stream.

Nick took the line in his left hand and pulled the trout, thumping tiredly against the current, to the surface. His back was mottled the clear, water-over-gravel color, his side flashing in the sun. The rod under his right arm, Nick stooped, dipping his right hand into the current. He held the trout, never still, with his moist right hand, while he unhooked the barb from his mouth, then dropped him back into the stream.

He hung unsteadily in the current, then settled to the bottom beside a stone. Nick reached down his hand to touch him, his arm to the elbow under water. The trout was steady in the moving stream resting on the gravel, beside a stone. As Nick's fingers touched him, touched his smooth, cool, underwater feeling, he was gone, gone in a shadow across the bottom of the stream.

He's all right, Nick thought. He was only tired.

He had wet his hand before he touched the trout, so he would not disturb the delicate mucus that covered him. If a trout was touched with a dry hand, a white fungus attacked the unprotected spot. Years before when he had fished crowded streams, with fly fishermen ahead of him and behind him, Nick had again and again come on dead trout furry with white fungus, drifted against a rock, or floating belly up in some pool. Nick did not like to fish with other men on the river. Unless they were of your party, they spoiled it.

He wallowed down the stream, above his knees in the current, through the fifty yards of shallow water above the pile of logs that crossed the stream. He did not rebait his hook and held it in his hand as he waded. He was certain he could catch small trout in the shallows, but he did not want them. There would be no big trout in the shallows this time of day.

Now the water deepened up his thighs sharply and coldly. Ahead was the smooth dammed-back flood of water above the logs. The water was smooth and dark; on the left, the lower edge of the meadow; on the right the swamp.

Nick leaned back against the current and took a hopper from the bottle. He threaded the hopper on the hook and spat on him for good luck. Then he pulled several yards of line from the reel and tossed the hopper out ahead onto the fast, dark water. It floated down towards the logs, then the weight of the line pulled the bait under the surface. Nick held the rod in his right hand, letting the line run out through his fingers.

There was a long tug. Nick struck and the rod came alive and dangerous, bent double, the line tightening, coming out of water, tightening, all in a heavy, dangerous, steady pull. Nick felt the moment when the leader would break if the strain increased and let the line go.

The reel ratcheted into a mechanical shriek as the line went out in a rush. Too fast. Nick could not check it, the line rushing out, the reel note rising as the line ran out.

With the core of the reel showing, his heart feeling stopped with the excitement, leaning back against the current that mounted icily his thighs, Nick thumbed the reel hard with his left hand. It was awkward getting his thumb inside the fly reel frame.

As he put on pressure the line tightened into sudden hardness and beyond the logs a huge trout went high out of water. As he jumped, Nick lowered the tip of the rod. But he felt, as he dropped the tip to ease the strain, the moment when the strain was too great, the hardness too tight. Of course, the leader had broken. There was no mistaking the feeling when all spring left the line and it became dry and hard. Then it went slack.

His mouth dry, his heart down, Nick reeled in. He had never seen so big a trout. There was a heaviness, a power not to be held, and then the bulk of him, as he jumped. He looked as broad as a salmon.

Nick's hand was shaky. He reeled in slowly. The thrill had been too much. He felt, vaguely, a little sick, as though it would be better to sit down.

The leader had broken where the hook was tied to it. Nick took it in his hand. He thought of the trout somewhere on the bottom, holding himself steady over the gravel, far down below the light, under the logs, with the hook in his jaw. Nick knew the trout's teeth would cut through the snell of the hook. The hook would imbed itself in his jaw. He'd bet the trout was angry. Anything that size would be angry. That was a trout. He had been solidly hooked. Solid as a rock. He felt like a rock, too, before he started off. By God, he was a big one. By God, he was the biggest one I ever heard of.

Nick climbed out onto the meadow and stood, water running down his trousers and out of his shoes, his shoes squelchy. He went over and sat on the logs. He did not want to rush his sensations any.

He wriggled his toes in the water, in his shoes, and got out a cigarette from his breast pocket. He lit it and tossed the match into the fast water below the logs. A tiny trout rose at the match, as it swung around in the fast current. Nick laughed. He would finish the cigarette.

He sat on the logs, smoking, drying in the sun, the sun warm on his back, the river shallow ahead entering the woods, curving into the woods, shallows, light glittering, big water-smooth rocks, cedars along the bank and white birches, the logs warm in the sun, smooth to sit on, without bark, gray to the touch; slowly the feeling of disappointment left him. It went away slowly, the feeling of disappointment that came sharply after the thrill that made his shoulders ache. It was all right now. His rod lying out on the logs, Nick tied a new hook on the leader, pulling the gut tight until it grimped into itself in a hard knot.

He baited up, then picked up the rod and walked to the far end of the logs to get into the water, where it was not too deep. Under and beyond the logs was a deep pool. Nick walked around the shallow shelf near the swamp shore until he came out on the shallow bed of the stream.

On the left, where the meadow ended and the woods began, a great elm tree was uprooted. Gone over in a storm, it lay back into the woods, its roots clotted with dirt, grass growing in them, raising a solid bank beside the stream. The river cut to the edge of the uprooted tree. From where Nick stood he could see deep channels, like ruts, cut in the shallow bed of the stream by the flow of the current. Pebbly where he stood and pebbly and full of boulders beyond; where it curved near the tree roots, the bed of the stream was marly and between the ruts of deep water green weed fronds swung in the current.

Nick swung the rod back over his shoulder and forward, and the line, curving forward, laid the grasshopper down on one of the deep channels in the weeds. A trout struck and Nick hooked him.

Holding the rod far out toward the uprooted tree and sloshing backward in the current, Nick worked the trout, plunging, the rod bending alive, out of the danger of the weeds into the open river. Holding the rod, pumping alive against the current, Nick brought the trout in. He rushed, but always came, the spring of the rod yielding to the rushes, sometimes jerking under water, but always bringing him in. Nick eased downstream with the rushes. The rod above his head he led the trout over the net, then lifted.

The trout hung heavy in the net, mottled trout back and silver sides in the meshes. Nick unhooked him; heavy sides, good to hold, big undershot jaw, and slipped him, heaving and big sliding, into the long sack that hung from his shoulders in the water.

Nick spread the mouth of the sack against the current and it filled, heavy with water. He held it up, the bottom in the stream, and the water poured out through the sides. Inside at the bottom was the big trout, alive in the water.

Nick moved downstream. The sack out ahead of him sunk heavy in the water, pulling from his shoulders.

It was getting hot, the sun hot on the back of his neck.

Nick had one good trout. He did not care about getting many trout. Now the stream was shallow and wide. There were trees along both banks. The trees of the left bank made short shadows on the current in the forenoon sun. Nick knew there were trout in each shadow. In the afternoon, after the sun had crossed toward the hills, the trout would be in the cool shadows on the other side of the stream.

The very biggest ones would lie up close to the bank. You could always pick them up there on the Black. When the sun was down they all moved out into the current. Just when the sun made the water blinding in the glare before it went down, you were liable to strike a big trout anywhere in the current. It was almost impossible to fish then, the surface of the water was blinding as a mirror in the sun. Of course, you could fish upstream, but in a stream like the Black, or this, you had to wallow against the current and in a deep place, the water piled up on you. It was no fun to fish upstream with this much current.

Nick moved along through the shallow stretch watching the balks for deep holes. A beech tree grew close beside the river, so that the branches hung down into the water. The stream went back in under the leaves. There were always trout in a place like that.

Nick did not care about fishing that hole. He was sure he would get hooked in the branches.

It looked deep though. He dropped the grasshopper so the current took it under water, back in under the overhanging branch. The line pulled hard and Nick struck. The trout threshed heavily, half out of water in the leaves and branches. The line was caught. Nick pulled hard and the trout was off. He reeled in and holding the hook in his hand walked down the stream.

Ahead, close to the left bank, was a big log. Nick saw it was hollow; pointing up river the current entered it smoothly, only a little ripple spread each side of the log. The water was deepening. The top of the hollow log was gray and dry. It was partly in the shadow.

Nick took the cork out of the grasshopper bottle and a hopper clung to it. He picked him off, hooked him and tossed him out. He held the rod far out so that the hopper on the water moved into the current flowing into the hollow log. Nick lowered the rod and the hopper floated in. There was a heavy strike. Nick swung the rod against the pull. It felt as though he were hooked into the log itself, except for the live feeling.

He tried to force the fish out into the current. It came, heavily.

The line went slack and Nick thought the trout was gone. Then he saw him, very near, in the current, shaking his head, trying to get the hook out. His mouth was clamped shut. He was fighting the hook in the clear flowing current.

Looping in the line with his left hand, Nick swung the rod to make the line taut and tried to lead the trout toward the net, but he was gone, out of sight, the line pumping. Nick fought him against the current, letting him thump in the water against the spring of the rod. He shifted the rod to his left hand, worked the trout upstream, holding his weight, fighting on the rod, and then let him down into the net. He lifted him clear of the water, a heavy half circle in the net, the net dripping, unhooked him and slid him into the sack.

He spread the mouth of the sack and looked down in at the two big trout alive in the water.

Through the deepening water, Nick waded over to the hollow log. He took the sack off, over his head, the trout flopping as it came out of water, and hung it so the trout were deep in the water. Then he pulled himself up on the log and sat, the water from his trousers and boots running down into the stream. He laid his rod down, moved along to the shady end of the log and took the sandwiches out of his pocket. He dipped the sandwiches in the cold water. The current carried away the crumbs. He ate the sandwiches and dipped his hat full of water to drink, the water running out through his hat just ahead of his drinking.

It was cool in the shade, sitting on the log. He took a cigarette out and struck a match to light it. The match sunk into the gray wood, making a tiny furrow. Nick leaned over the side of the log, found a hard place and lit the match. He sat smoking and watching the river.

Ahead the river narrowed and went into a swamp. The river became smooth and deep and the swamp looked solid with cedar trees, their trunks close together, their branches solid. It would not be possible to walk through a swamp like that. The branches grew so low. You would have to keep almost level with the ground to move at all. You could not crash through the branches. That must be why the animals that lived in swamps were built the way they were, Nick thought.

He wished he had brought something to read. He felt like reading. He did not feel like going on into the swamp. He looked down the river. A big cedar slanted all the way across the stream. Beyond that the river went into the swamp.

Nick did not want to go in there now. He felt a reaction against deep wading with the water deepening up under his armpits, to hook big trout in places impossible to land them. In the swamp the banks were bare, the big cedars came together overhead, the sun did not come through, except in patches; in the fast deep water, in the half-light, the fishing would be tragic. In the swamp fishing was a tragic adventure. Nick did not want it. He did not want to go up the stream any further today.

He took out his knife, opened it and stuck it in the log. Then he pulled up the sack, reached into it and brought out one of the trout. Holding him near the tail, hard to hold, alive, in his hand, he whacked him against the log. The trout quivered, rigid. Nick laid him on the log in the shade and broke the neck of the other fish the same way. He laid them side-by-side on the log. They were fine trout.

Nick cleaned them, slitting them from the vent to the tip of the jaw. All the insides and the gills and tongue came out in one piece. They were both males; long gray-white strips of milt, smooth and clean. All the insides clean and compact, coming out all together. Nick took the offal ashore for the minks to find.

He washed the trout in the stream. When he held them back up in the water, they looked like live fish. Their color was not gone yet. He washed his hands and dried them on the log. Then he laid the trout on the sack spread out on the log, rolled them up in it, tied the bundle and put it in the landing net. His knife was still standing, blade stuck in the log. He cleaned it on the wood and put it in his pocket.

Nick stood up on the log, holding his rod, the landing net hanging heavy, then stepped into the water and splashed ashore. He climbed the bank and cut up into the woods, toward the high ground. He was going back to camp. He looked back. The river just showed through the trees. There were plenty of days coming when he could fish the swamp.

"The Intruder"

ROBERT TRAVER

R obert Traver (1903–1991) was the pen name of John D. Voelker, a
lawyer and State Supreme Court Justice representing Michigan's
remote Upper Peninsula, where he was born in the town of Ishpeming,
not far from Lake Superior. Voelker began his writing career with the
memoir *Trouble-Shooter: The Story of a Northwoods Prosecutor* (1943), in
which he informs his readers that "by the time you finish this book I
may be devoting all my time to hunting and fishing." Voelker went on
to write legal novels, eventually achieving fame for his bestseller *Anatomy of a Murder* (1958), adapted for the screen by Otto Preminger. Only
then did he retire as a judge to spend half his year fly-fishing and the
other half writing. For fifty-two years, during angling season Voelker
kept notes and logs from which he drew material for his stories and
essays. His writing appeared both in magazines dedicated to the sport
(*Fly Rod & Reel, Fly Fisherman, Field & Stream*) and in general interest
magazines (*Esquire, Life*). *Trout Madness: Being a Dissertation on the
Symptoms and Pathology of This Incurable Disease by One of Its Victims*
(1960), *Anatomy of a Fisherman* (1964), and *Trout Magic* (1974)—his
three fishing books—secured Voelker's national reputation as North
America's premier author of fly-fishing tales. More than an evangelist
of what he called "trout wisdom," Voelker was also an environmental-
ist who used his stories to share the innate beauty of a wilderness that
had, for generations, been hacked away by lumber and steel barons. As
both a fisherman and a writer, Voelker closely guarded the locations of
his favorite trout fishing sites, hidden among "the brooding hills and
gloomy swamps and endless waterways" of the rugged land area border-
ing Lake Superior and Lake Michigan. Beloved among anglers, Voelker's 1960 story "The Intruder," from *Trout Madness,* celebrates the lore
of the secret fishing spot, and the considerable solitude and comfort it
can bring, even if the conflicts of the world cannot be banished forever.

"The Intruder"

ROBERT TRAVER

It was about noon when I put down my fly rod and sculled the little cedar boat with one hand and ate a sandwich and drank a can of beer with the other, just floating and enjoying the ride down the beautiful broad main Escanaba River. Between times I watched the merest speck of an eagle tacking and endlessly wheeling far up in the cloudless sky. Perhaps he was stalking my sandwich or even, dark thought, stalking me . . . The fishing so far had been poor; the good trout simply weren't rising. I rounded a slow double bend, with high gravel banks on either side, and there stood a lone fisherman—the first person I had seen in hours. He was standing astride a little feeder creek on a gravel point on the left downstream side, fast to a good fish, his glistening rod hooped and straining, the line taut, the leader vibrating and sawing the water, the fish itself boring far down out of sight.

Since I was curious to watch a good battle and anxious not to interfere, I eased the claw anchor over the stern—*plop*—and the little boat hung there, gurgling and swaying from side to side in the slow deep current. The young fisherman either did not hear me or, hearing, and being a good one, kept his mind on his work. As I sat watching he shifted the rod to his left hand, shaking out his right wrist as though it were asleep, so I knew then that the fight had been a long one and that this fish was no midget. The young fisherman fumbled in his shirt and produced a cigarette and lighter and lit up, a real cool character. The fish made a sudden long downstream run and the fisherman raced after him, prancing through the water like a yearling buck, gradually coaxing and working him back up to the deeper slow water across from the gravel bar. It was a nice job of handling and I wanted to cheer. Instead I coughed discreetly and he glanced quickly upstream and saw me.

"Hi," he said pleasantly, turning his attention back to his fish.

"Hi," I answered.

"How's luck?" he said, still concentrating.

"Fairish," I said. "But I haven't raised anything quite like you seem to be on to. How you been doin'—otherwise, I mean?"

"Fairish," he said. "This is the third good trout in this same stretch—all about the same size."

"My, my," I murmured, thinking ruefully of the half-dozen-odd barely legal brook trout frying away in my sunbaked creel. "Guess I've just been out floating over the good spots."

"Pleasant day for a ride, though," he said, frowning intently at his fish.

"Delightful," I said wryly, taking a slow swallow of beer.

"Yep," the assured young fisherman went on, expertly feeding out line as his fish made another downstream sashay. "Yep," he repeated, nicely taking up slack on the retrieve, "that's why I gave up floating this lovely river. Nearly ten years ago, just a kid. Decided then 'twas a hell of a lot more fun fishing a hundred yards of her carefully than taking off on these all-day floating picnics."

I was silent for a while. Then: "I think you've got something there," I said, and I meant it. Of course he was right, and I was simply out joy-riding past the good fishing. I should have brought along a girl or a camera. On this beautiful river if there was no rise a float was simply an enforced if lovely scenic tour. If there was a rise, no decent fisherman ever needed to float. Presto, I now had it all figured out . . .

"Wanna get by?" the poised young fisherman said, flipping his cigarette into the water.

"I'll wait," I said. "I got all day. My pal isn't meeting me till dark—'way down at the old burned logging bridge."

"Hm . . . trust you brought your passport—you really are out on a voyage," he said. "Perhaps you'd better slip by, fella—by the feel of this customer it'll be at least ten-twenty minutes more. Like a smart woman in the mood for play, these big trout don't like to be rushed. C'mon, just bear in sort of close to me, over here, right under London Bridge. It won't bother us at all."

My easy young philosopher evidently didn't want me to see how really big his fish was. But being a fisherman myself I knew, I knew. "All right," I said, lifting the anchor and sculling down over his way and under his throbbing line. "Thanks and good luck."

"Thanks, chum," he said, grinning at me. "Have a nice ride and good luck to you."

"Looks like I'll need it," I said, looking enviously back over my shoulder at his trembling rod tip. "Hey," I said, belatedly remembering my company manners, "want a nice warm can of beer?"

Smiling: "Despite your glowing testimonial, no thanks."

"You're welcome," I said, realizing we were carrying on like a pair of strange diplomats.

"And one more thing, please," he said, raising his voice a little to be heard over the burbling water, still smiling intently at his straining fish. "If you don't mind, please keep this little stretch under your hat—it's been all mine for nearly ten years. It's really something special. No use kidding you—I see you've spotted my bulging creel and I guess by now you've got a fair idea of what I'm on to. And anyway I've got to take a little trip. But I'll be back—soon I hope. In the meantime try to be good to the place. I know it will be good to you."

"Right!" I shouted, for by then I had floated nearly around the downstream bend. "Mum's the word." He waved his free hand and then was blotted from view by a tall doomed spruce leaning far down out across the river from a crumbling water-blasted bank. The last thing I saw was the gleaming flash of his rod, the long taut line, the strumming leader. It made a picture I've never forgotten.

That was the last time ever that I floated the Big Escanaba River. I had learned my lesson well. Always after that when I visited this fabled new spot I hiked in, packing my gear, threading my way down river through a pungent needled maze of ancient deer trails, like a fleeing felon keeping always slyly away from the broad winding river itself. My strategy was twofold: to prevent other sly fishermen from finding and deflowering the place, and to save myself an extra mile of walking.

Despite the grand fishing I discovered there, I did not go back too often. It was a place to hoard and save, being indeed most good to me, as advertised. And always I fished it alone, for a fisherman's pact had been made, a pact that became increasingly hard to keep as the weeks rolled into months, the seasons into years, during which I never again encountered my poised young fisherman. In the morbid pathology of trout fishermen such a phenomenon is mightily disturbing. What had become of my fisherman? Hadn't he ever got back from his trip? Was he sick or had he moved away? Worse yet, had he died? How could such a consummate young artist have possibly given up fishing such an enchanted spot? Was he one of that entirely mad race of eccentric fishermen who cannot abide the thought of sharing a place, however fabulous, with even one other fisherman?

By and by, with the innocent selfishness possessed by all fishermen, I dwelt less and less upon the probable fate of my young fisherman and instead came smugly to think it was I who had craftily discovered the place. Nearly twenty fishing seasons slipped by on golden wings, as fishing seasons do, during which time I, fast getting no sprightlier, at last found it expedient to locate and hack out a series of abandoned old logging roads to let me drive within easier walking distance of my secret spot. The low cunning of middle age was replacing the hot stamina of youth . . . As a road my new trail was strictly a spring-breaking bronco-buster, but at least I was able to sit and ride, after a fashion, thus saving my aging legs for the real labor of love to follow.

Another fishing season was nearly done when, one afternoon, brooding over that gloomy fact, I suddenly tore off my lawyer-mask and fled my office, heading for the Big Escanaba, bouncing and bucking my way in, finally hitting the Glide—as I had come to call the place—about sundown. For a long time I just stood there on the high bank, drinking in the sights and pungent river smells. No fish were rising, and slowly, lovingly, I went through the familiar ritual of rigging up: scrubbing out a fine new leader, dressing the tapered line, jointing the rod and threading the line, pulling on the tall patched waders, anointing myself with fly dope. No woman dressing for a ball was more fussy . . . Then I composed myself on my favorite fallen log and waited. I smoked a slow pipe and sipped a can of beer, cold this time, thanks to the marvels of dry ice and my new road. My watching spot overlooked a wide bend and commanded a grand double view: above, the deep slow velvet glide with its little feeder stream where I first met my young fisherman; below a sporty and productive broken run of white water stretching nearly a half-mile. The old leaning spruce that used to be there below me had long since bowed in surrender and been swept away by some forgotten spring torrent. As I sat waiting the wind had died, the shadowing waters had taken on the brooding blue hush of evening, the dying embers of sundown suddenly lit a great blazing forest fire in the tops of the tall spruces across river from me, and an unknown bird that

I have always called simply the "lonely" bird sang timidly its ancient haunting plaintive song. I arose and took a deep breath like a soldier advancing upon the enemy.

The fisherman's mystic hour was at hand.

First I heard and then saw a young buck in late velvet slowly, tentatively splashing his way across to my side, above me and beyond the feeder creek, ears twitching and tall tail nervously wigwagging. Then he winded me, freezing in midstream, giving me a still and liquid stare for a poised instant; then came charging on across in great pawing incredibly graceful leaps, lacquered flanks quivering, white flag up and waving, bounding up the bank and into the anonymous woods, the sounds of his excited blowing fading and growing fainter and then dying away.

In the meantime four fair trout had begun rising in the smooth tail of the glide just below me. I selected and tied on a favorite small dry fly and got down below the lowest riser and managed to take him on the first cast, a short dainty float. Without moving I stood and lengthened line and took all four risers, all nice firm brook trout upwards of a foot, all the time purring and smirking with increasing complacency. The omens were good. As I relit my pipe and waited for new worlds to conquer I heard a mighty splash above me and wheeled gaping at the spreading magic ring of a really good trout, carefully marking the spot. Oddly enough he had risen just above where the young buck had just crossed, a little above the feeder creek. Perhaps, I thought extravagantly, perhaps he was after the deer . . . I waited, tense and watchful, but he did not rise again.

I left the river and scrambled up the steep gravelly bank and made my way through the tall dense spruces up to the little feeder creek. I slipped down the bank like a footpad, stealthily inching my way out to the river in the silted creek itself, so as not to scare the big one, my big one. I could feel the familiar shock of icy cold water suddenly clutching at my ankles as I stood waiting at the spot where I had first run across my lost fisherman. I quickly changed to a fresh fly in the same pattern, carefully snubbing the knot. Then the fish obediently rose again, a savage easy engulfing roll, again the undulant outgoing ring, just where I had marked him, not more than thirty feet from me and a little beyond the middle and obliquely upstream. Here was, I saw, a cagey selective riser, lord of his pool, and one who would not suffer fools gladly. So I commanded myself to rest him before casting. "Twenty-one, twenty-two, twenty-three . . ." I counted.

The cast itself was indecently easy and, finally releasing it, the little Adams sped out on its quest, hung poised in midair for an instant, and then settled sleepily upon the water like a thistle, uncurling before the leader like the languid outward folding of a ballerina's arm. The fly circled a moment, uncertainly, then was caught by the current. Down, down it rode, closer, closer, then—clap!—the fish rose and kissed it, I flicked my wrist and he was on, and then away he went roaring off downstream, past feeder creek and happy fisherman, the latter hot after him.

During the next mad half-hour I fought this explosive creature up and down the broad stream, up and down, ranging at least a hundred feet each way, or so it seemed, without ever once seeing him. This meant, I figured, that he was either a big brown or a brook. A rainbow would surely have leapt a dozen times by now. Finally I worked him into the deep safe water off the feeder creek where he sulked nicely while I panted and rested my benumbed rod arm. As twilight receded into dusk with no sign of his tiring I began vaguely to wonder just who had latched on to whom. For the fifth or sixth time I rested my aching arm by transferring the rod to my left hand, professionally shaking out my tired wrist just as I had once seen a young fisherman do.

Nonchalantly I reached in my jacket and got out and tried to light one of my rigidly abominable Italian cigars. My fish, unimpressed by my show of aplomb, shot suddenly away on a powerful zigzag exploratory tour upstream, the fisherman nearly swallowing his unlit cigar as he scrambled up after him. It was then that I saw a lone man sitting quietly in a canoe, anchored in midstream above me. The tip of his fly rod showed over the stern. My heart sank: after all these years my hallowed spot was at last discovered.

"Hi," I said, trying to convert a grimace of pain into an amiable grin, all the while keeping my eye on my sulking fish. The show must go on.

"Hi," he said.

"How you doin'?" I said, trying to make a brave show of casual fish talk.

"Fairish," he said, "but nothing like you seem to be on to."

"Oh, he isn't so much," I said, lying automatically if not too well.

"I'm working a fine leader and don't dare to bull him." At least that was the truth.

The stranger laughed briefly and glanced at his wristwatch. "You've been on to him that I know of for over forty minutes—and I didn't see you make the strike. Let's not try to kid the Marines. I just moved down a bit closer to be in on the finish. I'll shove away if you think I'm too close."

"Nope," I answered generously, delicately snubbing my fish away from a partly submerged windfall. "But about floating this lovely river," I pontificated, "there's nothing in it, my friend. Absolutely nothing. Gave it up myself eighteen-twenty years ago. Figured out it was better working one stretch carefully than shoving off on these floating picnics. Recommend it to you, comrade."

The man in the canoe was silent. I could see the little red moon of his cigarette glowing and fading in the gathering gloom. Perhaps my gratuitous pedagogical ruminations had offended him; after all, trout fishermen are a queer proud race. Perhaps I should try diversionary tactics. "Wanna get by?" I inquired silkily. Maybe I could get him to go away before I tried landing this unwilling porpoise. He still remained silent. "Wanna get by?" I repeated. "It's perfectly okay by me. As you see—it's a big roomy river."

"No," he said dryly. "No thanks." There was another long pause. Then: "If you wouldn't mind too much I think I'll put in here for the night. It's getting pretty late—and somehow I've come to like the looks of this spot."

"Oh," I said in a small voice—just "Oh"—as I disconsolately watched him lift his anchor and expertly push his canoe in to the near gravelly shore, above me, where it grated halfway in and scraped to rest. He sat there quietly, his little neon cigarette moon glowing, and I felt I just had to say something more. After all I didn't own the river. "Why sure, of course, it's a beautiful place to camp, plenty of pine knots for fuel, a spring-fed creek for drinking water and cooling your beer," I ran on gaily, rattling away like an hysterical realtor trying to sell the place. Then I began wondering how I would ever spirit my noisy fish car out of the woods without the whole greedy world of fishermen learning about my new secret road to this old secret spot. Maybe I'd even have to abandon it for the night and hike out . . . Then I remembered there was an uncooperative fish to be landed, so I turned my full attention to the unfinished and uncertain business at hand. "Make yourself at home," I lied softly.

"Thanks," the voice again answered dryly, and again I heard the soft chuckle in the semidarkness.

My fish had stopped his mad rushes now and was busily boring the bottom, the long leader vibrating like the plucked string of a harp. For the first time I found I was able gently to pump him up for a cautious look. And again I almost swallowed my still unlit stump of cigar as I beheld his dorsal fin cleaving the water nearly a foot back from the fly. He wallowed and shook like a dog and then rolled on his side, then recovered and fought his way back down and away on another run, but shorter this time. With a little pang I knew then that my fish was done, but the pang quickly passed—it always did—and again I gently, relentlessly pumped him up, shortening line, drawing him in to the familiar daisy hoop of landing range, kneeling and stretching and straining out my opposing aching arms like those of an extravagant archer. The net slipped fairly under him on the first try and, clenching my cigar, I made my pass and lo! lifted him free and dripping from the water. "Ah-h-h . . ." He was a glowing superb spaniel-sized brown. I staggered drunkenly away from the water and sank anywhere to the ground, panting like a winded miler.

"Beautiful, beautiful," I heard my forgotten and unwelcome visitor saying like a prayer. "I've dreamed all this—over a thousand times I've dreamed it."

I tore my feasting eyes away from my fish and glowered up at the intruder. He was half standing in the beached canoe now, one hand on the side, trying vainly to wrest the cap from a bottle, of all things, seeming in the dusk to smile uncertainly. I felt a sudden chill sense of concern, of vague nameless alarm.

"Look, chum," I said, speaking lightly, very casually, "is everything all okay?"

"Yes, yes, of course," he said shortly, still plucking away at his bottle. "There . . . I—I'm coming now."

Bottle in hand he stood up and took a resolute broad step out of the canoe, then suddenly, clumsily he lurched and pitched forward, falling heavily, cruelly, half in the beached canoe and half out upon the rocky wet shore. For a moment I sat staring ruefully, then I scrambled up and started running toward him, still holding my rod and the netted fish, thinking this fisherman was indubitably potted. "No, no, no!" he shouted at me, struggling and scrambling to his feet in a kind of wild urgent frenzy. I halted, frozen, holding my sagging dead fish as the intruder limped toward me, in a curious sort of creaking stiffly mechanical limp, the uncorked but still intact bottle held triumphantly aloft in one muddy wet hand, the other hand reaching gladly toward me.

"Guess I'll never get properly used to this particular battle stripe," he said, slapping his thudding and unyielding right leg. "But how are you, stranger?" he went on, his wet eyes glistening, his bruised face smiling. "How about our having a drink to glorious trout—and still another to reunion at our old secret fishing spot?"

"They Find the Drowned"

MELINDA MOUSTAKIS

Melinda Moustakis (b. 1982), a native of Fairbanks, Alaska, was raised in California. Her short-story collection, *Bear Down, Bear North: Alaska Stories* (2011), garnered Moustakis the Flannery O'Connor Award for Short Fiction and the Maurice Prize, and led the National Book Foundation to name her one of their 5 Under 35 Writers to watch. Moustakis writes about Alaska's wilderness as though it were a family member, whose warmth and care represents both a blessing and a curse. A daughter and descendant of Alaskan homesteaders, she explains her writing as "a fusion of memories and stories of Alaska" and "a reckoning of family mythology or heritage based on survival." Moustakis, who counts Pam Houston as a formative literary mentor, also credits family campfire tales about fishing and hunting for teaching her how to write voice and dialogue, as well as how to structure narrative tension in her own stories. In wilderness writing, she observes, a landscape has a voice, just like a character. The germ for her story "They Find the Drowned," which won a 2013 O. Henry short-story prize, was a moose tale told to the author by her uncle. Her fiction, written in a style the author characterizes as "Northern Gothic," simultaneously pays affectionate homage to the resilient homesteaders who live on the banks of the Kenai River, once known for its clean water, abundant rainbow trout, and great salmon runs. Moustakis's story uses snapshots in prose to tell the tale of the river's endangered wild ecosystem, its native fish, fauna, animals, and local fishing communities, all still struggling to recover from the environmental disaster of the 1989 *Exxon Valdez* oil spill. Herself an experienced fly-fisher, Moustakis has fittingly entitled her new novel *Homestead*.

"They Find the Drowned"

MELINDA MOUSTAKIS

HUMPIES

Oncorhynchus gorbuscha

A river loses strength, loses water. Scientists catch the humpies and put them into tanks and drive to the Kenai River. The humpies are released near the mouth when the reds are running. The humpies don't know where to go—they don't know the Kenai and they don't follow the reds. They don't recognize the currents of the river, or the smells, or the way the light refracts into the water and bounces off the bottom. The reds run up while the dead humpies float down. They die because they have the wrong memories.

OUTHOUSE

A woman with long, dark hair falls asleep with throbbing shoulders from fishing all day. She sits up and rummages in the cabinets for aspirin. She can't find the bottle and she doesn't want to wake the others. But her daughter wakes up and tugs her shirt.

The woman takes the girl's hand and they tiptoe out the cabin door. The girl forgets and the door slams shut.

They wince and wait for the others to stir, but no one does. They walk the short trail to the outhouse and the girl goes first, the mother standing outside. She hears a rustle and a low, throated moan. And then nothing.

The woman looks around. The girl takes a long time so the mother raps her knuckle on the door. "Shouldn't take this long."

The rustle comes closer. She sees a large, dark creature in the woods. And then nothing.

She knocks hard on the door. "Are you in there? Answer me." Did her daughter think this was a game? She stops knocking to listen. "I said answer me."

The rustle creeps closer. "Open this door." The woman kicks the door in with her unlaced boot. The wood splinters from the force.

"Stop," says the girl from inside. She opens the door. Her eyes marvel at her mother.

An animal bursts out of the bushes and the woman shoves the girl behind her. A grizzly charges toward them, running as if he's going to knock them over. The woman holds her ground. Then he stops. Sniffs the air. Walks toward the river. The bear wades into the Kenai, crossing water to reach the mainland. When they see him climb the bank on the other side, they hurry back to the cabin.

The woman remembers the first aid kit has packets of aspirin and swallows two tablets. She puts the girl back to bed. "Don't do that again."

The girl, thinking of the broken door, is soon asleep.

LOON
Gavia immer

A loon drifts down the current. The bird has a daggered beak and with his black, black head, red eyes, and white-striped wings, he's easy to spot. The loon dives down and disappears and the scientist times him, scanning for the breach. After a minute and eleven seconds, the loon reappears upstream, shakes the water off his head. There are loons and there are ducks. Ducks are never alone.

STORM

The woman's husband knocks on the door. They were looking for him. He has blood soaked down the front of his shirt. They hadn't heard a gun. Maybe the axe, but there isn't a wound. A thick, familiar smell calms them.

He stumbles over the doorway and falls. Two of his buddies carry him to the boat and he's vomiting red into the river. The woman watches the boat leave her and the island and the blood behind. "This is the last time," she says. She nods as she's nodded before, lays towels over the mess and wipes the blood with the toe of her boot. Then she dips the towels into the river, wrings them out.

The woman sits on a stump near the bank. In the stillwater, the smolt move like a storm of comets. The terns swoop down with their pitchfork tails and scoop up small fish. Seagulls on the gravel bar bicker over scraps.

THE SCIENTISTS

The scientists sit in a boat and dip tubes into the river. "Turquoise," says one, noting the color of the water. "Green," says another.

"Glacier blood."

"Crushed sky."

"Kenai Blue."

They test levels of sediment from the ice fields.

LIFE JACKET

The neighbors across the river have a big family. Grandma has a whip of a cast, a fluid flick of line into the water. Grandpa wears his white underwear to swim—his barrel of belly hanging out. The grandchildren scream and splash about in their life jackets. There are five boys and their shouts echo and amplify through the spruce, scaring away the moose and the mosquitoes, if mosquitoes could be scared away. The boys swim out past the dock and let the current carry their floating heads downriver. They stay in the shallow, where they can put their feet down and climb the bank. But if their feet miss, they can grab the net rope fixed to an orange buoy. Sometimes they swim farther across and spend an afternoon on the gravel bar with the gulls.

SPRUCE BARK BEETLE
Dendroctonus rufipennis

The scientists call it the plague—the outbreak of spruce bark beetles that has infested the forests of the Kenai Peninsula for over ten years. A couple of warm summers and the beetles became a blight. They have eaten through two million acres of white, lutz, black, and sitka spruce.

They are the length of a small bullet and they thrive in dryness and heat. The scientists hope for a summer of rain to contain them. The beetles burrow through the bark and chew a path to the cambium layer, the only part of the tree that is alive. They tunnel a gallery inside the host tree and lay eggs. The scientists set pheromone traps and watch as the forest turns into firewood, the dead outnumbering the green.

ROLL

The woman hunches over the reel and her long hair falls forward. Her hip's bruised blue from fishing, but she's got to anchor down with the rod. Boats move out and make a clear path as they drift down.

"Everyone wants to be you with this big ol' fish," says her husband.

They pass the end of the drift and he takes a side channel to avoid the backtrollers.

"Let's get this one in," he says.

She reels in slow and steady. The spinner flashes and he strikes with the net. The king thrashes. He slips to one knee, loses the handle. The king rolls, fifty pounds of fish wrestles out of the net. He steps in and grabs the handle, then grasps at the mesh. She reels but the hook springs loose.

"A hen," she says. "Could've used those eggs."

"Don't jaw me," he says. He throws down the empty net. "I know."

MOOSE

Alces alces gigas

The scientist has a favorite—he calls her A1 and every once in a while he'll sit on the river near Bing's Landing and look for her. She has twins now and crosses to the island at night when the river is quiet. He found her on the side of the road after she'd been hit by a truck on Sterling Highway. The driver died and he didn't think she was going to pull through. The scientist visited her when she was bandaged and bruised—he'd talk to her. "Listen," he'd say. "You're the first thing I've been good to in a long time."

YELLOW PATCHES

He and his buddies cut the trees that were turning brown from the blight, where bark beetles eat and weaken the tree from the inside. The diseased trees are yellow patches in a quilt of green. They are also dangerous. The woman is afraid the closer trees might fall over and crash into their cabin. But they're laughing and she calls them a bunch of idiots with axes.

One by one, the trees crack and fall away from the cabin. They splash into the Kenai and the current pushes them toward the bank.

But one won't fall. His axe wedges into the diagonal cut. The tree teeters toward cabin and land, not water. Women and kids scatter. After the boom, the cabin stands untouched. They are unharmed. He raises a bottle of beer to his good fortune.

RAINBOW TROUT
Oncorhynchus mykiss

Rainbows are the shimmering litmus, the indicator fish. If anything goes wrong in the Kenai, the rainbows tell the scientists. If there is pollution, they die. If the temperature changes too much, they die. If a feeder stream stops feeding, they die. Kiss a rainbow, the scientists say, and you'll know all the river's secrets.

A SIXTY-POUNDER

Across the river, Mom and Dad and Grandma and Grandpa play rummy and drink beer from an ice chest. They don't see the boy slide out of his life jacket on a dare. There's struggling and a shout. Dad dives in and emerges empty-fisted. Grandpa, in his white underwear, jumps into the boat and Grandma follows. They drive to the sinking boy and Grandma holds out the king net to him. When the boy doesn't grab, she scoops him with the net. He's a sixty-pounder and Grandpa has to help heave the net aboard. Grandma pinches the boy's nose—her nails making moon indents in his skin. She forces air into his icy mouth and presses his chest. The boy chokes on air and Grandma turns his head to the side. She brushes her tears away. "You little shit," she says. She pats his back. The boy spits the river.

EAGLE
Haliaeetus leucocephalus

The eagle is perched up in the tree, singing. His call jumps octaves, runs with scales. The scientist records the eagle's sounds and writes down the time of day. A boat drifts down Superhole and stops near the scientist.

"Isn't that something?" says the fisherman. He and the woman both wait for an answer.

The scientist holds up his recorder and points. "Shhhh."

"Well, if you knew anything, you'd know they sing all the time." The fisherman's boat starts downriver. "They sing opera."

THE WALTZ

Her husband has sprawled in her absence. She lies on her elbow and hip in the narrow space and unbraids her long, dark hair. The bed is high—there are storage cabinets built underneath. Blankets and waders are stashed in the gap between her side of the mattress and the wall. He rolls closer and gains inches of mattress.

"Move over," she says. "I don't have any room."

He moves, but he rolls toward her and knocks her off the bed.

The gap is narrow enough to be a problem. "Help me up," she says. She pats around in the shadows and feels fur. And a snout. Teeth.

She screams and scrambles to dislodge herself. He grabs her legs, pulls her up. She finds footing on the mattress and runs out of the room and then outside. The whole cabin wakes with the commotion.

Her husband stands on the deck with a bear head. "I was saving it for the teeth and claws." He unfolds the skin. "Harmless," he says and puts the bear head over his shoulder and fanfares off the porch. Then he waltzes, hand to paw, around the campfire. Man and bear nod in rhythm, in step.

HALF LIFE

Oncorhynchus nerka

The red swims a slow, stilted speed as if worming through sand. He swims outside the current, keeping to the edges with the smolt. His tail is white with rotting and layers of skin hang in silken scarves. A bite? Raked by the claw of a bear? The fish should be dead. The scientist steps closer and wades into the water, aiming with the net. The fish darts away.

BEETLEKILL

"We survived the oil spill and now this," says the scientist. There's division—no one agrees on how to separate the living from the dead.

The canopy has thinned by seventy percent and everything under it is changing—a beetle gnaws through the bark of a tree and the salmon count drops and then a fisherman drinks himself into a ditch.

LOGGING

The boys swim strapped inside the life jackets. The jackets float up near their ears. The river brings a tree to them and they swim to the uprooted trunk lodged near the gravel bar—the amputated branches silky with moss. Three boys straddle the tree as if they were riding a horse. The other boys grab the broken-off branches and shove and push. The river catches the tree and the boys shove more. "Go," they say. "Go." The three riders wave their arms when the current takes the tree. Grandma and Grandpa clap. Mom and Dad grab the camera and start the boat. The boys are waving for the picture as they ride downriver. The fisherman starts his boat, drives fast and waits below Mom and Dad. Naptowne Rapids waits behind him.

"One snag," he yells. "And the tree will roll."

HEN

Oncorhynchus tshawytscha

The scientist hovers over the dead hen, a female king, with tweezers. He pinches a scale from the head, the side, and the tail, measures the length and girth.

"Ain't she pretty?" says the fisherman.

The scientist holds one scale up to the light—the sheer skin of a pearl. Kneeling, the fisherman leans over the scientist's shoulders, puzzled about the lengthy examination. "It's a fish."

"Yes," says the scientist.

CRUTCH

He breaks things—doors, glass, plates. He breaks bones, but only his own, and punches the walls of the cabin. Most of the time he comes home wobbly and soft and puts his arm around her and she crutches him to the couch, hoping he doesn't wake their daughter. "I love my girls," he says. "I love my girls."

BODIES

The scientists come across a body while doing research. They need to count salmon and a human disrupts the day. A human can last six minutes to six hours in the water depending on the temperature. They find the drowned don't have liquid in their lungs—they gasp in the cold water until their tracheas collapse.

CPR

The woman and her husband walk a trail along the edge of the Kenai. The husband watches her long, dark hair swoosh across her back as he follows behind with two poles and a tackle box. She stomps ahead not thinking about where they are going. He follows because he has always chased after her. This is what they do. He has not touched her hair in two months. She has not wanted him to touch her in two months. They have no children, not yet. They have a cabin and two trucks and a long-standing argument about who should drive which truck. The woman trips over a root and there is a little blood on her knee.

"Are you okay?" he asks.

"I'm fine," she says and keeps walking. Her jade ring feels tight on her finger.

The man's hand begins to sweat around the handle of the tackle box. "Pick a spot so we can fish," he says. He wishes that her hair wasn't beautiful, with tinges of red, in the sun.

She walks a minute to make a point, and then stops. "Here."

A low-throated call makes them look upriver. A moose calf is struggling against the current. His head sinks and then pops up, then sinks again.

"He's drowning," she says.

"No he isn't," he says.

The calf gains footing for a brief moment and then falls.

"He's being swept away." She starts to walk up the trail.

"Where are you going?" he asks.

She runs. She wades out into the river. He's still holding the poles and the tackle box. The calf isn't struggling anymore. He's floating. "Please," she says. "Bring him this way." She goes in up to her waist. She grabs the calf by the neck and finds the riverbed with her feet. "Help me," she says to her husband.

They both haul the calf to the shore.

She puts her face near the moose's nose. "He's not breathing."

"He's dead then."

The woman covers the moose's nostrils with her hand. She puts her lips on the moose's mouth and blows air. "Where's his heart? Where do moose put their hearts?"

"I don't know," he says. "The chest seems right."

The woman compresses the chest and tries more air. "Go get help," she says.

The man runs up the trail. If only she were willing him to live, pressing her mouth to his. Her hair falling over his face. He finds another fisherman and the fisherman tells someone to call the rangers and Fish and Game.

The calf's mouth feels like a stubbled cheek. She cups the jaw and focuses the air stream. One. Two. She crosses her hands over the chest. The ears twitch. She pumps and hears a gurgle and water spills out. She tilts his head to allow the water to drain.

When the man returns to his wife, there is a crowd. The calf's side heaves with signs of life.

His wife looks up at him and says, "I think he might be breathing."

Fish and Game comes with oxygen. "You saved the calf's life," they say.

"*We* saved the calf's life." She looks directly at her husband. Then someone hands her a bottle of water and she swishes out her mouth.

The man and woman gather their gear. They walk the trail as before. But when they're away from everyone else she turns to face him. He's holding the poles and the tackle box so he stands there and she wraps one arm around his neck and puts her mouth on his. She kisses him and he kisses her and she puts one hand on his chest where his pulse quickens under her palm. This is what they do.

DEGREES OF NORTH

Here, the scientists know north is eighteen degrees on a compass. Not zero. They don't wander into the woods without a map. Or directions. Walking from camp, following the trail of moose—they don't lose their way. Losing, as they say, is not scientific.

"Memorial Days"

WAYNE KARLIN

Wayne Karlin (b. 1945) entered the U.S. Marine Corps in 1963. A recipient of multiple decorations for his service, Karlin is known for his compassionate writing on the Vietnam War's aftermath as experienced by soldiers and civilians alike, stories told both in his fiction (*Prisoners*, 1998) and in his creative nonfiction (*War Movies: Journeys to Viet Nam,* 2005). To date he has produced three works of nonfiction and eight novels, and he has won several writing awards, including the Paterson Prize (1999), the Vietnam Veterans of America Excellence in the Arts Award (2005), and most recently the Juniper Prize for his novel *A Wolf by the Ears* (2020), a story of escaped slaves from Southern Maryland fighting to secure their freedom. *The Wished-For Country* (2002), a previous work of fiction equally rich in the history and ecology of Maryland, depicts the founding of the colony from the perspectives of White, Black, and Indigenous peoples (as well as one panther). In an interview at the College of Southern Maryland, where Karlin taught for more than thirty years, he described the cultural and environmental landscape of the area, its trees, creeks, and marshlands offering "a microcosm of America with its history close to the surface, and the contradictions, strengths, choices, and problems of that history—its consequences—clearly visible." Karlin's 2020 short story "Memorial Days" brings some of those consequences home, as his protagonist, a veteran of two wars, jokingly refuses to be a Hemingway character. If Nick Adams and his many fictional heirs go to the northern rivers to fish and forget, Karlin's narrator kayaks through the southern marshes to remember and mourn. Tim O'Brien described Karlin as "one of the most gifted writers to emerge from the Vietnam War." He continues to write and reside in Southern Maryland.

"Memorial Days"

WAYNE KARLIN

I will use the day to remember Dennis.

At the point from which I start to paddle, the channel is only a few yards wide and the water shallow and brown over a bottom of mud, pebbles, matted leaves, and branches. Some of the branches scrape like fingernails along the kayak's bottom and an escort of panicked darters dance over the surface of the water, in front of and alongside me. The banks are tangled with bushes and holly and the branches of the syca-mores and elms and oaks arch and interweave overhead. In the shaded spots the water is transparent, and where sun spots filter through the shifting leaves they touch off, like paint dissipating from the tip of a brush, amoebic milky shapes on the surface and when I shift my eyes off one of them and take in the surrounding water, swirled with fallen leaves, it turns into a shifting tan and white camouflage.

As the woods close around me, I feel bands of tension I haven't even been aware of loosen from my forehead and chest. The light that breaks through the lace of leaves runs along with me as I paddle, the sparkle awakening as if the brush of my sight on the water created it. As I round a bend I see a blue heron, large as a five-year-old child. Fish-ing. It looks up, gives an impatient squawk, and does its disjointed, mechanical-toy heron takeoff, soaring from awkwardness to grace as it enters its element and wings downstream, following the cambering of the creek and staying low. It is his kingdom, and I call out that I am just a visitor, mean him no harm, something I'd learned from Dennis, picked up from a children's book Dennis had liked, though, even at eight years old a mythmaker, he had first claimed it as local legend.

I am in the country of childhood now, in a child's dream that I could enter through some portal in a tree or in a wardrobe, pass over into the shadowlands. Gliding into the country of memory, coached by the day's memorial purpose. I follow the heron's flight until the night I'd met Ashley and lost Dennis assembles for me, my perception con-jugating to an endless flowing present tense; I am again in Bledsoe's Bar and Dennis is telling me he has joined the Marines and I am rigid with an anger that is partly envy and partly an anticipation of the grief I feel now.

How does your father feel about it, I ask him.

Dennis keeps grinning silently, through a wreath of smoke, through the thin curtain of marsh grass, through the scrim of heat-mist rising off the surface of the water. He leans forward, coming out of the mist and the barroom gloom, clarifying. In the strobing neon bar signs sometimes he looks like his Vietnamese mother, an Asian cast to his cheekbones and eyes, his hair black and straight, but he has his father's size, bulk, and broad shoulders and sometimes he is taken for a Wesort, usurping the mix that flows in my own family's blood from the runaway Brit indentureds, renegade Piscataways, and escaped African slaves who once found refuge together in the Southern Maryland marshes. He doesn't answer my question.

I don't blame him, I say. *He doesn't want you to become him.*

Dennis's grin widens. *What's wrong with my father?*

Same thing was wrong with mine.

Your dad was a better man because of Vietnam. It gave him the guts to check out when he had to.

It gave him the reason to do it. That fucking year in his life pressed like a lid on all the rest of his years.

The creek widens and the dip of the paddle propels me back to the slipping present. I pass farther into marshland, the forest opening to acres of undulating cord grass, jeweled with dew-flecked spider webs and picketed here and there with looming hundred-foot sentinels of loblolly pine, some of them standing dead and white and skeletal. The tide line is a little low, exposing the muddied bottoms of the grass stalks. Clusters of small brown snails cling to the stalks and I remember how Dennis once told me that his mother would cook and eat the tiny snails that she chose to see as emissaries from her own shadowland of memories, shelled inhabitants of a Mekong she could sometimes transpose over Southern Maryland scenes, coax the water lilies into brilliant lotus blossoms that floated on the billowing green robes of water fairies, rooted in mud and petalling in sun. Whenever Dennis went fishing, he would gather snails for her, though when we were kids, he made me promise not to tell any of our classmates. It was one of the secrets that knit us, that existed to knit us, like our fantasy of the shadowlands, and Dennis's middle, Vietnamese, name that no one else could know.

Tough to be the children of myths, I say to Dennis.

Tough titty. The only way, my friend, to escape the legend, is to make your own legend.

The marsh stretches around me, the fetid smell of it thickening in my nostrils whenever my paddle brings up gobs of mud. I round a bend, paddle away from the tendrils of memories, my father's stories of his war floating into my memories of Dennis's mother, Xuân, and the secret name Dennis told me must never be pronounced, or a ghost would drown him. This marsh had been our Vietnam when we were kids, trying to be our fathers, humping the wetlands with plastic rifles and later BB guns, enduring the heat and insect bites. Though Dennis, more often than not, played being Viet Cong, his father's old enemies. I like winners, he said to me. The games we played, waiting impatiently for the chance to bring the real thing into our lives. I miss him, and I miss my father and the country I float through once again diffuses and transforms in the heat haze into that country whose name was never uttered except as the name of a war or the name of a curse. Vietnam-the-war drawn like a gauze veil over everything I—and Dennis and his sister Tuyết and Ashley—saw, as if that were our inheritance.

I can no longer see bottom, only a ghost crest of wavering grass beneath the surface of the creek.

I dig the paddle in, left and right, finding a rhythm, the motion rocking me to another memory of my father: Jack had sneered at the kayak, called it a yuppie toy. The SS *Minnow*. You've gone over to the enemy, boy. I shut my eyes, my skim over the water the glide my father had taken into another country where I couldn't follow. No more than I could follow Dennis's Humvee as it rose impossibly on an expanding bubble of gas and flame and tipped into a scum-rimed, garbage-clogged canal running alongside a street in some shithole town in Anbar Province: my friend from this estuarine place where we had both grown up, drowning, as if a ghost had found his secret name. Drowning in that trash-filled, reed-choked alien water now somehow confluent to the creek upon which I have now come to commemorate him on this Memorial Day.

I paddle harder, racing against ghosts. In Bledsoe's Bar it is the night I lost Dennis and, within minutes of his telling me he would leave for the war, found the woman who would become Ashley and in my life. She turns and looks at me from across the marsh grass, from across the space between our tables in the barroom gloom, a slim, blond woman whose eyes flit past mine and then back and then don't look away. Her eyes are gray and full of intelligence, her face shadowed and then lit by the sputter of a neon Old Boh sign on the wall behind the bar. She flicks her tongue nervously at the beer foam on her lips and a little frisson runs through my veins, a jolt of recognition that for a time afterwards I will like to think of as a premonition, our future together folding back in time to touch and inform that moment. Though what I understand now is it was our fathers' war that linked us. The same unrequested history that tied me to Dennis. Filtered that night through the war waiting for Dennis. She smiles at me. I think I see her nod slightly, as if approving my words. My anger at Dennis for going to the war. Dennis catches my stare. Sees what I see in it. Winks at Ruth, his girl that night, and then grins, swivels toward Ashley.

Darlene, I'd like you to meet my good friend Hunter.

My name's not Darlene.

Well, hell, I'm half right.

She stares at him. I can see her trying to repress a smile; Dennis's inevitable effect. *Why on Earth are you going into the Marines,* she asks him, then flushes. *I'm sorry. I wasn't eavesdropping.*

Dennis grins again, pats the empty chair next to mine.

Sure you were. Come on over. You kids were made for each other.

She smiles at me.

Is that right?

I hope so, I say, with no humor at all. She blinks quickly, a stalker-warning flickering in her eyes, and I smile, trying to silently reassure her that I am sane.

Come on over, Dennis says again.

You may not like what I have to say.

Hell, you already threw the chum in the water, honey.

He pats the seat next to me again.

Come over, sit on down. Speak your mind.

She hesitates a moment and then gives a what-the-hell shrug, rises, picks up her beer, joins us.

The question is, she says, *whether or not you really believe in the war.*

He will if he has to, I say.

Hey, I'm proud of him, we're fighting fanatics, Ruth says.

You know what the aim of fanaticism is, Ashley says.

My aim is fine, Dennis says. *Best thing about me.*

At least nobody's going to spit on him when he comes back, Ruth says.

I support the soldiers. Anyway, that's such an urban myth, Ashley says.

I had an uncle, Ruth says.

I have a father, Ashley says.

Support the troops, Dennis says, grinning wickedly. *Whoop, whoop, whoop. Support the troops. That's the trick. With stickers and bumpers and ribbons, oh my.*

He and Ruth begin to sing it.

Stickers and bumpers and ribbons, oh my.
Stickers and bumpers and ribbons, oh my.
Stickers and bumpers and ribbons, oh my.

Bullshit, Ashley says. She glares at me. *I support them by wanting to get them home safe.*

Sure thing, I say. I would have said anything to keep her next to me. To have her back. To have him back. I am mourning both of them. I'm in a fucking swamp mourning two losses. Though the distance between Ashley and me is only the distance of failed love and fading time. She is still alive, exists somewhere beyond the cage of my memories; Dennis is only the mist pierced like a tattered white curtain by the reeds around me.

Still, I lost them both to the war.

Your name is Hunter? Well, isn't that reassuring.

It's an old county name, I say defensively, and then think of another. *At least it's not Minor.*

Beer explodes from Dennis's nostrils. *Minor Dobson. Seventh Grade. What a tool.*

Ashley giggles. *Minor? As in Major?*

That's right. Anyway what kind of name is Ashley? Lady Ashley? Your parents into Hemingway?

Fucking Hunter, Dennis says. *Like everyone in the world gets his references. Like anybody reads books.*

My father, Ashley says primly, *is a funeral director.*

Oh shit, Dennis says. *The General. I heard of him.* He salutes her.

Least I don't want to be a Hemingway character, Den, I say.

A flat-bottomed wooden skiff is anchored among the cord grass in a small side stream that is hidden by the reeds until I am almost up on it. An Amish girl, in her bonnet and homespun cotton dress, is standing in the bow, fishing with a bamboo pole; at the stern a straw-hatted, beardless boy sits baiting a hook. They could be brother and sister. Both are motionless; they fasten me into a silent past I want to keep wrapped around myself. As if complicit in the need, they ignore me. I am an impossible intrusion from a future century, an awkward slip in time. Seeing myself through their eyes. Through my Wesort eyes, my father would have said, calling up the occasional shifts in sight descendants of that blood mix supposedly experienced. Peripheral glimpses of the fragmented past that would suddenly float front and center in my vision. An ability I never let myself believe in except when it was happening to me, and it only happened here, in this place my family had lived, in my father's words, since Christ was a corporal. *We've lived here since Christ was a Corporal,* I say to Ashley, and she smiles; it is a term, she tells me later, she has heard her father use.

An empty, dusty, bottle of Yoo-hoo in the stern of the Amish skiff fastens my eyes back to the present, floods me with a sense of relief that the Amish kids are really there, really here, really now.

'You kids were made for each other,' I assure the pair. They nod at me.

Here you go, Lady Ashes, Dennis says, passing a joint to her. She draws in the smoke, exhales, hands it to me, and I put my lips where her lips were. We are both drunk, but not that much, and in the back seat of Dennis's Camry, the warm skin of her arm against mine, her hip pressed against mine, she smiles and presses in harder and when our eyes meet there is the hint of a promise between us that we both know is as delicate as a strand in a spider web bowed up in a breeze. Later Ashley would say it was only because of what I'd said about fathers and she was a soldier's daughter and we were talking about the war and it was Dennis's last night before the Marines that she had sat with me, and then, when Bledsoe's closed, went with us to the Point. As if Dennis leaving for the war gave us a crazy kind of permission. As if instead of Dennis it was me acting out the cliché of grabbing at the quick of life before descending into the fire.

I turn the kayak into a slot in the saw grass, follow it back into forested country, gliding through a seemingly impassable curtain of reeds that I know is just a fringe. In the growing dusk I see my paddle trail a thread of phosphorescence in the water. I glide forward. The Camry barely stops when Dennis is out of the door whooping and running zigzag down a bluff over the river. By the time we catch up with him, he is already bare-assed and splashing in the water. *Ain't he beautiful,* Ruth chuckles, and runs down to join him. Ashley and I sit in the sand at the foot of the large concrete cross that marks the place the first colonists landed and I tell her inanely how they were welcomed warmly by the Piscataway Indians who thought to stick these hapless newcomers here between themselves and their Susquehannock enemies and she says yes, yes, she knows, and we hear Dennis and Ruth splashing in the river and we smoke again and we both know we are getting high not to lose inhibitions but to give us the excuse that we had done so. The cross stands ghostly, seemingly insubstantial in the night mist hovering over the river and I lean over to her or she leans over to me and we kiss and later, minutes or hours later, Ashley grins the same to-hell-with-it way she had before she'd jumped to our table in Bledsoe's and we go into the river, shifting, crystalline wisps of that mist weaving around and over us, beading on our bodies, sometimes parting and letting the full moon shine through to lay shifting, silvery scales on the black water. Her body rising out of that water to me, skin streaked with glows of phosphorescence and she laughs at the sight of me, at how much I want her, nothing minor there, she says, and when we come together I feel an estuarine blend of sensations I try to memorize even as they slip past: the cold of that river on my skin and the warmth inside her and the current pushing at our legs as she shudders and comes back to herself and pushes me away and we stand laughing, like delighted children, watching a luminescent cloud pulse out of me, ignited by the phosphorescence that always waits like ghosts in that dark water.

I push the bow of the kayak up a few inches onto the bank, and then get out and pull it to shore. Little has changed since the last time I was here. The pin oak stands in a hushed clearing. It is probably a hundred feet tall, and so thick two adults could not have wrapped their extended arms around it. It is a presence. Dennis and Tuyêt had first taken me here when I was ten years old, the memory, like all my memories this Memorial Day, a palimpsest over the geography in front of my eyes now, past borne into borderless present. Shaded by the tree is a small, grass-covered hillock, about fifteen feet long and five feet high, swelling strangely out of otherwise flat ground; it is, according to Emmett Wheeler, a Native American burial mound. We had accepted his assessment when we were kids because we wanted it to be true; even at ten years old we recognized wishful thinking. But over the years we'd become more certain that their dad was correct, as we found buried arrowheads and faint cryptic symbols carved into the trunk of the tree, spirals and circles and squares, stretched out and their lines distorted by the tree's growth. Emmett had refused to report the site to the archaeologists at the college; he would not have, he said, whoever was buried there disturbed. One of the few times I saw him and Xuân Wheeler truly angry was when the three of us decided to dig into the mound, using our bare hands. I had gotten deep enough to close my hand around something smooth and long and narrow that could have been a bone or a stick, when they caught us at it. Emmett screamed. But it was the tight-lipped expression on Xuân Wheeler's face, her silent rage, the slight tremble in her hands, that stopped us cold, an expression I had never taken as literal until that moment. A chill went through my blood. Tuyết began to cry.

But Dennis, staring at his mother, just grinned. Man, he said, patting the mound, when I die, this is the place.

Said as a joke, a way to annoy his mother, I had thought. He loved to tease her, and—most of the time—she loved being teased by him. But over the years, he had repeated that request whenever we came here, the mound and the tree always the end point for all our games, though Tuyết stopped coming with us after that day. The last time he said it to me was after boot camp and just before he was deployed, the two of us drinking cans of Old Boh beer and ceremonially tossing the cans onto the mound, our backs against the tree. It was a promise that of course I could not fulfill. Per the Wheeler family tradition, half his ashes had been interred at St. Inigoes Church and the rest scattered over the river. And even then, I wasn't sure if he was being serious or just being Dennis, presenting me with a dramatic last request before the war, an ironic acknowledgment of our shared vocabulary from the war movies that informed our childhood and that he was going to act out with his own life. Dennis the Menace.

I have brought a small knapsack with me. I unsling it at the base of the tree and draw out a small, blue tablecloth. I spread it between two knotted roots that disappear underground for a few feet and then muscle up out of the earth again as they reach the burial mound. I reach back into the knapsack and pull out the rest of the objects I've brought: a framed photo of Dennis in his green and gold colored gown at our high school graduation; I'd cropped myself out of the picture. A can of Old Boh beer. Two mandarin oranges and two apples. A Hershey chocolate bar. A small bowl. A hand spade. A stack of hell money and a bundle of incense sticks I'd bought from the Asian grocery in town.

I rest the photo against the trunk of the tree, its right edge touching one of those connecting roots, pick up the small bowl, go to the mound and spade up some dirt and fill the bowl. I place it in front of the photo, and then arrange the fruit and chocolate on one side of the tablecloth, the can of Old Boh on the other.

Growing up, I was always invited to the Wheelers around mid-July—whenever the fifteenth day of the seventh month in the lunar calendar fell—when Xuân Wheeler performed Trung Nguyen, the Day of Wandering Souls, ceremonies at a table covered with food, fruit, flowers, a small plate covered with coins and dollar bills, and smoldering incense sticks, their sweet sharp scent diffusing into the air, mixing with and sharpening the heavy scent of the bougainvillea she'd planted around the house. The table was set outside. It was the custom to feed the hungry ghosts who were said to wander the earth that day. But wise not to bring them into your house. There were hundreds of thousands of wandering souls left from the war, Emmett Wheeler had told us, the Vietnamese soldiers missing in action or civilians killed with no place nor family to give them rest, all doomed to roam and starve because their remains were never recovered and buried in ancestral ground. Xuân Wheeler's brother was one of them, Emmett once told us; his name had been given to Dennis. The part of the ceremony we three kids liked best was its ending, when Xuân and Emmett would toss the food and money on the table at us, and we would, per the custom, fight each other for it. Enthusiastically. Having grown up Catholic, I liked to imagine being in church and watching parishioners punch each other out as they scrambled for the wafer. This is my body, fight for it. We would wait anxiously while Xuân Wheeler prayed. Once the incense sticks burned down, she would kneel, her hands in front of her chest, bowing until her forehead touched the ground, weeping for her brother, burning a stack of hell money to send to him. But as soon as she looked up and spotted us, she would beam, her face transforming instantly. She would hold up the money plate and start by flinging the coins and bills at us, and then start pelting us with sugar cane, oranges, and chocolate bars. We grabbed at the offerings, punching, pushing, screeching with excitement while she and Emmett Wheeler laughed their asses off. Welcome to VC Halloween, Dennis would always whisper to me, at some point.

I try now to remember and imitate what I would see Xuân Wheeler do as she prayed at that table for lost souls.

I unwrap and light the incense, holding the bundle in one hand and fanning the flame with the other. Pressing the incense between both palms, I close my eyes and slowly bring it up to my forehead and then down again, three times. *The only way, my friend, to escape the legend, is to make your own legend.* I stick the bottoms of the incense sticks into the bowl. I am culturally appropriating like hell, and probably offending both sundry Vietnamese hungry ghosts and whatever Native American spirits rest in that mound. Dennis was not a wandering soul. Not technically. His remains had been returned and commemorated. The ghost I was bringing here was the ghost of our childhood. Dennis would understand. We made things our own. We were our own country. What I always took and treasured from being invited yearly to that wandering souls ceremony was the same gratitude I had felt when Dennis and Tuyết sealed me to themselves by bringing me here, to this secret and sacred place. It is the same way I felt when Dennis told me his secret name.

I watch as the incense sticks burn down, their long fingers transmuted into fragile ash replicas of their original form. A breeze picks up the ash and scatters it.

PART 6

HUNTER AND HUNTED

Unlike the talking woodland creatures that figure so prominently in folktales and fairy tales, wilderness tales typically place people at the center of the action while aiming for more realistic portrayals of wild animals. Not all adult hunting stories can entirely resist the lure of anthropomorphism; some attribute to birds and animals distinctly human feelings and thoughts—a rhetorical practice that may have originally offered hunters a means to better understand their prey. Behind the stories featured in this section is a shared invitation to acknowledge, respect, and protect the integrity and unknowability of the wild. Writers who were also experienced game hunters found the wilderness tale a suitable vehicle for championing the intelligence of wild animals and the importance of maintaining their habitats. Influenced by early wildlife advocacy groups like the Sierra Club (1892), the Wildlife Conservation Society (1895), and the National Audubon Society (1905), many hunters themselves sought to rein in the sport, using their wilderness tales as platforms to warn against the excesses of market and trophy hunters. The modern hunting tale's historical roots in conservationism also account for what the best stories in this genre still seek to do: challenge readers to come to terms with the complex ethics of hunting by exploring it from multiple perspectives—cultural, spiritual, emotional, and environmental.

"A White Heron"

SARAH ORNE JEWETT

Sarah Orne Jewett (1849–1909), the daughter of a country physician, was born in South Berwick, Maine, an industrial town on the banks of the Salmon Falls River, which powered sawmills and grist mills. Jewett's best fiction, produced in the waning decades of the nineteenth century, features the areas she knew best: the endangered mill towns and country towns of rural and coastal Down East Maine. The author of three novels—*A Country Doctor* (1884), *A Marsh Island* (1885), and *The Tory Lover* (1901)—Jewett today is better known for her short stories and sketches. *The Country of Pointed Firs* (1896) remains her most widely taught story collection, although it is "A White Heron," the lead story in Jewett's *A White Heron and Other Stories* (1886), that can now claim the greatest historical relevance for its early conservation concerns. Jewett wrote her coastal tale at a time when many wading birds, especially tree-nesting egrets and herons, were being hunted close to extinction, pursued by hunters as rare additions to their private taxidermy collections, and equally prized by milliners for the market value of their plumes, used to adorn women's fashionable hats. As if in response to Jewett's 1886 story, the Maine Ornithological Society was founded eleven years later to protect nongame birds as well as their wetland and forest habitats. Jewett lived with the Boston writer Annie Adams Field, with whom she shared a "Boston Marriage" for twenty-eight years. As Jewett's health deteriorated, the couple opted to return to Maine, where Jewett died of a stroke at the family homestead, in the same bedroom where she was born. Today, Jewett's story of an elusive white heron stands as American literature's earliest avian preservation tale.

"A White Heron"

SARAH ORNE JEWETT

I

The woods were already filled with shadows one June evening, just before eight o'clock, though a bright sunset still glimmered faintly among the trunks of the trees. A little girl was driving home her cow, a plodding, dilatory, provoking creature in her behavior, but a valued companion for all that. They were going away from whatever light there was, and striking deep into the woods, but their feet were familiar with the path, and it was no matter whether their eyes could see it or not.

There was hardly a night the summer through when the old cow could be found waiting at the pasture bars; on the contrary, it was her greatest pleasure to hide herself away among the huckleberry bushes, and though she wore a loud bell she had made the discovery that if one stood perfectly still it would not ring. So Sylvia had to hunt for her until she found her, and call Co'! Co'! with never an answering Moo, until her childish patience was quite spent. If the creature had not given good milk and plenty of it, the case would have seemed very different to her owners. Besides, Sylvia had all the time there was, and very little use to make of it. Sometimes in pleasant weather it was a consolation to look upon the cow's pranks as an intelligent attempt to play hide and seek, and as the child had no playmates she lent herself to this amusement with a good deal of zest. Though this chase had been so long that the wary animal herself had given an unusual signal of her whereabouts, Sylvia had only laughed when she came upon Mistress Moolly at the swamp-side, and urged her affectionately homeward with a twig of birch leaves. The old cow was not inclined to wander farther, she even turned in the right direction for once as they left the pasture, and stepped along the road at a good pace. She was quite ready to be milked now, and seldom stopped to browse. Sylvia wondered what her grandmother would say because they were so late. It was a great while since she had left home at half-past five o'clock, but everybody knew the difficulty of making this errand a short one. Mrs. Tilley had chased the horned torment too many summer evenings herself to blame any one else for lingering, and was only thankful as she waited that she had Sylvia, nowadays, to give such valuable assistance. The good woman suspected that Sylvia loitered occasionally on her own account; there never was such a child for straying about out-of-doors since the world was made! Everybody said that it was a good change for a little maid who had tried to grow for eight years in a crowded manufacturing town, but, as for Sylvia herself, it seemed as if she never had been alive at all before she came to live at the farm. She thought often with wistful compassion of a wretched geranium that belonged to a town neighbor.

"'Afraid of folks,'" old Mrs. Tilley said to herself, with a smile, after she had made the unlikely choice of Sylvia from her daughter's houseful of children, and was returning to the farm. "'Afraid of folks,' they said! I guess she won't be troubled no great with 'em up to the old place!" When they reached the door of the lonely house and stopped to unlock it, and the cat came to purr loudly, and rub against them, a deserted pussy, indeed, but fat with young robins, Sylvia whispered that this was a beautiful place to live in, and she never should wish to go home.

The companions followed the shady wood-road, the cow taking slow steps and the child very fast ones. The cow stopped long at the brook to drink, as if the pasture were not half a swamp, and Sylvia stood still and waited, letting her bare feet cool themselves in the shoal water, while the great twilight moths struck softly against her. She waded on through the brook as the cow moved away, and listened to the thrushes with a heart that beat fast with pleasure. There was a stirring in the great boughs overhead. They were full of little birds and beasts that seemed to be wide awake, and going about their world, or else saying good-night to each other in sleepy twitters. Sylvia herself felt sleepy as she walked along. However, it was not much farther to the house, and the air was soft and sweet. She was not often in the woods so late as this, and it made her feel as if she were a part of the gray shadows and the moving leaves. She was just thinking how long it seemed since she first came to the farm a year ago, and wondering if everything went on in the noisy town just the same as when she was there, the thought of the great red-faced boy who used to chase and frighten her made her hurry along the path to escape from the shadow of the trees.

Suddenly this little woods-girl is horror-stricken to hear a clear whistle not very far away. Not a bird's-whistle, which would have a sort of friendliness, but a boy's whistle, determined, and somewhat aggressive. Sylvia left the cow to whatever sad fate might await her, and stepped discreetly aside into the bushes, but she was just too late. The enemy had discovered her, and called out in a very cheerful and persuasive tone, "Halloa, little girl, how far is it to the road?" and trembling Sylvia answered almost inaudibly, "A good ways."

She did not dare to look boldly at the tall young man, who carried a gun over his shoulder, but she came out of her bush and again followed the cow, while he walked alongside.

"I have been hunting for some birds," the stranger said kindly, "and I have lost my way, and need a friend very much. Don't be afraid," he added gallantly. "Speak up and tell me what your name is, and whether you think I can spend the night at your house, and go out gunning early in the morning."

Sylvia was more alarmed than before. Would not her grandmother consider her much to blame? But who could have foreseen such an accident as this? It did not seem to be her fault, and she hung her head as if the stem of it were broken, but managed to answer "Sylvy," with much effort when her companion again asked her name.

Mrs. Tilley was standing in the doorway when the trio came into view. The cow gave a loud moo by way of explanation.

"Yes, you'd better speak up for yourself, you old trial! Where'd she tucked herself away this time, Sylvy?" But Sylvia kept an awed silence; she knew by instinct that her grandmother did not comprehend the gravity of the situation. She must be mistaking the stranger for one of the farmer-lads of the region.

The young man stood his gun beside the door, and dropped a lumpy game-bag beside it; then he bade Mrs. Tilley good-evening, and repeated his wayfarer's story, and asked if he could have a night's lodging.

"Put me anywhere you like," he said. "I must be off early in the morning, before day; but I am very hungry, indeed. You can give me some milk at any rate, that's plain."

"Dear sakes, yes," responded the hostess, whose long slumbering hospitality seemed to be easily awakened. "You might fare better if you went out to the main road a mile or so, but you're welcome to what we've got. I'll milk right off, and you make yourself at home. You can sleep on husks or feathers," she proffered graciously. "I raised them all myself. There's good pasturing for geese just below here towards the ma'sh. Now step round and set a plate for the gentleman, Sylvy!" And Sylvia promptly stepped. She was glad to have something to do, and she was hungry herself.

It was a surprise to find so clean and comfortable a little dwelling in this New England wilderness. The young man had known the horrors of its most primitive housekeeping, and the dreary squalor of that level of society which does not rebel at the companionship of hens. This was the best thrift of an old-fashioned farmstead, though on such a small scale that it seemed like a hermitage. He listened eagerly to the old woman's quaint talk, he watched Sylvia's pale face and shining gray eyes with ever growing enthusiasm, and insisted that this was the best supper he had eaten for a month, and afterward the new-made friends sat down in the door-way together while the moon came up.

Soon it would be berry-time, and Sylvia was a great help at picking. The cow was a good milker, though a plaguy thing to keep track of, the hostess gossiped frankly, adding presently that she had buried four children, so Sylvia's mother, and a son (who might be dead) in California were all the children she had left. "Dan, my boy, was a great hand to go gunning," she explained sadly. "I never wanted for pa'tridges or gray squer'ls while he was to home. He's been a great wand'rer, I expect, and he's no hand to write letters. There, I don't blame him, I'd ha' seen the world myself if it had been so I could.

"Sylvy takes after him," the grandmother continued affectionately, after a minute's pause. "There ain't a foot o' ground she don't know her way over, and the wild creaturs counts her one o' themselves. Squer'ls she'll tame to come an' feed right out o' her hands, and all sorts o' birds. Last winter she got the jay-birds to bangeing here, and I believe she'd 'a' scanted herself of her own meals to have plenty to throw out amongst 'em, if I hadn't kep' watch. Anything but crows, I tell her, I'm willin' to help support—though Dan he had a tamed one o' them that did seem to have reason same as folks. It was round here a good spell after he went away. Dan an' his father they didn't hitch, but he never held up his head ag'in after Dan had dared him an' gone off."

The guest did not notice this hint of family sorrows in his eager interest in something else.

"So Sylvy knows all about birds, does she?" he exclaimed, as he looked round at the little girl who sat, very demure but increasingly sleepy, in the moonlight. "I am making a collection of birds myself. I have been at it ever since I was a boy." (Mrs. Tilley smiled.) "There are two or three very rare ones I have been hunting for these five years. I mean to get them on my own ground if they can be found."

"Do you cage 'em up?" asked Mrs. Tilley doubtfully, in response to this enthusiastic announcement.

"Oh no, they're stuffed and preserved, dozens and dozens of them," said the ornithologist, "and I have shot or snared every one myself. I caught a glimpse of a white heron a few miles from here on Saturday, and I have followed it in this direction. They have never been found in this district at all. The little white heron, it is," and he turned again to look at Sylvia with the hope of discovering that the rare bird was one of her acquaintances.

But Sylvia was watching a hop-toad in the narrow footpath.

"You would know the heron if you saw it," the stranger continued eagerly. "A queer tall white bird with soft feathers and long thin legs. And it would have a nest perhaps in the top of a high tree, made of sticks, something like a hawk's nest."

Sylvia's heart gave a wild beat; she knew that strange white bird, and had once stolen softly near where it stood in some bright green swamp grass, away over at the other side of the woods. There was an open place where the sunshine always seemed strangely yellow and hot, where tall, nodding rushes grew, and her grandmother had warned her that she might sink in the soft black mud underneath and never be heard of more. Not far beyond were the salt marshes just this side the sea itself, which Sylvia wondered and dreamed much about, but never had seen, whose great voice could sometimes be heard above the noise of the woods on stormy nights.

"I can't think of anything I should like so much as to find that heron's nest," the handsome stranger was saying. "I would give ten dollars to anybody who could show it to me," he added desperately, "and I mean to spend my whole vacation hunting for it if need be. Perhaps it was only migrating, or had been chased out of its own region by some bird of prey."

Mrs. Tilley gave amazed attention to all this, but Sylvia still watched the toad, not divining, as she might have done at some calmer time, that the creature wished to get to its hole under the door-step, and was much hindered by the unusual spectators at that hour of the evening.

No amount of thought, that night, could decide how many wished-for treasures the ten dollars, so lightly spoken of, would buy.

The next day the young sportsman hovered about the woods, and Sylvia kept him company, having lost her first fear of the friendly lad, who proved to be most kind and sympathetic. He told her many things about the birds and what they knew and where they lived and what they did with themselves. And he gave her a jack-knife, which she thought as great a treasure as if she were a desert-islander. All day long he did not once make her troubled or afraid except when he brought down some unsuspecting singing creature from its bough. Sylvia would have liked him vastly better without his gun; she could not understand why he killed the very birds he seemed to like so much. But as the day waned, Sylvia still watched the young man with loving admiration. She had never seen anybody so charming and delightful; the woman's heart, asleep in the child, was vaguely thrilled by a dream of love. Some premonition of that great power stirred and swayed these young creatures who traversed the solemn woodlands with soft-footed silent care. They stopped to listen to a bird's song; they pressed forward again eagerly, parting the branches—speaking to each other rarely and in whispers; the young man going first and Sylvia following, fascinated, a few steps behind, with her gray eyes dark with excitement.

She grieved because the longed-for white heron was elusive, but she did not lead the guest, she only followed, and there was no such thing as speaking first. The sound of her own unquestioned voice would have terrified her—it was hard enough to answer yes or no when there was need of that. At last evening began to fall, and they drove the cow home together, and Sylvia smiled with pleasure when they came to the place where she heard the whistle and was afraid only the night before.

II

Half a mile from home, at the farther edge of the woods, where the land was highest, a great pine-tree stood, the last of its generation. Whether it was left for a boundary mark, or for what reason, no one could say; the woodchoppers who had felled its mates were dead and gone long ago, and a whole forest of sturdy trees, pines and oaks and maples, had grown again. But the stately head of this old pine towered above them all and made a landmark for sea and shore miles and miles away. Sylvia knew it well. She had always believed that whoever climbed to the top of it could see the ocean; and the little girl had often laid her hand on the great rough trunk and looked up wistfully at those dark boughs that the wind always stirred, no matter how hot and still the air might be below. Now she thought of the tree with a new excitement, for why, if one climbed it at break of day, could not one see all the world, and easily discover from whence the white heron flew, and mark the place, and find the hidden nest?

What a spirit of adventure, what wild ambition! What fancied triumph and delight and glory for the later morning when she could make known the secret! It was almost too real and too great for the childish heart to bear.

All night the door of the little house stood open and the whippoor-wills came and sang upon the very step. The young sportsman and his old hostess were sound asleep, but Sylvia's great design kept her broad awake and watching. She forgot to think of sleep. The short summer night seemed as long as the winter darkness, and at last when the whip-poorwills ceased, and she was afraid the morning would after all come too soon, she stole out of the house and followed the pasture path through the woods, hastening toward the open ground beyond, listen-ing with a sense of comfort and companionship to the drowsy twitter of a half-awakened bird, whose perch she had jarred in passing. Alas, if the great wave of human interest which flooded for the first time this dull little life should sweep away the satisfactions of an existence heart to heart with nature and the dumb life of the forest!

There was the huge tree asleep yet in the paling moonlight, and small and silly Sylvia began with utmost bravery to mount to the top of it, with tingling, eager blood coursing the channels of her whole frame, with her bare feet and fingers, that pinched and held like bird's claws to the monstrous ladder reaching up, up, almost to the sky itself. First she must mount the white oak tree that grew alongside, where she was almost lost among the dark branches and the green leaves heavy and wet with dew; a bird fluttered off its nest, and a red squirrel ran to and fro and scolded pettishly at the harmless housebreaker. Sylvia felt her way easily. She had often climbed there, and knew that higher still one of the oak's upper branches chafed against the pine trunk, just where its lower boughs were set close together. There, when she made the dangerous pass from one tree to the other, the great enterprise would really begin.

She crept out along the swaying oak limb at last, and took the daring step across into the old pine-tree. The way was harder than she thought; she must reach far and hold fast, the sharp dry twigs caught and held her and scratched her like angry talons, the pitch made her thin little fingers clumsy and stiff as she went round and round the tree's great stem, higher and higher upward. The sparrows and robins in the woods below were beginning to wake and twitter to the dawn, yet it seemed much lighter there aloft in the pine-tree, and the child knew she must hurry if her project were to be of any use.

The tree seemed to lengthen itself out as she went up, and to reach farther and farther upward. It was like a great main-mast to the voyaging earth; it must truly have been amazed that morning through all its ponderous frame as it felt this determined spark of human spirit wending its way from higher branch to branch. Who knows how steadily the least twigs held themselves to advantage this light, weak creature on her way! The old pine must have loved his new dependent. More than all the hawks, and bats, and moths, and even the sweet voiced thrushes, was the brave, beating heart of the solitary gray-eyed child. And the tree stood still and frowned away the winds that June morning while the dawn grew bright in the east.

Sylvia's face was like a pale star, if one had seen it from the ground, when the last thorny bough was past, and she stood trembling and tired but wholly triumphant, high in the tree-top. Yes, there was the sea with the dawning sun making a golden dazzle over it, and toward that glorious east flew two hawks with slow-moving pinions. How low they looked in the air from that height when one had only seen them before far up, and dark against the blue sky. Their gray feathers were as soft as moths; they seemed only a little way from the tree, and Sylvia felt as if she too could go flying away among the clouds. Westward, the woodlands and farms reached miles and miles into the distance; here and there were church steeples, and white villages, truly it was a vast and awesome world.

The birds sang louder and louder. At last the sun came up bewilderingly bright. Sylvia could see the white sails of ships out at sea, and the clouds that were purple and rose-colored and yellow at first began to fade away. Where was the white heron's nest in the sea of green branches, and was this wonderful sight and pageant of the world the only reward for having climbed to such a giddy height? Now look down again, Sylvia, where the green marsh is set among the shining birches and dark hemlocks; there where you saw the white heron once you will see him again; look, look! A white spot of him like a single floating feather comes up from the dead hemlock and grows larger, and rises, and comes close at last, and goes by the landmark pine with steady sweep of wing and outstretched slender neck and crested head. And wait! Wait! Do not move a foot or a finger, little girl, do not send an arrow of light and consciousness from your two eager eyes, for the heron has perched on a pine bough not far beyond yours, and cries back to his mate on the nest and plumes his feathers for the new day!

The child gives a long sigh a minute later when a company of shouting cat-birds comes also to the tree, and vexed by their fluttering and lawlessness the solemn heron goes away. She knows his secret now, the wild, light, slender bird that floats and wavers, and goes back like an arrow presently to his home in the green world beneath. Then Sylvia, well satisfied, makes her perilous way down again, not daring to look far below the branch she stands on, ready to cry sometimes because her fingers ache and her lamed feet slip. Wondering over and over again what the stranger would say to her, and what he would think when she told him how to find his way straight to the heron's nest.

"Sylvy, Sylvy!" called the busy old grandmother again and again, but nobody answered, and the small husk bed was empty and Sylvia had disappeared.

The guest waked from a dream, and remembering his day's pleasure hurried to dress himself that it might sooner begin. He was sure from the way the shy little girl looked once or twice yesterday that she had at least seen the white heron, and now she must really be made to tell. Here she comes now, paler than ever, and her worn old frock is torn and tattered, and smeared with pine pitch. The grandmother and the sportsman stand in the door together and question her, and the splendid moment has come to speak of the dead hemlock-tree by the green marsh.

But Sylvia does not speak after all, though the old grandmother fretfully rebukes her, and the young man's kind, appealing eyes are looking straight in her own. He can make them rich with money; he has promised it, and they are poor now. He is so well worth making happy, and he waits to hear the story she can tell.

No, she must keep silence! What is it that suddenly forbids her and makes her dumb? Has she been nine years growing and now, when the great world for the first time puts out a hand to her, must she thrust it aside for a bird's sake? The murmur of the pine's green branches is in her ears, she remembers how the white heron came flying through the golden air and how they watched the sea and the morning together, and Sylvia cannot speak; she cannot tell the heron's secret and give its life away.

Dear loyalty, that suffered a sharp pang as the guest went away disappointed later in the day, that could have served and followed him and loved him as a dog loves! Many a night Sylvia heard the echo of his whistle haunting the pasture path as she came home with the loitering cow. She forgot even her sorrow at the sharp report of his gun and the sight of thrushes and sparrows dropping silent to the ground, their songs hushed and their pretty feathers stained and wet with blood. Were the birds better friends than their hunter might have been, who can tell? Whatever treasures were lost to her, woodlands and summertime, remember! Bring your gifts and graces and tell your secrets to this lonely country child!

"Trail's End"

SIGURD OLSON

Sigurd Olson (1899–1982), raised in northern Wisconsin, was a wilderness canoe guide, wilderness writer, and wilderness conservationist, eventually serving as president of the National Parks Association as well as president of the Wilderness Society. For decades, Olson fought to protect from logging, mining, and prospecting the pristine lake country of Quetico-Superior in the Minnesota/Canada border region, an area of rivers, lakes, and forests extending one hundred and fifty miles across the U.S.–Canadian border. His labor was rewarded just four years before his death with the passage of the Boundary Waters Canoe Area Wilderness Act of 1978. Olson also helped to draft the congressional Wilderness Act of 1964, which pledged to "secure for present and future generations the benefits of wilderness." He lived most of his adult life in Ely, Minnesota, near a one-hundred-mile canoe route. When he wasn't hiking or canoeing, he was writing, in a small cabin, personal, often lyrical prose meditations on the sounds, shadows, moods, and mysteries of the canoe country of northern Minnesota. Olson's nine nature books—which include *The Singing Wilderness* (1956), *Listening Point* (1958), and *Reflections from the North Country* (1976)—celebrate the beauty of the forgotten North Woods and its endangered wildlife and wetlands. In "Trail's End," one of his only fiction stories, the start of the hunting season in northern Minnesota's boundary waters finds a swamp buck and his mate pursued by a group of relentless market hunters and an equally determined pack of hungry wolves. Encouraging readers to identify with the hunted and not the hunter, Olson (himself a hunter) chose to publish his 1933 tale in *Sports Afield,* attracted by the outdoor magazine's then credo: "We believe in sane conservation, we oppose pollution, and stand for the enforcement of our game laws."

"Trail's End"

SIGURD OLSON

It was early morning in the northern wilderness, one of those rare breathless mornings, that come only in November, and though it was not yet light enough to see, the birds were stirring. A covey of partridge whirred up from their cozy burrows in the snow and lit in the top of a white birch, where they feasted noisily upon the frozen brown buds. The rolling tattoo of a downy woodpecker, also looking for his breakfast, reverberated again and again through the timber.

They were not the only ones astir however, for far down the trail leading from the Tamarack Swamp to Kennedy Lake browsed a big buck. He worked his way leisurely along, stopping now and then to scratch away the fresh snow and nibble daintily the still tender green things underneath. A large buck he was, even as deer run, and as smooth and sleek as good feeding could make him. His horns, almost too large, were queerly shaped, for instead of being rounded as in other deer, they were broad and palmate, the horns of a true swamp buck.

The eastern skyline was just beginning to tint with lavender as he reached the summit of the ridge overlooking the lake. He stopped for his usual morning survey of the landscape below him. For some reason, ever since his spike-buck days, he had always stopped there to look the country over before working down to water. He did not know that for countless generations before him, in the days when the pine timber stood tall and gloomy round the shores of the lake, other swamp bucks had also stopped, to scent the wind and listen, before going down to drink.

As he stood on the crest of the ridge, his gaze took in the long reaches of dark blue water far below him, the ice rimmed shores with long white windfalls reaching like frozen fingers out into the shallows, and the mottled green and gray of the brush covered slopes. His attention was finally centered on a little log cabin tucked away on the opposite shore in a clump of second growth spruce and balsam. Straight above it rose a thin wreath of pale blue smoke, almost as blue as the clear morning air. The metallic chuck, chuck of an axe ringing on a dry log came clearly across the water, and a breath of air brought to him strange odors that somehow filled him with a vague misgiving.

He was fascinated by the cabin and could not take his gaze from it. On other mornings, it had seemed as much a part of the shoreline as the trees themselves, but now it was different. A flood of almost forgotten memories surged back to him, of days long ago, when similar odors and sounds had brought with them a danger far greater than that of any natural enemy. He rubbed the top of a low hazel bush and stamped his forefeet nervously, undecided what to do. Then, in a flash, the full realization came to him. He understood the meaning of it all. This was the season of the year when man was no longer his friend, and it was not safe to be seen in the logging roads or in the open clearings near the log houses. He sniffed the air keenly a moment longer, to be sure, then snorted loudly as if to warn all the wilderness folk of their danger, and bounded back up the trail the way he had come.

Not until he had regained the heavy protecting timber of the Tamarack Swamp, north of Kennedy Lake, did he feel safe. What he had seen made him once again the wary old buck who had lived by his cunning and strength through many a hunting season. Although he was safe for the time being, he was too experienced not to know that, before many days had passed, the Tamarack Swamp would no longer be a haven of refuge.

As he worked deeper into the heavy moss hung timber, he stopped frequently to look into the shadows. The trail here was knee-deep in moss and criss-crossed by a labyrinth of narrow rabbit runways. Soon his search was rewarded, for a sleek yearling doe met him at a place where two trails crossed. After nosing each other tenderly, by way of recognition, they began feeding together on the tender shoots of blueberries and still green tufts of swamp grass underneath the protecting blanket of snow.

All that morning they fed leisurely and when the sun was high in the heavens, they worked cautiously over to the edge of the swamp. Here was a warm sunny opening hedged in by huge windfalls grown over with a dense tangle of blackberry vines. They often came here for their afternoon sunning, as the ice-encrusted ovals in the snow attested. Leaping a big windfall that guarded the entrance to the opening, they carefully examined the ground, then picked their beds close together.

There they rested contentedly with the warm sun shining upon them, little thinking that soon their peace would be broken.

The snow had fallen early that autumn and good feed had been scarce everywhere, except in the depths of the Tamarack Swamp, where the protecting timber had sheltered the grass and small green things. The plague had killed off most of the rabbits, and the few which survived were already forced to feed upon the bark of the poplar. The heavy crust, forming suddenly the night after the first heavy snow, had imprisoned countless partridge and grouse in their tunnels. As a result, small game was scarce and the wolves were lean and gaunt, although it was yet hardly winter. The stark famine months ahead gave promise of nothing but starvation and death, and the weird discordant music of the wolf pack had sounded almost every night since the last full moon.

The swamp buck and his doe had not as yet felt the pinch of hunger, but instinct told them to keep close to the shelter of the Tamarack Swamp, so except for the morning strolls of the buck to the shore of Kennedy Lake, they had seldom ventured far from the timber. They had often heard the wolf pack, but always so far away that there was little danger as long as they stayed under cover.

Several days had passed since the buck had been to the shore of Kennedy Lake. As yet the silence of the swamp had been unbroken except for the crunching of their own hoofs through the icy crust on the trails, and the buck was beginning to wonder if there was really anything to fear. Then one day, as they were again leisurely working their way over to the sunning place in the clearing, they were startled by the strange noises far toward the east end of the swamp. They stopped, every nerve on edge. At times they could hear them quite plainly, then again they would be so faint as to be almost indistinguishable from the other sounds of the forest.

The two deer were not much concerned at first. After satisfying themselves that there was no real danger, they started again down the trail toward the clearing. They could still hear the noises occasionally, but could not tell whether they were coming closer or going further away.

Then just as they neared the edge of the swamp, the sound of heavy footsteps seemed suddenly to grow louder and more distinct. Once more they stopped and stood with heads high, ears pricked up, listening intently. This time they were thoroughly alarmed. Closer and closer came the racket. Now they could hear distinctly the crunching of snow and the crackling of twigs, and then the whole east end of the timber seemed to be fairly alive with tumult, and the air reeked with danger.

The buck ran in a circle, sniffing keenly. The same scent that had come to him from the cabin, now rankled heavily in the air, and he knew the time had come to leave the shelter of the Tamarack Swamp. He hesitated, however, not knowing which way to turn. Back and forth he ran, stopping now and then to paw the ground, or to blow the air through his nostrils with the sharp whistling noise that all deer use when in danger.

A branch cracked sharply close at hand, and the scent came doubly strong from the east. With a wild snort the buck wheeled and led the way toward the western end of the swamp followed closely by the doe. Their only hope lay in reaching a heavy belt of green hemlock timber which they knew was separated from the western end of the Tamarack Swamp by a broad stretch of barren, burned-over slashing. As they neared the edge of the swamp they stopped, dreading to leave its protection. From where they stood they could see the dark wall of timber half a mile away. A brushy gully ran diagonally toward it across the open slashing, offering some protection, but the hills on either side were as stark and bare as an open field.

Again came the crack and crunch, now so close that the very air burned with danger. It was time to go. They bounded out of the timber, their white flags waving defiance, and were soon in the brush gully, going like the wind. Just as they sailed over a windfall, the buck caught a glimpse of something moving on a big black pine stump on top of the ridge to their right. Then the quiet was shattered by a succession of rending crashes and strange singing and whining sounds filled the air above them.

Again and again came the crashes. Suddenly the little doe stopped dead in her tracks. She gave a frightened baa-aa-a of pain and terror as the blood burst in a stream from a jagged wound in her throat. The buck stopped and ran back to where she stood, head down and swaying unsteadily. He watched her a moment, then, growing nervous, started down the trail again. The doe tried bravely to follow, but fell half way across a windfall too high for her to clear. Again the buck stopped and watched her anxiously. The snow by the windfall was soon stained bright red with blood, and the head of the little doe sank lower and lower in spite of her brave efforts to hold it up.

Hurriedly the buck looked about him. Several black figures were coming rapidly down the ridge. He nosed his doe gently, but this time she did not move. Raising his head he looked toward the approaching figures. Danger was close, but he could not leave his mate.

A spurt of smoke came from one of the figures, followed by another crash. This time the buck felt a blow so sharp that it made him stumble. Staggering to his feet, he plunged blindly down the gully. His flag was down, the sure sign of a wounded deer. Again and again came the crashes and the air above him whined and sang as the leaden pellets searched for their mark. The bark flew from a birch tree close by, spattering him with fragments. In spite of his wound, he ran swiftly and was soon out of range in the protecting green timber. He knew that he would not be tracked for at least an hour, as his pursuers would wait for him to lie down and stiffen.

He was bleeding badly from a long red scar cutting across his flank, and his back trail was sprinkled with tiny red dots. Where he stopped to rest and listen, little puddles of blood would form that quickly turned bluish black in the snow. For two hours he ran steadily, and then was so weakened by loss of blood that at last he was forced to lie down.

After a short rest, he staggered to his feet, stiffened badly. The bed he had melted in the snow was stained dark red from his bleeding flank. The cold, however, had contracted the wound and had stopped the bleeding a little. He limped painfully down the trail, not caring much which direction it led. Every step was torture. Once when crossing a small gully, he stumbled and fell on his wounded leg. It rested him to lie there, and it was all he could do to force himself on.

While crossing a ridge, the wind bore the man scent strongly to him, and he knew that now he was being trailed. Once, he heard the brush crack behind him, and was so startled that the wound was jerked open and the bleeding started afresh. He watched his back trail nervously, expecting to see his pursuer at any moment and hear again the rending crash that would mean death.

He grew steadily weaker and knew that unless night came soon, he would be overtaken. He had to rest more often now, and when he did move it was to stagger aimlessly down the trail, stumbling on roots and stubs. It was much easier now to walk around the windfalls, than to try to jump over as he had always done before.

The shadows were growing longer and longer, and in the hollows it was already getting dusk. If he could last until nightfall he would be safe. But the man scent was getting still stronger, and he realized at last that speed alone could not save him. Strategy was the only course. If this pursuer could be thrown off the trail, only long enough to delay him half an hour, darkness would be upon the wilderness and he could rest.

So waiting until the trail ran down onto a steep ravine filled with brush and windfalls, the buck suddenly turned and walked back on his own trail as far as he dared. It was the old trick of back tracking that deer have used for ages to elude their pursuers. Then stopping suddenly, he jumped as far to the side as his strength would permit, landing with all four feet tightly bunched together in the very center of a scrubby hazel bush. From there, he worked his way slowly into a patch of scrub spruce and lay down exhausted under an old windfall. Weakened as he was from loss of blood and from the throbbing pain in his flank, it was all he could do to keep his eyes riveted on his back trail, and his ears strained for the rustling and crunching that he feared would come, unless darkness came first.

It seemed that he had barely lain down, when without warning, the brush cracked sharply, and not 100 yards away appeared a black figure. The buck was petrified with terror. His ruse had failed. He shrank as far down as he could in the grass under the windfall and his eyes almost burst from their sockets. Frantically he thought of leaving his hiding place, but knew that would only invite death. The figure came closer and closer, bending low over the trail and peering keenly into the spruce thicket ahead. In the fading light the buck was well hidden by the windfall, but the blood spattered trail led straight to his hiding place. Discovery seemed certain.

The figure picked its way still nearer. It was now within 30 feet of the windfall. The buck watched, hardly daring to breathe. Then, in order to get a better view into the thicket, the hunter started to climb a snow covered stump close by. Suddenly, losing his balance, he slipped and plunged backwards into the snow. The buck saw his chance. Gathering all his remaining strength, he dashed out of his cover and was soon hidden in the thick growth of spruce.

It was almost dark now and he knew that as far as the hunter was concerned, he was safe. Circling slowly around, he soon found a sheltered hiding place in a dense clump of spruce where he could rest and allow his wound to heal.

Night came swiftly, bringing with it protection and peace. The stars came out one by one, and a full November moon climbed into the sky, flooding the snowy wilderness with its radiance.

Several hours had passed since the buck had lain down to rest in the spruce thicket. The moon was now riding high in the heavens and in the open places it was almost as light as day. Although well hidden, he dozed fitfully, waking at times with a start, thinking that again he was being trailed. He would then lie and listen, with nerves strained to the breaking point, for any sounds of the wild that might mean danger. An owl hooted over in a clump of timber, and the new forming ice on the shores of Kennedy Lake, half a mile away, rumbled ominously. Then he heard a long quavering call, so faint and far away that it almost blended with the whispering of the wind. The coarse hair on his shoulders bristled as he recognized the hunting call of the age-old enemy of his kind. It was answered again and again. The wolf pack was gathering, and for the first time in his life, the buck knew fear. In the shelter of the Tamarack Swamp there had been little danger, and even if he had been driven to the open, his strength and speed would have carried him far from harm. Now, sorely wounded and far from shelter, he would have hardly a fighting chance should the pack pick up his trail.

They were now running in full cry, having struck a trail in the direction of the big swamp far to the west. To the buck, the weird music was as a song of death. Circling and circling, for a time they seemed to draw no nearer. As yet he was not sure whether it was his own blood bespattered trail that they were unraveling, or that of some other one of his kind. Then, suddenly, the cries grew in fierceness and volume and sounded much closer than before. He listened spellbound as he finally realized the truth it was his own trail they were following. The fiendish chorus grew steadily louder and more venomous, and now had a new note of triumph in it that boded ill for whatever came in its way.

He could wait no longer and sprang to his feet. To his dismay, he was so stiffened and sore, that he could hardly take a step. Forcing himself on, he hobbled painfully through the poplar brush and clumps of timber in the direction of the lake. Small windfalls made him stumble, and having to walk around hummocks and hollows made progress slow and difficult. How he longed for his old strength and endurance. About two-thirds of the distance to the lake had been covered and already occasional glimpses of water appeared between the openings.

Suddenly the cries of the pack burst out in redoubled fury behind him, and the buck knew they had found his warm blood-stained bed. Plunging blindly on, he used every ounce of strength and energy that he had left, for now the end was only a matter of minutes. The water was his only hope, for by reaching that he would at least escape being torn to shreds by the teeth of the pack. He could hear them coming swiftly down the ridge behind him and every strange shadow he mistook for one of the gliding forms of his pursuers. They were now so close that he could hear their snarls and yapping. Then a movement caught his eye in the checkered moonlight. A long gray shape had slipped out of the darkness and was easily keeping pace with him. Another form crept in silently on the other side and both ran like phantoms with no apparent effort. He was terror stricken, but kept on desperately. Other ghost-like shapes filtered in from the timber, but still they did not close. The water was just ahead. They would wait till he broke from the brush that lined the shore. With a crash, he burst through the last fringe of alders and charged forward. As he did so, a huge gray form shot out of the shadows and launched itself at his throat. He saw the movement in time and caught the full force of the blow on his horns. A wild toss and the snarling shape splashed into the ice rimmed shallows. At the same instant the two that had been running alongside closed, one for his throat and the other for his hamstrings. The first he hit a stunning blow with his sharp front hoof, but as he did so the teeth of the other fastened on the tendon of his hind leg. A frantic leap loosened his hold and the buck half plunged and half slid over the ice into the waters of Kennedy Lake. Then the rest of the pack tore down to the beach with a deafening babble of snarls and howls, expecting to find their quarry down or at bay. When they realized that they had been outwitted, their anger was hideous and the air was rent with howls and yaps.

The cold water seemed to put new life into the buck and each stroke was stronger than the one before. Nevertheless, it was a long hard swim, and before he was half way across the benumbing cold had begun to tell. He fought on stubbornly, his breath coming in short, choking sobs and finally, after what seemed ages, touched the hard sandy bottom of the other shore. Dragging himself painfully out, he lay down exhausted in the snow. All sense of feeling had left his tortured body, but the steady lap, lap of the waves against the tinkling shore ice soothed him into sleep.

When he awoke, the sun was high in the heavens. For a long time he lay as in a stupor, too weak and sorely stiffened to move. Then with a mighty effort he struggled to his feet, and stood motionless, bracing himself unsteadily. Slowly his strength returned and leaving his bed, he picked his way carefully along the beach, until he struck the trail, down which he had so often come to drink. He followed it to the summit of the ridge overlooking the lake.

The dark blue waters sparkled in the sun, and the rolling spruce covered ridges were green as they had always been. Nothing had really changed, yet never again would it be the same. He was a stranger in the land of his birth, a lonely fugitive where once he had roamed at will, his only choice to leave forever the ancient range of his breed. For a time he wavered torn between his emotions, then finally turned to go. Suddenly an overwhelming desire possessed him, to visit again the place where last he had seen his mate. He worked slowly down the trail to the old Tamarack Swamp and did not stop until he came to the old meeting place deep in the shadows where the two trails crossed. For a long time he did not move, then turned and headed into the north to a new wilderness far from the old, a land as yet untouched, the range of the Moose and Caribou.

"The Old People"

WILLIAM FAULKNER

William Faulkner (1897–1962) was born in New Albany, Mississippi, but raised in nearby Oxford, the town where he learned how to fish and hunt, and on which he based the setting for his fictional Mississippi county, Yoknapatawpha. Faulkner's most celebrated novels, *The Sound and the Fury* (1929), *As I Lay Dying* (1930), *Light in August* (1932), and *Absalom, Absalom!* (1936), in addition to more than fifty short stories, take place in Yoknapatawpha, the original Chickasaw name for one of the Tallahatchie River's tributaries. "The Old People," "The Bear," and "Delta Autumn," three wilderness tales in Faulkner's interrelated story collection *Go Down, Moses* (1942), are each set against the backdrop of the slow environmental degradation of the Mississippi River Delta area—the destruction of its wetlands, undergrowth, and riverbanks brought about by the agricultural cannibalization of its native trees. Faulkner's hunting tales read like elegies, memorializing what his story "The Bear" describes as "that doomed wilderness whose edges were being constantly and punily gnawed at by men with plows and axes who feared it because it was wilderness." First appearing in 1940 in *Harper's Magazine*, "The Old People" also explores race, place, and the complex relation between them against the melancholy disappearance of the big woods and its majestic animals. The story's depiction of Mississippi's old-growth forest as a brooding, secret, tremendous presence that waits, watches, and breathes remains among the most lyrical wilderness descriptions in modern fiction. Faulkner took home the 1949 Nobel Prize in Literature, though he nearly missed the ceremony in Sweden, refusing to cancel his yearly hunt at a Mississippi Delta deer camp. As a teenager Faulkner had killed his first buck at a deer camp and, in a coming-of-age ritual, had his face consecrated with the animal's fresh blood.

"The Old People"

WILLIAM FAULKNER

I

At first there was nothing. There was the faint, cold, steady rain, the gray and constant light of the late November dawn, with the voices of the hounds converging somewhere in it and toward them. Then Sam Fathers, standing just behind the boy as he had been standing when the boy shot his first running rabbit with his first gun and almost with the first load it ever carried, touched his shoulder and he began to shake, not with any cold. Then the buck was there. He did not come into sight; he was just there, looking not like a ghost but as if all of light were condensed in him and he were the source of it, not only moving in it but disseminating it, already running, seen first as you always see the deer, in that split second after he has already seen you, already slanting away in that first soaring bound, the antlers even in that dim light look-ing like a small rocking-chair balanced on his head.

"Now," Sam Fathers said, "shoot quick, and slow."

The boy did not remember that shot at all. He would live to be eighty, as his father and his father's twin brother and their father in his turn had lived to be, but he would never hear that shot nor remember even the shock of the gun-butt. He didn't even remember what he did with the gun afterward. He was running. Then he was standing over the buck where it lay on the wet earth still in the attitude of speed and not looking at all dead, standing over it shaking and jerking, with Sam Fathers beside him again, extending the knife. "Don't walk up to him in front," Sam said. "If he ain't dead, he will cut you all to pieces with his feet. Walk up to him from behind and take him by the horn first, so you can hold his head down until you can jump away. Then slip your other hand down and hook your fingers in his nostrils."

The boy did that—drew the head back and the throat taut and drew Sam Fathers' knife across the throat and Sam stooped and dipped his hands in the hot smoking blood and wiped them back and forth across the boy's face. Then Sam's horn rang in the wet gray woods and again and again; there was a boiling wave of dogs about them, with

Tennie's Jim and Boon Hogganbeck whipping them back after each had had a taste of the blood, then the men, the true hunters—Walter Ewell whose rifle never missed, and Major de Spain and old General Compson and the boy's cousin, McCaslin Edmonds, grandson of his father's sister, sixteen years his senior and, since both he and McCaslin were only children and the boy's father had been nearing seventy when he was born, more his brother than his cousin and more his father than either—sitting their horses and looking down at them: at the old man of seventy who had been a Negro for two generations now but whose face and bearing were still those of the Chickasaw chief who had been his father; and the white boy of twelve with the prints of the bloody hands on his face, who had nothing to do now but stand straight and not let the trembling show.

"Did he do all right, Sam?" his cousin McCaslin said.

"He done all right," Sam Fathers said.

They were the white boy, marked forever, and the old dark man sired on both sides by savage kings, who had marked him, whose bloody hands had merely formally consecrated him to that which, under the man's tutelage, he had already accepted, humbly and joy-fully, with abnegation and with pride too; the hands, the touch, the first worthy blood which he had been found at last worthy to draw, joining him and the man forever, so that the man would continue to live past the boy's seventy years and then eighty years, long after the man himself had entered the earth as chiefs and kings entered it—the child, not yet a man, whose grandfather had lived in the same country and in almost the same manner as the boy himself would grow up to live, leaving his descendants in the land in his turn as his grandfather had done, and the old man past seventy whose grandfathers had owned the land long before the white men ever saw it and who had vanished from it now with all their kind, what of blood they left behind them running now in another race and for a while even in bondage and now drawing toward the end of its alien and irrevocable course, barren, since Sam Fathers had no children.

His father was Ikkemotubbe himself, who had named himself Doom. Sam told the boy about that—how Ikkemotubbe, old Isse-tibbeha's sister's son, had run away to New Orleans in his youth and returned seven years later with a French companion calling himself the Chevalier Soeur-Blonde de Vitry, who must have been the Ikkemotubbe of his family too and who was already addressing Ikkemotubbe as *Du Homme;*—returned, came home again, with his foreign Aramis and the quadroon slave woman who was to be Sam's mother, and a gold-laced hat and coat and a wicker wine-hamper containing a litter of month-old puppies and a gold snuff-box filled with a white powder resembling fine sugar. And how he was met at the River landing by three or four companions of his bachelor youth, and while the light of a smoking torch gleamed on the glittering braid of the hat and coat Doom squatted in the mud of the land and took one of the puppies from the hamper and put a pinch of the white powder on its tongue and the puppy died before the one who was holding it could cast it away. And how they returned to the Plantation where Issetibbeha, dead now, had been succeeded by his son, Doom's fat cousin Moketubbe, and the next day Moketubbe's eight-year-old son died suddenly and that afternoon, in the presence of Moketubbe and most of the others (the People, Sam Fathers called them) Doom produced another puppy from the wine-hamper and put a pinch of the white powder on its tongue and Moketubbe abdicated and Doom became in fact The Man which his French friend already called him. And how on the day after that, during the ceremony of accession, Doom pronounced a marriage between the pregnant quadroon and one of the slave men which he had just inherited (that was how Sam Fathers got his name, which in Chickasaw had been Had-Two-Fathers) and two years later sold the man and woman and the child who was his own son to his white neighbor, Carothers McCaslin.

That was seventy years ago. The Sam Fathers whom the boy knew was already sixty—a man not tall, squat rather, almost sedentary, flabby-looking though he actually was not, with hair like a horse's mane which even at seventy showed no trace of white and a face which showed no age until he smiled, whose only visible trace of Negro blood was a slight dullness of the hair and the fingernails, and something else which you did notice about the eyes, which you noticed because it was not always there, only in repose and not always then—something not in their shape nor pigment but in their expression, and the boy's cousin McCaslin told him what that was: not the heritage of Ham, not the mark of servitude but of bondage; the knowledge that for a while that part of his blood had been the blood of slaves. "Like an old lion or a bear in a cage," McCaslin said. "He was born in the cage and has been in it all his life; he knows nothing else. Then he smells something. It might be anything, any breeze blowing past anything and then into his nostrils. But there for a second was the hot sand or the cane-brake that he never even saw himself, might not even know if he did see it and probably does know he couldn't hold his own with it if he got back to it. But that's not what he smells then. It was the cage he smelled. He hadn't smelled the cage until that minute. Then the hot sand or the brake blew into his nostrils and blew away, and all he could smell was the cage. That's what makes his eyes look like that."

"Then let him go!" the boy cried. "Let him go!"

His cousin laughed shortly. Then he stopped laughing, making the sound that is. It had never been laughing. "His cage ain't McCaslin's," he said. "He was a wild man. When he was born, all his blood on both sides, except the little white part, knew things that had been tamed out of our blood so long ago that we have not only forgotten them, we have to live together in herds to protect ourselves from our own sources. He was the direct son not only of a warrior but of a chief. Then he grew up and began to learn things, and all of a sudden one day he found out that he had been betrayed, the blood of the warriors and chiefs had been betrayed. Not by his father," he added quickly. "He probably never held it against old Doom for selling him and his mother into slavery, because he probably believed the damage was already done before then and it was the same warriors' and chiefs' blood in him and Doom both that was betrayed through the black blood which his mother gave him. Not betrayed by the black blood and not wilfully betrayed by his mother, but betrayed by her all the same, who had bequeathed him not only the blood of slaves but even a little of the very blood which had enslaved it; himself his own battleground, the scene of his own vanquishment and the mausoleum of his defeat. His cage ain't us," McCaslin said. "Did you ever know anybody yet, even your father and Uncle Buddy, that ever told him to do or not do anything that he ever paid any attention to?"

That was true. The boy first remembered him as sitting in the door of the plantation blacksmith-shop, where he sharpened plow-points and mended tools and even did rough carpenter-work when he was not in the woods. And sometimes, even when the woods had not drawn him, even with the shop cluttered with work which the farm waited on, Sam would sit there, doing nothing at all for half a day or a whole one, and no man, neither the boy's father and twin uncle in their day nor his cousin McCaslin after he became practical though not yet titular master, ever to say to him, "I want this finished by sundown" or "Why wasn't this done yesterday?" And once each year, in the late fall, in November, the boy would watch the wagon, the hooped canvas top erected now, being loaded—the food, hams and sausage from the smokehouse, coffee and flour and molasses from the commissary, a whole beef killed just last night for the dogs until there would be meat in camp, the crate containing the dogs themselves, then the bedding, the guns, the horns and lanterns and axes, and his cousin McCaslin and Sam Fathers in their hunting clothes would mount to the seat and with Tennie's Jim sitting on the dog-crate they would drive away to Jefferson, to join Major de Spain and General Compson and Boon Hogganbeck and Walter Ewell and go on into the big bottom of the Tallahatchie where the deer and bear were, to be gone two weeks. But before the wagon was even loaded the boy would find that he could watch no longer. He would go away, running almost, to stand behind the corner where he could not see the wagon and nobody could see him, not crying, holding himself rigid except for the trembling, whispering to himself: "Soon now. Soon now. Just three more years" (or two more or one more) "and I will be ten. Then Cass said I can go."

White man's work, when Sam did work. Because he did nothing else: farmed no allotted acres of his own, as the other ex-slaves of old Carothers McCaslin did, performed no field-work for daily wages as the younger and newer Negroes did—and the boy never knew just how that had been settled between Sam and old Carothers, or perhaps with old Carothers' twin sons after him. For, although Sam lived among the Negroes, in a cabin among the other cabins in the quarters, and consorted with Negroes (what of consorting with anyone Sam did after the boy got big enough to walk alone from the house to the blacksmith-shop and then to carry a gun) and dressed like them and talked like them and even went with them to the Negro church now and then, he was still the son of that Chickasaw chief and the Negroes knew it. And, it seemed to the boy, not only Negroes. Boon Hogganbeck's grandmother had been a Chickasaw woman too, and although the blood had run white since and Boon was a white man, it was not chief's blood. To the boy at least, the difference was apparent immediately you saw Boon and Sam together, and even Boon seemed to know it was there—

even Boon, to whom in his tradition it had never occurred that anyone might be better born than himself. A man might be smarter, he admitted that, or richer (luckier, he called it) but not better born. Boon was a mastiff, absolutely faithful, dividing his fidelity equally between Major de Spain and the boy's cousin McCaslin, absolutely dependent for his very bread and dividing that impartially too between Major de Spain and McCaslin, hardy, generous, courageous enough, a slave to all the appetites and almost unratiocinative. In the boy's eyes at least it was Sam Fathers, the Negro, who bore himself not only toward his cousin McCaslin and Major de Spain but toward all white men, with gravity and dignity and without servility or recourse to that impenetrable wall of ready and easy mirth which Negroes sustain between themselves and white men, bearing himself toward his cousin McCaslin not only as one man to another but as an older man to a younger.

He taught the boy the woods, to hunt, when to shoot and when not to shoot, when to kill and when not to kill, and better, what to do with it afterward. Then he would talk to the boy, the two of them sitting beneath the close fierce stars on a summer hilltop while they waited for the hounds to bring the fox back within hearing, or beside a fire in the November or December woods while the dogs worked out a coon's trail along the creek, or fireless in the pitch dark and heavy dew of April mornings while they squatted beneath a turkey-roost. The boy would never question him; Sam did not react to questions. The boy would just wait and then listen and Sam would begin, talking about the old days and the People whom he had not had time ever to know and so could not remember (he did not remember ever having seen his father's face), and in place of whom the other race into which his blood had run supplied him with no substitute.

And as he talked about those old times and those dead and vanished men of another race from either that the boy knew, gradually to the boy those old times would cease to be old time and would become a part of the boy's present, not only as if they had happened yesterday but as if they were still happening, the men who walked through them actually walking in breath and air and casting an actual shadow on the earth they had not quitted. And more: as if some of them had not happened yet but would occur tomorrow, until at last it would seem to the boy that he himself had not come into existence yet, that none of his race nor the other subject race which his people had brought with them into the land had come here yet; that although it had been his grand-father's and then his father's and uncle's and was now his cousin's and some day would be his own land which he and Sam hunted over, their hold upon it actually was as trivial and without reality as the now faded and archaic script in the chancery book in Jefferson which allocated it to them and that it was he, the boy, who was the guest here and Sam Fathers' voice the mouthpiece of the host.

Until three years ago there had been two of them, the other a full-blood Chickasaw, in a sense even more incredibly lost than Sam Fathers. He called himself Jobaker, as if it were one word. Nobody knew his history at all. He was a hermit, living in a foul little shack at the forks of the creek five miles from the plantation and about that far from any other habitation. He was a market hunter and fisherman and he consorted with nobody, black or white; no Negro would even cross his path and no man dared approach his hut except Sam. And perhaps once a month the boy would find them in Sam's shop—two old men squatting on their heels on the dirt floor, talking in a mixture of negroid English and flat hill dialect and now and then a phrase of that old tongue which as time went on and the boy squatted there too listening, he began to learn. Then Jobaker died. That is, nobody had seen him in some time. Then one morning Sam was missing, nobody, not even the boy, knew when nor where, until that night when some Negroes hunting in the creek bottom saw the sudden burst of flame and approached. It was Jobaker's hut, but before they got anywhere near it, someone shot at them from the shadows beyond it. It was Sam who fired, but nobody ever found Jobaker's grave.

The next morning, sitting at breakfast with his cousin, the boy saw Sam pass the dining-room window and he remembered then that never in his life before had he seen Sam nearer the house than the blacksmith-shop. He stopped eating even; he sat there and he and his cousin both heard the voices from beyond the pantry door, then the door opened and Sam entered, carrying his hat in his hand but without knocking as anyone else on the place except a house servant would have done, entered just far enough for the door to close behind him and stood looking at neither of them—the Indian face above the n—— clothes, looking at something over their heads or at something not even in the room.

"I want to go," he said. "I want to go to the Big Bottom to live."

"To live?" the boy's cousin said.

"At Major de Spain's and your camp, where you go to hunt," Sam said. "I could take care of it for you all while you ain't there. I will build me a little house in the woods, if you rather I didn't stay in the big one."

"What about Isaac here?" his cousin said. "How will you get away from him? Are you going to take him with you?" But still Sam looked at neither of them, standing just inside the room with that face which showed nothing, which showed that he was an old man only when it smiled.

"I want to go," he said. "Let me go."

"Yes," the cousin said quietly. "Of course. I'll fix it with Major de Spain. You want to go soon?"

"I'm going now," Sam said. He went out. And that was all. The boy was nine then; it seemed perfectly natural that nobody, not even his cousin McCaslin, should argue with Sam. Also, since he was nine now, he could understand that Sam could leave him and their days and nights in the woods together without any wrench. He believed that he and Sam both knew that this was not only temporary but that the exigencies of his maturing, of that for which Sam had been training him all his life some day to dedicate himself, required it. They had settled that one night last summer while they listened to the hounds bringing a fox back up the creek valley; now the boy discerned in that very talk under the high, fierce August stars a presage, a warning, of this moment today. "I done taught you all there is of this settled country," Sam said. "You can hunt it good as I can now. You are ready for the Big Bottom now, for bear and deer. Hunter's meat," he said. "Next year you will be ten. You will write your age in two numbers and you will be ready to become a man. Your pa" (Sam always referred to the boy's cousin as his father, establishing even before the boy's orphanhood did that relation between them not of the ward to his guardian and kinsman and chief and head of his blood, but of the child to the man who sired his flesh and his thinking too) "promised you can go with us then." So the boy could understand Sam's going. But he couldn't understand why now, in March, six months before the moon for hunting.

"If Jobaker's dead like they say," he said, "and Sam hasn't got any-body but us at all kin to him, why does he want to go to the Big Bottom now, when it will be six months before we get there?"

"Maybe that's what he wants," McCaslin said. "Maybe he wants to get away from you a little while."

But that was all right. McCaslin and other grown people often said things like that and he paid no attention to them, just as he paid no attention to Sam saying he wanted to go to the Big Bottom to live. After all, he would have to live there for six months, because there would be no use in going at all if he was going to turn right around and come back. And, as Sam himself had told him, he already knew all about hunting in this settled country that Sam or anybody else could teach him. So it would be all right. Summer, then the bright days after the first frost, then the cold and himself on the wagon with McCaslin this time and the moment would come and he would draw the blood, the big blood which would make him a man, a hunter, and Sam would come back home with them and he too would have outgrown the child's pursuit of rabbits and 'possums. Then he too would make one before the winter fire, talking of the old hunts and the hunts to come as hunters talked.

So Sam departed. He owned so little that he could carry it. He walked. He would neither let McCaslin send him in the wagon, nor take a mule to ride. No one saw him go even. He was just gone one morning, the cabin which had never had very much in it, vacant and empty, the shop in which there never had been very much done, standing idle. Then November came at last, and now the boy made one—himself and his cousin McCaslin and Tennie's Jim, and Major de Spain and General Compson and Walter Ewell and Boon and old Uncle Ash to do the cooking, waiting for them in Jefferson with the other wagon, and the surrey in which he and McCaslin and General Compson and Major de Spain would ride.

Sam was waiting at the camp to meet them. If he was glad to see them, he did not show it. And if, when they broke camp two weeks later to return home, he was sorry to see them go, he did not show that either. Because he did not come back with them. It was only the boy who returned, returning solitary and alone to the settled familiar land, to follow for eleven months the childish business of rabbits and such while he waited to go back, having brought with him, even from his brief first sojourn, an unforgettable sense of the big woods—not a quality dangerous or particularly inimical, but profound, sentient, gigantic and brooding, amid which he had been permitted to go to and fro at will, unscathed, why he knew not, but dwarfed and, until he had drawn honorably blood worthy of being drawn, alien.

Then November, and they would come back. Each morning Sam would take the boy out to the stand allotted him. It would be one of the poorer stands of course, since he was only ten and eleven and twelve and he had never even seen a deer running yet. But they would stand there, Sam a little behind him and without a gun himself, as he had been standing when the boy shot the running rabbit when he was eight years old. They would stand there in the November dawns, and after a while they would hear the dogs. Sometimes the chase would sweep up and past quite close, belling and invisible; once they heard the two heavy reports of Boon Hogganbeck's old gun with which he had never killed anything larger than a squirrel and that sitting, and twice they heard the flat unreverberant clap of Walter Ewell's rifle, following which you did not even wait to hear his horn.

"I'll never get a shot," the boy said. "I'll never kill one."

"Yes you will," Sam said. "You wait. You'll be a hunter. You'll be a man."

But Sam wouldn't come out. They would leave him there. He would come as far as the road where the surrey waited, to take the riding horses back, and that was all. The men would ride the horses and Uncle Ash and Tennie's Jim and the boy would follow in the wagon with Sam, with the camp equipment and the trophies, the meat, the heads, the antlers, the good ones, the wagon winding on among the tremendous gums and cypresses and oaks where no axe save that of the hunter had ever sounded, between the impenetrable walls of cane and brier—the two changing yet constant walls just beyond which the wilderness whose mark he had brought away forever on his spirit even from that first two weeks seemed to lean, stooping a little, watching them and listening, not quite inimical because they were too small, even those such as Walter and Major de Spain and old General Compson who had killed many deer and bear, their sojourn too brief and too harmless to excite to that, but just brooding, secret, tremendous, almost inattentive.

Then they would emerge, they would be out of it, the line as sharp as the demarcation of a doored wall. Suddenly skeleton cotton- and corn-fields would flow away on either hand, gaunt and motionless beneath the gray rain; there would be a house, barns, fences, where the hand of man had clawed for an instant, holding, the wall of the wilderness behind them now, tremendous and still and seemingly impenetrable in the gray and fading light, the very tiny orifice through which they had emerged apparently swallowed up. The surrey would be waiting, his cousin McCaslin and Major de Spain and General Compson and Walter and Boon dismounted beside it. Then Sam would get down from the wagon and mount one of the horses and, with the others on a rope behind him, he would turn back. The boy would watch him for a while against that tall and secret wall, growing smaller and smaller against it, never looking back. Then he would enter it, returning to what the boy believed, and thought that his cousin McCaslin believed, was his loneliness and solitude.

II

So the instant came. He pulled trigger and Sam Fathers marked his face with the hot blood which he had spilled and he ceased to be a child and became a hunter and a man. It was the last day. They broke camp that afternoon and went out, his cousin and Major de Spain and General Compson and Boon on the horses, Walter Ewell and the Negroes in the wagon with him and Sam and his hide and antlers. There could have been (and were) other trophies in the wagon. But for him they did not exist, just as for all practical purposes he and Sam Fathers were still alone together as they had been that morning. The wagon wound and jolted between the slow and shifting yet constant walls from beyond and above which the wilderness watched them pass, less than inimical now and never to be inimical again since the buck still and forever leaped, the shaking gun-barrels coming constantly and forever steady at last, crashing, and still out of his instant of immortality the buck sprang, forever immortal; the wagon jolting and bouncing on, the moment of the buck, the shot, Sam Fathers and himself and the blood with which Sam had marked him forever one with the wilderness which had accepted him since Sam said that he had done all right, when suddenly Sam reined back and stopped the wagon and they all heard the unmistakable and unforgettable sound of a deer breaking cover.

Then Boon shouted from beyond the bend of the trail and while they sat motionless in the halted wagon, Walter and the boy already

reaching for their guns, Boon came galloping back, flogging his mule
with his hat, his face wild and amazed as he shouted down at them.
Then the other riders came around the bend, also spurring.

"Get the dogs!" Boon cried. "Get the dogs! If he had a nub on his
head, he had fourteen points! Laying right there by the road in that
pawpaw thicket! If I'd a knowed he was there, I could have cut his
throat with my pocket knife!"

"Maybe that's why he run," Walter said. "He saw you never had
your gun." He was already out of the wagon with his rifle. Then the
boy was out too with his gun, and the other riders came up and Boon
got off his mule somehow and was scrabbling and clawing among the
duffel in the wagon, still shouting, "Get the dogs! Get the dogs!" And
it seemed to the boy too that it would take them forever to decide what
to do—the old men in whom the blood ran cold and slow, in whom
during the intervening years between them and himself the blood had
become a different and colder substance from that which ran in him
and even in Boon and Walter.

"What about it, Sam?" Major de Spain said. "Could the dogs bring
him back?"

"We won't need the dogs," Sam said. "If he don't hear the dogs
behind him, he will circle back in here about sundown to bed."

"All right," Major de Spain said. "You boys take the horses. We'll
go on out to the road in the wagon and wait there." He and General
Compson and McCaslin got into the wagon and Boon and Walter and
Sam and the boy mounted the horses and turned back and out of the
trail. Sam led them for an hour through the gray and unmarked afternoon whose light was little different from what it had been at dawn and
which would become darkness without any graduation between. Then
Sam stopped them.

"This is far enough," he said. "He'll be coming upwind, and he
don't want to smell the mules." They tied the mounts in a thicket. Sam
led them on foot now, unpathed through the markless afternoon, the
boy pressing close behind him, the two others, or so it seemed to the
boy, on his heels. But they were not. Twice Sam turned his head slightly
and spoke back to him across his shoulder, still walking: "You got time.
We'll get there 'fore he does."

So he tried to go slower. He tried deliberately to decelerate the
dizzy rushing of time in which the buck which he had not even seen

was moving, which it seemed to him must be carrying the buck farther and farther and more and more irretrievably away from them even
though there were no dogs behind him now to make him run, even
though, according to Sam, he must have completed his circle now
and was heading back toward them. They went on; it could have been
another hour or twice that or less than half, the boy could not have said.
Then they were on a ridge. He had never been in here before and he
could not see that it was a ridge. He just knew that the earth had risen
slightly because the underbrush had thinned a little, the ground sloping
invisibly away toward a dense wall of cane. Sam stopped. "This is it,"
he said. He spoke to Walter and Boon: "Follow this ridge and you will
come to two crossings. You will see the tracks. If he crosses, it will be at
one of these three."

Walter looked about for a moment. "I know it," he said. "I've
even seen your deer. I was in here last Monday. He ain't nothing but a
yearling."

"A yearling?" Boon said. He was panting from the walking. His face
still looked a little wild. "If the one I saw was any yearling, I'm still in
kindergarten."

"Then I must have seen a rabbit," Walter said. "I always heard you
quit school altogether two years before the first grade."

Boon glared at Walter. "If you don't want to shoot him, get out of
the way," he said. "Set down somewhere. By God, I——"

"Ain't nobody going to shoot him standing here," Sam said quietly.

"Sam's right," Walter said. He moved, slanting the worn, silver-
colored barrel of his rifle downward to walk with it again. "A little
more moving and a little more quiet too. Five miles is still Hogganbeck
range, even if we wasn't downwind." They went on. The boy could still
hear Boon talking, though presently that ceased too. Then once more
he and Sam stood motionless together against a tremendous pin oak in
a little thicket, and again there was nothing. There was only the soaring
and sombre solitude in the dim light, there was the thin murmur of the
faint cold rain which had not ceased all day. Then, as if it had waited for
them to find their positions and become still, the wilderness breathed
again. It seemed to lean inward above them, above himself and Sam
and Walter and Boon in their separate lurking-places, tremendous,
attentive, impartial and omniscient, the buck moving in it somewhere,
not running yet since he had not been pursued, not frightened yet and

never fearsome but just alert also as they were alert, perhaps already circling back, perhaps quite near, perhaps conscious also of the eye of the ancient immortal Umpire. Because he was just twelve then, and that morning something had happened to him: in less than a second he had ceased forever to be the child he was yesterday. Or perhaps that made no difference, perhaps even a city-bred man, let alone a child, could not have understood it; perhaps only a country-bred one could comprehend loving the life he spills. He began to shake again.

"I'm glad it's started now," he whispered. He did not move to speak; only his lips shaped the expiring words: "Then it will be gone when I raise the gun——"

Nor did Sam. "Hush," he said.

"Is he that near?" the boy whispered. "Do you think——"

"Hush," Sam said. So he hushed. But he could not stop the shaking. He did not try, because he knew it would go away when he needed the steadiness—had not Sam Fathers already consecrated and absolved him from weakness and regret too?—not from love and pity for all which lived and ran and then ceased to live in a second in the very midst of splendor and speed, but from weakness and regret. So they stood motionless, breathing deep and quiet and steady. If there had been any sun, it would be near to setting now; there was a condensing, a densifying, of what he had thought was the gray and unchanging light until he realised suddenly that it was his own breathing, his heart, his blood—something, all things, and that Sam Fathers had marked him indeed, not as a mere hunter, but with something Sam had had in his turn of his vanished and forgotten people. He stopped breathing then; there was only his heart, his blood, and in the following silence the wilderness ceased to breathe also, leaning, stooping overhead with its breath held, tremendous and impartial and waiting. Then the shaking stopped too, as he had known it would, and he drew back the two heavy hammers of the gun.

Then it had passed. It was over. The solitude did not breathe again yet; it had merely stopped watching him and was looking somewhere else, even turning its back on him, looking on away up the ridge at another point, and the boy knew as well as if he had seen him that the buck had come to the edge of the cane and had either seen or scented them and faded back into it. But the solitude did not breathe again. It should have suspired again then but it did not. It was still facing, watching, what it had been watching and it was not here, not where he and Sam stood; rigid, not breathing himself, he thought, cried *No! No!*, knowing already that it was too late, thinking with the old despair of two and three years ago: *I'll never get a shot.* Then he heard it—the flat single clap of Walter Ewell's rifle which never missed. Then the mellow sound of the horn came down the ridge and something went out of him and he knew then he had never expected to get the shot at all.

"I reckon that's it," he said. "Walter got him." He had raised the gun slightly without knowing it. He lowered it again and had lowered one of the hammers and was already moving out of the thicket when Sam spoke.

"Wait."

"Wait?" the boy cried. And he would remember that—how he turned upon Sam in the truculence of a boy's grief over the missed opportunity, the missed luck. "What for? Don't you hear that horn?"

And he would remember how Sam was standing. Sam had not moved. He was not tall, squat rather and broad, and the boy had been growing fast for the past year or so and there was not much difference between them in height, yet Sam was looking over the boy's head and up the ridge toward the sound of the horn and the boy knew that Sam did not even see him; that Sam knew he was still there beside him but he did not see the boy. Then the boy saw the buck. It was coming down the ridge, as if it were walking out of the very sound of the horn which related its death. It was not running, it was walking, tremendous, unhurried, slanting and tilting its head to pass the antlers through the undergrowth, and the boy standing with Sam beside him now instead of behind him as Sam always stood, and the gun still partly aimed and one of the hammers still cocked.

Then it saw them. And still it did not begin to run. It just stopped for an instant, taller than any man, looking at them; then its muscles suppled, gathered. It did not even alter its course, not fleeing, not even running, just moving with that winged and effortless ease with which deer move, passing within twenty feet of them, its head high and the eye not proud and not haughty but just full and wild and unafraid, and Sam standing beside the boy now, his right arm raised at full length, palm-outward, speaking in that tongue which the boy had learned from listening to him and Joe Baker in the blacksmith-shop, while up the ridge Walter Ewell's horn was still blowing them into a dead buck.

"Oleh, Chief," Sam said. "Grandfather."

When they reached Walter, he was standing with his back toward them, quite still, bemused almost, looking down at his feet. He didn't look up at all.

"Come here, Sam," he said quietly. When they reached him he still did not look up, standing above a little spike buck which had still been a fawn last spring. "He was so little I pretty near let him go," Walter said. "But just look at the track he was making. It's pretty near big as a cow's. If there were any more tracks here besides the ones he is laying in, I would swear there was another buck here that I never even saw."

III

It was dark when they reached the road where the surrey waited. It was turning cold, the rain had stopped, and the sky was beginning to blow clear. His cousin and Major de Spain and General Compson had a fire going. "Did you get him?" Major de Spain said.

"Got a good-sized swamp-rabbit with spike horns," Walter said. He slid the little buck down from his mule. The boy's cousin McCaslin looked at it.

"Nobody saw the big one?" he said.

"I don't even believe Boon saw it," Walter said. "He probably jumped somebody's straw cow in that thicket." Boon started cursing, swearing at Walter and at Sam for not getting the dogs in the first place and at the buck and all.

"Never mind," Major de Spain said. "He'll be here for us next fall. Let's get started home."

It was after midnight when they let Walter out at his gate two miles from Jefferson and later still when they took General Compson to his house and then returned to Major de Spain's, where he and McCaslin would spend the rest of the night, since it was still seventeen miles home. It was cold, the sky was clear now; there would be a heavy frost by sunup and the ground was already frozen beneath the horses' feet and the wheels and beneath their own feet as they crossed Major de Spain's yard and entered the house, the warm dark house, feeling their way up the dark stairs until Major de Spain found a candle and lit it, and into the strange room and the big deep bed, the still cold sheets until they began to warm to their bodies and at last the shaking stopped and suddenly he was telling McCaslin about it while McCaslin listened, quietly until he had finished. "You don't believe it," the boy said. "I know you don't——"

"Why not?" McCaslin said. "Think of all that has happened here, on this earth. All the blood hot and strong for living, pleasuring, that has soaked back into it. For grieving and suffering too, of course, but still getting something out of it for all that, getting a lot out of it, because after all you don't have to continue to bear what you believe is suffering; you can always choose to stop that, put an end to that. And even suffering and grieving is better than nothing; there is only one thing worse than not being alive, and that's shame. But you can't be alive forever, and you always wear out life long before you have exhausted the possibilities of living. And all that must be somewhere; all that could not have been invented and created just to be thrown away. And the earth is shallow; there is not a great deal of it before you come to the rock. And the earth don't want to just keep things, hoard them; it wants to use them again. Look at the seed, the acorns, at what happens even to carrion when you try to bury it: it refuses too, seethes and struggles too until it reaches light and air again, hunting the sun still. And they—" the boy saw his hand in silhouette for a moment against the window beyond which, accustomed to the darkness now, he could see sky where the scoured and icy stars glittered "—they don't want it, need it. Besides, what would it want, itself, knocking around out there, when it never had enough time about the earth as it was, when there is plenty of room about the earth, plenty of places still unchanged from what they were when the blood used and pleasured in them while it was still blood?"

"But we want them," the boy said. "We want them too. There is plenty of room for us and them too."

"That's right," McCaslin said. "Suppose they don't have substance, can't cast a shadow——"

"But I saw it!" the boy cried. "I saw him!"

"Steady," McCaslin said. For an instant his hand touched the boy's flank beneath the covers. "Steady. I know you did. So did I. Sam took me in there once after I killed my first deer."

"The Hunter's Wife"

ANTHONY DOERR

Anthony Doerr (b. 1973) is the author of a memoir, two collections of short stories, and three novels. From the beginning of his career Doerr's fiction has been widely recognized for its originality. His individual essays and stories to date have won five O. Henry Prizes and four Pushcart Prizes; his first short-story collection, *The Shell Collector* (2002), received the Barnes & Noble Discover Prize and the New York Public Library's Young Lions Fiction Award; his second collection, *Memory Wall* (2010), was awarded The Story Prize; and his most famous work, *All the Light We Cannot See* (2014), won the Pulitzer Prize for Fiction and the Andrew Carnegie Medal for Excellence in Fiction. Doerr's most recent novel, *Cloud Cuckoo Land* (2021), continues the themes of natural history, human frailty, and species connection that shape much of his storytelling. Across local, international, and even cosmic settings, Doerr writes like a naturalist, crafting expressive story environments memorable for their descriptive beauty. From seashores to forests, mountains to stars, his fiction explores how powerfully wild places and wild things define us. Doerr has said that his 2001 story "The Hunter's Wife" (an O. Henry Prize winner) was born out of his interest in animals that hibernate and a particular curiosity about them: Do hibernating animals dream? The remote Montana river valley in "The Hunter's Wife" invites our simultaneous identification with the hunter and the hunted, bringing us deep inside a border wilderness where animal and human, life and death, are not so far apart. Doerr currently resides in Boise, Idaho, with his wife and twin sons.

"The Hunter's Wife"

ANTHONY DOERR

It was the hunter's first time outside of Montana. He woke, stricken still with the hours-old vision of ascending through rose-lit cumulus, of houses and barns like specks deep in the snowed-in valleys, all the scrolling country below looking December—brown and black hills streaked with snow, flashes of iced-over lakes, the long braids of a river gleaming at the bottom of a canyon. Above the wing the sky had deepened to a blue so pure he knew it would bring tears to his eyes if he looked long enough.

Now it was dark. The airplane descended over Chicago, its galaxy of electric lights, the vast neighborhoods coming clearer as the plane glided toward the airport—streetlights, headlights, stacks of buildings, ice rinks, a truck turning at a stoplight, scraps of snow atop a warehouse and winking antennae on faraway hills, finally the long converging parallels of blue runway lights, and they were down.

He walked into the airport, past the banks of monitors. Already he felt as if he'd lost something, some beautiful perspective, some lovely dream fallen away. He had come to Chicago to see his wife, whom he had not seen in twenty years. She was there to perform her magic for a higher-up at the state university. Even universities, apparently, were interested in what she could do.

Outside the terminal the sky was thick and gray and hurried by wind. Snow was coming. A woman from the university met him and escorted him to her Jeep. He kept his gaze out the window.

They were in the car for forty-five minutes, passing first the tall, lighted architecture of downtown, then naked suburban oaks, heaps of ploughed snow, gas stations, power towers, and telephone wires. The woman said, So you regularly attend your wife's performances?

No, he said. Never before.

She parked in the driveway of an elaborate and modern mansion with square balconies suspended at angles over two trapezoidal garages, huge triangular windows in the facade, sleek columns, domed lights, a steep shale roof.

Inside the front door about thirty name tags were laid out on a table. His wife was not there yet. No one, it seemed, was there yet. He found his tag and pinned it to his sweater. A silent girl in a tuxedo appeared and disappeared with his coat.

The foyer was all granite, flecked and smooth, backed with a grand staircase that spread wide at the bottom and tapered at the top. A woman came down. She stopped four or five steps from the bottom and said, Hello, Anne, to the woman who had driven him there and, You must be Mr. Dumas, to him. He took her hand, a pale bony thing, weightless, like a featherless bird.

Her husband, the university's chancellor, was just knotting his bow tie, she said, and laughed sadly to herself, as if bow ties were something she disapproved of. Beyond the foyer spread a vast parlor, high-windowed and carpeted. The hunter moved to a bank of windows, shifted aside the curtain, and peered out.

In the poor light he could see a wooden deck encompassing the length of the house, angled and stepped, never the same width, with a low rail. Beyond it, in the blue shadows, a small pond lay encircled by hedges, with a marble birdbath at its center. Behind the pond stood leafless trees—oaks, maples, a sycamore white as bone. A helicopter shuttled past, winking a green light.

It's snowing, he said.

Is it? asked the hostess, with an air of concern, perhaps false. It was impossible to tell what was sincere and what was not. The woman who drove him there had moved to the bar where she cradled a drink and stared into the carpet.

He let the curtain fall back. The chancellor came down the staircase. Other guests fluttered in. A man in gray corduroy, with BRUCE MAPLES on his name tag, approached him. Mr. Dumas, he said, your wife isn't here yet?

You know her? the hunter asked.

Oh no, Maples said, and shook his head. No I don't. He spread his legs and swiveled his hips as if stretching before a foot race. But I've read about her.

The hunter watched as a tall, remarkably thin man stepped through the front door. Hollows behind his jaw and beneath his eyes made him appear ancient and skeletal—as if he were visiting from some other leaner world. The chancellor approached the thin man, embraced him, and held him for a moment.

That's President O'Brien, Maples said. A famous man, actually, to people who follow those sorts of things. So terrible, what happened to his family. Maples stabbed the ice in his drink with his straw.

The hunter nodded, unsure of what to say. For the first time he began to think he should not have come.

Have you read your wife's books? Maples asked.

The hunter nodded.

In her poems her husband is a hunter.

I guide hunters. He was looking out the window to where snow was settling on the hedges.

Does that ever bother you?

What?

Killing animals. For a living, I mean.

The hunter watched snowflakes disappear as they touched the window. Was that what hunting meant to people? Killing animals? He put his fingers to the glass. No, he said. It doesn't bother me.

The hunter met his wife in Great Falls, Montana, in the winter of 1972. That winter arrived immediately, all at once—you could watch it come. Twin curtains of white appeared in the north, white all the way to the sky, driving south like the end of all things. They drove the wind before them and it ran like wolves, like floodwater through a cracked dike. Cattle galloped the fence-lines, bawling. Trees toppled; a barn roof tumbled over the highway. The river changed directions. The wind flung thrushes screaming into the gorge and impaled them on the thorns in grotesque attitudes.

She was a magician's assistant, beautiful, sixteen years old, an orphan. It was not a new story: a glittery red dress, long legs, a traveling magic show performing in the meeting hall at the Central Christian Church. The hunter had been walking past with an armful of groceries when the wind stopped him in his tracks and drove him into the alley behind the church. He had never felt such wind; it had him pinned. His face was pressed against a low window, and through it he could see the show. The magician was a small man in a dirty blue cape. Above him a sagging banner read THE GREAT VESPUCCI. But the hunter watched only the girl; she was graceful, young, smiling. Like a wrestler the wind held him against the window.

The magician was buckling the girl into a plywood coffin that was painted garishly with red and blue bolts of lightning. Her neck and head stuck out one end, her ankles and feet the other. She beamed; no one had ever before smiled so broadly at being locked into a coffin. The magician started up an electric saw and brought it noisily down through the center of the box, sawing her in half. Then he wheeled her apart, her legs going one way, her torso another. Her neck fell back, her smile waned, her eyes showed only white. The lights dimmed. A child screamed. Wiggle your toes, the magician ordered, flourishing his magic wand, and she did; her disembodied toes wiggled in glittery high-heeled pumps. The audience squealed with delight.

The hunter watched her pink fine-boned face, her hanging hair, her outstretched throat. Her eyes caught the spotlight. Was she looking at him? Did she see his face pressed against the window, the wind slashing at his neck, the groceries—onions, a sack of flour—tumbled to the ground around his feet? Her mouth flinched; was it a smile, a flicker of greeting?

She was beautiful to him in a way that nothing else had ever been beautiful. Snow blew down his collar and drifted around his boots. The wind had fallen off but the snow came hard and still the hunter stood riveted at the window. After some time the magician rejoined the severed box halves, unfastened the buckles, and fluttered his wand, and she was whole again. She climbed out of the box and curtsied in her glittering slit-legged dress. She smiled as if it were the Resurrection itself.

Then the storm brought down a pine tree in front of the courthouse and the power winked out, streetlight by streetlight, all over town. Before she could move, before ushers began escorting the crowd out with flashlights, the hunter was slinking into the hall, making for the stage, calling for her.

He was thirty years old, twice her age. She smiled at him, leaned over from the dais in the red glow of the emergency exit lights and shook her head. Show's over, she said. In his pickup he trailed the magician's van through the blizzard to her next show, a library fundraiser in Butte. The next night he followed her to Missoula. He rushed to the stage after each performance. Just eat dinner with me, he'd plead. Just tell me your name. It was hunting by persistence. She said yes in Bozeman. Her name was plain, Mary Roberts. They had rhubarb pie in a hotel restaurant.

I know how you do it, he said. The feet in the sawbox are dummies. You hold your legs against your chest and wiggle the dummy feet with a string.

She laughed. Is that what you do? she asked. Follow a girl to four towns to tell her her magic isn't real?

No, he said. I hunt.

You hunt. And when you're not hunting?

I dream about hunting. She laughed again. It's not funny, he said.

You're right, she said, and smiled. It's not funny. I'm that way with magic. I dream about it. I dream about it all the time. Even when I'm not asleep.

He looked into his plate, thrilled. He searched for something he might say. They ate. But I dream bigger dreams, you know, she said afterward, after she had eaten two pieces of pie, carefully, with a spoon. Her voice was quiet and serious. I have magic inside of me. I'm not going to get sawed in half by Tony Vespucci all my life.

I don't doubt it, the hunter said.

I knew you'd believe me, she said.

But the next winter Vespucci brought her back to Great Falls and sawed her in half in the same plywood coffin. And the winter after that. After both performances the hunter took her to the Bitterroot Diner where he watched her eat two pieces of pie. The watching was his favorite part: a hitch in her throat as she swallowed, the way the spoon slid cleanly out from her lips, the way her hair fell over her ear.

Then she was eighteen, and after pie she let him drive her to his cabin, forty miles from Great Falls, up the Missouri, then east into the Smith River valley. She brought only a small vinyl purse. The truck skidded and sheered as he steered it over the unplowed roads, fishtailing in the deep snow, but she didn't seem afraid or worried about where he might be taking her, about the possibility that the truck might sink in a drift, that she might freeze to death in her peacoat and glittery magician's-assistant dress. Her breath plumed out in front of her. It was twenty degrees below zero. Soon the roads would be snowed over, impassable until spring.

At his one-room cabin with furs and old rifles on the walls, he unbolted the crawlspace and showed her his winter hoard: a hundred smoked trout, skinned pheasant, and venison quarters hanging frozen from hooks. Enough for two of me, he said. She scanned his books over the fireplace, a monograph on grouse habits, a series of journals on upland game birds, a thick tome titled simply *Bear*. Are you tired? he asked. Would you like to see something? He gave her a snowsuit, strapped her boots into a pair of leather snowshoes, and took her to hear the grizzly.

She wasn't bad on snowshoes, a little clumsy. They went creaking over wind-scalloped snow in the nearly unbearable cold. The bear denned every winter in the same hollow cedar, the top of which had been shorn off by a storm. Black, three-fingered, and huge, in the starlight it resembled a skeletal hand thrust up from the ground, a ghoulish visitor scrabbling its way out of the underworld.

They knelt. Above them the stars were knife points, hard and white. Put your ear here, he whispered. The breath that carried his words crystallized and blew away, as if the words themselves had taken on form but expired from the effort. They listened, face-to-face, their ears over woodpecker holes in the trunk. She heard it after a minute, tuning her ears into something like a drowsy sigh, a long exhalation of slumber. Her eyes widened. A full minute passed. She heard it again.

We can see him, he whispered, but we have to be dead quiet. Grizzlies are light hibernators. Sometimes all you do is step on twigs outside their dens and they're up.

He began to dig at the snow. She stood back, her mouth open, eyes wide. Bent at the waist, he bailed snow back through his legs. He dug down three feet and then encountered a smooth icy crust covering a large hole in the base of the tree. Gently he dislodged plates of ice and lifted them aside. The opening was dark, as if he'd punched through to some dark cavern, some netherworld. From the hole the smell of bear came to her, like wet dog, like wild mushrooms. The hunter removed some leaves. Beneath was a shaggy flank, a brown patch of fur.

He's on his back, the hunter whispered. This is his belly. His forelegs must be up here somewhere. He pointed to a place higher on the trunk.

She put one hand on his shoulder and knelt in the snow above the den. Her eyes were wide and unblinking. Her jaw hung open. Above her shoulder a star separated itself from the galaxy and melted through the sky. I want to touch him, she said. Her voice sounded loud and out of place in that wood, under the naked cedars.

Hush, he whispered. He shook his head no. You have to speak quietly.

Just for a minute.

No, he hissed. You're crazy. He tugged at her arm. She removed the mitten from her other hand with her teeth and reached down. He pulled at her again but lost his footing and fell back, clutching an empty mitten. As he watched, horrified, she turned and placed both hands, spread-fingered, in the thick shag of the bear's chest. Then she lowered her face, as if drinking from the snowy hollow, and pressed her lips to the bear's chest. Her entire head was inside the tree. She felt the soft, silver tips of its fur brush her cheeks. Against her nose one huge rib flexed slightly. She heard the lungs fill and then empty. She heard blood slug through veins.

Want to know what he dreams? she asked. Her voice echoed up through the tree and poured from the shorn ends of its hollowed branches. The hunter took his knife from his coat. Summer, her voice echoed. Blackberries. Trout. Dredging his flanks across river pebbles.

I'd have liked, she said later, back in the cabin as he built up the fire, to crawl all the way down there with him. Get into his arms. I'd grab him by the ears and kiss him on the eyes.

The hunter watched the fire, the flames cutting and sawing, each log a burning bridge. Three years he had waited for this. Three years he had dreamed this girl by his fire. But somehow it had ended up different from what he had imagined; he had thought it would be like a hunt—like waiting hours beside a wallow with his rifle barrel on his pack to see the huge antlered head of a bull elk loom up against the sky, to hear the whole herd behind him inhale, then scatter down the hill. If you had your opening you shot and walked the animal down and that was it. All the uncertainty was over. But this felt different, as if he had no choices to make, no control over any bullet he might let fly or hold back. It was exactly as if he was still three years younger, stopped outside the Central Christian Church and driven against a low window by the wind or some other, greater force.

Stay with me, he whispered to her, to the fire. Stay the winter.

Bruce Maples stood beside him jabbing the ice in his drink with his straw.

I'm in athletics, Bruce offered. I run the athletic department here.

You mentioned that.

Did I? I don't remember. I used to coach track. Hurdles.

Hurdles, the hunter repeated.

You bet.

The hunter studied him. What was Bruce Maples doing here? What strange curiosities and fears drove him, drove any of these people filing now through the front door, dressed in their dark suits and black gowns? He watched the thin, stricken man, President O'Brien, as he stood in the corner of the parlor. Every few minutes a couple of guests made their way to him and took O'Brien's hands in their own.

You probably know, the hunter told Maples, that wolves are hurdlers. Sometimes the people who track them will come to a snag and the prints will disappear. As if the entire pack just leaped into a tree and vanished. Eventually they'll find the tracks again, thirty or forty feet away. People used to think it was magic—flying wolves. But all they did was jump. One great coordinated leap.

Bruce was looking around the room. Huh, he said. I wouldn't know about that.

She stayed. The first time they made love, she shouted so loudly that coyotes climbed onto the roof and howled down the chimney. He rolled off her, sweating. The coyotes coughed and chuckled all night, like children chattering in the yard, and he had nightmares. Last night you had three dreams and you dreamed you were a wolf each time, she whispered. You were mad with hunger and running under the moon.

Had he dreamed that? He couldn't remember. Maybe he talked in his sleep.

In December it never got warmer than fifteen below. The river froze—something he'd never seen. Christmas Eve he drove all the way to Helena to buy her figure skates. In the morning they wrapped themselves head to toe in furs and went out to skate the river. She held him by the hips and they glided through the blue dawn, skating hard up the frozen coils and shoals, beneath the leafless alders and cottonwoods, only the bare tips of creek willow showing above the snow. Ahead of them vast white stretches of river faded on into darkness. An owl hunkered on a branch and watched them with its huge eyes. Merry Christmas, Owl! she shouted into the cold. It spread its huge wings, dropped from the branch, and disappeared into the forest.

In a wind-polished bend they came upon a dead heron, frozen by its ankles into the ice. It had tried to hack itself out, hammering with its beak first at the ice entombing its feet and then at its own thin and scaly legs. When it finally died, it died upright, wings folded back, beak parted in some final, desperate cry, legs rooted like twin reeds in the ice.

She fell to her knees and knelt before the bird. Its eye was frozen and cloudy. It's dead, the hunter said, gently. Come on. You'll freeze too.

No, she said. She slipped off her mitten and closed the heron's beak in her fist. Almost immediately her eyes rolled back in her head. Oh wow, she moaned. I can *feel* her. She stayed like that for whole minutes, the hunter standing over her, feeling the cold come up his legs, afraid to touch her as she knelt before the bird. Her hand turned white and then blue in the wind.

Finally she stood. We have to bury it, she said. He chopped the bird out with his skate and buried it in a drift.

That night she lay stiff and would not sleep. It was just a bird, he said, unsure of what was bothering her but bothered by it himself. We can't do anything for a dead bird. It was good that we buried it, but tomorrow something will find it and dig it out.

She turned to him. Her eyes were wide; he remembered how they had looked when she put her hands on the bear. When I touched her, she said, I saw where she went.

What?

I saw where she went when she died. She was on the shore of a lake with other herons, a hundred others, all facing the same direction, and they were wading among stones. It was dawn and they watched the sun come up over the trees on the other side of the lake. I saw it as clearly as if I was there.

He rolled onto his back and watched shadows shift across the ceiling. Winter is getting to you, he said. In the morning he resolved to make sure she went out every day. It was something he'd long believed: go out every day in winter or your mind will slip. Every winter the paper was full of stories about ranchers' wives, snowed in and crazed with cabin fever, who had dispatched their husbands with cleavers or awls.

The next night he drove her all the way north to Sweetgrass, on the Canadian border, to see the northern lights. Great sheets of violet, amber, and pale green rose from the distances. Shapes like the head of a falcon, a scarf, and a wing rippled above the mountains. They sat in the truck cab, the heater blowing on their knees. Behind the aurora the Milky Way burned.

That one's a hawk! she exclaimed.

Auroras, he explained, occur because of Earth's magnetic field. A wind blows all the way from the sun and gusts past the earth, moving charged particles around. That's what we see. The yellow-green stuff is oxygen. The red and purple at the bottom there is nitrogen.

No, she said, shaking her head. The red one's a hawk. See his beak? See his wings?

Winter threw itself at the cabin. He took her out every day. He showed her a thousand ladybugs hibernating in an orange ball hung in a river-bank hollow; a pair of dormant frogs buried in frozen mud, their blood crystallized until spring. He pried a globe of honeybees from its hive, slow-buzzing, stunned from the sudden exposure, each bee shimmy-ing for warmth. When he placed the globe in her hands she fainted, her eyes rolled back. Lying there she saw all their dreams at once, the winter reveries of scores of worker bees, each one fiercely vivid: bright trails through thorns to a clutch of wild roses, honey tidily brimming a hundred combs.

With each day she learned more about what she could do. She felt a foreign and keen sensitivity bubbling in her blood, as though a seed planted long ago was just now sprouting. The larger the animal, the more powerfully it could shake her. The recently dead were virtual mines of visions, casting them off with a slow-fading strength like a long series of tethers being cut, one by one. She pulled off her mittens and touched everything she could: bats, salamanders, a cardinal chick tumbled from its nest, still warm. Ten hibernating garter snakes coiled beneath a rock, eyelids sealed, tongues stilled. Each time she touched some frozen insect, some slumbering amphibian, anything just dead, her eyes rolled back and its visions, its heaven, went shivering through her body.

Their first winter passed like that. When he looked out the cabin window he saw wolf tracks crossing the river, owls hunting from the trees, six feet of snow like a quilt ready to be thrown off. She saw burrowed dreamers nestled under the roots against the long twilight, their dreams rippling into the sky like auroras.

With love still lodged in his heart like a splinter, he married her in the first muds of spring.

Bruce Maples gasped when the hunter's wife finally arrived. She moved through the door like a show horse, demure in the way she kept her eyes down but assured in her step; she brought each tapered heel down and struck it against the granite. The hunter had not seen his wife for twenty years, and she had changed—become refined, less wild, and somehow, to the hunter, worse for it. Her face had wrinkled around the eyes, and she moved as if avoiding contact with anything near her, as if the hall table or closet door might suddenly lunge forward to snatch at her lapels. She wore no jewelry, no wedding ring, only a plain black suit, double-breasted.

She found her name tag on the table and pinned it to her lapel. Everyone in the reception room looked at her then looked away. The hunter realized that she, not President O'Brien, was the guest of honor. In a sense they were courting her. This was their way, the chancellor's way—a silent bartender, tuxedoed coat girls, big icy drinks. Give her pie, the hunter thought. Rhubarb pie. Show her a sleeping grizzly.

They sat for dinner at a narrow and very long table, fifteen or so high-backed chairs down each side and one at each head. The hunter was seated several places away from his wife. She looked over at him finally, a look of recognition, of warmth, and then looked away again. He must have seemed old to her—he must always have seemed old to her. She did not look at him again.

The kitchen staff, in starched whites, brought onion soup, scampi, poached salmon. Around the hunter guests spoke in half whispers about people he did not know. He kept his eyes on the windows and the blowing snow beyond.

The river thawed and drove huge saucers of ice toward the Missouri. The sound of water running, of release, of melting, clucked and purled through the open windows of the cabin. The hunter felt that old stirring, that quickening in his soul, and he would rise in the wide pink dawns, take his fly rod and hurry down to the river. Already trout were rising through the chill brown water to take the first insects of spring. Soon the telephone in the cabin was ringing with calls from clients, and his guiding season was on.

Occasionally a client wanted a lion or a trip with dogs for birds, but late spring and summer were for trout. He was out every morning before dawn, driving with a thermos of coffee to pick up a lawyer, a widower, a politician with a penchant for native cutthroat. After dropping off clients he'd hustle back out to scout for the next trip. He scouted until dark and sometimes after, kneeling in willows by the river and waiting for a trout to rise. He came home stinking of fish gut and woke her with his eager stories, cutthroat trout leaping fifteen-foot cataracts, a stubborn rainbow wedged under a snag.

By June she was bored and lonely. She wandered through the woods, but never very far. The summer woods were dense and busy, nothing like the quiet graveyard feel of winter. You couldn't see twenty feet in the summer. Nothing slept for very long; everything was emerging from cocoons, winging about, buzzing, multiplying, having litters, gaining weight. Bear cubs splashed in the river. Chicks screamed for worms. She longed for the stillness of winter, the long slumber, the bare sky, the bone-on-bone sound of bull elk knocking their antlers against trees. In August she went to the river to watch her husband cast flies with a client, the loops lifting from his rod like a spell cast over the water. He taught her to clean fish in the river so the scent wouldn't linger. She made the belly cuts, watched the viscera unloop in the current, the final, ecstatic visions of trout fading slowly up her wrists, running out into the river.

In September the big-game hunters came. Each client wanted something different: elk, antelope, a bull moose, a doe. They wanted to see grizzlies, track a wolverine, even shoot sandhill cranes. They wanted the heads of seven-by-seven royal bulls for their dens. Every few days he came home smelling of blood, with stories of stupid clients, of the Texan who sat, wheezing, too out of shape to get to the top of a hill for his shot. A bloodthirsty New Yorker claimed only to want to photograph black bears, then pulled a pistol from his boot and fired wildly at two cubs and their mother. Nightly she scrubbed blood out of the hunter's coveralls, watched it fade from rust to red to rose in the river water.

He was gone seven days a week, all day, home long enough only to grind sausage or cut roasts, clean his rifle, scrub out his meat pack, answer the phone. She understood very little of what he did, only that he loved the valley and needed to move in it, to watch the ravens and kingfishers and herons, the coyotes and bobcats, to hunt nearly everything else. There is no order in that world, he told her once, waving vaguely toward Great Falls, the cities that lay to the south. But here there is. Here I can see things I'd never see down there, things most folks are blind to. With no great reach of imagination she could see him fifty years hence, still lacing his boots, still gathering his rifle, all the world to see and him dying happy having seen only this valley.

She began to sleep, taking long afternoon naps, three hours or more. Sleep, she learned, was a skill like any other, like getting sawed in half and reassembled, or like divining visions from a dead robin. She taught herself to sleep despite heat, despite noise. Insects flung themselves at the screens, hornets sped down the chimney, the sun angled hot and urgent through the southern windows; still she slept. When he came home each autumn night, exhausted, forearms stained with blood, she was hours into sleep. Outside, the wind was already stripping leaves from the cottonwoods—too soon, he thought. He'd lie down and take her sleeping hand. Both of them lived in the grips of forces they had no control over—the November wind, the revolutions of the earth.

That winter was the worst he could remember: from Thanksgiving on they were snowed into the valley, the truck buried under six-foot drifts. The phone line went down in December and stayed down until April. January began with a chinook followed by a terrible freeze. The next morning a three-inch crust of ice covered the snow. On the ranches to the south cattle crashed through and bled to death kicking their way out. Deer punched through with their tiny hooves and suffocated in the deep snow beneath. Trails of blood veined the hills.

In the mornings he'd find coyote tracks written in the snow around the door to the crawlspace, two inches of hardwood between them and all his winter hoard hanging frozen now beneath the floorboards. He reinforced the door with baking sheets, nailing them up against the wood and over the hinges. Twice he woke to the sound of claws scrabbling against the metal, and charged outside to shout the coyotes away.

Everywhere he looked something was dying ungracefully, sinking in a drift, an elk keeling over, an emaciated doe clattering onto ice like a drunken skeleton. The radio reported huge cattle losses on the southern ranches. Each night he dreamt of wolves, of running with them, soaring over fences and tearing into the steaming, snow-matted bodies of cattle.

Still the snow fell. In February he woke three times to coyotes under the cabin, and the third time mere shouting could not send them running; he grabbed his bow and knife and dashed out into the snow barefoot, already his feet going numb. This time they had gone in under the door, chewing and digging the frozen earth under the foundation. He unbolted what was left of the door and swung it free.

A coyote hacked as it choked on something. Others shifted and panted. Maybe there were ten. Elk arrows were all he had, aluminum shafts tipped with broadheads. He squatted in the dark entryway—their only exit—with his bow at full draw and an arrow nocked. Above him he could hear his wife's feet pad silently over the floorboards. A coyote made a coughing sound. He began to fire arrows steadily into the dark. He heard some bite into the foundation blocks at the back of the crawlspace, others sink into flesh. He spent his whole quiver: a dozen arrows. The yelps of speared coyote went up. A few charged him, and he lashed at them with his knife. He felt teeth go to the bone of his arm, felt hot breath on his cheeks. He lashed with his knife at ribs, tails, skulls. His muscles screamed. The coyote were in a frenzy. Blood bloomed from his wrist, his thigh.

Upstairs she heard the otherworldly screams of wounded coyotes come through the floorboards, his grunts and curses as he fought. It sounded as if an exit had been tunneled all the way up from hell to open under their house, and what was now pouring out was the worst violence that place could send up. She knelt before the fireplace and felt the souls of coyote as they came through the boards on their way skyward.

He was blood-soaked and hungry and his thigh had been badly bitten but he worked all day digging out the truck. If he did not get food, they would starve, and he tried to hold the thought of the truck in his mind. He lugged slate and tree bark to wedge under the tires, excavated a mountain of snow from the truck bed. Finally, after dark, he got the engine turned over and ramped the truck up onto the frozen, wind-crusted snow. For a brief, wonderful moment he had it careening over the icy crust, starlight washing through the windows, tires spinning, engine churning, what looked to be the road unspooling in the head-lights. Then he crashed through. Slowly, painfully, he began digging it out again.

It was hopeless. He would get it up and then it would crash through a few miles later. Hardly anywhere was the sheet of ice atop the snow thick enough to support the truck's weight. For twenty hours he revved and slid the truck over eight-foot drifts. Three more times it broke through and sank to the windows. Finally he left it. He was ten miles from home, thirty miles from town.

He made a weak and smoky fire with cut boughs and lay beside it and tried to sleep but couldn't. The heat from the fire melted snow and trickles ran slowly toward him but froze solid before they reached him. The stars twisting in their constellations above had never seemed farther or colder. In a state that was neither fully sleep nor fully waking, he watched wolves lope around his fire, just outside the reaches of light, slavering and lean. A raven dropped through the smoke and hopped to him. He thought for the first time that he might die if he did not get warmer. He managed to kneel and turn and crawl for home. Around him he could feel the wolves, smell blood on them, hear their nailed feet scrape across the ice.

He traveled all that night and all the next day, near catatonia, some-times on his feet, more often on his elbows and knees. At times he thought he was a wolf and at times he thought he was dead. When he finally made it to the cabin, there were no tracks on the porch, no sign that she had gone out. The crawlspace door was still flung open and shreds of the siding and door frame lay scattered about as though some wounded devil had clawed its way out of the cabin's foundation and galloped into the night.

She was kneeling on the floor, ice in her hair, lost in some kind of hypothermic torpor. With his last dregs of energy he constructed a fire and poured a mug of hot water down her throat. As he fell into sleep, he watched himself as from a distance, weeping and clutching his near-frozen wife.

They had only flour, a jar of frozen cranberries, and a few crackers in the cupboards. He went out only to split more wood. When she could speak her voice was quiet and far away. I have dreamt the most amazing things, she murmured. I have seen the places where the coyotes go when they are gone. I know where spiders go, and geese. . . .

Snow fell incessantly. He wondered if some ice age had befallen the entire world. Night was abiding; daylight passed in a breath. Soon the whole planet would become a white and featureless ball hurtling through space, lost. Whenever he stood up his eyesight fled in slow, nauseating streaks of color.

Icicles hung from the cabin's roof and ran all the way to the porch, pillars of ice barring the door. To exit he had to hack his way out with an axe. He went out with lanterns to fish, shoveled down to the river ice, drilled through with a hand auger and shivered over the hole jigging a ball of dough on a hook. Sometimes he brought back a trout, frozen stiff in the short snowshoe from the river to the cabin. Other times they ate a squirrel, a hare, once a famished deer whose bones he cracked and boiled and finally ground into meal, or only a few handfuls of rose hips. In the worst parts of March he dug out cattails to peel and steam the tubers.

She hardly ate, sleeping eighteen, twenty hours a day. When she woke it was to scribble on notebook paper before plummeting back into sleep, clutching at the blankets as if they gave her sustenance. There was, she was learning, strength hidden at the center of weakness, ground at the bottom of the deepest pit. With her stomach empty and her body quieted, without the daily demands of living, she felt she was making important discoveries. She was only nineteen and had lost twenty pounds since marrying him. Naked she was all rib cage and pelvis.

He read her scribbled dreams but they read like senseless poems and gave him no clues to her: *Snail,* she wrote,

sleds down blades in the rain.
Owl: fixed his eyes on hare, dropping as if from the moon.
Horse: rides across the plains with his brothers . . .

Eventually he hated himself for bringing her there, for quarantining her in a cabin winterlong. This winter was making her crazy—making them both crazy. All that was happening to her was his fault.

In April the temperature rose above zero and then above twenty. He strapped the extra battery to his pack and went to dig out the truck. Its excavation took all day. He drove it slowly back up the slushy road in the moonlight, went in and asked if she'd like to go to town the next morning. To his surprise, she said yes. They heated water for baths and dressed in clothes they hadn't worn in six months. She threaded twine through her belt loops to keep her trousers up.

Behind the wheel his chest filled up to have her with him, to be moving out into the country, to see the sun above the trees. Spring was coming; the valley was dressing up. Look there, he wanted to say, those geese streaming over the road. The valley lives. Even after a winter like that.

She asked him to drop her off at the library. He bought food—a dozen frozen pizzas, potatoes, eggs, carrots. He nearly wept at seeing bananas. He sat in the parking lot and drank a half gallon of milk. When he picked her up at the library, she had applied for a library card and borrowed twenty books. They stopped at the Bitterroot for hamburgers and rhubarb pie. She ate three pieces. He watched her eat, the spoon sliding out of her mouth. This was better. This was more like he dreamed it would be.

Well, Mary, he said. I think we made it.

I love pie, she said.

As soon as the lines were repaired the phone began to ring. He took his fishing clients down the river. She sat on the porch, reading, reading.

Soon her appetite for books could not be met by the Great Falls Public Library. She wanted other books, essays about sorcery, primers on magic-working and conjury that had to be mail-ordered from New Hampshire, New Orleans, even Italy. Once a week the hunter drove to town to collect a parcel of books from the post office: *Arcana Mundi, The Seer's Dictionary, Paragon of Wizardry, Occult Science Among the Ancients.* He opened one to a random page and read, *bring water, tie a soft fillet around your altar, burn it on fresh twigs and frankincense. . . .*

She regained her health, took on energy, no longer lay under furs dreaming all day. She was out of bed before him, brewing coffee, her nose already between pages. With a steady diet of meat and vegetables her body bloomed, her hair shone; her eyes and cheeks glowed. After supper he'd watch her read in the firelight, blackbird feathers tied all through her hair, a heron's beak hanging between her breasts.

In November he took a Sunday off and they cross-country skied. They came across a bull elk frozen to death in a draw, ravens shrieking at them as they skied to it. She knelt by it and put her palm on its leathered skull. Her eyes rolled back in her head. There, she moaned. I feel him.

What do you feel? he asked, standing behind her. What is it?

She stood, trembling. I feel his life flowing out, she said. I see where he goes, what he sees.

But that's impossible, he said. It's like saying you know what I dream.

I do, she said. You dream about wolves.

But that elk's been dead at least a day. It doesn't go anywhere. It goes into the crops of those ravens.

How could she tell him? How could she ask him to understand such a thing? How could anyone understand? The books she read never told her that.

More clearly than ever she could see that there was a fine line between dreams and wakefulness, between living and dying, a line so tenuous it sometimes didn't exist. It was always clearest for her in winter. In winter, in that valley, life and death were not so different. The heart of a hibernating newt was frozen solid but she could warm and wake it in her palm. For the newt there was no line at all, no fence, no River Styx, only an area between living and dying, like a snowfield between two lakes: a place where lake denizens sometimes met each other on their way to the other side, where there was only one state of being, neither living nor dead, where death was only a possibility and visions rose shimmering to the stars like smoke. All that was needed was a hand, the heat of a palm, the touch of fingers.

That February the sun shone during the days and ice formed at night—slick sheets glazing the wheat fields, the roofs and roads. He dropped her off at the library, the chains on the tires rattling as he pulled away, heading back up the Missouri toward Fort Benton.

Around noon Marlin Spokes, a snowplow driver the hunter knew from grade school, slid off the Sun River Bridge in his plow and dropped forty feet into the river. He was dead before they could get him out of the truck. She was reading in the library a block away and heard the plow crash into the riverbed like a thousand dropped girders. When she got to the bridge, sprinting in her jeans and T-shirt, men were already in the water—a telephone man from Helena, the jeweler, the butcher in his apron, all of them scrambling down the banks, wading in the rapids, prying the door open. She careened down the snow-covered slope beneath the bridge and splashed to them. The men lifted Marlin from the cab, stumbling as they carried him. Steam rose from their shoulders and from the crushed hood of the plow. Her hand on the jeweler's arm, her leg against the butcher's leg, she reached for Marlin's ankle.

When her finger touched Marlin's body, her eyes rolled immediately back and a single vision leapt to her: Marlin Spokes pedaling a bicycle, a child's seat mounted over the rear tire with a helmeted boy—Marlin's own son—strapped into it. Spangles of light drifted over the riders as they rolled down a lane beneath giant sprawling trees. The boy reached for Marlin's hair with one small fist. Fallen leaves turned over in their wake. In the glass of a storefront window their reflection flashed past. This quiet vision—like a ribbon of rich silk—ran out slowly and fluidly, with great power, and she shook beneath it. It was she who pedaled the bike. The boy's fingers pulled through her hair.

The men who were touching her or touching Marlin saw what she saw, felt what she felt. They tried not to talk about it, but after the funeral, after a week, they couldn't keep it in. At first they spoke of it only in their basements, at night, but Great Falls was not a big town and this was not something one kept locked in a basement. Soon they talked about it everywhere, in the supermarket, at the gasoline pumps. People who didn't know Marlin Spokes or his son or the hunter's wife or any of the men in the river that morning soon spoke of the event like experts. All you had to do was *touch* her, a barber said, and you saw it too. The most beautiful lane you've ever dreamed, raved a deli owner. Giant trees bigger'n you've ever imagined. You didn't just pedal his son around, movie ushers whispered, you *loved* him.

He could have heard anywhere. In the cabin he built up the fire, flipped idly through a stack of her books. He couldn't understand them—one of them wasn't even in English.

After dinner she took the plates to the sink.

You read Spanish now? he asked.

Her hands in the sink stilled. It's Portuguese, she said. I only understand a little.

He turned his fork in his hands. Were you there when Marlin Spokes was killed?

I helped pull him out of the truck. I don't think I was much good.

He looked at the back of her head. He felt like driving his fork through the table. What tricks did you play? Did you hypnotize people?

Her shoulders tightened. Her voice came out furious: Why can't you— she began, but her voice fell off. It wasn't tricks, she muttered. I helped carry him.

When she started to get phone calls, he hung up on the callers. But they were relentless: a grieving widow, an orphan's lawyer, a reporter from the *Great Falls Tribune*. A blubbering father drove all the way to the cabin to beg her to come to the funeral parlor, and finally she went. The hunter insisted on driving her. It wasn't right, he declared, for her to go alone. He waited in the truck in the parking lot, engine rattling, radio moaning.

I feel so alive, she said afterward as he helped her into the cab. Her clothes were soaked through with sweat. Like my blood is fizzing through my body. At home she lay awake, far away, all night.

She got called back and called back, and each time he drove her. Some days he'd take her after a whole day of scouting for elk and he'd pass out from exhaustion while he waited in the truck. When he woke she'd be beside him, holding his hand, her hair damp, her eyes wild.

You dreamt you were with the wolves and eating salmon, she said. They were washed up and dying on the shoals. It was right outside the cabin.

It was well after midnight and he'd be up before four the next day. The salmon used to come here, he said. When I was a boy. There'd be so many you could stick your hand in the river and touch one. He drove them home over the dark fields. He tried to soften his voice. What do you do in there? What really?

I give them solace. I let them say goodbye to their loved ones. I help them know something they'd never otherwise know.

No, he said. I mean what kind of tricks? How do you do it?

She turned her hands palm up. As long as they're touching me they see what I see. Come in with me next time. Go in there and hold hands. Then you'll know.

He said nothing. The stars above the windshield seemed fixed in their places.

Families wanted to pay her; most wouldn't let her leave until they did. She would come out to the truck with fifty, a hundred—once four hundred—dollars folded into her pocket. She grew her hair out, obtained talismans to dramatize her performances: a bat wing, a raven's beak, a fistful of hawk's feathers bound with a sprig of cheroot. A cardboard box full of candle stubs. Then she went off for weekends, disappearing in the truck before he was up, a fearless driver. She stopped for roadkill and knelt by it—a crumpled porcupine, a shattered deer. She pressed her palm to the truck's grille where a hundred husks of insects smoked. Seasons came and went. She was gone half the winter. Each of them was alone. They never spoke. On longer drives there were times she was tempted to keep the truck pointed away and never return.

In the first thaws he would go out to the river, try to lose himself in the rhythm of casting, in the sound of pebbles driven downstream, clacking together. But even fishing had gone lonely for him. Everything, it seemed, was out of his hands—his truck, his wife, the course of his own life.

As hunting season came on his mind wandered. He was botching opportunities—getting upwind of elk or telling a client to call it quits thirty seconds before a pheasant burst from cover and flapped slowly, untroubled, into the sky. When a client missed his mark and pegged an antelope in the neck, the hunter berated him for being careless, knelt over its tracks, and clutched at the bloody snow. Do you understand what you've done? he shouted. How the arrow shaft will knock against the trees, how the animal will run and run, how the wolves will trot behind it to keep it from resting? The client was red-faced, huffing. Wolves? the client said. There haven't been wolves here for twenty years.

She was in Butte or Missoula when he discovered her money in a boot: six thousand dollars and change. He canceled his trips and stewed for two days, pacing the porch, sifting through her things, rehearsing his arguments. When she saw him, the sheaf of bills jutting from his shirt pocket, she stopped halfway to the door, her bag over her shoulder, her hair brought back. The light came across his shoulders and fell onto the yard.

It's not right, he said.

She walked past him into the cabin. I'm helping people. I'm doing what I love. Can't you see how good I feel afterward?

You take advantage of them. They're grieving, and you take their money.

They *want* to pay me, she shrieked. I help them see something they desperately want to see.

It's a grift. A con.

She came back out on the porch. No, she said. Her voice was quiet and strong. This is real. As real as anything: the valley, the river, the trees, your trout hanging in the crawlspace. I have a talent. A gift.

He snorted. A gift for hocus-pocus. For swindling widows out of their savings. He lobbed the money into the yard. The wind caught the bills and scattered them over the snow.

She hit him, once, hard across the mouth. How dare you? she cried. You, of all people, should understand. You who dream of wolves every night.

He went out alone the next evening and she tracked him through the snow. He was up on a deer platform under a blanket. He was wearing white camouflage; he'd tiger-striped his face with black paint. She crouched a hundred yards away, for four hours or more, damp and trembling in the snow behind his tree stand. She thought he must have dozed off when she heard an arrow sing down from the platform and strike a doe she hadn't even noticed in the chest. The doe looked around, wildly surprised, and charged off, galloping through the trees. She heard the aluminum shaft of the arrow knocking against branches, heard the deer plunge through a thicket. The hunter sat a moment, then climbed down from his perch and began to follow. She waited until he was out of sight, then followed.

She didn't have far to go. There was so much blood she thought he must have wounded other deer, which must all have come charging down this same path, spilling out the quantities of their lives. The doe lay panting between two trees, the thin shaft of the arrow jutting from her shoulder. Blood so red it was almost black pulsed down its flank. The hunter stood over the animal and slit its throat.

Mary leapt forward from where she squatted, her legs all pins and needles, dashed across the snow in her parka and, lunging, grabbed the doe by its still-warm foreleg. With her other hand she seized the hunter's wrist and held on. His knife was still inside the deer's throat and as he pulled away blood spread thickly into the snow. Already the doe's vision was surging through her body—fifty deer wading a sparkling brook, their bellies in the current, craning their necks to pull leaves from overhanging alders, light pouring around their bodies, a buck raising its antlered head like a king. A silver bead of water hung from its muzzle, caught the sun, and fell.

What? the hunter gasped. He dropped his knife. He was pulling away, pulling from his knees with all his strength. She held on; one hand on his wrist, the other clamped around the doe's foreleg. He dragged them across the snow and the doe left her blood as she went. Oh, he whispered. He could feel the world—the grains of snow, the stripped bunches of trees—falling away. The taste of alder leaves was in his mouth. A golden brook rushed under his body; light spilled onto him. The buck was raising its head, meeting his eyes. All the world washed in amber.

The hunter gave a last pull and was free. The vision sped away. No, he murmured. No. He rubbed his wrist where her fingers had been and shook his head as if shaking off a blow. He ran.

Mary lay in the blood-smeared snow a long time, the warmth of the doe running up her arm until finally the woods had gone cold and she was alone. She dressed the doe with his knife and quartered the carcass and ferried it home over her shoulders. Her husband was in bed. The fireplace was cold. Don't come near me, he said. Don't touch me. She built the fire and fell asleep on the floor.

In the months that followed she left the cabin more frequently and for longer durations, visiting homes, accident sites, and funeral parlors all over central Montana. Finally she pointed the truck south and didn't turn back. They had been married five years.

Twenty years later, in the Bitterroot Diner, he looked up at the ceiling-mounted television and there she was, being interviewed. She lived in Manhattan, had traveled the world, written two books. She was in demand all over the country. Do you commune with the dead? the interviewer asked. No, she said, I help people. I commune with the living. I give people peace.

Well, the interviewer said, turning to speak into the camera, I believe it.

The hunter bought her books at the bookstore and read them in one night. She had written poems about the valley, written them to the animals: you rampant coyote, you glorious bull. She had traveled to Sudan to touch the backbone of a fossilized stegosaur, and wrote of her frustration when she divined nothing from it. A TV network flew her to Kamchatka to embrace the huge shaggy forefoot of a mammoth as it was airlifted from the permafrost—she had better luck with that one, describing an entire herd slogging big-footed through a slushy tide, tearing at sea grass and bringing it to their mouths with their trunks. In a handful of poems there were even vague allusions to him—a brooding, blood-soaked presence that hovered outside the margins, like storms on their way, like a killer hiding in the basement.

The hunter was fifty-eight years old. Twenty years was a long time. The valley had diminished slowly but perceptibly: roads came in, and the grizzlies left, seeking higher country. Loggers had thinned nearly every accessible stand of trees. Every spring runoff from logging roads turned the river chocolate-brown. He had given up on finding a wolf in that country although they still came to him in dreams and let him run with them, out over frozen flats under the moon. He had never been with another woman. In his cabin, bent over the table, he set aside her books, took a pencil, and wrote her a letter.

A week later a Federal Express truck drove all the way to the cabin. Inside the envelope was her response on embossed stationery. The handwriting was hurried and efficient. *I will be in Chicago,* it said, *day after tomorrow. Enclosed is a plane ticket. Feel free to come. Thank you for writing.*

After sherbet the chancellor rang his spoon against a glass and called his guests into the reception room. The bar had been dismantled; in its place three caskets had been set on the carpet. The caskets were mahogany, polished to a deep luster. The one in the center was larger than the two flanking it. A bit of snow that had fallen on the lids— they must have been kept outside—was melting, and drops ran onto the carpet where they left dark circles. Around the caskets cushions had been placed on the floor. A dozen candles burned on the mantel. There were the sounds of staff clearing the dining room. The hunter leaned against the entryway and watched guests drift uncomfortably into the room, some cradling coffee cups, others gulping at gin or vodka in deep tumblers. Eventually everyone settled onto the floor.

The hunter's wife came in then, elegant in her dark suit. She knelt and motioned for O'Brien to sit beside her. His face was pinched and inscrutable. Again the hunter had the impression that he was not of this world but of a slightly leaner one.

President O'Brien, his wife said. I know this is difficult for you. Death can seem so final, like a blade dropped through your center. But the nature of death is not at all final; it is not some dark cliff off which we leap. I hope to show you it is merely a fog, something we can peer into and out of, something we can know and face and not necessarily fear. By each life taken from our collective lives we are diminished. But even in death there is much to celebrate. It is only a transition, like so many others.

She moved into the circle and unfastened the lids of the caskets. From where he sat the hunter could not see inside. His wife's hands fluttered around her waist like birds. Think, she said. Think hard about something you would like resolved, some matter, gone now, which you wish you could take back—perhaps with your daughters, a moment, a lost feeling, a desperate wish.

The hunter lidded his eyes. He found himself thinking of his wife, of their long gulf, of dragging her and a bleeding doe through the snow. Think now, his wife was saying, of some wonderful moment, some fine and sunny minute you shared, your wife and daughters, all of you together. Her voice was lulling. Beneath his eyelids the glow of the candles made an even orange wash. He knew her hands were reaching for whatever—whoever—lay in those caskets. Somewhere inside him he felt her extend across the room.

His wife said more about beauty and loss being the same thing, about how they ordered the world, and he felt something happening—a strange warmth, a flitting presence, something dim and unsettling like a feather brushed across the back of his neck. Hands on both sides of him reached for his hands. Fingers locked around his fingers. He wondered if she was hypnotizing him, but it didn't matter. He had nothing to fight off or snap out of. She was inside him now; she had reached across and was poking about.

Her voice faded, and he felt himself swept up as if rising toward the ceiling. Air washed lightly in and out of his lungs; warmth pulsed in the hands that held his own. In his mind he saw a sea emerging from fog. The water was broad and flat and glittered like polished metal. He could feel dune grass moving against his shins, and wind coming over his shoulders. The sea was very bright. All around him bees shuttled over the dunes. Far out a shorebird was diving for crabs. He knew that a few hundred yards away a pair of girls were building castles in the sand; he could hear their song, soft and lilting. Their mother was with them, reclined under an umbrella, one leg bent, the other straight. She was drinking iced tea and he could taste it in his mouth, sweet and bitter with a trace of mint. Each cell in his body seemed to breathe. He became the girls, the diving bird, the shuttling bees; he was the mother of the girls and the father; he could feel himself flowing outward, richly dissolving, paddling into the world like the very first cell into the great blue sea. . . .

When he opened his eyes he saw linen curtains, women in gowns kneeling. Tears were visible on many people's cheeks—O'Brien's and the chancellor's and Bruce Maples's. His wife's head was bowed. The hunter gently released the hands that held his and walked out into kitchen, past the sudsy sinks, the stacks of dishes. He let himself out a side door and found himself on the long wooden deck that ran the length of the house, a couple inches of snow already settled on it.

He felt drawn toward the pond, the birdbath, and the hedges. He walked to the pond and stood at its rim. The snow was falling easily and slowly and the undersides of the clouds glowed yellow with reflected light from the city. Inside the house the lights were all down and only the dozen candles on the mantel showed, trembling and winking through the windows, a tiny, trapped constellation.

Before long his wife came out onto the deck and walked through the snow and came down to the pond. There were things he had been preparing to say: something about a final belief, about his faithfulness to the idea of her, an expression of gratitude for providing a reason to leave the valley, if only for a night. He wanted to tell her that although the wolves were gone, may always have been gone, they still came to him in dreams. That they could run there, fierce and unfettered, was surely enough. She would understand. She had understood long before he did.

But he was afraid to speak. He could see that speaking would be like dashing some very fragile bond to pieces, like kicking a dandelion gone to seed; the wispy, tenuous sphere of its body would scatter in the wind. So instead they stood together, the snow fluttering down from the clouds to melt into the water where their own reflected images trembled like two people trapped against the glass of a parallel world, and he reached, finally, to take her hand.

PART 7

MYTH AND MAGIC

I n folklore and fantasy tales set in the North American wild, wilderness emerges as a dynamic place of imagination, transformation, and enchantment. Distinctions among different animals, or between human and animal, remain more or less intact in the larger tradition of wilderness tales, but an important subset of stories within this canon—myth and magic tales—choose to question cultural oppositions between civilized and wild. Leaving literary realism behind, fantasy tales of cross-species transformation engage freely in the anthropomorphic in order to emphasize close connections among people, wildlife, and nature. Nearly all myth and magic tales are cast as adventure or survival stories, and they are as likely to highlight conflicts and competition between species as to imagine possibilities for cooperation and communication among them. The many human-to-wild metamorphoses that populate these North American tales owe less to the European werewolf, a folktale figure brought to North America by the colonists, and more to the shape-shifters of Indigenous oral storytelling traditions. Themes of trust and trickery, modernity and tradition, mutation and adaptation animate these tales. Whether addressed to children or to adult audiences, the appeal of these stories flows from their collective conjuring of a sometimes dangerous and always wondrous world—a world in which all living creatures are understood as kin.

"The King of the Polar Bears"

L. FRANK BAUM

L. Frank Baum (1856–1919) wrote short stories, novels, poems, plays, songs, and even scripts, but is best known for his bestselling children's book *The Wonderful Wizard of Oz* (1900), which he viewed as a "modernized fairy tale." For Oz, Baum called on his happy childhood memories of the deep woods in Upstate New York for his creation of a fantastical forest, populated by a tin woodsman, fighting trees, and personified animals. For the more realistic representation of Kansas, Baum similarly drew on prior experience as a South Dakota newspaper editor chronicling the severe dust storms of one of the most terrible drought periods to hit the Great Plains. In 1901, after the success of his first Oz novel, Baum began writing fanciful stories, some carrying moral lessons, for newspapers and published them the same year in book form under the title *American Fairy Tales,* the first collection of fairy tales by an American author. The most conservation-minded of the tales, "The King of the Polar Bears," tells the story of a wise old polar bear rumored by the other Arctic creatures to be a great magician. Baum's prime motivation to write this North Country tale was his deep personal distaste for the commercial harvesting of polar bear hides, which by the 1890s had become a valuable luxury commodity, aggressively hunted by both Arctic whalers and Hudson Bay Company fur traders. This magical transformation tale was also likely influenced by Sioux animal folktales that the author heard while living and working in the Dakota Territory, and by the publication of Yankton Dakota writer Zitkala-Ša's *Old Indian Legends,* which appeared the same year Baum produced his collection of fairy tales. Dying shortly before the publication of his fourteenth and final Oz book, *Glinda of Oz* (1920), Baum never lived to see the first book of his popular fantasy series made into a Hollywood musical, ranked by the American Film Institute as one of the greatest American movies ever made.

"The King of the Polar Bears"

L. FRANK BAUM

The King of the Polar Bears lived among the icebergs in the far north country. He was old and monstrous big; he was wise and friendly to all who knew him. His body was thickly covered with long, white hair that glistened like silver under the rays of the midnight sun. His claws were strong and sharp, that he might walk safely over the smooth ice or grasp and tear the fishes and seals upon which he fed.

The seals were afraid when he drew near, and tried to avoid him; but the gulls, both white and gray, loved him because he left the remnants of his feasts for them to devour.

Often his subjects, the polar bears, came to him for advice when ill or in trouble; but they wisely kept away from his hunting grounds, lest they might interfere with his sport and arouse his anger.

The wolves, who sometimes came as far north as the icebergs, whispered among themselves that the King of the Polar Bears was either a magician or under the protection of a powerful fairy. For no earthly thing seemed able to harm him; he never failed to secure plenty of food, and he grew bigger and stronger day by day and year by year.

Yet the time came when this monarch of the north met man, and his wisdom failed him.

He came out of his cave among the icebergs one day and saw a boat moving through the strip of water which had been uncovered by the shifting of the summer ice. In the boat were men.

The great bear had never seen such creatures before, and therefore advanced toward the boat, sniffing the strange scent with aroused curiosity and wondering whether he might take them for friends or foes, food or carrion.

When the king came near the water's edge a man stood up in the boat and with a queer instrument made a loud "bang!" The polar bear felt a shock; his brain became numb; his thoughts deserted him; his great limbs shook and gave way beneath him and his body fell heavily upon the hard ice.

That was all he remembered for a time.

When he awoke he was smarting with pain on every inch of his huge bulk, for the men had cut away his hide with its glorious white hair and carried it with them to a distant ship.

Above him circled thousands of his friends the gulls, wondering if their benefactor were really dead and it was proper to eat him. But when they saw him raise his head and groan and tremble they knew he still lived, and one of them said to his comrades:

"The wolves were right. The king is a great magician, for even men cannot kill him. But he suffers for lack of covering. Let us repay his kindness to us by each giving him as many feathers as we can spare."

This idea pleased the gulls. One after another they plucked with their beaks the softest feathers from under their wings, and, flying down, dropped them gently upon the body of the King of the Polar Bears.

Then they called to him in a chorus:

"Courage, friend! Our feathers are as soft and beautiful as your own shaggy hair. They will guard you from the cold winds and warm you while you sleep. Have courage, then, and live!"

And the King of the Polar Bears had courage to bear his pain and lived and was strong again.

The feathers grew as they had grown upon the bodies of the birds and covered him as his own hair had done. Mostly they were pure white in color, but some from the gray gulls gave his majesty a slight mottled appearance.

The rest of that summer and all through the six months of night the king left his icy cavern only to fish or catch seals for food. He felt no shame at his feathery covering, but it was still strange to him, and he avoided meeting any of his brother bears.

During this period of retirement he thought much of the men who had harmed him, and remembered the way they had made the great "bang!" And he decided it was best to keep away from such fierce creatures. Thus he added to his store of wisdom.

When the moon fell away from the sky and the sun came to make the icebergs glitter with the gorgeous tintings of the rainbow, two of the polar bears arrived at the king's cavern to ask his advice about the hunting season. But when they saw his great body covered with feathers instead of hair they began to laugh, and one said:

"Our mighty king has become a bird! Whoever before heard of a feathered polar bear?"

Then the king gave way to wrath. He advanced upon them with deep growls and stately tread and with one blow of his monstrous paw stretched the mocker lifeless at his feet.

The other ran away to his fellows and carried the news of the king's strange appearance. The result was a meeting of all the polar bears upon a broad field of ice, where they talked gravely of the remarkable change that had come upon their monarch.

"He is, in reality, no longer a bear," said one; "nor can he justly be called a bird. But he is half bird and half bear, and so unfitted to remain our king."

"Then who shall take his place?" asked another.

"He who can fight the bird-bear and overcome him," answered an aged member of the group. "Only the strongest is fit to rule our race."

There was silence for a time, but at length a great bear moved to the front and said:

"I will fight him; I—Woof—the strongest of our race! And I will be King of the Polar Bears."

The others nodded assent, and dispatched a messenger to the king to say he must fight the great Woof and master him or resign his sovereignty.

"For a bear with feathers," added the messenger, "is no bear at all, and the king we obey must resemble the rest of us."

"I wear feathers because it pleases me," growled the king. "Am I not a great magician? But I will fight, nevertheless, and if Woof masters me he shall be king in my stead."

Then he visited his friends, the gulls, who were even then feasting upon the dead bear, and told them of the coming battle.

"I shall conquer," he said, proudly. "Yet my people are in the right, for only a hairy one like themselves can hope to command their obedience."

The queen gull said:

"I met an eagle yesterday, which had made its escape from a big city of men. And the eagle told me he had seen a monstrous polar bear skin thrown over the back of a carriage that rolled along the street. That skin must have been yours, oh king, and if you wish I will send a hundred of my gulls to the city to bring it back to you."

"Let them go!" said the king, gruffly. And the hundred gulls were soon flying rapidly southward.

For three days they flew straight as an arrow, until they came to scattered houses, to villages, and to cities. Then their search began.

The gulls were brave, and cunning, and wise. Upon the fourth day they reached the great metropolis, and hovered over the streets until a carriage rolled along with a great white bear robe thrown over the back seat. Then the birds swooped down—the whole hundred of them— and seizing the skin in their beaks flew quickly away.

They were late. The king's great battle was upon the seventh day, and they must fly swiftly to reach the Polar regions by that time.

Meanwhile the bird-bear was preparing for his fight. He sharpened his claws in the small crevasses of the ice. He caught a seal and tested his big yellow teeth by crunching its bones between them. And the queen gull set her band to pluming the king bear's feathers until they lay smoothly upon his body.

But every day they cast anxious glances into the southern sky, watching for the hundred gulls to bring back the king's own skin.

The seventh day came, and all the Polar bears in that region gathered around the king's cavern. Among them was Woof, strong and confident of his success.

"The bird-bear's feathers will fly fast enough when I get my claws upon him!" he boasted; and the others laughed and encouraged him.

The king was disappointed at not having recovered his skin, but he resolved to fight bravely without it. He advanced from the opening of his cavern with a proud and kingly bearing, and when he faced his enemy he gave so terrible a growl that Woof's heart stopped beating for a moment, and he began to realize that a fight with the wise and mighty king of his race was no laughing matter.

After exchanging one or two heavy blows with his foe, Woof's courage returned, and he determined to dishearten his adversary by bluster.

"Come nearer, bird-bear!" he cried. "Come nearer, that I may pluck your plumage!"

The defiance filled the king with rage. He ruffled his feathers as a bird does, till he appeared to be twice his actual size, and then he strode forward and struck Woof so powerful a blow that his skull crackled like an egg-shell and he fell prone upon the ground.

While the assembled bears stood looking with fear and wonder at their fallen champion the sky became darkened.

A hundred gulls flew down from above and dropped upon the king's body a skin covered with pure white hair that glittered in the sun like silver.

And behold! the bears saw before them the well-known form of their wise and respected master, and with one accord they bowed their shaggy heads in homage to the mighty King of the Polar Bears.

This story teaches us that true dignity and courage depend not upon outward appearance, but come rather from within; also that brag and bluster are poor weapons to carry into battle.

"A Human Kayak"

OHAYOHOK

Ohayohok (dates unknown) was a skilled storyteller in the village of Kingigin (or Keengegan), one of the oldest villages in the Bering Strait, located at the tip of what is now also known as Wales, Alaska, the nearest spot to Siberia from the American mainland. Having survived the devastating 1918 flu pandemic, which reduced the village population by more than half, Ohayohok was one of four now forgotten community storytellers recorded in the 1930s by educator and scientist Clark M. Garber. For eight years, Garber served as Superintendent of the Western District of Alaska, responsible for overseeing schools, medical relief, and reindeer herds. A product of his time, Garber, trained in colonial ethnology, traveled to Alaska to educate "the Eskimo" but left his post condemning the efforts of "selfish and unseeing missionaries and teachers to obliterate" the Inuits' languages, songs, dances, and stories. These "aggressive" and "damaging" attempts to eradicate Inuit culture propelled Garber to work with village elders to preserve their folklore, a collaboration that resulted in the thirty-one myths and legends translated and published in Garber's *Stories and Legends of the Bering Straits Eskimos* (1940). Ohayohok's "A Human Kayak" begins as a hunting tale and morphs into a transformation tale. It is one of a number of Inuit, Yup'ik, and Inupiat folktales from northern Alaska and Canada that explore the mystical unifying power of all living things. These fantastical stories of hunting, sealing, fishing, and often of storytelling itself encode the area's long history of migration and commerce across the North American and Siberian sides of the Bering Strait.

"A Human Kayak"

OHAYOHOK

This is the story of two brothers who lived in the south part of the village of Keengegan. They had just passed the tests that would permit them to be considered among the regular hunters of the village. After each had brought home a seal and delivered it to the old chief, who would cut it up and pass the meat around to all the homes, they became producers instead of dependents. It was in the spring of the year. The warm south winds had broken up the great ice fields and had brought with them a great abundance of seal to become the prey of *Innuit* hunters. On this particular day the two brothers agreed to go out to the edge of the shore ice and hunt seal. How proud their old father, the Chief, would be to see his two sons dragging their first seal over the ice to the village. Thereafter, they would be considered full-fledged hunters and would take their place with the other hunters.

Taking their bows, arrows, spears, *pooksaks,* and other necessary hunting equipment, they traveled almost half of the day before they came to the edge of the shore ice. Around the open patches of water, they hunted until darkness began to overtake them. This brought them to the realization that they had better return to the village regardless of the fact that they had failed to kill a single seal and would be the subjects of many chiding remarks and laughter when they reached the village empty-handed. When they came to a point about halfway on their homeward journey, they discovered that they were on a very large pan of ice which had broken away from the shore and had already left a wide stretch of water between them and the village. The wind and current carried them farther and farther away on their enormous raft of ice. As darkness fell, they could see the land gradually disappearing from sight.

Their plight offered no serious difficulties to the problem of procuring food. They could always rely on their bows and arrows and spears to provide the food they would need. But they realized that unless their ice raft brought them again to land they would finally find themselves in the land of Peeleeuktuk, the land of missing men, from which no man ever returned. Then their relatives and friends would hear of them no more. In their feather parkas and fur pants and *mukluks* they could not freeze, or even suffer from the cold. As long as they could kill seal or other game, they were in no danger of starving.

The boys could hardly wait for daylight to come the next morning so they could set to work building a shelter of snow and ice blocks. In this kind of a shelter, even though it were small, they would be safe from the blizzards which so often raged across the ocean ice. In their little snow hut they lived for many days while their big raft of ice carried them farther and farther from home. Apparently the spirits of the sea were unfavorable to them, because they had been so careless as to get caught on the drifting ice. Therefore the seal and other game animals failed to come near them. It was not long until they became very hungry. One day, when the older boy returned from a hunt for food he found his brother had fallen sick in their snow hut. Thereupon a great fear began to creep into their hearts. A longing to return to their father's *innie* possessed them and made them very sad.

On the following day, the younger brother said, "One has conversed with the spirits during the night. They have said that one's body will turn cold in death before two more suns pass."

On the second day thereafter, the older brother went to their customary lookout on top of a large ice ridge to search with his keen eyes the endless expanse of ice for some sign of land. Toward midday, he sighted a low dark streak of land. Waiting long enough to be sure that they were approaching the shore, he rushed back to the snow hut thinking that such glad tidings would bring rapid recovery to his brother. When he entered the hut, he found his brother dead. Thus his brother's body had turned cold in death just as he had said it would. What could he do now? Land was in sight and the big ice raft on which he was drifting would soon touch the shore. He could not leave his brother's body on the drifting ice. That would offend the spirits of the sea animals beyond repair and would bring famine upon all his people.

There was only one thing to do. Dragging his brother's body by the parka hood, he came as quickly as possible to the edge of the ice nearest to the land. But, here he was again thwarted in his purpose. The large ice floe had already touched the shore and was again drifting away from the land. How to get to land across the rapidly widening open water, and at the same time take his brother's body ashore, gave him a problem almost beyond his ability to solve. At length, after many trials and failures, he struck upon the plan of using his brother's body as a means to reach the shore. With his hunting knife he quickly opened the body of his brother and removed the viscera. Then he lashed the shaft of his harpoon to the back of the corpse in order to hold it rigid. He then placed the corpse in the water with the face turned up, and carefully assumed a position within the body cavity, as he would sit in his kayak. In this manner, he had converted the body of his brother into a human kayak. After much hard paddling with his bare hands and very slow progress, he finally reached the shore ice safely.

By this time he was becoming very weak from hunger. However he managed, by great will power and effort, to drag his brother's body to the mountain side and bury it among the rocks. Then he began journeying along the beach in the direction of his home. Day after day he walked slowly along the rock strewn shore and sandy beach. After many days of slow and difficult traveling with nothing to eat but bits of decaying matter which he picked up along the beach, he came upon a village. When he first caught sight of the village, his strength suddenly left him and he fell prone upon the ground. By sheer will power he forced himself to crawl along on his hands and knees. In this manner he came to the first *innie* of the village. Darkness had fallen, so there were no people about to witness his slow and laborious approach. When he crawled into the entrance of the *innie,* he came upon a mother dog with a litter of pups. There his progress was halted with great commotion.

The *innie* door opened and out through the tunnel-like entrance came a beautiful girl to discover the cause of such an unusual disturbance. No sooner did she discover the young man in his weak and starving condition than she sounded an alarm and summoned help from within. Her father came to help her, and soon the young man was lying upon a soft bed of skins noisily devouring a large dish of *okpone,* blood stew. Under the kind treatment of these good people and the excellent food, which the very nice girl prepared for him, his strength soon returned. In a few days, he was ready to add his hunting skill to the problem of keeping food supplied for the family. It was not long until he had become the best hunter in the village. Thereupon he married the lovely girl who had saved him and had nursed him back to health. Thereafter, for a long time, he lived with his wife's people and became the main support of her family.

Until many moons later, life ran along smoothly for the young hunter and his wife. One day his wife came to him and said with much concern, "One's man is a very good hunter. Every time he goes hunting he returns after a short time with a very fine catch. How does one do it?"

"Someday one will tell his woman all about it," replied the young husband.

When another moon had passed, his wife again asked him about his wonderful skill as a hunter. To her query he replied, "First you must get your man some water from the ocean." With her small pail, she hastened to the beach and dipped it full of salty brine. Returning quickly to the *innie,* she placed the pail of water on the floor before her husband. From his parka sleeve her husband drew the skin of a bird. He wet the bird skin in his mouth and then stretched it over his body thereby transforming himself into a bird. Then he began to fly about inside of the *innie.* After flying about the *innie* for a while, he suddenly dived into the pail of water and came out with a small fish in his beak. Flying as high as possible in the *innie,* he dropped the little fish onto the floor. To the great amazement of his wife, the little fish suddenly turned into a seal. Again the bird man dived into the pail of water and this time brought up a larger fish. This one turned into an *oogrook* when dropped upon the floor. Suddenly the bird man flew through the window of the *innie.* His wife called to him, "Come back my husband. Come back my man. Do not leave your woman in this way."

"This is why one did not wish to tell his lovely wife about his hunting skill. Now one must leave his woman and never return," replied the young bird-like husband, as he flew over the *innie* endeavoring to find his bearings.

In his bird plumage, the young hunter began the journey to his own home. When he arrived in the village of his own people after many days of flying along the coast, his people did not know him from the other birds which flew about the village. Many times, he slept near his mother's *innie* but she did not know that this little bird was one of her long lost sons. All the time, the little bird stayed near the window of his mother's *eeah,* kitchen, where the smoke from the seal oil lamps and stoves came out. At length the smoke and soot had turned his plumage black so that he looked like a raven.

One day, he fell asleep while perched on the edge of the *eeah* window, and fell into the kitchen. His mother struck him with a wooden spoon with which she was stirring the *okpone,* blood stew. The blow burst the bird plumage open and out stepped her son. His mother's feelings at finding her long lost son so unexpectedly brought tears of joy which were mingled with sobs of sorrow when she learned about the death of her other son.

Thereafter, the young man used the bird skin when hunting food for his own people. It brought him great success, and soon he was a very rich man. At length he found himself a wife among his own people. Unfortunately, she gave him nothing but girl babies but she was a very devoted wife and kept his *innie* in good order. As his fortune increased his desire for sons became greater. He must have sons to carry on his skill and position among the people. Eventually, he took a second wife who was especially skilled at sewing, tanning and making fur garments. His second wife gave him four sons who, like their father, grew to be famous hunters.

"Spotted Eagle and Black Crow"

JENNY LEADING CLOUD

J enny Leading Cloud (dates unknown) was a member of the White River Sioux, in South Dakota, and a tribal storyteller. Cloud's retelling of the Sioux tale "Spotted Eagle and Black Crow" was recorded in 1967 by Richard Erdoes at the White River, Rosebud Indian Reservation in south-central South Dakota. Together with another Native American folklorist and activist, Alfonso Ortiz, Erdoes gathered one hundred and sixty-six tales from the Native peoples and nations of North America for their book *American Indian Myths and Legends* (1984), part of Pantheon Books' Fairy Tale and Folklore Library. A gifted storyteller, Jenny Leading Cloud is the source for seven of the Plains Indian stories in the volume: four battle tales, two trickster tales, and one end-of-the-world tale. In her battle tale "Spotted Eagle and Black Crow," human characters have avian names and avian characters have human agency. As in many Indigenous folktales, the people, birds, animals, and plants that share the Great Plains are equal in the eyes of its creator, the "Great Spirit," a spiritual force that unifies all living things. In Sioux culture the eagle is the highest flying and most sacred of birds, a medicine bird that can transport prayers to the Great Spirit, while the crow is a bird of great intelligence and skill, though also a trickster capable of deception. Richard Erdoes, whose audiocassettes, photographs, and books sought to document and preserve the storytelling heritage of the Dakotas and other tribes, presents Jenny Leading Cloud's spiritual and cultural view of human-animal relations this way: "Man is just another animal. The buffalo and the coyote are our brothers; the birds, our cousins. White people see man as nature's master and conqueror, but Indians, who are close to nature, know better." Cloud's oral telling of "Spotted Eagle and Black Crow" reminds audiences that the western landscapes of North America were never empty spaces waiting to be populated but rather living theaters in which earth's creatures play out, in competition and in cooperation, the everyday dramas of living and dying.

"Spotted Eagle and Black Crow"

JENNY LEADING CLOUD

*This story of two warriors, of jealousy, and of eagles was first
told by the great Mapiya Luta.*

—CHIEF RED CLOUD OF THE OGLALAS

Many lifetimes ago there lived two brave warriors. One was named
Wanblee Gleshka, Spotted Eagle. The other was Kangi Sapa,
Black Crow. They were friends but, as it happened, were also in love
with the same girl, Zintkala Luta Win—Red Bird. She was beautiful as
well as accomplished in tanning and quillwork, and she liked Spotted
Eagle best, which made Black Crow unhappy and jealous.

Black Crow went to his friend and said: "Let's go on a war party
against the Pahani. We'll get ourselves some fine horses and earn eagle
feathers."

"Good idea," said Spotted Eagle, and the two young men purified
themselves in a sweat bath. They got out their war medicine and their
shields, painted their faces, and did all that warriors should do before a
raid. Then they rode out against the Pahani.

The raid did not go well. The Pahani were watchful, and the young
warriors could not get near the herd. Not only did they fail to capture
any ponies, they even lost their own mounts while they were trying
to creep up to the enemy's herd. Spotted Eagle and Black Crow had a
hard time escaping on foot because the Pahani were searching for them
everywhere. At one time the two had to hide underwater in a lake and
breathe through long, hollow reeds which were sticking up above the
surface. But at least they were clever at hiding, and the Pahani finally
gave up the hunt.

Traveling on foot made the trip home a long one. Their moccasins
were tattered, their feet bleeding. At last they came to a high cliff. "Let's
go up there," said Black Crow, "and find out whether the enemy is

following us." Clambering up, they looked over the countryside and saw that no one was on their trail. But on a ledge far below them they spied a nest with two young eagles in it. "Let's get those eagles, at least," Black Crow said. There was no way to climb down the sheer rock wall, but Black Crow took his rawhide lariat, made a loop in it, put the rope around Spotted Eagle's chest, and lowered him.

When his friend was on the ledge with the nest, Black Crow said to himself: "I can leave him there to die. When I come home alone, Red Bird will marry me." He threw his end of the rope down and went away without looking back or listening to Spotted Eagle's cries.

At last it dawned on Spotted Eagle that his friend had betrayed him, that he had been left to die. The lariat was much too short to lower himself to the ground; an abyss of three hundred feet lay beneath him. He was alone with the two young eagles, who screeched angrily at the strange, two-legged creature that had invaded their home.

Black Crow returned to his village. "Spotted Eagle died a warrior's death," he told the people. "The Pahanis killed him." There was loud wailing throughout the village, because everybody had liked Spotted Eagle. Red Bird slashed her arms with a sharp knife and cut her hair to make her sorrow plain to all. But in the end because life must go on, she became Black Crow's wife.

Spotted Eagle, however, did not die on his lonely ledge. The eagles got used to him, and the old eagles brought plenty of food—rabbits, prairie dogs, and sage hens—which he shared with the two chicks. Maybe it was the eagle medicine in his bundle which he carried on his chest that made the eagles accept him. Still, he had a very hard time on that ledge. It was so narrow that he had to tie himself to a little rock sticking out of the cliff to keep from falling off in his sleep. In this way he spent some uncomfortable weeks; after all, he was a human being and not a bird to whom a crack in the rock face is home.

At last the young eagles were big enough to practice flying. "What will become of me now?" thought the young man. "Once the fledglings have flown the nest, the old birds won't bring any more food." Then he had an inspiration, and told himself, "Perhaps I'll die. Very likely I will. But I won't just sit here and give up."

Spotted Eagle took his little pipe out of his medicine bundle, lifted it up to the sky, and prayed: "Wakan Tanka, *onshimala ye:* Great Spirit, pity me. You have created man and his brother, the eagle. You have given me the eagle's name. Now I will try to let the eagles carry me to the ground. Let the eagles help me; let me succeed."

He smoked and felt a surge of confidence. Then he grabbed hold of the legs of the two young eagles. "Brothers," he told them, "you have accepted me as one of your own. Now we will live together, or die together. Hoka-hey!" and he jumped off the ledge.

He expected to be shattered on the ground below, but with a mighty flapping of wings, the two young eagles broke his fall and the three landed safely. Spotted Eagle said a prayer of thanks to the ones above. Then he thanked the eagles and told them that one day he would be back with gifts and have a giveaway in their honor.

Spotted Eagle returned to his village. The excitement was great. He had been dead and had come back to life. Everybody asked him how it happened that he was not dead, but he wouldn't tell them. "I escaped," he said, "that's all." He saw his love married to his treacherous friend and bore it in silence. He was not one to bring strife and enmity to his people, to set one family against the other. Besides, what had happened could not be changed. Thus he accepted his fate.

A year or so later, a great war party of the Pahani attacked his village. The enemy outnumbered the Sioux tenfold, and Spotted Eagle's band had no chance for victory. All the warriors could do was fight a slow rear-guard action to give the aged, the women, and the children time to escape across the river. Guarding their people this way, the handful of Sioux fought bravely, charging the enemy again and again, forcing the Pahani to halt and regroup. Each time, the Sioux retreated a little, taking up a new position on a hill or across a gully. In this way they could save their families.

Showing the greatest courage, exposing their bodies freely, were Spotted Eagle and Black Crow. In the end they alone faced the enemy. Then, suddenly, Black Crow's horse was hit by several arrows and collapsed under him. "Brother, forgive me for what I have done," he cried to Spotted Eagle, "let me jump on your horse behind you."

Spotted Eagle answered: "You are a Kit Fox member, a sash wearer. Pin your sash as a sign that you will fight to the finish. Then, if you survive, I will forgive you; and if you die, I will forgive you also."

Black Crow answered: "I am a Fox. I shall pin my sash. I will win here or die here." He sang his death song. He fought stoutly. There was no one to release him by unpinning him and taking him up on a horse.

He was hit by lances and arrows and died a warrior's death. Many Pahani died with him.

Spotted Eagle had been the only one to watch Black Crow's last fight. At last he joined his people, safe across the river, where the Pahani did not follow them. "Your husband died well," Spotted Eagle told Red Bird.

After some time had passed, Spotted Eagle married Red Bird. And much, much later he told his parents, and no one else, how Black Crow had betrayed him. "I forgive him now," he said, "because once, long ago, he was my friend, and because he died as a warrior should, fighting for his people, and also because Red Bird and I are happy now."

After a long winter, Spotted Eagle told his wife when spring came again: "I must go away for a few days to fulfill a promise. And I have to go alone." He rode off by himself to that cliff and stood again at its foot, below the ledge where the eagles' nest had been. He pointed his sacred pipe to the four directions, then down to Grandmother Earth and up to the Grandfather, letting the smoke ascend to the sky, calling out: "Wanblee, Mishunkala, little Eagle Brothers, hear me."

High above in the clouds appeared two black dots, circling. These were the eagles who had saved his life. They came at his call, their huge wings spread royally. Swooping down, uttering a shrill cry of joy and recognition, they alighted at his feet. He stroked them with his feather fan, thanked them many times, and fed them choice morsels of buffalo meat. He fastened small medicine bundles around their legs as a sign of friendship, and spread sacred tobacco offerings around the foot of the cliff. Thus he made a pact of friendship and brotherhood between Wanblee Oyate—the eagle nation—and his own people. Afterwards the stately birds soared up again into the sky, circling motionless, carried by the wind, disappearing into the clouds. Spotted Eagle turned his horse's head homeward, going back to Red Bird with deep content.

"St. Lucy's Home for Girls Raised by Wolves"

KAREN RUSSELL

Karen Russell (b. 1981) was born and raised in Miami, Florida, a state that has influenced much of her fiction. She is the author of the critically acclaimed short-story collections *St. Lucy's Home for Girls Raised by Wolves* (2006), *Vampires in the Lemon Grove* (2014), and *Orange World and Other Stories* (2019), as well as the novella *Sleep Donation* (2020). Winner of a MacArthur "Genius Grant," Russell also wrote the gator-wrestling theme park novel *Swamplandia!* (2011), a finalist for the Pulitzer Prize. A fan of L. Frank Baum's hallucinatory yet familiar wonderland of Oz, Russell describes her attraction to the dreamlike and dangerous tropical wetlands of South Florida in similar terms: "as if you're standing in a mythic and a real space at once." In Russell's genre-defying work—part science fiction, part Gothic horror, part magical realism—wilderness often serves as a catalyst for encounters with the mythical and the phantasmal. From the sun-drenched swamps of the Florida Everglades to the mossy forests of the Pacific Northwest, Russell's fiction captures humanity's unnatural relationship with the natural from coast to coast. Her story "St. Lucy's Home for Girls Raised by Wolves," first published in 2006 in the literary magazine *Granta,* is a wilderness myth that takes the form of an animal fable. Using comic and fantasy motifs to make a serious point, this imaginative transformation tale of wolf-girl "rehabilitation" offers up a sly critique of efforts to domesticate and tame the wildness out of animals (including animals of the human variety) by using behavioral modification to alienate them from their natural sympathies and animal selves. Karen Russell currently resides in Portland, Oregon, with her husband and two children.

"St. Lucy's Home for Girls Raised by Wolves"

KAREN RUSSELL

STAGE 1: The initial period is one in which everything is new, exciting, and interesting for your students. It is fun for your students to explore their new environment.

—from *The Jesuit Handbook on Lycanthropic Culture Shock*

At first, our pack was all hair and snarl and floor-thumping joy. We forgot the barked cautions of our mothers and fathers, all the promises we'd made to be civilized and ladylike, couth and kempt. We tore through the austere rooms, overturning dresser drawers, pawing through the neat piles of the Stage 3 girls' starched underwear, smashing lightbulbs with our bare fists. Things felt less foreign in the dark. The dim bedroom was windowless and odorless. We remedied this by spraying exuberant yellow streams all over the bunks. We jumped from bunk to bunk, spraying. We nosed each other midair, our bodies buckling in kinetic laughter. The nuns watched us from the corner of the bedroom, their tiny faces pinched with displeasure.

"*Ay caramba,*" Sister Maria de la Guardia sighed. "*Que barbaridad!*" She made the Sign of the Cross. Sister Maria came to St. Lucy's from a halfway home in Copacabana. In Copacabana, the girls are fat and languid and eat pink slivers of guava right out of your hand. Even at Stage 1, their pelts are silky, sun-bleached to near invisibility. Our pack was hirsute and sinewy and mostly brunette. We had terrible posture. We went knuckling along the wooden floor on the calloused pads of our fists, baring row after row of tiny, wood-rotted teeth. Sister Josephine sucked in her breath. She removed a yellow wheel of floss from under her robes, looping it like a miniature lasso.

"The girls at our facility are *backwoods,*" Sister Josephine whispered to Sister Maria de la Guardia with a beatific smile. "You must be patient with them." I clamped down on her ankle, straining to close my jaws around the woolly XXL sock. Sister Josephine tasted like sweat and freckles. She smelled easy to kill.

We'd arrived at St. Lucy's that morning, part of a pack fifteen-strong. We were accompanied by a mousy, nervous-smelling social worker; the baby-faced deacon; Bartholomew, the blue wolfhound; and four burly woodsmen. The deacon handed out some stale cupcakes and said a quick prayer. Then he led us through the woods. We ran past the wild apiary, past the felled oaks, until we could see the white steeple of St. Lucy's rising out of the forest. We stopped short at the edge of a muddy lake. Then the deacon took our brothers. Bartholomew helped him to herd the boys up the ramp of a small ferry. We girls ran along the shore, tearing at our new jumpers in a plaid agitation. Our brothers stood on the deck, looking small and confused.

Our mothers and fathers were werewolves. They lived an outsider's existence in caves at the edge of the forest, threatened by frost and pitchforks. They had been ostracized by the local farmers for eating their silled fruit pies and terrorizing the heifers. They had ostracized the local wolves by having sometimes-thumbs, and regrets, and human children. (Their condition skips a generation.) Our pack grew up in a green purgatory. We couldn't keep up with the purebred wolves, but we never stopped crawling. We spoke a slab-tongued pidgin in the cave, inflected with frequent howls. Our parents wanted something better for us; they wanted us to get braces, use towels, be fully bilingual. When the nuns showed up, our parents couldn't refuse their offer. The nuns, they said, would make us naturalized citizens of human society. We would go to St. Lucy's to study a better culture. We didn't know at the time that our parents were sending us away for good. Neither did they.

That first afternoon, the nuns gave us free rein of the grounds. Everything was new, exciting, and interesting. A low granite wall surrounded St. Lucy's, the blue woods humming for miles behind it. There was a stone fountain full of delectable birds. There was a statue of St. Lucy. Her marble skin was colder than our mother's nose, her pupilless eyes rolled heavenward. Doomed squirrels gamboled around her stony toes. Our diminished pack threw back our heads in a celebratory howl—an exultant and terrible noise, even without a chorus of wolf brothers in the background. There were holes everywhere!

We supplemented these holes by digging some of our own. We

interred sticks, and our itchy new jumpers, and the bones of the friendly, unfortunate squirrels. Our noses ached beneath an invisible assault. Everything was smudged with a human odor: baking bread, petrol, the nuns' faint woman-smell sweating out beneath a dark perfume of tallow and incense. We smelled one another, too, with the same astounded fascination. Our own scent had become foreign in this strange place.

We had just sprawled out in the sun for an afternoon nap, yawning into the warm dirt, when the nuns reappeared. They conferred in the shadow of the juniper tree, whispering and pointing. Then they started toward us. The oldest sister had spent the past hour twitching in her sleep, dreaming of fatty and infirm elk. (The pack used to dream the same dreams, back then, as naturally as we drank the same water and slept on the same red scree.) When our oldest sister saw the nuns approaching, she instinctively bristled. It was an improvised bristle, given her new, human limitations. She took clumps of her scraggly, nut-brown hair and held it straight out from her head.

Sister Maria gave her a brave smile.

"And what is your name?" she asked.

The oldest sister howled something awful and inarticulable, a distillate of hurt and panic, half-forgotten hunts and eclipsed moons. Sister Maria nodded and scribbled on a yellow legal pad. She slapped on a name tag: HELLO, MY NAME IS _____! "Jeanette it is."

The rest of the pack ran in a loose, uncertain circle, torn between our instinct to help her and our new fear. We sensed some subtler danger afoot, written in a language we didn't understand.

Our littlest sister had the quickest reflexes. She used her hands to flatten her ears to the side of her head. She backed toward the far corner of the garden, snarling in the most menacing register that an eight-year-old wolf-girl can muster. Then she ran. It took them two hours to pin her down and tag her: HELLO, MY NAME IS MIRABELLA!

"Stage 1," Sister Maria sighed, taking careful aim with her tranquilizer dart. "It can be a little overstimulating."

> STAGE 2: After a time, your students realize that they must work to adjust to the new culture. This work may be stressful and students may experience a strong sense of dislocation. They may miss certain foods. They may spend a lot

of time daydreaming during this period. Many students feel isolated, irritated, bewildered, depressed, or generally uncomfortable.

Those were the days when we dreamed of rivers and meat. The full-moon nights were the worst! Worse than cold toilet seats and boiled tomatoes, worse than trying to will our tongues to curl around our false new names. We would snarl at one another for no reason. I remember how disorienting it was to look down and see two square-toed shoes instead of my own four feet. Keep your mouth shut, I repeated during our walking drills, staring straight ahead. Keep your shoes on your feet. Mouth shut, shoes on feet. Do not chew on your new penny loafers. Do not. I stumbled around in a daze, my mouth black with shoe polish. The whole pack was irritated, bewildered, depressed. We were all uncomfortable, and between languages. We had never wanted to run away so badly in our lives; but who did we have to run back to? Only the curled black grimace of the mother. Only the father, holding his tawny head between his paws. Could we betray our parents by going back to them? After they'd given us the choicest part of the woodchuck, loved us at our hairless worst, nosed us across the ice floes and abandoned us at St. Lucy's for our own betterment?

Physically, we were all easily capable of clearing the low stone walls. Sister Josephine left the wooden gates wide open. They unslatted the windows at night so that long fingers of moonlight beckoned us from the woods. But we knew we couldn't return to the woods; not till we were civilized, not if we didn't want to break the mother's heart. It all felt like a sly, human taunt.

It was impossible to make the blank, chilly bedroom feel like home. In the beginning, we drank gallons of bathwater as part of a collaborative effort to mark our territory. We puddled up the yellow carpet of old newspapers. But later, when we returned to the bedroom, we were dismayed to find all trace of the pack musk had vanished. Someone was coming in and erasing us. We sprayed and sprayed every morning; and every night, we returned to the same ammonia eradication. We couldn't make our scent stick here; it made us feel invisible. Eventually we gave up. Still, the pack seemed to be adjusting on the same timetable. The advanced girls could already alternate between two speeds: "slouch" and "amble." Almost everybody was fully bipedal.

Almost.

The pack was worried about Mirabella.

Mirabella would rip foamy chunks out of the church pews and replace them with ham bones and girl dander. She loved to roam the grounds wagging her invisible tail. (We all had a hard time giving that up. When we got excited, we would fall to the ground and start pumping our backsides. Back in those days we could pump at rabbity velocities. *Que horror!* Sister Maria frowned, looking more than a little jealous.) We'd give her scolding pinches. "Mirabella," we hissed, imitating the nuns. "No." Mirabella cocked her ears at us, hurt and confused.

Still, some things remained the same. The main commandment of wolf life is Know Your Place, and that translated perfectly. Being around other humans had awakened a slavish-dog affection in us. An abasing, belly-to-the-ground desire to please. As soon as we realized that someone higher up in the food chain was watching us, we wanted only to be pleasing in their sight. Mouth shut, I repeated, shoes on feet. But if Mirabella had this latent instinct, the nuns couldn't figure out how to activate it. She'd go bounding around, gleefully spraying on their gilded statue of St. Lucy, mad-scratching at the virulent fleas that survived all of their powders and baths. At Sister Maria's tearful insistence, she'd stand upright for roll call, her knobby, oddly muscled legs quivering from the effort. Then she'd collapse right back to the ground with an ecstatic *oomph!* She was still loping around on all fours (which the nuns had taught us to see looked unnatural and ridiculous—we could barely believe it now, the shame of it, that we used to locomote like that!), her fists blue-white from the strain. As if she were holding a secret tight to the ground. Sister Maria de la Guardia would sigh every time she saw her. *"Caramba!"* She'd sit down with Mirabella and pry her fingers apart. "You see?" she'd say softly, again and again. "What are you holding on to? Nothing, little one. Nothing."

Then she would sing out the standard chorus, "Why can't you be more like your sister Jeanette?"

The pack hated Jeanette. She was the most successful of us, the one furthest removed from her origins. Her real name was GWARR!, but she wouldn't respond to this anymore. Jeanette spiffed her penny loafers until her very shoes seemed to gloat. (Linguists have since traced the colloquial origins of "goody two-shoes" back to our facilities.) She could even growl out a demonic-sounding precursor to "Pleased to meet you." She'd delicately extend her former paws to visitors, wearing white kid gloves.

"Our little wolf, disguised in sheep's clothing!" Sister Ignatius liked to joke with the visiting deacons, and Jeanette would surprise everyone by laughing along with them, a harsh, inhuman, barking sound. Her hearing was still twig-snap sharp. Jeanette was the first among us to apologize; to drink apple juice out of a sippy cup; to quit eyeballing the cleric's jugular in a disconcerting fashion. She curled her lips back into a cousin of a smile as the traveling barber cut her pelt into bangs. Then she swept her coarse black curls under the rug. When we entered a room, our nostrils flared beneath the new odors: onion and bleach, candle wax, the turnipy smell of unwashed bodies. Not Jeanette. Jeanette smiled and pretended like she couldn't smell a thing.

I was one of the good girls. Not great and not terrible, solidly middle of the pack. But I had an ear for languages, and I could read before I could adequately wash myself. I probably could have vied with Jeanette for the number one spot, but I'd seen what happened if you gave in to your natural aptitudes. This wasn't like the woods, where you had to be your fastest and your strongest and your bravest self. Different sorts of calculations were required to survive at the home.

The pack hated Jeanette, but we hated Mirabella more. We began to avoid her, but sometimes she'd surprise us, curled up beneath the beds or gnawing on a scapula in the garden. It was scary to be ambushed by your sister. I'd bristle and growl, the way that I'd begun to snarl at my own reflection as if it were a stranger.

"Whatever will become of Mirabella?" we asked, gulping back our own fear. We'd heard rumors about former wolf-girls who never adapted to their new culture. It was assumed that they were returned to our native country, the vanishing woods. We liked to speculate about this before bedtime, scaring ourselves with stories of catastrophic bliss. It was the disgrace, the failure that we all guiltily hoped for in our hard beds. Twitching with the shadow question: *Whatever will become of me?*

We spent a lot of time daydreaming during this period. Even Jeanette. Sometimes I'd see her looking out at the woods in a vacant way. If you interrupted her in the midst of one of these reveries, she would lunge at you with an elder-sister ferocity, momentarily forgetting her human catechism. We liked her better then, startled back into being foamy old Jeanette.

In school, they showed us the St. Francis of Assisi slideshow, again and again. Then the nuns would give us bags of bread. They never announced these things as a test; it was only much later that I realized that we were under constant examination. "Go feed the ducks," they urged us. "Go practice compassion for all God's creatures." *Don't pair me with Mirabella,* I prayed, *anybody but Mirabella.* "Claudette"— Sister Josephine beamed—"why don't you and Mirabella take some pumpernickel down to the ducks?"

"Ohhkaaythankyou," I said. (It took me a long time to say anything; first I had to translate it in my head from the Wolf.) It wasn't fair. They knew Mirabella couldn't make bread balls yet. She couldn't even undo the twist tie of the bag. She was sure to eat the birds; Mirabella didn't even try to curb her desire to kill things—and then who would get blamed for the dark spots of duck blood on our Peter Pan collars? Who would get penalized with negative Skill Points? Exactly.

As soon as we were beyond the wooden gates, I snatched the bread away from Mirabella and ran off to the duck pond on my own. Mirabella gave chase, nipping at my heels. She thought it was a game. "Stop it," I growled. I ran faster, but it was Stage 2 and I was still unsteady on my two feet. I fell sideways into a leaf pile, and then all I could see was my sister's blurry form, bounding toward me. In a moment, she was on top of me, barking the old word for tug-of-war. When she tried to steal the bread out of my hands, I whirled around and snarled at her, pushing my ears back from my head. I bit her shoulder, once, twice, the only language she would respond to. I used my new motor skills. I threw dirt, I threw stones. "Get away!" I screamed, long after she had made a cringing retreat into the shadows of the purple saplings. "Get away, get away!"

Much later, they found Mirabella wading in the shallows of a distant river, trying to strangle a mallard with her rosary beads. I was at the lake; I'd been sitting there for hours. Hunched in the long cattails, my yellow eyes flashing, shoving ragged hunks of bread into my mouth.

I don't know what they did to Mirabella. Me they separated from my sisters. They made me watch another slideshow. This one showed images of former wolf-girls, the ones who had failed to be rehabilitated. Long-haired, sad-eyed women, limping after their former wolf packs in white tennis shoes and pleated culottes. A wolf-girl bank teller, her makeup smeared in oily rainbows, eating a raw steak on the deposit slips while her colleagues looked on in disgust. Our parents. The final slide was a bolded sentence in St. Lucy's prim script: DO YOU WANT TO END UP SHUNNED BY BOTH SPECIES?

After that, I spent less time with Mirabella. One night she came to me, holding her hand out. She was covered with splinters, keening a high, whining noise through her nostrils. Of course I understood what she wanted; I wasn't that far removed from our language (even though I was reading at a fifth-grade level, halfway into Jack London's *The Son of the Wolf*).

"Lick your own wounds," I said, not unkindly. It was what the nuns had instructed us to say; wound licking was not something you did in polite company. Etiquette was so confounding in this country. Still, looking at Mirabella—her fists balled together like small, white porcupines, her brows knitted in animal confusion—I felt a throb of compassion. *How can people live like they do?* I wondered. Then I congratulated myself. This was a Stage 3 thought.

> STAGE 3: It is common that students who start living in a new and different culture come to a point where they reject the host culture and withdraw into themselves. During this period, they make generalizations about the host culture and wonder how the people can live like they do. Your students may feel that their own culture's lifestyle and customs are far superior to those of the host country.

The nuns were worried about Mirabella too. To correct a failing, you must first be aware of it as a failing. And there was Mirabella, shucking her plaid jumper in full view of the visiting cardinal. Mirabella, battling a raccoon under the dinner table while the rest of us took dainty bites of peas and borscht. Mirabella, doing belly flops into compost.

"You have to pull your weight around here," we overheard Sister Josephine saying one night. We paused below the vestry window and peered inside.

"Does Mirabella try to earn Skill Points by shelling walnuts and polishing Saint-in-the-Box? No. Does Mirabella even know how to say the word *walnut*? Has she learned how to say anything besides a sinful 'HraaaHA!' as she commits frottage against the organ pipes? No."

There was a long silence.

"Something must be done," Sister Ignatius said firmly. The other nuns nodded, a sea of thin, colorless lips and kettle-black brows. "Something must be done," they intoned. That ominously passive construction; a something so awful that nobody wanted to assume responsibility for it.

I could have warned her. If we were back home, and Mirabella had come under attack by territorial beavers or snow-blind bears, I would have warned her. But the truth is that by Stage 3 I wanted her gone. Mirabella's inability to adapt was taking a visible toll. Her teeth were ground down to nubbins; her hair was falling out. She hated the spongy, long-dead foods we were served, and it showed—her ribs were poking through her uniform. Her bright eyes had dulled to a sour whiskey color. But you couldn't show Mirabella the slightest kindness anymore—she'd never leave you alone! You'd have to sit across from her at meals, shoving her away as she begged for your scraps. I slept fitfully during that period, unable to forget that Mirabella was living under my bed, gnawing on my loafers.

It was during Stage 3 that we met our first purebred girls. These were girls raised in captivity, volunteers from St. Lucy's School for Girls. The apple-cheeked fourth-grade class came to tutor us in playing. They had long golden braids or short, severe bobs. They had frilly-duvet names like Felicity and Beulah; and pert, bunny noses; and terrified smiles. We grinned back at them with genuine ferocity. It made us nervous to meet new humans. There were so many things that we could do wrong! And the rules here were different depending on which humans we were with: dancing or no dancing, checkers playing or no checkers playing, pumping or no pumping.

The purebred girls played checkers with us.

"These girl-girls sure is dumb," my sister Lavash panted to me between games. "I win it again! Five to none."

She was right. The purebred girls were making mistakes on purpose, in order to give us an advantage. "King me," I growled, out of turn. *"I say king me!"* and Felicity meekly complied. Beulah pretended not to mind when we got frustrated with the oblique, fussy movement from square to square and shredded the board to ribbons. I felt sorry for them. I wondered what it would be like to be bred in captivity, and always homesick for a dimly sensed forest, the trees you've never seen.

Jeanette was learning how to dance. On Holy Thursday, she mastered a rudimentary form of the Charleston. *"Brava!"* The nuns clapped. *"Brava!"*

Every Friday, the girls who had learned how to ride a bicycle celebrated by going on chaperoned trips into town. The purebred girls sold seven hundred rolls of gift-wrap paper and used the proceeds to buy us a yellow fleet of bicycles built for two. We'd ride the bicycles uphill, a sanctioned pumping, a grim-faced nun pedaling behind each one of us. "Congratulations!" the nuns would huff. "Being human is like riding this bicycle. Once you've learned how, you'll never forget." Mirabella would run after the bicycles, growling out our old names. HWRAA! GWARR! TRRRRRRR! We pedaled faster.

At this point, we'd had six weeks of lessons, and still nobody could do the Sausalito but Jeanette. The nuns decided we needed an inducement to dance. They announced that we would celebrate our successful rehabilitations with a Debutante Ball. There would be brothers, ferried over from the Home for Man-Boys Raised by Wolves. There would be a photographer from the *Gazette Sophisticate*. There would be a three-piece jazz band from West Toowoomba, and root beer in tiny plastic cups. The brothers! We'd almost forgotten about them. Our invisible tails went limp. I should have been excited; instead, I felt a low mad anger at the nuns. They knew we weren't ready to dance with the brothers; we weren't even ready to talk to them. Things had been so much simpler in the woods. That night I waited until my sisters were asleep. Then I slunk into the closet and practiced the Sausalito two-step in secret, a private mass of twitch and foam. Mouth shut—shoes on feet! Mouth shut—shoes on feet! Mouthshutmouthshut . . .

One night I came back early from the closet and stumbled on Jeanette. She was sitting in a patch of moonlight on the windowsill, reading from one of her library books. (She was the first of us to sign for her library card too.) Her cheeks looked dewy.

"Why you cry?" I asked her, instinctively reaching over to lick Jeanette's cheek and catching myself in the nick of time.

Jeanette blew her nose into a nearby curtain. (Even her mistakes annoyed us—they were always so well intentioned.) She sniffled and pointed to a line in her book: "The lake-water was reinventing the forest and the white moon above it, and wolves lapped up the cold reflection of the sky." But none of the pack besides me could read yet, and I wasn't ready to claim a common language with Jeanette.

The following day, Jeanette golfed. The nuns set up a miniature putt-putt course in the garden. Sister Maria dug four sandtraps and got old Walter, the groundskeeper, to make a windmill out of a lawn mower engine. The eighteenth hole was what they called a "doozy," a minuscule crack in St. Lucy's marble dress. Jeanette got a hole in one.

On Sundays, the pretending felt almost as natural as nature. The chapel was our favorite place. Long before we could understand what the priest was saying, the music instructed us in how to feel. The choir director—aggressively perfumed Mrs. Valuchi, gold necklaces like pineapple rings around her neck—taught us more than the nuns ever did. She showed us how to pattern the old hunger into arias. Clouds moved behind the frosted oculus of the nave, glass shadows that reminded me of my mother. The mother, I'd think, struggling to conjure up a picture. A black shadow, running behind the watery screen of pines.

We sang at the chapel annexed to the home every morning. We understood that this was the humans' moon, the place for howling beyond purpose. Not for mating, not for hunting, not for fighting, not for anything but the sound itself. And we'd howl along with the choir, hurling every pitted thing within us at the stained glass. "Sotto voce." The nuns would frown. But you could tell that they were pleased.

> STAGE 4: As a more thorough understanding of the host culture is acquired, your students will begin to feel more comfortable in their new environment. Your students feel more at home, and their self-confidence grows. Everything begins to make sense.

"Hey, Claudette," Jeanette growled to me on the day before the ball. "Have you noticed that everything's beginning to make sense?"

Before I could answer, Mirabella sprang out of the hall closet and snapped through Jeanette's homework binder. Pages and pages of words swirled around the stone corridor, like dead leaves off trees.

"What about you, Mirabella?" Jeanette asked politely, stooping to pick up her erasers. She was the only one of us who would still talk to Mirabella; she was high enough in the rankings that she could afford to talk to the scruggliest wolf-girl. "Has everything begun to make more sense, Mirabella?"

Mirabella let out a whimper. She scratched at us and scratched at us, raking her nails along our shins so hard that she drew blood. Then she rolled belly-up on the cold stone floor, squirming on a bed of spelling-bee worksheets. Above us, small pearls of light dotted the high, tinted window.

Jeanette frowned. "You are a late bloomer, Mirabella! Usually, everything's begun to make more sense by Month Twelve at the latest." I noticed that she stumbled on the word *bloomer*. HraaaHA! Jeanette could never fully shake our accent. She'd talk like that her whole life, I thought with a gloomy satisfaction, each word winced out like an apology for itself.

"Claudette, help me," she yelped. Mirabella had closed her jaws around Jeanette's bald ankle and was dragging her toward the closet. "Please. Help me to mop up Mirabella's mess."

I ignored her and continued down the hall. I had only four more hours to perfect the Sausalito. I was worried only about myself. By that stage, I was no longer certain of how the pack felt about anything.

At seven o'clock on the dot, Sister Ignatius blew her whistle and frog-marched us into the ball. The nuns had transformed the rectory into a very scary place. Purple and silver balloons started popping all around us. Black streamers swooped down from the eaves and got stuck in our hair like bats. A full yellow moon smirked outside the window. We were greeted by blasts of a saxophone, and fizzy pink drinks, and the brothers.

The brothers didn't smell like our brothers anymore. They smelled like pomade and cold, sterile sweat. They looked like little boys. Someone had washed behind their ears and made them wear suspendered dungarees. Kyle used to be a blustery alpha male, BTWWWR!, chewing through rattlesnakes, spooking badgers, snatching a live trout out of a grizzly's mouth. He stood by the punch bowl, looking pained and out of place.

"My stars!" I growled. "What lovely weather we've been having!"

"Yeees," Kyle growled back. "It is beginning to look a lot like Christmas." All around the room, boys and girls raised by wolves were having the same conversation. Actually, it had been an unseasonably warm and brown winter, and just that morning a freak hailstorm had sent Sister Josephina to an early grave. But we had only gotten up to Unit 7: Party

Dialogue; we hadn't yet learned the vocabulary for Unit 12: How to Tactfully Acknowledge Disaster. Instead, we wore pink party hats and sucked olives on little sticks, inured to our own strangeness.

The nuns swept our hair back into high, bouffant hair styles. This made us look more girlish and less inclined to eat people, the way that squirrels are saved from looking like rodents by their poofy tails. I was wearing a white organdy dress with orange polka dots. Jeanette was wearing a mauve organdy dress with blue polka dots. Linette was wearing a red organdy dress with white polka dots. Mirabella was in a dark corner, wearing a muzzle. Her party culottes were duct-taped to her knees. The nuns had tied little bows on the muzzle to make it more festive. Even so, the jazz band from West Toowoomba kept glancing nervously her way.

"You smell astooooounding!" Kyle was saying, accidentally stretching the diphthong into a howl and then blushing. "I mean—"

"Yes, I know what it is that you mean," I snapped. (That's probably a little narrative embellishment on my part; it must have been months before I could really "snap" out words.) I didn't smell astounding. I had rubbed a pumpkin muffin all over my body earlier that morning to mask my natural, feral scent. Now I smelled like a purebred girl, easy to kill. I narrowed my eyes at Kyle and flattened my ears, something I hadn't done for months. Kyle looked panicked, trying to remember the words that would make me act like a girl again. I felt hot, oily tears squeezing out of the red corners of my eyes. *Shoesonfeet!* I barked at myself. I tried again. "My! What lovely weather—"

The jazz band struck up a tune.

"The time has come to do the Sausalito," Sister Maria announced, beaming into the microphone. "Every sister grab a brother!" She switched on Walter's industrial flashlight, struggling beneath its weight, and aimed the beam in the center of the room.

Uh-oh. I tried to skulk off into Mirabella's corner, but Kyle pushed me into the spotlight. "No," I moaned through my teeth, "noooooo." All of a sudden the only thing my body could remember how to do was pump and pump. In a flash of white-hot light, my months at St. Lucy's had vanished, and I was just a terrified animal again. As if of their own accord, my feet started to wiggle out of my shoes. *Mouth shut,* I gasped, staring down at my naked toes, *mouthshutmouthshut.*

"Ahem. The time has come," Sister Maria coughed, "to do the Sausalito." She paused. "The Sausalito," she added helpfully, "does not in any way resemble the thing that you are doing."

Beads of sweat stood out on my forehead. I could feel my jaws gaping open, my tongue lolling out of the left side of my mouth. What were the steps? I looked frantically for Jeanette; she would help me, she would tell me what to do.

Jeanette was sitting in the corner, sipping punch through a long straw and watching me pant. I locked eyes with her, pleading with the mute intensity that I had used to beg her for weasel bones in the forest. "What are the steps?" I mouthed.

"The steps!"

"The steps?" Then Jeanette gave me a wide, true wolf smile. For an instant, she looked just like our mother. "Not for you," she mouthed back.

I threw my head back, a howl clawing its way up my throat. I was about to lose all my Skill Points, I was about to fail my Adaptive Dancing test. But before the air could burst from my lungs, the wind got knocked out of me. *Oomph!* I fell to the ground, my skirt falling softly over my head. Mirabella had intercepted my eye-cry for help. She'd chewed through her restraints and tackled me from behind, barking at unseen cougars, trying to shield me with her tiny body. *"Caramba!"* Sister Maria squealed, dropping the flashlight. The music ground to a halt. And I have never loved someone so much, before or since, as I loved my littlest sister at that moment. I wanted to roll over and lick her ears, I wanted to kill a dozen spotted fawns and let her eat first.

But everybody was watching; everybody was waiting to see what I would do. "I wasn't talking to you," I grunted from underneath her. "I didn't want your help. Now you have ruined the Sausalito! You have ruined the ball!" I said more loudly, hoping the nuns would hear how much my enunciation had improved.

"You have ruined it!" my sisters panted, circling around us, eager to close ranks. "Mirabella has ruined it!" Every girl was wild-eyed and itching under her polka dots, punch froth dribbling down her chin. The pack had been waiting for this moment for some time. "Mirabella cannot adapt! Back to the woods, back to the woods!"

The band from West Toowoomba had quietly packed their instruments into black suitcases and were sneaking out the back. The boys had fled back toward the lake, bow ties spinning, snapping suspenders in their haste. Mirabella was still snarling in the center of it all, trying to figure out where the danger was so that she could defend me against it. The nuns exchanged glances.

In the morning, Mirabella was gone. We checked under all the beds. I pretended to be surprised. I'd known she would have to be expelled the minute I felt her weight on my back. Walter came and told me this in secret after the ball, "So you can say yer goodbyes." I didn't want to face Mirabella. Instead, I packed a tin lunch pail for her: two jelly sandwiches on saltine crackers, a chloroformed squirrel, a gilt-edged placard of St. Bolio. I left it for her with Sister Ignatius, with a little note: "Best wishes!" I told myself I'd done everything I could.

"Hooray!" the pack crowed. "Something has been done!"

We raced outside into the bright sunlight, knowing full well that our sister had been turned loose, that we'd never find her. A low roar rippled through us and surged up and up, disappearing into the trees. I listened for an answering howl from Mirabella, heart thumping—what if she heard us and came back? But there was nothing.

We graduated from St. Lucy's shortly thereafter. As far as I can recollect, that was our last communal howl.

STAGE 5: At this point your students are able to interact effectively in the new cultural environment. They find it easy to move between the two cultures.

One Sunday, near the end of my time at St. Lucy's, the sisters gave me a special pass to go visit the parents. The woodsman had to accompany me; I couldn't remember how to find the way back on my own. I wore my best dress and brought along some prosciutto and dill pickles in a picnic basket. We crunched through the fall leaves in silence, and every step made me sadder. "I'll wait out here," the woodsman said, leaning on a blue elm and lighting a cigarette.

The cave looked so much smaller than I remembered it. I had to duck my head to enter. Everybody was eating when I walked in. They all looked up from the bull moose at the same time, my aunts and uncles, my sloe-eyed, lolling cousins, the parents. My uncle dropped a thighbone from his mouth. My littlest brother, a cross-eyed wolf-boy who has since been successfully rehabilitated and is now a dour, balding children's book author, started whining in terror. My mother recoiled from me, as if I was a stranger. TRRR? She sniffed me for a long moment. Then she sank her teeth into my ankle, looking proud and sad. After all the tail wagging and perfunctory barking had died down, the parents sat back on their hind legs. They stared up at me expectantly, panting in the cool gray envelope of the cave, waiting for a display of what I had learned.

"So," I said, telling my first human lie. "I'm home."

PART 8

PAST AND PRESENT

Perceptions of the wild shifted in the modern period with the emergence of numerous wilderness conservation groups. Dedicated to protecting and preserving a wild no longer viewed as Gothic or Romantic but as chiefly environmental, organizations like the National Parks Conservation Association (1919), the Wilderness Society (1935), the National Wildlife Federation (1936), and the Nature Conservancy (1951) were all founded to arrest or undo the ecological mistakes of the past. At the same time that both land and wildlife conservation were becoming, for many, a pressing public priority, new fictional tales emerged underscoring deep personal connections to wilderness. Struggling to adjust to disappearing wild places and vanishing ways of life, writers began to consider the lasting import of wilderness through the lens of individual or family history, a form of personal and often generational reckoning that relies on the emotional power of memory to sort through the complex meanings of what has been lost or what might be due. Stories in this section, pervaded by feelings of guilt or nostalgia, feature characters looking back on the wild natural landscapes of their ancestral or individual past as they seek reconciliation, redemption, or resolution in their present.

"The Third Generation"

MARJORIE PICKTHALL

Marjorie Pickthall (1883–1922) was born in West London in 1883 and raised mainly in Toronto, Ontario, where she was celebrated in her youth for her precociously accomplished poetry. But it is her posthumously published short-story collection *Angels' Shoes* (1923) that represents her best writing. Pickthall, who worked as a secretary, a vegetable grower, an assistant librarian, and a mechanic during World War I, shifted from writing poems to writing periodical and magazine short stories because they were more lucrative, ultimately publishing more than two hundred of them. She also composed three Canadian frontier adventure novels for children, beginning with *Dick's Desertion: A Boy's Adventures in Canadian Forests* (1905), and three adult novels, most prominently *The Bridge: A Story of the Great Lakes* (1922)—books that, like many of her short stories, dramatize journeys into the uncharted and mysterious interiors of the Canadian wild. Her tale "The Third Generation" travels deep into the region's abundant lakes and rivers for a sobering reckoning. Appearing in the literary magazine the *Bellman* on December 14, 1918, at the very height of the great flu pandemic, Pickthall's story confronts readers with the colonial legacy and deadly impact of another highly infectious virus, smallpox. Unique for its time, this story goes well beyond the typical expedition adventure narrative, instead raising meaningful and far-reaching questions of historical guilt and generational atonement by asking whether the sins of the fathers might yet be visited on their descendants. Pickthall, who had suffered ill health since childhood, moved to the west coast of Vancouver Island to live out her life among members of the Ditidaht First Nation, but soon after died of an embolism at the age of thirty-eight.

"The Third Generation"

MARJORIE PICKTHALL

No shanty fires shall cheer them,
No comrades march beside,
But the northern lights shall beckon
And the wandering winds shall guide.
They shall cross the silent waters
By a trail that is wild and far.
To the place of the lonely lodges
Under a lonely star.

—LA LONGUE TRAVERSE

B ob, is this Lake Lemaire?"

Bob Lemaire, leaning against a wind-twisted tamarack on the ridge above the portage, looked long and very long at the desolate country spread out beneath them. Then he looked at a map, drawn on parchment in faded ink, which he had just unfolded from a waterproof case. "I can't identify it," he confessed at last, "but I think—"

"If you say another word," groaned Barrett, "about the reliability of your grandfather, I—I'll heave rocks at you." Lemaire smiled slowly, and the smile transfigured his lean, serious face; he folded the map and replaced it in the little case. "Well," he answered, comfortingly, "we can't mistake P'tite Babiche, anyway, when we come to it."

"If the thing exists . . . Oh, I know your grandfather said he found it, and stuck it on his map. But no one else has ever found it since."

"No one else," said Lemaire, quietly, "has been so far west from the Gran' Babiche."

He looked again at the land, one of the most desolate in the world, across which they must go. Lake, rapid, river; rock, scrub, pine, and caribou moss—here the world held only these things, repeated to infinity. But as Lemaire's grave eyes rested on them, those eyes showed nothing but stillness and a strange content. And Barrett, who had been watching his friend and not the new chain of lakes ahead, cried suddenly, "Bob, I believe you like it!"

"Yes, I like it—if like is the word."

"O gosh! And you never saw it till five years ago?"

"No."

"And your father never saw it at all?"

"No. He married young, you know, and had no money. He worked in an office all his life. My mother said he used to talk in his sleep of— all this—which he had never seen. And when I saw it, it just seemed to—come natural." He smiled again. "We've three—four—more portages," he went on, "before we camp."

"And it's along of having Forbes Lemaire for a grandfather," groaned Barrett, as he limped after Lemaire's light stride, down the rocky slope to the little beach where they had left their canoe.

They launched the canoe, thigh deep in the rush of the ice-clear water, and put out into yet another of that endless chain of unknown and uncharted lakes whose course they were following. Only one map in the world showed these lakes, those low iron hills, that swamp—the map made by Bob Lemaire's grandfather fifty years before; as far as was known, only one white man before themselves had ever tried the journey from the Gran' Babiche due west to the P'tite Babiche, that mythical river; and that had been Forbes Lemaire. As Barrett said, it was a tour personally conducted by the ghost of a grandfather.

Another wet portage—tripping and sliding under a low cliff among fallen shale and willow bushes—another lake, as wide, as lonely, as the former one. So for three hours. And then the afternoon shut down in drive on drive of damp gray mist; and they edged the canoe inshore, and beached it at last upon a dun ridge of sand, the shadows of dwarfed bullpines promising firing.

Too tired to speak, they made their camp, deftly, as long practice had taught them. Tinned beef, flapjacks and coffee had power, however, to change the very aspect of the weather. And Barrett, smoking the pipe of repletion, under a wisp of tent, had time to admire the Japanese effect of the writhed pines in the fog, to hear a sort of wild music in the voices of rain and water, and to meditate on the chances of an ouananiche for the morning's meal.

The shadows of the fog were changing to the shadows of night, and the silent Lemaire rose and flung wood on the fire. It sent out a warm glow; and as if it had been a signal, a living shadow crept from the shadow of the rocks, and very timidly approached the light.

Both men rose with an exclamation; for they had not seen a human being for nearly a month. Barrett said, "An Indian," and sank back on his blanket, leaving Lemaire to ask questions. Lemaire went round the fire, and stooped over the queer huddled shadow on the ground.

"Well?" Barrett called after him at last.

"A Montagnais," Lemaire answered after a pause, some trouble in his voice. "About the oldest old Indian I've ever seen; they aren't long-lived . . . He seems a bit wrong in the head. He doesn't seem to know his name or where he comes from. But—he says he's going to a big encampment many days' journey west. He says he's been following us. He says he's a friend of mine."

"Is he?"

"I never saw him before . . . That's all I can get out of him. He's probably been cast off by his tribe. Why? Oh, too old to be useful."

"Cruel brutes."

"Not so cruel as some white men," said Lemaire, half to himself. He had come back to the firelight, and was rummaging among their stores, none too plentiful. He returned to the old Indian, carrying food; and presently Barrett heard snapping sounds, as of a hungry dog feeding. Lemaire came again to his nook under the tent; and Barrett smoked out his pipe in silence. Then, as he knocked the ashes, fizzling, into a little pool of rain, he said gently, "Bob, what makes you so uncommonly good to the Indians?"

Quiet Lemaire did not attempt to evade the direct question. But a rather shy flush rose to his dark, lean cheeks as he said diffidently, "I suppose—because I feel my family—any one of my name—owes 'em something."

"The grandfather again, eh?"

"Yes . . . Men had no souls in those days, Barrett. I think the tremendous loneliness—the newness—the lack of responsibility—something killed their souls . . . Wait."

Leaning forward, he flung more wood on the fire. And the red light flickered on his strong and gentle face. He glanced at his friend, and went on abruptly. "I've my grandfather's maps and journals, you know—what my father called the shameful records of his fame. He was absolutely explicit in 'em. I never saw them in father's lifetime, but he left them to me, saying I could read them or not, as I liked. I was very proud of them. I read them. And upon my word—though from them I got the hints that may lead us to the rediscovery of the Lost Babiche—I'm almost sorry I did. It leaves a bad taste in the mind, if you know what I mean, to think that one's father's father was such a heroic scoundrel."

"A bad record, Bobby?"

"Bad even for those days. Listen to me. While he was on this very expedition we're on now, he was taken sick. He was very sick, and going to be worse. He knew what it was. He was near the big summer camp of a tribe of Indians that had been very kind to him, coast Indians, come inland for the caribou hunting; he went to them. He was sick, and they took him in, and nursed him. And all the time he knew what it was he had. It was the smallpox.

"You know what La Picotte is in the wilds. They've a song about it still, down along the Lamennais . . . For of all that tribe, only one family, they say, escaped. All the others died; they died as if the Angel of Destruction had come among them with his sword—they died like flies, they died in heaps. And over the bones of the dead the tepees stood for years, ragged, blowing in the winds. And then the skins rotted, and the bare poles stood, gleaming white, over the rotting bones that covered an acre of ground, they say. No one ever went to that place any more. It was cursed . . . because of my grandfather."

"Monsieur Forbes made his get-away?"

"Yes, or I shouldn't be telling you about it." Lemaire summoned a smile, but his eyes were sombre. "And so I guess—that's one reason why. One among many."

"You're a likeable old freak," murmured Barrett affectionately, "but—*you* ain't responsible, you know!"

"As I look at it, we're all responsible."

"Well—anyway, I wouldn't give that old scarecrow too much of our grubstake, old man. We've none too much, if the Babiche doesn't turn up according to schedule."

"Probably we won't see any more of him. He'll be gone by the morning."

He was gone with the morning. But as day followed weary day, and there was still no sign of the lakes narrowing to the long-sought river, Barrett was increasingly conscious that the old man was close upon their trail. Sometimes, in the brief radiance of the September dawns, he would see, far and far behind on the wrinkled silver water, a warped canoe paddling feebly. They always hauled away, by miles, from that decrepit canoe. But always, some time in the dark hours, it crept up again. Sometimes, he would see, in the sunset, a wavering thread of smoke arising from the site of their last-camp-but-one. It irritated him at last; the thought of that ragged, cranky canoe, paddled by the ragged, dirty, old imbecile, forever following them—creeping, creeping, under the great gaunt stars, creeping, creeping, under the flying dawns, the stormy moons; when he found Lemaire leaving little scraps of precious tobacco, a pinch of flour in a screw of paper, or a fresh-caught fish beside the trodden ashes of their cooking-place, he exploded.

"I can't help it," Lemaire apologized, "I *know* I'm all kinds of a fool, Barrett. But the poor old wretch is nearly blind—from long-ago small-pox, I should think. He can't catch things for himself much."

Barrett, aware that wisdom was on his side, yet felt sorry for his explosion. He said nothing more. Soon he forgot the matter, having much else to think about.

For the Lost Babiche, the once-discovered river, did not "turn up according to schedule." The chain of lakes they had been follow-ing turned due south. They left them, and, after a terrible portage, launched the canoe in a stream that ran west. Here their progress was very slow, for there were rapids, and consequent portages, every mile or so. This stream, instead of feeding another lake, died out in impassable quaking mosses. They saw a range of low hills some four or five miles ahead; so again they left the canoe and struck out for them on foot, half-wading, half-walking. It was exhausting work. At last they climbed the barren spurs and saw beyond, under a flaring yellow sunset, a world of interlacing waterways, unvisited and unknown, that seemed then as if they smoked under the vast clouds and spirals of wildfowl settling homeward to the reeds. The two men watched that wonderful sight in silence.

At last, "They're gathering to go south," said Lemaire briefly. And Barrett answered, "D'you know what date it is? It's the day on which we said we'd turn back if we hadn't found the Lost Babiche. It's the fifteenth of September."

"Well . . . are we going back?"

"Not till we've found our river," cried Barrett, with half a laugh and half a curse. They gripped hands, smiling rather grimly. They made a miserable, fireless camp, and went back the next day, carrying canoe and supplies, in four toilsome trips, across the hills; repacking and relaunching the second day on a new lake, where in all probability no white man—but one—had ever before dipped paddle.

They had been in the wilderness so long that they had fallen into the habit of carrying on conversations as if the lapse of two or three days had been as many minutes. Barrett knew to what Lemaire referred when he said abruptly, "After all, it isn't as if you were ignorant of the risks."

"I guess I know just as much about them as you," said Barrett, cheerily. "We're taking chances on the grub, aren't we? If we find the Lost Babiche before the game moves, we'll be alright, though our own supplies won't take us there. Once there, Bob, we're pretty sure to find friendly Indians when we link up with the Silver Fork—which we do seventy miles down the P'tite Babiche if your grandpa's map's correct. Well there are a good many 'ifs' in the programme, but don't you worry. We'll get through or out, somehow. There's always fish. I've a feeling that this country *can't* go back on a Lemaire!"

They went on to a pleasant camp that night on a sandy islet overgrown with dwarf willow, and a wild-duck supper. The current of these new lakes went west with such increasing strength that Lemaire thought they were feeling the "pull" of some big river into which the system drained; and if so, it could be no river but the Lost Babiche. They slept, all a-tingle with the fever of discovery and re-made maps in their dreams.

Behind them many miles, a wandering smoke arose from the ashes of their last camp. The old Indian, about whom they had almost forgotten, had gained on them while they packed their supplies over the hills. Now he was close upon them again.

The life of that old savage seemed thin and wavering as the smoke of the fire he made. All night he sat in the ashes, motionless as a stone. Only once, just before the fierce dawn, he rose to his feet with an inarticulate cry, stirred to some instinctive excitement. For in a moment the vast, chill dusk was filled with a musical thrill, a tremendous clamour and rush of life, as thousand by thousand after their kinds, teal and widgeon, mallard and sheldrake, lifted from the reeds and fled before the coming cold. As the old man dimly watched, two delicate things fell and touched his face; one was a feather, the second was a flake of snow.

In those few delicate flakes, Lemaire and Barrett seemed to feel for the first time the ever-present hostility of nature; with such a brief, exquisite touch were they first made aware of the powers against which they strove. The new waterways seemed to stretch interminably. Each time they cleared one of the deep-cut channels which linked lake with lake as regularly as a thread links beads, they looked ahead with the same question. Each time they saw the same expanse of gray water, low islets, barren shores; the country passed them changing and unchanging as a dream. They seemed to be moving in a dream, conscious of nothing but the pressure of the current on their paddles.

Then came the mist.

It shut them into a circle ten feet wide, a pearl-white prison. Outside the circle were shadows, wandering voices, trees as men walking. For two days they felt their way westward through this fog; two nights they shivered over a damp-wood fire, hearing nothing but water beading and dripping everywhere with a sound of grief. It strangely broke Lemaire's steel nerve. On the second night he said, restlessly, "We must turn back tomorrow."

"Bob!"

He flung out a tanned hand passionately. "I know . . . But can't you feel it? Things have turned against us. These things." He pointed at the veiled sky, the milky water. "I daren't go on. If we don't find the river tomorrow, we'll go back. And then . . . the land will have done for me what it never did for my grandfather."

"What, Bob, old fellow?"

"Beaten me," said Lemaire, and rolled into his blankets without another word.

He woke next morning with the touch of clear sunlight on his eyelids. He leaped to his feet silently, without waking Barrett, and as he did so, ice broke and tinkled like glass where the edge of the blankets had lain in a little pool of moisture. The last of the fog was draining in golden smoke from the low, dark hills. He strode to the edge of the water, and stopped, shaking suddenly as if he were cold. Then he went to Barrett, and stooped over him.

"Hullo, Bob is it morning?" Then, as he saw Lemaire's face, "My God, what is it?"

Twice Lemaire tried to speak. Then he pointed eastward to three high rocky islands which lay across the water, exactly spaced, like the ruined spans of a great bridge which once had stretched from shore to shore.

"Barrett," he said huskily, "We entered the Lost Babiche yesterday in the fog, and never knew. Those islands are ten miles down the river on Forbes Lemaire's map."

They faced each other in silence, too much moved to speak. Their hands met in a long grip. Then Barrett said suddenly, "Anything else."

"Yes. It's freezing hard."

"But . . . we've won, Bob, we've won!"

"Not yet," said the man whose fathers had been bred in the wilderness, and wed to it. "Not yet. It's still against us."

But there was no talk now of turning back.

The Lost Babiche—lost no more—was a noble river; a gray and ice-clear stream winding in generous curves between high cliffs of slate-coloured rock. These cliffs were much cut into ravines and gullies, where grew timber of fine size for that country. But as their tense excitement lessened a little, they were struck by the absence of all life; even in the deep rock-shadows they saw no fish. Of human life there was not a sign; though in Forbes Lemaire's days the country had supported many Indians. And now—"Not a soul but ourselves," said Barrett, in an awed voice; "not a living soul . . ."

Yes. One soul yet living. Far behind them, in the staggering old canoe, the old Indian paddled valiantly on their trail. But he had forgotten them now, as they had long forgotten him. He stopped no more for the offal of their camps. A stronger instinct even than that of hunger was drawing him on the way they also went; down the Lost Babiche. Had they looked, they would not have seen him. And soon, between him and them, the clouds which had been gathering all day dropped a curtain of fine snow.

The first sting of the tiny balled flakes on his knuckles was to Lemaire like the thunder of guns, the opening of a battle.

He had no need to speak to Barrett. They bent over the paddles and the canoe surged forward. It was a race; a race between the early winter and themselves. If the cold weather set in so soon, if they found no Indians on the little-known Silver Fork—there were a dozen "ifs" in their minds as, mile after mile, they fled down the P'tite Babiche. Even as they fled from the winter, so that other white man long ago had fled from the sickness; seen those stark bluffs unrolling; viewed perhaps those very trees.

They made a record distance that day. "We're winning, Bob, we're winning," said Barrett over the fire that night. Lemaire had not the heart to contradict him; but Lemaire's instincts, inherited from generations, told him that the wilderness was still mysteriously their enemy. He sat smoking, silent, hearing nothing but the faint, innumerable hiss of the snowflakes falling into the flames.

The snow was thickening in the morning, and by noon a bitter wind arose, blowing in their faces and against the stream. Soon the canoe was smack-smack-smacking on the waves, and the snow was driving almost level. The continual pressure of wind and snow drugged their senses. They never heard the voice of the rapids until, rounding an abrupt bend, the raveled water seemed to leap at them from under the very bow of the canoe.

There was only one thing to be done, and—"Let her go!" yelled Lemaire, crouching tense as a spring above the steering paddle.

Now for the trained eye, the strong hand—the eye to see the momentary chance, the hand to obey without a falter.

Now for the sleeping instincts of a brain inherited from far generations of wanderers and voyageurs. Flash on flash of leaping water, the drive of spray and snow, the canoe staggering and checking like a thing hurt, but always recovering.

Barrett, in the bows, paddled blindly. His life lay in Bob Lemaire's hands, and he was content to leave it there during those roaring moments. But those hands failed—by an inch.

They were in smooth water. Barrett would have paused to take breath, but Lemaire's voice barked at him from the stern. He obeyed. The canoe drove forward again—forward in great leaps, towards the point of a small island ahead, dimly seen through the snow— something wrong, though, thought Barrett, grunting; he could get no "beef" on the thing—it dragged; you'd have thought Bob was paddling against him. Then, suddenly, he understood. He called up the last of his strength, drove the paddle in, once, twice—again—heard a shout, flung himself overside into water waist-deep, and just as the canoe was sinking under them, he and Lemaire caught it and ran it ashore. Then, dripping, they looked each other in the face, and each seemed to see the face of disaster.

"It was a rock," said Lemaire at last, very quietly, "a few inches below the surface. It has almost cut the canoe in two."

"What's to be done?"

"Find shelter, I suppose."

They were very quiet about it. There was no shelter on their islet but a few rocks and a dead spruce in the middle. Here they set up their tent as a wind-break. It was bitterly cold; the island was sheathed with white ice, for the spray from the rough water froze now as it fell; everything in the canoe was wet; they were wet to their waists. They tried to induce the dead tree to burn, but the wood was so rotted with wet it only smoldered and went out. They had a little cooking-lamp and a few squares of compressed fuel for it; they lighted this, and Lemaire made tea with numbed hands. It renewed the life in them, but could not dry them. They huddled against the little lamp in silence, waiting—waiting.

After some time Lemaire heard a curious sound from Barrett; his teeth were chattering. Lemaire saw that his face had taken a waxy white hue. He spoke to him, and Barrett looked up, but his eyes were dim and glazed. "It'll be all right," he said, thickly, "we'll get through, somehow. I've a feeling that this country can't go back on a Lemaire."

They were the first symptoms of collapse. Lemaire groaned. He got to his feet, and staggered across the slippery rocks. He shook his fist in the implacable face of the desolation. He shouted, foolish rage and defiance, caught back at his sanity; shouted again . . . This time he thought he heard a faint cry in the snow. It whipped him back to self-control. He splashed out into the curdling shallows, shouting desperately.

Out of the gray drive of snow loomed the ghost of a canoe, paddled, as it seemed, by a ghost. It was the old Indian, whom Lemaire had long forgotten; the weather had not hindered him, the rapids had not wrecked him. At Lemaire's cry he raised his head, and the canoe put inshore, waveringly. Lemaire splashed to meet it, met the incurious gaze of the half-blind old eyes under the scarred lids, and read into the wrinkled, foul old face, a sort of animal kindness.

Five minutes later he was desperately trying to rouse Barrett. Barrett looked at him at last, and Lemaire saw that the brief delirium was past. "What is it, Bob?" he asked, weakly. And Lemaire broke into a torrent of words.

"The old Indian—the old Indian you said was a hoodoo—don't you remember? He's here. He has caught us up, God knows how. He says his canoe'll hold three. He says that a very little way on there's a big camp, and that he'll take us there—in a very little while. He says his tribe is always kind to strangers, to white men . . . I can't make out all he says, he's queer in his head. But he's dead sure of the encampment. He says it's always there."

Still talking eagerly, Lemaire snatched together a few things, got an arm round Barrett, lifted him up to his feet, got him reeling to the canoe, laid him in the bottom, and helped the old Indian push off. There was no second paddle. There was no need of it. The current took them at once.

The cold was increasing, as the wind died and the snow thinned. Lemaire ceased to be conscious of the passing of time, but within himself the stubborn life burned; he was strongly curious to know the end, to discover what it was the wilderness had in store for him after five years, to read the riddle of that relationship with himself which had called him from the cities to this.

He was aware, at last, of a vast, golden light. The clouds were parting behind the snow, and the sunset was gleaming through. It turned the snow into a mist of rose and molten gold. The old Indian feebly turned the canoe. It crept toward the shore.

"The lodges of my people," muttered the old Indian. He stood erect, and pointed with his bleached paddle. "They are very many—a very strong tribe."

Lemaire also looked, and saw.

Silently, the canoe took the half-frozen sand. Silently, very slowly, Lemaire stepped out. The old Indian waited for him. It seemed that the whole world was waiting for him.

He, like a man in a dream, moved slowly into the midst of a level stretch of sand, and stood there. All about him, covering the whole level, were the ridgepoles of wigwams, but the coverings had long fallen away and rotted, and the sunset glowed through the gaunt poles. Lemaire stretched out his hand, and touched the nearest; they fell into dust and rot . . . Under his feet he crushed the bones of the dead—the dead, who had died fifty years before, and had waited for him here ever since, under the blown sand and the ground willows . . . "They've a song about it, down along the Lamennais. For of all that tribe, only one family, they say, escaped. All the others died . . . they died like flies, they died in heaps. And over the bones of the dead the tepees stood for years . . . No one ever went to that place any more. It was cursed . . . because of my grandfather. . . ."

He went back to the canoe. Whining like an old animal, the old Indian was busied above Barrett. "The lodges of my people," he muttered, "a very strong tribe, and kind to the white men."

Very gently, Lemaire put aside the blind old hands that touched Barrett's unconscious face. "Don't wake him," he said.

"The Wind and the Snow of Winter"

WALTER VAN TILBURG CLARK

Walter Van Tilburg Clark (1909–1971) was born in Maine but is known as an unconventional writer of the people and landscapes of the American West. Setting nearly all his fiction in Nevada, the place where he was raised, Clark published his major works across a single decade: *The Ox-Bow Incident* (1940), a story of 1885 vigilante injustice on the western plain; *The City of Trembling Leaves* (1945), a bildungsroman of growing up in Reno in the 1920s and '30s; and *The Track of the Cat* (1949), a survival narrative featuring a cattle ranch family stalked by a mountain lion. *The Ox-Bow Incident* and *The Track of the Cat* were both made into Hollywood Westerns directed by William A. Wellman. Inspired by the land, sky, and climate of the West, Clark's fiction explores how natural environments shape people. Five of his short stories won O. Henry Prizes from 1941 to 1945, a remarkable consecutive run that ended with a first-prize win for "The Wind and the Snow of Winter," published in the *Yale Review* in 1944. Clark thought of his story as an "in memoriam" to a near-vanished western breed, the old-time walking prospector. Traveling alone with their burros, walking prospectors spent most of the year searching for gold or silver ore across vast expanses of land and territory, often wintering in towns out West. Clark's affecting story of a figure lost to time brings us back to the wilderness roots of the word "bewilderment," in which the embedded verb "wilder" etymologically signifies "to lose one's way, as in a wild or unknown place." Clark's short stories appeared together in his 1950 collection *The Watchful Gods,* his last book. He was buried in Nevada's Virginia City, an old silver-mining town, having abruptly and mysteriously ceased publishing fiction two decades earlier.

"The Wind and the Snow of Winter"

WALTER VAN TILBURG CLARK

It was near sunset when Mike Braneen came onto the last pitch of the old wagon road which had led into Gold Rock from the east since the Comstock days. The road was just two ruts in the hard earth, with sagebrush growing between them, and was full of steep pitches and sharp turns. From the summit it descended even more steeply into Gold Rock in a series of short switchbacks down the slope of the canyon. There was a paved highway on the other side of the pass now, but Mike never used that. Cars coming from behind made him uneasy, so that he couldn't follow his own thoughts long, but had to keep turning around every few minutes, to see that his burro, Annie, was staying out on the shoulder of the road, where she would be safe. Mike didn't like cars anyway, and on the old road he could forget about them, and feel more like himself. He could forget about Annie too, except when the light, quick tapping of her hoofs behind him stopped. Even then he didn't really break his thoughts. It was more as if the tapping were another sound from his own inner machinery, and when it stopped, he stopped too, and turned around to see what she was doing. When he began to walk ahead again at the same slow, unvarying pace, his arms scarcely swinging at all, his body bent a little forward from the waist, he would not be aware that there had been any interruption of the memory or the story that was going on in his head. Mike did not like to have his stories interrupted except by an idea of his own, something to do with his prospecting, or the arrival of his story at an actual memory which warmed him to close recollection or led into a new and more attractive story.

An intense, golden light, almost liquid, fanned out from the peaks above him and reached eastward under the gray sky, and the snow which occasionally swarmed across this light was fine and dry. Such little squalls had been going on all day, and still there was nothing like real snow down, but only a fine powder which the wind swept along until it caught under the brush, leaving the ground bare. Yet Mike Braneen was not deceived. This was not just a flurrying day; it was the beginning of winter. If not tonight, then tomorrow, or the next day, the snow would begin which shut off the mountains, so that a man might as well be on a great plain for all he could see, perhaps even the snow which blinded a man at once and blanketed the desert in an hour. Fifty-two years in this country had made Mike Braneen sure about such things, although he didn't give much thought to them, but only to what he had to do because of them. Three nights before, he had been awakened by a change in the wind. It was no longer a wind born in the near mountains, cold with night and altitude, but a wind from far places, full of a damp chill which got through his blankets and into his bones. The stars had still been clear and close above the dark humps of the mountains, and overhead the constellations had moved slowly in full panoply, unbroken by any invisible lower darkness, yet he had lain there half awake for a few minutes, hearing the new wind beat the brush around him, hearing Annie stirring restlessly and thumping in her hobble. He had thought drowsily, "Smells like winter this time," and then, "It's held off a long time this year, pretty near the end of December." Then he had gone back to sleep, mildly happy because the change meant he would be going back to Gold Rock. Gold Rock was the other half of Mike Braneen's life. When the smell of winter came, he always started back for Gold Rock. From March or April until the smell of winter, he wandered slowly about among the mountains, any-where between the White Pines and the Virginias, with only his burro for company. Then there would come the change, and they would head back for Gold Rock.

Mike had travelled with a good many burros during that time, eighteen or twenty, he thought, although he was not sure. He could not remember them all, but only those he had had first, when he was a young man and always thought most about seeing women when he got back to Gold Rock, or those with something queer about them, like Baldy, who'd had a great, pale patch, like a bald spot, on one side of his belly, or those who'd had something queer happen to them, like Maria. He could remember just how it had been that night. He could remember it as if it were last night. It had been in Hamilton. He had felt unhappy, because he could remember Hamilton when the whole hollow was full of people and buildings, and everything was new and active. He had gone to sleep in the empty shell of the Wells Fargo Build-ing, hearing an old iron shutter banging against the wall in the wind. In the morning, Maria had been gone. He had followed the scuffing track she made on account of her loose hobble, and it had led far up the old snow-gullied road to Treasure Hill, and then ended at one of the black shafts that opened like mouths right at the edge of the road. A man remembered a thing like that. There weren't many burros that foolish. But burros with nothing particular about them were hard to remember, especially those he'd had in the last twenty years or so, when he had gradually stopped feeling so personal about them, and had begun to call all the jennies Annie and all the burros Jack.

The clicking of the little hoofs behind him stopped, and Mike stopped too, and turned around. Annie was pulling at a line of yellow grass along the edge of the road.

"Come on, Maria," Mike said patiently. The burro at once stopped pulling at the dead grass and came on up towards him, her small black nose working, the ends of the grass standing out on each side of it like whiskers. Mike began to climb again, ahead of her.

It was a long time since he had been caught by a winter, too. He could not remember how long. All the beginnings ran together in his mind, as if they were all the beginning of one winter so far back that he had almost forgotten it. He could still remember clearly, though, the winter he had stayed out on purpose, clear into January. He had been a young man then, thirty-five or forty or forty-five, somewhere in there. He would have to stop and try to bring back a whole string of memories about what had happened just before, in order to remember just how old he had been, and it wasn't worth the trouble. Besides, sometimes even that system didn't work. It would lead him into an old camp where he had been a number of times, and the dates would get mixed up. It was impossible to remember any other way, because all his comings and goings had been so much alike. He had been young, anyhow, and not much afraid of anything except running out of water in the wrong place; not even afraid of the winter. He had stayed out because he'd thought he had a good thing, and he had wanted to prove it. He could remember how it felt to be out in the clear winter weather on the mountains, the piñon trees and the junipers weighted down with feathery snow, and making sharp, blue shadows on the white slopes. The hills had made blue shadows on one another too, and in the still air his pick had made the beginning of a sound like a bell's. He knew he had been young, because he could remember taking a day off now and then, just to go tramping around those hills, up and down the white and through the blue shadows, on a kind of holiday. He had pretended to his common sense that he was seriously prospecting, and had carried his hammer, and even his drill along, but he had really just been gallivanting, playing colt. Maybe he had been even younger than thirty-five, though he could still be stirred a little, for that matter, by the memory of the kind of weather which had sent him gallivanting. High-blue weather, he called it. There were two kinds of high-blue weather, besides the winter kind, which didn't set him off very often, spring and fall. In the spring it would have a soft, puffy wind and soft, puffy white clouds which made separate shadows that traveled silently across hills that looked soft too. In the fall it would be still, and there would be no clouds at all in the blue, but there would be something in the golden air and the soft, steady sunlight on the mountains that made a man as uneasy as the spring blowing, though in a different way, more sad and not so excited. In the spring high-blue, a man had been likely to think about women he had slept with, or wanted to sleep with, or imaginary women made up with the help of newspaper pictures of actresses or young society matrons, or of the old oil paintings in the Lucky Boy Saloon, which showed pale, almost naked women against dark, sumptuous backgrounds, women with long hair or braided hair, calm, virtuous faces, small hands and feet, and ponderous limbs, breasts, and buttocks. In the fall high-blue, though it had been much longer since he had seen a woman, or heard a woman's voice, he was more likely to think about old friends, men, or places he had heard about, or places he hadn't seen for a long time. He himself thought most often about Goldfield the way he had last seen it in the summer in nineteen-twelve. That was as far south as Mike had ever been in Nevada. Since then, he had never been south of Tonopah. When the high-blue weather was past, though, and the season worked toward winter, he began to think about Gold Rock. There were only three or four winters out of the fifty-two when he hadn't gone home to Gold Rock, to his old room at Mrs. Wright's, up on Fourth Street, and to his meals in the dining room at the International House, and to the Lucky Boy, where he could talk to Tom Connover and his other friends, and play cards, or have a drink to hold in his hand while he sat and remembered.

This journey had seemed a little different from most, though. It had started the same as usual, but as he had come across the two vast valleys, and through the pass in the low range between them, he hadn't felt quite the same. He'd felt younger and more awake, it seemed to him, and yet, in a way, older too, suddenly older. He had been sure that there was plenty of time, and yet he had been a little afraid of getting caught in the storm. He had kept looking ahead to see if the mountains on the horizon were still clearly outlined, or if they had been cut off by a lowering of the clouds. He had thought more than once, how bad it would be to get caught out there when the real snow began, and he had been disturbed by the first flakes. It had seemed hard to him to have to walk so far, too. He had kept thinking about distance. Also the snowy cold had searched out the regions of his body where old injuries had healed. He had taken off his left mitten a good many times, to blow on the fingers which had been frosted the year he was sixty-three, so that now it didn't take much cold to turn them white and stiffen them. The queer tingling, partly like an itch and partly like a pain, in the patch on his back that had been burned in that old powder blast, was sharper than he could remember its ever having been before. The rheumatism in his joints, which was so old a companion that it usually made him feel no more than tight-knit and stiff, and the place where his leg had been broken and torn when that ladder broke in ninety-seven, ached, and had a pulse he could count. All this made him believe that he was walking more slowly than usual, although nothing, probably not even a deliberate attempt, could actually have changed his pace. Sometimes he even thought, with a moment of fear, that he was getting tired.

On the other hand, he felt unusually clear and strong in his mind. He remembered things with a clarity which was like living them again, nearly all of them events from many years back, from the time when he had been really active and fearless and every burro had had its own name. Some of these events, like the night he had spent in Eureka with the little, brown-haired whore, a night in the fall in eighteen eighty-eight or nine, somewhere in there, he had not once thought of for years. Now he could remember even her name. Armandy she had called herself, a funny name. They all picked names for their business, of course, romantic names like Cecily or Rosamunde or Belle or Claire, or hard names like Diamond Gert or Horseshoe Sal, or names that were pinned on them, like Indian Kate or Roman Mary, but Armandy was different.

He could remember Armandy as if he were with her now, not the way she had behaved in bed; he couldn't remember anything particular about that. In fact, he couldn't be sure that he remembered anything about that at all. There were others he could remember more clearly for the way they had behaved in bed, women he had been with more often. He had been with Armandy only that one night. He remembered little things about being with her, things that made it seem good to think of being with her again. Armandy had a room upstairs in a hotel. They could hear a piano playing in a club across the street. He could hear the tune, and it was one he knew, although he didn't know its name. It was a gay tune that went on and on the same, but still it sounded sad when you heard it through the hotel window, with the lights from the bars and hotels shining on the street, and the people coming and going through the lights, and then, beyond the lights, the darkness where the mountains were. Armandy wore a white silk dress with a high waist, and a locket on a gold chain. The dress made her look very brown and like a young girl. She used a white powder on her face, that smelled like violets, but this could not hide her brownness. The locket was heart-shaped, and it opened to show a cameo of a man's hand holding a woman's hand very gently, just their fingers laid out long together, and the thumbs holding, the way they were sometimes on tombstones. There were two little gold initials on each hand, but Armandy wouldn't tell what they stood for, or even if the locket was really her own. He stood in the window, looking down at the club from which the piano music was coming, and Armandy stood beside him, with her shoulders against his arm, and a glass of wine in her hand. He could see the toe of her white satin slipper showing from under the edge of her skirt. Her big hat, loaded with black and white plumes, lay on the dresser behind him. His own leather coat, with the sheepskin lining, lay across the foot of the bed. It was a big bed, with a knobby brass foot and head. There was one oil lamp burning in the chandelier in the middle of the room. Armandy was soft-spoken, gentle, and a little fearful, always looking at him to see what he was thinking. He stood with his arms folded. His arms felt big and strong upon his heavily muscled chest. He stood there, pretending to be in no hurry, but really thinking eagerly about what he would do with Armandy, who had something about her which tempted him to be cruel. He stood there, with his chin down into his heavy dark beard, and watched a man come riding down the middle of the street from the west. The horse was a fine black, which lifted its head and feet with pride. The man sat very straight, with a high rein, and something about his clothes and hat made him appear to be in uniform, although it wasn't a uniform he was wearing. The man also saluted friends upon the sidewalks like an officer, bending his head just slightly, and touching his hat instead of lifting it. Mike Braneen asked Armandy who the man was, and then felt angry because she could tell him, and because he was an important man who owned a mine that was in bonanza. He mocked the airs with which the man rode, and his princely greetings. He mocked the man cleverly, and Armandy laughed and repeated what he said, and made him drink a little of her wine as a reward. Mike had been drinking whisky, and he did not like wine anyway, but this was not the moment in which to refuse such an invitation.

Old Mike remembered all this, which had been completely forgotten for years. He could not remember what he and Armandy had said, but he remembered everything else, and he felt very lonesome for Armandy, and for the room with the red, figured carpet and the brass chandelier with oil lamps in it, and the open window with the long tune coming up through it, and the young summer night outside on the mountains. This loneliness was so much more intense than his familiar loneliness that it made him feel very young. Memories like this had come up again and again during these three days. It was like beginning life over again. It had tricked him into thinking, more than once, "Next summer I'll make the strike, and this time I'll put it into something safe for the rest of my life, and stop this fool wandering around while I've still got some time left," a way of thinking which he had really stopped a long time before.

It was getting darker rapidly in the pass. When a gust of wind brought the snow against Mike's face so hard that he noticed the flakes felt larger, he looked up. The light was still there, although the fire was dying out of it, and the snow swarmed across it more thickly. Mike remembered God. He did not think anything exact. He did not think about his own relationship to God. He merely felt the idea as a comforting presence. He'd always had a feeling about God whenever he looked at a sunset, especially a sunset which came through under a stormy sky. It had been the strongest feeling left in him until these memories like the one about Armandy had begun. Even in this last pass, his strange fear of the storm had come on him again a couple of times, but now that he had looked at the light and thought of God, it was gone. In a few minutes he would come to the summit and look down into his lighted city. He felt happily hurried by this anticipation.

He would take the burro down and stable her in John Hammersmith's shed, where he always kept her. He would spread fresh straw for her, and see that the shed was tight against the wind and snow, and get a measure of grain for her from John. Then he would go up to Mrs. Wright's house at the top of Fourth Street, and leave his things in the same room he always had, the one in front, which looked down over the roofs and chimneys of his city, and across at the east wall of the canyon, from which the sun rose late. He would trim his beard with Mrs. Wright's shears, and shave the upper part of his cheeks. He would bathe out of the blue bowl and pitcher, and wipe himself with the towel with yellow flowers on it, and dress in the good, dark suit and the good, black shoes with the gleaming box toes, and the good, black hat which he had left in the chest in his room. In this way he would perform the ceremony which ended the life of the desert and began the life of Gold Rock. Then he would go down to the International House, and greet Arthur Morris in the gleaming bar, and go into the dining room and eat the best supper they had, with fresh meat and vegetables, and new-made pie, and two cups of hot, clear coffee. He would be served by the plump, blonde waitress who always joked with him, and gave him many little extra things with his first supper, including the drink which Arthur Morris always sent in from the bar.

At this point Mike Braneen stumbled in his mind, and his anticipation wavered. He could not be sure that the plump, blonde waitress would serve him. For a moment he saw her in a long skirt, and the dining room of the International House, behind her, had potted palms standing in the corners, and was full of the laughter and loud, manly talk of many customers who wore high vests and mustaches and beards. These men leaned back from tables covered with empty dishes. They patted their tight vests and lighted expensive cigars. He knew all their faces. If he were to walk down the aisle between the tables on his side, they would all speak to him. But he also seemed to remember the dining room with only a few tables, with oilcloth on them instead of linen, and with moody young men sitting at them in their work clothes, strangers who worked for the highway department or were just passing through, or talked mining in terms which he did not understand or which made him angry.

No, it would not be the plump, blonde waitress. He did not know who it would be. It didn't matter. After supper he would go up Canyon Street under the arcade to the Lucky Boy Saloon, and there it would be the same as ever. There would be the laurel wreaths on the frosted-glass panels of the doors, and the old sign upon the window, the sign that was older than Tom Connover, almost as old as Mike Braneen himself. He would open the door and see the bottles and the white women in the paintings, and the card table in the back corner and the big stove and the chairs along the wall. Tom would look around from his place behind the bar.

"Well, now," he would roar, "look who's here, boys. Now will you believe it's winter?" he would roar at them.

Some of them would be the younger men, of course, and there might even be a few strangers, but this would only add to the dignity of his reception, and there would also be his friends. There would be Henry Bray with the gray walrus mustache, and Mark Wilton and Pat Gallagher. They would all welcome him loudly.

"Mike, how are you anyway?" Tom would roar, leaning across the bar to shake hands with his big, heavy, soft hand with the diamond ring on it.

"And what'll it be, Mike? The same?" he'd ask, as if Mike had been in there no longer ago than the night before.

Mike would play that game too. "The same," he would say.

Then he would really be back in Gold Rock: never mind the plump, blonde waitress.

Mike came to the summit of the old road and stopped and looked down. For a moment he felt lost again, as he had when he'd thought about the plump, blonde waitress. He had expected Canyon Street to look much brighter. He had expected a lot of orange windows close together on the other side of the canyon. Instead there were only a few scattered lights across the darkness, and they were white. They made no communal glow upon the steep slope, but gave out only single, white needles of light, which pierced the darkness secretly and lonesomely, as if nothing could ever pass from one house to another over there. Canyon Street was very dark, too. There it went, the street he loved, steeply down into the bottom of the canyon, and down its length there were only the few street lights, more than a block apart, swinging in the wind and darting about that cold, small light. The snow whirled and swooped under the nearest street light below.

"You are getting to be an old fool," Mike Braneen said out loud to himself, and felt better. This was the way Gold Rock was now, of course, and he loved it all the better. It was a place that grew old with a man, that was going to die some time too. There could be an understanding with it.

He worked his way slowly down into Canyon Street, with Annie slipping and checking behind him. Slowly, with the blown snow behind them, they came to the first built-up block, and passed the first dim light showing through a smudged window under the arcade. They passed the dark places after it, too, and the second light. Then Mike Braneen stopped in the middle of the street, and Annie stopped beside him, pulling her rump in and turning her head away from the snow. A highway truck, coming down from the head of the canyon, had to get way over onto the wrong side of the street to pass them. The driver leaned out as he went by, and yelled, "Pull over, Pop. You're in town now."

Mike Braneen didn't hear him. He was staring at the Lucky Boy. The Lucky Boy was dark, and there were boards nailed across the big window that had shown the sign. At last Mike went over onto the board walk to look more closely. Annie followed him, but stopped at the edge of the walk and scratched her neck against a post of the arcade. There was the other sign, hanging crossways under the arcade, and even in that gloom Mike could see that it said Lucky Boy and had a Jack of Diamonds painted on it. There was no mistake. The Lucky Boy sign, and others like it under the arcade, creaked and rattled in the wind.

There were footsteps coming along the boards. The boards sounded hollow, and sometimes one of them rattled. Mike Braneen looked down slowly from the sign and peered at the approaching figure. It was a man wearing a sheepskin coat with the collar turned up round his head. He was walking quickly, like a man who knew where he was going, and why, and where he had been. Mike almost let him pass. Then he spoke.

"Say, fella—"

He even reached out a hand as if to catch hold of the man's sleeve, though he didn't touch it. The man stopped, and asked, impatiently, "Yeah?" and Mike let the hand down again slowly.

"Well, what is it?" the man asked.

"I don't want anything," Mike said. "I got plenty."

"Okay, okay," the man said. "What's the matter?"

Mike moved his hand towards the Lucky Boy. "It's closed," he said.

"I see it is, Dad," the man said. He laughed a little. He didn't seem to be in quite so much of a hurry now.

"How long has it been closed?" Mike asked.

"Since about June, I guess," the man said. "Old Tom Connover, the guy that ran it, died last June."

Mike waited for a moment. "Tom died?" he asked.

"Yup. I guess he'd just kept it open out of love of the place anyway. There hasn't been any real business for years. Nobody cared to keep it open after him."

The man started to move on, but then he waited, peering, trying to see Mike better.

"This June?" Mike asked finally.

"Yup. This last June."

"Oh," Mike said. Then he just stood there. He wasn't thinking anything. There didn't seem to be anything to think.

"You know him?" the man asked.

"Thirty years," Mike said. "No, more'n that," he said, and started to figure out how long he had known Tom Connover, but lost it, and said, as if it would do just as well, "He was a lot younger than I am, though."

"Hey," said the man, coming closer, and peering again. "You're Mike Braneen, aren't you?"

"Yes," Mike said.

"Gee, I didn't recognize you at first. I'm sorry."

"That's all right," Mike said. He didn't know who the man was, or what he was sorry about.

He turned his head slowly, and looked out into the street. The snow was coming down heavily now. The street was all white. He saw Annie with her head and shoulders in under the arcade, but the snow settling on her rump.

"Well, I guess I'd better get Molly under cover," he said. He moved toward the burro a step, but then halted.

"Say, fellow . . ."

The man had started on, but he turned back. He had to wait for Mike to speak.

"I guess this about Tom's mixed me up."

"Sure," the man said. "It's tough, an old friend like that."

"Where do I turn to get to Mrs. Wright's place?"

"Mrs. Wright's?"

"Mrs. William Wright," Mike said. "Her husband used to be a foreman in the Aztec. Got killed in the fire."

"Oh," the man said. He didn't say anything more, but just stood there, looking at the shadowy bulk of old Mike.

"She's not dead, too, is she?" Mike asked slowly.

"Yeah, I'm afraid she is, Mr. Braneen," the man said.

"Look," he said more cheerfully. "It's Mrs. Branley's house you want right now, isn't it? Place where you stayed last winter?"

Finally Mike said, "Yeah. Yeah, I guess it is."

"I'm going up that way. I'll walk up with you," the man said.

After they had started, Mike thought that he ought to take the burro down to John Hammersmith's first, but he was afraid to ask about it. They walked on down Canyon Street, with Annie walking along beside them in the gutter. At the first side street they turned right and began to climb the steep hill toward another of the little street lights dancing over a crossing. There was no sidewalk here, and Annie followed right at their heels. That one street light was the only light showing up ahead.

When they were halfway up to the light, Mike asked, "She die this summer, too?"

The man turned his body half around, so that he could hear inside his collar.

"What?"

"Did she die this summer, too?"

"Who?"

"Mrs. Wright," Mike said.

The man looked at him, trying to see his face as they came up towards the light. Then he turned back again, and his voice was muffled by the collar.

"No, she died quite a while ago, Mr. Braneen."

"Oh," Mike said finally.

They came up onto the crossing under the light, and the snow-laden wind whirled around them again. They passed under the light, and their three lengthening shadows before them were obscured by the innumerable tiny shadows of the flakes.

"Death by Landscape"

MARGARET ATWOOD

Margaret Atwood (b. 1939) is one of Canada's most prolific and celebrated authors, read widely for her novels, stories, poetry, essays, criticism, and children's literature written across a span of sixty years. Born in Ottawa, Ontario, Atwood as a child often accompanied her father, an entomologist, into the deep woods of northern Quebec and Ontario. Environmental concerns have been present in Atwood's fiction at least as early as the radioactive wasteland referenced in her most famous novel, *The Handmaid's Tale* (1985), and expanding to its sequel, *The Testaments* (2019), her second Booker Prize–winning novel after *The Blind Assassin* (2000). Atwood's environmentally dystopic fictions, *Oryx and Crake* (2003), *The Year of the Flood* (2009), and *Madd-Addam* (2013)—collectively known as the MaddAddam Trilogy—take up directly the themes of ecological catastrophe and human extinction. Her long-standing interest in the Far North—its geographical, mythological, and literary mappings—also appears in her first book of nonfiction, *Survival: A Thematic Guide to Canadian Literature* (1972), and almost twenty years later in her *Strange Things: The Malevolent North in Canadian Literature* (1995). Atwood's tale "Death by Landscape," which first appeared in 1989 in Canada's oldest general magazine, *Saturday Night,* is reprinted in the author's aptly named *Wilderness Tips* (1991), one of ten short-fiction collections Atwood has published during her equally prolific career as a short-story writer. In "Death by Landscape" a woman who privately collects wilderness paintings seeks a clearer picture of two summers she spent at a Canadian girls' camp, an experience marked by campfire sing-alongs and overnight canoe trips. No less than stories of boys coming of age in the wilderness, tales of girls transitioning from childhood into adulthood in the outdoors can reflect the considerable power of wild places to indelibly shape both memory and identity. Margaret Atwood currently lives in Toronto.

"Death by Landscape"

MARGARET ATWOOD

Now that the boys are grown up and Rob is dead, Lois has moved to a condominium apartment in one of Toronto's newer waterfront developments. She is relieved not to have to worry about the lawn, or about the ivy pushing its muscular little suckers into the brickwork, or the squirrels gnawing their way into the attic and eating the insulation off the wiring, or about strange noises. This building has a security system, and the only plant life is in pots in the solarium.

Lois is glad she's been able to find an apartment big enough for her pictures. They are more crowded together than they were in the house, but this arrangement gives the walls a European look: blocks of pictures, above and beside one another, rather than one over the chesterfield, one over the fireplace, one in the front hall, in the old acceptable manner of sprinkling art around so it does not get too intrusive. This way has more of an impact. You know it's not supposed to be furniture.

None of the pictures is very large, which doesn't mean they aren't valuable. They are paintings, or sketches and drawings, by artists who were not nearly as well known when Lois began to buy them as they are now. Their work later turned up on stamps, or as silk-screen reproductions hung in the principals' offices of high schools, or as jigsaw puzzles, or on beautifully printed calendars sent out by corporations as Christmas gifts, to their less important clients. These artists painted mostly in the twenties and thirties and forties; they painted landscapes. Lois has two Tom Thompsons, three A. Y. Jacksons, a Lawren Harris. She has an Arthur Lismer, she has a J. E. H. MacDonald. She has a David Milne. They are pictures of convoluted tree trunks on an island of pink wave-smoothed stone, with more islands behind; of a lake with rough, bright, sparsely wooded cliffs; of a vivid river shore with a tangle of bush and two beached canoes, one red, one gray; of a yellow autumn woods with the ice-blue gleam of a pond half-seen through the interlaced branches.

It was Lois who'd chosen them. Rob had no interest in art, although he could see the necessity of having something on the walls. He left all the decorating decisions to her, while providing the money, of course. Because of this collection of hers, Lois's friends—especially the men— have given her the reputation of having a good nose for art investments.

But this is not why she bought the pictures, way back then. She bought them because she wanted them. She wanted something that was in them although she could not have said at the time what it was. It was not peace: she does not find them peaceful in the least. Looking at them fills her with a wordless unease. Despite the fact that there are no people in them or even animals, it's as if there is something, or someone, looking back out.

When she was thirteen, Lois went on a canoe trip. She'd only been on overnights before. This was to be a long one, into the trackless wilderness, as Cappie put it. It was Lois's first canoe trip, and her last.

Cappie was the head of the summer camp to which Lois had been sent ever since she was nine. Camp Manitou, it was called; it was one of the better ones, for girls, though not the best. Girls of her age whose parents could afford it were routinely packed off to such camps, which bore a generic resemblance to one another. They favored Indian names and had hearty, energetic leaders, who were called Cappie or Skip or Scottie. At these camps you learned to swim well and sail, and paddle a canoe, and perhaps ride a horse or play tennis. When you weren't doing these things you could do Arts and Crafts, and turn out dingy, lumpish clay ashtrays for your mother—mothers smoked more, then—or bracelets made of colored braided string.

Cheerfulness was required at all times, even at breakfast. Loud shouting and the banging of spoons on the tables were allowed, and even encouraged, at ritual intervals. Chocolate bars were rationed, to control tooth decay and pimples. At night, after supper, in the dining hall or outside around a mosquito-infested campfire ring for special treats, there were singsongs. Lois can still remember all the words to "My Darling Clementine," and to "My Bonnie Lies Over the Ocean," with acting-out gestures: a rippling of the hands for "the ocean," two hands together under the cheeks for "lies." She will never be able to forget them, which is a sad thought.

Lois thinks she can recognize women who went to these camps, and were good at it. They have a hardness to their handshakes, even now; a way of standing, legs planted firmly and farther apart than usual; a way of sizing you up, to see if you'd be any good in a canoe—the front, not the back. They themselves would be in the back. They would call it the stern.

She knows that such camps still exist, although Camp Manitou does not. They are one of the few things that haven't changed much. They now offer copper enameling, and functionless pieces of stained glass baked in electric ovens, though judging from the productions of her friends' grandchildren the artistic standards have not improved.

To Lois, encountering it in the first year after the war, Camp Manitou seemed ancient. Its log-sided buildings with the white cement in between the half logs, its flagpole ringed with whitewashed stones, its weathered gray dock jutting out into Lake Prospect, with its woven rope bumpers and its rusty rings for tying up, its prim round flowerbed of petunias near the office door, must surely have been there always. In truth, it dated only from the first decade of the century; it had been founded by Cappie's parents, who'd thought of camping as bracing to the character, like cold showers, and had been passed along to her as an inheritance, and an obligation.

Lois realized later that it must have been a struggle for Cappie to keep Camp Manitou going, during the Depression and then the war, when money did not flow freely. If it had been a camp for the very rich, instead of the merely well-off, there would have been fewer problems. But there must have been enough Old Girls, ones with daughters, to keep the thing in operation, though not entirely shipshape; furniture was battered, painted trim was peeling, roofs leaked. There were dim photographs of these Old Girls dotted around the dining hall, wearing ample woolen bathing suits and showing their fat, dimpled legs, or standing, arms twined, in odd tennis outfits with baggy skirts.

In the dining hall, over the stone fireplace that was never used, there was a huge molting stuffed moose head, which looked somehow carnivorous. It was a sort of mascot; its name was Monty Manitou. The older campers spread the story that it was haunted, and came to life in the dark, when the feeble and undependable lights had been turned off or, due to yet another generator failure, had gone out. Lois was afraid of it at first, but not after she got used to it.

Cappie was the same: you had to get used to her. Possibly she was forty, or thirty-five, or fifty. She had fawn-colored hair that looked as if it was cut with a bowl. Her head jutted forward, jigging like a chicken's as she strode around the camp, clutching notebooks and checking things off in them. She was like Lois's minister in church: both of them smiled a lot and were anxious because they wanted things to go well; they both had the same over-washed skins and stringy necks. But all this disappeared when Cappie was leading a singsong or otherwise leading. Then she was happy, sure of herself, her plain face almost luminous. She wanted to cause joy. At these times she was loved, at others merely trusted.

There were many things Lois didn't like about Camp Manitou, at first. She hated the noisy chaos and spoon-banging of the dining hall, the rowdy singsongs at which you were expected to yell in order to show that you were enjoying yourself. Hers was not a household that encouraged yelling. She hated the necessity of having to write dutiful letters to her parents claiming she was having fun. She could not complain, because camp cost so much money.

She didn't much like having to undress in a roomful of other girls, even in the dim light, although nobody paid any attention, or sleeping in a cabin with seven other girls, some of whom snored because they had adenoids or colds, some of whom had nightmares, or wet their beds and cried about it. Bottom bunks made her feel closed in, and she was afraid of falling out of top ones; she was afraid of heights. She got homesick, and suspected her parents of having a better time when she wasn't there than when she was, although her mother wrote to her every week saying how much they missed her. All this was when she was nine. By the time she was thirteen she liked it. She was an old hand by then.

Lucy was her best friend at camp. Lois had other friends in the winter, when there was school and itchy woolen clothing and darkness in the afternoons, but Lucy was her summer friend.

She turned up the second year, when Lois was ten, and a Bluejay. (Chickadees, Bluejays, Ravens, and Kingfishers—these were the names Camp Manitou assigned to the different age groups, a sort of totemic clan system. In those days, thinks Lois, it was birds for girls, animals for boys: wolves, and so forth. Though some animals and birds were suitable and some were not. Never vultures, for instance; never skunks, or rats.)

Lois helped Lucy to unpack her tin trunk and place the folded clothes on the wooden shelves, and to make up her bed. She put her in the top bunk right above her, where she could keep an eye on her. Already she knew that Lucy was an exception to a good many rules; already she felt proprietorial.

Lucy was from the United States, where the comic books came from, and the movies. She wasn't from New York or Hollywood or Buffalo, the only American cities Lois knew the names of, but from Chicago. Her house was on the lakeshore and had gates to it, and grounds. They had a maid, all of the time. Lois's family only had a cleaning lady twice a week.

The only reason Lucy was being sent to *this* camp (she cast a look of minor scorn around the cabin, diminishing it and also offending Lois, while at the same time daunting her) was that her mother had been a camper here. Her mother had been a Canadian once, but had married her father, who had a patch over one eye, like a pirate. She showed Lois the picture of him in her wallet. He got the patch in the war. "Shrapnel," said Lucy. Lois, who was unsure about shrapnel, was so impressed she could only grunt. Her own two-eyed, unwounded father was tame by comparison.

"My father plays golf," she ventured at last.

"*Everyone* plays golf," said Lucy. "My *mother* plays golf."

Lois's mother did not. Lois took Lucy to see the outhouses and the swimming dock and the dining hall with Monty Manitou's baleful head, knowing in advance they would not measure up.

This was a bad beginning; but Lucy was good-natured, and accepted Camp Manitou with the same casual shrug with which she seemed to accept everything. She would make the best of it, without letting Lois forget that this was what she was doing.

However, there were things Lois knew that Lucy did not. Lucy scratched the tops off all her mosquito bites and had to be taken to the infirmary to be daubed with Ozonol. She took her T-shirt off while sailing, and although the counselor spotted her after a while and made her put it back on, she burned spectacularly, bright red, with the X of her bathing-suit straps standing out in alarming white; she let Lois peel the sheets of whispery thin burned skin off her shoulders. When they sang

"Alouette" around the campfire, she did not know any of the French words. The difference was that Lucy did not care about the things she didn't know, whereas Lois did.

During the next winter, and subsequent winters, Lucy and Lois wrote to each other. They were both only children, at a time when this was thought to be a disadvantage, so in their letters they pretended to be sisters, or even twins. Lois had to strain a little over this, because Lucy was so blond, with translucent skin and large blue eyes like a doll's, and Lois was nothing out of the ordinary, just a tallish, thinnish, brownish person with freckles. They signed their letters LL, with the *L*'s entwined together like the monograms on a towel. (Lois and Lucy, thinks Lois. How our names date us. Lois Lane, Superman's girlfriend, enterprising female reporter; *I Love Lucy*. Now we are obsolete, and it's little Jennifers, little Emilys, little Alexandras and Carolines and Tiffanys.)

They were more effusive in their letters than they ever were in person. They bordered their pages with *X*'s and *O*'s, but when they met again in the summers it was always a shock. They had changed so much, or Lucy had. It was like watching someone grow up in jolts. At first it would be hard to think up things to say.

But Lucy always had a surprise or two, something to show, some marvel to reveal. The first year she had a picture of herself in a tutu, her hair in a ballerina's knot on the top of her head; she pirouetted around the swimming dock, to show Lois how it was done, and almost fell off. The next year she had given that up and was taking horseback riding. (Camp Manitou did not have horses.) The next year her mother and father had been divorced, and she had a new stepfather, one with both eyes, and a new house, although the maid was the same. The next year, when they had graduated from Bluejays and entered Ravens, she got her period, right in the first week of camp. The two of them snitched some matches from their counselor, who smoked illegally, and made a small fire out behind the furthest outhouse, at dusk, using their flashlights. They could set all kinds of fires by now; they had learned how in Campcraft. On this fire they burned one of Lucy's used sanitary napkins. Lois is not sure why they did this, or whose idea it was. But she can remember the feeling of deep satisfaction it gave her as the white fluff singed and the blood sizzled, as if some wordless ritual had been fulfilled.

They did not get caught, but then they rarely got caught at any of their camp transgressions. Lucy had such large eyes, and was such an accomplished liar.

This year Lucy is different again: slower, more languorous. She is no longer interested in sneaking around after dark, purloining cigarettes from the counselor, dealing in black market candy bars. She is pensive, and hard to wake in the mornings. She doesn't like her stepfather, but she doesn't want to live with her real father either, who has a new wife. She thinks her mother may be having a love affair with a doctor; she doesn't know for sure, but she's seen them smooching in his car, out in the driveway, when her stepfather wasn't there. It serves him right. She hates her private school. She has a boyfriend, who is sixteen and works as a gardener's assistant. This is how she met him: in the garden. She describes to Lois what it is like when he kisses her—rubbery at first, but then your knees go limp. She has been forbidden to see him, and threatened with boarding school. She wants to run away from home.

Lois has little to offer in return. Her own life is placid and satisfactory, but there is nothing much that can be said about happiness. "You're so lucky," Lucy tells her, a little smugly. She might as well say *boring* because this is how it makes Lois feel.

Lucy is apathetic about the canoe trip, so Lois has to disguise her own excitement. The evening before they are to leave, she slouches into the campfire ring as if coerced, and sits down with a sigh of endurance, just as Lucy does.

Every canoe trip that went out of camp was given a special send-off by Cappie and the section leader and counselors, with the whole section in attendance. Cappie painted three streaks of red across each of her cheeks with a lipstick. They looked like three-fingered claw marks. She put a blue circle on her forehead with fountain-pen ink, tied a twisted bandanna around her head and stuck a row of frazzle-ended feathers around it, and wrapped herself in a red and black Hudson's Bay blanket. The counselors, also in blankets but with only two streaks of red, beat on tom-toms made of round wooden cheese boxes with leather stretched over the top and nailed in place. Cappie was Chief Cappeosota. They all had to say "How!" when she walked into the circle and stood there with one hand raised.

Looking back on this, Lois finds it disquieting. She knows too much about Indians. She knows, for instance, that they should not even be called Indians, and that they have enough worries without other people taking their names and dressing up as them. It has all been a form of stealing.

But she remembers, too, that she was once ignorant of this. Once she loved the campfire, the flickering of light on the ring of faces, the sound of the fake tom-toms, heavy and fast like a scared heartbeat; she loved Cappie in a red blanket and feathers, solemn, as a Chief should be, raising her hand and saying, "Greetings, my Ravens." It was not funny, it was not making fun. She wanted to be an Indian. She wanted to be adventurous and pure, and aboriginal.

"You go on big water," says Cappie. This is her idea—all their ideas—of how Indians talk. "You go where no man has ever trod. You go many moons." This is not true. They are only going for a week, not many moons. The canoe route is clearly marked, they have gone over it on a map, and there are prepared campsites with names that are used year after year. But when Cappie says this—and despite the way Lucy rolls up her eyes—Lois can feel the water stretching out, with the shores twisting away on either side, immense and a little frightening.

"You bring back much wampum," says Cappie. "Do good in war, my braves, and capture many scalps." This is another of her pretenses: that they are boys, and bloodthirsty. But such a game cannot be played by substituting the word squaw. It would not work at all.

Each of them has to stand up and step forward and have a red line drawn across her cheeks by Cappie. She tells them they must follow in the paths of their ancestors (who most certainly, thinks Lois, looking out the window of her apartment and remembering the family stash of daguerreotypes and sepia-colored portraits on her mother's dressing table, the stiff-shirted, black-coated, grim-faced men and the beflounced women with their severe hair and their corseted respectability, would never have considered heading off onto an open lake, in a canoe, just for fun).

At the end of the ceremony they all stood and held hands around the circle and sang taps. This did not sound very Indian, thinks Lois. It sounded like a bugle call at a military post, in a movie. But Cappie was never one to be much concerned with consistency, or with archaeology.

After breakfast the next morning they set out from the main dock, in four canoes, three in each. The lipstick stripes have not come off completely, and still show faintly pink, like healing burns. They wear their white denim sailing hats, because of the sun, and thin-striped T-shirts, and pale baggy shorts with the cuffs rolled up. The middle one kneels, propping her rear end against the rolled sleeping bags. The counselors going with them are Pat and Kip. Kip is no-nonsense; Pat is easier to wheedle, or fool.

There are white puffy clouds and a small breeze. Glints come from the little waves. Lois is in the bow of Kip's canoe. She still can't do a J-stroke very well, and she will have to be in the bow or the middle for the whole trip. Lucy is behind her; her own J-stroke is even worse. She splashes Lois with her paddle, quite a big splash.

"I'll get you back," says Lois.

"There was a stable fly on your shoulder," Lucy says.

Lois turns to look at her, to see if she's grinning. They're in the habit of splashing each other. Back there, the camp has vanished behind the first long point of rock and rough trees. Lois feels as if an invisible rope has broken. They're floating free, on their own, cut loose. Beneath the canoe the lake goes down, deeper and colder than it was a minute before.

"No horsing around in the canoe," says Kip. She's rolled her T-shirt sleeves up to the shoulder; her arms are brown and sinewy, her jaw determined, her stroke perfect. She looks as if she knows exactly what she is doing.

The four canoes keep close together. They sing, raucously and with defiance; they sing "The Quartermaster's Store," and "Clementine," and "Alouette." It is more like bellowing than singing.

After that the wind grows stronger, blowing slantwise against the bows, and they have to put all their energy into shoving themselves through the water.

. . .

Was there anything important, anything that would provide some sort of reason or clue to what happened next? Lois can remember everything, every detail; but it does her no good.

They stopped at noon for a swim and lunch, and went on in the afternoon. At last they reached Little Birch, which was the first campsite for overnight. Lois and Lucy made the fire, while the others pitched the heavy canvas tents. The fireplace was already there, flat stones piled into a U shape. A burned tin can and a beer bottle had been left in it. Their fire went out, and they had to restart it. "Hustle your bustle," said Kip. "We're starving."

The sun went down, and in the pink sunset light they brushed their teeth and spat the toothpaste froth into the lake. Kip and Pat put all the food that wasn't in cans into a packsack and slung it into a tree, in case of bears.

Lois and Lucy weren't sleeping in a tent. They'd begged to be allowed to sleep out; that way they could talk without the others hearing. If it rained, they told Kip, they promised not to crawl dripping into the tent over everyone's legs: They would get under the canoes. So they were out on the point.

Lois tried to get comfortable inside her sleeping bag, which smelled of musty storage and of earlier campers, a stale, salty sweetness. She curled herself up, with her sweater rolled up under her head for a pillow and her flashlight inside her sleeping bag so it wouldn't roll away. The muscles of her sore arms were making small pings, like rubber bands breaking.

Beside her Lucy was rustling around. Lois could see the glimmering oval of her white face.

"I've got a rock poking into my back," said Lucy.

"So do I," said Lois. "You want to go into the tent?" She herself didn't, but it was right to ask.

"No," said Lucy. She subsided into her sleeping bag. After a moment she said, "It would be nice not to go back."

"To camp?" said Lois.

"To Chicago," said Lucy. "I hate it there."

"What about your boyfriend?" said Lois. Lucy didn't answer. She was either asleep or pretending to be.

There was a moon, and a movement of the trees. In the sky there were stars, layers of stars that went down and down. Kip said that when the stars were bright like that instead of hazy, it meant bad weather later on. Out on the lake there were two loons, calling to each other in their insane, mournful voices. At the time it did not sound like grief. It was just background.

The lake in the morning was flat calm. They skimmed along over the glassy surface, leaving V-shaped trails behind them; it felt like flying. As the sun rose higher it got hot, almost too hot. There were stable flies in the canoes, landing on a bare arm or leg for a quick sting. Lois hoped for wind.

They stopped for lunch at the next of the named campsites, Lookout Point. It was called this because, although the site itself was down near the water on a flat shelf of rock, there was a sheer cliff nearby and a trail that led up to the top. The top was the lookout, although what you were supposed to see from there was not clear. Kip said it was just a view.

Lois and Lucy decided to make the climb anyway. They didn't want to hang around waiting for lunch. It wasn't their turn to cook, though they hadn't avoided much by not doing it, because cooking lunch was no big deal. It was just unwrapping the cheese and getting out the bread and peanut butter, though Pat and Kip always had to do their woodsy act and boil up a billy tin for their own tea.

They told Kip where they were going. You had to tell Kip where you were going, even if it was only a little way into the woods to get dry twigs for kindling. You could never go anywhere without a buddy.

"Sure," said Kip, who was crouching over the fire, feeding driftwood into it. "Fifteen minutes to lunch."

"Where are they off to?" said Pat. She was bringing their billy tin of water from the lake.

"Lookout," said Kip.

"Be careful," said Pat. She said it as an afterthought, because it was what she always said.

"They're old hands," Kip said.

Lois looks at her watch: it's ten to twelve. She is the watch-minder; Lucy is careless of time. They walk up the path, which is dry earth and rocks, big rounded pinky-gray boulders or split-open ones with jagged edges. Spindly balsam and spruce trees grow to either side; the lake is blue fragments to the left. The sun is right overhead; there are no shadows anywhere. The heat comes up at them as well as down. The forest is dry and crackly.

It isn't far, but it's a steep climb and they're sweating when they reach the top. They wipe their faces with their bare arms, sit gingerly down on a scorching-hot rock, five feet from the edge but too close for Lois. It's a lookout all right, a sheer drop to the lake and a long view over the water, back the way they've come. It's amazing to Lois that they've traveled so far, over all that water, with nothing to propel them but their own arms. It makes her feel strong. There are all kinds of things she is capable of doing.

"It would be quite a dive off here," says Lucy.

"You'd have to be nuts," says Lois.

"Why?" says Lucy. "It's really deep. It goes straight down." She stands up and takes a step nearer the edge. Lois gets a stab in her midriff, the kind she gets when a car goes too fast over a bump. "Don't," she says.

"Don't what?" says Lucy, glancing around at her mischievously. She knows how Lois feels about heights. But she turns back. "I really have to pee," she says.

"You have toilet paper?" says Lois, who is never without it. She digs in her shorts pocket.

"Thanks," says Lucy.

They are both adept at peeing in the woods: doing it fast so the mosquitoes don't get you, the underwear pulled up between the knees, the squat with the feet apart so you don't wet your legs, facing downhill; the exposed feeling of your bum, as if someone is looking at you from behind. The etiquette when you're with someone else is not to look. Lois stands up and starts to walk back down the path, to be out of sight.

"Wait for me?" says Lucy.

Lois climbed down, over and around the boulders, until she could not see Lucy; she waited. She could hear the voices of the others, talking and laughing, down near the shore. One voice was yelling, "Ants! Ants!" Someone must have sat on an anthill. Off to the side, in the woods, a raven was croaking, a hoarse single note.

She looked at her watch: it was noon. This is when she heard the shout.

She has gone over and over it in her mind since, so many times that the first, real shout has been obliterated, like a footprint trampled by other footprints. But she is sure (she is almost positive, she is nearly certain) that it was not a shout of fear. Not a scream. More like a cry of surprise, cut off too soon. Short, like a dog's bark.

"Lucy?" Lois said. Then she called. "Lucy!" By now she was clambering back up, over the stones of the path. Lucy was not up there. Or she was not in sight.

"Stop fooling around," Lois said. "It's lunchtime." But Lucy did not rise from behind a rock or step out, smiling, from behind a tree. The sunlight was all around; the rocks looked white. "This isn't funny!" Lois said, and it wasn't. Panic was rising in her, the panic of a small child who does not know where the bigger ones are hidden. She could hear her own heart. She looked quickly around; she lay down on the ground and looked over the edge of the cliff. It made her feel cold. There was nothing.

She went back down the path, stumbling; she was breathing too quickly; she was too frightened to cry. She felt terrible—guilty and dismayed, as if she had done something very bad, by mistake. Something that could never be repaired. "Lucy's gone," she told Kip.

Kip looked up from her fire, annoyed. The water in the billy tin was boiling. "What do you mean, 'Gone'?" she said. "Where did she go?"

"I don't know," said Lois. "She's just gone."

No one had heard the shout, but then no one had heard Lois calling either. They had been talking among themselves, by the water.

Kip and Pat went up to the lookout and searched and called and blew their whistles. Nothing answered.

Then they came back down, and Lois had to tell exactly what had happened. The other girls all sat in a circle and listened to her. Nobody said anything. They all looked frightened, especially Pat and Kip. They were the leaders. You did not just lose a camper like this, for no reason at all.

"Why did you leave her alone?" said Kip.

"I was just down the path," said Lois. "I told you. She had to go to the bathroom." She did not say pee in front of people older than herself.

Kip looked disgusted.

"Maybe she just walked off into the woods and got turned around," said one of the girls.

"Maybe she's doing it on purpose," said another.

Nobody believed either of these theories.

They took the canoes and searched around the base of the cliff, and peered down into the water. But there had been no sound of falling rock; there had been no splash. There was no clue, nothing at all. Lucy had simply vanished.

That was the end of the canoe trip. It took them the same two days to go back that it had taken coming in, even though they were short a paddler. They did not sing.

After that, the police went in a motorboat, with dogs; they were the Mounties and the dogs were German shepherds, trained to follow trails in the woods. But it had rained since, and they could find nothing.

Lois is sitting in Cappie's office. Her face is bloated with crying, she's seen that in the mirror. By now she feels numbed; she feels as if she has drowned. She can't stay here. It has been too much of a shock. Tomorrow her parents are coming to take her away. Several of the other girls who were on the canoe trip are also being collected. The others will have to stay, because their parents are in Europe, or cannot be reached.

Cappie is grim. They've tried to hush it up, but of course everyone in camp knows. Soon the papers will know too. You can't keep it quiet, but what can be said? What can be said that makes any sense? "Girl vanishes in broad daylight, without a trace." It can't be believed. Other things, worse things, will be suspected. Negligence, at the very least. But they have always taken such care. Bad luck will gather around Camp Manitou like a fog; parents will avoid it, in favor of other, luckier places. Lois can see Cappie thinking all this, even through her numbness. It's what anyone would think.

Lois sits on the hard wooden chair in Cappie's office, beside the old wooden desk, over which hangs the thumbtacked bulletin board of normal camp routine, and gazes at Cappie through her puffy eyelids.

Cappie is now smiling what is supposed to be a reassuring smile. Her manner is too casual: she's after something. Lois has seen this look on Cappie's face when she's been sniffing out contraband chocolate bars, hunting down those rumored to have snuck out of their cabins at night.

"Tell me again," says Cappie, "from the beginning."

Lois has told her story so many times by now, to Pat and Kip, to Cappie, to the police, that she knows it word for word. She knows it, but she no longer believes it. It has become a story. "I told you," she says. "She wanted to go to the bathroom. I gave her my toilet paper. I went down the path, I waited for her. I heard this kind of shout . . ."

"Yes," says Cappie, smiling confidingly, "but before that. What did you say to one another?"

Lois thinks. Nobody has asked her this before. "She said you could dive off there. She said it went straight down."

"And what did you say?"

"I said you'd have to be nuts."

"Were you mad at Lucy?" says Cappie, in an encouraging voice.

"No," says Lois. "Why would I be mad at Lucy? I wasn't ever mad at Lucy." She feels like crying again. The times when she has in fact been mad at Lucy have been erased already. Lucy was always perfect.

"Sometimes we're angry when we don't know we're angry," says Cappie, as if to herself. "Sometimes we get really mad and we don't even know it. Sometimes we might do a thing without meaning to, or without knowing what will happen. We lose our tempers."

Lois is only thirteen, but it doesn't take her long to figure out that Cappie is not including herself in any of this. By *we* she means Lois. She is accusing Lois of pushing Lucy off the cliff. The unfairness of this hits her like a slap. "I didn't!" she says.

"Didn't what?" says Cappie softly. "Didn't what, Lois?"

Lois does the worst thing, she begins to cry. Cappie gives her a look like a pounce. She's got what she wanted.

Later, when she was grown up, Lois was able to understand what this interview had been about. She could see Cappie's desperation, her need for a story, a real story with a reason in it; anything but the senseless vacancy Lucy had left for her to deal with. Cappie wanted Lois to supply the reason, to be the reason. It wasn't even for the newspapers or

the parents, because she could never make such an accusation without proof. It was for herself: something to explain the loss of Camp
Manitou and of all she had worked for, the years of entertaining spoiled
children and buttering up parents and making a fool of herself with
feathers stuck in her hair. Camp Manitou was in fact lost. It did not
survive.

Lois worked all this out, twenty years later. But it was far too late. It
was too late even ten minutes afterwards, when she'd left Cappie's office
and was walking slowly back to her cabin to pack. Lucy's clothes were
still there, folded on the shelves, as if waiting. She felt the other girls in
the cabin watching her with speculation in their eyes. *Could she have
done it? She must have done it.* For the rest of her life, she has caught
people watching her in this way.

Maybe they weren't thinking this. Maybe they were merely sorry
for her. But she felt she had been tried and sentenced, and this is what
has stayed with her: the knowledge that she has been singled out, condemned for something that was not her fault.

Lois sits in the living room of her apartment, drinking a cup of tea.
Through the knee-to-ceiling window she has a wide view of Lake
Ontario, with its skin of wrinkled blue-gray light, and of the willows of
Toronto Island shaken by a wind that is silent at this distance, and on
this side of the glass. When there isn't too much pollution she can see
the far shore, the foreign shore, though today it is obscured.

Possibly she could go out, go downstairs, do some shopping; there
isn't much in the refrigerator. The boys say she doesn't get out enough.
But she isn't hungry, and moving, stirring from this space, is increasingly an effort.

She can hardly remember, now, having her two boys in the hospital, nursing them as babies; she can hardly remember getting married,
or what Rob looked like. Even at the time she never felt she was paying
full attention. She was tired a lot, as if she was living not one life but
two: her own, and another, shadowy life that hovered around her and
would not let itself be realized—the life of what would have happened
if Lucy had not stepped sideways, and disappeared from time.

She would never go up north, to Rob's family cottage or to any
place with wild lakes and wild trees and the calls of loons. She would

never go anywhere near. Still, it was as if she was always listening for another voice, the voice of a person who should have been there but was not. An echo.

While Rob was alive, while the boys were growing up, she could pretend she didn't hear it, this empty space in sound. But now there is nothing much left to distract her.

She turns away from the window and looks at her pictures. There is the pinkish island, in the lake, with the intertwisted trees. It's the same landscape they paddled through, that distant summer. She's seen travelogues of this country, aerial photographs; it looks different from above, bigger, more hopeless: lake after lake, random blue puddles in dark green bush, the trees like bristles.

How could you ever find anything there, once it was lost? Maybe if they cut it all down, drained it all away, they might find Lucy's bones, sometime, wherever they are hidden. A few bones, some buttons, the buckle from her shorts.

But a dead person is a body; a body occupies space, it exists somewhere. You can see it; you put it in a box and bury it in the ground, and then it's in a box in the ground. But Lucy is not in a box, or in the ground. Because she is nowhere definite, she could be anywhere.

And these paintings are not landscape paintings. Because there aren't any landscapes up there, not in the old, tidy European sense, with a gentle hill, a curving river, a cottage, a mountain in the background, a golden evening sky. Instead there's a tangle, a receding maze, in which you can become lost almost as soon as you step off the path. There are no backgrounds in any of these paintings, no vistas; only a great deal of foreground that goes back and back, endlessly, involving you in its twists and turns of tree and branch and rock. No matter how far back in you go, there will be more. And the trees themselves are hardly trees; they are currents of energy, charged with violent color.

Who knows how many trees there were on the cliff just before Lucy disappeared? Who counted? Maybe there was one more, afterwards.

Lois sits in her chair and does not move. Her hand with the cup is raised halfway to her mouth. She hears something, almost hears it: a shout of recognition or of joy.

She looks at the paintings, she looks into them. Every one of them is a picture of Lucy. You can't see her exactly, but she's there, in behind the pink stone island or the one behind that. In the picture of the cliff she is hidden by the clutch of fallen rocks toward the bottom; in the one of the river shore she is crouching beneath the overturned canoe. In the yellow autumn woods she's behind the tree that cannot be seen because of the other trees, over beside the blue sliver of pond; but if you walked into the picture and found the tree, it would be the wrong one, because the right one would be farther on.

Everyone has to be somewhere, and this is where Lucy is. She is in Lois's apartment, in the holes that open inward on the wall, not like windows but like doors. She is here. She is entirely alive.

"Happiness"

RON CARLSON

Ron Carlson (b. 1947) is the author of six novels and five short-story collections and a recipient of the 2009 Aspen Prize for Literature. The great western outdoors inspires much of Carlson's work, particularly his novels *Five Skies* (2007) and *The Signal* (2009), both featuring lyric descriptions of the mountains, woods, rivers, canyons, and high deserts of Idaho and Wyoming. In his short-story collections, as well, numerous tales are set in Carlson's home state of Utah, where wilderness might serve as a site of solitude and sanctuary or of drama and danger. Carlson is a skilled practitioner of the art of the short story, and his tales are notable for their perfect pacing, relatable characters, and haunting themes. Three of Carlson's story collections, *Plan B for the Middle Class* (1992), *The Hotel Eden* (1997), and *At the Jim Bridger* (2002), have been named a Best Book or a Notable Book of the Year by the *New York Times* or the *Los Angeles Times*. His stories have been included in *Best American Short Stories, The O. Henry Prize Series, The Pushcart Prize Anthology,* and *The Norton Anthology of Short Fiction*. Of all the modern wilderness tales that draw deeply on the power of memory, Carlson's story "Happiness" stands apart in fully embracing the restorative effects of both nature and family. Published in 2014 in *Ecotone,* a magazine devoted to place-based writing, this O. Henry Prize–winning story narrates a family reunion at a remote cabin in Utah. Embracing the persistence of the past within the present, while investing the presence of place with deep emotional resonance, Carlson's touching wilderness narrative is that rarest of literary short stories: a tale of true happiness.

"Happiness"

RON CARLSON

We had ten pillows. It was the first thing my son Nick said when we entered the motel room and we were tired from traveling all day and surprised by the deep cold as we got out of the rental car, five degrees or so, and the warm room was perfectly cozy, the two big beds and the large television, and when he said we had ten pillows we both just laughed. Most of the time ten pillows are too many, but now with the trip and the dark and the cold, I wanted all my pillows.

It was wonderful to park our small cases on the bureau and turn on the television. It was October and it was game three of the World Series. Things were working out. The bathroom was big and well lighted and there was all kinds of soap and a coffeemaker. "Are we going over there?" Nick said, meaning Wally's, the burger place we'd seen across the street.

"We've got to," I said. "Wear your jacket."

Outside, the parking lot was full of trucks with fans of mud along the doors and bumpers, big trucks with all kinds of oil gear and toolboxes in the beds. If it hadn't been so cold, there would have been dogs in a few of the trucks, but now I knew the motel was full of smart shepherds and collies. I loved seeing the trucks and I loved seeing our little rental car in its place; we arrived late and still got a room full of pillows.

The cold was like metal in our noses and we tucked our chins and walked across the old empty highway to the little glassed building: Wally's, Home of the Wally Burger. In the street Nick kept bumping into me and laughing. On the sign each of the red letters had a big blue-painted shadow and the Wally Burger had been painted there, big as a car, beautiful and steaming and dripping and sort of vibrating by the depiction. Beneath the burger was the phrase: FRESH-CUT FRIES. Nick opened the door for me. He had read it all and was happy.

Inside there was a couple, a man and a woman who were my age, sitting in one of the little plastic booths by a coin-operated video game with a plastic rifle attached to it. It was called Big Game. The man had a huge white mustache, and they were both eating their Wally Burgers in the bright light. They still wore their coats and I wondered if it was a date. They had a paper between them, spread with the beautiful french fries.

The two teenage boys at the counter in their white paper hats were waiting for us. There wasn't a line. It was so great. I wanted to get a bag of this fine food and get back to the ball game. One kid wrote it all down: two Wally Burgers with everything, two cones of fries. When I ordered I said, "fresh-cut fries," and there was pleasure in it. In the old days I would have asked if Wally was around and Nick would have ducked in embarrassment at his old man, but I stopped that years ago. I turned and saw there were fringes of condensation frozen in the corners of the big front window, but it was warm in Wally Burger and I loosened my scarf.

The bag was hot and we hustled it across the dark highway and into the motel parking lot. The cold was over everything, the great arctic cold that had slid over Wyoming. In the warm motel room, we each sat on a bed picking at the greasy brown fries which were heavy and salty and delicious. The Wally Burger took some skill so that the onion and tomato didn't slide out. It was like food from the fifties and we ate without talking while the game unfolded. This was the game in St. Louis in which Albert Pujols hit a home run and then he came up again and hit a home run. Nick was lying on his bed watching the game and I put on my pajamas and was watching the game. After a while Nick said, "Why do they keep pitching to him?"

I was tired and full of fresh-cut fries, so I turned out the lights so just the game was on and I washed my face with great satisfaction and started sorting my pillows. They had been a terrific help while I was sitting up, but now there were too many. I didn't like putting pillows on the floor. Nick's pillows were all on the floor. Nick was sleeping in his clothes and I reached across to his bed and put my hand on his shoulder. I didn't need to say anything; he turned and undressed in one minute and crawled into bed.

I'd been at home in Southern California that morning and Nick had been in Phoenix with his mother. There wasn't a fall in my little beach town. The ocean layer thickened and the air grew damp and the days short. I'd met Nick in the Salt Lake City airport and we'd motored northeast to Evanston, Wyoming, for the first night of our fishing trip. I grew up in this part of the west, Utah and Wyoming, and I'd loved walking across that old highway in the dark. I found the remote control in the covers of my bed and watched the television for another minute. Nick was lost in sleep. They pitched to Albert Pujols and he hit a third home run.

We got up early and even so all of the trucks in the motel parking lot were gone. The sun was clear and sharp, shooting across the sides of things and catching in the yellow leaves in the bottom of the trees and on the street. There was frost in the shadows.

The interstate highway was full of trucks and Nick drove us east among them toward the Continental Divide. The bright sunlight was on the sage hills and the day was opening. At the great valley of Bar Hat Road, we came over the crest to see the highway descend in a straight line and rise up the far side, and Nick said, "Seven point two miles," which is just the distance. I've known it since this big road was just two lanes sixty years ago and my father used to ask how far I thought it was and I'd say twenty miles.

A little farther on we came to the big green fireworks sign in the high desert and the abandoned Fireworks shop where we'd stopped so many times. There was only one building at the exit, and Nick's mother called me the Mayor of Fireworks because I let the kids buy all sorts of armaments in the bright-colored packages. We drove past that summit, both of us now feeling the trip had really begun; we were far from home and would be at the cabin in three hours.

Twenty miles east, we left the interstate and drove into the Bridger Valley and stopped at Fort Bridger, the frontier garrison. The parking lot for the old territorial military base was empty, banked with leaves against the low fences. Nick had his camera and went ahead of me taking his long steps out onto the grounds by the old wooden schoolhouse and the grave of the famous dog who saved the barracks from the midnight fire. Across the lawn I could see the ancient steel bear trap and the antique buckboard; the museum was down the lane. We'd been in it a few times and I remembered they had a Hotchkiss machine gun. Today there was a wind and it was tricky to decide in the fragile sunlight if it was warm or cold. This little town always thrilled me, isolated as it was in the broad valley, and now watching my son drift among the old white-board buildings in the sharp fall day, it was as lovely as it could ever be. I went back and climbed in the rental car and was pleased at the sun warm on the seats.

At the four-way stop in Lyman, where there used to be two buffalo behind the Thunderbird station, we turned south. The buffalo, which Nick's mother and I saw the day after we were married forty years ago, are gone and the Thunderbird station is gone.

The mountains you can see from the town of Mountain View are the great Uinta Range running there along the northern edge of Utah, a thin and magnificent white line along the horizon, all the distant peaks covered in snow. It was a lot to look at and I was excited. You try not to hurry on such trips to the real mountains, but it is hard not to hurry, and as you get out of your car in the parking lot of the Benedict's Market in Mountain View, you walk toward the store with the measured steps of someone who is not hurrying and it is a kind of happiness in the sunny October day. We filled two carts with supplies: rib-eye steaks and big cans of stew and two bags of sourdough bread and big deep-green cucumbers and a block of sharp cheddar cheese and milk and half-and-half and a box of fresh chocolate chip cookies from their bakery and candy and a bag of potatoes and four onions and tomatoes and two kinds of apples and some soda and beer and bottled water and English muffins and salted butter and paper plates and coffee and hot chocolate and tea and a tub of coleslaw the guy spooned up for us and a bag of green beans and two packages of bacon and four of sliced ham and little cans of green chiles and two dozen eggs and a butternut squash. We checked out and I couldn't help myself and I told her we were going fishing and she said, "Good luck. You've got the day for it." Above the front windows of the big supermarket were fine examples of taxidermy, an antelope and a coyote, and above the woman and our groceries was a mountain lion rearing to reach for a pheasant. The big yellow cat's claw was just touching the bird's tail feathers, frozen in the air. The whole story.

We drove south out of town and then east into the badlands above Lonetree. It was on some of these lonely roads in this barren place where we'd set off plenty of fireworks twenty years before. There was an amazing kind of mortar box you could buy at Fireworks and it had six sleeves and six small balls each with a fuse. It was big stuff for our two boys. You light the fuse, drop the ball in the sleeve, and run back. The running back was everything.

From the badlands, Nick and I drove into the low willow meadows outside of Lonetree, the creeks full and amber, the real streams you see on such a drive. The old Lonetree general store closed twenty years ago, but I was in it as a child. It is where we stopped to use the outhouses behind the old school and to buy a lime pop out of the cooler in the wooden-floored store. The last time I was there was with my father and he admired the old clock on the back wall, a clock made in Winsted, Connecticut. The thing everyone remembers about Lonetree is that there is a parking meter in front of the store by the wooden hitching post. Every time I saw that meter in my lifetime, I was with someone I loved.

Now we were up along the northern slope of the Uinta Mountains, a mile from the Utah state line, and we drove along the beautiful hay-fields of the last farms parallel to the state line and below the state and federal land. To our right we could see the great white peaks getting closer behind the foothills.

Yesterday, we had met at the airport and we'd rented this Subaru and the October light in my old hometown wanted to break my heart. We drove up past the university and along Foothill Drive and there at Parley's Way Nick pointed and I said, "Yeah. It's the church where I married your mother."

Now the fields were tall with grass and we passed the old ruined trailer and the neat log-cabin house and tiny abandoned cabin as old as anything in the region, and then we rounded a shoulder on the hillside and crossed back into Utah, though nothing changed.

A minute later the town of Manila, Utah, came into view, the scattered buildings and the blue of the lake behind it. We would fish tomorrow on the far shore.

The entire trip in a straight drive takes just four hours, Salt Lake to the cabin, and every town, every turn has a story: the flat tire and the crushed fishing pole, the herd of deer jumping the wire fence in the moonlight, the mountain sheep, the flood, the bear and her two cubs, the moose, the elk. Going through Manila, Nick had tried to find the Mexican restaurant we'd eaten at after coming out of the mountains on the backpacking trip when he was sixteen. It had been a double-wide trailer and the combination platters were killer, so good, but that place was long gone. Now we drove through the afternoon sunlight without talking. After the last hayfield in Manila, we turned in at the tipped stone canyons and there were two Fish and Game vehicles in the turn-out with their orange traffic cones. There was a big black Ford pickup parked there and the hunters were showing the officers the buck. We could see the pink tag on the antlers. I had long ago told Nick of the times that I had deer hunted, all of them three-part stories, pretty good, especially the time when I was a kid and my dad and I woke to a snow-storm and decided to break camp and drive home a day early, but ran into a guy who had shot his hand and my father helped him fix a proper bandage. It wasn't a terrible wound, but I remember blood on the man's canvas trousers and my father working quietly with his first aid kit and the medical tape on the man's hand. My father hated accidents and was angry. When he came back to our truck, I asked him what had hap-pened and all he said was, "There are two ends of a gun, always." I never heard him tell the story again.

On the radio, the football game came and went. Nick and I drove up the sage switchbacks above the massive blue lake and stopped at the rest area, which was abandoned this late in the year. The big loneliness of the planet was part of it now, and even in the nourishing sunlight I felt the wind tucking at us; it was fall. Farther, the canyon walls that plunged into the water were red and yellow and gave the whole reser-voir its name.

After the promontory we crossed into the real mountains and the pines, past the road to Spirit Lake, the place I learned to fish when I was seven. The forest along the back of the mountains is still thick and green, not ruined yet by the bark beetle. It is like a vast garden, a mil-lion pine trees, fir and ponderosa and piñon growing down to the road. This time of day and after three weeks of elk and deer hunting there would be no danger of game on the road. The first feeling in this place is always also the last: We're here. Everything else is gravy.

Nick could sense it too. "Where do you think Colin and Regan are?"

"North of Moab," I said, thinking of desolate Highway 191 as it cuts through the wasteland. I could imagine the connector to Interstate 70 and the fifty miles of that before the Loma turnoff. "No, they're farther. They'll cross into Colorado any time now and then climb over the summit." My son Colin and my brother Regan were driving today from Arizona and would meet us tonight at the cabin. "I hope we can get everything working," I said. "If the water is frozen, it will be a tough night."

I hadn't been to the cabin for a year and a half, and nothing was certain. Now driving with the sunlight holding, everything was still rinsed with optimism, but the bright edge of the short day was crumbling and the shadows of the thick tall pines cut at the roadway in a dizzying serrated shadow that wanted to put me to sleep. When we came to the junction for the lake and the lodge, Nick asked, "Are you hungry?"

"Sort of." We were both thinking of the Flaming Gorge Burger with bacon and cheese which had grown bigger in memory; it had been a while. It was always stunning to eat at the lodge, to sit in a chair and have the salty chili fries set before us on a plate. "But let's go set up and make a pot of spaghetti. They'll arrive sometime about eight."

"Root beer float," Nick said as we passed the turnoff.

"I'm going to get one tomorrow."

Now we drove up the long hill which was the eastern shoulder of the Uinta Mountains and at the top we followed the old highway south through the forest and felt the light change. This was a section of road I sometimes imagined when I could not sleep: each frost heave, turnout, campground, the old corral fence. Nick eased the rental car down to the steel-pipe gate and I stood out in the shadow of the mountain. The sun was golden on the green hills behind us and the brook was talking where it crossed under the road. There has never been in my life a feeling of homecoming like this: unlocking the gate, swinging it wide for the car. When I'd secured the gate again, Nick drove us slowly along the gravel lane. We could see our little cabin from across the loop and it looked like a cabin in a story, a house a child would draw, the window, the door, the chimney. It was sweet not to hurry and Nick drove slowly so that he could point again to each place he'd had a bike accident, and the slash field, and how big the one hill had seemed twenty years ago and so small now. Our entry was marked with the sign my father cut out of stainless steel, the outline of a little moose along with the number 15, our number, set on the cedar post I'd dug in fifteen years ago. The long tree-lined driveway was grown with tall grass, which you want to see in a place, a thing which makes a house look abandoned and full of ghosts, and after driving on the gravel, our approach became very silent as Nick rolled down into the dooryard. The long woodpile lined one side of the grassy driveway, and I had to say again, "I've had every stick in that stack in my hand."

"I know," Nick said.

"Your kids will burn that wood." When I used to say that, Nick would come back, "I don't think so," or "Who are you talking about?" But now we stood out of the car and he looked at the wall of stove-length logs and he said, "They probably will. I'll be sure to tell them what you did."

The cabin stood before us shuttered and silent like a big puzzle box we were about to open. There was work to do. Nick opened the front door and we went in and found the old good smell of firewood and burned coffee and the dry smell of the books. Nick opened all the blinds, copper Levolors. I remember the summer they came. Then we carried outdoor stuff: the ladder, the bicycles, the mower, the barbe-cue, the picnic table, and the two butterfly chairs onto the tall grass behind the cabin. I turned on the electricity and the lights came on in the gloom and the radio roared with static and the fridge chugged and began to grind forward. It was forty years old.

Outside against the cabin wall I opened the small wooden lid over the waterworks and removed the insulating carpet and Nick and I looked at the blue valve that held our success. It was all as I had left it two years ago. I knelt and said, "Listen for it," and opened the valve turn by turn.

Nick ran inside and I called, "Anything?" I could not hear water running.

He appeared a minute later. "I can hear it filling the water heater, but no leaks under the sinks." I looked at the old blue valve and the piping in the ground. It was all working.

"Man," was all I could say, standing up. The feeling now was like being airborne. The meadow in front of the cabin was all yellow sage grass in shadow and the high friction of the air moving in the trees sounded like water over a spillway. The sun was still flat gold against the hills to the east and every time I looked up, walking back and forth from the car to the cabin, the line of shade had advanced. When you know your brother and your other son are on their way, it gives you great reason to assess your groceries again and plan out the spaghetti with thick tomato sauce and hot Italian sausage and big wedges of let-tuce with stripes of blue cheese and burned toast and ginger ale. They would have now passed through Rangely, Colorado, through the oil field and the antelope, and they'd be driving into the last low angle of sunlight, the shadow of Regan's Blazer sixty yards behind them.

Nick went out and turned the car around, parking it nose-out in the dooryard, and then he came back in the cabin and found me sitting on the couch. I could feel the altitude a little. It was pleasant looking over the meadow though we knew there would be no deer tonight; they were all in the high country. In the summers, there were deer every night and one summer a moose had tried to head-butt our dear dog Max. Max's tags were in an antique mason jar on the bookshelf.

"How soon will they get here?" Nick said.

"Just after eight, if I know Regan," I said. "We'll go down and meet them."

"Do we need to cook now?"

"Not for an hour."

Nick took the kindling bucket and stood in the doorway. "I'm going to get some sticks and start a fire." We could feel the chill now that the sun was gone. He opened the closet and drew out a pillow from the shelf. "Why don't you lie down there?"

The pillow was perfect. I remembered the old pillowcase pattern from early in my marriage, and I laid out on the long couch and felt the blood beat in my knees while I listened to Nick break sticks and open the stove door and start the fire. I'd napped here a hundred times. Max would find me and lay his chin on my stomach for a minute before curling on the rag rug beside the old couch under the wagon-wheel ceiling light.

One November night twenty-five years ago my father and I put the woodburning stove in the fireplace. It was a great stove with a big glass door and the draft vents made lighting a fire easy and then, when engaged, it heated the whole room. Many times during storms when we'd lost power, Nick's mother would move all the pans to the wood-stove top and make a pot of a soup she called slumgullion with knots of sausage and thick carrot coins and tomatoes, and she'd set the teakettle there for hot chocolate or tea. The cabin would fill with steam and sweet smells, and there'd come a moment late in the middle of the night in the dark with everyone asleep when the fridge would suddenly chug and the radio spit static and it was always an odd disappointment: the power was back on. We'd made soup and had an evening of card games in candlelight.

Now I lived four blocks from the Pacific Ocean and it was fresh there, *fresh* being the word I used for the wet cold which captured many an evening at my cottage. The boys' mother had given me an electric mattress pad I used most nights. I had never lived near the coast, and it was a good place. I could hear the concussions of the surf from my room, and I had a good bicycle which I used every day. I once had a wife and two sons and a good dog, and now I had some tenacious plants and that bicycle. I had survived the pinching loneliness and now I was just alone and, I would admit, a little proud of it. I couldn't cook very well, but I got around that by cooking selectively or riding my bicycle out for Thai food or fish tacos or Mexican food or what there was. I carried a book and rode my bicycle to dinner here and there. Some nights when I rode home from the restaurants in the village, I rode down the middle of the empty streets and I breathed the fresh air deeply under the few stars and remembered being a boy in Utah. In some ways they were the same days: I was just independent, a boy with his bicycle, and now I was an old man alone who rode his bicycle everywhere he could.

I woke warm; the yellow flames fluttered in the glass stove front and it was dark. Nick was on the other couch looking at his iPhone in the gloom, his face lighted by the screen.

"Colin called. They left Vernal fifteen minutes ago."

"Okay then," I said, swinging my feet to the floor. I could feel my heart in my forehead, the altitude, and I let it subside before I tied my shoes.

"What's that?" I said, pointing where the big frying pan steamed on the stove.

"I just fried those sausages and cut them up into the spaghetti sauce."

"Smells good."

Nick adjusted the stove to low simmer and we went out into the cold mountain dark. The stars were coming out a million at a time and it was quiet in the meadow. If you stood still, you could sense the heavy layers of worlds above us. Nick pointed and pointed again at satellites sliding among the stars. I said: "That's your phone company making sure you have reception."

"Or UFOs," he said. We got in the car. "I should have warmed it up," Nick said. "Sorry."

"We're good," I said. "The radio stations will be popping up and maybe we can get something."

He drove us up the narrow grassy drive to the circle road and we crept the mile to the gate. I got out of the car and was clamped by the still cold as I wandered back of the car to pee. The stars piled on my shoulders and the great silence flooded the sky. It was a big night in the world and we were waiting for a rendezvous.

They'd been driving ten hours. Headlights came north and Nick, who had the best eyes of anyone I've ever met, said, "That's Regan's Blazer." I felt a tension let go in my back, and I climbed out again and unlocked the gate, waving at Regan's headlights and waving them through.

"Hello, boys," I said to Colin's open window.

"Hey, Dad."

"Go on to the cabin. We'll be right there."

The cabin was warm against the frozen evening, and Nick took two more logs for the stove when we went inside. You want to hear someone say, "Smells good," when you enter the only warm room in the mountains and Regan said it. "That's spicy spaghetti sauce." We were all standing around and Colin peeled off his fleece jacket and stored his gear on one side of the wood box and Regan began to put his gear away, and I boiled the water and dumped in the pasta and fired up the toaster with sourdough bread and unwrapped the butter and sliced four thick wedges off the cheddar. Nick pulled cases on the pillows and after a while we all sat at the old table in the big room. The silverware drawer was an inventory of the ages. The spoons were silver soup spoons from the Ambassador Club, gone thirty years now, forty, and the forks were heavy and perfect for the spaghetti. We ate and talked about the day's travel, and Regan said my chainsaw was in his car, and we decided not to do the tree work tomorrow, but to fish in the morning over by the state line at Antelope Flats. We had two full days and everyone was talking like you do when you're rich that way.

Nick banked the stove and we made a campsite of the room, pulling out the giant sofa beds and throwing down our sleeping bags. The old couch beds had always been noisy and tilted and crazy to sleep on, even when new, but we were all tired, which improves a bed. We groaned a little bit, I did, but it was all show and led the way to sleep. In the dark cabin every edge caught the orange glow of the pulsing fire.

The cabin percolator was a tall silver pot, elegant and sixty years old. It was the kind of thing that in 1958 looked like the distant future. When it first chugged, the water would start to flush into the glass topper, and the smell of coffee filled the room. It was cold now in the cabin in the morning, thirty-nine. I stepped carefully over all the gear and around the couches and out the front door. The day was like a slap; it was twenty degrees outside and the meadow was frosted white. Inside again, it felt warm. Nick had seen to the fire. I fried the big pan of bacon and dropped eight eggs into the hot grease. Colin was up and he loaded and reloaded the toaster. Regan sorted his gear and got his boots on and then he and Nick put the room away so we could do some good. Everyone was drinking lots of water from the old jelly-jar glasses and even so I could still feel the pressure in my head from the altitude. In ten minutes the kitchen table was wall-to-wall dishes and cups.

"Some coffeepot," Colin said. The percolator rocked and a column of bright steam shot from the spout. We already had the half-and-half on the table.

"We'll stop at the lodge and get licenses and drive across to the flats." We all dipped buttered toast into the thick milky coffee and drank orange juice out of paper cups as old as the boys.

"Sounds good," Regan said. "We'll see if that fish is over there." He went out and came back with the chainsaw and set it on the wood box. "You keep this thing clean as a violin," he said.

"I always did," I said. It was a good saw and I'd gone right by the book with it. We were here to cut down one big dead tree and to remove two that the Forest Service had already dropped. Their annual letter outlined what we needed to do to keep the lease. Colin picked up the saw and looked at me. "We can do this," he said.

"Tomorrow you'll be a lumberjack," I told him. It was a weird thing, passing the saw. I'd cut three hundred trees in twenty-five years, half of them standing dead from beetle kill. I'd loved the work in the summers, writing all morning and then a tree or two in the afternoon.

Nick put the big pot full of water on the stove to boil to do the dishes. I remembered seeing his mother there at the big steel sink bathing both boys at once, a naked little boy on each side. Outside the front window the meadow filled with light and now the first gold grass showed the sun. I knew this light as well as any in the world.

All along the drive down the mountain, the sun burned off the frost and the day opened into broad Indian summer. With the deer hunt concluded, the lodge parking lot was empty, a rare sight. With the few yellow leaves in the two maples, it made a lonely place. Summers there were always big pickups hauling pleasure boats. We already had a big bag of lunch in the car, so we bought licenses and candy bars and big cups of coffee. On the store bulletin board Colin studied the dozens of Polaroid photographs of all the big lake trout being held up by fishermen. On the little magazine rack, Nick saw the copy of a sports journal with my story in it and showed it to Regan; it was the story about a trip Regan and I had made three years before and a fish we did not catch.

I went out into the day. The sun on the mountain downslope and the layered plains of Wyoming in the distance filled me with hope. Nick came out of the store with our goods in a brown paper bag, then Regan with a twelve of Coca-Cola, and then Colin reading his fishing license.

The drive to Antelope Flats was a sinuous switchback descent to the big blue lake, past the marina and then over the silver bridge and then twenty miles per hour over the Flaming Gorge Dam. Now there were two highway patrol cars in the visitors' center parking lot, side by side, as part of Homeland Security. The reservoir here was always a stunning sight: the vast blue-water lake brimming against the huge curved dam and on the other side the red-rock canyon drawing down on the Green River way below. The road wound up and over through where the huge forest and brush fire burned ten years before, past the hamlet of Dutch John, and spooling out around the tendrils of the reservoir and between the rock gaps.

A mile before the Wyoming state line, Nick turned our car down the gravel road that runs down the broad ridge to Antelope Flats.

"Look for my hubcap," I said, because I always said it. That was five years ago or six. Nick drove twenty-five miles per hour down the broad washboard track, sun everywhere in the pale sage. The water was bluer than the sky. Across the huge expanse of the lake, we could see the village of Manila. As we neared the lake, we saw the little campground shelters, each with a cooking grill on a steel post.

"Do you even still have that car?" Regan said.

"No, but look for my hubcap."

Colin said, "There they are," and he pointed to the hill beyond the campground where the antelope stood in clusters.

There were more antelope along the top of the big empty parking lot by the boat ramp. They were all lying down and took little notice of us and we stopped and opened all the doors and organized our chairs and the lunch and then we geared up the fishing poles. They watched us for a while but none of the antelope moved. The air was still here and it was warm in the sun. "I'm going to sit in the car for a minute," I told them.

"You feel okay?" Nick asked.

"Good," I said. "I just want to rest. I'm glad to be here. Catch a fish."

Nick led Colin and Regan over the sage hill and down to the water. I'd first fished here forty-five years before on a trip with two friends the last week of high school. There had been no campsites then, just clearings in the sage; the dam and the reservoir were new. I had waded in my Levi's and later dried them by the fire, burning up a pair of good wool socks. It was warm in the car and I lowered the window a few inches; the sun in October was a blanket of its own.

The road from Manila, old Utah Route 43, used to connect to Antelope Flats. It was just one mile straight on the highway. Then the year I was sixteen, they finished the dam and the water backed up and now with this lake it was fifty miles to drive around. The old two-lane road was still down there somewhere under the lake. For years they used it as a boat ramp on both sides.

Sometimes a little nap is just the ticket and I don't know how long I slept, half an hour perhaps, and when I stood in the slanted daylight all the antelope were gone.

At the lake Nick had caught two fish. I loved this desolate place, the ridged mountains rising out of the water across the lake in a way I'd memorized years ago, their geologic layers tipped in a clear display, a place I saw once a year all these years and always unchanged. Regan had his sleeves rolled up in the sunshine and Nick came over to me with the sunblock. "Where's your hat?"

"In the car." I had forgotten it. "It's okay. We won't be here that long. It's October." I tied a swivel on my line.

Colin had his ball cap pulled low because of the late-day glare. The water was silver for two hundred yards.

Spin casting into the glittering lake seemed a perfect activity. We fished for an hour and Regan, Colin, and Nick each took a fish and Nick two more. I unpacked the lunch and handed out the ham sandwiches with the wedges of cheddar and just enough mayo to make the tomatoes slippery. "Too much pepper?" I asked Nick.

He smiled, my pepperhound. We had apple slices and salty chips and bottles of water. Regan and I propped our poles on the shoreline willows and sat in the gravel of the beach. The sun was at us pretty good. "I never caught a fish without the pole in my hand," Regan said, getting up and reeling in for another cast.

"I did," I said, "and I was unhappy about it. He ate the thing, some little fish, and I had to kill him." I reeled and reset my gear and put it out there thirty yards, the lure making a little sound when it hit: *loop!* I stood fishing until my legs ached, casting, and then I walked up and down the bank stretching.

"Three more casts," I said.

"Well, give it a good go," Colin said. "Because this is as far from home as we're going to get and when we turn for the cars, we're headed back."

I knew he was making fun of me, the thing I always said on our trips, but it didn't sound like mockery. It sounded like my son letting me know the news. I'd said it first on our backpacking trip into the Uinta Mountains, Island Lake, a ten-mile hike. It was a magnificent trip and when we fished Island Lake, a deer, a small doe, followed us like a dog. I'd never seen that before. We caught a lot of fish, putting back all we could, and finally we had to stop ourselves. When Nick had lifted the last cutthroat trout from the water, Colin had said, "That's ten we're keeping." The rocks we stood on were wet and Nick had looked at me to see if we should begin hiking back around to our camp. I said then, "Here we go. Every step now takes us toward home and your dear mother." We had a feast that night in the high mountain camp, frying the trout and dropping the filets into the thick trout chowder we made from leek and mushroom soup. How many times in a life do you have a day where the food is a match for the effort?

The sun fell over the broken red cliffs until we were looking at a world that was only silver and shadow, huge shifting sheets of glittering water. Regan said, "Oh oh," the way our father used to and I turned to see his rod bend and start to dance. Regan was walking along the sand being led by his pole.

"He's a big," Colin said.

"Is that the one?" I asked Regan.

"We'll see," he said. "Maybe he'll have your hubcap. Grab that net, Nick."

Regan walked straight back up the bank hauling his fish in, sliding it on the sand and Nick netted him, a silver rainbow sixteen inches.

"A big fat fish," Regan said. "Let's keep him and have a fry."

"Perfect," I said.

Colin pulled the stringer from the lake with the other fish on it and we knelt and began cleaning and rinsing the fish. Nick took a picture of Regan's fish.

"He's not the one, so we'll have to come back next year."

Nick's arms were sunburned. "What a day," he said. "This is like summer."

"We were lucky," I said.

"It's been like this every year, Nick," Regan said. "It's a secret, this last week in October." We were walking up the narrow winding dirt path over the first sage hump to the big parking lot in the high desert wilderness.

"Parking hasn't been a problem for the fishermen today," Regan said.

We lodged the fish in the cooler and Colin passed out some ginger ale and Regan grabbed his Coke. It was a pleasure being in the car, sitting, and Nick did a slow U-turn and eased onto the gravel road.

"Check," Colin said, pointing ahead.

"Slow down and they won't run," I said, and Nick slowed to five miles an hour and we drove through the middle of the loitering tribe of antelope.

As we drove back up the slope into the forest and along the mountain meadow, the evening wind was up and the temperature had dropped fifteen or twenty degrees and low clouds were moving in tatters around the mountains. We were all a little sunburned and we could feel the cold. "This could put a wrinkle in our plans to fish at East Canyon tomorrow," Regan said.

We stopped at the empty lodge and it was dark in the café; they hadn't turned the lights on in the late afternoon. We stood at the counter there long enough for the waitress who had been working at the desk over a pile of motel receipts to come pour Regan and me big coffees to go and set out all the creamers and spoons and we made a little mess and before I could strike, Nick nabbed a Coke for himself and Colin and put three fives on the counter and ushered us back into the changing day. "You are required to overtip in the territories," he said. Having the coffee was like treasure. Nick drove us up to 191 and then turned up the mountain. We had the windows up and Nick had the heater on.

Colin unlocked the gate, and as he bent to it, I wondered again at all of it, of the days before the great lake filled, before I met the boys' mother in Miss Porter's class, where we read *Silas Marner* and I read my poem after which she spoke to me in the hallway of the old Union Building, and two years before the two of us camped above Kamas with the smallest campfire in the history of Utah, and before I ever had sons and now they were grown and one was driving the car and the other swung the gate open and wheeled his arm and called, "Move it out, buddy!" and we drove through. I could see our little cabin in the trees.

The wind bit at us when we climbed out of the car. It was loud in the trees and the sky was banking up with slow-moving clouds in the deep dusk. Regan put the fish in the sink and rinsed them again, and we hauled firewood into the firebox. Any place out of the wind was warm and our sunburns bloomed when we went indoors.

"We'll bake these trout and my beautiful squash," I said. I looked at my watch. "In about two hours."

Nick banked the stove and in ten minutes the glass front was orange flames and the circulating fan was pumping out waves of heat, a blessing. Colin came in the front door and announced: "It's twenty-five degrees. How can that be?"

Everyone had staked a lamp and part of a couch. Nick was reading a stack of magazines and kids' books that he and Colin had read years ago including an utterly wrong-headed book called *Desperate Dan,* which I had bought in England thirty years before at the seven-story Foyles Bookshop by the Tottenham tube stop, and I had told their mother that I was buying *Desperate Dan* for her kids who were that day still eight years from being people. Regan was sorting his gear, and Colin was going through the floor of the closet to see if there were any boots he could wear should it snow.

"It's going to snow," Regan said. "Can you smell it?"

I'd just put the squash in the oven and could only smell the clean smell of the oven heating up after two years.

"What about these?" Colin said, pulling my old Chippewas out of the tangle of shoes.

"Try them on. They've been here ten years, fifteen. I caught a lot of fish in those shoes. I caught a ten-inch cutthroat on a bare hook in Dime Lake."

I stepped past him and went out the front door in the dark. By the light from the window I could read the thermometer on the porch post: twenty degrees. Now I could smell the dry frozen promise of snow and I could feel the low clouds. There wasn't a star available on such a night. Inside the window everything glowed in lamplight and the fire pulsed.

I peppered the fish and sliced lemon and sweet onion inside of each and laid them on the broiling pan to bake. Nick was reading sections from the scurrilous children's book aloud and laughing and Colin was walking around my father's wagon-wheel coffee table in his new shoes. It was the last Thursday night in October of a year in the mountain cabin with my brother and my sons.

We slathered the steaming squash with butter and we each had a piece big as a cake and a trout which fell apart on our plates and came cleanly away from the bones. The skin was crisp and salty and we ate it with our fingers. Nick wiped the plates with his wadded paper napkin and then slid them into the warm dishwater. Colin opened the couches and pulled out the beds.

"I'm sleeping with my head this way," Regan said, meaning toward the fire. We had already stood four round stove logs on the hearth to load in the middle of the night.

The old poker caddy was full of three kinds of mongrel chips all clay and older than me, fun to handle, and we divvied up four stacks and dealt the old blue Bicycle cards. Nick was talking poker, big blinds and small blinds and being on the button, and Regan said, "Let's just play cards," and so we did that: seven-card stud. Immediately Colin distinguished himself as a bluffer, ten if not twenty every turn, bet and raise, and he got clipped early but wouldn't stop. We played almost an hour. Nobody wanted any ice cream.

"Hey," I said, examining the king of diamonds in my hand. "One of these cards is torn."

"King of diamonds," Nick said.

"You didn't know that?" Regan said.

"A marked deck," I said. I lay the red king on the table.

"That black two has a folded corner," Colin said, and now he was all in and after a minute he showed a seven high, the lowest hand in the history of the cabin.

He stood up. "So close," he said.

Nick and I took a minute and sorted the old chips into the slots and boxed the damaged cards.

"I'll remember that king," I said.

"Wouldn't it be nice if we could," Regan said. "It'll take us an hour next time to figure it out."

"That time, we'll have a big blind and a small blind."

"I'm blind right now," Regan said. He'd put his glasses on the driftwood table beside this bedroll which he was struggling into. "Fire up the stove, Nick."

"I will." Nick was rolling out his bag on our bed. "Think we can get the game?"

"That's right," I said, "they're playing tonight in St. Louis."

It was an old black plastic General Electric AM/FM radio, a small console that had been my parents', in their first kitchen. Days it would get the station from Vernal that advertised auto glass all day long and played eighties songs, but nights the radio stations came out like stars and sizzled against each other, rising and fading.

"Let's see." I leaned against the couch and turned the AM dial up loud and began to drift through the stations.

"They all sound like the ball game," Colin said. And they did, each with its static roar. All the self-help and political bullies were on the clear stations and then just before ten on the dial, I got it. We heard the announcer say, ". . . coming to the plate . . ." and then it faded. I got scientific with my tuning, a whisker, a whisker and we could hear him in there under all the noise, but we couldn't hear what he was saying. I held the radio up and tilted it this way a little and then over there.

"You're a terrible antenna," Nick said. We had done this before on summer nights, the radio dance. Then I tuned in a channel so clear it sounded like someone talking at the table. "It's the UFO guy," Nick said. "Listen."

"What would it take," the baritone voice pleaded. "What would it take to believe they are among us? One convincing crash. Just one. And how many do we have?"

Somebody else, it must have been a caller, said, "I don't know. How many?"

"Fifty-two," the expert said. "We've got fifty-two documented crashes and there are still skeptics. Oh, it's a tough road, my friends."

Regan turned his lamp off and now the cabin was dark except for the fluttering orange glow from the stove fire. I was still holding out the radio.

"Well, let me ask," the caller said. "If these extraterrestrials are so advanced, why are they always crashing?"

The expert didn't miss a beat: "Oh man, come on. Do you think they're sending their best equipment to this planet? They're working with some off-brand airships; it only makes sense."

"Makes sense to me," Regan said.

After Nick and Colin saw the alien visitor movie *Fire in the Sky*, when they were nine and ten, Nick would not sleep outside on the trampoline anymore. His mother had asked him why not, and he said, "It's too easy to get us. We're like snacks on a plate."

I put the radio back on the shelf by the boys' old Lego constructions: jet fighters and battleships. I could feel my forehead sunburned. I was tired in the way you are when a day uses you and it felt good; the room in the muffled light was good.

In the morning, despite the thick gray cloud cover, it was only nine degrees outside. Nick fired up the stove and turned the blower on high while I fried up the bacon and burned a pan of hash browns. We could feel the wind working at the cabin and behind Regan out the front window, I saw the dots commence as it started to snow.

"You guys can tell me how it was at East Canyon," Regan said, stirring cream into his coffee. He was using the white enamel mug we called spidercup, which when you told the story, it made you shudder. "I'll be here reading a book. That place, that trip was as cold as I'll ever want to be."

We'd had a trip four years ago in such wind and snow at that reservoir that I had trouble opening the car doors, and Regan went out to the whitecap water and caught a fish. When he came back up, his eyelashes were iced up. We have a picture somewhere.

"We could do that tree work unless the snow gets too heavy."

Colin had folded his bacon into the sourdough toast, pressed it with his big hands and took a bite. He nodded at me. "Let's do it and learn about this saw."

We laid the saw out on newspapers on the kitchen table and I went through it with Colin. Nick said from the couch, "Teach him and if I need to know it, he'll tell me."

We disassembled the saw and Regan said, "I can't believe how clean that thing is." There were the caps, oil and gas, and there was the trigger and the choke. Regan gave one of the new sharp chains from the bag to Colin. They were lightly oiled and had been in storage for three years. Regan pinched one of the small blades and held it up for Colin. "This is the cutting edge. Set it on the drive rail so this is forward." I stepped back. It was funny about the saw; it was hard not to have it in my hands, but now I knew it was long gone.

"He's got it," Regan said. "Let's do some good."

Nick was wrapping his scarf on and he had his gloves in his hand. We had a lot of gear hanging from the ceiling wagon wheel to dry and I took my jacket off a hanger and pulled it on.

In the meadow, the wind had subsided and the crazy snowflakes were crossing wildly as they descended. It would last all day. We had two hours before it got too deep to work these trees. I checked the toolshed and found the mixed gas and the bar oil right where I put them two years ago. I showed both bottles to Regan knowing he'd appreciate my providence. Colin pulled his glove off to handle the gas and he pulled an envelope out of his back pocket and turned to me and said, "Oh yeah, Mom sent this for you." I recognized her blue stationery and I put the letter in my front pocket, so it wouldn't get wet. We just stood back and let Colin fill the reservoirs in the saw and then adjust the choke and pull the starter rope. He was a big man and made the saw look much lighter than I ever did. It snorted alive on the third pull. Colin stood with the idling saw, adjusting the fuel feed with the trigger. When the rpm dropped to a hum, I said, "You're good to go." There was one fifty-foot jack pine standing dead with its cowl of rusty branches, and he knelt to it. I showed him to make one front cut horizontal to the ground and perpendicular to the fall line, then the angled wedge cut, which he did in less than a minute, kicking out the wedge with his boot easily. We all stepped clear and he ran the saw in the back of the tree and it tilted sweetly, silently in the falling snow and fell alongside of the driveway. Colin looked at me and we talked for a moment about how to limb it up, cutting each branch at the trunk, no hurry. The three of us stood back and watched him walk up the tree, left right left right, sending the limbs into the grass. Nick took more pictures.

"He looks like he's been doing this for a while," Regan said. And it was true. Colin was now bucking up the log, cutting the trunk into stove-length pieces, and we hauled the logs to the old woodpile, the bright yellow ends sharp against the gray wood. The whole job, something that would have taken me two hours, took twenty minutes and we had nothing but a stump and two piles of slash.

There were two more trees, old giants that had been cut down by the power company last summer, and which we'd been instructed to remove. Colin limbed both big trees and we made haystacks of the branches and then he started cutting each log into lengths. They were each almost the diameter of the length of his blade but he didn't force it, letting the saw find its way, and he finished the last tree in half an hour.

We were all red-faced in the snow and Colin turned off the saw and carried a log down to the stack with his other arm.

"What now?" he said, and we all felt it. We wanted more. We needed another tree standing dead or leaning or even downed, but there were none. The trees towering above us had been knee-high twenty years ago. A tree that Nick replanted as a seedling was now thirty feet tall at the corner of the meadow. It was the old feeling: The day is young and we're good for it, and I laughed. The snow was still general, but we could see it wouldn't trap the vehicles or snow us in.

Inside, Nick heated a big pot of Dinty Moore stew, cutting one of our onions into it and simmering it until the brown gravy bubbled, and then he imbedded bread-and-butter pickles in some grilled cheese sandwiches which he fried until they smoked in the pan. The fire had slumped while we were outside and I opened the woodstove and laid in three fresh logs and I closed the glass door and it filled with bright fire. With the fire stoked we ate salty vinegar chips at the table, crunching on the sandwiches, dunking the corners into the potato-thick stew, drinking ice-cold ginger ale. We had one more day.

After lunch, Colin cleaned the saw, taking it apart and wiping it clean and storing it in newspapers in an open cardboard box on the closet shelf. Nick stared out at the snow in the meadow. The snow itself now was not flakes but a steady dusting.

"What do you want?" Nick looked at me. "You want to go for a walk?"

"Yeah, Dad," Colin said. "Let's go. You can show us this place."

Regan had already pulled his boots off and he had his plastic tray of flies on his lap, sorting them for tomorrow. We knew as soon as he lifted his feet onto the wagon-wheel table, he would be asleep. "Have fun, boys."

It was funny going out into the great day. I wasn't sure I was ready.

We walked around the cabin and already the places we had tracked up were covered with snow, the slash piles snowy heaps. The boys would have to haul all those sticks next summer.

"Up the dead end," I said. "And then across the marmot ranch and into the trees."

At the top of the spur road, I led up across the rock spill where all the marmots lived in the summer and they were certainly back in their chambers now. At the far side, I slipped and knocked my knee on the last rock. Colin grabbed my arm and held me up.

"You okay?"

"I'm good." There were no tracks, but across and into the trees, we merged onto a game trail already marked by two deer or three, fresh tracks in the snow. When we were in the trees, Nick said from the rear, "This is just a little weird."

"Not really," I said.

When we approached the big red sandstone boulders, I turned and said, "Do you know where you are? Can you find this place?"

We looked back, marking the grove of trees.

"It's not even half a mile."

"Got it," Colin said.

"We've been here before," Nick said. He was standing next to me and then closer and he bumped me like he always did.

"A couple times," I said. "Remember when we saw the coyotes, the mother and the pups, and we had to stop so Max wouldn't catch the scent?"

"Right," Nick said. "These are those big red-rock rooms." We walked the corridor between the rocks each as big as a bus, and I stopped. It was strange to be here in the snow. Once, twenty years ago, I'd surprised forty elk here and they'd stood and disappeared like vapor. That was when I knew the spot. Now it was quiet in the space between the rocks and the snow fell silently in the odd shelter.

"This is it," I told the boys. "Stand up there on those rocks and let me go." You could see our breath in the spotty snow, the gray afternoon. Nick had come up and grabbed hold of me, just a hug.

"Good idea," Colin said and grabbed me, such big men. "You want us to mark it? Should I make a steel tag, your initials?"

"No need," I said. "You guys will know. That's enough."

"Good deal," Colin said. "We've got it. It's a great place." My son looked at me. "You want to say something? You're the guy with words."

"Not really," I said. "It's sweet to be here." Then I added, "You boys."

"Let's go back," Nick said. "We'll fish that lake tomorrow, but every step from here starts to take us home."

"You lead," I told him. "So I know you know the way."

PART 9

ENDANGERMENT AND EXTINCTION

One of the oldest types of environmental writing, wilderness literature has assumed in the contemporary period even greater social and cultural relevance. According to the 2019 United Nations' Global Report on Biodiversity and Ecosystem Services, one million wild animal and plant species currently face extinction as a result of unsustainable human population growth. So many species are threatened that the International Union for Conservation of Nature has, since it began its global inventory of disappearing species in 1964, needed to specify and scale its "red list" into seven ascending categories: least concern, near threatened, vulnerable, endangered, critically endangered, extinct in the wild, and extinct. Many recent wilderness stories derive much of their narrative and ethical force from growing public concern over biodiversity decline and the planet's vanishing wildlife, caused variously by habitat loss, infectious disease, unchecked pollution, excessive hunting, overfishing, and human-induced climate change. Today's wilderness stories participate in the global effort to sound the alarm, and they remind us along the way that by failing to conserve our natural resources we too are a vulnerable species at future risk of extinction. Under the cloud of a new mass extinction, the environmentally conscious wilderness tale now has a new aim: highlighting the plight of countless imperiled species while simultaneously mourning the ones already lost.

"The Fog Horn"

RAY BRADBURY

Ray Bradbury (1920–2012) was born in Illinois along the shores of Lake Michigan, in the city of Waukegan, the fictional "Green Town" described in Bradbury's tales of small-town midwestern life. He started writing fiction as a teenager in Los Angeles, and over a seventy-five-year writing career he composed novels, stories, plays, and screenplays, frequently seeing his work adapted for radio, theater, film, and television. Bradbury's twenty-seven novels include the dystopic *The Martian Chronicles* (1950), a postwar apocalyptic narrative set on Mars, and *Fahrenheit 451* (1953), a satire of McCarthy-era book burning and censorship that was itself banned by some school boards. Belatedly recognized for the enduring power and influence of his science fiction and fantasy literature, Bradbury was awarded the National Book Foundation's Medal for Distinguished Contribution to American Letters in 2000, the National Medal of Arts in 2004, and a special Pulitzer Prize citation in 2007. The asteroid 9766 Bradbury was named in his honor, as was Bradbury Landing, NASA's rover landing site on Mars. The author won his first O. Henry Prize in 1947 (for the story "Homecoming"), and he went on to write more than six hundred short stories. His 1951 story "The Beast from 20,00 Fathoms," which first appeared in the *Saturday Evening Post,* inspired the 1953 atomic-era "creature feature" film by the same title, provoking an irritated Bradbury to change his original story title to "The Fog Horn" for his collection *The Golden Apples of the Sun* (1953). A fantasy tale, "The Fog Horn" introduces two conjoined themes that over time became distinctive markers of endangerment and extinction tales: loneliness and lastness. Science fiction and fantasy fiction are often confused, but as Bradbury shrewdly explained the difference, "fantasies are things that can't happen, and science fiction is about things that can happen." By the time he died at the age of ninety-one, Ray Bradbury was North America's most acclaimed writer in both genres.

"The Fog Horn"

RAY BRADBURY

Out there in the cold water, far from land, we waited every night for the coming of the fog, and it came, and we oiled the brass machinery and lit the fog light up in the stone tower. Feeling like two birds in the gray sky, McDunn and I sent the light touching out, red, then white, then red again, to eye the lonely ships. And if they did not see our light, then there was always our Voice, the great deep cry of our Fog Horn shuddering through the rags of mist to startle the gulls away like decks of scattered cards and make the waves turn high and foam.

"It's a lonely life, but you're used to it now, aren't you?" asked McDunn.

"Yes," I said. "You're a good talker, thank the Lord."

"Well, it's your turn on land tomorrow," he said, smiling, "to dance the ladies and drink gin."

"What do you think, McDunn, when I leave you out here alone?"

"On the mysteries of the sea." McDunn lit his pipe. It was a quarter past seven of a cold November evening, the heat on, the light switching its tail in two hundred directions, the Fog Horn bumbling in the high throat of the tower. There wasn't a town for a hundred miles down the coast, just a road which came lonely through dead country to the sea, with few cars on it, a stretch of two miles of cold water out to our rock, and rare few ships.

"The mysteries of the sea," said McDunn thoughtfully. "You know, the ocean's the biggest damned snowflake ever? It rolls and swells a thousand shapes and colors, no two alike. Strange. One night, years ago, I was here alone, when all of the fish of the sea surfaced out there. Something made them swim in and lie in the bay, sort of trembling and staring up at the tower light going red, white, red, white across them so I could see their funny eyes. I turned cold. They were like a big peacock's tail, moving out there until midnight. Then, without so much as a sound, they slipped away, the million of them was gone. I kind of think maybe, in some sort of way, they came all those miles to worship. Strange. But think how the tower must look to them, standing seventy feet above the water, the God-light flashing out from it, and the tower declaring itself with a monster voice. They never came back, those fish, but don't you think for a while they thought they were in the Presence?"

I shivered. I looked out at the long gray lawn of the sea stretching away into nothing and nowhere.

"Oh, the sea's full." McDunn puffed his pipe nervously, blinking. He had been nervous all day and hadn't said why. "For all our engines and so-called submarines, it'll be ten thousand centuries before we set foot on the real bottom of the sunken lands, in the fairy kingdoms there, and know *real* terror. Think of it, it's still the year 300,000 Before Christ down under there. While we've paraded around with trumpets, lopping off each other's countries and heads, they have been living beneath the sea twelve miles deep and cold in a time as old as the beard on a comet."

"Yes it's an old world."

"Come on. I got something special I've been saving up to tell you."

We ascended the eighty steps, talking and taking our time. At the top, McDunn switched off the room lights so there'd be no reflection in the plate glass. The great eye of the light was humming, turning easily in its oiled socket. The Fog Horn was blowing steadily, once every fifteen seconds.

"Sounds like an animal, don't it?" McDunn nodded to himself. "A big lonely animal crying in the night. Sitting here on the edge of ten million years calling out to the deeps, I'm here, I'm here, I'm here. And the Deeps do answer, yes, they do. You been here now for three months Johnny, so I better prepare you. About this time of year," he said, studying the murk and fog, "something comes to visit the lighthouse."

"The swarms of fish like you said?"

"No, this is something else. I've put off telling you because you might think I'm daft. But tonight's the latest I can put it off, for if my calendar's marked right from last year, tonight's the night it comes. I won't go into detail, you'll have to see it yourself. Just sit down there. If you want, tomorrow you can pack your duffel and take the motorboat in to land and get your car parked there at the dinghy pier on the cape and drive on back to some little inland town and keep your lights burning nights, I won't question or blame you. It's happened three years now, and this is the only time anyone's been here with me to verify it. You wait and watch."

Half an hour passed with only a few whispers between us. When we grew tired waiting, McDunn began describing some of his ideas to me. He had some theories about the Fog Horn itself.

"One day many years ago a man walked along and stood in the sound of the ocean on a cold sunless shore and said, 'We need a voice to call across the water, to warn ships; I'll make one. I'll make a voice like all of time and all of the fog that ever was; I'll make a voice that is like an empty bed beside you all night long, and like an empty house when you open the door, and like trees in autumn with no leaves. A sound like the birds flying south, crying, and a sound like November wind and the sea on the hard, cold shore. I'll make a sound that's so alone that no one can miss it, that whoever hears it will weep in their souls, and hearths will seem warmer, and being inside will seem better to all who hear it in the distant towns. I'll make me a sound and an apparatus and they'll call it a Fog Horn and whoever hears it will know the sadness of eternity and the briefness of life.'"

The Fog Horn blew.

"I made up that story," said McDunn quietly, "to try to explain why this thing keeps coming back to the lighthouse every year. The fog horn calls it, I think, and it comes . . ."

"But—" I said.

"Sssst!" said McDunn. "There!" He nodded out to the Deeps.

Something was swimming towards the lighthouse tower.

It was a cold night, as I have said; the high tower was cold, the light coming and going, and the Fog Horn calling and calling through the raveling mist. You couldn't see far and you couldn't see plain, but there was the deep sea moving on its way about the night earth, flat and quiet, the color of gray mud, and here were the two of us alone in the high tower, and there, far out at first, was a ripple, followed by a wave, a rising, a bubble, a bit of froth. And then, from the surface of the cold sea came a head, a large head, dark-colored, with immense eyes, and then a neck. And then—not a body—but more neck and more! The head rose a full forty feet above the water on a slender and beautiful dark neck. Only then did the body, like a little island of black coral and shells and crayfish, drip up from the subterranean. There was a flicker of tail. In all, from head to tip of tail, I estimated the monster at ninety or a hundred feet.

I don't know what I said. I said something.

"Steady, boy, steady," whispered McDunn.

"It's impossible!" I said.

"No, Johnny, *we're* impossible. *It's* like it always was ten million years ago. *It* hasn't changed. It's *us* and the land that've changed, become impossible, *Us!*"

It swam slowly and with a great dark majesty out in the icy waters, far away. The fog came and went about it, momentarily erasing its shape. One of the monster eyes caught and held and flashed back our immense light, red, white, red, white, like a disc held high and sending a message in primeval code. It was as silent as the fog through which it swam.

"It's a dinosaur of some sort!" I crouched down, holding to the stair rail.

"Yes, one of the tribe."

"But they died out!"

"No, only hid away in the Deeps. Deep, deep down in the deepest Deeps. Isn't *that* a word now, Johnny, a real word, it says so much: the Deeps. There's all the coldness and darkness and deepness in a word like that."

"What'll we do?"

"Do? We got our job, we can't leave. Besides, we're safer here than in any boat trying to get to land. That thing's as big as a destroyer and almost as swift."

"But here, why does it come *here*?"

The next moment I had my answer.

The Fog Horn blew.

And the monster answered.

A cry came across a million years of water and mist. A cry so anguished and alone that it shuddered in my head and my body. The monster cried out at the tower. The Fog Horn blew. The monster roared again. The Fog Horn blew. The monster opened its great toothed mouth and the sound that came from it was the sound of the Fog Horn itself. Lonely and vast and far away. The sound of isolation, a viewless sea, a cold night, apartness. That was the sound.

"Now," whispered McDunn, "do you know why it comes here?"

I nodded.

"All year long, Johnny, that poor monster there lying far out, a thousand miles at sea, and twenty miles deep maybe, biding its time, perhaps it's a million years old, this one creature. Think of it, waiting a million years; could *you* wait that long? Maybe it's the last of its kind. I sort of think that's true. Anyway, here come men on land and build this lighthouse, five years ago. And set up their Fog Horn and sound it and sound it out towards the place where you bury yourself in sleep and sea memories of a world where there were thousands like yourself, but now you're alone, all alone in a world not made for you, a world where you have to hide.

"But the sound of the Fog Horn comes and goes, comes and goes, and you stir from the muddy bottom of the Deeps, and your eyes open like the lenses of two-foot cameras and you move, slow, slow, for you have the ocean sea on your shoulders, heavy. But that Fog Horn comes through a thousand miles of water, faint and familiar, and the furnace in your belly stokes up, and you begin to rise, slow, slow. You feed yourself on minnows, great slakes of cod and minnow, on rivers of jellyfish, and you rise slow through the autumn months, through September when the fogs started, through October with more fog and the horn still calling you on, and then, late in November, after pressurizing yourself day by day, a few feet higher every hour, you are near the surface and still alive. You've got to go slow; if you surfaced all at once you'd explode. So it takes you all of three months to surface, and then a number of days to swim through the cold waters to the lighthouse. And there you are, out there, in the night, Johnny, the biggest damned monster in creation. And here's the lighthouse calling to you, with a long neck like your neck sticking way up out of the water, and a body like your body, and, most important of all, a voice like your voice. Do you understand now, Johnny, do you understand?"

The Fog Horn blew.

The monster answered.

I saw it all, I knew it all—the million years of waiting alone, for someone to come back who never came back. The million years of isolation at the bottom of the sea, the insanity of time there, while the skies cleared of reptile-birds, the swamps dried on the continental lands, the sloths and saber-tooths had their day and sank in tar pits, and men ran like white ants upon the hills.

The Fog Horn blew.

"Last year," said McDunn, "that creature swam round and round, round and round, all night. Not coming too near, puzzled, I'd say.

Afraid, maybe. And a bit angry after coming all this way. But the next day, unexpectedly, the fog lifted, the sun came out fresh, the sky was as blue as a painting. And the monster swam off away from the heat and the silence and didn't come back. I suppose it's been brooding on it for a year now, thinking it over from every which way."

The monster was only a hundred yards off now, it and the Fog Horn crying at each other. As the lights hit them, the monster's eyes were fire and ice, fire and ice.

"That's life for you," said McDunn. "Someone always waiting for someone who never comes home. Always someone loving some thing more than that thing loves them. And after a while you want to destroy whatever that thing is, so it can't hurt you no more."

The monster was rushing at the lighthouse.

The Fog Horn blew.

"Let's see what happens," said McDunn.

He switched the Fog Horn off.

The ensuing minute of silence was so intense that we could hear our hearts pounding in the glassed area of the tower, could hear the slow greased turn of the light.

The monster stopped and froze. Its great lantern eyes blinked. Its mouth gaped. It gave a sort of rumble, like a volcano. It twitched its head this way and that, as if to seek the sounds now dwindled off into the fog. It peered at the lighthouse. It rumbled again. Then its eyes caught fire. It reared up, threshed the water, and rushed at the tower, its eyes filled with angry torment.

"McDunn!" I cried. "Switch on the horn!"

McDunn fumbled with the switch. But even as he switched it on, the monster was rearing up. I had a glimpse of its gigantic paws, fish-skin glittering in webs between the finger-like projections, clawing at the tower. The huge eye on the right side of its anguished head glittered before me like a caldron into which I might drop, screaming. The tower shook. The Fog Horn cried; the monster cried. It seized the tower and gnashed at the glass, which shattered in upon us.

McDunn seized my arm. "Downstairs!"

The tower rocked, trembled, and started to give. The Fog Horn and the monster roared. We stumbled and half fell down the stairs. "Quick!"

We reached the bottom as the tower buckled down towards us.

We ducked under the stairs into the small stone cellar. There were a thousand concussions as the rocks rained down; the Fog Horn stopped abruptly. The monster crashed upon the tower. The tower fell. We knelt together, McDunn and I, holding tight, while our world exploded.

Then it was over, and there was nothing but darkness and the wash of the sea on the raw stones.

That and the other sound.

"Listen," said McDunn quietly. "Listen."

We waited a moment. And then I began to hear it. First a great vacuumed sucking of air, and then the lament, the bewilderment, the loneliness of the great monster, folded over and upon us, above us, so that the sickening reek of its body filled the air, a stone's thickness away from our cellar. The monster gasped and cried. The tower was gone. The light was gone. The thing that had called to it a million years was gone. And the monster was opening its mouth and sending out great sounds. The sounds of a Fog Horn, again and again. And ships far at sea, not finding the light, not seeing anything, but passing and hearing late that night, must've thought: There it is, the lonely sound, the Lonesome Bay horn. All's well. We've rounded the cape.

And so it went for the rest of that night.

The sun was hot and yellow the next afternoon when the rescuers came out to dig us from our stoned-under cellar.

"It fell apart, is all," said Mr. McDunn gravely. "We had a few bad knocks from the waves and it just crumbled." He pinched my arm.

There was nothing to see. The ocean was calm, the sky blue. The only thing was a great algaic stink from the green matter that covered the fallen tower stones and the shore rocks. Flies buzzed about. The ocean washed empty on the shore.

The next year they built a new lighthouse, but by that time I had a job in the little town and a wife and a good small warm house that glowed yellow on autumn nights, the doors locked, the chimney puffing smoke. As for McDunn, he was master of the new lighthouse, built to his own specifications, out of steel-reinforced concrete. "Just in case," he said.

The new lighthouse was ready in November. I drove down alone one evening late and parked my car and looked across the gray waters and listened to the new horn sounding, once, twice, three, four times a minute far out there, by itself.

The monster?

It never came back.

"It's gone away," said McDunn. "It's gone back to the Deeps. It's learned you can't love anything too much in this world. It's gone into the deepest Deeps to wait another million years. Ah, the poor thing! Waiting out there, and waiting out there, while man comes and goes on this pitiful little planet. Waiting and waiting."

I sat in my car, listening. I couldn't see the lighthouse or the light standing out in Lonesome Bay. I could only hear the Horn, the Horn, the Horn. It sounded like the monster calling.

I sat there wishing there was something I could say.

"After the Plague"

T. C. BOYLE

T C. Boyle (b. 1948) has lived in Montecito, California, for decades. He is the author of eleven collections of short fiction and eighteen novels, most recently *Outside Looking In* (2019), a novel of the 1960s psychedelic revolution, and *Talk to Me* (2021), a story of interspecies communication. Boyle, who counts science, nature, and ecology among his passions, draws on his considerable creative and observational powers to write about a range of environmental issues, including global warming and deforestation in *A Friend of the Earth* (2000), wildlife preservation and species extinction in *When the Killing's Done* (2011), and natural disasters and eco-survivalists in *The Terranauts* (2016). In a 2003 interview, Boyle noted: "Probably the theme that has interested me the most throughout all of my work is human kindness, an animal species living on a planet with limited resources." Boyle took home the 1988 PEN/Faulkner Award for *World's End* (1987), a novel that recounts three hundred years of Hudson Valley history and that fittingly begins with an epigraph from Washington Irving's "Rip Van Winkle": "He began to doubt whether he and the world around him were not bewitched." Winner of five O. Henry Awards for his short stories, Boyle also received the 2014 Henry David Thoreau Prize for Literary Excellence in Nature Writing. "After the Plague" appeared on either side of the millennium, first in the September 1999 issue of *Playboy* and next as the concluding story in Boyle's 2001 collection *After the Plague*. This eerily prescient tale begins in the High Sierras and moves down to coastal Montecito as a fast-moving global pandemic rearranges the landscape. In Boyle's apocalyptic vision, California condors and beluga whales may not be the only endangered species on the planet. Boyle continues to reside in Montecito.

"After the Plague"

T. C. BOYLE

After the plague—it was some sort of Ebola mutation passed from hand to hand and nose to nose like the common cold—life was different. More relaxed and expansive, more natural. The rat race was over, the freeways were clear all the way to Sacramento, and the poor dwindling ravaged planet was suddenly big and mysterious again. It was a kind of miracle really, what the environmentalists had been hoping for all along, though of course even the most strident of them wouldn't have wished for his own personal extinction, but there it was. I don't mean to sound callous—my parents are long dead and I'm unmarried and siblingless, but I lost friends, colleagues and neighbors, the same as any other survivor. What few of us there are, that is. We're guessing it's maybe one in ten thousand, here in the States anyway. I'm sure there are whole tribes that escaped it somewhere in the Amazon or the interior valleys of Indonesia, meteorologists in isolated weather stations, fire lookouts, goatherds and the like. But the president's gone, the vice president, the cabinet, Congress, the joint chiefs of staff, the chairmen of the boards and CEOs of the Fortune 500 companies, along with all their stockholders, employees, and retainers. There's no TV. No electricity or running water. And there won't be any dining out anytime soon.

Actually, I'm lucky to be here to tell you about it—it was sheer serendipity, really. You see, I wasn't among my fellow human beings when it hit—no festering airline cabins or snaking supermarket lines for me, no concerts, sporting events, or crowded restaurants—and the closest I came to intimate contact was a telephone call to my on-and-off girlfriend, Danielle, from a gas station in the Sierra foothills. I think I may have made a kissing noise over the wire, my lips very possibly coming into contact with the molded plastic mouthpiece into which hordes of strangers had breathed before me, but this was a good two weeks before the first victim carried the great dripping bag of infection that was himself back from a camcorder safari to the Ngorongoro Crater or a conference on economic development in Malawi. Danielle, whose voice was a drug I was trying to kick, at least temporarily, promised to come join me for a weekend in the cabin after my six weeks of self-imposed isolation were over, but sadly, she never made it. Neither did anyone else.

I *was* isolated up there in the mountains—that was the whole point—and the first I heard of anything amiss was over the radio. It was a warm, full-bodied day in early fall, the sun caught like a child's ball in the crown of the Jeffrey pine outside the window, and I was washing up after lunch when a smooth melodious voice interrupted *Afternoon Classics* to say that people were bleeding from the eyeballs and vomiting up bile in the New York subways and collapsing en masse in the streets of the capital. The authorities were fully prepared to deal with what they were calling a minor outbreak of swine flu, the voice said, and people were cautioned not to panic, but all at once the announcer seemed to chuckle deep in his throat, and then, right in the middle of the next phrase, he sneezed—a controlled explosion hurtling out over the airwaves to detonate ominously in ten million trembling speakers—and the radio fell silent. Somebody put on a CD of Richard Strauss's *Death and Transfiguration,* and it played over and over through the rest of the afternoon.

I didn't have access to a telephone—not unless I hiked two and a half miles out to the road where I'd parked my car and then drove another six to Fish Fry Flats, pop. 28, and used the public phone at the bar/restaurant/gift shop/one-stop grocery/gas station there—so I ran the dial up and down the radio to see if I could get some news. Reception is pretty spotty up in the mountains—you never knew whether you'd get Bakersfield, Fresno, San Luis Obispo, or even Tijuana—and I couldn't pull in anything but white noise on that particular afternoon, except for the aforementioned tone poem, that is. I was powerless. What would happen would happen, and I'd find out all the sordid details a week later, just as I found out about all the other crises, scandals, scoops, coups, typhoons, wars, and cease-fires that held the world spellbound while I communed with the ground squirrels and woodpeckers. It was funny. The big events didn't seem to mean much up here in the mountains, where life was so much more elemental and immediate and the telling concerns of the day revolved around priming the water pump and lighting the balky old gas stove without blowing the place up. I picked up a worn copy of John Cheever's stories somebody had left in the cabin during one of its previous incarnations and forgot all about the news out of New York and Washington.

Later, when it finally came to me that I couldn't live through another measure of Strauss without risk of permanent impairment, I flicked off the radio, put on a light jacket, and went out to glory in the way the season had touched the aspens along the path out to the road. The sun was leaning way over to the west now, the shrubs and ground litter gathering up the night, the tall trees trailing deep blue shadows. There was the faintest breath of a chill in the air, a premonition of winter, and I thought of the simple pleasures of building a fire, preparing a homely meal, and sitting through the evening with a book in one hand and a scotch and Drambuie in the other. It wasn't until nine or ten at night that I remembered the bleeding eyeballs and the fateful sneeze, and though I was half-convinced it was a hoax or maybe one of those fugitive terrorist attacks with a colorless, odorless gas—sarin or the like—I turned on the radio, eager for news.

There was nothing, no Strauss, no crisp and efficient NPR correspondent delivering news of riots in Cincinnati and the imminent collapse of the infrastructure, no right-wing talk, no hip-hop, no jazz, no rock. I switched to AM, and after a painstaking search I hit on a weak signal that sounded as if it were coming from the bottom of Santa Monica Bay. *This is only a test,* a mechanical voice pronounced in what was now just the faintest whispering squeak, *in the event of an actual emergency please stay tuned to . . .* and then it faded out. While I was fumbling to bring it back in, I happened upon a voice shouting something in Spanish. It was just a single voice, very agitated, rolling on tirelessly, and I listened in wonder and dread until the signal went dead just after midnight.

I didn't sleep that night. I'd begun to divine the magnitude of what was going on in the world below me—this was no hoax, no casual atrocity or ordinary attrition; this was the beginning of the end, the Apocalypse, the utter failure and ultimate demise of all things human. I felt sick at heart. Lying there in the fastness of the cabin in the absolute and abiding dark of the wilderness, I was consumed with fear. I lay on my stomach and listened to the steady thunder of my heart pounding through the mattress, attuned to the slightest variation, waiting like a condemned man for the first harrowing sneeze.

Over the course of the next several days, the radio would sporadically come to life (I left it switched on at all times, day and night, as if I were going down in a sinking ship and could shout "Mayday!" into the receiver at the first stirring of a human voice). I'd be pacing the floor or spooning sugar into my tea or staring at a freshly inserted and eternally blank page in my ancient manual typewriter when the static would momentarily clear and a harried newscaster spoke out of the void to provide me with the odd and horrific detail: an oceanliner had run aground off Cape Hatteras and nothing left aboard except three sleek and frisky cats and various puddles of flesh swathed in plaid shorts, polo shirts, and sunglasses; no sound or signal had come out of South Florida in over thirty-six hours; a group of survivalists had seized Bill Gates's private jet in an attempt to escape to Antarctica, where it was thought the infection hadn't yet reached, but everyone aboard vomited black bile and died before the plane could leave the ground. Another announcer broke down in the middle of an unconfirmed report that every man, woman, and child in Minneapolis was dead, and yet another came over the air early one morning shouting, "It kills! It kills! It kills in three days!" At that point, I jerked the plug out of the wall.

My first impulse, of course, was to help. To save Danielle, the frail and the weak, the young and the old, the chairman of the social studies department at the school where I teach (or taught), a student teacher with cropped red hair about whom I'd had several minutely detailed sexual fantasies. I even went so far as to hike out to the road and take the car into Fish Fry Flats, but the bar/restaurant/gift shop/one-stop grocery/gas station was closed and locked and the parking lot deserted. I drove round the lot three times, debating whether I should continue on down the road or not, but then a lean furtive figure darted out of a shed at the corner of the lot and threw itself—himself—into the shadows beneath the deck of the main building. I recognized the figure immediately as the splay-footed and pony-tailed proprietor of the place, a man who would pump your gas with an inviting smile and then lure you into the gift shop to pay in the hope that the hand-carved Tule Indian figurines and Pen-Lite batteries would prove irresistible. I saw his feet protruding from beneath the deck, and they seemed to be jittering or trembling as if he were doing some sort of energetic new

contra-dance that began in the prone position. For a long moment I sat
there and watched those dancing feet, then I hit the lock button, rolled
up the windows, and drove back to the cabin.

What did I do? Ultimately? Nothing. Call it enlightened self-
interest. Call it solipsism, self-preservation, cowardice, I don't care.
I was terrified—who wouldn't be?—and I decided to stay put. I had
plenty of food and firewood, fuel for the generator and propane for the
stove, three reams of twenty-five percent cotton fiber bond, correction
fluid, books, board games—Parcheesi and Monopoly—and a complete
set of *National Geographic*, 1947–1962. (By way of explanation, I should
mention that I am—or was—a social studies teacher at the Montecito
School, a preparatory academy in a pricey suburb of Santa Barbara,
and that the serendipity that spared me the fate of nearly all my fellow
men and women was as simple and fortuitous a thing as a sabbatical
leave. After fourteen years of unstinting service, I applied for and was
granted a one-semester leave at half-salary for the purpose of writing a
memoir of my deprived and miserable Irish-Catholic upbringing. The
previous year a high school teacher from New York—the name escapes
me now—had enjoyed a spectacular *succès d'estime,* not to mention
d'argent, with a memoir about his own miserable and deprived Irish-
Catholic boyhood, and I felt I could profitably mine the same territory.
And I got a good start on it too, until the plague hit. Now I ask myself
what's the use—the publishers are all dead. Ditto the editors, agents,
reviewers, booksellers, and the great congenial book-buying public
itself. What's the sense of writing? What's the sense of anything?)

At any rate, I stuck close to the cabin, writing at the kitchen table
through the mornings, staring out the window into the ankles of the
pines and redwoods as I summoned degrading memories of my alcoholic mother, father, aunts, uncles, cousins, and grandparents, and in
the afternoons I hiked up to the highest peak and looked down on
the deceptive tranquility of the San Joaquin Valley spread out like a
continent below me. There were no planes in the sky overhead, no
sign of traffic or movement anywhere, no sounds but the calling of the
birds and the soughing of the trees as the breeze sifted through them. I
stayed up there past dark one night and felt as serene and terrible as a
god when I looked down at the velvet expanse of the world and saw no
ray or glimmer of light. I plugged the radio back in that night, just to

hear the fading comfort of man-made noise, of the static that emanates from nowhere and nothing. Because there was nothing out there, not anymore.

It was four weeks later—just about the time I was to have ended my hermitage and enjoyed the promised visit from Danielle—that I had my first human contact of the new age. I was at the kitchen window, beating powdered eggs into a froth for dinner, one ear half-attuned to the perfect and unbroken static hum of the radio, when there was a heavy thump on the deteriorating planks of the front deck. My first thought was that a branch had dropped out of the Jeffrey pine—or worse, that a bear had got wind of the corned beef hash I'd opened to complement the powdered eggs—but I was mistaken on both counts. The thump was still reverberating through the floorboards when I was surprised to hear a moan and then a curse—a distinctly human curse. "Oh, shit-fuck!" a woman's voice cried. "Open the goddamned door! Help, for shit's sake, help!"

I've always been a cautious animal. This may be one of my great failings, as my mother and later my fraternity brothers were always quick to point out, but on the other hand, it may be my greatest virtue. It's kept me alive when the rest of humanity has gone on to a quick and brutal extinction, and it didn't fail me in that moment. The door was locked. Once I'd got wind of what was going on in the world, though I was devastated and the thought of the radical transformation of every-thing I'd ever known gnawed at me day and night, I took to locking it against just such an eventuality as this. "Shit!" the voice raged. "I can hear you in there, you son of a bitch—I can *smell* you!"

I stood perfectly still and held my breath. The static breathed dismally through the speakers and I wished I'd had the sense to disconnect the radio long ago. I stared down at the half-beaten eggs.

"I'm dying out here!" the voice cried. "I'm starving to death—hey, are you deaf in there or what? I said, I'm *starving*!"

And now of course I was faced with a moral dilemma. Here was a fellow human being in need of help, a member of a species whose value had just vaulted into the rarefied atmosphere occupied by the gnatcatcher, the condor and the beluga whale by virtue of its rarity.

Help her? Of course I would help her. But at the same time, I knew if I opened that door I would invite the pestilence in and that three days hence both she and I would be reduced to our mortal remains.

"Open up!" she demanded, and the tattoo of her fists was the thunder of doom on the thin planks of the door.

It occurred to me suddenly that she couldn't be infected—she'd have been dead and wasted by now if she were. Maybe she was like me, maybe she'd been out brooding in her own cabin or hiking the mountain trails, utterly oblivious and immune to the general calamity. Maybe she was beautiful, nubile, a new Eve for a new age, maybe she would fill my nights with passion and my days with joy. As if in a trance, I crossed the room and stood at the door, my fingers on the long brass stem of the bolt. "Are you alone?" I said, and the rasp of my own voice, so long in disuse, sounded strange in my ears.

I heard her draw in a breath of astonishment and outrage from the far side of the thin panel that separated us. "What the hell do you think, you son of a bitch? I've been lost out here in these stinking woods for I don't know how long and I haven't had a scrap for days, not a goddamn scrap, not even bark or grass or a handful of soggy trail mix. *Now will you fucking open this door?!*"

Still, I hesitated.

A rending sound came to me then, a sound that tore me open as surely as a surgical knife, from my groin to my throat: she was sobbing. Gagging for breath, and sobbing. "A frog," she sobbed, "I ate a goddamn slimy little putrid *frog!*"

God help me. God save and preserve me. I opened the door.

Sarai was thirty-eight years old—that is, three years older than I—and she was no beauty. Not on the surface anyway. Even if you discounted the twenty-odd pounds she'd lost and her hair that was like some crushed rodent's pelt and the cuts and bites and suppurating sores that made her skin look like a leper's, and tried, by a powerful leap of the imagination, to see her as she once might have been, safely ensconced in her condo in Tarzana and surrounded by all the accoutrements of feminine hygiene and beauty, she still wasn't much.

This was her story: she and her live-in boyfriend, Howard, were nature enthusiasts—at least Howard was, anyway—and just before the plague hit they'd set out to hike an interlocking series of trails in the Golden Trout Wilderness. They were well provisioned, with the best of everything—Howard managed a sporting goods store—and for the first three weeks everything went according to plan. They ate delicious freeze-dried fettuccine Alfredo and shrimp couscous, drank cognac from a bota bag, and made love wrapped in propylene, Gore-Tex, and nylon. Mosquitoes and horseflies sampled her legs, but she felt good, born again, liberated from the traffic and the smog and her miserable desk in a miserable corner of the electronics company her father had founded. Then one morning, when they were camped by a stream, Howard went off with his day pack and a fly rod and never came back. She waited. She searched. She screamed herself hoarse. A week went by. Every day she searched in a new direction, following the stream both ways and combing every tiny rill and tributary, until finally she got herself lost. All streams were one stream, all hills and ridges alike. She had three Kudos bars with her and a six-ounce bag of peanuts, but no shelter and no freeze-dried entrées—all that was back at the camp she and Howard had made in happier times. A cold rain fell. There were no stars that night, and when something moved in the brush beside her she panicked and ran blindly through the dark, hammering her shins and destroying her face, her hair, and her clothes. She'd been wandering ever since.

I made her a package of Top Ramen, gave her a towel and a bar of soap, and showed her the primitive shower I'd rigged up above the ancient slab of the tub. I was afraid to touch her or even come too close to her. Sure I was skittish. Who wouldn't be when ninety-nine percent of the human race had just died off on the tailwind of a simple sneeze? Besides, I'd begun to adopt all the habits of the hermit—talking to myself, performing elaborate rituals over my felicitous stock of food-stuffs, dredging bursts of elementary school songs and beer jingles out of the depths of my impacted brain—and I resented having my space invaded. *Still.* Still, though, I felt that Sarai had been delivered to me by some higher power and that she'd been blessed in the way that I was—we'd escaped the infection. We'd survived. And we weren't just errant members of a selfish, suspicious, and fragmented society, but the very foundation of a new one. She was a woman. I was a man.

At first, she wouldn't believe me when I waved a dismissive hand at the ridge behind the cabin and all that lay beyond it and informed her that the world was depeopled, that the Apocalypse had come and that she and I were among the solitary survivors—and who could blame her? As she sipped my soup and ate my flapjacks and treated her cuts and abrasions with my Neosporin and her hair with my shampoo, she must have thought she'd found a lunatic as her savior. "If you don't believe me," I said, and I was gloating, I was, sick as it may seem, "try the radio."

She looked up at me out of the leery brooding eyes of the one sane woman in a madhouse of impostors, plugged the cord in the socket, and calibrated the dial as meticulously as a safecracker. She was rewarded by static—no dynamics even, just a single dull continuum—but she glared up at me as if I'd rigged the thing to disappoint her. "*So*," she spat, skinny as a refugee, her hair kinked and puffed up with my shampoo till it devoured her parsimonious and disbelieving little sliver of a face, "that doesn't prove a thing. It's broken, that's all."

When she got her strength back, we hiked out to the car and drove into Fish Fry Flats so she could see for herself. I was half-crazy with the terrible weight of the knowledge I'd been forced to hold inside me, and I can't describe the irritation I felt at her utter lack of interest—she treated me like a street gibberer, a psychotic, Cassandra in long pants. She condescended to me. She was *humoring* me, for God's sake, and the whole world lay in ruins around us. But she would have a rude awakening, she would, and the thought of it was what kept me from saying something I'd regret—I didn't want to lose my temper and scare her off, but I hate stupidity and willfulness. It's the one thing I won't tolerate in my students. Or wouldn't. Or didn't.

Fish Fry Flats, which in the best of times could hardly be mistaken for a metropolis, looked now as if it had been deserted for a decade. Weeds had begun to sprout up through invisible cracks in the pavement, dust had settled over the idle gas pumps and the windows of the main building were etched with grime. And the animals—the animals were everywhere, marmots waddling across the lot as if they owned it, a pair of coyotes asleep in the shade of an abandoned pickup, ravens cawing and squirrels chittering. I cut the engine just as a bear the color of cinnamon toast tumbled stupendously through an already shattered window and lay on his back, waving his bloodied paws in the air as if he were drunk, which he was. As we discovered a few minutes later—once he'd lurched to his feet and staggered off into the bushes—a whole host of creatures had raided the grocery, stripping the candy display right down to the twisted wire rack, scattering Triscuits and Doritos, shattering jars of jam and jugs of port wine, and grinding the hand-carved Tule Indian figurines underfoot. There was no sign of the formerly sunny proprietor or of his dancing feet—I could only imagine that the ravens, coyotes, and ants had done their work.

But Sarai—she was still an unbeliever, even after she dropped a quarter into the public telephone and put the dead black plastic receiver to her ear. For all the good it did her, she might as well have tried coaxing a dial tone out of a stone or a block of wood, and I told her so. She gave me a sour look, the sticks of her bones briefly animated beneath a sweater and jacket I'd loaned her—it was the end of October and getting cold at seventy-two hundred feet—and then she tried another quarter, and then another, before she slammed the receiver down in a rage and turned her seething face on me. "The lines are down, that's all," she sneered. And then her mantra: "It doesn't prove a thing."

While she'd been frustrating herself, I'd been loading the car with canned goods, after entering the main building through the broken window and unlatching the door from the inside. "And what about all this?" I said, irritated, hot with it, sick to death of her and her thick-headedness. I gestured at the bloated and lazy coyotes, the hump in the bushes that was the drunken bear, the waddling marmots, and the proprietary ravens.

"I don't know," she said, clenching her jaws. "And I don't care." Her eyes had a dull sheen to them. They were insipid and bovine, exactly the color of the dirt at her feet. And her lips—thin and stingy, collapsed in a riot of vertical lines like a dried-up mud puddle. I hated her in that moment, godsend or no. Oh, how I hated her.

"What are you *doing*?" she demanded as I loaded the last of the groceries into the car, settled into the driver's seat, and turned the engine over. She was ten feet from me, caught midway between the moribund phone booth and the living car. One of the coyotes lifted its head at the vehemence of her tone and gave her a sleepy, yellow-eyed look.

"Going back to the cabin," I said.

"You're *what*?" Her face was pained. She'd been through agonies. I was a devil and a madman.

"Listen, Sarai, it's all over. I've told you time and again. You don't have a job anymore. You don't have to pay rent, utility bills, don't have to make car payments or remember your mother's birthday. It's over. Don't you get it?"

"You're insane! You're a shithead! I hate you!"

The engine was purring beneath my feet, fuel awasting, but there was infinite fuel now, and though I realized the gas pumps would no longer work, there were millions upon millions of cars and trucks out there in the world with full tanks to siphon, and no one around to protest. I could drive a Ferrari if I wanted, a Rolls, a Jag, anything. I could sleep on a bed of jewels, stuff the mattress with hundred-dollar bills, prance through the streets in a new pair of Italian loafers, and throw them into the gutter each night and get a new pair in the morning. But I was afraid. Afraid of the infection, the silence, the bones rattling in the wind. "I know it," I said. "I'm insane. I'm a shithead. I admit it. But I'm going back to the cabin and you can do anything you want—it's a free country. Or at least it used to be."

I wanted to add that it was a free world now, a free universe, and that God was in the details, the biblical God, the God of famine, flood, and pestilence, but I never got the chance. Before I could open my mouth she bent for a stone and heaved it into the windshield, splintering me with flecks and shards of safety glass. "Die!" she shrieked. "*You* die, you shit!"

That night we slept together for the first time. In the morning, we packed up a few things and drove down the snaking mountain road to the charnel house of the world.

I have to confess that I've never been much of a fan of the apocalyptic potboiler, the doomsday film shot through with special effects and asinine dialogue or the cyberpunk version of a grim and relentless future. What these entertainments had led us to expect—the roving gangs, the inhumanity, the ascendancy of machines, and the redoubled pollution and ravaging of the earth—wasn't at all what it was like. There were no roving gangs—they were all dead, to a man, woman, and tattooed punk—and the only machines still functioning were the automobiles and weed whippers and such that we the survivors chose to put into prosaic action. And a further irony was that the survivors were the least likely and least qualified to organize anything, either for better or worse. We were the fugitive, the misfit, the recluse, and we were so widely scattered we'd never come into contact with one another anyway—and that was just the way we liked it. There wasn't even any looting of the supermarkets—there was no need. There was more than enough for everybody who ever was or would be.

Sarai and I drove down the mountain road, through the deserted small town of Springville and the deserted larger town of Porterville, and then we turned south for Bakersfield, the Grapevine, and Southern California. She wanted to go back to her apartment, to Los Angeles, and see if her parents and her sisters were alive still—she became increasingly vociferous on that score as the reality of what had happened began to seep through to her—but I was driving and I wanted to avoid Los Angeles at all costs. To my mind, the place had been a pit before the scourge hit, and now it was a pit heaped with seven million moldering corpses. She carped and moaned and whined and threatened, but she was in shock too and couldn't quite work herself up to her usual pitch, and so we turned west and north on Route 126 and headed toward Montecito, where for the past ten years I'd lived in a cottage on one of the big estates there—the DuPompier place, *Mírame.*

By the way, when I mentioned earlier that the freeways were clear, I was speaking metaphorically—they were free of traffic, but cluttered with abandoned vehicles of all sorts, take your pick, from gleaming choppers with thousand-dollar gold-fleck paint jobs to sensible family cars, Corvettes, Winnebagos, eighteen-wheelers, and even fire engines and police cruisers. Twice, when Sarai became especially insistent, I pulled alongside one or another of these abandoned cars, swung open her door, and said, "Go ahead. Take this Cadillac"—or BMW or whatever—"and drive yourself any damn place you please. Go on. What are you waiting for?" But her face shrank till it was as small as a doll's and her eyes went stony with fear: those cars were catacombs, each and every one of them, and the horror of that was more than anybody could bear.

So we drove on, through a preternatural silence and a world that already seemed primeval, up the Coast Highway and along the frothing bright boatless sea and into Montecito. It was evening when we arrived, and there wasn't a soul in sight. If it weren't for that—and a certain creeping untended look to the lawns, shrubs, and trees—you wouldn't have noticed anything out of the ordinary. My cottage, built in the twenties of local sandstone and draped in wisteria till it was all but invisible, was exactly as I'd left it. We pulled into the silent drive with the great house looming in the near distance, a field of dark reflective glass that held the blood of the declining sun in it, and Sarai barely glanced up. Her thin shoulders were hunched and she was staring at a worn place on the mat between her feet.

"We're here," I announced, and I got out of the car.

She turned her eyes to me, stricken, suffering, a waif. "Where?"

"Home."

It took her a moment, but when she responded she spoke slowly and carefully, as if she were just learning the language. "I have no home," she said. "Not anymore."

So. What to tell you? We didn't last long, Sarai and I, though we were pioneers, though we were the last hope of the race, drawn together by the tenacious glue of fear and loneliness. I knew there wouldn't be much opportunity for dating in the near future, but we just weren't suited to each other. In fact, we were as unsuited as any two people could ever be, and our sex was tedious and obligatory, a ballet of mutual need and loathing, but to my mind at least, there was a bright side— here was the chance to go forth and be fruitful and do what we could to repopulate the vast and aching sphere of the planet. Within the month, however, Sarai had disabused me of that notion.

It was a silky, fog-hung morning, the day deepening around us, and we'd just gone through the mechanics of sex and were lying exhausted and unsatisfied in the rumple of my gritty sheets (water was a problem and we did what laundry we could with what we were able to haul down from the estate's swimming pool). Sarai was breathing through her mouth, an irritating snort and burble that got on my nerves, but before I could say anything, she spoke in a hard shriveled little nugget of a voice. "You're no Howard," she said.

"Howard's dead," I said. "He deserted you."

She was staring at the ceiling. "Howard was gold," she mused in a languid, reflective voice, "and you're shit."

It was childish, I know, but the dig at my sexual performance really stung—not to mention the ingratitude of the woman—and I came back at her. "You came to me," I said. "I didn't ask for it—I was doing fine out there on the mountain without you. And where do you think you'd be now if it wasn't for me? Huh?"

She didn't answer right away, but I could feel her consolidating in the bed beside me, magma becoming rock. "I'm not going to have sex with you again," she said, and still she was staring at the ceiling. "Ever. I'd rather use my finger."

"You're no Danielle," I said.

She sat up then, furious, all her ribs showing and her shrunken breasts clinging to the remains of them like an afterthought. "Fuck Danielle," she spat. "And fuck you."

I watched her dress in silence, but as she was lacing up her hiking boots I couldn't resist saying, "It's no joy for me either, Sarai, but there's a higher principle involved here than our likes and dislikes or any kind of animal gratification, and I think you know what I'm talking about—"

She was perched on the edge of a leather armchair I'd picked up at a yard sale years ago, when money and things had their own reality. She'd laced up the right boot and was working on the left, laces the color of rust, blunt white fingers with the nails bitten to the quick. Her mouth hung open slightly and I could see the pink tip of her tongue caught between her teeth as she worked mindlessly at her task, reverting like a child to her earliest training and her earliest habits. She gave me a blank look.

"Procreation, I mean. If you look at it in a certain way, it's—well, it's our duty."

Her laugh stung me. It was sharp and quick, like the thrust of a knife. "You idiot," she said, and she laughed again, showing the gold in her back teeth. "I hate children, always have—they're little monsters that grow up to be uptight fussy pricks like you." She paused, smiled, and released an audible breath. "I had my tubes tied fifteen years ago."

That night she moved into the big house, a replica of a Moorish castle in Seville, replete with turrets and battlements. The paintings and furnishings were exquisite, and there were some twelve thousand square feet of living space, graced with carved wooden ceilings, colored tiles, rectangular arches, a loggia, and formal gardens. Nor had the DuPompiers spoiled the place by being so thoughtless as to succumb inside— they'd died, Julius, Eleanor, and their daughter, Kelly, under the arbor in back, the white bones of their hands eternally clasped. I wished Sarai good use of the place. I did. Because by that point I didn't care if she moved into the White House, so long as I didn't have to deal with her anymore.

Weeks slipped by. Months. Occasionally I would see the light of Sarai's Coleman lantern lingering in one of the high windows of *Mírame* as night fell over the coast, but essentially I was as solitary— and as lonely—as I'd been in the cabin in the mountains. The rains came and went. It was spring. Everywhere the untended gardens ran wild, the lawns became fields, the orchards forests, and I took to walking round the neighborhood with a baseball bat to ward off the packs of feral dogs for which Alpo would never again materialize in a neat bowl in the corner of a dry and warm kitchen. And then one afternoon, while I was at Vons, browsing the aisles for pasta, bottled marinara, and Green Giant asparagus spears amid a scattering of rats and the lingering stench of the perished perishables, I detected movement at the far end of the next aisle over. My first thought was that it must be a dog or a coyote that had somehow managed to get in to feed on the rats or the big twenty-five-pound bags of Purina Dog Chow, but then, with a shock, I realized I wasn't alone in the store.

In all the time I'd been coming here for groceries, I'd never seen a soul, not even Sarai or one of the six or seven other survivors who were out there occupying the mansions in the hills. Every once in a while I'd see lights shining in the wall of the night—someone had even managed to fire up a generator at Las Tejas, a big Italianate villa half a mile away—and every so often a car would go helling up the distant freeway, but basically we survivors were shy of one another and kept to ourselves. It was fear, of course, the little spark of panic that told you the contagion was abroad again and that the best way to avoid it was to avoid all human contact. So we did. Strenuously.

But I couldn't ignore the squeak and rattle of a shopping cartwheeling up the bottled water aisle, and when I turned the corner, there she was, Felicia, with her flowing hair and her scared and sorry eyes. I didn't know her name then, not at first, but I recognized her—she was one of the tellers at the Bank of America branch where I cashed my checks. Formerly cashed them, that is. My first impulse was to back wordlessly away, but I mastered it—how could I be afraid of what was human, so palpably human, and appealing? "Hello," I said, to break the tension, and then I was going to say something stupid like "I see you made it too" or "Tough times, huh?" but instead I settled for "Remember me?"

She looked stricken. Looked as if she were about to bolt—or die on the spot. But her lips were brave and they came together and uttered my name. "Mr. Halloran?" she said, and it was so ordinary, so plebeian, so real.

I smiled and nodded. My name is—was—Francis Xavier Halloran III, a name I've hated since Tyrone Johnson (now presumably dead) tormented me with it in kindergarten, chanting "Francis, Francis, Francis" till I wanted to sink through the floor. But it was a new world now, a world burgeoning and bursting at the seams to discover the lineaments of its new forms and rituals. "Call me Jed," I said.

Nothing happens overnight, especially not in plague times. We were wary of each other, and every banal phrase and stultifying cliché of the small talk we made as I helped her load her groceries into the back of her Range Rover reverberated hugely with the absence of all the multitudes who'd used those phrases before us. Still, I got her address that afternoon—she'd moved into Villa Ruscello, a mammoth place set against the mountains, with a creek, pond, and Jacuzzi for fresh water—and I picked her up two nights later in a Rolls Silver Cloud and took her to my favorite French restaurant. The place was untouched and pristine, with a sweeping view of the sea, and I lit some candles and poured us each a glass of twenty-year-old Bordeaux, after which we feasted on canned crab, truffles, cashews, and marinated artichoke hearts.

I'd like to tell you that she was beautiful, because that's the way it should be, the way of the fable and the fairy tale, but she wasn't—or not conventionally anyway. She was a little heavier than she might have been ideally, but that was a relief after stringy Sarai, and her eyes were ever so slightly crossed. Yet she was decent and kind, sweet even, and more important, she was available.

We took walks together, raided overgrown gardens for lettuce, tomatoes, and zucchini, planted strawberries and snow peas in the middle of the waist-high lawn at Villa Ruscello. One day we drove to the mountains and brought back the generator so we could have lights and refrigeration in the cottage—ice cubes, now there was a luxury—and begin to work our way through the eight thousand titles at the local video store. It was nearly a month before anything happened between us—anything sexual, that is. And when it did, she first felt obligated, out of a sense of survivor's guilt, I suppose, to explain to me how she came to be alive and breathing still when everyone she'd ever known had vanished off the face of the earth. We were in the beamed living room of my cottage, sharing a bottle of Dom Pérignon 1970, with the three-hundred-ten-dollar price tag still on it, and I'd started a fire against the gathering night and the wet raw smell of rain on the air. "You're going to think I'm an idiot," she said.

I made a noise of demurral and put my arm round her.

"Did you ever hear of a sensory deprivation tank?" She was peering up at me through the scrim of her hair, gold and red highlights, health in a bottle.

"Yeah, sure," I said. "But you don't mean—?"

"It was an older one, a model that's not on the market anymore—one of the originals. My roommate's sister—Julie Angier?—she had it out in her garage on Padaro, and she was really into it. You could get in touch with your inner self, relax, maybe even have an out-of-body experience, that's what she said, and I figured why not?" She gave me a look, shy and passionate at once, to let me know that she was the kind of girl who took experience seriously. "They put salt water in it, three hundred gallons, heated to your body temperature, and then they shut the lid on you and there's nothing, absolutely nothing there—it's like going to outer space. Or inner space. Inside yourself."

"And you were in there when—?"

She nodded. There was something in her eyes I couldn't read—pride, triumph, embarrassment, a spark of sheer lunacy. I gave her an encouraging smile.

"For days, I guess," she said. "I just sort of lost track of everything, who I was, where I was—you know? And I didn't wake up till the water started getting cold"—she looked at her feet—"which I guess is when the electricity went out because there was nobody left to run the power plants. And then I pushed open the lid and the sunlight through the window was like an atom bomb, and then, then I called out Julie's name, and she . . . well, she never answered."

Her voice died in her throat and she turned those sorrowful eyes on me. I put my other arm around her and held her. "Hush," I whispered, "it's all right now, everything's all right." It was a conventional thing to say, and it was a lie, but I said it, and I held her and felt her relax in my arms.

It was then, almost to the precise moment, that Sarai's naked sliver of a face appeared at the window, framed by her two uplifted hands and a rock the size of my Webster's unabridged. "What about *me,* you son of a bitch!" she shouted, and there it was again, everlasting stone and frangible glass, and not a glazier left alive on the planet.

I wanted to kill her. It was amazing—three people I knew of had survived the end of everything, and it was one too many. I felt vengeful. Biblical. I felt like storming Sarai's ostentatious castle and wringing her chicken neck for her, and I think I might have if it weren't for Felicia. "Don't let her spoil it for us," she murmured, the gentle pressure of her fingers on the back of my neck suddenly holding my full attention, and we went into the bedroom and closed the door on all that mess of emotion and glass.

In the morning, I stepped into the living room and was outraged all over again. I cursed and stomped and made a fool of myself over heaving the rock back through the window and attacking the shattered glass as if it were alive—I admit I was upset out of all proportion to the crime. This was a new world, a new beginning, and Sarai's nastiness and negativity had no place in it. Christ, there were only three of us— couldn't we get along?

Felicia had repaired dozens of windows in her time. Her little brothers (dead now) and her fiancé (dead too) were forever throwing balls around the house, and she assured me that a shattered window was nothing to get upset over (though she bit her lip and let her eyes fill at the mention of her fiancé, and who could blame her?). So we consulted the Yellow Pages, drove to the nearest window glass shop and broke in as gently as possible. Within the hour, the new pane had been installed and the putty was drying in the sun, and watching Felicia at work had so elevated my spirits I suggested a little shopping spree to celebrate.

"Celebrate what?" She was wearing a No Fear T-shirt and an Anaheim Angels cap and there was a smudge of off-white putty on her chin.

"You," I said. "The simple miracle of you."

And that was fine. We parked on the deserted streets of downtown

Santa Barbara and had the stores to ourselves—clothes, the latest (and last) bestsellers, CDs, a new disc player to go with our newly electrified house. Others had visited some of the stores before us, of course, but they'd been polite and neat about it, almost as if they were afraid to betray their presence, and they always closed the door behind them. We saw deer feeding in the courtyards and one magnificent tawny mountain lion stalking the wrong way up a one-way street. By the time we got home, I was elated. Everything was going to work out, I was sure of it.

The mood didn't last long. As I swung into the drive, the first thing I saw was the yawning gap where the new window had been, and beyond it, the undifferentiated heap of rubble that used to be my living room. Sarai had been back. And this time she'd done a thorough job, smashing lamps and pottery, poking holes in our cans of beef stew and chili con carne, scattering coffee, flour, and sugar all over everything, and dumping sand in the generator's fuel tank. Worst of all, she'd taken half a dozen pairs of Felicia's panties and nailed them to the living room wall, a crude *X* slashed across the crotch of each pair. It was hateful and savage—human, that's what it was, human—and it killed all the joy we'd taken in the afternoon and the animals and the infinite and various riches of the mall. Sarai had turned it all to shit.

"We'll move to my place," Felicia said. "Or any place you want. How about an oceanfront house—didn't you say you'd always wanted to live right on the ocean?"

I had. But I didn't want to admit it. I stood in the middle of the desecrated kitchen and clenched my fists. "I don't want any other place. This is my home. I've lived here for ten years and I'll be damned if I'm going to let *her* drive me out."

It was an irrational attitude—again, childish—and Felicia convinced me to pack up a few personal items (my high school yearbook, my reggae albums, a signed first edition of *For Whom the Bell Tolls,* a pair of deer antlers I'd found in the woods when I was eight) and move into a place on the ocean for a few days. We drove along the coast road at a slow, stately pace, looking over this house or that, until we finally settled on a grand modern place that was all angles and glass and broad sprawling decks. I got lucky and caught a few perch in the surf, and we barbecued them on the beach and watched the sun sink into the western bluffs.

The next few days were idyllic, and we thought about little beyond love and food and the way the water felt on our skin at one hour of the day or another, but still, the question of Sarai nagged at me. I was reminded of her every time I wanted a cold drink, for instance, or when the sun set and we had to make do with candles and kerosene lanterns— we'd have to go out and dig up another generator, we knew that, but they weren't exactly in demand in a place like Santa Barbara (in the old days, that is) and we didn't know where to look. And so yes, I couldn't shake the image of Sarai and the look on her face and the things she'd said and done. And I missed my house, because I'm a creature of habit, like anybody else. Or more so. Definitely more so.

Anyway, the solution came to us a week later, and it came in human form—at least it appeared in human form, but it was a miracle and no doubt about it. Felicia and I were both on the beach—naked, of course, as naked and without shame or knowledge of it as Eve and Adam— when we saw a figure marching resolutely up the long curving finger of sand that stretched away into the haze of infinity. As the figure drew closer, we saw that it was a man, a man with a scraggly salt-and-pepper beard and hair the same color trailing away from a bald spot worn into his crown. He was dressed in hiking clothes, big-grid boots, a bright blue pack riding his back like a second set of shoulders. We stood there, naked, and greeted him.

"Hello," he said, stopping a few feet from us and staring first at my face, then at Felicia's breasts, and finally, with an effort, bending to check the laces of his boots. "Glad to see you two made it," he said, speaking to the sand.

"Likewise," I returned.

Over lunch on the deck—shrimp salad sandwiches on Felicia-baked bread—we traded stories. It seems he was hiking in the mountains when the pestilence descended—"The mountains?" I interrupted. "Whereabouts?"

"Oh," he said, waving a dismissive hand, "up in the Sierras, just above this little town—you've probably never heard of it—Fish Fry Flats?"

I let him go on a while, explaining how he'd lost his girlfriend and wandered for days before he finally came out on a mountain road and appropriated a car to go on down to Los Angeles—"One big cemetery"—and how he'd come up the coast and had been wandering ever since. I don't think I've ever felt such exhilaration, such a rush of excitement, such perfect and inimitable a sense of closure.

I couldn't keep from interrupting him again. "I'm clairvoyant," I said, raising my glass to the man sitting opposite me, to Felicia and her breasts, to the happy fishes in the teeming seas and the birds flocking without number in the unencumbered skies. "Your name's Howard, right?"

Howard was stunned. He set down his sandwich and wiped a fleck of mayonnaise from his lips. "How did you guess?" he said, gaping up at me out of eyes that were innocent and pure, the newest eyes in the world.

I just smiled and shrugged, as if it were my secret. "After lunch," I said, "I've got somebody I want you to meet."

"The Great Silence"

TED CHIANG

Ted Chiang (b. 1967) is a computer scientist and technical writer who also writes creative short fiction—stories that are more like "elaborate thought experiments" in the view of Joyce Carol Oates, "riddles, concerned with asking rather than answering difficult questions." The thinking person's fantasy writer, Chiang's questions are pointedly philosophical, unafraid to address big-picture issues: technology, species, being, time, truth, life, fate. He is the author of two short-story collections: *Stories of Your Life and Others* (2002) and *Exhalation: Stories* (2019). Praised by Barack Obama as "the best kind of science fiction," Chiang's short stories and novellas have won four Hugo Awards, four Nebula Awards, and four Locust Awards. "The Great Silence" was included in *Best American Short Stories of 2016,* the same year Chiang's other tale of alien communication, "Story of Your Life," was made into the film *Arrival* by the director Denis Villeneuve. "The Great Silence" originally accompanied a video installation by the same title, in collaboration with artists Allora & Calzadilla for the 56th Venice Biennale. It is the only story in this volume not set on the North American mainland but rather on the island of Puerto Rico, a U.S. territory. In 1974, Puerto Rico's Arecibo Observatory, then the largest radio telescope in the world, directed a transmission twenty-five thousand light-years away in search of intelligent life. In December 2020, five years after Chiang's story first appeared in the arts journal *e-flux,* the telescope crashed when its ageing cables broke. Giving voice to a critically endangered Puerto Rican parrot (a species driven to near extinction by deforestation), Chiang wonders why we are more interested in contacting extraterrestrials than in learning to communicate with the nonhuman species closest to us. He currently lives in Bellevue, Washington.

"The Great Silence"

TED CHIANG

The humans use Arecibo to look for extraterrestrial intelligence. Their desire to make a connection is so strong that they've created an ear capable of hearing across the universe.

But I and my fellow parrots are right here. Why aren't they interested in listening to our voices?

We're a nonhuman species capable of communicating with them. Aren't we exactly what humans are looking for?

The universe is so vast that intelligent life must surely have arisen many times. The universe is also so old that even one technological species would have had time to expand and fill the galaxy. Yet there is no sign of life anywhere except on Earth. Humans call this the Fermi paradox.

One proposed solution to the Fermi paradox is that intelligent species actively try to conceal their presence, to avoid being targeted by hostile invaders.

Speaking as a member of a species that has been driven nearly to extinction by humans, I can attest that this is a wise strategy.

It makes sense to remain quiet and avoid attracting attention. The Fermi paradox is sometimes known as the Great Silence. The universe ought to be a cacophony of voices, but instead it is disconcertingly quiet.

Some humans theorize that intelligent species go extinct before they can expand into outer space. If they're correct, then the hush of the night sky is the silence of a graveyard.

Hundreds of years ago, my kind was so plentiful that the Río Abajo Forest resounded with our voices. Now we're almost gone. Soon this rainforest may be as silent as the rest of the universe.

·   ·   ·

There was an African gray parrot named Alex. He was famous for his cognitive abilities. Famous among humans, that is.

A human researcher named Irene Pepperberg spent thirty years studying Alex. She found that not only did Alex know the words for shapes and colors, he actually understood the concepts of shape and color.

Many scientists were skeptical that a bird could grasp abstract concepts. Humans like to think they're unique. But eventually Pepperberg convinced them that Alex wasn't just repeating words, that he understood what he was saying.

Out of all my cousins, Alex was the one who came closest to being taken seriously as a communication partner by humans.

Alex died suddenly, when he was still relatively young. The evening before he died, Alex said to Pepperberg, "You be good. I love you."

If humans are looking for a connection with a nonhuman intelligence, what more can they ask for than that?

Every parrot has a unique call that it uses to identify itself; biologists refer to this as the parrot's "contact call."

In 1974, astronomers used Arecibo to broadcast a message into outer space intended to demonstrate human intelligence. That was humanity's contact call.

In the wild, parrots address each other by name. One bird imitates another's contact call to get the other bird's attention.

If humans ever detect the Arecibo message being sent back to Earth, they will know someone is trying to get their attention.

Parrots are vocal learners: we can learn to make new sounds after we've heard them. It's an ability that few animals possess. A dog may understand dozens of commands, but it will never do anything but bark.

Humans are vocal learners too. We have that in common. So humans and parrots share a special relationship with sound. We don't simply cry out. We pronounce. We enunciate.

Perhaps that's why humans built Arecibo the way they did. A receiver doesn't have to be a transmitter, but Arecibo is both. It's an ear for listening, and a mouth for speaking.

.   .   .

Humans have lived alongside parrots for thousands of years, and only recently have they considered the possibility that we might be intelligent.

I suppose I can't blame them. We parrots used to think humans weren't very bright. It's hard to make sense of behavior that's so different from your own.

But parrots are more similar to humans than any extraterrestrial species will be, and humans can observe us up close; they can look us in the eye. How do they expect to recognize an alien intelligence if all they can do is eavesdrop from a hundred light years away?

It's no coincidence that "aspiration" means both hope and the act of breathing.

When we speak, we use the breath in our lungs to give our thoughts a physical form. The sounds we make are simultaneously our intentions and our life force.

I speak, therefore I am. Vocal learners, like parrots and humans, are perhaps the only ones who fully comprehend the truth of this.

There's a pleasure that comes with shaping sounds with your mouth. It's so primal and visceral that, throughout their history, humans have considered the activity a pathway to the divine.

Pythagorean mystics believed that vowels represented the music of the spheres, and chanted to draw power from them.

Pentecostal Christians believe that when they speak in tongues, they're speaking the language used by angels in Heaven.

Brahmin Hindus believe that by reciting mantras, they are strengthening the building blocks of reality.

Only a species of vocal learners would ascribe such importance to sound in their mythologies. We parrots can appreciate that.

According to Hindu mythology, the universe was created with a sound: "om." It is a syllable that contains within it everything that ever was and everything that will be.

When the Arecibo telescope is pointed at the space between stars, it hears a faint hum.

Astronomers call that the "cosmic microwave background." It's the residual radiation of the Big Bang, the explosion that created the universe fourteen billion years ago.

But you can also think of it as a barely audible reverberation of that original "om." That syllable was so resonant that the night sky will keep vibrating for as long as the universe exists.

When Arecibo is not listening to anything else, it hears the voice of creation.

We Puerto Rican Parrots have our own myths. They're simpler than human mythology, but I think humans would take pleasure from them.

Alas, our myths are being lost as my species dies out. I doubt the humans will have deciphered our language before we're gone.

So the extinction of my species doesn't just mean the loss of a group of birds. It's also the disappearance of our language, our rituals, our traditions. It's the silencing of our voice.

Human activity has brought my kind to the brink of extinction, but I don't blame them for it. They didn't do it maliciously. They just weren't paying attention.

And humans create such beautiful myths; what imaginations they have. Perhaps that's why their aspirations are so immense. Look at Arecibo. Any species who can build such a thing must have greatness within them.

My species probably won't be here for much longer; it's likely that we'll die before our time and join the Great Silence. But before we go, we are sending a message to humanity. We just hope the telescope at Arecibo will enable them to hear it.

The message is this:

You be good. I love you.

"Woodland"

LYDIA MILLET

Lydia Millet (b. 1968) was born in Boston, Massachusetts, and grew up in Toronto, Ontario. She is the author of thirteen novels, including three for young adults, and two short-story collections: *Love in Infant Monkeys* (2009), a Pulitzer Prize finalist, and *Fight No More* (2018), a *Library Journal* best book of the year. Millet's interests in ecology, extinction, and endangerment unify her books *How the Dead Dream* (2008), *Ghost Lights* (2011), and *Magnificence* (2012), a novel cycle the writer Jonathan Lethem lauded as "a tapestry of vast implication and ethical urgency, something as large as any writer could attempt: a kind of allegorical elegy for life on a dying planet." A finalist for the National Book Award for Fiction, Millet's novel *A Children's Bible* (2020) vividly imagines the consequences of climate change, as does her story "Woodland," published a year before in the arts and politics journal *Guernica*. A company theme park in the Pacific Northwest, the fictional Woodland advertises itself as wilderness Americana for wealthy nature tourists nostalgic for the forest greenery and wild animal life the national parks once protected. Posing moral questions for the present, this futuristic tale directly links the reality of vanishing North American wildlife to the erosion of fundamental human liberties. Millet, who holds a master's degree from Duke University in environmental policy, works and writes for the Center for Biological Diversity, a nonprofit organization dedicated both to protecting endangered species and their habitats and to fighting climate change. The best art should come out of desperation, Millet has commented. Climate emergencies, species extinctions, existential threats—these are the crises the author deftly navigates in her fiction, urging readers to take note and take action. Millet lives with her children in the desert in Tucson, Arizona.

"Woodland"

LYDIA MILLET

I first saw this place through the eye of a drone. Footage taken in summer, when the grass at the edge of the sea cliffs turns gold.

It was three panels of color on my screen, from left to right: blue, yellow, and green. Ocean, sand and field, forest. One long white line unfurled after another, over the blue to the yellow. And faded.

The marshy springs at the camp were mostly flats of cracked mud, so the largest body of water I'd ever seen was our rainwater tank. A dirty white goliath lifted up from the ground on squat legs.

Inland, where I grew up, a dry wash cut through the walls of a canyon. The trees around it were skeletons, the ghosts of cottonwoods and willows. Their roots were frail and had long since ceased to clutch the earth: we once pushed one over easily. But looking at the fallen tree, its broken roots delicate and spidery, we resolved never to push down another. Even standing there dead, they were good company.

Old timers called the wash a river. It too was a ghost.

My baby brother liked to run straight down the steep banks, feet sliding, spindly arms windmilling as he sped up. I'd feel my stomach clutch, afraid that he might slip. Even small injuries could be bad at the camp. Now and then a nurse or a midwife came through, but we had seen their efforts fail.

Where we lived, everything was brown. I gazed at the colors of that footage on our device and realized place was all there was.

"From savannas and evergreen forests," said the ad copy on the site, "to the soaring cliffs and rocky pinnacles of this unspoiled gem of the Pacific coast, clients are treated to a spectacular landscape. And beautiful wildlife roaming free."

There were pictures of forest animals—a fawn browsing in the grass, a hawk with wings outspread. A bobcat with kittens.

Posts were available there, at the leisure facility. I decided to take the online course and tests, and if I passed them, submit my file. I would apply no matter how slim the odds: I wanted nothing more than to go where trees lived and water flowed.

Mo would come with me; that was our dream. In select cases, if an applicant scored high enough, the facility would make room for a family member.

Our parents meant well, but they worked so hard they were shadows. They spoke only when spoken to.

Meanwhile, home was the screen. Movies from the camp's archives. Tales of lives from the past, some true and some invented. Our favorite time was evening, when we finished our chores and nestled together on our thin mattress, heads bent over our device, in a bright trance.

Mo chose to watch shows, and I watched with him. After he fell asleep, I ran the practice tests.

Once, the screen went black and couldn't be fixed. It took us months of scavenging to save up for a new device. We could use the camp's shared console from time to time, but children were low on the list. So we had little to do, after our tasks were completed, but dig for trade.

In the landfill we had a precious advantage—it dated from olden times and held a trove of riches. Adults lacked the patience and time to dig down as far as we did. We found a hand-cranked wooden box our parents said was for grinding the beans of an energy drink. We found pieces of jewelry and birth-control and pain pills, years since expired, but holding some value still. Silver-plated forks, a brand-new doll in a box, a stroller, a copper kettle, lighters, a two-burner gas stove. All told, we collected forty-six things to trade with the peddlers.

Waiting for them to arrive, we read paper books from the common tent. Mo looked at the maps of old countries in a large, shabby world atlas, pronouncing their exotic names. "Pakistan, Bangladesh," he would say, and point to them on the page.

Looks were a major factor in work applications: only attractive candidates would have a chance at selection. Photos were needed for the file, with a time and GPS stamp. Clients didn't want to be served by hardscrabble who reminded them of the derelicts. I took to wearing a wide-brimmed hat to keep my skin from wrinkling in the sun. Next to our device, that hat was my most prized possession. My mother didn't wear a hat, and her face looked like leather.

Our long days of work ran together, one much the same as the next. The springs gave off a sulfurous smell. There were chickens to feed in a faded red henhouse, fenced high and sharp to keep out the coyotes and feral dogs. There were ragged goats to tend, with dung clinging to their underbellies and tails. The goats were bad-tempered. One was such a vicious biter we weren't even sad when he went under the knife.

His meat was tough. But nourishing.

The camp was a cluster of rust-stained trailers, tires sunk into the mud. Tents and outbuildings and metal rain gutters strung together, with satellite dishes rising above. Generators that made noise when there was fuel to run them. A precious solar array guarded by teens with shotguns.

Mo was too young to be entrusted with a gun. His duties were gathering eggs and patching tent holes, sweeping sand out of the tents and pulling up weeds in the vegetable gardens.

The facility's ad site reminded me of pictures I'd found browsing. Photos of lit-up window boxes in a historic museum. I'd shown the pictures to Mo and we read about these buildings, which anyone had been allowed to go into. The lit-up windows were artificial landscapes behind large panels of glass.

Each of the windows was a scene. I preferred the winter scenes, with snow-capped peaks painted on their back walls, and in the foreground, life-sized replicas of extinct animals. White bears and brown wolverines. Mo's favorite landscape contained hulking ocean mammals with tusks. *Walrus,* said a plaque. "Big funny teeth," said Mo. "And they're so fat!" They'd looked like grave elderly men. They even had whiskers. He laughed at those whiskers, delighted.

Sometimes the artists had made their life-sized models with the animals' own skins. I learned that but didn't tell Mo. I didn't want to have to say, *Don't cry, you tender-hearted boy.*

Terrible. But lovely.

· · ·

Woodland is a remote stretch of country twenty miles from the main leisure complex. Supplies were delivered to us in mud-spattered vans, rattling over dirt roads that could be deeply rutted. After one of the powerful coastal storms, the roads got so uneven they had to bring diggers in. Trucks dragging chains.

Field staff had an all-terrain vehicle to drive, and I had to learn quickly. I loved driving. We lived together in a log cabin, fine and solid. It sits in a clearing surrounded by trees and has a rustic appearance.

The decor here was based on old America, its wilderness and parks. At one trailhead a sign stands even now, battered by time and weather, with a friendly cartoon bear on it wearing a hat. A faded, mysterious fragment of speech beside him. "Only YOU   forest fires."

At the beginning, Management used helicopters to fly in the clients, but the noise of these brought down the ratings, and by the time I got here, clients arrived by jeep or boat.

I marveled at these personal transports. When I got hired, a bolt from the blue that still surprises me when I recall it, they gave me one week to report for duty. It was touch and go whether I'd make it. I'd waited years for an offer. All but given up.

My parents were more silent than ever, having to say goodbye. Yet they took up a collection of trade items to pay for my bus trains. I'd send back my wages, in food and medicine, to repay the debt.

The real trains had gone out of service route by route, tracks fallen into disrepair. Buses traveled together in caravans, armed guards at the front and rear, picking up and delivering passengers and cargo among the camps and citadels. I had to make eight connections to get to the leisure facility, with detours for buckling, impassable asphalt. I slept on the ground at the nexus points. In the end, I was three days over the week they'd allowed, but they accepted me anyway.

Luckily I'd had nothing on me to be stolen while I slept. My father had read reports of assaults: he'd knotted my hair and streaked my face with dirt to make me unappealing. Draped me in a long coat that smelled of goat manure and urine.

And Mo wasn't with me to protect. My posting had come too late for him.

During training they drove us around the grounds, with maps to orient ourselves on company-owned devices. One stop was at the cliffs. I stood at the edge of the cliffs and gazed at the ocean.

It wasn't blue and open. Near the shore, beneath us, structures of jetties and nets jutted into the water. Fish farms, the driver told me. I realized the footage I'd watched had been outdated.

Far beyond the jetties the ocean stretched to the horizon. I couldn't get close to it.

But at least I could see.

Next to us was a hunting service. When Management bought the land, in former times a national forest, they split it in two and ran half of it as a service for nature visitors. The other half was given to Chasseur. French for *hunter*. The other leisure companies offered services with similar names—"Elegant Chase," "Country Squire," "Field and Stream."

Chasseur clients wished to have the aura of gentlemen. The ad site said, "to the manor born." They stayed in a lodge modeled on an ancient French château and ate together at long tables, served their dinner off platters by staff. They hunted herds of elk and bighorn sheep with the help of trained dogs. Sometimes, when I drew near the boundary, I could hear hounds baying faintly in the distance.

There was a stable of captive-bred animals here: raccoons, skunks, possums, even beavers. I helped to feed, water, and care for them. Furbearers do live wild on the grounds, but they could be elusive. We had to stage-manage, since clients were promised they'd see forest creatures. We couldn't leave it up to chance.

Some of the animals shared their dens with cockroaches. They didn't seem to mind. It was the beavers I wished Mo could've met. There'd been a family of them in a favorite picture book I'd read to him when he was six. In it, beavers and rabbits wore clothing and had the power of speech. They went on picnics and played games and said things human children might say.

I understood they *were* children, only with different faces and bodies. But Mo assumed that long ago the animals *had* spoken. Not chickens or goats, but wild ones. He was hopeful their descendants would be willing to talk also.

The only wild animals at the camp were pack rats, coyotes, and vultures. A few times he hovered near the henhouse at dusk waiting for coyotes to approach, planning a conversation.

"Real wild creatures don't talk," I had to tell him finally.

For a while after that he was annoyed by the picture book. "It's all made up," he said bitterly.

But soon his bitterness softened and he asked for the story again. Mo was a cheerful little boy. He never stayed angry.

The citadels where clients lived were luxe but sterile, I was told. Some of them missed the unfenced world and cherished an idea of wilderness: the branches of massive trees that swayed in the breeze. Sunbeams that dappled the leaves.

And for the steep price of a safari, they could see that dappled light. But there were risks: mosquitos that carried disease, blackflies, rattlesnakes. Maybe a large predator, though these were seldom seen. Smaller hazards like twisted ankles, thirst, and exhaustion. When clients requested alone time they had to be monitored. A staff surgeon was always on call.

I felt peace descend as I followed one at a distance, rambling along a stream or spotting birds through field glasses. Their presence comforted me. It proved that some people still did exactly as they wished.

But clients came less often. Economies were made, stricter and stricter. Our salaries dwindled until we earned only room and board. We didn't know if this was occurring at all the facilities or only our own. The company blocked access to the ad sites of their competition—they didn't want employees comparing notes.

In the waning years, many staff left, abandoning their posts without notice. I took on more and more responsibility, and the service was stripped down to its basics.

With fewer employees, accidents got more frequent. In Chasseur, one client was mauled by a mountain lion. The few lions that remained had no fondness for people. Company ratings took a hit.

Another was killed by gunshot at the hand of a fellow hunter. They all signed documents that said Management couldn't be blamed. But we knew supervision had turned lax.

At the end it was just me and a man named Charlie in the cabin. He was tough, a former soldier who taught me many tricks for living. How to make fires and fix broken tools. Which mushrooms and berries could be safely eaten. I depended on his wisdom.

Our last client had none of the confidence of those I'd guided before. She had an attitude of defeat.

She talked to me as we walked through the forest. I didn't know what animals we might encounter, since the last of the captives had been released—I couldn't care for them all myself, and Charlie worried about sickness and malnutrition. So we had set them free.

This was her swan song, she said. She'd wanted to be somewhere green. To remember, now that she had nothing. Her children were gone, she said. She'd lost track of them. Her husband was gone too. He had left to look for them, and then also disappeared.

She'd had to abandon their home, she said. A wildfire had torn through her citadel, and after that she'd had to move to another, and was assigned a new device with new digits. The registries rarely got updated. Her family might be out there, but she had given up on finding them.

We walked for hours without seeing a single animal. All we heard was the chatter of birds up in the canopy.

"It's all right," said the client. "The trees are enough."

Charlie pitched a tent for her among the pines. We cooked her evening meal. She'd brought a bottle of wine and offered to share it with us. She was generous.

One glass was enough to make me light-headed, though, as Charlie advised, I drank it slowly. I hadn't tasted such an expensive drink before. And haven't since.

Over the campfire the client told us of her many adventures, and later these memories would sustain me. In slow times I still run over them in my head. As though they are my own.

She told how once she'd gone climbing in tall mountains halfway across the globe, known as the Himalayas. That was in the era of chartered jet flights. Only the oligarchs still flew, she said. Another time she'd danced in a great hall with enormous jeweled lights that hung from the ceiling. People wore special clothes for the occasion. Clothes they would only wear that night, she said, and probably not wear again.

Once she'd even had a pet. A large, amiable dog. Not trained for hunting or feral. When her daughter was born, the dog had been jealous. The dog had barked at the baby. But over time he'd come to love her. He had been fiercely protective of that baby until the day he died.

In the morning, she left. And no one came after her.

When the facility was shuttered I stayed here, on the grounds. A few of us did; we had nowhere else to go.

They warned us we'd be wide open. No electricity or security. No uplink to connect us, and anyway our devices would soon lose their power and turn to scrap. The orchards that gave us fruit would go untended. Well water could not be pumped, without power. We'd only have water from the creeks, and a few chemical filters.

Eventually scavengers would wander in from the derelicts.

We said we'd take our chances. Charlie had his eye on an A-frame a couple of miles away that was standing empty. He liked the location. So he left the cabin to me.

Now we live spaced out across the vast acreage, the ones who lasted. On the first day of each month we hike in from our separate dwellings to Charlie's house. There we trade from our gardens. Matches or First Aid items. Sometimes a can of beans or soup left over from the days of abundance.

I find myself thinking of Mo, how it would have been to have him here with me. If he hadn't fallen ill back then.

Mo will always be a small boy.

But what if you'd grown up? I ask his memory. *And weren't a boy forever?*

One time I saw a movement in the trees, and for a split-second my heart beat fast. As though it could be him. Come back to me.

But it was a black bear. Limping and very thin.

We'd sit here at the end of a day and drink our cups of tea. I make it with fragrant herbs Charlie taught me to gather. We'd rock on the porch swing on my cabin deck, just the two of us, and gaze out to where the clearing meets the forest. Beneath our feet these soft, gray, weathered planks.

The sun paints the sky at dusk, clouds lit up pink and red over the trees. Sometimes deer amble into the clearing. A doe with her fawn. Or a stag dips his head to drink from the creek, and his antlers look so heavy I can hardly believe he bears their weight.

When I walk through the woods in the right season, I find the shed antlers. I've picked up so many they make a lacework on the shelf over the fireplace.

Maybe, with all this time on your hands, you would have learned their language, I say to my little brother. *Maybe they would have spoken to you after all.*

PART 10

CLIMATES AND FUTURES

In 2019, scientists undertook a study to determine how many wilderness areas are left in the world. Using global satellite technology, they reported in the journal *One Earth* that only four countries (Australia, Brazil, Canada, and Russia) show any sizable remaining terrestrial wilderness—land without a human footprint. Just two hundred years after Washington Irving inaugurated the wilderness short story, North America has become de-wildered, having lost most of its intact ecosystems. Today's wilderness short stories take up an urgent question: If wilderness disappears, then what? Extreme weather events, precipitated by the effects of greenhouse gases on wind, water, rain, and temperature, motivate most climate change stories—tales that seem to verge on the apocalyptic but rarely cross into the terrain of fantasy. Instead, they offer speculative fictions about a dying planet, envisioning environmental situations that could actually happen and dystopic futures that are by no means impossible. The ecological scenarios at the center of climate change stories—persistent droughts, infertile soils, evaporating freshwaters, rising seas, intensifying storms—are in fact all happening now, demonstrating how powerfully environmental fiction can sharpen our awareness of a future that has already begun. Attentive to the painful realities of class inequality and social unrest, climate change fiction is also social justice fiction, narratives that shine a bright spotlight on the historical failure to protect wilderness spaces and their natural resources, and thus invite a moral reckoning on the profound costs of that neglect for the most vulnerable among us.

"Luvina"

JUAN RULFO

Juan Rulfo (1917–1986) was born in Mexico's west-central state of Jalisco. Before becoming a writer, Rulfo (born Juan Nepomuceno Carlos Pérez Rulfo Vizcaíno) was an immigration clerk and a traveling sales agent who covered the territory of southern Mexico. The natural environments and remote villages Rulfo discovered on the job inspire the settings for his 1955 novel *Pedro Páramo* and tales in his 1953 story collection *El llano en llamas* (*The Plain in Flames*); the two books established Rulfo's enduring literary reputation. Early-twentieth-century conflicts over land rights, agrarian reforms, and religious education provide the political backdrops for Rulfo's exploration of the destructive effects of war and climate on rural life, a story he chose to tell through two mediums: photography and fiction. Rulfo's stark black-and-white photographs find their literary counterpart in his stripped-down prose style, together painting a portrait of Mexico's postrevolutionary villages as ghostly places, marked by the violence of the Mexican Revolution and the Cristero Rebellion. The extreme weather of south-central Mexico's most rugged terrain is the subject of one of Rulfo's best and most haunting stories, "Luvina" (1953). A village perched on a bald mountain ridge, Luvina bears the brunt of a harsh, unforgiving wind, a force so powerful, and in the end allegorical, it becomes a character in its own right. Rulfo's portrait of a dying community made desolate by little rain and barren soil is an early example of a central concern in climate change fiction: the effects, both physical and psychological, of inhospitable climates on the poor. Rulfo, who wrote most of his fiction in Mexico City, devoted the last twenty-four years of his life to directing the editorial department of Mexico's National Institute for Indigenous Studies.

"Luvina"

JUAN RULFO

Of all the high ranges in the south, the one in Luvina is the highest and rockiest. It's full of that gray stone from which they make lime, but in Luvina they don't make lime from it nor do they put it to any good use. They call it crude stone there, and the incline that rises toward Luvina is called Crude Stone Hill. The wind and sun have taken care of breaking it down, so the earth around there is white and shining, as if it were bedewed with morning dew; though all this is just words, because in Luvina the days are as cold as the nights and the dew grows thick in the sky before it manages to reach the earth.

. . . And the earth is steep. It slashes everywhere into deep ravines, so far down that they disappear, that's how far down they go. People in Luvina say dreams rise out of those ravines; but the only thing I ever saw rise up from there was the wind, whirling, as if it had been imprisoned down below in reed pipes. A wind that doesn't even let bittersweet grow: those sad little plants can barely live, holding on for all they're worth to the side of the cliffs in these hills, as if they were smeared onto the earth. Only at times, where there's a little shade, hidden among the rocks, can the *chicalote* bloom with its white poppies. But the *chicalote* soon withers. Then one hears it scratching the air with its thorny branches, making a noise like a knife on a whetstone.

"You'll see that wind blowing over Luvina. It's gray. They say that's because it carries volcanic sand; but the truth is, it's a black air. You'll see. It settles on Luvina, clinging to things as if it were biting them. And on many days it carries off the roofs of houses as if it were carrying off a straw hat, leaving the walls unprotected and bare. Then it scratches, as if it had nails: one hears it morning and night, hour after hour, without rest, scraping the walls, tearing off strips of soil, gouging under the doors with its pointy spade, until one feels it roiling inside oneself, as if it were trying to rattle the hinges of our very bones. You'll see."

The man who was talking remained quiet for a while, looking outside.

The sound of the river passing its rising waters over the *camichín* boughs reached them; the rumor of the air softly moving the almond-tree leaves, and the screams of the children playing in the little space illuminated by the light coming out of the store.

Termites came in and bounced against the oil lamp, falling to the ground with their wings scorched. And night still advanced outside.

"Hey, Camilo, give us two more beers!" the man went on. Then he added:

"Something else, señor. In Luvina you'll never see a blue sky. The whole horizon is colorless; always cloudy with a caliginous stain that never disappears. The whole ridge bald, without a single tree, without a single green thing for your eyes to rest on; everything enveloped in the ash-cloud of lime. You'll see: those hills, their lights darkened as if they were dead, and Luvina at the very top, crowning it with its white houses as if it were the crown of a dead man . . ."

The children's screams got closer until they were inside the store. That made the man stand up, go to the door, and say to them: "Get away from here! Stop interrupting! Go on playing, but without making a ruckus."

Then, heading back to the table, he sat down and said:

"So yes, as I was saying. It rains very little there. By midyear a bunch of storms arrive and lash the earth, ripping it up, leaving nothing but a sea of stones floating on the crust. Then it's nice to see how the clouds crawl along, the way they wander from one hill to another making noise as if they were swollen bladders; ricocheting and thundering just as if they were breaking apart on the edge of the ravines. But after ten or twelve days they leave and don't come back until the following year, and sometimes it happens they don't come back for a few years . . .

". . . Yes, rain is scarce. Little or next to nothing, to the point that the earth, in addition to being dry and shrunken like old leather, is full of cracks and that thing they call '*pasojos de agua*' there, which are nothing but dirt clods hardened into sharp-edged stones that pierce your feet when you walk, as if the land itself had grown thorns there. As if it were like that."

He drank the beer until only foam bubbles were left in the bottle and then went on talking:

"No matter how you look at it, Luvina is a very sad place. Now that you're going there, you'll see what I mean. I would say it's the place where sadness nests. Where smiles are unknown, as if everyone's faces had gone stiff. And, if you want, you can see that sadness at every turn. The wind that blows there stirs it up but never carries it away. It's there, as if it had been born there. You can even taste it and feel it, because it's always on you, pressed against you, and because it's oppressive like a great poultice on your heart's living flesh.

". . . People there say that when the moon is full, they see the shape of the figure of the wind wandering the streets of Luvina, dragging a black blanket; but the thing I always came to see, when the moon was out in Luvina, was the image of despair . . . always.

"But drink your beer. I see you haven't even tried it. Drink. Or perhaps you don't like it as it is, at room temperature. There's no other option here. I know it tastes bad like that; that it takes on a flavor like donkey's pee. You get used to it around here. Keep in mind that over there you can't even get this. You'll miss it when you get to Luvina. Over there you won't be able to get anything but mescal, which people make with an herb called *hojasé,* and after the first few swallows you'll be going round and round as if you had been beaten up. Better drink your beer. I know what I'm talking about."

Outside you could still hear the river struggle. The rumor of wind. Children playing. It seemed as if it were still early in the night.

Once again the man had gone to look out the door and had come back.

Now he was saying:

"It's easy to look at things from over here, merely recalled from memory, where there's no similarity. But I have no problem going on telling you what I know in regard to Luvina. I lived there. I left my life there . . . I went to that place with my illusions intact and came back old and used up. And now you're going there . . . All right. I seem to remember the beginning. I put myself in your shoes and think . . . Look, when I first got to Luvina . . . But first can I have your beer? I see you're not paying any attention to it. And it'll be good for me. It's healing for me. I feel as if my head were being rinsed with camphor oil . . . Well, as I was telling you, when I first arrived in Luvina, the mule driver that took us there didn't even want the beasts to rest. As soon as we were on the ground, he turned around:

" 'I'm going back,' he said.

" 'Wait, you won't let your animals take a rest? They're beaten up.'

" 'They would end up even more messed up here,' he said. 'I better get back.'

"And he left, dropping us at Crude Stone Hill, spurring his horses as if he were fleeing from a place of the devil.

"We, my wife and three children, remained there, standing in the middle of the plaza, with all our belongings in our arms. In the middle of that place where you heard only the wind . . .

"Nothing but the plaza, without a single plant to break the wind. We stayed there.

"Then I asked my wife:

" 'What country are we in, Agripina?'

"And she shrugged her shoulders.

" 'Well, if you don't mind, go look for someplace to eat and some-place to spend the night. We'll wait for you here,' I said to her.

"She took the youngest of our children and left. But she didn't come back.

"At dusk, when the sun lit up only the hilltops, we went looking for her. We walked along the narrow streets of Luvina, until we found her inside the church: sitting right in the middle of that lonely church, with the child asleep between her legs.

" 'What are you doing here, Agripina?'

" 'I came in to pray,' she said to us.

" 'What for?' I asked.

"She shrugged her shoulders.

"There was nothing to pray to there. It was an empty shack, with no doors, just some open galleries and a broken ceiling through which the air filtered like a sieve.

" 'Where's the inn?'

" 'There is no inn.'

" 'And the hostel?'

" 'There is no hostel.'

" 'Did you see anyone? Does anyone live here?' I asked her.

" 'Yes, right opposite . . . Some women . . . I can still see them. Look, behind the cracks in that door I see the eyes watching us, shin-ing . . . They have been staring at us . . . Look at them. I see the shining balls of their eyes . . . But they have nothing to give us to eat. Without even sticking their heads out, they told me there's no food in this town . . . Then I came here to pray, to ask God on our behalf.'

" 'Why didn't you come back? We were waiting for you.'

" 'I came here to pray. I haven't finished yet.'

" 'What country is this, Agripina?'

"And she shrugged her shoulders again.

"That night we settled down to sleep in a corner of the church, behind the dismantled altar. Even there you could feel the wind, though not quite as strong. We kept hearing it passing above us, with its long howls; we kept hearing it coming in and going out through the hollow concavities of the doors; hitting the crosses in the stations of the cross with its hands of wind: big, strong crosses made of mesquite wood that hung from the walls over the length of the church, tied with wires that grated each time the wind shook them as if it were the grating of teeth.

"The children were crying because they were too frightened to sleep. And my wife was trying to hold them all in her arms. Hugging her bouquet of children. And I was there, not knowing what to do.

"The wind calmed down a bit before sunrise. Later on it came back. But there was a moment at dawn when everything became still, as if the sky and the earth had joined together, crushing all sounds with their weight . . . You could hear the children breathing, now more relaxed. I could hear my wife breathing heavily next to me:

" 'What's that?' she said to me.

" 'What's what?' I asked her.

" 'That. That noise.'

" 'It's silence. Go to sleep. Rest, even if only a little bit, because it will be dawn soon.'

"But soon I heard it, too. It was like bats flitting in the darkness, very close to us. Like bats with their long wings sweeping against the floor. I got up and the sounds of wings beating became stronger, as if the colony of bats had been frightened and they were flying toward the holes in the doors. Then I tiptoed over there, feeling that muffled whispering in front of me. I stopped in the doorway and I saw them. I saw all the women of Luvina with water jugs on their shoulders, with their shawls hanging from their heads and their dark silhouettes against the black depths of the night.

" 'What do you want?' I asked them. 'What are you looking for at this time of night?'

"One of them responded:

" 'We're going to get water.'

"I saw them standing in front of me, watching me. Then, as if they were shadows, they started walking down the street with their black water jars.

"No, I'll never forget that first night I spent in Luvina.

". . . Don't you think this deserves another drink? If only so I can get rid of the bad taste of the memory."

"I believe you asked me how many years I was in Luvina, right? . . . Truth is, I don't know. I lost any sense of time once the fever got me all turned around; but it must have been an eternity . . . And that's because time is very long there. No one keeps count of hours, nor is anyone interested in how the years mount up. Days start and end. Then night comes. Just day and night until the day you die, which for them is a kind of hope.

"You must think I'm harping on the same idea. And yes, it's true, señor . . . To sit on the doorstep, watching the sun rise and set, raising and lowering your head, until the springs go slack and then everything comes to a halt, without time, as if one lived forever in eternity. That's what the old men do over there.

"Because only old people live in Luvina and those who aren't yet born, as people say . . . And women with no strength, just skin and bones, they're so thin. The children who were born there have left . . . No sooner do they see the light of dawn than they become men. As people say, they jump from their mother's breast to the hoe and they disappear from Luvina. That's how things are there.

"Only very old men remain and abandoned women, or women with a husband who is God only knows where . . . They return every so often like the storms I was telling you about; you can hear the whole town whispering when they come back and something like a grunt when they leave . . . They leave behind a sack of provisions for the old and plant another child in their wife's womb, and then no one knows anything about them again until next year, and sometimes never . . . That's the custom. Over there it's called the law, but it's the same thing. Their children spend their lives working for their parents the way they did for theirs and as who knows how many before them behaved in accordance with that law . . .

"Meanwhile, the old people wait for them and for the day of their death, sitting in their doorways, with their arms at their sides, moved only by the grace that is a child's gratitude . . . Alone, in that solitude of Luvina.

"One day I tried convincing them to go elsewhere, where the soil was good. 'Let's leave this place,' I said. 'We'll find a way to settle somewhere else. The government will help us.'

"They listened to me without batting an eye, looking at me from the depths of their eyes, from which only a little light emerges from deep inside.

" 'You say the government will help us, professor? Are you acquainted with the government?'

"I told them I was.

" 'We know it, too. It so happens that we do. What we know nothing about is the government's mother.'

"I told them it was the fatherland. They shook their heads to say no. And they laughed. It was the only time I saw the people from Luvina laugh. They bared their ruined teeth and told me no, the government had no mother.

"And you know what? They're right. The government man only remembers them when one of his young men has done something wrong down here. Then he sends to Luvina for him and they kill him. Beyond that, they don't even know that they exist.

" 'You want to tell us we should leave Luvina because, according to you, it's enough being hungry with no need to be,' they said to me. 'But if we leave, who'll carry our dead? They live here and we can't leave them behind.'

"And they're still there. You'll see them once you get there. Chewing dry mesquite pulp and swallowing their saliva in order to outwit hunger. You'll see them passing by like shadows, hugging the walls of houses, almost dragged along by the wind.

" 'Don't you hear that wind?' I finally told them. 'It'll be the end of you.'

" 'You endure what you have to endure. It's God's mandate,' they answered me. 'It's bad when the wind stops blowing. When that happens, the sun presses close to Luvina and sucks our blood and the little water we have in our hides. The wind makes the sun stay up there. It's better that way.'

"I said nothing more. I left Luvina and I haven't gone back nor do I think I will.

". . . But look at the somersaults the world is doing. You're going there now, in a few hours. It's probably fifteen years since I was told the same thing: 'You're going to San Juan Luvina.'

"In those days I was strong. I was full of ideas . . . You know that ideas infuse us all. And one goes with a burden on one's shoulders to make something out of one's self. But it didn't work out in Luvina. I did the experiment and it came undone . . .

"San Juan Luvina. The name sounded celestial to me. But it's Purgatory. A moribund place where even the dogs have died and there's not even anyone to bark at the silence; because the moment one gets used to the winds that blow there, one hears nothing but that silence that exists in all solitudes. And that uses you all up. Look at me. It used me up. You're going, and you'll understand what I'm saying very soon . . .

"What do you think if we ask that man to put together some *mezcalitos* for us? With beer one needs to get up all the time and that interrupts the conversation. Listen, Camilo, send us over some mezcals right away!

"So yes, as I was telling you . . ."

But he didn't say anything. He kept staring at a fixed point on the table where the termites, now without wings, circled like naked little worms.

Outside one could hear the night advancing. The water of the river splashing against the trunks of the *camichines*. The already distant shouting of children. Through the small sky of the doorway one could see the stars.

The man who was watching the termites slumped over the table and fell asleep.

"The Tamarisk Hunter"

PAOLO BACIGALUPI

Paolo Bacigalupi (b. 1972) was born in Paonia, Colorado. While he has written stories on subjects as diverse as news, baseball, magic, and zombies, he is primarily a speculative and science fiction author who writes powerful dystopic novels on global warming, food bioengineering, environmental degradation, and water rationing. Bacigalupi has won numerous prizes for his fiction, including Nebula and Hugo Awards, as well as Locus Awards for *Pump Six and Other Stories* (2008) and *The Windup Girl* (2009). Water crisis constitutes the central drama informing Bacigalupi's "The Tamarisk Hunter," a 2006 short story that first appeared in *High Country News,* a magazine devoted to the ecological and political issues of the Mountain West. Bacigalupi's desert tale is set in the near future of 2030, when the waters of the Colorado River Basin have been forcibly redirected for the use of Californians alone, leaving residents from the Southwestern United States and Northern Mexico prohibited both from drinking their own river water and from crossing into California. Contemplating the extreme regional, class, and social inequalities that could reshape the landscape of the West in a time of perpetual drought, "The Tamarisk Hunter" later became the basis for Bacigalupi's bestselling book *The Water Knife* (2015), a novel variously described as cli-fi, industrial noir, or biopunk. Speaking of the dangers posed by a rapidly warming climate, the author has explained that the most important job of science fiction is to ask: "If this goes on, what will the world look like?" Just six years after *The Water Knife* appeared, Bacigalupi came to the realization that his best estimation of what could go wrong came up depressingly short, his speculative scenarios neither cynical nor extreme enough. Bacigalupi continues to reside in western Colorado.

"The Tamarisk Hunter"

PAOLO BACIGALUPI

A big tamarisk can suck 73,000 gallons of river water a year. For $2.88 a day, plus water bounty, Lolo rips tamarisk all winter long.

Ten years ago, it was a good living. Back then, tamarisk shouldered up against every riverbank in the Colorado River Basin, along with cottonwoods, Russian olives, and elms. Ten years ago, towns like Grand Junction and Moab thought they could still squeeze life from a river.

Lolo stands on the edge of a canyon, Maggie the camel his only companion. He stares down into the deeps. It's an hour's scramble to the bottom. He ties Maggie to a juniper and starts down, boot-skiing a gully. A few blades of green grass sprout neon around him, piercing juniper-tagged snow clods. In the late winter, there is just a beginning surge of water down in the deeps; the ice is off the river edges. Up high, the mountains still wear their ragged snow mantles. Lolo smears through mud and hits a channel of scree, sliding and scattering rocks. His jugs of tamarisk poison gurgle and slosh on his back. His shovel and rockbar snag on occasional junipers as he skids by. It will be a long hike out. But then, that's what makes this patch so perfect. It's a long way down, and the riverbanks are largely hidden.

It's a living; where other people have dried out and blown away, he has remained: a tamarisk hunter, a water tick, a stubborn bit of weed. Everyone else has been blown off the land as surely as dandelion seeds, set free to fly south or east, or most of all north where watersheds sometimes still run deep and where even if there are no more lush ferns or deep cold fish runs, at least there is still water for people.

Eventually, Lolo reaches the canyon bottom. Down in the cold shadows, his breath steams.

He pulls out a digital camera and starts shooting his proof. The Bureau of Reclamation has gotten uptight about proof. They want different angles on the offending tamarisk, they want each one photographed before and after, the whole process documented, GPS'd, and uploaded directly by the camera. They want it done on-site. And then they still sometimes come out to spot check before they calibrate his headgate for water bounty.

But all their due diligence can't protect them from the likes of Lolo. Lolo has found the secret to eternal life as a tamarisk hunter. Unknown to the Interior Department and its BuRec subsidiary, he has been seeding new patches of tamarisk, encouraging vigorous brushy groves in previously cleared areas. He has hauled and planted healthy root balls up and down the river system in strategically hidden and inaccessible corridors, all in a bid for security against the swarms of other tamarisk hunters that scour these same tributaries. Lolo is crafty. Stands like this one, a quarter-mile long and thick with salt-laden tamarisk, are his insurance policy.

Documentation finished, he unstraps a folding saw, along with his rockbar and shovel, and sets his poison jugs on the dead salt bank. He starts cutting, slicing into the roots of the tamarisk, pausing every thirty seconds to spread Garlon 4 on the cuts, poisoning the tamarisk wounds faster than they can heal. But some of the best tamarisk, the most vigorous, he uproots and sets aside, for later use.

$2.88 a day, plus water bounty.

It takes Maggie's rolling bleating camel stride a week to make it back to Lolo's homestead. They follow the river, occasionally climbing above it onto cold mesas or wandering off into the open desert in a bid to avoid the skeleton sprawl of emptied towns. Guardie choppers buzz up and down the river like swarms of angry yellowjackets, hunting for porto-pumpers and wildcat diversions. They rush overhead in a wash of beaten air and gleaming National Guard logos. Lolo remembers a time when the guardies traded potshots with people down on the riverbanks, tracer-fire and machine-gun chatter echoing in the canyons. He remembers the glorious hiss and arc of a Stinger missile as it flashed across red rock desert and blue sky and burned a chopper where it hovered.

But that's long in the past. Now, guardie patrols skim up the river unmolested.

Lolo tops another mesa and stares down at the familiar landscape of an eviscerated town, its curving streets and subdivision cul-de-sacs all sitting silent in the sun. At the very edge of the empty town, one-acre ranchettes and snazzy five-thousand-square-foot houses with dead-stick trees and dust-hill landscaping fringe a brown tumbleweed golf course. The sandtraps don't even show anymore.

When California put its first calls on the river, no one really worried. A couple towns went begging for water. Some idiot newcomers with bad water rights stopped grazing their horses, and that was it. A few years later, people started showering real fast. And a few after that, they showered once a week. And then people started using the buckets. By then, everyone had stopped joking about how "hot" it was. It didn't really matter how "hot" it was. The problem wasn't lack of water or an excess of heat, not really. The problem was that 4.4 million acre-feet of water were supposed to go down the river to California. There was water; they just couldn't touch it.

They were supposed to stand there like dumb monkeys and watch it flow on by.

"Lolo?"

The voice catches him by surprise. Maggie startles and groans and lunges for the mesa edge before Lolo can rein her around. The camel's great padded feet scuffle dust and Lolo flails for his shotgun where it nestles in a scabbard at the camel's side. He forces Maggie to turn, shotgun half-drawn, holding barely to his seat and swearing.

A familiar face, tucked amongst juniper tangle.

"Goddamnit!" Lolo lets the shotgun drop back into its scabbard. "Jesus Christ, Travis. You scared the hell out of me."

Travis grins. He emerges from amongst the junipers' silver bark rags, one hand on his gray fedora, the other on the reins as he guides his mule out of the trees. "Surprised?"

"I could've shot you!"

"Don't be so jittery. There's no one out here 'cept us water ticks."

"That's what I thought the last time I went shopping down there. I had a whole set of new dishes for Annie and I broke them all when I ran into an ultralight parked right in the middle of the main drag."

"Meth flyers?"

"Beats the hell out of me. I didn't stick around to ask."

"Shit. I'll bet they were as surprised as you were."

"They almost killed me."

"I guess they didn't."

Lolo shakes his head and swears again, this time without anger. Despite the ambush, he's happy to run into Travis. It's lonely country, and Lolo's been out long enough to notice the silence of talking to Maggie. They trade ritual sips of water from their canteens and make camp together. They swap stories about BuRec and avoid discussing where they've been ripping tamarisk and enjoy the view of the empty town far below, with its serpentine streets and quiet houses and shining untouched river.

It isn't until the sun is setting and they've finished roasting a magpie that Lolo finally asks the question that's been on his mind ever since Travis's sunbaked face came out of the tangle. It goes against etiquette, but he can't help himself. He picks magpie out of his teeth and says, "I thought you were working downriver."

Travis glances sidelong at Lolo and in that one suspicious uncertain look, Lolo sees that Travis has hit a lean patch. He's not smart like Lolo. He hasn't been reseeding. He's got no insurance. He hasn't been thinking ahead about all the competition, and what the tamarisk endgame looks like, and now he's feeling the pinch. Lolo feels a twinge of pity. He likes Travis. A part of him wants to tell Travis the secret, but he stifles the urge. The stakes are too high. Water crimes are serious now, so serious Lolo hasn't even told his wife, Annie, for fear of what she'll say. Like all of the most shameful crimes, water theft is a private business, and at the scale Lolo works, forced labor on the Straw is the best punishment he can hope for.

Travis gets his hackles down over Lolo's invasion of his privacy and says, "I had a couple cows I was running up here, but I lost 'em. I think something got 'em."

"Long way to graze cows."

"Yeah, well, down my way even the sagebrush is dead. Big Daddy Drought's doing a real number on my patch." He pinches his lip, thoughtful. "Wish I could find those cows."

"They probably went down to the river."

Travis sighs. "Then the guardies probably got 'em."

"Probably shot 'em from a chopper and roasted 'em."

"Californians."

They both spit at the word. The sun continues to sink. Shadows fall across the town's silent structures. The rooftops gleam red, a ruby cluster decorating the blue river necklace.

"You think there's any stands worth pulling down there?" Travis asks.

"You can go down and look. But I think I got it all last year. And someone had already been through before me, so I doubt much is coming up."

"Shit. Well, maybe I'll go shopping. Might as well get something out of this trip."

"There sure isn't anyone to stop you."

As if to emphasize the fact, the thud-thwap of a guardie chopper breaks the evening silence. The black-fly dot of its movement barely shows against the darkening sky. Soon it's out of sight and cricket chirps swallow the last evidence of its passing.

Travis laughs. "Remember when the guardies said they'd keep out looters? I saw them on TV with all their choppers and Humvees and them all saying they were going to protect everything until the situation improved." He laughs again. "You remember that? All of them driving up and down the streets?"

"I remember."

"Sometimes I wonder if we shouldn't have fought them more."

"Annie was in Lake Havasu City when they fought there. You saw what happened." Lolo shivers. "Anyway, there's not much to fight for once they blow up your water treatment plant. If nothing's coming out of your faucet, you might as well move on."

"Yeah, well, sometimes I think you still got to fight. Even if it's just for pride." Travis gestures at the town below, a shadow movement. "I remember when all that land down there was selling like hotcakes and they were building shit as fast as they could ship in the lumber. Shopping malls and parking lots and subdivisions, anywhere they could scrape a flat spot."

"We weren't calling it Big Daddy Drought, back then."

"Forty-five thousand people. And none of us had a clue. And I was a real estate agent." Travis laughs, a self-mocking sound that ends quickly. It sounds too much like self-pity for Lolo's taste. They're quiet again, looking down at the town wreckage.

"I think I might be heading north," Travis says finally.

Lolo glances over, surprised. Again he has the urge to let Travis in on his secret, but he stifles it. "And do what?"

"Pick fruit, maybe. Maybe something else. Anyway, there's water up there."

Lolo points down at the river. "There's water."

"Not for us." Travis pauses. "I got to level with you, Lolo. I went down to the Straw."

For a second, Lolo is confused by the non sequitur. The statement is too outrageous. And yet Travis's face is serious. "The Straw? No kidding? All the way there?"

"All the way there." He shrugs defensively. "I wasn't finding any tamarisk, anyway. And it didn't actually take that long. It's a lot closer than it used to be. A week out to the train tracks, and then I hopped a coal train, and rode it right to the interstate, and then I hitched."

"What's it like out there?"

"Empty. A trucker told me that California and the Interior Department drew up all these plans to decide which cities they'd turn off when." He looks at Lolo significantly. "That was after Lake Havasu. They figured out they had to do it slow. They worked out some kind of formula: how many cities, how many people they could evaporate at a time without making too much unrest. Got advice from the Chinese, from when they were shutting down their old communist industries. Anyway, it looks like they're pretty much done with it. There's nothing moving out there except highway trucks and coal trains and a couple truck stops."

"And you saw the Straw?"

"Oh sure, I saw it. Out toward the border. Big old mother. So big you couldn't climb on top of it, flopped out on the desert like a damn silver snake. All the way to California." He spits reflexively. "They're spraying with concrete to keep water from seeping into the ground and they've got some kind of carbon-fiber stuff over the top to stop the evaporation. And the river just disappears inside. Nothing but an empty canyon below it. Bone-dry. And choppers and Humvees everywhere, like a damn hornet's nest. They wouldn't let me get any closer than a half mile on account of the eco-crazies trying to blow it up. They weren't nice about it, either."

"What did you expect?"

"I dunno. It sure depressed me, though: They work us out here and toss us a little water bounty and then all that water next year goes right down into that big old pipe. Some Californian's probably filling his swimming pool with last year's water bounty right now."

Cricket-song pulses in the darkness. Off in the distance, a pack of coyotes starts yipping. The two of them are quiet for a while. Finally, Lolo chucks his friend on the shoulder. "Hell, Travis, it's probably for the best. A desert's a stupid place to put a river, anyway."

Lolo's homestead runs across a couple acres of semi-alkaline soil, conveniently close to the river's edge. Annie is out in the field when he crests the low hills that overlook his patch. She waves, but keeps digging, planting for whatever water he can collect in bounty.

Lolo pauses, watching Annie work. Hot wind kicks up, carrying with it the scents of sage and clay. A dust devil swirls around Annie, whipping her bandana off her head. Lolo smiles as she snags it; she sees him still watching her and waves at him to quit loafing.

He grins to himself and starts Maggie down the hill, but he doesn't stop watching Annie work. He's grateful for her. Grateful that every time he comes back from tamarisk hunting she is still here. She's steady. Steadier than the people like Travis who give up when times get dry. Steadier than anyone Lolo knows, really. And if she has nightmares sometimes, and can't stand being in towns or crowds and wakes up in the middle of the night calling out for family she'll never see again, well, then it's all the more reason to seed more tamarisk and make sure they never get pushed off their patch like she was pushed.

Lolo gets Maggie to kneel down so he can dismount, then leads her over to a water trough, half-full of slime and water skippers. He gets a bucket and heads for the river while Maggie groans and complains behind him. The patch used to have a well and running water, but like everyone else, they lost their pumping rights and BuRec stuffed the well with Quikrete when the water table dropped below the Minimum Allowable Reserve. Now he and Annie steal buckets from the river, or, when the Interior Department isn't watching, they jump up and down on a footpump and dump water into a hidden underground cistern he built when the Resource Conservation and Allowable Use Guidelines went into effect.

Annie calls the guidelines "RaCAUG" and it sounds like she's hawking spit when she says it, but even with their filled-in well, they're lucky. They aren't like Spanish Oaks or Antelope Valley or River Reaches: expensive places that had rotten water rights and turned to dust, money or no, when Vegas and L.A. put in their calls. And they didn't have to bail out of Phoenix Metro when the Central Arizona Project got turned off and then had its aqueducts blown to smithereens when Arizona wouldn't stop pumping out of Lake Havasu.

Pouring water into Maggie's water trough, and looking around at his dusty patch with Annie out in the fields, Lolo reminds himself how lucky he is. He hasn't blown away. He and Annie are dug in. Calies may call them water ticks, but fuck them. If it weren't for people like him and Annie, they'd dry up and blow away the same as everyone else. And if Lolo moves a little bit of tamarisk around, well, the Calies deserve it, considering what they've done to everyone else.

Finished with Maggie, Lolo goes into the house and gets a drink of his own out of the filter urn. The water is cool in the shadows of the adobe house. Juniper beams hang low overhead. He sits down and connects his BuRec camera to the solar panel they've got scabbed onto the roof. Its charge light blinks amber. Lolo goes and gets some more water. He's used to being thirsty, but for some reason he can't get enough today. Big Daddy Drought's got his hands around Lolo's neck today.

Annie comes in, wiping her forehead with a tanned arm. "Don't drink too much water," she says. "I haven't been able to pump. Bunch of guardies around."

"What the hell are they doing around? We haven't even opened our headgates yet."

"They said they were looking for you."

Lolo almost drops his cup.

They know.

They know about his tamarisk reseeding. They know he's been splitting and planting root-clusters. That he's been dragging big healthy chunks of tamarisk up and down the river. A week ago he uploaded his claim on the canyon tamarisk—his biggest stand yet—almost worth an acre-foot in itself in water bounty. And now the guardies are knocking on his door.

Lolo forces his hand not to shake as he puts his cup down. "They say what they want?" He's surprised his voice doesn't crack.

"Just that they wanted to talk to you." She pauses. "They had one of those Humvees. With the guns."

Lolo closes his eyes. Forces himself to take a deep breath. "They've always got guns. It's probably nothing."

"It reminded me of Lake Havasu. When they cleared us out. When they shut down the water treatment plant and everyone tried to burn down the BLM office."

"It's probably nothing." Suddenly he's glad he never told her about his tamarisk hijinks. They can't punish her the same. How many acre-feet is he liable for? It must be hundreds. They'll want him, all right. Put him on a Straw work crew and make him work for life, repay his water debt forever. He's replanted hundreds, maybe thousands of tamarisk, shuffling them around like a card sharp on a poker table, moving them from one bank to another, killing them again and again and again, and always happily sending in his "evidence."

"It's probably nothing," he says again.

"That's what people said in Havasu."

Lolo waves out at their newly tilled patch. The sun shines down hot and hard on the small plot. "We're not worth that kind of effort." He forces a grin. "It probably has to do with those enviro crazies who tried to blow up the Straw. Some of them supposedly ran this way. It's probably that."

Annie shakes her head, unconvinced. "I don't know. They could have asked me the same as you."

"Yeah, but I cover a lot of ground. See a lot of things. I'll bet that's why they want to talk to me. They're just looking for eco-freaks."

"Yeah, maybe you're right. It's probably that." She nods slowly, trying to make herself believe. "Those enviros, they don't make any sense at all. Not enough water for people, and they want to give the river to a bunch of fish and birds."

Lolo nods emphatically and grins wider. "Yeah. Stupid." But suddenly he views the eco-crazies with something approaching brotherly affection. The Californians are after him too.

Lolo doesn't sleep all night. His instincts tell him to run, but he doesn't have the heart to tell Annie, or to leave her. He goes out in the morning hunting tamarisk and fails at that as well. He doesn't cut a single stand all day. He considers shooting himself with his shotgun, but chickens out when he gets the barrels in his mouth. Better alive and on the run than dead. Finally, as he stares into the twin barrels, he knows that he has to tell Annie, tell her he's been a water thief for years and that he's got to run north. Maybe she'll come with him. Maybe she'll see reason.

They'll run together. At least they have that. For sure, he's not going to let those bastards take him off to a labor camp for the rest of his life.

But the guardies are already waiting when Lolo gets back. They're squatting in the shade of their Humvee, talking. When Lolo comes over the crest of the hill, one of them taps the other and points. They both stand. Annie is out in the field again, turning over dirt, unaware of what's about to happen. Lolo reins in and studies the guardies. They lean against their Humvee and watch him back.

Suddenly Lolo sees his future. It plays out in his mind the way it does in a movie, as clear as the blue sky above. He puts his hand on his shotgun. Where it sits on Maggie's far side, the guardies can't see it. He keeps Maggie angled away from them and lets the camel start down the hill.

The guardies saunter toward him. They've got their Humvee with a .50 caliber on the back and they've both got M-16s slung over their shoulders. They're in full bulletproof gear and they look flushed and hot. Lolo rides down slowly. He'll have to hit them both in the face. Sweat trickles between his shoulder blades. His hand is slick on the shotgun's stock.

The guardies are playing it cool. They've still got their rifles slung, and they let Lolo keep approaching. One of them has a wide smile. He's maybe forty years old, and tanned. He's been out for a while, picking up a tan like that. The other raises a hand and says, "Hey there, Lolo."

Lolo's so surprised he takes his hand off his shotgun. "Hale?" He recognizes the guardie. He grew up with him. They played football together a million years ago, when football fields still had green grass and sprinklers sprayed their water straight into the air. Hale. Hale Perkins. Lolo scowls. He can't shoot Hale.

Hale says. "You're still out here, huh?"

"What the hell are you doing in that uniform? You with the Calies now?"

Hale grimaces and points to his uniform patches: Utah National Guard.

Lolo scowls. Utah National Guard. Colorado National Guard. Arizona National Guard. They're all the same. There's hardly a single member of the "National Guard" that isn't an out-of-state mercenary. Most of the local guardies quit a long time ago, sick to death of goose-stepping family and friends off their properties and sick to death of trading potshots with people who just wanted to stay in their homes. So even if there's still a Colorado National Guard, or an Arizona or a Utah, inside those uniforms with all their expensive night-sight gear and their brand-new choppers flying the river bends, it's pure California.

And then there are a few like Hale.

Lolo remembers Hale as being an okay guy. Remembers stealing a keg of beer from behind the Elks Club one night with him. Lolo eyes him. "How you liking that Supplementary Assistance Program?" He glances at the other guardie. "That working real well for you? The Calies a big help?"

Hale's eyes plead for understanding. "Come on, Lolo. I'm not like you. I got a family to look after. If I do another year of duty, they let Shannon and the kids base out of California."

"They give you a swimming pool in your backyard too?"

"You know it's not like that. Water's scarce there too."

Lolo wants to taunt him, but his heart isn't in it. A part of him wonders if Hale is just smart. At first, when California started winning its water lawsuits and shutting off cities, the displaced people just followed the water—right to California. It took a little while before the bureaucrats realized what was going on, but finally someone with a sharp pencil did the math and realized that taking in people along with their water didn't solve a water shortage. So the immigration fences went up.

But people like Hale can still get in.

"So what do you two want?" Inside, Lolo's wondering why they haven't already pulled him off Maggie and hauled him away, but he's willing to play this out.

The other guardie grins. "Maybe we're just out here seeing how the water ticks live."

Lolo eyes him. This one, he could shoot. He lets his hand fall to his shotgun again. "BuRec sets my headgate. No reason for you to be out here."

The Calie says, "There were some marks on it. Big ones."

Lolo smiles tightly. He knows which marks the Calie is talking about. He made them with five different wrenches when he tried to dismember the entire headgate apparatus in a fit of obsession. Finally he gave up trying to open the bolts and just beat on the thing, banging the steel of the gate, smashing at it, while on the other side he had plants withering. After that, he gave up and just carried buckets of water to his plants and left it at that. But the dents and nicks are still there, reminding him of a period of madness. "It still works, don't it?"

Hale holds up a hand to his partner, quieting him. "Yeah, it still works. That's not why we're here."

"So what do you two want? You didn't drive all the way out here with your machine gun just to talk about dents in my headgate."

Hale sighs, put-upon, trying to be reasonable. "You mind getting down off that damn camel so we can talk?"

Lolo studies the two guardies, figuring his chances on the ground. "Shit." He spits. "Yeah, okay. You got me." He urges Maggie to kneel and climbs off her hump. "Annie didn't know anything about this. Don't get her involved. It was all me."

Hale's brow wrinkles, puzzled. "What are you talking about?"

"You're not arresting me?"

The Calie with Hale laughs. "Why? Cause you take a couple buckets of water from the river? Cause you probably got an illegal cistern around here somewhere?" He laughs again. "You ticks are all the same. You think we don't know about all that crap?"

Hale scowls at the Calie, then turns back to Lolo. "No, we're not here to arrest you. You know about the Straw?"

"Yeah." Lolo says it slowly, but inside, he's grinning. A great weight is suddenly off him. They don't know. They don't know shit. It was a good plan when he started it, and it's a good plan still. Lolo schools his face to keep the glee off, and tries to listen to what Hale's saying, but he can't, he's jumping up and down and gibbering like a monkey. They don't know—

"Wait." Lolo holds up his hand. "What did you just say?"

Hale repeats himself. "California's ending the water bounty. They've got enough Straw sections built up now that they don't need the program. They've got half the river enclosed. They got an agreement from the Department of Interior to focus their budget on seep and evaporation control. That's where all the big benefits are. They're shutting down the water bounty payout program." He pauses. "I'm sorry, Lolo."

Lolo frowns. "But a tamarisk is still a tamarisk. Why should one of those damn plants get the water? If I knock out a tamarisk, even if Cali doesn't want the water, I could still take it. Lots of people could use the water."

Hale looks pityingly at Lolo. "We don't make the regulations, we just enforce them. I'm supposed to tell you that your headgate won't get opened next year. If you keep hunting tamarisk, it won't do any good." He looks around the patch, then shrugs. "Anyway, in another couple years they were going to pipe this whole stretch. There won't be any tamarisk at all after that."

"What am I supposed to do, then?"

"California and BuRec is offering early buyout money." Hale pulls a booklet out of his bulletproof vest and flips it open. "Sort of to soften the blow." The pages of the booklet flap in the hot breeze. Hale pins the pages with a thumb and pulls a pen out of another vest pocket. He marks something on the booklet, then tears off a perforated check. "It's not a bad deal."

Lolo takes the check. Stares at it. "Five hundred dollars?"

Hale shrugs sadly. "It's what they're offering. That's just the paper codes. You confirm it online. Use your BuRec camera phone, and they'll deposit it in whatever bank you want. Or they can hold it in trust until you get into a town and want to withdraw it. Any place with a BLM office, you can do that. But you need to confirm before April 15. Then BuRec'll send out a guy to shut down your headgate before this season gets going."

"Five hundred dollars?"

"It's enough to get you north. That's more than they're offering next year."

"But this is my patch."

"Not as long as we've got Big Daddy Drought. I'm sorry, Lolo."

"The drought could break any time. Why can't they give us a couple more years? It could break any time." But even as he says it, Lolo doesn't believe. Ten years ago, he might have. But not now. Big Daddy Drought's here to stay. He clutches the check and its keycodes to his chest.

A hundred yards away, the river flows on to California.

"the river"

ADRIENNE MAREE BROWN

adrienne maree brown (b. 1978) was born in El Paso, Texas, and educated in Georgia, New York, and California, as well as in Germany, where her father served in the military. brown attributes her interest in the literature of science fiction and the politics of racial justice to her family's return to the United States and her introduction to the pervasiveness of White supremacy. In her book *Emergent Strategy: Shaping Change, Changing Worlds* (2017), she notes the appeal of futuristic writing: "Science fiction is simply a way [of] . . . practicing futures together, practicing justice together, living into new stories." The stories brown tells, both fictional and nonfictional, exemplify her commitment to creating new worlds. Her 2015 anthology *Octavia's Brood: Science Fiction from Social Justice Movements* (coedited with Walidah Imarisha) and her guides *Pleasure Activism: The Politics of Feeling Good* (2019) and *We Will Not Cancel Us: And Other Dreams of Transformative Justice* (2020) all use storytelling to explore the close connections among social, racial, economic, and environmental justice. A resident of Detroit, Michigan, brown drew on her training and experience as a doula to write her novel *Grievers* (2021), a pandemic book that grapples with Black death and mourning. Her 2015 Afrofuturist short story "the river," revised in 2020 for the ecological journal *Dark Mountain,* is also set in Detroit. It focuses on the city's main waterway—in the nineteenth century a part of the Great Lakes Wilderness and a final stop on the Underground Railroad for fugitive slaves fleeing across the border to Canada, and in the twentieth century an industrial dumping ground for dangerous pollutants and toxic chemicals. brown's visionary story dares to dream of a future in which the Detroit River's former wild ecosystem and natural beauty might be reclaimed.

"the river"

ADRIENNE MAREE BROWN

Something in the river haunted the island between the city and the border. she felt it, when she was on the waves in the little boat. she didn't say anything, because what could be said, and to whom?

but she felt it. and she felt it growing.

made a sort of sense to her that something would grow there. nuff things went in for something to have created itself down there.

she was a water woman, had learned to boat as she learned to walk, and felt rooted in the river. she'd learned from her grandfather, who'd told her his life lessons on the water. he'd said, "black people come from a big spacious place, under a great big sky. this little country here, we have to fight for any inches we get. but the water has always helped us get free one way or another."

sunny days, she took paying passengers over by the belle isle bridge to see the cars in the water. mostly, you couldn't see anything. but sometimes, you'd catch a glimpse of something shiny, metal, not of the river—something big and swallowed, that had a color of cherry red, of 1964 american-made dream.

these days, the river felt like it had back then, a little too swollen, too active, too attentive.

too many days, she sat behind the wheel of the little boat, dialing down her apprehension. she felt a restlessness in the weeds and shadows that held detroit together. belle isle, an overgrown island, housed the ruins of a zoo, an aquarium, a conservatory, and the old yacht club. down the way were the abandoned, squatted towers of the renaissance center, the tallest ode to economic crisis in the world.

she had been born not too far from the river, chalmers, on the east side. as a child she played along the riverbanks. she could remember when a black person could only dock a boat at one black-owned harbor. she remembered it because all she'd ever wanted was to be on that river, especially after her grandfather passed. when she was old enough, she'd purchased the little boat, motor awkward on its backside, and named her *bessie* after her mama. her mama had taught her important things:

how to love detroit, that gardening in their backyard was not a hobby but a strategy, and to never trust a man for the long haul.

mostly, she'd listened to her mama. and when she'd gone astray, she'd always been able to return to the river.

now she was forty-three, and the river was freedom. in that boat she felt liberated all day. she loved to anchor near the underground railroad memorial and imagine runaway slaves standing on one bank and how good—terrifying, but good—that water must have felt, under the boat, or all over the skin, or frozen under the feet.

this was a good river for boating. you wouldn't jump in for any money. no one would.

she felt the same way about eating out of the river, but it was a hungry time. that morning she'd watched a fisherman reel in something, slow, like he didn't care at all. what he pulled up, a long slender fish, had an oily sheen on its scales. she'd tried to catch his eye with her disgust, offer a side eye warning to this stranger, but he turned with his catch, headed for the ice box.

she was aware of herself as a kind of outsider. she loved the city desperately and the people in it. but she mostly loved them from her boat. lately she wore her overalls, kept her greying hair short and natural, her sentences short. her routine didn't involve too many humans. when she tried to speak, even small talk, there was so much sadness and grief in her mouth for the city disappearing before her eyes that it got hard to breathe.

next time she was out on the water, on a stretch just east of chene park, she watched two babies on the rocks by the river, daring each other to get closer. the mothers were in deep and focused gossip, while also minding a grill that uttered a gorgeous smell over the river waves. the waves were moving aggressive today, and she wanted to yell to the babies or the mamas but couldn't get the words together.

you can't yell just any old thing in detroit. you have to get it right. folks remember.

as she watched, one baby touched his bare toe in, his trembling ashy mocha body stretched out into the rippling nuclear aquamarine green surface. then suddenly he jumped up and backed away from the river, spooked in every limb. he took off running past his friend, all the way to his mama's thighs, which he grabbed and buried himself in, babbling incoherent confessions to her flesh.

the mother didn't skip a beat or a word, just brushed him aside, ignoring his warning.

she didn't judge that mama, though. times were beyond tough in detroit. a moment to pause, to vent, to sit by the river and just talk, that was a rare and precious thing.

off the river, out of the water, she found herself in an old friend's music studio, singing her prettiest sounds into his machines. he was as odd and solitary as she was, known for his madness, his intimate marrow-deep knowledge of the city, and his musical genius.

she asked him: *what's up with the river?*

he laughed first. she didn't ask why.

here is what he said: *your river? man, detroit is in that river. the whole river and the parts of the river. certain parts, it's like an ancestral burying ground. it's like a holy vortex of energy.*

like past the island? in the deep shits where them barges plow through? that was the hiding place, that was where you went if you loose tongue about the wrong thing or the wrong people. man, all kinds of sparkling souls been weighted down all the way into the mud in there. s'why some folks won't anchor with the city in view. might hook someone before they ghost! takes a while to become a proper ghost.

he left it at that.

she didn't agree with his theory. didn't feel dead, what she felt in the river. felt other. felt alive and other.

peak of the summer was scorch that year. the city could barely get dressed. the few people with jobs sat in icy offices watching the world waver outside. people without jobs survived in a variety of ways that all felt like punishment in the heat.

seemed like every morning there'd be bodies, folks who'd lost darwinian struggles during the sweaty night. bodies by the only overnight shelter, bodies in the fake downtown garden sponsored by coca-cola, bodies in potholes on streets strung with christmas lights because the broke city turned off the streetlights.

late one sunday afternoon, after three weddings took place on the island, she heard a message come over the river radio: four pale bodies found floating in the surrounding river, on the far side. she tracked the story throughout the day. upon being dragged out of the water and onto the soil by gloved official hands, it was clear that the bodies, of two adults and two teenagers, were recently dead, hardly bloated, each one bruised as if they'd been in a massive struggle before the toxic river filled their lungs.

they were from pennsylvania.

on monday she motored past the spot she'd heard the coast guard going on about over the radio. the water was moving about itself, swirling without reason. she shook her head, knowing truths that couldn't be spoken aloud were getting out of hand.

she tried for years to keep an open heart to the new folks, most of them white. the city needed people to live in it and job creation, right? and some of these new folk seemed to really care.

but it could harden her heart a little each day, to see people showing up all the time with jobs, or making new work for themselves and their friends, while folks born and raised here couldn't make a living, couldn't get investors for business. she heard entrepreneurs on the news speak of detroit as this exciting new blank canvas. she wondered if the new folks just couldn't see all the people there, the signs everywhere that there was history and there was a people still living all over that canvas.

the next tragedy came tuesday, when a passel of new local hipsters were out at the island's un-secret swimming spot on an inner waterway of belle isle. this tragedy didn't start with screams, but that was the first thing she heard—a wild cacophony of screaming through the thick reeds.

by the time she doubled back to the sliver entrance of the waterway and made it to the place of the screaming sounds, there was just a whimper, just one whimpering white kid and an island patrol, staring into the water.

she called out: *what happened?*

the patrol, a white kid himself, looked up, terrified and incredulous and trying to be in control. *well, some kids were swimming out here. now they're missing, and this one says a wave ate them!*

the kid turned away from the river briefly to look up at the patrol, slack-mouthed and betrayed. then the damp confused face turned to her and pointed at the water: it took them.

she looked over the side of the boat then, down into the shallows and seaweed. the water and weeds moved innocently enough, but there were telltale signs of guilt: a mangled pair of aviator glasses, three strips of natty red board shorts, the back half of a navy-striped tom's shoe, a tangle of bikini, and an unlikely pile of clean new bones of various lengths and origins.

she gathered these troubled spoils with her net, clamping her mouth down against the lie "I told you so," cause who had she told? and even now, as more kinds of police and coast guard showed up, what was there to say?

something impossible was happening.

she felt bad for these hipsters. she knew some of their kind from her favorite bars in the city and had never had a bad experience with any of them. she had taken boatloads of them on her river tours over the years. it wasn't their fault there were so many of them. hipsters and entrepreneurs were complicated locusts. they ate up everything in sight, but they meant well.

they should have shut down the island then, but these island bodies were only a small percentage of the bodies of summer, most of them stabbed, shot, strangled, stomped, starved. authorities half-heartedly posted ambiguous warning flyers around the island as swimmers, couples strolling on the river walk paths, and riverside picnickers went missing without explanation.

no one else seemed to notice that the bodies the river was taking that summer were not the bodies of detroiters. perhaps because it was a diverse body of people, all ages, all races. all folks who had come more recently, drawn by the promise of empty land and easy business, the opportunity available among the ruins of other peoples' lives.

she wasn't much on politics, but she hated the shifts in the city, the way it was fading as it filled with people who didn't know how to see it. she knew what was coming, what always came with pioneers: strip malls and sameness. she'd seen it nuff times.

so even though the river was getting dangerous, she didn't take it personally.

she hated strip malls too.

then something happened that got folks' attention.

the mayor's house was a mansion with a massive yard and covered dock on the river, overlooking the midwestern jungle of belle isle, and farther on, the shore of gentle canada.

this was the third consecutive white mayor of the great black city, this one born in grand rapids, raised in new york, and appointed by the governor. he'd entered office with economic promises on his lips, as usual, but so far he had just closed a few schools and added a third incinerator tower to expand detroit's growing industry as leading trash processor of north america.

the mayor had to entertain at home a few times a year, and his wife's job was to orchestrate elegance using the mansion as the backdrop. people came, oohed and aahed, and then left the big empty place to the couple. based on the light patterns she observed through the windows on her evening boat rides, she suspected the two spent most of their time out of the public eye happily withdrawn to opposite wings.

she brought the boat past the yard and covered dock every time she was out circling the island looking for sunset. as the summer had gone on, island disappearances had put the spook in her completely, and she circled farther and farther from the island's shores, closer and closer to the city.

which meant that on the evening of the mayor's august cocktail party, she was close to his yard. close enough to see it happen.

dozens of people coated the yard with false laughter, posing for cameras they each assumed were pointed in their direction. members of the press were there, marking themselves with cameras and tablets and smartphones, with the air of journalists covering something relevant. the mayor was aiming for dapper, a rose in his lapel.

as she drifted through the water, leaving no wake, the waves started to swell erratically. in just a few moments, the water began thrashing wildly, bucking her. it deluged the front of her little boat as she tried to find an angle to cut through. looking around, she saw no clear source of disruption, just a single line of waves moving out from the island behind her, clear as a moonbeam on a midnight sea.

she doubled the boat around until she was out of the waves, marveling at how the water could be smooth just twenty feet east. she looked back and saw that the waves continued to rise and roll, smacking against the wall that lined the mayor's yard.

the guests, oblivious to the phenomenon, shouted stories at each other and heimlich-maneuvered belly laughter over the sound of an elevator jazz ensemble.

again she felt the urge to warn them, and again she couldn't think of what to say. could anyone else even see the clean line of rising waves? maybe all this time alone on the boat was warping her mind.

as she turned to move along with her boat, feeling the quiet edge of sanity, the elevator music stopped, and she heard the thumping of a microphone being tested. there he was, slick, flushed, wide and smiling. he stood on a little platform with his back to the river, his guests and their champagne flutes all turned toward him. the media elbowed each other half-heartedly, trying to manifest an interesting shot.

that's when it happened.

first thing was a shudder, just a bit bigger than the quake of summer 2010, which had shut down work on both sides of the river. and then one solitary and massive wave, a sickly bright green whip up out of the blue river, headed toward the mayor's back.

words were coming out her mouth, incredulous screams twisted with a certain glee: *the island's coming! the river is going to eat all you carpetbaggers right up!*

when she heard what she was saying she slapped her hand over her mouth, ashamed, but no one even looked in her direction. and if they had they would have seen naught but an old black water woman, alone in a boat.

the wave was over the yard before the guests noticed it, looking up with grins frozen on their faces. it looked like a trick, an illusion. the mayor laughed at their faces before realizing with an animated double take that there was something behind him.

as she watched, the wave crashed over the fence, the covered dock, the mayor, the guests, and the press, hitting the house with its full force. with a start, a gasp of awe, she saw that the wave was no wider than the house.

nothing else was even wet.

the wave receded as fast as it had come. guests sprawled in all manner of positions, river water dripping down their supine bodies, some tossed through windows of the house, a few in the pear tree down the yard.

frantically, as humans do after an incident, they started checking themselves and telling the story of what had just happened. press people lamented over their soaked equipment, guests straightened their business casual attire into wet order, and security detail blew their cover as they desperately looked for the mayor.

she felt the buoys on the side of her boat gently bump up against the river wall and realized that her jaw had dropped and her hands fallen from the wheel. the water now was utterly calm in every direction.

still shocked, she gunned the engine gently back toward the mansion.

the mayor was nowhere to be seen. nor was his wife. and others were missing. she could see the smallness of the remaining guests. all along the fence was party detritus, similar to that left by the swallowed hipsters. heeled shoes, pieces of dresses and slacks. on the surface of the water near the mansion, phones and cameras floated.

on the podium, the rose from the mayor's lapel lay, looking as if it had just bloomed.

the city tried to contain the story, but too many journalists had been knocked about in the wave, felt the strange all-powerful nature of it, saw the post-tsunami yard full of only people like themselves, from detroit.

plus the mayor was gone.

the crazy, impossible story made it to the public, and the public panicked.

she watched the island harbor empty out, the island officially closed with cement blockades across the only bridge linking it to the city. the newly sworn-in mayor was a local who had been involved in local gardening work, one of the only people willing to step up into the role. he said this was an opportunity, wrapped in a crisis, to take the city back.

she felt the population of the city diminish as investors and pioneers packed up, looking for fertile new ground.

and she noticed who stayed, and it was the same people who had
always been there. a little unsure of the future maybe, but too deeply
rooted to move anywhere quickly. for the first time in a long time, she
knew what to say.

it never did touch us y'know. maybe, maybe it's a funny way to do
it, but maybe it's a good thing we got our city back?

and folks listened, shaking their heads as they tried to understand,
while their mouths agreed: it ain't how I'd have done it, but the thing
is done.

she still went out in her boat, looking over the edges near the island,
searching inside the river, which was her most constant companion,
for some clue, some explanation. and every now and then, squinting
against the sun's reflection, she'd see through the blue, something swallowed, caught, held down so the city could survive. something that
never died.

something alive.

"New Jesus"

TOMMY ORANGE

Tommy Orange (b. 1982) was born in Oakland, California, where much of his fiction is set. He is a member of the Cheyenne and Arapaho Tribes, and he received his MFA from the Institute of American Indian Arts in Santa Fe, New Mexico, where he has also taught. Orange's novel *There There* (2018) was named by more than a dozen review outlets as one of the best books of the year. Celebrated as "a new kind of American epic," this ambitious and widely praised debut novel went on to win the American Book Award and the PEN/Hemingway Award, and was a finalist for the Pulitzer Prize. In his prologue to *There There,* Orange includes himself in the generation of city-born "Urban Indians." He notes: "We know the sound of the freeway better than we do rivers, the howl of distant trains better than wolf howls." And yet, he clarifies, cities too are a part of the living earth: "Being an Indian has never been about returning to the land. The land is everywhere or nowhere." A short-story writer as well as a novelist, Orange returns to this theme in a 2019 story composed for the literary journal *McSweeney's.* Their special issue "2040 A.D." features creative responses to the United Nations 2018 Climate Report and its sobering predictions for the future, should greenhouse gas emissions fail to be cut dramatically by the year 2040. Orange's "New Jesus," another potent climate change tale in which the future may already have arrived, envisions a society of mountain elevation dwellers and sea level dwellers, two social groups confronting in different ways a new environmental reality capable of generating new belief systems. Suspended between two worlds—inundated city and distant mountain—Orange's story presses us to consider whether the end of the world will arrive "not with a bang but with a whimper, or a series of minor disasters." Currently, Orange is writing a sequel to *There There,* which he began before the first book was published. He lives with his wife and son in Angels Camp, California, an old Gold Rush town at the base of the Sierra Nevada Mountains.

"New Jesus"

TOMMY ORANGE

My niece Tina was visiting us from the mountains for the summer and couldn't understand that we just walk in water now. It's not a big deal, but Tina is young and entitled and one of these new mountain elevation people who don't see eye to eye with us sea-level dwellers, we the coastal flooded. The first day she was here her socks got soaked and she sneezed excessively in the evening to the point that I thought she was trying to make us feel bad.

"You can't make yourself sneeze, Herold," my wife Dolorothie said to me.

"You can if you yank nose hairs out, that makes *me* sneeze," I said.

"She wasn't yanking nose hairs out with tweezers while we weren't looking to make us *feel* bad," Dolorothie said, looking out the kitchen window like there was something wrong out there, but what was wrong was in us, was me.

"You don't need tweezers, you can do it with your fingers, you just have to simulate tweezer-grip by putting your fingernails together and yanking."

"Yanking?"

Dolorothie was right, of course. Tina's feet had just gotten too wet, and the cold in Oakland seeps into your bones, the moisture gets through, she's used to high mountain air, thin against human skin it can't penetrate, so yes, Tina had maybe caught the beginning of a cold, but wasn't she emphasizing the sneezes in an unnatural way? This made me distinctly upset, this not knowing if she was leaning into her sneezes or if she really was getting sick.

I should clarify about how much water we walk in. It's not as if we always walk in water, it's that the tide has risen, comes higher when it comes. There's not always water we have to walk in but it's there more often than it's not. We'd wanted to leave, but couldn't afford to just up and go. We got used to it, got used to the storms and floods and the heat, got used to knowing the end of the world had finally arrived not with a bang but a whimper, or a series of minor disasters. Actually too many people call it the end of the world when the world, the earth, would be just fine without us, better off actually, give or take an era or eon or age or whatever amount of time the world might need to get over us.

We hung Tina's socks out on the drying line in the backyard, and I told her she'd be better off not wearing socks outside during her visit. Tina's my estranged sister Valerie's only daughter.

"I'm so many things I'm not even a thing," Tina told me and Dolorothie regarding her background, her heritage, or her blood, because I'd asked her if we were from the same tribe.

"But are you enrolled in our tribe? It's not about blood, it's about having citizenship in a sovereign nation. That's what it used to mean, anyway."

"Citizenship in a sovereign nation?" Tina said, with a distrustful look in her eyes.

"Your mom didn't explain any of it to you?"

"It's that my dad is Chinese and Thai and Italian and other white things. I can't even remember all of them."

"I'm not even sure the tribe's still together and organized in Oklahoma anymore," I said. Tina wasn't the least bit interested in what I was talking about.

"So what do *you* do when your feet get cold?" she asked my wife, avoiding my eyes. Most people around here don't wear socks, and not even shoes either but porous rubber clogs. There's a saying from Hammon, Oklahoma, the small town where my dad grew up, and it goes, "It's Hammon, man, no socks." I'm not sure what sense it made for my dad, or for my Cheyenne relatives in Oklahoma, but here in Oakland, in the year 2040, it makes utter sense. We live wet lives but our feet need not stay wet with socks. There are wood-burning stoves to warm our feet by and socks inside—we wear socks in the house, we're not insane people. The future turned out not to be as futuristic as everyone thought. The weather slowed everything down. Anyone who *could* leave left for higher, stormless ground a long time ago. Tina was *born* in the mountains, so this is her first time down to the coast. Everyone's gotten so used to it here we don't even talk about it anymore. The water. People walk their dogs in it, their babies in strollers with aquadynamic design. Jogging is doable most of the time. Sometimes it's so shallow that if the light hits it right it looks like we're walking on water. No one even talks about Jesus anymore. The end of the world came and went too many times and Jesus failed to show, or it was because science proved to be right about climate change, and had always stood diametrically opposed to religion. Or we lost the need or ability to have faith. I don't really know.

Down from the mountains, Tina brought word of a New Jesus. At first I thought it seemed like lazy naming, New Jesus, but then for the books it's just the Old then New Testament so it makes a kind of sense. My dad always used the word *Creator*. This was often the Native stand-in name for Jesus. He would use *Creator, God,* or *Jesus* interchangeably. Christianity had been shoved down the throats of Native people since contact but in worse and worse ways; the tighter and more normalized the government's grip became, the more effectively Christianity through colonization exercised its control. That's why I would never be a Christian, had never considered it. Even though my dad believed that when he died he would be in heaven with Jesus. The old one. Indian stuff is complex.

"New Jesus lives in each of us and is our action," Tina said. No one had asked her to elaborate on New Jesus. "New Jesus is our cooperation with each other and with the earth. We all become new in New Jesus when we take care of and love one another. The whole world is New Jesus waiting to be realized."

"Gobbledygook," I said without meaning to say it out loud. Tina didn't back down or get her feelings hurt like I thought she might, she came straight for me.

"I'm sorry, Herold, if we still believe in goodness, and don't want to let the ethical murkiness that got us into this mess flood our lives with ruin." She really said that.

Flood our lives with ruin. I laughed and Dolorothie looked at me with something nestled between deep concern and pity.

"Why does it have to be Jesus again?" Dolorothie asked Tina. I liked Dolorothie's line of questioning.

"Yeah, and what makes New Jesus new?" I asked.

"We aren't waiting for him to come back anymore. We've redefined his holy location. It's here. It's like he talked about. The kingdom of God is here. Now."

"All this talk of him, and kingdom, it feels so . . . outdated. Why give god gender at all?" Dolorothie said.

"That's the beauty of it all, and part of why it's New Jesus—it's matriarchal. And by still using Jesus we've been able to recruit people we wouldn't have been able to recruit before. It's like how Christians adopted pagan rituals to be more appealing. A belief system needs to be big enough for there to be community. We need each other."

"Interesting," Dolorothie said. At that point Tina and I both said, "What is?" in an overeager way. We were both worried about which side of interest she fell on. I didn't want the conversation to continue.

"Remember we have that thing tomorrow, early, Dolorothie, we should get some sleep," I said, and gestured with my head toward the stairs leading up to our bedroom. We really did have a thing. We were helping friends pack up their house; they were moving. I wasn't looking forward to it. They were more Dolorothie's friends than mine, but it worked as an excuse to leave Tina in the kitchen alone with her New Jesus.

We left Tina at home to help our friends move. We found out that day that they were moving onto a boat to try their hand at seafaring. This was something people are doing, living on the water. Fishing for sustenance. It makes a kind of sense. One of the first movies I ever saw in the theater was *Waterworld,* with Kevin Costner. It was right after I saw him save so many Indians in *Dances with Wolves,* at which time he was briefly a hero of mine. Our world is not like *Waterworld,* with pirates and filtering pee for drinking water and white girls with dreads, but more and more people are living on boats and dependent on sustenance from fishing. This also means fish is one of our main sources of protein, is more often than not the only meat to eat.

Dolorothie felt bad leaving Tina to herself all day so we took her out to dinner when we got home. Mainly it was fruit and seafood, a combination we've come to master, which it seems strange now was never a thing before, it pairs so well. Raspberries and salmon, tuna and mango, strawberry trout, it just works. Tina didn't *trust* the fish so she only ate the fruit. Blackberries. When we went for a walk after dinner, Tina continued to complain about the water, this time about the murkiness, how she didn't like not being able to see what she was stepping in.

"Too much water breeds bad life," Tina said to us.

"What kind of bad life do you mean?" I said.

"This bad life," she said, pointing all around us.

"Now that's going a little too far, from someone who . . . We've invited you into our home, now you take that back, Tina," I said. When she didn't I called her a hillbilly. Dolorothie really didn't like that I said that, felt that I'd stooped to outdated insults. I went upstairs, afraid I'd say something worse, afraid I was undoing our life by opening my mouth, by letting Tina get to me, by letting my insecurities get to me about what Dolorothie might really think about the way we lived, whether she thought of it as good or bad.

After sulking in the bedroom, trying but failing to read, to focus enough to comprehend anything from the several novels I keep on my desk, waiting for Dolorothie to possibly come tend to me, I went downstairs and heard Tina and Dolorothie talking.

"It's really all about finding a way to love everything," Tina was saying.

"I don't know if that's healthy," Dolorothie said.

"You have to rethink your thought patterns, you have to redo thinking altogether, you have to become New," Tina said.

"What does becoming new do for you?" Dolorothie said.

"Everything, just everything, Auntie," Tina said. I'd had enough.

"D'you care for some coffee or tea, dear?" I said to Dolorothie, strolling into the living room. Tina seemed startled, then recovered.

"I'd love some," Tina said to Dolorothie.

"No, thank you," Dolorothie said to me.

"Which one?" I asked Dolorothie about what Tina wanted.

"Tea," Tina said to Dolorothie. I went and made her tea. Their conversation about New Jesus did not continue that night, but over the following weeks, if I left the house, whenever I came back the two of them would go quiet around me like they didn't want me to know they had been talking. Could this have been paranoia? The thing about paranoia is that as soon as you start getting paranoid about paranoia you're lost. You have to follow through with conviction. But Dolorothie had become quieter about Tina. Less vocal about Tina's presence, with her ideas about life in the mountains.

"You're not really buying into this New Jesus business, are you?" I asked Dolorothie in our bedroom before bed one night.

"Buying in . . . business . . . interesting," Dolorothie said, keeping her head down in a book.

"What does *that* mean?" I said. "What book is that?"

"None of your *business*," she said.

"Tina's leaving in a few days, I was thinking we should have some friends over and give her a farewell party."

"You sound ridiculous," Dolorothie said. Something was wrong. Further along than I thought. Dolorothie had always been a little sad, a little susceptible to beliefs requiring faith, but these had been related to her garden, or to aesthetic theories regarding interior design, never religion, and never like this.

Lying there next to my wife that night I got it into my head to tie Tina up in our flooded basement, to convince her she was wrong about how much better life was in the mountains, and to tell Dolorothie she had changed her mind and come around to see things the way we see them. I would get her down there by convincing her to come see the family of albino smooth newts that had showed up one day to stay, probably because it's so cool and moist down there. I would use the albino smooth newts, claiming they were poisonous to make her promise she'd have one of her talks with my wife, only this time to convince her that *we* had the good life and that mountain life was the bad life and that she was leaving immediately to go get her stuff and move down here and renounce New Jesus.

"You're going to have to do something about the roof," Dolorothie said to me before turning out the light to go to sleep. There was an audible drip in the corner of the room. That *I* was going to have to do something about the roof concerned me. We normally used the royal we concerning the house, anything related to the life we lived together.

"There's a new sealant I heard about that's supposed to be pretty long-lasting," I said. But she was already asleep.

The next day I slept in until noon. I never sleep in, much less that late. I suspected them of drugging me right away. But how? Had I stayed up all night worried in bed? Yes, but I must have gotten some sleep at some point. That I didn't know should have worried me more.

I checked the closet and found Dolorothie's clothes mostly gone. I borrowed a neighbor's car and headed out for Copperopolis, the town where Tina lives. It was two hours away. We'd only been there once years ago for my sister's wedding. I remember Dolorothie saying more than once that she loved it up there. I hadn't thought of it again until then. We were maybe not the happiest couple, not the happiest people, but we had our life together and it was not a bad one. I'd never imagined her wanting to leave. My neighbor's car had no radio so I was stuck with my own head and the sound of the wind moving through the car, the low rumble of the road. I searched my memory for clues about Dolorothie's unhappiness. I knew she didn't like the storms and the floods and that she was palpably happier when the sun was out. Had I ever asked if she wanted to move? Never mind that we couldn't afford it. Though maybe that's why I'd never asked, why the subject had never been broached until Tina came down and made it all possible. Tina's mom had a nice piece of land up there. Just a trailer on the land but land nonetheless, with oak trees and wild horses, chickens in a coop and wandering deer. Turkeys. But Jesus. New Jesus. She would have invited us up when the shit started hitting the proverbial fan years ago but for that she knew I wasn't and would never be a believer. As much as it was supposed to be new and about love, it was still a sin to live with worldly people, even if they were family. End-of-the-worldly people like Dolorothie and me would never have been accepted up there.

I was maybe halfway there when it started raining. Hard. Out of nowhere. I swore the sky'd been cloudless, blue. Maybe not. Either way it came down so hard I had to pull over. Where I pulled over was not ideal, as it was next to a ditch and kind of sunken in even where I'd parked. The rain was so loud and relentless. It was coming down in sheets. Gallons of rain pounding the car. It's not like I hadn't been in a heavy rain before. It was how loud it was against the roof of the car, it was being so alone and desperate, it was feeling like someone or something from above was telling me something. Did I think it was New Jesus? Not at all. But after half an hour of relentless rain, I was afraid. What if it didn't stop? What if there was nothing but rain now? There were places that got weird weather like that and ended up underwater, noncoastal towns. I felt bad for being in a car. I'd sworn them off after everything that happened had seemed so based on cars. Cars and cows and planes and men. The rain kept coming at the same rate and volume. Dumping. And I'd been dumped. That's what had happened. Taking your clothes and leaving and not saying anything was dumping someone. Did I think I would save her? She was being saved by New Jesus. I told myself that if the rain would just let up, I'd do the same, I'd turn around and go home, let Dolorothie do what she wanted, come home or not. Dolorothie didn't need me saving her any more than Indians ever needed Kevin Costner types to save them. I could let go of the fact that I wouldn't get closure if she didn't come back, that we wouldn't have our last words together. If this was about god, about New Jesus, who was I to interfere? But the rain didn't stop. At one point I got out of the car and fell to the ground from the water pressure. That's what it felt like, like weight pushing me down. I couldn't see five feet in front of me in any direction. The rain was roaring. I got back in the car and thought about who I would pray to if I were to pray. Help from where? I closed my eyes and leaned my head against the steering wheel. I remembered my first time seeing the ocean. My dad brought me to Half Moon Bay and told me that the first time he'd seen the ocean he was already a father. I couldn't believe how big it was, how vast, and how it came at the land with such force, such power, the waves. I asked my dad what made it do that. He told me Creator.

As the rain continued to pour down I felt a kind of softening in my heart for Tina, who had been raised up Christian, too, and was so many things she wasn't even a thing. She was Indian, too, even if she was so many things besides, even if she wasn't enrolled. She didn't know better. I couldn't blame Tina. Dolorothie was bigger than that.

I'm not sure how much time passed. It seemed like the rain couldn't possibly keep up its intensity for much longer, which made time seem to pass impossibly slow, or not pass at all. At one point I opened the car door again and saw that the water was almost a foot up, that the rain had collected in this sunken area along the highway along the Altamont Pass where there used to be windmills as far as the eye could see. When I closed the door I thought I felt the car slip a little. Was it sinking? I thought of the ocean again, and of my dad, and his belief. Then I did something I'd never done before. I wouldn't call it praying, but that's probably what it was. With all the windows rolled up, I said, almost as if to the car, I said, *Thank you for what I've had, how I've managed with what I haven't been allowed, and thank you for getting me this far. I'm sorry I haven't done more.* It felt good. Like I'd done something good for someone I loved. Not for myself. Some bigger body I'm a part of. I half expected to be thanked, for the rain to let up a little, or altogether, but it didn't. I don't know what it was about the fact that the water was rising and I didn't care that it was. I'd never felt such a sense of dread and possible freedom at the same time before. I laughed a laugh that turned into a cry that made me so sad I wanted to fall asleep. Something had been wrong for a long time. And it was me.

Suggested Further Wilderness Reading

Since the last decades of the twentieth century, scholars have debated and recast the meaning of wilderness. Here are twenty-five books and anthologies that provide additional historical, social, cultural, and environmental frameworks in which to interpret wilderness tales.

Brinkley, Douglas. *The Wilderness Warrior: Theodore Roosevelt and the Crusade for America*. New York: HarperCollins, 2009.

Callicott, J. Baird, and Michael P. Nelson, eds. *The Great New Wilderness Debate*. Athens: University of Georgia Press, 1998.

Cronon, William. *Changes in the Land: Indians, Colonists, and the Ecology of New England*. 2nd ed. New York: Hill & Wang, 2003.

Cronon, William, ed. *Uncommon Ground: Rethinking the Human Place in Nature*. New York: W. W. Norton & Company, 1995.

den Otter, A. A. *Civilizing the Wilderness: Culture and Nature in Pre-Confederation Canada and Rupert's Land*. Edmonton: University of Alberta Press, 2012.

Dixon, Melvin. *Ride Out the Wilderness: Geography and Identity in Afro-American Literature*. Champaign: University of Illinois Press, 1987.

Farrell, Justin. *Battle for Yellowstone: Morality and the Sacred Roots of Environmental Conflict*. Princeton, NJ: Princeton University Press, 2015.

Finch, Robert, and John Elder, eds. *The Norton Book of Nature Writing*. New York: W. W. Norton & Company, 2002.

Finney, Caroline. *Black Faces, White Places: Reimagining the Relationship of African Americans to the Great Outdoors*. Chapel Hill: University of North Carolina Press, 2014.

Harvey, Mark. *Wilderness Forever: Howard Zahniser and the Path to the Wilderness Act*. Seattle: University of Washington Press, 2005.

Kimmerer, Robin Wall. *Braiding Sweetgrass: Indigenous Wisdom, Scientific Knowledge, and the Teaching of Plants*. Minneapolis, MN: Milkweed Editions, 2013.

Lewis, Michael, ed. *American Wilderness: A New History*. New York: Oxford University Press, 2007.

McKibben, Bill, ed. *American Earth: Environmental Writing Since Thoreau*. New York: The Library of America, 2008.

Miles, John C. *Wilderness in National Parks: Playground or Preserve*. Seattle: University of Washington Press, 2009.

Morgan, Ted. *Wilderness at Dawn: The Settling of the North American Continent*. New York: Simon & Schuster, 1993.

Nash, Roderick Frazier. *Wilderness and the American Mind*. 5th ed. New Haven, CT: Yale University Press, 2014.

Nelson, Michael P., and J. Baird Callicott, eds. *The Wilderness Debate Rages On: Continuing the Great New Wilderness Debate*. Athens: University of Georgia Press, 2008.

Newell, Margaret Ellen. *Brethren by Nature: New England Indians, Colonists, and the Origins of American Slavery*. Ithaca, NY: Cornell University Press, 2015.

Oelschlaeger, Max. *The Idea of Wilderness: From Prehistory to the Age of Ecology*. New Haven, CT: Yale University Press, 1991.

Powell, Miles A. *Vanishing America: Species Extinction, Racial Peril, and the Origins of Conservation*. Cambridge, MA: Harvard University Press, 2016.

Schullery, Paul. *Searching for Yellowstone: Ecology and Wonder in the Last Wilderness*. Boston: Houghton Mifflin, 1997.

Shoalts, Adam. *A History of Canada in Ten Maps: Epic Stories of Charting a Mysterious Land*. Toronto: Penguin Canada, 2018.

Spence, Mark David. *Dispossessing the Wilderness: Indian Removal and the Making of National Parks*, rev. ed. New York: Oxford University Press, 1999.

Turner, James Morton. *The Promise of Wilderness: American Environmental Politics Since 1964*. Seattle: University of Washington Press, 2013.

Van Horn, Gavin, and John Hausdoerffer, eds. *Wildness: Relations of People and Place*. Chicago: University of Chicago Press, 2017.

Suggested Further Story Reading

The archive of North American wilderness tales is broad and deep. Here are fifty more short stories of note, listed in order of their original publication dates.

ABRAHAM PANTHER, "AN ACCOUNT OF A BEAUTIFUL YOUNG LADY"
Perhaps a short story avant la lettre, this widely disseminated eighteenth-century tale by a pseudonymous author is a strange hybrid of sentimental romance, Indian captivity tale, lost-in-the-wilderness saga, and hermit story. The tale appeared in multiple versions, one of the earliest in a 1787 Middletown Connecticut pamphlet, the first story featured in Charles L. Crow's *American Gothic: An Anthology 1787–1916* (Blackwell Publishers, 1999).

NATHANIEL HAWTHORNE, "THE MAN OF ADAMANT"
Hawthorne's allegorical portrait of a stern and intolerant Puritan who retreats to a forest cave and gradually becomes one with his environment. First published anonymously in Samuel Griswold Goodrich's annual Christmas gift book *The Token and Atlantic Souvenir* (Charles Bowen, 1837) and reprinted in Hawthorne's *The Snow-Image and Other Twice-Told Tales* (Ticknor, Reed & Fields, 1852).

JOHN NEAL, "IDIOSYNCRASIES"
This story of a family caught in a mountain avalanche is part wilderness tale, part family melodrama, and part legal drama. First published in two installments in the magazine *Brother Jonathan* 5 (May 6 and July 8, 1843) and reprinted in *The Genius of John Neal: Selections from His Writings,* edited by Benjamin Lease and Hans-Joachim Lang (Peter Lang, 1978).

EDGAR ALLAN POE, "A TALE OF THE RAGGED MOUNTAIN"
A bizarre Gothic tale of mesmerism, morphine, mosques, minarets, and monkeys set in the Virginia mountains. First published in *Godey's Lady's Book* (April 1844) and reprinted in Poe's *Tales* (Wiley and Putnam, 1845).

HARRIET PRESCOTT SPOFFORD, "THE MOONSTONE MASS"

A man sets sail on a ship called the *Albatross* in search of the Northwest Passage. First published in *Harper's Magazine* (October 1868). Republished in *The Amber Gods and Other Stories,* edited by Alfred Bendixen (Rutgers University Press, 1989).

MARK TWAIN, "CANNIBALISM IN THE CARS"

A comic political satire featuring travelers on a train, stranded by snow on the Midwestern prairie and contemplating cannibalism. First published in the literary miscellany the *Broadway Annual* (November 1868) and reprinted in Twain's *Sketches, New and Old* (American Pub. Co., 1875).

AMBROSE BIERCE, "DEATH OF HALPIN FRAYSER"

With echoes of Hawthorne and Poe, this dark psychological tale of a man lost in a haunted wood at the base of California's Mount St. Helena appears to introduce North America's first literary zombie. First published in the San Francisco magazine the *Wave* (December 19, 1891) and reprinted in Bierce's collection *Can Such Things Be?* (Cassell, 1893).

WILLA CATHER, "ON THE DIVIDE"

As another brutal winter descends on the Nebraska plain, an isolated and lonely Swedish immigrant forces a woman to marry him. "On the Divide" is Cather's first published story, edited by one of her professors and submitted for publication without her consent. First published in *Overland Monthly* 27 (January 1896) and reprinted in *Willa Cather's Short Fiction, 1892–1912* (University of Nebraska Press, 1965).

CHARLES G. D. ROBERTS, "THE PANTHER AT THE PARSONAGE"

Influenced by earlier women-and-panther stories, this tale of a young frontier mother protecting her infant from a predatory panther is one of several panther attack tales in Roberts's wilderness fiction. In Roberts's *Around the Camp Fire* (Thomas Y. Crowell & Company, Publishers, 1896).

H. TUKEMAN, "THE KILLING OF THE MAMMOTH"

Written at the end of the nineteenth century when public interest in zoology was high, this story follows two adventurers through a hidden valley as they pursue a prehistoric mammoth, the last of its species. Another first-person wilderness short story that readers widely assumed to be a true account. In *McClure's Magazine* 13, no. 6 (October 1899).

JACK LONDON, "LOVE OF LIFE"

As winter approaches in the Canadian Barrens, an irrepressible instinct to survive keeps an injured Klondiker fighting to beat the odds. In London's *Love of Life and Other Stories* (Macmillan and Company, 1907).

O. HENRY, "TO HIM WHO WAITS"

Tragicomic romantic satire about a fictional "Hermit on the Hudson." First published in *Collier's* 42, no. 18 (January 23, 1909) and reprinted in O. Henry's *Options* (Harper & Brothers, 1909).

SHERWOOD ANDERSON, "DEATH IN THE WOODS"

Offering a striking counterpoint to the classic survival tales of men out-doors, Anderson pens a domestic tale of a woman's dangerous winter walk home. First published in Anderson's *Death in the Woods and Other Stories* (Boni & Liveright, 1933), with an earlier version embedded in his fictional memoir *Tar: A Midwest Childhood* (Boni & Liveright, 1926).

TOM WHITECLOUD, "BLUE WINDS DANCING"

Riding the rails from a New Mexico college town all the way to the northern lights of a Wisconsin reservation, Whitecloud's autobiograph-ical Depression-era tale dramatizes the magnetic power of the real true north—the families we leave behind. In *Scribner's Magazine* (February 1938).

HOWARD O'HAGAN, "A MOUNTAIN JOURNEY"

In O'Hagan's best-known story, a Canadian fur trapper encounters the "cold hand of wilderness" after falling through ice. First published in *Queen's Quarterly* 46 (January 1, 1939) and reprinted in O'Hagan's *The Woman Who Got on at Jasper Station & Other Stories* (Talonbooks, 1977).

WALTER VAN TILBURG CLARK, "HOOK"

An abandoned hawk gains, then loses, each of the three "hungers" of the wild—flying, killing, and mating—but continues to follow its will to endure. First published in the *Atlantic Monthly* (1940) and reprinted in Clark's *The Watchful Gods and Other Stories* (Random House, 1950) and in *Great Western Short Stories*, edited by J. Golden Taylor (The American West Publishing Company, 1967).

ETUKEOK, "THE BOY WHO WAS RAISED BY A BEAR"

Raised in a mountain cave by a bear without cubs, a boy begins to question the motives of the mother bear. Recorded and translated by Clark M. Garber, *Stories and Legends of the Bering Strait Eskimos* (Christopher Publishing House, 1940).

WILLIAM FAULKNER, "THE BEAR"

Faulkner's famous tale recounts the hunt for legendary Old Ben, the last living bear in the remaining wilderness of Yoknapatawpha County. First published, in four parts, in the *Saturday Evening Post* 214, no. 45 (May 9, 1942), this lengthy story expands to five parts in Faulkner's collection *Go Down, Moses* (Random House, 1942) but appears in its original form in Faulkner's book of hunting tales, *Big Woods* (Random House, 1955).

ZORA NEALE HURSTON, "HURRICANE"

Hurston drew on her firsthand knowledge of the Florida Everglades, a network of wetlands fed by Lake Okeechobee, to write the famous hurricane scene in her 1937 novel *Their Eyes Were Watching God*. Almost ten years later, this powerful account of the real-life 1928 hurricane that flooded the Glades was excerpted and published as a short story in Ann Watkin's *Taken at the Flood: The Human Drama as Seen by Modern American Novelists* (Harper & Brothers, 1946).

RAY B. WEST JR., "THE LAST OF THE GRIZZLY BEARS"

A father recalls his childhood days as a Boy Scout, learning about the bears of the Ohio valley and listening to an old trapper's tale of battling a fierce grizzly. First published in *Epoch* magazine (1951). Reprinted in *The Best American Short Stories of 1951*, edited by Martha Foley (Houghton Mifflin, 1951), and in *Great Western Short Stories*, edited by J. Golden Taylor (The American West Publishing Company, 1967).

JOYCE MARSHALL, "THE OLD WOMAN"

A wife rejoins her husband at an isolated power station in Northern Quebec, only to find him acting strangely. Written in 1952 and reprinted in Marshall's *A Private Place* (Oberon Press, 1975) and *Any Time at All and Other Stories* (New Canadian Library, 1993).

JUAN RULFO, "THE PLAIN IN FLAMES"

Government soldiers pursue rural revolutionaries across the Great Plain and mountainous regions of Mexico. In *El llano en llamas* (Fondo de Cultura Económica, 1953). Translated by Ilan Stavans with Harold Augenbraum in *The Plain in Flames* (University of Texas Press, 2012).

RAYMOND CARVER, "THE CABIN"

A man returns in winter to a favorite fishing camp but is threatened by juvenile boys. This story about a wilderness retreat (that turns out not to be one) is the inverse of Hemingway's "Big Two-Hearted River." "The Cabin," first published in *Granta* 12 (June 1, 1984), is a revised version of Carver's earlier tale "Pastoral." Both stories can be found in Carver's *Collected Stories* (The Library of America, 2009).

DAVID MICHAEL KAPLAN, "DOE SEASON"

A different kind of coming-of-age hunting story, this time told from the perspective of a young girl. First published in the *Atlantic* (November 1985) and reprinted in *The Best American Short Stories, 1986,* edited by Raymond Carver and Shannon Ravenel (Houghton Mifflin, 1986), and in Kaplan's collection *Comfort* (Viking, 1987).

ALISTAIR MACLEOD, "AS BIRDS BRING FORTH THE SUN"

On Nova Scotia's Cape Breton Island a dog who disappears and returns to the wild becomes a family superstition down the generations. First published in *Cape Breton's Magazine* 42 (June 1, 1986) and reprinted in MacLeod's *As Birds Bring Forth the Sun & Other Stories* (McClelland & Stewart, 1986) and in *MacLeod's Island: The Complete Short Stories* (McClelland & Stewart, and W. W. Norton & Company, 2000).

DAVID LONG, "GREAT BLUE"

Family summer cabins by Lake Superior are the setting for a boy's first awareness of mortality, with a great blue heron carrying the story's theme. First published in Long's *The Flood of '64* (Ecco Press, 1987) and reprinted in *Passages West: Nineteen Stories of Youth and Identity,* edited by Hugh Nichols (Confluence Press, Inc., 1990).

TIM O'BRIEN, "ON THE RAINY RIVER"

After receiving his draft notice to fight in Vietnam, a terrified draftee flees northward through Minnesota, landing in an old fishing camp, where he must decide whether to cross the border into Canada. From O'Brien's *The Things They Carried* (Houghton Mifflin, 1990).

RANDALL KENAN, "LET THE DEAD BURY THEIR DEAD"

An oral history of an antebellum Maroon society founded by slaves seeking refuge in the wooded, swampy, and mountainous areas of North Carolina. The final tale in a linked story collection by the same title, about the residents of a fictional town called Tim's Creek. In Kenan's *Let the Dead Bury Their Dead* (Harcourt, Inc., 1992).

ALICE MUNRO, "A WILDERNESS STATION"

Mystery tale set in Canada's North Woods, told mostly through letters that span more than a century. First published in the *New Yorker* (April 27, 1992) and reprinted in Munro's *Open Secrets* (Vintage, 1994).

ANNA LEE WALTERS, "CHE"

Walking on a windy prairie, a young couple wonders if the elders' descriptions of the prairie as being once black with buffalo could be true. First published in Walters's *Talking Indian* (Firebrand Books, 1992) and reprinted in *Stories for a Winter's Night: Short Fiction by Native Americans,* edited by Maurice Kenny (White Pine Press, 2000).

DARRYL BABE WILSON, "AKUN, JIKI WALU, GRANDFATHER MAGICIAN"

Composed by a member of the Pit River Nation in Northeastern California, this tale of two adventurous young brothers, impatient to learn how to shoot magic bows and arrows, draws on an Achumawe creation myth in which magicians create the natural features of the earth. In *Earth Song, Sky Spirit: Short Stories of Contemporary Native American Experience,* edited by Clifford E. Trafzer (Anchor Books, 1993).

STEPHEN KING, "THE MAN IN THE BLACK SUIT"

In a contemporary spin on Hawthorne's "Young Goodman Brown," a dying man recalls a terrifying encounter when he was a nine-year-old boy fishing alone on the banks of a forked stream. Set before the

Great War, when the isolated woods of Western Maine were still full of "snakes and secrets," King's homage to Hawthorne's wilderness Gothic tale suggests that, as in any dark fairy tale, no one is safe in the woods, especially children. First published in the *New Yorker* (October 31, 1994) and reprinted in two of King's story collections: *Six Stories* (Philtrum Press, 1997) and *Everything's Eventual* (Scribner, 2002).

RICK BASS, "THE HERMIT'S STORY"

Traveling to Saskatchewan in the winter, a dog trainer delivers six hunting dogs to a man named Gray Owl living alone on the icy northern tundra. First published in the *Paris Review* 147 (Summer 1998) and revised and reprinted in Bass's collection *For a Little While: New and Selected Stories* (Little, Brown and Company, 2016).

ANTHONY DOERR, "SO MANY CHANCES"

A daughter of Hispanic immigrants finds release and freedom fly-fishing the cold ocean waters of Maine. A rare fishing tale from a teenage girl's point of view. First published in *Sycamore Review* and *Fly Rod & Reel* and reprinted in Doerr's *The Shell Collector: Stories* (Scribner, 2002).

RON RASH, "SOMETHING RICH AND STRANGE"

A girl wanders away from a vacation outing in the Appalachian Mountains. First published in *Shade: An Anthology, 2004,* edited by David Dodd Lee (Four Way Books, 2003) and reprinted in Rash's *Something Rich and Strange: Selected Stories* (Ecco, 2014).

EDDIE CHUCULATE, "GALVESTON BAY, 1826"

Chuculate's story, winner of an O. Henry story prize, follows four young men from an inland tribe as they adventure west through unfamiliar landscape to see the "Great Lake" they've heard so much about, encountering both the natural beauty and the sudden danger the power of an ocean storm can bring. First published in *MĀNOA* (Winter 2004) and reprinted in Chuculate's *Cheyenne Madonna* (David R. Godine, Publisher, 2010).

BILL ROORBACH, "THE GIRL OF THE LAKE"

A touching story of generational change and coming-of-age at a family lake house. First published in *Ecotone* 1, no. 1 (Winter/Spring 2005) and reprinted in Roorbach's *The Girl of the Lake: Stories* (Algonquin Books, 2017).

EMMA DONOGHUE, "SNOWBLIND"

In 1896, two men stake a claim together in the Yukon, struggling to survive a brutal winter and finding something other than gold. First published in *The Faber Book of Best New Irish Stories,* edited by David Marcus (Faber, 2007), and reprinted in Donoghue's *Astray* (Little, Brown and Company, 2012).

YASUKO THANH, "FLOATING LIKE THE DEAD"

Left alone on a forested island with only minimal provisions, three men with leprosy must battle exile, loneliness, and despair in their quest to survive. This tale is based on the true history of Canada's D'Arcy Island in the Halo Straits, a barren island where, beginning in 1891, Chinese immigrants with leprosy were quarantined. First published in *Vancouver Review* and reprinted in *The Journey Prize: Stories* 21 (McClelland & Stewart, 2009) and in Thanh's *Floating Like the Dead* (McClelland & Stewart, 2012).

WELLS TOWER, "RETREAT"

On a remote mountain in Maine's North Woods, two estranged brothers reunite and contemplate their futures. First published in *McSweeney's* 30 (March 2009) and reprinted in Tower's *Everything Ravaged, Everything Burned: Stories* (Farrar, Straus & Giroux, 2009).

LYDIA MILLET, "ZOOGOING"

A man visiting an Arizona zoo unexpectedly develops feelings of kinship with a rare Mexican wolf. He breaks into its enclosure that night, leading to more nights, and more zoogoing, as he silently contemplates the world's vanishing species. In *I'm with the Bears: Short Stories from a Damaged Planet,* edited by Mark Martin (Verso, 2011), extracted from Millet's novel *How the Dead Dream* (Counterpoint, 2008).

THOMAS MCGUANE, "RIVER CAMP"

A fishing trip in the wild turns dangerous for two anglers and their guide. First published in *McSweeney's* 41 (2012) and reprinted in McGuane's *Cloudbursts: Collected and New Stories* (Alfred A. Knopf, 2018).

SHIRLEY JACKSON, "THE MAN IN THE WOODS"

Another allegorical tale about a strange meeting in the woods. Recently discovered in the Library of Congress, this unpublished Jackson story of unspecified date was posthumously published in the *New Yorker* (April 28, 2014) and reprinted in *Shirley Jackson, Let Me Tell You: New Stories, Essays, and Other Writings,* edited by Laurence Jackson Hyman and Sarah Hyman DeWitt (Random House, 2015).

TONI JENSEN, "IN THE TIME OF ROCKS"

As fracking threatens to despoil the high plains of West Texas, a young Métis girl and her friend map their beloved wild canyons. In *Ecotone* 11, no. 1 (Fall/Winter 2015).

J. R. MCCONVEY, "HOW THE GRIZZLY CAME TO HANG IN THE ROYAL OAK HOTEL"

A traumatized war veteran must remove from a posh Canadian hotel a bewildered and angry bear, plucked from the Yukon for a film shoot. In *Event* 44, no. 1 (Spring/Summer 2015) and reprinted in *The Journey Prize: Stories* 28 (McClelland & Stewart, 2016).

HEATHER O'NEILL, "THE WOLF-BOY OF NORTHERN QUEBEC"

In a tale of wilderness lost, a feral child who lived among wolves becomes internationally famous while the wolves that raised him are relegated to a zoo. In O'Neill's *Daydreams of Angels* (Farrar, Straus and Giroux, 2015).

HELEN PHILLIPS, "THE BEEKEEPER"

A cli-fi story about species infertility, in which both pollinating bees and girls of reproductive age suddenly go missing. In Phillips's *Some Possible Solutions: Stories* (Henry Holt and Company, 2016).

OLIVIA CLARE, "EYE OF WATER"

This climate change story set in the desert community of Las Vegas, where water is rationed, flowers are banned, and birds have disappeared, explores the psychological consequences of living in a world without greenery or wildlife. In Clare's *Disasters in the First World: Stories* (Black Cat, 2017).

CLINTON PETERS, "ECOTONES"

Featuring the viewpoints of both a rare Florida panther and the animal activist who seeks to save her, this story poses ethical questions about wildlife management and human efforts to prevent species extinction. In *Cold Mountain Review* (Fall 2017) in a special issue on extinction.

LUIS ALBERTO URREA, "THE NIGHT DRINKER"

As the world burns, a historian of religion in Mexico City witnesses a wave of climate refugees seeking higher ground, as well as a reemergence of belief in the ancient Aztec gods. In *McSweeney's* 58 (2019).

Acknowledgments

During the years of putting this anthology together, I have read countless magazines, newspapers, journals, books, and collections published over the past two hundred years, in which I uncovered numerous tales and short stories about the North American wild. A group of colleagues, students, friends, and family have followed my research adventures, offering information, counsel, and companionship on many a hike and journey along the way. I am especially indebted to James Eatroff for his wilderness wisdom, to Jeffrey Stylos for his tech savvy, and to Paul Schorin for his literary acumen. At Princeton, I credit John Orluk Lacombe for helping me bring the project home. For their generous feedback and support I thank Patricia Crain, Carolyn Dean, William Gleason, Martha Howell, Heather Love, Sharon Marcus, Francesca Trivellato, and Judith Walkowitz. To my test readers—Clarissa Carson Rose, Jeremy Colvin, Joanna Curry, Kathryn Didion, Alison Duerwald, Emma Hopkins, Alex Hsia, Will Lentz, John (Jack) Lohmann, Dan Petticord, Justin Sansone, Paul Schorin, Madison Shorty, Michael Tummarello, and Charlie Van Allen—I have greatly valued your excitement, candor, and input. Finally, I thank Peter Bernstein for his early guidance and for his introduction to the team at Knopf, where my sharp-eyed editor, Victoria Wilson, and her assistant, Marc Jaffee, along with permission managers Beau Sullivan and Sherri Marmon, made a daunting task both easier and more enjoyable.

Permissions

Permissions are listed in the order in which the stories appear in the volume.

SIGURD OLSON, "TRAIL'S END"

"Trail's End," by Sigurd Olson, first printed in *Sports Afield,* copyright © 1933. Used by permission of Sigurd F. Olson Publications and courtesy of Dr. David J. Backes.

WILLIAM FAULKNER, "THE OLD PEOPLE"

"The Old People" from *The Big Woods* by William Faulkner, copyright © 1931, 1940, 1942, 1951, 1955 by William Faulkner. Copyright © 1930, 1934, 1954, 1955 by The Curtis Publishing Company. Copyright renewed 1958, 1959 by William Faulkner. Copyright renewed 1962, 1968, 1970 by Estelle Faulkner and Jill Faulkner Summers. Copyright renewed 1979, 1982, 1983 by Jill Faulkner Summers. Used by permission of Random House, an imprint and division of Penguin Random House LLC, and by permission of W. W. Norton & Company, Inc. All rights reserved.

ANTHONY DOERR, "THE HUNTER'S WIFE"

"The Hunter's Wife" from *The Shell Collector* by Anthony Doerr, copyright © 2002 by Anthony Doerr. First printed in the *Atlantic Monthly.* Reprinted with the permission of Scribner, a division of Simon & Schuster, Inc. And with the permission of ICM Partners. All rights reserved.

JENNY LEADING CLOUD, "SPOTTED EAGLE AND BLACK CROW"

"Spotted Eagle and Black Crow" told by Jenny Leading Cloud in White River, Rosebud Indian Reservation, South Dakota, 1967. Recorded by Richard Erdoes; from *American Indian Myths and Legends* by Richard Erdoes and Alfonso Ortiz, copyright © 1984 by Richard Erdoes and Alfonso Ortiz. Used by permission of Pantheon Books, an imprint of the Knopf Doubleday Publishing Group, a division of Penguin Random House LLC. All rights reserved. And from *American Indian Myths & Legends* by Richard Erdoes and Alfonso Oritz published by Pimlico. Copyright © 1997 by Richard Erdoes and Alfonso Oritz. Reprinted by permission of The Random House Group Limited.

KAREN RUSSELL, "ST. LUCY'S HOME FOR GIRLS RAISED BY WOLVES"

"St. Lucy's Home for Girls Raised by Wolves" from *St. Lucy's Home for Girls Raised by Wolves: Stories* by Karen Russell, copyright © 2006 by

A NOTE ON THE TYPE

This book was set in Adobe Garamond. Designed for the Adobe Corporation by Robert Slimbach, the fonts are based on types first cut by Claude Garamond (ca. 1480–1561). Garamond was a pupil of Geoffroy Tory and is believed to have followed the Venetian models, although he introduced a number of important differences, and it is to him that we owe the letter we now know as "old style." He gave to his letters a certain elegance and feeling of movement that won their creator an immediate reputation and the patronage of Francis I of France.

Typeset by Scribe,
Philadelphia, Pennsylvania

Printed and bound by Berryville Graphics,
Berryville, Virginia

Designed by Soonyoung Kwon